LOOK 'N UP INVASION

AN EXERCISE IN EMPATHY

Janice Carr Smith

Look 'N Up Publishing, Lewiston, CA

Look 'N Up Publishing
Lewiston, CA
www.looknup.us
looknupsmiths@gmail.com

This book is a work of fiction. Names, characters, places, and incidents are a product of the author's imagination. Any resemblance to actual people, living or dead, or to businesses, companies, events, institutions, or locales is completely coincidental.

Copyright © 2023 by Janice Carr Smith

Book Layout © 2022 BookDesignTemplates.com
Editorial Services by Sage Taylor Kingsley
www.SageforYourPage.com
Cover Design by Angelotti

Look'N Up Invasion/ Janice Carr Smith. – 2nd edition.
ISBN 979-8-9875179-1-8 (ebook)
ISBN 979-8-9875179-0-1 (pbk)

For Kip

That's
Ed Pacheco,
The most Look 'N Up person I've ever known.

CONTENTS

1. First Pomegranate Day

Baput could feel the people's excitement, and their fear, when he arrived at the Great Hall as part of the Holy Entourage. His friends Bazu and Pindrad were standing with their families across the plaza paved with flat rocks. Pindrad's 17th-year sister and Baput's betrothed, Tamaya, stared at Baput with appraising eyes below arched eyebrows in a high forehead the color of the soft, thick moss that grew on the cold, dark side of the rocks in the forest.

Uncle Felsic left the Holy Family and crossed the plaza to join his 8th-year daughter, Trillella, who shared his olive skin and purple freckles, and his wife, Aunt Peratha, pale as a peeled cucumber. All 25 families were there, their skins the color of spring grass, or the leaves of the mighty oaks, or the needles of the lofty pines.

The Holy Family filed across the West Trench on a simple wooden bridge to reach the stage, a temporary platform in the center of the rectangle formed by the four battle trenches in front of the Great Hall. Baput followed behind the *Akash*, but he could not join him on the platform, because he was only 12. He was to stand on the bloodstained ground in front of the stage with his parents, Salistar, who was *Tether* to and daughter of Akash, Valko, Guard of Akash, and G-Pa's dog, Shastina, a wolf-like creature in lavender with deep purple highlights.

When everyone was in place, the singing abruptly stopped, and Baput's G-Pa, the Holy Akash, took center stage, his legs apart, his arms open, his longstick held aloft, bedecked with strings of beads and feathers. His heavy robe of woven *yal* grass, dried to a bleached white, framed his wirey form. Scrawny wrists and neck extended from the baggy tunic and drawstring pants he wore beneath the robe. Of the same woven grass, in a simpler weave, the undergarments were identical to those of his loyal subjects, man and woman alike.

His shriveled green skin, silvery grey like the leaves of the willows by the river, was turning yellow along the wrinkles, just like those leaves were doing now in the crisp fall air. His hair, once lush and black as Baput's, and his beard, once an impenetrable ebony like Valko's, were now sparse strings of faded lavender. He began to recite the First Pomegranate Day Litany, or was it?

"People, this shall be a First Pomegranate Day like no man has ever seen before. On this day, I shall defeat the *nimblies* and the *bumblies* with the weapon that I found in the Holy Cave and assembled personally at great self-sacrifice, for you, my people. I tell you, on this day, the nimblies and bumblies shall be no more!"

"No more nimblies! No more bumblies!" the crowd chanted. The men shook spears and longsticks above their heads, their faces, dark as ivy, light as lichen, and every shade in between, were smeared with white zinc and black magnesium war paint. When the chanting died down, the Akash continued.

"You men go enjoy the wine. No need to occupy the trenches. You women will not see your sons die on this day, or tomorrow. Celebrate, people! The curse of the nimblies and bumblies shall end this day. I shall do this. You and your sons shall sing my name into the future for all time."

Dark brown eyes blinked long black eyelashes. Faces the colors of pale mullein, delicate basil, and deep forest shade stared, motionless.

"Well, go on, now, celebrate!" the Akash roared the order. Still, no one moved.

Baput gestured frantically at his G-Pa from the ground below. The old man bent down to him, the stiff strings of his lavender beard falling in the boy's face. Baput brushed it aside with respectful indulgence and whispered, "G-Pa, you must speak The Litany!"

The Akash groaned, straightened up and ambled back to center stage. He recited the familiar words in a monotone before the silent crowd.

"I have been to the *Akashic Plane*, the River of Sight, the Neverending Flow. The Plane bears all the knowledge of the past, present, and future to any man with the wisdom to seek it. I cast a hopeful mold of the future into it, so that the power manifested there will give us another *cycle*, another three years of living together and loving one another. The vibrations of all who went before us remain there, part of the eternal energy of the Akashic Plane. Those who fall in battle this cycle will join them with pride."

He went off script again. "Except none of you will die this cycle. Not by nimbly today nor bumbly tonight, and not for the next two tomorrows, for I alone shall defeat them all today. By midnight tonight, we shall have forever won the right to continue planting the Holy Seed. Pomegranates shall continue! We shall continue. We shall be forever!"

"No more nimblies! No more bumblies! Not ever! No more!" The crowd echoed the gleeful chant from the Tale of Yanzoo, which had not yet come true.

"They have awakened!" The Akash suddenly bellowed over the jubilant chanting. The gleeful chant crystallized to silence. The Great Horn sounded.

The men sprang into action. They ran for their weapons: their longsticks, wooden poles up to seven feet long, with tips of knapped stone or carbonized wood. They grabbed their shields, made of wooden stakes lashed together with ropes of woven grass. Some had blowguns and darts, and some wielded clubs. Others had short throwing spears or long-handled rackets for swatting the beasts from the air. Each man was trained to his weapon from the age of three. Even the men who held other professions besides warrior had trained on some weapon, and they all fought during the Season.

"They are so early!" the women whispered to one another.

"The men didn't even get to eat!" worried Baput's mother, Salistar, as she hurried into the Great Hall to her usual station. As Tether to Akash, she was in charge of the women's vital battle support operation during the three-day Season. But not this time.

Baput followed his momama into the Great Hall. Women scurried back and forth carrying food to the tables to quickly feed the warriors, which included every able-bodied man of at least 15 years, or five three-year *cycles*. They grabbed grape leaves stuffed with purple beans and dark red beets, red peppers stuffed with peas and black rice, rolls of protein-rich sprouted pomegranate-seed bread, and a ceremonial taste of Uncle Felsic's famous *kip* wine, made from the culls of the vital pomegranates they called kips.

But Rakta, the War Chief, allowed only one ceremonial drink for each warrior. The men would need to keep their wits about them. The food was not just a harvest feast; it was preparation for a siege. A three-day nightmare that recurred every three years, right at harvest time.

As the men filed through, the women packed the rest of the food into fragile clay meal boxes that the *ganeesh* would carry out to the men at their posts whenever the bumblies and nimblies allowed. Enormous and highly intelligent, the elephant-like creatures were each trained to a battle station. They could find their way there in the pitch dark, surrounded by a cloud of bumblies. The purple-grey leather of an adult ganeesh could not be penetrated by the savage needle of a nimbly, nor ripped by the razor-sharp horn of a bumbly.

Men did not enter kitchens, not even one who is the Apprentice Akash and the son of the accustomed chief of that kitchen. Baput stopped at the kitchen door.

Salistar turned to face him, her heavy black eyebrows knotted in her basil forehead. Her lush, dark purple-black hair was tied back tightly, but errant strands dangled on either side of her face. Baput hadn't noticed the lavender grey highlights before.

"Check the ganeesh stalls. Make sure *she* secures them," she directed her son.

Baput was startled by the order. The Apprentice Akash did not concern himself with woman's matters, even if the woman was his momama. The venom in his momama's voice and the bitter look below those wrinkled brows were even more disconcerting. His hand shook a little when he raised it to cup her cheek, sweet and soft as the new grass after the first fall rain. "I will, Momama," he gulped.

She squeaked, a small, helpless sound that was more unusual still, and rushed into the kitchen where he could not follow.

The scent of the freshly limed but still pungent vault toilets assaulted Baput as he approached the stables at the back of the Great Hall. Tamaya was there, swiftly packing a ganeesh for battle. He scanned the unfamiliar rigging with no idea if it was right or not, until the ganeesh pointed to a loose strap with her trunk—and maybe winked at Baput. It was hard to tell.

Tamaya grabbed the loose strap and yanked hard, staring defiantly at Baput as she did.

Breaking that stare, Baput scanned the other stalls. All empty. All in battle already, except old Heffala here. No tender-skinned *babbets*, not anymore. He shuddered, and his eyes wandered back to Tamaya's.

"Are you scared?" she asked, those deep brown eyes probing.

"N-no," he replied, more curtly and less honestly than he wanted to. "Are you?"

"Not if you're here," she said serenely, making Baput even more scared. He was afraid of the nimblies and bumblies, of course, but right then he felt more scared of those eyes of hers and the desire they showed for something that, on his 12th birthday, he couldn't quite identify and wasn't ready to give.

"It'll be alright," he promised lamely.

"Do you see that? In the future?" she asked.

Was she trying to sound hopeful? It sounded more like a challenge.

"I can't see the future. Not until I am Akash. In three years, I will ascend, and then I will see all the way to forever," he bragged, looking up at her. Was she impressed? Or was she making fun of him? He couldn't tell. In three years, she would be his wife.

They returned to the main hall, where they were surprised to find Rakta, the War Chief, arguing with the Akash. To do so was almost unheard of, and it took more courage than fighting the nimblies and bumblies. Women rushed past them, sometimes bumping the War Chief, but never the Akash. Tamaya rushed away into the kitchen.

Baput crouched behind the spiral staircase to the East Turret to watch this unprecedented event. Shastina appeared at his side and stood rigid, her tail straight up and vibrating. Rakta's dog, Wenzel, stood with bared teeth next to Rakta's son and First Commander, Rakted.

"First, you tell the men not to fight!" Rakta shouted at the holy man! "Fortunately, the warriors obey me, not you. They know what to do." Squat and green as a bullfrog, Rakta circled the Akash like a sparring partner. Women stopped, holding their loads, and watched. The men gathered around, whispering.

"Now you want to take your whole family to the Holy Cave! We must all stay together in the Great Hall. We need Valko and Salistar. Salistar is in charge of the food. Valko must fight. As must Felsic. You know we need all hands. You should take only the boy, like last time."

"I told you there will be no battle here!" The Akash stated, as if it were an undeniable fact. "It will all be over tonight."

Rakta thumped the butt of his longstick on the floor. "What if it isn't?" he grunted.

The Akash stood as tall as he could. The burly war chief, with his bulging muscles, wide frame, broad face as dark as the pines of the forest that had sacrificed themselves for this Great Hall, and his pile of dense, dark hair, dwarfed him in every way. Even so, Rakta took a step back.

The Akash swooped in, right eye first, invading the space Rakta had vacated. "Salistar is my Tether. We will be at the Holy Cave for the entire battle. If it is three days, in that unlikely event, we will need a food supply."

Stepping forward further, forcing Rakta back another step, the small but mighty Akash continued explaining his plan to Rakta. "Your Tether, Azuray, will take charge of the women here. As for Valko, his position is to guard me and the Akashic family. We will all be at the Cave. Therefore, Valko must be there. And we need Felsic's strong legs to pedal the contraption."

"You play with fire, old man. You know you play with forbidden forces, yet you take our key manpower away during the Season."

"We will kill more nimblies and bumblies with that thing in the Holy Cave than a hundred men with longsticks ever could. But we must go now. The nimblies are awake already. Salistar is packing Heffala."

"You want a ganeesh, too?"

"Just Heffala, the old mother. She has no taste for battle, after last time. She can get us there safely, if we go now."

Rakta didn't like it, but he could not tell the Akash what to do, even if he was breaking the rules. The Holy One had powers he couldn't even begin to understand. His Evil Eye could bring instant death or a slow, painful one, just by looking at a man. Rakta shuddered inside his ganeesh-skin armor. No one questioned the Akash's wisdom. Not even secretly, in their innermost thoughts. Besides, in his hidden, truthful thoughts, Rakta agreed with the old man. They needed something new to fight the nimblies and bumblies. They increased with every passing cycle, and the people grew fewer.

Every three years, during the three days of constant struggle, they lost at least four or five young men, often more. In a village of only 100 people, those losses added up. But why not take it one step further? Why commit the sin of *Shavarandu* by messing with that contraption the Akash found in the Cave, but not *Insitucide*, the seemingly simpler task of killing the beasts in the caves while they slept, which also was forbidden? Rakta shook his head, glad he was not the Akash. War decisions made sense. The Akash had to obey all the rules handed down from the Old Ones, sometimes for no conceivable reason.

"Take what you need. I can't stop you," Rakta grumbled, hurrying off to tend to the remaining forces. This would take some adjustments! Who would take charge of Valko's troops? His mind ran through the remaining men for a substitute commander for the West Trench, their final line of defense before the Great Hall full of their women, children, and food.

The Akash stood motionless amidst the bustle. He rested on his longstick, far more ornate than Rakta's. His ceremonial robe flowed around him, beautifully woven and beaded by Salistar.

Baput approached cautiously. "G-Pa, the ganeesh is ready. Are Momama and Popa coming? Uncle Felsic?"

"Yes, Grandson." The Akash turned, burying his recent argument behind him. "Go get them and tell them it is time. We must hurry."

The Battle

Four boys under 15, too young for battle, stood ready to close the heavy doors made of whole logs lashed together. Baput ran through them, out onto the battlefield where the men were quickly disassembling the stage where the Akash had just delivered his sermon. They were taking its planks to the trenches for bridges, and for the bit of cover they would provide.

The Akash was right beside Baput, his two-toned purple dog, Shastina, at his heels. Baput could hear the heavy footsteps of his large, heavily bearded popa, and the much lighter steps of his petite momama. Uncle Felsic's clumsy steps faltered.

Someone squealed, "Popa!"

The Akash kept going, but Baput turned back to see his little cousin, Trillella, running to her popa, arms outstretched, crying, "Popa, don't go! Take me with you!"

Felsic's wife, Aunt Peratha, was right behind her. "Trillella! No! You stay here with me!"

Trillella threw herself into Felsic's arms. Peratha reached them, and the little family huddled together on the open battlefield while the boys closed the doors to the Great Hall.

Baput's giant popa, Valko, rushed over to his younger brother's family, swallowing them up in his great bulk. He plucked his little niece out of the group, carried her to where Baput and Salistar waited with the ganeesh, and placed her gently on the ground. Felsic and Peratha rushed to join them and they all ran along the edge of the battlefield while the warriors piled into the trenches with their clubs, darts, and spears.

Heffala, the ganeesh, loaded with three days' supply of food and supplies, galloped ahead of them. They all ran closely behind her, obscured by her dust. Valko brought up the rear, towering over his family like a mighty oak, his long, black hair flying behind him. They left the battlefield and started up a worn trail that lead east, out of the village.

They caught up with the Akash at the east end of the orchard. On the right, willow-clad hummocks sloped away to the river, concealing the underground chambers of the Lair of the Unmarriageables. Ahead, the Holy Cave beckoned from its spire of pink dolomite framed in the eternal upriver mist.

As they grew closer, Baput could see the smoke from last night's fire still trickling from the chimney, a tiny hole high in the side that faced west, toward the Great Hall. He, G-Pa, Popa, and Uncle Felsic had been there long into the night, setting up the mysterious weapon.

The main entrance to the Holy Cave faced the river. It was large enough for two ganeesh to enter side by side, but only after climbing, single file, 30 feet of steep, narrow staircase hewn from solid rock. At the top, a flat stone porch spread out in front of the wide, arched entrance.

The men tightened the straps on her load, and Heffala lumbered up the stairs ahead of them, with Shastina scrambling up at her heels. The rest clambered after the animals, the Akash in the lead, Peratha and Trillella bringing up the rear.

The Akash stopped the last two at the door. "These females cannot enter!" he bellowed. He stood at the doorway, feet spread and hands on his hips, as if his thin frame could block the wide opening.

Peratha and Trillella stood before him, eyes pleading.

Felsic ran over. "You must let them in! The nimblies are coming! The animals are allowed in, but not my family? Let them pass!"

The Akash stood firm. "My dog can stay. She is family. The ganeesh must go. Salistar is my daughter and my Tether. But these two are not of Akashic blood and have no right here."

Felsic surprised everyone by becoming the second person today to argue with the Akash. "I am not Akashic either. Nor is Valko." He glanced anxiously at his big brother. Would Valko be mad? No, Valko came right to Felsic's side.

"You two are men," the Akash said, as if they were idiots. "Besides, I need you. But low-born females," he sneered, "can *never* enter the Holy Cave!"

"They need to help Salistar with the food," Valko was ready to argue with the old man, as well.

Salistar didn't need any help, but she wanted Peratha and Trillella safely inside the Cave, so she stilled her pride and kept quiet.

"They stay outside, with the ganeesh," the Akash replied coldly. "The ganeesh will protect them."

"But we will be here at night when the bumblies come. Surely they can come in then!" Valko persisted.

"We'll see," the Akash muttered cryptically. "Now go! Off with you!" He shooed the woman, girl, and elephant down the steep stairs to the ground far below.

Baput inhaled a slow, deep breath as he stepped inside the Holy Cave and stared down at the Holy Rock. Shiny, smooth, perfectly round and about eight feet in diameter, the metallic sphere lay half-buried in the floor. The Akash had told him that it gave the Holy Cave its power, but Baput still didn't understand how it worked.

Now it would provide the energy for a new weapon that would put an end to their symbiotic predators, the nimblies today and the bumblies tonight, and the Great Battle would be over forever. No more momamas and popas would bury their 16th-year sons. *No more nimblies, no more bumblies, not ever no more.* Baput heard the people's chant, their most fervent desire, repeating in his head. *G-Pa is right. If we don't follow all the rules, Kakeeche might be angry and make us fail. But what we're doing is against the rules! But it's so important!*

He hesitated, scanning the Cave. It was a large, open space, except for two tunnels that disappeared into the depths. Daylight gleamed weakly from what they called the chimney, an opening above the fireplace that collected the smoke into a horizontal tube that ran almost a hundred feet along the ceiling to the tiny hole on the west side of the dolomite bluff, facing the Great Hall. The other tunnel went straight back into the wall behind the Holy Rock. No hint of light emerged from that chamber, where they had found all these strange objects and the cryptic instructions for their assembly into a weapon.

Baput shuddered at the darkness and turned back toward the Cave entrance, preferring to face the horror he understood: the approaching nimblies.

But instead, he faced another unfamiliar horror. Uncle Felsic, wordless but obviously furious, stormed past him and the Holy Rock toward the back of Cave and into that dark tunnel, where a stationary bicycle stood, with a thick black cord dangling from the back. With one muscular arm, he hoisted the heavy apparatus roughly and hauled it to the front of the Cave, dragging the wire, yanking impatiently when it caught on every rock and bump along the way.

"Careful, you idiot!" the Akash barked.

Ignoring the holy man, Felsic slammed the bicycle down just inside the Cave entrance where he could see Peratha and Trillella, huddled together with the loyal ganeesh. He looked down at his family. "OK?" he asked them. They nodded.

Baput didn't think they looked OK at all, nor did Felsic. He grasped his uncle's shoulder. "Are you ready?" he asked, seeking Felsic's eyes. He held them for a moment, breathing deeply and softly, until those wild eyes finally focused. "We'll kill them all," he promised rashly. "They don't stand a chance," he squeezed Felsic's shoulder. "Now, it's time. I will connect the strands."

Baput picked up the end of the bicycle's cord and took it to the levers he was to attend. He uncoiled two more wires and connected one to the cord from the stationary bicycle. He plugged the other one into the Net, a feather-light weave of fine, stiff, silvery white fibers that covered the Holy Rock like a crinkly queen-sized satin sheet.

A heavy metal tube, about eight inches across and polished to a reddish shine, protruded from under the Net, pointed at the Cave entrance. Baput knew how heavy that tube was. Even Popa could only lift one end of it. They never could have set all this up without Heffala. *Now she's banished outside, with my aunt and my little cousin.* Once again, Baput fought back his budding doubts. Surely, his G-Pa, the Akash, knew what was best.

He suddenly realized the Rock was humming.

And the Cave walls were humming back.

Had this ever-increasing hum already been there? Had he not noticed it over all the arguing on the porch? The Net still lay lifelessly over the Rock, over the copper pipe.

"Now, Felsic," Baput ordered, pointing at the bike and pulling the first lever.

Felsic grudgingly began to pedal the wheel that turned the belt that spun the cylinder that generated the fearsome and forbidden Shavarandu that powered the weapon.

The Rock hummed louder. It began to glow. The pitch rose higher, and the Net lifted off the Rock. Paralleling the Rock's perfectly curved shape, it hung suspended about six inches above it on a cloud of white light.

Baput could hear the nimblies thrumming the air upriver.

"Peratha, Trillela, get back against the wall. Stay still!" Felsic urged, pedaling harder. His family flattened themselves against the wall. Heffala pressed against them, covering them with her tough hide.

Valko lifted the end of the heavy pipe that stuck out from the Net. He ran his fingers over the astounding material, smooth, uniform— and hard as rock! He aimed it at the first swarm of nimblies that appeared out of the upriver mist on their ravenous journey to the Great Hall.

There were 100 nimblies, in neat rows of 10. They resembled giant dragonflies, eight inches long with a double set of 12-inch wings, today. They would be even bigger tomorrow. Decked in a brindle pattern of muted yellow and orange, with wings of rust-colored lace, they could blend with the fall foliage, but they didn't spend much time hiding in the trees.

Their fearsome faces were more mosquito than dragonfly, featuring two multifaceted eyes over a needle-like proboscis that could easily pierce a man to his heart and drain it in minutes, if given the time. If not, their stingers delivered a paralyzing poison that left the victim helpless when the bumblies came that night.

Baput pushed the next lever. The room darkened a bit, and the humming was muted as part of the energy that had collected between the Rock and the Net was directed into the tube. It poured out the other end as a laser of light and vibration.

Valko pointed the tube at the nimblies. Felsic pedaled as hard as he could, increasing the pitch even more. It hurt his ears, but he just pedaled harder.

The first row of nimblies flew straight past the Cave entrance, on their age-old migration route to the Great Hall. They did not seem to notice the Akashic family in the Cave, or Peratha, Trillella, and Heffala, whose grayish purple hide blended with the cliff below the Cave.

The concentrated beam shot straight out from the Cave entrance, hitting the closest nimbly in the first row. It exploded with a loud pop, black-red guts flying everywhere. Felsic hooted and Salistar ran to the front of the Cave to see the results.

The remainder of the first row continued without a pause, but Valko was ready for the second row. He pointed the stream just ahead of the row, and as they entered the beam they popped, the closest one first, then all the way down the row, as if the beam travelled right through one victim to penetrate the next one.

"It's working!" the Akash cried gleefully, dancing around the Holy Rock and shaking his fist at his lifelong enemies as they disappeared before his eyes, his dream coming true.

Five more rows went by, fifty more nimblies died, but the sixth row of nimblies veered suddenly and flew right toward the Cave entrance.

Felsic pedaled even harder as Valko blasted the first three arrivals in quick succession.

In a single, fluid movement, the Akash flung off his beaded robe and cast it toward the entrance, trying to catch the invading insects, or at least knock them down. The robe flew out the door, and the nimblies backed out of the Cave, spinning off course. With a satisfied snort, the Akash leapt onto the Rock, landing at the peak of the perfectly rounded surface, in the middle of the floating white Net, pressing it down with his longstick and his feet so it made contact with the Rock's smooth surface.

There was a blinding flash.

The light no longer streamed the cave mouth, and the loud hum stopped abruptly. There was only a weird ringing sound as the metal tube Valko had been holding fell to the stone floor of the porch above them. Peratha and Trillella peeked up at the Cave mouth from between the sweaty pillars of Heffala's legs, then quickly retreated as some huge flying thing fluttered to the ground.

"The Akash's robe!" Peratha whispered. She had helped Salistar with that elaborate beadwork he'd insisted on.

Peratha dared to stick her head out again. The closest nimblies were diving and swirling out of control. She winced as one ran full speed into the outer wall of the Cave and fell to the ground, twitching. The last few rows staggered away in ragged spirals, then regrouped over the river and resumed their migration to the Great Hall.

Peratha grabbed Trillella's shoulder and they struggled free from Heffala's heaving side. Squinting up at the wide, dark, silent hole at the top of the steep rock stairs, Peratha called, "Felsic?"

"Popa?" Trillella peeped.

Suddenly, Heffala snatched the little girl up by the waist with her trunk and placed her firmly on her broad back. Then she put her trunk around Peratha's slumped shoulders and gently urged her ahead. Together, they climbed the stairs to the Holy Cave that had been forbidden to them. Peratha wasn't sure if a ganeesh could override an Akashic order, but it didn't matter. There was no one in the Cave. No Akash, no Felsic or Valko, no Salistar or Baput. There was just the Holy Rock, draped with the soft, white Net, the power crank Felsic had pedaled, the tube Valko had held, lying on the floor, and the food boxes Salistar had been unpacking.

"Where are they?" squeaked a befuddled Trillella.

"I don't know, Sweetie," Peratha replied with little comfort.

"What do we do now, Momama?"

Peratha looked at the stash of food at the back of the Cave. Enough for five people, for the three-day Season. "We stay here," she replied, brightening. "Look! There's gup cake, just for us!"

The Passage

The pressure passed into Baput like a wave, but it did not pass through him. It stayed, incomprehensible and unbearable. He couldn't breathe, and his head felt like it was in a pomegranate-seed press. He felt the Akashic Plane tighten to a line and stretch away from him. He could feel his friends, Bazu and Pindrad, and his betrothed, Tamaya, moving farther and farther away, and then, with a gut-wrenching snap, they were gone. For the first time in his life, Baput could not feel his people, or any of the animals and birds of home. He couldn't feel the village at all. He could only feel his parents, grandfather, Uncle Felsic, and Shastina.

The Akash let out a howl like a stuck bumbly. "I've lost something," he muttered over and over. "I've lost something."

"Akash?" Valko croaked groggily.

Shastina let out a short, whiny howl.

Suddenly Uncle Felsic was screaming, "Peratha! Trillella!"

Baput opened his eyes. Cold blue light stabbed his head. His family lay sprawled on the ground in awkward positions. Everyone who had been inside the Holy Cave. But where were Peratha and little Trillella? Shastina, their dog, was here, but where was Heffala?

They were no longer inside the Cave, but outside on a bare spot of flat, rocky ground. There was no cave anywhere. Just a steep cliff above them, draped in dense green vines. Below them, on the other side of the wide, flat area, was a steep bank that dropped to a dry riverbed. *What happened to the river?* Baput wondered, and as his eyes focused he could see water glinting behind a clump of willows on the other side of a wide gravel expanse. The familiar river was so low! His eyes scanned to the left, upriver, where the stream bent northward and the water got closer, just like at home. The upriver distance was concealed by the mists, as usual.

"Baput! Baput! Come to me, Boy! I've lost something! I've lost everything!" the Akash continued to rant.

Baput led the Akash away from the others as they staggered to their feet. Shastina followed them faithfully. "Did you feel it, G-Pa?" He used the familial address, as if they were safe in their private home. "It broke! I can't feel anyone except those who are with us. What happened, G-Pa?"

"I don't know," G-Pa whined. "Come, meditate with me."

Baput looked back at the others. His parents were trying to console Felsic over the apparent disappearance of his wife and daughter. Popa looked over and nodded to Baput.

Steadying his G-Pa, Baput noticed the Akash had lost his robe somewhere. He wore only a simple grass tunic over woven drawstring pants like the rest of them. He looked smaller, somehow.

They walked upriver toward that bend where they could see the water glinting in the hazy distance. The others staggered after them without speaking.

The river veered toward the closer bank. Sunlight flashed off the tepid flow topped with green algae as it slugged its way reluctantly downriver. They found a clear spot and sat down on the bank. G-Pa reached out and took Baput's hand. They sat cross-legged, silently staring at the river and feeling the ever-changing frequencies of light and sound and the currents in the air. They inhaled long breaths that filled their chests and bellies, held for a few seconds, and then breathed all the way out through their noses, squeezing their chests and bellies tight.

Baput concentrated hard, prepared to ascend to the familiar Akashic Plane, as G-Pa had taught him. The Plane wasn't a real, physical place. You couldn't really go there, or see it in the sky. It was a place of the mind where a river of thought flowed constantly, always bringing wisdom if you just watched and waited in deep meditation. The Plane never failed to provide exactly what was needed, just at the right time, to one patient enough to wait and wise enough to recognize it.

By the ancient method he had been taught, Baput stilled his soul and his mind. He let his worries fall away, all his thoughts; even his body seemed to drop like a shed skin as his sprit rose into the sky to the place where the Constant Comfort flowed.

But this time it was different. He found himself on a sterile-looking plane that flashed with sparks of blue light. He wasn't connected to it. It hummed in a way that irritated him. He couldn't concentrate. He thought he heard voices, but he couldn't understand what they said. It didn't feel like the Plane at all. But it was energy, and it had knowledge that they desperately needed. He pulled out of G-Pa's cold hand and rose, walking to the left, up the river, Shastina at his heels. G-Pa rose worriedly and waved his hands at the others. They scurried over to him, exchanging muddled glances.

"He goes upriver?" Valko questioned.

"Into the mists?" Salistar whispered fearfully, moving closer to Valko.

The Akash said nothing but followed his apprentice. They all trudged upriver with their heads down, except for occasional, habitual scans of the sky, up and to the left.

A willow tree with a trunk the size of a grandfather kip tree grew almost horizontally along the riverbank. It had been tied down as a supple child and trained to lie flat for about six feet before rising in a graceful "S" curve. A thick, raggedy rope still restrained its constant efforts to be straight.

And on that sideways tree trunk sat the strangest creature Baput had ever seen.

It was a kid, about his age, with skin the color of very dry grass, no color at all, it seemed to Baput. His hair was a shinier yellow, like morning sunlight, and it flopped over where his left eye should be. His right eye was an astounding blue. Baput had never seen anyone who didn't have green skin, black or lavender hair, and deep brown eyes like his.

The creature looked up at them, straight into Baput's eyes. Baput felt sudden, inexplicable relief.

"Hello!" the strange boy said. Baput understood the intent as a greeting, but he had never heard the word before.

"Ha-low...?" he repeated hesitantly.

The light-colored boy looked past Baput to his family. Then he brushed his hair back with his left hand, revealing a second amazing blue eye. Baput could see that something was puzzling him.

"Are you here for the job?" the strange boy asked.

"The job." Baput again repeated the sounds. Why were this boy's words so strange? Baput had never heard any of these words before.

"Yeah, the pomegranate job." The boy enunciated the strange words slowly and carefully.

"Pom-o-gran-it!" Baput repeated. He brightened as a picture of a kip popped into his mind. "Pomegranate!" he repeated loudly, perfectly.

"Kip!" He turned around shouting, "Momama, Popa! Kip! Pom-o-gran-it!"

They all repeated it back, even G-Pa: "Pom-o-gran-it."

"Yes!" whooped the pale boy, catching their enthusiasm.

"Yes!" mimicked Baput.

They followed their beige host up a narrow foot trail along the river, occasionally glancing up at the sky. Baput walked by G-Pa's side, trying to hear what he was mumbling. He mostly seemed to be saying, "It's gone! It's gone! I can't get it back!" over and over.

Had G-Pa completely lost his connection with the Plane? Baput couldn't imagine that. He still felt the Plane, far above him, but that alien surface lay between him and it. It was interfering, and it was getting stronger. It bombarded his third eye with a staggering onslaught of images. New knowledge, all downloaded in an unsorted jumble with no reference, no handle to even begin to sort it out. He focused his eyes on the back of the tawny head of the boy they followed into the unknown. He couldn't read the strange boy's mind, but he could feel his world, his feelings, and his knowledge. And when he said a word, Baput could find the picture in his head. Baput found this disconcerting, but somehow reassuring.

2. The Look'N Up

Jerry led the green aliens who had just appeared out of nowhere, apparently in search of work, straight to the farmhouse where his parents waited desperately for help with the harvest. On the way, he tried to empathize. It was the Look'N Up Way to try to imagine what the other person was feeling. "Walk in their shoes," his parents always said. He looked down at the green people's patchwork sandals of dark red leather, or was that pomegranate skin? Well, he couldn't imagine where they came from, not yet. Probably not Earth, based on their color, but he hadn't seen a spaceship. He found he couldn't imagine being green without knowing where they came from, but he could imagine what it would be like to be in a strange land and not understand the language.

That green kid was bigger than him but he seemed to be about the same age. He beckoned to the boy with the avocado skin to walk with him. The kid gave him a look that made him feel uncomfortably like a boss, then he joined him at the front of the line.

Jerry pointed to things and named them, having the burly green kid repeat each word. He started by pointing to himself with his thumb. "Jerry." Before the alien kid could answer, he pointed to the awesome dog at his side, a German shepherd in two tones of lavender. "Dog," he said. "Tree. Rock. Hill. Sky. Sun. River. Bird."

"Zebkin!" the lighter-green woman cried with wary delight, pointing as a deer sprang from willows by the river.

"Deer." Jerry translated patiently.

Around a bend in the river, the valley opened up to a wide, green expanse with a cluster of wooden buildings. Behind those, row upon row of pomegranate trees gleamed red with fruit, even from this distance. The huge dark green guy with the lavish beard stared at the faraway trees for a long time.

"Here's the ranch." Jerry stopped at the vista. Brushing his hair away from his left eye again, he cocked his head, looked up and to the left and pointed that way, his left arm and forefinger fully extended.

The green people all jerked their heads in that direction and cringed. Except for the kid. His dark eyes grew wide as they fixed on an invisible point in the blank gray sky, as if he saw something wonderful there.

"Welcome to the Look'N Up Pomegranate Ranch," Jerry declared formally, knowing they wouldn't recognize his ritual salutation no matter where they were from.

They scanned the sky more frequently when they reached the open grass. Suddenly, the beardless guy with the olive skin let out a bloodcurdling whoop. They all ducked and covered their heads.

Jerry looked up. A jetliner was passing by, high in the overcast sky. *What?* Jerry wondered. *They've never seen aircraft before? But they're aliens! How did they get here?*

The green kid was on the ground, huddled under his own arms. Jerry coaxed him to his feet and forced him to look. He was shivering. "Airplane," Jerry pronounced slowly.

Baput's face brightened with recognition. "Plane?" He looked at Jerry hopefully, then back up at the airplane.

The others were slowly emerging to look at the airplane with wonder and alarm.

Jerry tried to explain. "People ride inside of it. They go places, far away, really fast. Don't you have airplanes where you're from?"

Those words flew as high over Baput's head as the airplane had. But the pale boy didn't seem to be afraid of the flying monster. In fact, as he spoke, it grew smaller and smaller, as if he were talking it out of existence. Now it was just a shiny speck, barely visible in the foggy eastern sky.

Baput shuddered and looked at each of his family members in turn. "The mists," they whispered in their language, shivering.

Felsic and Valko flanked the Akash, supporting him by the elbows, along a slender trail through the grass. As they passed a tiny square building made of stone, G-Pa struggled away from them, as if drawn to it.

Valko clamped his large hand over G-Pa's stick-like arm. "Come on, Old Man!" he roared in his native tongue from behind the shiny black beard that covered most of his face, neck, and massive chest. Unlike his naked-faced little brother, Felsic, Valko never scraped his face with a bumbly horn to remove the thick black hair that sprang so eagerly from his proud chin.

He looked at the sky again. Nearly dragging the struggling old man, he and Felsic caught up with the rest as the ground turned from soft grass to small, angular pebbles that poked the soles of their pomegranate-leather shoes annoyingly.

Jerry beckoned them toward a rustic but homey structure where a middle-aged couple in rumpled flannel shirts and cargo jeans stood crookedly in the doorway. The man straightened as they approached. His right hand moved to his hip and rested there.

"Come and meet my parents," Jerry invited. "They own this place."

By this time, Baput had learned enough English to describe this immediate world. He understood "parents," but couldn't translate "own," not only because it didn't come with a picture, but because he didn't know the concept. They filed up the stairs, Baput behind Jerry, with Shastina at his heels, the rest dragging behind.

Shastina's hackles rose at a roar of barks that came from inside the house. A male dog as big as her burst through the front screen door. His hair was the same odd yellowish color as Jerry's. His ears flopped down and he had a square snout, unlike Shastina's pointy ears and fine, needle-like snout. Shastina roared back, rushing forward until the dogs were nose to nose, tails straight up, vibrating with tension. Once the right odors were exchanged, the tails broke into enthusiastic wags. Roars simmered down to whimpers, and they scampered off the porch together to chase each other in circles on the gravel driveway.

Jerry laughed. "That's Brodey. Mom says his bark is worse than his bite. Come on in." They followed Jerry's parents into the house.

"Dad! Mom! These people are here for the job."

"Did they apply?" snapped Jerry's dad.

"We still haven't got any applications," said Jerry's mom.

Baput, sensing something was going wrong, mustered all his new English and sputtered, "We know pom-o-gran-its."

"Pom-o-gran-its!" the strange family repeated, perfectly and in unison. The big, dark, hairy guy came forward and unleashed a tirade in his native tongue, gesticulating wildly in the direction of the orchards.

Jerry's dad, who came to about mid-beard on the giant, took a step back. His right hand twitched again toward his empty hip, then dropped. "What's that?" he demanded, hackles raised.

Baput stepped up boldly. "The trees are cut, um, pruned, it is wrong!" He stretched his arms apart vertically. "They have only one stalk." He spread his arms horizontally. "They should be like, um, a bush, with many stalks." He held up seven thick, green fingers. "You cut them wrong!"

"Huh," Jerry's dad considered. Arms folded in front of him, his gray eyes looked up at Valko, clouded by defensiveness, anger, fear. "We prune just like the Ag Extension says to."

"Are you Indian?" asked Jerry's mom.

"Yes," Baput mimicked the word he didn't understand. "Indian."

"India Indian?" Jerry's dad asked.

"Yes. India Indian," Baput echoed, wondering why the word was repeated.

"That's how they prune them in India!" Jerry's mom remarked. "And they've been growing them a lot longer than we have."

Jerry's dad unfolded his arms. "India, huh?" he asked, looking sideways at the green-skinned group.

"Yes," Baput said automatically.

"You got papers?" the light-skinned man asked suddenly, with more than a hint of hostility.

In his mind, Baput saw a stack of thin sheets, like the ancient books in the Holy Cave, but with no binding. But he had no idea what it meant. "Papers?"

Jerry's dad rolled his eyes and shook his head. He turned his back on everyone and ran his hand through his thinning hair, browner and crinklier than Jerry's. He mumbled to himself, or to someone Baput couldn't see, for what seemed like a very long time. Finally, he turned and faced the anxious group, who were holding their breath.

"OK." Exhales all around, starting with Jerry's mom. The new boss went on. "Cash and room and board. Well, room anyway. Your whole family will work, yes?"

"Yes," Baput said again, almost understanding.

"What about Grandpa, here?"

"G-Pa is our Akash," Baput said plainly, as if it explained everything.

There was an awkward pause, felt by everyone, no matter what color they were.

Eventually Jerry's dad repeated, "Akash. Whatever. OK, so I get what, two men and one boy? And your mom, does she work on the pomegranates?"

"Momama takes care of us," Baput replied in rapidly improving English. "And, of course, most of all, she takes care of the Akash. She is Tether." He swelled with a sort of pride that he wasn't used to feeling, then suddenly felt like he'd betrayed her. "She also makes, um juice and oil from the pomegranate seeds." He crossed the room to where Felsic stood. "And Uncle Felsic, he makes the pomegranate wine. But he also helps with the harvest. We can tend the trees all year, if you want us."

Everyone marveled at Baput's rapidly increasing proficiency in English. Though halting at times, he spoke eloquently, and used all the right words. Baput marveled most of all. He had found a stream of information that seemed almost limitless, but not as infinite as the Plane. The signal was very clear to him now, like it was coming from somewhere much closer than the Plane that the Akash had taught him to feel and interpret. This stream of information was much easier for him to access, almost too easy. It came rushing into his head uninvited. It terrified him, but he knew he had to use it to protect his family.

Jerry's dad continued with his proposal: "I'll give you $400 each per forty-hour week. You can stay in the quarters. Three bedrooms, indoor plumbing and a kitchen so Mom there can make your weird Indian food."

"Elmer!" Jerry's mom barked.

Elmer lowered his head, just a bit. "Sorry," he apologized to the floor. Then he looked around, his eyes tight. He gulped and ran his hand through his hair again. "But I assume that's what you want. She cooks your food, like you're used to. You can raid our pantry for tonight. My wife, Frannie here, she'll show you around, Ms… Um, hey, I didn't even get your names. I'm Elmer."

Baput stood between his family and this strangely colored man. Kind of a pinky beige skin with that same pale hair and light eyes as his son and his wife and apparent tether, but their colors were not as bright and astounding as Jerry's. The parents had tawny, light brown hair and eyes of light gray-blue, like the sky in this colorless place.

"I am Baput," Baput said haltingly, but clearly and correctly. "This is my popa, Valko, and my Uncle Felsic, my popa's brother. And this is my momama, Salistar, and my G-Pa, who is Akash."

"Pleased to meet you," Elmer responded, extending his hand slowly. Valko grasped it firmly. Elmer stared up into those piercing dark eyes. He wanted to squeeze a warning, something to assert himself as the boss, but his hand felt like a baby bird inside the monstrous green paw, which released its grip only when Valko was done communicating his own wordless message.

Elmer moved on to shake Salistar's hand, but when he looked at her, she seemed to almost disintegrate with trembling, and there was a low growl coming out from under the big man's beard.

OK, cultural differences, he reminded himself, and quickly backed off. "I'm Elmer Musik. This is my wife, Francine–"

The woman and boy giggled.

"Call me Fran," Francine offered, to more giggles. She looked at Jerry. He just shrugged.

"You've met our son, Jerry," she said, beaming a sincere smile at the motley green family in their shoddy tunics of woven grass. "Welcome to the Look'N Up Pomegranate Ranch. Sign here. What's the date, Hon?"

"**September 27, 2014**," Jerry reported.

Valko, Felsic, and Baput made strange marks on the paper where Elmer pointed, glancing curiously at the tip of the pen before and after.

Francine led Salistar toward the pantry. "Come on, let's get you some food." Salistar stared at the canned goods blankly, but she eagerly selected some red potatoes and red onions, black beans, and wild rice.

Francine grabbed a bottle of olive oil and put it in the box. "For cooking," she explained. "I don't have pomegranate oil, but I can't wait to try yours. There are pots, pans, and dishes out in the quarters."

Fran opened the refrigerator. Salistar stood with her mouth hanging open in the cool, oddly lit air. Fran opened a drawer and pulled out fresh vegetables in soft, clear sacks: reddish-green lettuce, beets, tomatoes and summer squash. Salistar accepted the miraculous gifts without hesitation, but she asked Fran something in her native tongue.

"She says they are not in season," Baput translated from the doorway.

Fran shifted her gaze to him, realizing the boy understood English better than his elders, which was not unusual in the migrant families she'd worked with. "You don't eat meat, do you?" she asked, calling on what she knew about "India Indians."

A horrible image appeared in Baput's mind. Blood, hunks of flesh cut from a recently killed animal. It was like what the bumblies ate! Squirting blood everywhere, chunks of your loved one, your relative, every three years people you loved devoured, never knowing which cycle it would be you. The vision so horrified him that he cried, "No!" much too loudly. He didn't fully recover until everyone had stopped staring at him.

"OK, vegetables it is," Fran said soothingly.

On their way back from of the kitchen, they passed a box of freshly picked, early-ripe pomegranates. Salistar looked at them longingly in a way that touched Fran's heart.

"You want some?" Fran asked Salistar gently.

"Yes!" Salistar beamed, nodding her whole upper half.

"Hell, take 'em all if you'll use them." Elmer snapped from his recliner. "We'll be up to our ears in 'em soon enough!"

Fran nodded at the anxious basil-colored face with the innocent dark eyes etched with worry. Then she turned to the group in the living room. "Jerry! Get a bunch of blankets. Have someone help you," she ordered, indicating Felsic.

Valko started to walk past her toward the door. Fran handed him a heavy box of potatoes, beans, and rice while she rambled on to Salistar. "You got everything you need for tonight? Here are some towels to wash up with. There's a shower in there. We'll go to the store tomorrow."

Jerry emerged from the back of the house, barely visible behind a stack of blankets, followed closely by a similarly burdened Felsic. "Come on, uh, Baput, is it?" Jerry asked as they walked through the door Fran held open.

"Yes," Baput replied, smiling brightly and hoisting the full box of pomegranates. "Baput. And Jer-ree. Yes?"

"Yes, Jer-ree." Jerry replied as they walked down the porch steps.

Flushing

Fran's mind was racing as she entered the workers' quarters with pillows and toilet paper. *Green people? Maybe they all dyed themselves green, some kind of religious thing. Or maybe it's genetic? They're a family, maybe from an isolated population with a rare gene? But where on Earth…? Are they even from this world?*

Valko placed his box on the sill of a serving window that joined the kitchen to the dining area. Then he turned and sat heavily in the living room recliner, just like a human from Earth would do, it seemed to Fran.

The old man, the Akash, found a hard chair in a corner of the room where he rocked back and forth muttering. Their beautiful dog, like a German shepherd in blended tones of lavender, lay across his feet on her stomach, her dark eyes staring straight up from the top of her head. *And a purple dog. Is she dyed, too?* Fran wondered further.

"I need to show you the stove." Fran ushered Salistar into the kitchen and beckoned to Baput.

Baput paused, hand on the doorway, and turned his brown eyes to his popa, as if for permission.

Valko met Baput's gaze, shrugged and pointed to the kitchen.

Baput oozed into the room sticking to the wall like he was entering a dragon's lair.

As Francine had promised, the kitchen was well-stocked with pots, pans, plates, and all kinds of cooking tools. Salistar caressed the heavy cast-iron skillet and Dutch oven; familiar, but much more smooth and fine than her clay cookware. The thinner, lighter, shinier pots and pans mystified her. Wouldn't they melt in the cooking fire?

Fran pointed to the plastic handle of a stainless-steel saucepot Salistar held. "Not in the oven, OK?" she pointed to the oven and shook her head. The she pointed to some rectangular stainless-steel baking pans. "OK in the oven," she instructed, with a nod and thumbs-up.

"OK, oven," Salistar repeated the words.

Baput translated as Francine demonstrated the gas cookstove. "Always turn it off when you are done. Understand?" she said earnestly, crowding Salistar a little, turning the burner out slowly, pointing to the flame, and the dial. Baput repeated the phrase in their language. Salistar nodded, eyes fixed on the quick blue flame.

Fran opened the refrigerator. "It's not cold yet, but the power is on now. It's working, hear it?" Fran took the vegetables from the box and laid them in the crisper drawer, making sure Salistar could see. "They'll stay good, even though they are out of season," she assured the silent faces colored even more bizarrely by the harsh light. *Wherever they're from, I guess they don't have refrigeration yet.* She closed the door. The box hummed happily as if digesting its recent meal.

"Now, the bathroom." Grabbing a pack of toilet paper, she led Salistar and Baput down a narrow hallway, still talking, hoping they would understand. "I can't leave this stuff in an empty house or the mice eat it. If you see any mice around, let me know, and we'll get some traps. They'll go away now that you're here, anyway, especially with your beautiful dog."

She flipped a tiny lever on the wall, and an orb on the ceiling glowed bright white light with no flame, just like the Rock in the Holy Cave! Baput got between his mother and the mysterious light and put his arms around her.

Fran's smile wrinkled when she saw how they stared at the light. "It's OK. Light." She said the word, loud and clear.

Salistar looked over Baput's head and drew in a breath at the sight of the gleaming white fixtures. She gently pushed him to the side. Baput let her pass him, but he stuck close behind her.

Fran turned a knob at the sink. Salistar gasped in amazement. A stream of clean water came out, and it kept coming! *So much water! So easy!*

Fran moved to the shower and turned the faucet below it. "See? Just wait, it gets hot. You can take a bath—or," she flipped a lever, "a shower."

Salistar squeaked with surprise as the water cascaded from the shower nozzle. She slowly reached in, put her hand under it, and smiled.

"Feels good, huh?" Francine asked, smiling back.

Baput stared at the toilet. Sensing his unspoken question, Fran stood next to him before the porcelain throne. "See? You, ah, do your business," she offered, vaguely gesturing to where Baput's fly would be, seeing none in his drawstring pants. "Or you sit on it. Take your pants down."

Baput unabashedly dropped his coarsely woven drawers and sat on the toilet. He flinched, startled, as a tinkling sound emerged from beneath him.

"Good boy!" Fran exclaimed, flashing back to training Jerry. But this kid was as old as Jerry! He must have used only an outhouse before. "Use this if you need to, for, um," she gestured at the toilet paper and patted her own behind.

"*Boo!*" exclaimed Baput, laughing. "Momama!" he addressed Salistar, "It is a *boor.*"

"Boor," Fran repeated the foreign word.

"Yes, boor," Baput confirmed. "But I not boo now."

"OK. But when you do, use this paper," Fran recommended. She mounted the roll, then tore a few squares off, pretending to wipe herself. "Then put it in the boor with the um, boo. We call it a toilet, and um, poo." She looked at Salistar. "You might like to use it for, um, no boo, too. Yellow water. We call that pee."

"Get up, pull up your pants." She averted her eyes while Baput obeyed. "Now," she was excited to show the next part. "See this handle? Push it down."

Baput did. He and Salistar both jumped as the water rushed in noisily. Baput stared, tilting his head to the right as the water spiraled counterclockwise, made its own hole, and disappeared. *Where did it go? Is this the way home?* He wondered. The brave, brilliant young man who had just negotiated a livelihood for his family while learning English now looked like a lost little boy.

Fran stepped back and whispered to Salistar, "Be sure to tell the men to put the seat down for you. They often forget."

Salistar looked unbelievingly at Fran. *Tell the men...?*

"I will tell them," offered Baput.

Fran sensed tension. Suddenly, she grabbed the shy little woman and hugged her tightly.

Baput looked anxiously toward the living room as his momama melted in silent tears in the stranger's arms. Then Fran walked briskly out, wiping her eyes. Salistar returned to the kitchen to start chopping potatoes and onions for dinner and putting beans on to soak.

As soon as Fran left, the green family dove into the pomegranates like the refugees they were. Munching on the familiar seeds comforted the men while they sat around the table, and Salistar nibbled on a whole pomegranate as she cooked. For the first time since their world had disappeared and been replaced with this strange new one, they were left alone to have a conversation in their own language.

"Baput," Valko asked gently, "do you understand what they say? I can't understand them. I don't know their words."

Baput tried to explain. "When they say words, I see pictures. If I can make a picture, I learn the word. But some words don't come with pictures, and some have pictures I don't understand. Like, at the end, Jerry's popa said 'papers' and 'cash.' I see pictures, but I don't understand what they are. They look like sheets of parchment, and they, um, feel very important."

"Oh!" Momama suddenly shrieked from the kitchen.

Valko jumped from his seat and ran to her, daring to enter the forbidden room. "This potato!" she cried. "It is red on the outside, but no color on the inside! Completely blank!"

Valko grunted harshly. "Is that all, woman? We are in the worst mess of our lives, and she worries about potatoes!" He waved his hand impatiently without even looking at the offending root, then returned to the living room. Turning to Baput he asked, "So, we stay here?"

"Yes, Popa, we are to help with the kip harvest, the pom-o-gran-its."

"Pomegranates," Valko repeated.

"And we will have food and enough kips for oil?" Momama worried about potatoes from the serving window.

"I'll make sure, Momama," Baput reassured her, feeling a weight settle heavily on his shoulders. He glanced at G-Pa, still muttering in the corner, and took a deep breath. "We will help with harvest. Popa, me, and Uncle Felsic. I told them we know kips."

"There is no mill," Salistar reported. "We walked all along the river to here, and I did not see it."

"The mill is downriver. We walked upriver," Valko snapped.

"Why are the huts upriver?" Felsic wondered. "There are no huts upriver from the Holy Cave. Too close to the mists." His face fell. "Where is the press? I must make wine!"

Valko stared across the table at his brother until his silence drew Felsic's attention. "No drinking," he admonished in a deep tone that precluded argument.

Felsic's stubbly face perked up. "*Is* there any?"

"No," Valko answered sternly. "And good thing. Do not ask this man for any. He expects us to work!"

"I know!" whined Felsic. "I'll work hard. You know how hard I can work. But I could just use... because Peratha and Trillella!" he doubled over in his chair, sobbing silently.

Valko softened. "I know, Little Brother," he said, as gently as he could. "But do not dishonor them by using them as an excuse. They would want you to pull yourself together and do your best, so you can get home to them as soon as you can."

Felsic lifted a tear-stained face to Valko. "And just how am I supposed to do that?"

"Wait!" The Akash cried. He rose from his chair, eyes and voice suddenly clear. "Wait and watch. The Plane has put us, its feelers, into these strange surroundings to find something. Watch for it. Identify it. Obtain it. Then watch for your chance to go home." He sat back down.

"You mean 'our chance,' right, G-Pa?" Baput squeaked, resting his eyes on Shastina's soft orbs.

G-Pa was silent.

Valko pushed his hawk nose right into the old man's space and asked the unspoken question in the back of all their minds: "Will the bumblies come tonight?"

The Akash came back with a swift, definitive answer, like the Akash of, well, this morning. "No. There are none. No bumblies! No nimblies!"

They all repeated the refrain from the Tale of Yanzoo: "No more nimblies! No more bumblies! Not ever! No more!" The chant, usually joyful, hung dully in the air.

Baput peered into the eyes of his mentor. "G-Pa, are you sure?"

The dark beads under the faded lavender eyebrows dashed away from Baput's. Bright and focused, they shifted back and forth, dodging as he spoke. "There can't be. None came through. I know. I remember. I saw. I saw, the pain, the pressure, and it was gone! It's still gone! I can't feel it, Baput!" The Akash collapsed in the arms of his apprentice, mumbling "No more nimblies! No more bumblies!" over and over. Then he broke into a delirious smile and whispered, "I am Yanzoo!"

Shastina let out a long groan.

Baput turned a meaningful stare at Valko.

Salistar rushed from the kitchen to embrace her popa's limp form.

Valko crossed to the window and peered into the gathering darkness. He ran his broad finger down the glass, mystified by the clear, flat, solid. He wondered if it would keep out the six-inch diameter bumbly bats with their 24-inch wingspans. Black as the darkest night, those man-eating monsters had red eyes like the dying coals of dawn, and three-inch long horns on the ends of their hideous, sniffing snouts. Slicing with its razor sharp, rhino-like horn and biting with its long canines and incisors, a single bumbly could cut a grown man to shreds in about three minutes of extreme agony. Fortunately, they usually fed in packs.

"Jerry and his parents didn't say anything about it, like 'watch out, the nimblies and bumblies are out,'" offered Baput.

"Why would they say it?" Felsic figured. "Everybody knows what happens on First Pomegranate Day."

"We stay inside tonight," Valko ordered. "Woman! Are there boo pots?" Salistar giggled in the kitchen, drawing Valko's glare.

"Better, Popa! The boor is inside, like the Great Hall."

"Then there must be bumblies and nimblies," worried Felsic. "And we're supposed to work tomorrow?"

Valko turned his nose toward the back of the house and sniffed angrily. "I don't smell boors."

Baput replied, "I am to show you, come on."

The men headed into the bathroom, chattering loudly, Shastina wagging fully. "See how the water swirls around, and disappears?" Baput demonstrated to "oohs and aahs," but seeing the water disappear down the hole still sent chills down his spine. Then he explained about the seat, for Momama.

The quick dinner Salistar cooked for her exhausted family was getting cold by the time they ate, but they ate hungrily. When they were done, Salistar rose and started gathering the plates. She surprised them all with a wry smile. "What do I always say, family?"

They all recited in unison: "No matter what happens in life, there are always dishes to do."

"No matter what happens, indeed!" Valko rumbled. He didn't even consider helping her, nor did Baput or Felsic. Instead, they adjourned to the living room, where they stood in a ragged circle.

Valko looked sharply into Baput's face, grabbing his shoulder firmly. "Son, can you feel the Plane?" he asked, gently but gravely.

Baput's dark black eyebrows wrinkled. "I can," he replied, drawing a sigh of relief from the others, "but it's different. There is something weird about it, something... unnatural. I get flashes, pictures of information that I don't think come from the Plane. I hear their words being spoken in my head, and I don't understand. If it was the Plane, I would understand. The Plane is sending me the pictures, I think, helping me to learn these new words for everything."

"Can you access the Plane now, Son?" Valko demanded anxiously.

Baput sat cross-legged on the floor and closed his eyes. He placed his hands on his knees, palms up, and held his head high, his chin jutting out slightly. The room was silent except for Baput's deep, slow, even breathing and the distracting hum of the refrigerator. Then suddenly, his eyes jerked open in terror.

"They are beating each other with sticks like they're fighting bumblies! But it is people hitting other people with sticks! Some are wearing helmets and bearing shields, like they were expecting to beat and be beaten with sticks! What am I seeing?"

"I don't know, Son." Valko replied, hating this new feeling of helplessness.

Baput's hand was drawn to a tiny button on the front of the television. He pushed it. In a moment, a strange blue light glowed, and then suddenly, terrifyingly, the set came alive with a graphic news report. A line of men stood on one side, wearing helmets and carrying shields. Most of them had that same light-colored skin as Jerry and his family. They faced a line of people whose skins were darker. Some were deep, dark brown like the fertile soil in the orchards. Some were lighter, like the dried clay. A few were as light as Jerry. There was every shade of brown, but no green.

The brown people didn't have helmets and armor like the light-skinned group they opposed. Even so, the lesser-armed people advanced, throwing something at the armored ones. The well-equipped Jerry-skinned ones responded, and, in seconds they were all beating each other with clubs and fists, just as Baput had described. Something like smoke billowed around the ones that ran away.

The lost green family stood before the television with their mouths hanging open, unable to believe the image, to comprehend the technology that brought it to them, or even to wonder how Baput had seen it before he pressed the button.

The Musiks

Jerry tried to go straight to his room without talking to his parents.

"Jerry!" Elmer yelled. "What the…?"

"Oh, hey, Dad," Jerry gulped.

"Where did they come from?" Elmer demanded.

"I don't know. I was at the Horizontal Tree, and they came up the trail. I didn't see a spaceship. I guess they hitched a ride and got let off at the bridge, except I didn't hear a car door, either."

"Did you ask them why they're *green?*"

"Of course not, Dad. That would be rude, wouldn't it?"

Elmer scoffed.

Jerry asked, "Why didn't *you* ask them?"

Elmer found his words. "I've hired undocumenteds before. I'm not proud of it, but it's sure hard to get good help. But green? Bright green. Who the…? Where…? Well, people are gonna notice, is all I'm saying."

"Maybe nobody will say anything. Maybe they're like us. Nobody wants to be rude."

"Son," Elmer said slowly, "there are plenty of people in town who don't have any problem being rude. Especially to someone who's different! If we let 'em stay, and I ain't saying we will, they're gonna have to stay right here on the ranch all season, all the time, for their own good. And after the picking, they're gone!"

"But Elmer, they said they'd work year-round. Isn't that what we always wanted?" Fran pleaded.

Elmer shook his head violently. "No. Not these ones. I don't trust them, and it ain't cuz they're green. They seem kind of, um, furtive, you know? Like they're running from something. Why? Who's after them? And why are they green?"

"They've gotta be aliens," Jerry insisted. "I mean alien aliens, not from this planet."

"But green aliens are supposed to be little!" Elmer countered. "That guy reminds me of that old avocado-colored refrigerator we had in here when I was a kid."

"He's like the Hulk," Jerry brought a more up-to-date perspective.

"But better looking," Fran quipped with a grin.

"Oh, so you *like* the big guy," Elmer looked sideways at his wife.

"Maybe it's just genetic, like our thing, Dad," Jerry mused.

"Maybe so. But they all have it. Only half of us are messed up." Elmer shrugged.

Jerry was ready with an answer, as usual. "Yeah, if they were from here, their weird genes would be diluted by normal, dominant genes. They wouldn't all have it. But if they're from another planet, and this is their first encounter with us—"

"Cut the bullshit," Elmer snarled, raising his hands. "You didn't see a spaceship. Now, I just hired these aliens, and put them up in my workers' quarters, and I have no idea who they are or where they're from. What planet even! And I ain't sure that's a good idea."

"Oh, Elmer!" Fran cried, "Don't you see? They're lost and homeless, with a kid and a sick old man. They said they'd work. We need help. They need work, and a place to stay. Honey, please. Just give them a chance!"

Two pairs of hurt puppy eyes pleaded for the homeless alien strangers who had entered their lives just a couple hours ago.

Elmer growled, more like a kitten than a lion. "OK, we'll try 'em. They can hide out here for harvest, unless they don't work, or they make trouble, or we find out something bad about them, or the Men in Black show up. Then they're gone!"

"What about school?" Fran worried. "That boy is big, but look at his popa! He seems to me to be around Jerry's age. We don't know what their schooling is like, but he should be..."

"Yeah," Elmer guffawed... "The bright green kid with no papers shows up at school with my kid and says he's staying here. No, thanks!"

"I'll teach him, Mom," Jerry offered. "He's really smart. I already taught him English on the way here from the river."

"Good job, Son," Elmer replied, proud but skeptical. "That's a kind offer. Just don't let your tutoring him interfere with your work, or his. And keep an eye on them. See if you can find out their story. But be careful. If they say anything weird or dangerous, you gotta tell me right away. Hear me?"

"I was going to take Salistar shopping tomorrow," Fran blurted.

"No, Fran! We can't let anyone see them," Elmer put his foot down. "I'll give the kid time in the morning to help you talk to her, after I get the men started. Bring the laptop over and show them some pictures or something."

"The health food store has a good website," Fran brightened. "She can pick out what she wants, and I can run in and get it for her."

The TV Plane

The horrid pictures of the riot disappeared from the screen, and a man and woman appeared side by side behind a long table. They looked right at the lost green family and spoke their strange words calmly and incessantly. Baput pushed the button again, and the little people simply disappeared. Baput could feel the difference as the signal was cut, but there were more out there. More vibrations. More information. A second, artificial, plane between him and the real Plane!

With the TV off, he could still feel and see images, stories, facts, fiction, music, more violence and things he had never seen or dreamed of before and couldn't comprehend, like a wagon with no ganeesh to pull it, speeding so fast you couldn't quite see it, like the nimblies when they first come swarming to the Great Hall on First Pomegranate Day. All the images had people in them. So many people! More than he had ever seen. Many times the number of his whole village. Some had different-colored hair and skin than Jerry and his parents, but no one had green skin.

He sat back down on the floor and took several Akashic breaths to calm himself and sort out the signals he was receiving. Where was that feed he had tapped into before, with the words and their meanings? He couldn't find it anymore, so he began to teach his family the English he had already picked up, saying the English word and their word over and over.

Felsic groaned. "Why do they have to use these weird words? Why can't they just use regular words, like us?"

Baput had been thinking about this. "They have never seen us before. They learned to talk without us, so they had to make up their own words for things. Our words are just as strange to them," he explained.

By the time they went to bed, they all knew all the words Baput knew, except the ones that none of them understood, like "country" and "owner" as well as "cash" and "papers."

At last, they all went into the largest of the three bedrooms, where they would all sleep together until the Season was over. Jerry had made up the bunks, awkwardly communicating with Felsic about the sleeping arrangements. There were four bunk beds, each with two adult-sized sleeping surfaces; one at about knee level and the other at eye level, padded with thin mattresses and topped with sheets and blankets.

Felsic crawled onto the lower bunk of the unit to the left of the door, wrapped the blankets around himself and turned his face to the wall.

Two bunk beds had been pushed together to form a double bed for Valko and Salistar. Salistar burrowed under the blankets of the lower bunk behind Valko's protective bulk. The upper bunks provided a canopy, a bit of extra shelter from the bumblies.

The bunks to the right of the door were made up for Baput and the Akash. Baput climbed up into the top bunk, willing to brave the possible bat attack for the chance at such a novel adventure. People usually slept on mats stuffed with straw, either on the floor or on a low platform.

G-Pa stood staring at the lower bunk beneath Baput, then turned bewildered eyes up at him. Baput sighed, and climbed down beside G-Pa. He gently put his arm around the suddenly frail old man and indicated the mattress, pointed to the floor, then looked into those terrified eyes. Seeing G-Pa's terror sent Baput reeling as he realized, probably more than any of the others, just how lost they were, how powerless! With just a hint in the direction of G-Pa's eyes, Baput pulled the mattress onto the floor, tenderly covered the old man and climbed back into his roost on the upper bunk, where he could see out the high window.

G-Pa continued to mumble into the night. "It's gone...all gone... gone." Felsic began to snore softly. His parents were quiet, but Baput knew Popa was wide awake, listening for bumblies.

Baput lay flat on his back and closed his eyes, trying to meditate and reach the Plane. Strange, random images flowed through his mind. More violence. But now, instead of hitting each other with sticks, they simply pointed them at each other. Baput would hear a loud bang, and the person who the stick was pointed at simply fell over dead. He saw this many times. Sometimes one man shooting one other, sometimes many in neat rows facing and shooting at each other, or randomly struggling and shooting in all sorts of strange settings.

There was a slightly different vibration, where the warring figures didn't look real at all. They looked like the *rasta*, cartoon-like pictures of past heroes, war chiefs, and Akashes, drawn by Pindross, the artist, and his popa and G-Pa before him. These unreal images were engaging in even more violent activity that the more realistic ones.

Baput tried to rise above the chaos. He knew the real, Akashic Plane was there above it all. He willed himself to go higher, imagined he was light, so very light, floating up and out of the tide of disturbing images. When he looked back down, what he saw took his breath away. A boundless body of knowledge, information, art, music—and something frightening he had to look away from.

The current of conversation went on constantly. He didn't know enough words to keep up. Even with his limited English, he realized some conversations were not in English or his own tongue, but several other languages. *How can these people talk to each other when they all use different words? Why do they?* He tried to focus on a single conversation in English, but there were so many going on at once, and he was so tired.

Suddenly the live, violent images dropped from his mind. The cartoon images shut off a few minutes later. It was darker. He looked out the window. The lights at Jerry's house had been turned off. The images in his mind quieted, and now he could explore this second plane with its endless stream of human chatter and information. He tried to absorb as much knowledge as he could, like he had when he'd followed Jerry to his house. He focused his mind, like the Akash had taught him, filtering out the noise and mining the information.

He learned that the world he found himself in was called Earth. It had big patches of ground called continents and huge bodies of open water called oceans, not like rivers. More like huge ponds. Water farther than the eye could see. That seemed impossible; maybe it wasn't real, like those rasta images. Each continent had one or more countries on it, one of the words he hadn't understood before. He still didn't understand. Each country had a different "language," that was the English word for a set of words people used. He spent hours awake, just surfing along, learning as much as he could understand.

When he finally fell asleep, he dreamed of his betrothed, Tamaya, standing on the Rock in the Holy Cave with the Net billowing around her. *Standing in the very spot where we were, then we were not.* Even in meditation or dreams, his mind could not contain the thought.

Suddenly, G-Pa's mumbling was loud and clear. "The Queen was in the Chimney!" he snorted, then rolled over on his side and went silent.

Baput couldn't get back to sleep and was too tired to think anymore. He stared out the window as dawn turned the black sky into the dark purple of the pomegranates back home.

Sleepless Elmer

Fran was so excited about having possible aliens from another planet living in the workers' quarters, she had literally talked herself to sleep.

Elmer wished it had worked on him, too, but he was about as far from sleep as a man could be. He had long since given up closing his eyes. Whenever he did, he saw Valko's piercing black eyes above that hawk-like beak and raven beard, staring down on him. They were the eyes of a warrior. Elmer had no idea how he knew that, but surely, a warrior's eyes: brave and selfless, with a savagery easily triggered, and, once released, unstoppable. But in that same mystical way, Elmer could also tell that that savagery would only be unleashed in defense of the others.

And there was something else in that stare. Something that contradicted, no, completed, the warrior package. He dared close his eyes once more, invoking the image that was burned on his retinas. *The big guy's scared to death!* He was flooded with relief that quickly turned into more worry.

A trapped animal. A big one. With a family to protect. I have a family to protect, too. What if they have a disease? What if they're the first of a takeover? Shit! They're gonna set up their communications network under the quarters and contact the mother ship: "Yeah, these idiots set us up real good, come on down." I'd better disconnect the satellite out there.... Elmer drifted, not quite dreaming. *Even if the big guy's OK, that kid's got some kind of mental superpowers. And who knows what the old wizard can do? What am I thinking? Too much TV, I guess. But green aliens? So they're green, that don't mean they're homicidal, does it? Naw! It ain't the green. I'm not a racist. Am I? I always thought I wasn't. Dad taught me that real good. What would he do? He'd keep 'em. He'd hire 'em.*

A chuckle whispered from the side of his mouth when he thought about his grandfather. *Pop'd shoot 'em!* The smile faded. *No, he wouldn't. He'd let 'em stay. As long as they worked and didn't threaten this place, or this family. He'd have to take them. It's the Look 'N Up way, ever since Pop was a penniless, migrant Okie farm worker in the Depression. He was about the same age as that green kid when Mr. Richardson took them in. It wasn't charity, neither. They worked their tails off for him, but he kept them on, let them stay, and finally gave Pop the farm, free and clear.*

He was family by then, he had my dad on his lap, and we had a nice farm to grow up on. All because he looked up. That's what Dad called it. The cockeyed

Look 'N Up Way, up and to the left, like their crazy eyes. It means you pull your head out of wherever you like to tuck it and look around at the people around you. Feel them. Think about them. Consider them. How do those green people feel?

He rolled over roughly, not worrying about waking Fran, jealous of her bliss. He whispered, "What have you got us into, Babe?" He forced his eyes to close, turning his thoughts back to familiar terrain.

Old Pop always said this family owed the world a debt of gratitude. So now the payment's come due, eh? But is this payback for that one good man, that one good deed? Or is it going to be payback for all the others? The ones who beat Pop up and spat on him? The ones who made fun of him and my dad and my brother and now my sweet angel of a niece, because of their cocked-up eyes?

How about Patrick? He takes after our dad, not just on the outside. Literally won't hurt a fly. He'd give 'em free reign. Hmmm. Maybe he could take 'em! But he don't need workers. And what about my little niece? What if they went after Belinda? What would Patrick do? He don't even own a gun.

What would my crazy neighbor, Ian, do? He has just as much trouble getting help with his poms. He hires immigrants but treats 'em like dirt. Now, there's a racist! He'd shoot these weirdos on sight. No, he'd work 'em to death, then shoot 'em. I could send them over to him and let him take care of it.

He felt the ethereal burn of Fran's disapproval. He studied her face. Her eyelids were closed lightly over eyes that darted back and forth. Her lips turned up in a tiny, sweet smile. He knew she was dreaming of her new friends, imagining their wonderful world, where there were no guns, no evil wizards or mad warriors, no hating people because they're different. Nothing to fear from people who come out of nowhere, undocumented, completely unknown.

Savoring one last look at Fran's blissful face, he jerked the covers back and stepped across the room to shiver and gaze out at the silent workers' quarters. "Yeah," he whispered, "I'm fearing the unknown. You betcha."

First Work Day

The next morning, they ate more fried potatoes for breakfast, while Salistar mumbled apologies for the repetition.

"It's OK, Momama," Baput comforted her. "We'll get more food today."

G-Pa was worse this morning. He didn't touch his breakfast, he wouldn't look at anyone. He mumbled constantly, and inaudibly. Baput didn't have time to work with him.

As soon as they were done eating, Elmer called to them from outside. "Rise and shine, folks! Time to start picking poms!"

Baput exchanged a meaningful glance with his momama, who naturally shouldered her duty as Tether, and began spoon-feeding the Akash. The three workers rushed out to the porch, shoving each other in their hurry.

Elmer smiled at their eagerness to work. They looked ready, except for the flimsy shoes and the clothes made of... what, grass? He addressed his new crew. "Let's head over to the shop, where the truck is." Elmer gestured behind the quarters and strolled that way. Felsic, Valko, and Baput followed, habitually glancing at the sky.

The shop was a huge, gaping hulk of corrugated metal over steel beams. Big enough to store five trucks side by side, it contained an old two-ton dual-axle Ford farm truck, an even older Ford tractor covered with clutter and oily rags, a forklift, brush mower, lawn tractor, weed eater, four-wheeler, and a four-seater Jeep. A workbench ran along the back wall, with a vice, grinding wheel, and lathe mounted to it. Hand tools hung on pegs on the walls.

"Here's my shop," Elmer declared proudly. "Are any of you guys mechanically inclined?" The blank looks he got in response made him wonder if it was more than just the language barrier. It almost seemed like they had never seen any of this stuff before! He proceeded to the forklift with little hope. "Can any of you drive a forklift?"

Felsic walked tentatively over and put his finger on the engine behind the seat. "Fork. Lift."

"Guess not," muttered Elmer. "How about the truck?" He pointed to the old monster in the corner. On its door was a picture of a pomegranate with eyes. The left eye was much higher than the right, and the eyeball pointed up and to the left.

"Truck!" Felsic repeated, liking the sound of the word. "Truck!" He sprinted over to the driver's side of the cab and scrambled up. He fumbled with the door latch, and when he got it, the door opened outward and almost knocked him off the running board. Giggling, he climbed up in the seat behind the wheel.

"The keys are in her." Elmer instructed, "She should start right up, I had her going yesterday. Go ahead, give her a crank."

No response.

"Turn the key!" Elmer ordered, making the motion with his hand.

The truck let out a vicious cough and jumped forward two feet, almost swallowing Valko and noisily scattering a 55-gallon drum of scrap metal before choking itself to death. Valko lurched out of the way, and stood staring at the mess, a low rumble emanating from deep within him.

"Whoa!" Elmer yelled. "You gotta take it out of gear! Don't you know how to drive a stick? Come on down from there before you kill somebody!" Under his breath, he wondered: *Can't even drive? What am I gonna do with these guys?"*

He headed for the Jeep. Turning back to the shocked little group, he beckoned. "Come on, get in." He pointed to Felsic and patted the seat beside him, adding, "You, up front with me. You're gonna learn to drive a stick. You two in back. We're going for a tour of the orchard."

Felsic opened the passenger's side door, a little faster this time. Valko awkwardly climbed over the door into the rear seat of the open-topped Jeep, then grunted his way across the seat to the passenger side, where he crammed his legs behind Felsic's seat. Baput scrambled in, excited. Would it jump and howl, like the truck?

Elmer took them to the East Orchard, along the river. "These are the oldest trees, they ripen first. Let's check them."

Valko reached up as if to pick one, but he didn't touch it. He wrapped his giant hand around a good-sized pomegranate without contacting it at any point. He waved his nose back and forth across it, sniffing. "They are ripe. We should start picking today or tomorrow, if we can." His voice was certain, but his face was puzzled. He gazed into the hazy eastern sky for a long time.

On the way back toward the shop, Felsic observed, "The grass should be mowed." With Baput translating, he continued. "I saw mowing tools in the shed."

"Can you handle the mowers? I only have one walk-behind. And the weed eater, but there's too much ground to cover. That thing will wear you out, 'cuz the center of gravity is so far away, says my son."

"I saw two mowers," Valko corrected, through Baput.

"Well, yeah, there's a rider, but you have to drive it," Elmer said to silence, driving past the back of the shop to another orchard behind his house. "OK, here's the West Orchard. You're right, it could use a mow. I gotta get some work outta you guys. Come on, back to the shop." He grinned at Felsic. "You wanna drive?"

Felsic struggled past the gear shift to the driver's seat as Elmer climbed into the passenger seat. "Were you watching? Push in the clutch there, with your left foot. Now, put 'er in gear here, with this handle, now let out on the clutch, and step on the gas with the other foot. Other foot! Give it a little gas. Easy. Don't slip the clutch!"

Metal

Exhilarated by the jostling, lurching ride, Baput leapt over the Jeep door to the shop floor.

Far less overjoyed, Valko struggled to extract his legs from behind the seat and find the ground. "Mowers!" he rumbled in English. He headed for a back corner of the shop. Brushing back the cobwebs, he pulled two old hand scythes from pegs on the wall. Two blades of exquisitely shaped stone with a rough, red coating were bolted to two dried-out sticks that should have been replaced years ago. He shot Elmer a disdainful look and drew his finger across a dull blade.

He handed the splintery handles to Baput, who ran up to Elmer and asked, "Do you have wood for this?"

Elmer drew back, surprised, then pointed to a stack of three-inch logs that he hadn't yet cut into firewood. "Fetch a good straight one—"

Baput dashed off.

"And we'll fire up the lathe?" Elmer asked the empty air. He went back into the shop to unbury the wood lathe and check on the big guy.

Valko sat in Elmer's favorite folding chair, staring at a rusty scythe blade, running his fingers over it like he'd never seen metal before. Fascinated, Elmer handed him a file. Valko stared at it cluelessly.

"Are you serious?" Elmer huffed. He took the file back and demonstrated. "Go in this direction." Elmer sat down next to Valko, shaking his head and watching the man who'd never seen metal work the steel blade. Amusement overwhelmed his mounting impatience, for a while. But when Valko began to knock the burr off the second blade like an expert, Elmer left him to go show Felsic the walk-behind brush mower.

The quiet, bearded man used the file to break through the rust coating and reveal the metal below. So smooth! So uniform! So hard! Slowly, wondrously, he drew the file across the blade, and the amazing material formed to his will but held firm to its shape as he smoothed the pits and burrs into a blade more perfect and sharp than he had imagined possible. Suddenly, his reverie was exploded by the unfamiliar noise of a small engine firing and Felsic whooping like he'd never heard him whoop before, and he'd heard a lot of Felsic's whooping.

Baput rushed in, carrying two rough-hewn but perfectly fitted handles, one a bit longer than the other.

Elmer cut the engine. "Where did you get those, boy?"

"I make," Baput replied, first proud, then worried. "With the wood you told me OK."

"You were supposed to bring it to me. I would've shown you the lathe. How did you...?"

"My knife," Baput answered simply, producing a knapped stone with no handle from his pocket with an oversized hand, like a large-breed puppy's paw. His tough palm, silvery light green like a manzanita leaf, was spattered with reddish-brown blood.

"Holy crap!" Elmer sucked in his breath. "You guys are literally Stone Age! Get outta here! Um, go to lunch. Get that hand fixed up."

Valko quietly tapped his sharpened scythe blades into their new, perfectly fitted handles.

Lunch

"We are mowing," Valko told Salistar in their language as she spread crushed pomegranate seeds on Baput's wound. "There is good *yal* grass for weaving in the orchard by the river. How much do you need?"

"Do you need bags for picking?"

"I didn't see any," Valko replied, his lip curled. "Picking time and no bags ready? What kind of farmer is this man? You should have seen the condition of his mowers!"

Salistar placed her order. "Five bags, plus winter clothes for the five of us. We have nothing."

The statement was like a stab in Valko's heart, or was it in his pride?

Salistar calculated on her fingers. "Six bundles?"

"I will send the boy," Valko assured her.

Elmer burst into the kitchen, hungry for lunch and burning with frustration. "Franny, I swear! We're as bad off as we were yesterday, help-wise. These guys are literally Stone Age! Never seen a truck or a Jeep or a mower. Can you even believe that? It's 2014 for crying out loud! They want to mow with my Pop's old hand scythes! The big guy's got' em all sharpened up. It seemed like he'd never even seen metal before."

Fran was fascinated. "Where can they be from?"

"I'm a little afraid to ask them, and they're not real forthcoming. They'll tell us when they're ready, I guess. I don't much care, as long as they work, but they don't know nothing! I'm sorry, Fran, but I might need the boy to stay home from school tomorrow and help out. I know you hate that, but…"

Fran sighed. "OK, this time. He didn't want to go today, anyway. Said he'd learn more from the aliens."

"Yeah, well, these guys don't know much," Elmer repeated, then dove into his sandwich and potato salad.

"Be patient, Elmer. Give them a chance. A few more days to get settled. We don't know what they've been through."

"Well, they ain't been through the drive-through, that's for sure. It's harvest time. Now. I don't have a few more days. I'm supposed to be picking poms, and instead, I'm teaching the one guy to drive."

"Which one? The boy?"

"No, the uncle. Felsic. At least he's interested. But I don't have time for this. They ain't worth it."

"Worth what?" Fran demanded. "I don't even know how we're going to pay them. No papers, no bank accounts. Why, they can't even take cash to the store, if they can't be seen anywhere. I'll keep track of their hours and deduct what I buy for them, but, well, they're actually totally dependent on us."

Elmer chewed for far longer than the bite of boiled potatoes required before he gulped it down and met her eyes. "We ain't paying them for this morning, Fran. They ain't done nothing. Now if you go buying them food, they're gonna owe us."

Fran's face soured, then brightened. "Then they'll have to stay!"

Elmer sprung from his stool and began his habitual pacing. After winding himself up sufficiently, he spoke again. "It ain't the money, Fran. It's the risk."

"What risk?" Fran scoffed.

"The danger!"

"Danger? Did the big guy scare you?" Fran quipped without thinking.

Elmer puffed up. No fair. He couldn't be scared of anything in front of Fran, and she knew it. He grunted in self-defense. "Nah. He didn't do nothin'. Yet."

"They're just a family, Elmer. A family of people, I don't care what color they are. They have a kid, the same age as Jerry, and a doddering old man, and they're homeless and in trouble, for whatever reason."

Elmer looked at her silently like he was waiting for the point. When she stopped, his eyebrows went up, as if to say, "So?"

Fran turned away from him, scanned the pictures on the walls. "It's the Look'N Up Way, Elmer, you know that. You know you have to give them a chance. You can't just dismiss them. Where would they go?" She pictured the sad little group wandering down the county road, turning deep, hurt eyes back at the Look'N Up Ranch.

Elmer was smiling when he looked at her, like he'd finally come to his senses. "I got the guys to ride in the Jeep today. Maybe I could talk them into going on a little ride with me. Leave 'em off under a bridge somewhere. Tonight, when it's dark. At night all cats are gray, you know." He winked at Fran.

"Oooooof!" Fran exclaimed. She grabbed her laptop and left the house, slamming the front door.

Valko and Baput were leaving for the East Orchard with their crude "mowers" when Fran arrived at their quarters. She asked if Baput could stay.

"Meet me at the yal patch," Valko directed, and left.

Francine re-introduced herself, curious about those giggles from yesterday. "My name is Francine."

Sure enough, Salistar giggled.

"That is a man's name," Baput explained, "Only two sounds: Fran-cine. Like Ba-put or Fel-sic."

Salistar said her name slowly, clapping her hands softly to demonstrate. "Sal-is-tar. Three sounds for a woman."

"Syllables," offered Francine.

Salistar brightened and gently offered Fran her hand. "Syl-la-ble!" she said, delighted with the name. "Three sounds, yes."

"Uh, no." Fran answered. *Can't have her calling me Syllable. Kind of pretty, though.* "Fran-cin-a!" she offered, grasping Salistar's still extended hand. "But you can call me Fran, if you want to."

Salistar replied in a shy whisper, "Call me Star."

Fran opened the laptop. Baput felt a rush of energy as strong as the signal he had felt last night from that box across the room. But this flow was peaceful, like the strange new plane that had carried him through the night, teaching him.

Momama could see it, too! She leaned into the colorful photo of fresh vegetables, drawn like a moth to a flame. She pointed to an eggplant on the screen. Fran clicked the mouse, and Star jumped back as the picture changed to a selection of eggplants, long and lavender to round and almost black.

Baput helped translate as Star picked out all kinds of fruits and vegetables, preferring the red and purple varieties.

They couldn't find any pomegranate oil. "Did you say you make pomegranate oil?" Fran asked.

Baput answered for Star. "Oh, yes. My momama makes the best. Do you have a press?"

"No, but if you can show us how you do it, we can find a press that would work."

"Valko make," Star said proudly.

"Elmer will be glad to help," Fran volunteered. She closed the laptop and stood up. "I'll go to town and pick this stuff up for you,"

Salistar rose, too, speaking excitedly in her language.

"She wants to help pick," explained Baput.

Fran stood still for a second, gathering her thoughts. "This has all been picked for me already by someone else, and stored." With Baput translating, they seemed to be following. "When we want something, we go to the store and get it." They smiled. "And we pay money for it."

Whoosh! All understanding dropped from their faces.

"We do have a garden, though." Fran explained to Star as she stepped out onto the porch. "Not much in it now, it's almost October! I'll get some winter seed. Broccoli and cabbage, purple, if I can, and some winter greens. We'll do a winter garden together." Star's smile broadened as Baput translated. Fran gave Star a warm goodbye and headed for town.

Salistar stared as Fran climbed into a box with wheels that rolled down the driveway without a ganeesh or even a dog pulling it! Baput, already used to such things, grabbed his scythe and headed for the yal patch.

Weedeater

Elmer met Felsic at the shop after lunch. "You did OK driving, um, Felsic." He surveyed the clean-shaven olive-colored man cautiously. He was about his same size and age, but this guy had muscles! Yet, there was something unassuming about this Felsic. *Definitely beta*, Elmer mused. *I can use that. But he belongs to the big guy.* Out loud, it was, "Maybe I can put you on the orchard mower. But first I want to show you how this stuff works."

Felsic stood before him, dark eyes attentive, eager to learn.

Elmer went for the weed eater, a circular head with heavy plastic strings at the end of a long handle. He turned the head toward them. "See, these strings go round and round and cut the grass." He reversed the machine and held the handle, swinging the head back and forth just above the ground in front of him. "Let's go outside."

Felsic practiced swinging the weed eater, then reversed it and looked at the head again. "Cut?" he asked Elmer.

"You gotta fire it up, then these strings spin so fast they'll cut through anything."

"Anything?" wondered Felsic, looking up at the sky, as he had so many times today.

"Grass, small weeds. Put a steel blade on 'er and she'll cut down a bush or a small tree. Why? What do you want to cut?"

"Fire it up," said Felsic eagerly.

Elmer gave him a sidelong glance. *If I can't trust him with the mowers, what good is he?* Wondering if he was under some alien mind control, he slowly crossed the driveway to the pile of logs Baput had pilfered from that morning. He rested the weed eater's handle on the pile, keeping the head off the ground, and pulled the cord. Felsic whooped and held his ears when the noisy little engine fired. Elmer demonstrated, passing the head back and forth, cutting the weeds and grass along the driveway. Felsic followed, way too close to his left shoulder.

That reminded him. "Crap." Elmer snapped inaudibly, letting go of the trigger. "I can't be doing this without the face shields and earmuffs, and some gloves. I'll have Immigration *and* OSHA after me!" He wedged the idling instrument into the log pile with the head sticking up, vibrating mutedly and spinning weakly. "Stay! Don't touch!" he ordered Felsic and headed into the shop for two sets of safety gear.

As he reached for the equipment, he heard the weed eater rev to life. He whirled around to see Felsic raise the long-handled head with its spinning strings into the sky, waving it back and forth above and in front of him, screaming "Nimblies! Bumblies!" and something else in his language, over and over.

"Definitely not working out," Elmer hissed through clenched teeth as he donned his face shield-earmuff combo and gloves. Carrying Felsic's gear, he cringed behind a support beam as the strings assaulted its other side, right above his head.

Felsic's whoop pitched into a scream. He cleared the post and completed his arc, exposing his side to Elmer, a former high-school shortstop, who hurled a leather glove right into the crazed green face, then another.

Felsic giggled and backed up, trying to slice the assailing gloves.

"No, no!" Elmer yelled. "Don't cut those, you wear 'em." Elmer threw the face shield with the attached earmuffs past Felsic's whirling blades. Felsic turned in pursuit, striking it down with the handle of the weed eater. He bent over the strange creature he had just assailed, which now lay rocking on the ground.

With the green man's bent back toward him, Elmer launched himself from behind the post. He caught Felsic from behind and grabbed the long handle below Felsic's left hand, near the hot motor. He stuck his foot in the back of Felsic's right knee, forcing it to bend. Surprised, the muscular warrior lost his grip on his weapon and folded to the ground. Elmer took the sputtering tool, hit the kill switch, and set it down.

"Awww!" Felsic whined like a kid whose quarter had just run out.

"You done?" Elmer asked coldly. Felsic still knelt on the ground. Was he shaking? No, he was laughing! He looked up at Elmer like a kid on Christmas. When their eyes met, the exuberant face fell, melting like an overfilled ice cream cone on a hot summer day.

"Did I bad?" Felsic squeaked from his knees.

Elmer stood over him and stared down without flinching. He was done. Past trying them, past judging them, he was back to working on how to get rid of them. Preferably without attracting attention or blowing his marriage. He took his eyes off his kneeling captive long enough to glance at the bright red orbs that taunted from their laden trees. *And how am I gonna make the harvest without help? Or with it?*

Felsic's first words were inaudible. His lips moved, and he was breathing, but no words of any language came out. It looked like the effort pained him. Finally he squeaked, "I know. I am not worthy to touch your sacred weapon." He cast beseeching eyes up at his new boss, who continued his silent staring. "But we do not have such things. If we did, we could be like you!" Excited eyes eagerly searched Elmer's for understanding. Still nothing. "This is the Holy Weapon! This is how you did it!" Felsic babbled on in a barely intelligible mixture of English and whatever his language was.

"How I did what?"

"Got rid of them!"

"What?" Elmer repeated impatiently.

"The nimblies. The bumblies!" Felsic answered, just as impatiently. He sprung to his feet and stood in front of Elmer, a bit too close. He flapped his arms a few times, then put his right hand up to his face, with his forefinger pointing straight up from the tip of his nose. He stuck his chin out and nodded, thrusting on the up-nod. "Bumblies." He said it clearly, but there was no sign of recognition from Elmer.

Next, he stretched both arms out to the side without flapping, and hummed. He again brought his right hand to his nose and pointed his forefinger from there, this time straight out. He looked at it so he was cross-eyed, and leaned forward like he was trying to stick the finger into Elmer. Elmer leapt back, not liking this at all.

"Nim-blies," Felsic pronounced, slowly and perfectly. Still no recognition. A little fear, a lot of revulsion, but no recognition.

"Never heard of 'em," Elmer replied coldly.

Felsic inhaled a long, slow breath and wished Peratha and Trillella could see a world without nimblies and bumblies.

Elmer's thoughts were far less peaceful: *This guy is definitely crazy. I can't have Jerry out here either, if this guy is gonna be crazy. They can't work, he can't work, now I got nobody. What good are they? They're just gonna get us all killed. Sorry, Fran, they gotta go!*

He looked again at Felsic's olive face, now calm, reflecting some blissful illusion. In the silence of the standoff, Elmer heard a low, intermittent rumble and a soft, constant whoosh. "What the—?" he muttered.

Felsic looked even happier now. "It's Valko and Baput. They are done mowing East Orchard." He broke the standoff and ran to the north side of the shop.

Elmer followed on his heels, scanning for weapons as he passed. From the end of the shop, they could see part of the East Orchard. The grass was uniformly low and neat as a pin, all the way to where the ground sloped out of sight toward the river. Here came Valko and Baput, emerging from the last two rows, swinging those ancient hand scythes in wide arcs, not hitting each other, leaving not a blade of high grass behind them. They talked as they went, and every so often they would duck their heads and look up, like they had yesterday, as if they expected to be attacked by flying critters. They were moving at least as fast as the riding mower, making a swath twice as wide, and they didn't even look tired.

Elmer couldn't help but wonder, "Do they *pick* like that?"

Felsic's elation dampened a bit. "Valko is too big, and Baput is still learning, so they are a little slow. I can pick as much as they can, all by myself." He nodded confidently, sending Elmer into a productivity calculation that couldn't possibly be right.

Felsic waved urgently at the approaching pair. *Here it comes. He's gonna tell the big guy I tackled him,* Elmer surmised dismally, wondering if he should go for the pipe wrench or the nail gun. But the two cutters stayed on course, barely breaking their strides to return human-like waves. Elmer waved weakly, hoping it would keep the big guy away.

It did. The two finished the East Orchard and continued across the driveway into the West Orchard without stopping. Elmer watched them separate and vanish rapidly down the first two rows, their scythes swooshing invisibly without even rustling the leaves on the trees.

"Now what we do?" Felsic jarred Elmer from his thoughts. He was standing too close again, but the urge to yell in his face, to grab that filthy woven shirt and shake sense into the guy had flown from Elmer's bones. He looked into those simple, honest eyes that looked back with nothing but obsequious respect and an eagerness to please that he had never seen in Jerry or any of his other workers. *Why did I get so mad at him?* Elmer tried to remember. *Maybe he ain't crazy. Maybe they really do have flying monsters where he comes from. He didn't really try to weed eat me! He just got carried away.*

He put a hand on Felsic's wiry shoulder and turned him back toward the shop. "We're mowing grass," he pointed down, "on the ground." A noise drew his glance to the West Orchard, where Baput and Valko were already re-emerging from the third and fourth rows. "Looks like they got that covered." He looked back at Felsic, raised his left eyebrow questioningly. "Right?"

Felsic bobbed his head eagerly. "Yes, done soon!" he gushed. "Before dinner time." More head bobbing, and that goofy, eager-to-please look.

Elmer led his helper back to the farm truck, still sitting at its skewed angle since Felsic's first attempt at driving. "Climb up in 'er again. I'll show you. It's like the Jeep, kinda."

As Felsic scrambled up into the driver's seat, Elmer heard the buzz of another two-cycle engine. He thought it was Baput and Valko's mowers, until he remembered they were scythes. *No, that's Jerry, coming up the driveway from the school bus stop on his dirt bike.* "Even better," he whispered.

Jerry pulled off his helmet and dismounted. Baput and Valko came into view, approaching rapidly along the two middle rows of the West Orchard, silently cutting the grass with, what were those, scythes? They emerged onto the driveway just as the big truck lurched out of the shop, landing inches from where Valko froze in his tracks, scythe raised in defense.

Hanging onto the window frame with white knuckles, Elmer grinned at his new friend from the running board. "I'm gonna chalk that up to repressed aggression against your brother, and you feelin' this new power, right?" He winked playfully at Felsic, who happily agreed with whatever Elmer had said.

"Come on." Elmer reached in and put his arm around Felsic's shoulders. "Let's get down outta here for a minute. We gotta plan. You're still my driver." He turned to the gathering crowd. "Everybody, come here. Jerry, Baput." He was a little afraid to call Valko, but he came along sulkily anyway, giving the truck a wide berth.

When everyone was gathered, Elmer took charge. "We gotta set up the boxes in the rows for picking. You'll pick into your bags and then load into these boxes. We need someone to drive the truck, and someone to drive and operate the forklift. Jerry, do you think you can operate the forklift?"

Jerry looked down. "Not after last time, Dad."

"Not after last time?" Elmer jeered. "What kinda thinking is that? Why, Felsic here almost killed Valko twice already today, and he's still willing to get back on that horse, ain't ya, Felsic?" He slapped Felsic gently on the back. Felsic nodded happily at the attention.

Turning back to Jerry, Elmer asked, "Can you drive the truck?"

"I'm too small, Dad. I tried it."

"You are so negative!"

"Well, I can't. Physically. I have to stand on the clutch with all my weight, and then I can't steer."

"Well, you do know how to drive a stick, right, Son? I taught you enough times."

"Yeah, I know how to drive a stick."

"OK, well so does Felsic, sorta."

"I saw that."

"So you're gonna teach him how to drive that truck. Get up in there and ride with him," ordered Elmer.

"Are you sure it's safe?"

"Naw!" Elmer shook his head. "Not even close!"

Jerry stared at him. "But, Dad, you said—"

"Never mind what I said!" Elmer snapped. Then he winked his left eye and grinned. "Just keep it in low gear. You'll be fine. I think."

"Are we to pick now?" Baput asked Elmer.

Elmer addressed the group again. "No, it's too late. I don't like to leave them in the boxes overnight. Let's just get the boxes out and pick tomorrow. Valko and Baput, finish mowing, then you can go home. I just need Felsic and Jerry for now. I'll yell for you about 6:00 tomorrow morning. Felsic will be home by dinnertime."

Felsic caught on quickly in the truck, with Jerry telling him what pedal to press and how hard. They made lots of stops and starts, Elmer offloading a box at each stop with the forklift. It was great practice. When they finished, they headed to the West Orchard. It was mowed like a fairway, and Valko and Baput were long gone. By the time the late September sun was setting red in the west, the boxes were placed throughout both orchards, and Felsic could stop and start, use the clutch and shift gears as well as anybody. At least when Valko wasn't around.

The TV Plane

Back at their quarters, G-Pa continued to mumble, loyal Shastina at his feet. Star had to feed him dinner the same way she'd done breakfast, like a toddler. Valko, already irritated by his rough introduction to mechanized equipment, was further exasperated by this.

After dinner, Baput walked G-Pa to one of the unoccupied bedrooms. Star brought two cushions made of woven yal, like the picking bags she'd made, stuffed with softer grass.

Baput laid them on the floor. "G-Pa, come. Let's meditate."

Baput led the chanting and directed the breathing, and G-Pa followed. It was normally the reverse. Baput felt himself rising up and to the left, toward the first of the Earth planes. He envisioned grabbing G-Pa's hand. "Hold on tight, G-Pa!" he warned, knowing what to expect. G-Pa tottered beside him, as if buffeted by a great wind. A bright image assaulted them. No sticks and armor this time, just people talking. Baput didn't bother trying to figure out what they were talking about. It seemed whenever he came through this level, they were arguing and talking over one another, or shooting each other. He focused on a talk show, where a woman hosted three guests.

"Why, she's an odd color!" exclaimed G-Pa.

"We're the odd color, G-Pa," Baput corrected, then realized, "You see them?"

"Yes, a brown woman. She speaks boldly, for a woman."

"You see it! Good! It's the first Earth Plane." Baput was relieved to find a peaceful TV image to guide G-Pa through, and that the Akash was responding rationally, for now. "Now, try to look through the image. It's only a rasta; the people aren't really here. It's like the Plane, but it's not, um, real." At a loss to explain it, he just hoped G-Pa could stay here long enough to feel it for himself.

Two of the guests on the show started talking at the same time, trying to drown each other out. A young man with pale skin like Jerry's and dark hair like Baput's joined in, and soon all four people were talking at once, louder and louder.

Baput grabbed G-Pa's arm. "Hang on! Breathe! Look through them. They're OK. That's just the way they talk to each other. They aren't really there. They can't see or hurt you. Just look through, breathe through."

G-Pa relaxed a bit, just as the image shifted to a multi-story building in ruins. Sirens wailed. People with bleeding heads and missing limbs were being carried away on stretchers. In the dusty background, silhouettes searched the chunks of masonry for survivors.

"Ohhhh," G-Pa groaned and slumped on his cushion, not to be roused.

Baput sighed. *Why are these images always fighting?* Encouraged by the Akash's brief flash of lucidity, he resolved to try again tomorrow, wondering how he could protect his G-Pa from these violent assaults.

Elmer's Second Night

Exhausted but wide awake, Elmer lay on his back finishing that incredible poms-per-day calculation, checking it, still not believing it. He lost the thread, rolled over to face Fran's sleeping face and thought long thoughts.

So that's how you are, eh, Elmer Musik? All worried about the green people eating your family and taking over the world until you find out they'll make you more money? Now all of a sudden I trust them? That's how cons work! They play on your greed. A half-million poms a day? Ha! I can't even grow that many. We'll just have to see...

He chuckled out loud as another thought emerged unexpectedly. *That Felsic! If they're planning on doing us harm, I don't think he's in on it. He couldn't pull it off. He's got no guile. Not a bad bone in his body, that one. If I can win him over, get between him and his big brother...* He schemed as he drifted off to sleep.

A translucent Valko floated up from under the bed. He rose higher and higher, stretched taller and taller, glaring down at Elmer with that predator beak and those jet-black warrior eyes. He raised his right arm, a bloody scythe in his hand, and swung. Elmer's eyes jerked open and the apparition vanished, along with his last chance of sleeping that night.

Third Day

Baput emerged casually from the quarters when he heard Jerry's bike coming up the driveway from the school bus stop. Jerry removed his helmet and shook his blond hair so it fell back over his left eye, where it belonged. He grinned lopsidedly and greeted his friend. "Hey, Baput! Done picking already?"

"Yes," Baput replied. "Felsic drove the truck just fine as long as Popa stayed away from it. It was full by lunchtime. Your Popa drove it away and said we were done until tomorrow."

"Cool." Jerry smiled. "Let me change and tell my mom I'm home, and we can hang out. OK?"

"Yes!" Baput enthused, smiling more than he had since arriving.

Jerry came out in heavier pants and a plaid flannel shirt, his hair under a cap. Brodey bounced excitedly at his side.

They walked up the driveway, past Baput's quarters on the left and the dormant vegetable garden on the right, to a green expanse of lawn. The river bent around the grassy area, creating river frontage on two sides. Benches were scattered along the bank in gaps between willows.

It was the same trail through the grass they had come in on. There was the tiny house made of stone that G-Pa had been drawn to. Jerry approached it. "Come on."

With some effort, Jerry opened the swollen wooden door. They stepped inside. A weirdly familiar vibration stirred deep within Baput.

It was pitch dark, no windows. Spider webs crisscrossed the doorway and dangled from the ceiling. Jerry took something out of his pocket that made a blue light with no flame. He pointed the magical beam to the back of the tiny building. Baput could barely make out a black box with a tube attached to the top, leading up through the roof. Two wide wooden shelfs ran along the other three walls. "It's a sauna. My grandpa made it. They used to get all hot in here and sweat. They'd build a fire in that black box. That's a wood stove. Do you have those? Oh, yeah. My dad says you guys don't have metal. He says you still use stone tools, and you have a stone knife. Can I see? You guys have fire, though, right? You gotta have fire, or you couldn't live." Jerry continued his questioning, not waiting for answers.

They stepped out into the cool fall sunshine. Baput opened his scarred hand to show Jerry his knife. It was just a round stone, palm sized, with a sharp, knapped edge. Jerry produced his pocketknife and unfolded it, exposing the shiny metal blade. Baput inhaled sharply and reached out, dropping his stone tool.

"Careful," Jerry warned. "It's probably sharper than yours."

Baput touched the blade carefully, with the same wondrous look Valko had worn when he'd filed that rusty old scythe blade. *Stone-age people! How did they get here if they have no technology? It doesn't seem like they even know,* Jerry mused.

"Hey, Baput, remember where we met? At the Horizontal Tree?"

"Yes," replied Baput.

"Well, that's my spot. It's nofo, um, no cell phone reception. I go there to get away from it all, you know, like, hang out and think? Come on."

Jerry's mind was so full of questions, he didn't know where to start. They walked in awkward silence until he just asked it, straight out. "What happened to you guys?"

Baput told the story of how they excited a glowing rock while trying to kill some giant dragonflies that attacked every three years, right at pomegranate harvest time. And how they suddenly, unexpectedly went through some horrible pressure and woke up here, on that flat spot just down the trail. Jerry had a new question for every three words Baput spoke, but he didn't want to stop the story.

"But here, there are no nimblies or bumblies. It is now the third day. We should have had nimblies every day and bumblies every night. There are none! Felsic says you got rid of them with something called a Weed Eater. Can I see it?" Baput demanded excitedly, forgetting to be shy.

"The nimblies are the giant dragonfly things you were fighting, right? What are the bumblies?" Jerry asked.

"They are like your bats, but bigger." Baput held up his hands the size of a softball. "The first night they are this big. Just the body." He spread his hands about two feet apart. "This big with wings. They get even bigger over the three days. They have a horn at the end of their nose, sticking straight up, like your rhinoceros. The horn is only three inches long but very sharp, like your knife."

Baput nodded his head with a thrust on the upstroke, his finger at the end of his nose, pointing up, just like Felsic had done. "Cut a man to pieces. And big teeth to bite the flesh off his bones. They all swarm in and devour him in minutes." His face was drawn, with too many wrinkles for a boy his age.

Jerry pressed on. "What about the dragonfly things, the nimblies? Do they eat you, too?"

"Yes," Baput answered. "They drink you. They have a probe at the end of their nose like a needle. They stick it in you and suck all your blood, in seconds. They poison you at the same time, so you can't move. Even if they don't get all your blood, you are helpless and awake that night when the bumblies come and finish you. Then they go after the live people, my cousins, friends, brothers…" Baput's voice rose and his face turned a pale sage. "Sisters," he gulped.

Jerry, still burning with questions, stood respectfully silent while his new friend pulled himself together. Bravely, the alien boy went on.

"It happens every three years, on First Pomegranate Day, when the pomegranates are perfectly ripe. They must be picked, or they split and go bad."

Jerry nodded. He knew how fast that happened.

Baput went on, "But we cannot harvest for three days, because we have to fight all the time, night and day. The women and children all stay together in the Great Hall made of logs. The men go out to the trenches to fight and fight. When they finally stop coming, after three days, the pomegranates, kips, we call them, they are only good for shoes and linings and oil. And Uncle Felsic's wine."

Jerry looked down at Baput's shoes. They really *were* made of pom skins. "You never get to eat your pomegranates?" he asked. "They split and rot every year?"

"No, we would starve if they came every year. It is only every third year. On those years, after the three days of Nimbly Bumbly Season, we have Passascenday. Young men who are at least 15 ascend to their professions and marry their betrotheds, if they live through their first Season in battle.

"We plant new seeds then, and three years later, the little trees bear their first fruit. Then, that autumn, when the first pomegranates are ripe on the adult trees, it is First Pomegranate Day again, and the nimblies and bumblies come back. It will be Passascenday tomorrow."

Baput's brow furrowed as he tried to imagine the world back home. Was it still there? "They will dig a big hole and bury the dead." He wondered who it would be this time. Surely someone—if life went on at home at all. "They will harvest, or salvage, what they can. Some kips can be used for oil, some for wine. If too split and ripe, ganeesh will eat many."

Jerry couldn't resist. "Ganeesh? Is that the big creature you said carried your stuff to the Cave?"

"Like your elephant," Baput continued.

Jerry couldn't see what his dark eyes were looking at inwardly, but they glistened with such sadness!

"The rest of the spoiled pomegranates cover the dead in the hole, to sweeten the odor and sustain them on their trip to the stars. Then we cover them with dirt. All the dead from those three days. All together. Man, woman, child, dog, all but ganeesh. They take care of their own. Sometimes a ganeesh's family will give us their dead." His eyes zoomed in on Jerry. "Did you know a ganeesh's skin is impenetrable to nimblies and bumblies? If they give us their dead, we can make armor."

Jerry squinted for a second, then asked a most human question. "Do you ever kill a ganeesh for its skin?" He wished he hadn't.

Baput's eyes went to a very dark place. He moved away from Jerry, stumbling off the trail.

"Sorry, man," Jerry sputtered. "Of course you wouldn't kill one. Any more than I'd kill Brodey here."

Baput's face flushed, an ugly greenish brown. "A ganeesh is worth more than its skin!" he snarled with burning eyes. "A ganeesh is not a pet, either. He or she is more like a wise friend. A spiritual counselor. Wiser than most people, except the Akash, of course."

"That's your G-Pa, right?"

"Yes," Baput explained. "For one more cycle. Three more years. Then I will be 15. I will ascend to Akash."

"On next, passa, what?

"Pass-ascend-day," Baput repeated slowly.

"Awesome," Jerry let a respectful moment of silence pass, though it strained the patience of his avid curiosity. "So, you came here to find some way to get rid of the monsters?"

"No, I don't know why we came, um, here." He seemed to struggle with the simple word. "Or how. We weren't supposed to. We committed Shavarandu. Perhaps we were punished."

"What's Shavarandu?"

"The things we used to kill the nimblies. The wires, the thing Felsic pedaled, the net that lay across the Rock, the heavy tubes of that strange, shiny stuff you seem to have everywhere here, your knife…"

"Metal?"

"Yes. All these things are forbidden. But we used them anyway. We are so desperate to be rid of the bumblies and nimblies. We are dying! All of us! There are only 100 of us left, counting us five who are now…" Baput wore his G-Pa's confused look for an instant.

Jerry felt panic but said nothing while Baput recovered. It gave him a little time to take all this in. Then a roguish smile crept across his face. "I can't say I blame you for breaking that law, under the circumstances. But who says it's forbidden? Isn't your G-Pa the boss?"

"It has been forbidden by the Old Ones since the Beginning, even for the Akash," Baput pronounced in a monotone that made Jerry's skin crawl. He felt like a curtain had dropped between them. He had to push it away.

"If it's forbidden, how did you get it?" he grilled.

"It was… behind… the door," Baput answered haltingly, trailing off, head bowed low.

Jerry was silent until they reached the Horizontal Tree. He gently guided Baput by the shoulders to sit on the level trunk where Musiks had sat for four generations now, worn so smooth it gleamed in the dappled sun. The river sparkled just below them.

Baput sat staring at the water, breathing deeply. Jerry wondered if he was OK. *He's going into some kind of trance. Should I let him? As long as he's breathing, I guess.* Jerry watched his strange friend closely.

Time went by as usual on the Horizontal Tree, alone, but with a mind full of new thoughts and so many questions! After what seemed like forever, Baput emerged, a vague smile on his face.

"The Plane is good here."

"The Plane. What's that?"

"Don't you know? You people have your own plane. It's below our Plane, but it has much knowledge."

"You mean, the internet? But you're Stone Age! You don't have a computer or a cell phone. How can you access the internet?"

"A what or a what?" Baput grinned at his new friend. He looked much younger now. "I go there like I go to my Plane. With my mind. By meditating. My Plane is like your plane, because it gives information, but on my Plane, it comes into my mind just when I need it. Your plane, I must search."

"Is that how you learned our language so fast? How you know all about our bats and rhinos and dragonflies and elephants and stuff? I was wondering."

"Yes. I have spent the last two nights surfing your iPlane, learning as much as I can."

"The iPlane," Jerry smiled at the new name for the internet. Then it hit him. "Without a computer!"

Baput didn't seem to share the enthusiasm. "It gets in the way of our Plane, especially for G-Pa," he complained. "But your iPlane has helped me a lot. There are lower planes, too. You have many planes! The lower planes are, are violent! All the time! What *is* that? People hurting and killing each other..." There were tears in his deep, dark eyes.

Jerry wondered what it would be like to pick up television in his head, involuntarily. Did he even get to choose the channel? "Television. TV, we call it. Do you hear it now?"

"No. In the quarters, in the evening."

"When we watch TV. What did we watch last night?"

"The first night, they were wearing helmets and shields and beating each other with clubs."

"Yeah, that was probably one of those riots in Ferguson, Missouri. They're fighting 'cause the cops killed a black guy, Michael Brown." Jerry trailed off at Baput's uncomprehending face. How could he even begin to explain?

Baput nodded vaguely. "Yes, some of the people were brown, not black, but is that what you mean?" he mused with faraway eyes and wrinkled brow.

Shaking off his confusion, Baput switched to last night's graphic image. "Last night, I thought the world ended. I was afraid it was our home, but it didn't look like it. There was dust or smoke everywhere. I couldn't see clearly. There were buildings made of stone. They were all fallen down, just piles of stone with people picking through them. There were people being carried. One had one arm. Another's eye was gone, blood pouring out of the hole. The people were light brown, not like you, darker. Their hair was black, like ours.

"Yeah, that was real, too, unfortunately," Jerry replied gravely. "Probably a war in Syria or Afghanistan or something."

"So every day is something? A war? A riot?"

"Somewhere in the world, yeah," Jerry sighed. "And the TV brings it all home. But we watch movies and stuff, too. Those aren't real. Some are really fun. What movie did we watch last night?"

Baput had his forefinger sticking out and his thumb up, like a little kid playing cowboy. Then he lowered his thumb, just like that kid. "What is the bang-bang stick?"

Jerry threw back his head and laughed so hard he fell off the tree. He wriggled around on the ground while Brodey straddled him, trying to lick him. He pushed his dog aside and struggled to sit up. "It's called a gun. You're seeing our TV, alright. Maybe we should lay off on the bang-bang stick movies. That sure narrows it down..." His giggling ebbed to silence as he followed the thought. *Are we gonna have to give up TV for these guys?*

Baput had more complaints. "And there is the *rasta*. Like drawings, but they move."

"Cartoons? We don't watch cartoons."

"Big booms and flashes. Giant monsters."

"My videogames?" Jerry's heart was sinking fast. He had to think this over before he mentioned it to Mom and Dad. "Do the others pick it up too?"

"No. My popa and uncle are not of the Akashic line. They were trained as children to ascend to the Plane, like all the boys. But you must meditate, concentrate. It takes time and patience. Most men would rather tend the crops or practice fighting or make things of wood and stone. So they don't meditate. They wouldn't feel the TV or the iPlane unless they tried really hard."

"What about your mom? She's Akashic, right?" Jerry figured, if Baput was, and Valko wasn't, then…

Baput was looking at him like he was a complete idiot. "She is a woman!"

"What? She can't? Because she's female?!"

"Of course not!" Baput snapped as if disappointed in his new friend. Jerry was shocked into silence. Eventually, Baput spoke again. "It's quiet here."

Jerry brightened. "Yeah, it's nofo here. No internet. My phone doesn't even work. No EMFs, energy waves, except natural ones."

"And the river is here. Very good for meditating. Jerry, can I bring my G-Pa here?"

"You mean, at night, while we are watching TV?" Jerry was hoping for a deal, but he couldn't do that. "It might be dangerous. It's dark this time of year."

Share his spot or give up his TV and videogames? Jerry sighed as the weight of the Look'N Up Way fell on his shoulders for the first time. He had to empathize. He tried to imagine coming from a primitive land and being able to feel this whole crazy world all at once. *It must be blowing all his circuits! It's amazing he's doing this well!* Then he thought about the mumbling old man.

"Is that what's wrong with your G-Pa?" he gulped, dreading the answer. "Our TV? Our internet? Overwhelming him?"

Baput was staring at the water again. "Yes. Partly. But there's something else. He couldn't feel our Plane when we first arrived. Not even here, at this nofo place. I was confused by the iPlane and the TV. They were in the way, but I could still feel our Akashic Plane, too. He couldn't. Last night I led him in meditation. I am his apprentice! He is supposed to be teaching me! But he is so lost." Baput inhaled roughly. "We got to the TV plane. We did OK until we saw that Afgana-what? War? Then he fell off and went back to his mumbling."

Baput wept his frustration through his long, black, eyelashes. He was about four inches taller than Jerry and weighed a lot more. All muscle, like his dad and uncle. Jerry could see why, after seeing him cut that grass.

Jerry searched for a compromise. "Is he on the Plane all day? What did he normally do at home?"

Baput closed his eyes, trying to see that vanished homeland. "Usually, he goes to the Holy Cave in the morning after Momama gives him breakfast."

"OK, so in the morning he meditates for how long?"

"Lately, he was staying at the Holy Cave all day. But he wasn't meditating, not all day. He was committing Shavarandu!" This train of thought lead to a dark surge in Baput's heart, some seed of resentment that had burst out of its shell and begun its journey toward the light.

"Before that." Jerry derailed that train. "So, he needs what? All morning? And you need to be with him? But it's harvest, and Dad needs you to work. I bet after harvest, they'll give you time off in the morning for that. Mom will make Dad do that. And we don't watch TV or play games in the morning."

Baput looked up, eyebrows raised. "Momama make Popa?"

"You mean, your mom's not the boss of your house?" the strange boy asked.

"Of course not!" Baput snapped automatically. "Popa is the boss! Akash is overall boss, of course. But for the family, Popa is boss."

Jerry flashed his famous grin, the one that covered the bottom half of his face and went up higher on the left side, right up to where his golden hair covered his left eye. "Who makes the food?" he asked.

"Momama, of course."

"So, what if she doesn't? Can you cook? Can your Dad? Felsic?"

"Of course not! That is woman's work."

"Then if she decides not to cook, you're gonna starve. Think about it. Who has the real power?" That grin again. He gave a sidelong glance toward the houses. "Speaking of moms wielding their power by making us dinner, we better go." They rose and headed down the trail.

"Bring G-Pa out here tomorrow, when you get off work. And, Baput, um, is the TV bothering you? The video games?" Jerry asked one last time, holding his breath.

"I can get past them now, myself," Baput admitted. "But G-Pa cannot. He needs to be here. Or at home with no TV signal. I would like to show him your iPlane. He could learn from it, like I do."

They were approaching the grassy area with the stone shed. "Hey!" Jerry yelped, running over to the tiny square building of stacked tan rock with purple staining. "Maybe it's nofo in here!" He pulled his iPhone from his pocket. There was barely a bar outside. Inside, the display was red. It said, "No signal."

Jerry grinned, prattling on. "I know the Wi-Fi doesn't reach out here, 'cause I tried my iPod." He ran over to the benches by the river, phone in his outstretched hand, dogs at his heels. "No Wi-Fi here, either. The phone's a little better than in the shed, but not much."

Baput sat on the bench and closed his eyes. "No TV. I can feel the iPlane, but it is not as strong. I could get through it, to my Plane, easily. Especially here, with the river going by. I could teach G-Pa. But first, I need an all-nofo place."

They returned to the dark sauna house. Jerry shined his cell phone into it again. "We'll clean it up and get some light. It's an easy walk from the quarters. And it is stone nofo! Look, my phone doesn't even show the time!" Jerry babbled jubilantly. Problem solved! And without giving up TV or video games, or sharing his special spot! And best of all—he had a family of aliens living with him, with superpowers!

Refugees

"They're refugees." Jerry told his parents that night at dinner. "They're being wiped out by flying creatures that eat them."

Elmer calmly confirmed the bizarre statement. "Yeah, Felsic tried to tell me about 'em. Flying things with horns. I thought he was nuts, but I guess they're real, eh? Or else, they're all crazy."

"Dad, do you still think they're from Earth?"

"No, not really. They're too weird."

"So," began Scientist Jerry, "What do we know about extraterrestrial life?"

"Just what I see in the movies."

"None of that's real, Dad. So, how do you know they *don't* have flying things that eat them? I believe it. And they're getting seriously wiped out! They need help!" Jerry pleaded for his friend.

"So, how'd they get here?" Elmer demanded.

Jerry revealed the rest of the story with his mouth full. "They were fighting the daytime dragonfly ones, the nimblies. There was a rock in this cave. I'm thinking it was made of some really resonant material."

Elmer grunted. It was Elmer's mom who had brought science into the house. She had taught it at the same high school Elmer and his little brother Patrick attended. She taught Jerry a lot, too, before she departed. Elmer never took to it like Patrick and Jerry did. Now Jerry was getting just like her, always trying to teach him stuff.

"It vibrates good," Jerry said slowly.

"Jerry!" Fran snapped.

"It vibrates well?" he said it like a question.

Jerry finished the story, just as Baput had told it in his ever-improving English, but with his own scientific slant. "They made electricity. A coil rigged up to a stationary bike that Felsic pedaled. It got this big, smooth rock that sticks out of the floor of the Holy Cave to vibrate and glow. Valko captured whatever radiation was coming off of it in a heavy, metal pipe. Baput said it was red metal, maybe copper."

"But Valko ain't never seen metal! I could tell!" protested Elmer.

"Yeah, well, they found it behind some secret door. They weren't supposed to use it, but they're desperate!"

Their dinners went cold as they listened. Jerry told them all he knew about the predators, the weapon and the Rock. At last, he took a big bite, swallowed without chewing, and asked, "You know what else is cool? He can get on the internet without a computer."

"Who needs tech?" wondered Fran.

"It just gets you blasted to another planet!" finished Elmer.

"Or dimension," added Jerry, thinking hard. Should he tell them? *Mom will probably say give up TV! Then Dad will yell and they'll take my videogames away.* He took the riveting conversation in another direction.

"Can we fix up the sauna for Baput's G-Pa?"

"He wants to take a sauna?" Elmer asked, trying not to image the scrawny, wizened old man in the nude.

"No, he needs to meditate."

"Why out there?" Fran asked, worried about spiders.

"Um, well, he likes it. He's got a place like that at home. We're gonna fix it up. Can he build a fire in the woodstove? For staring at?"

"He can't stare at it. It's a wood stove. He'll smoke himself out. You know that," grumbled Elmer.

"He's not real, um, competent, you know," Fran objected. "But, sure. You wear long sleeves, a dust mask, and goggles when you clean that place out. Both of you."

"Both who?" Elmer retorted. "You and Baput will have plenty of time after school. If they pick like they did today, I'll have a full truck and be on my way to town by then." Elmer reckoned happily. "You know, I was worried about our late start yesterday. Now, today, I was the first truck to the buyer. Got top dollar. Maybe these green guys are gonna work out, after all. Boy, you should see those guys pick! The kid's all yours tomorrow when they're done. You'll see how fast he works."

"He needs to work with his G-Pa, too," Jerry kept up. "Morning is best, but not during harvest."

"Not during summer either, Son. Morning's the best time to work. If these guys are this fast at everything, I might let them off all afternoon every day. They work twice as fast as any crew I've seen. Picked like the dickens, all three of them! One o'clock in the afternoon, and there I was, first in line! They even left the unripe ones for another round! All picked at perfect ripeness, and they didn't bruise a one!"

Jerry jumped at the evidence. "It's 'cause when those creatures come, every three years, they come right at harvest time. So they can't get the harvest in. After three days, that would be tonight, they stop coming. So tomorrow, they would go out and pick like the dickens." Jerry grinned. "Then they bury their dead, what's left of 'em. Bones, mostly. They cover them with the rotten pomegranates and bury them all together. Except the elephants. No one knows where the elephants bury their dead."

Fran found her voice to muse softly, "The elephant's graveyard. Earth elephants do that, too."

"So he can take care of his G-Pa after work until I get home, then hang with me," Jerry hoped out loud.

Elmer agreed. "Sure, if you can get more of that kind of information, you can hang out with him after school."

"He has to help his G-Pa, if he can. That's the important thing, not your little spy network," Fran accused Elmer angrily.

"I'm not a spy, Mom. I'm his friend. I like him." Jerry promised. *And I can still watch TV and play videogames*! He kept that part to himself.

Third Night

"Tomorrow is Passascenday!" Salistar realized out loud while the green family ate their red beans and black rice on the final night of the Season. The last raid of the bumblies would be tonight. They would be full-grown, and at their most vicious. The exhausted men in the trenches would slap at them with long-handled swatters and poke them with longsticks, shoot darts at them with their blowguns and launch arrows with their slings.

At dawn, the bumblies, gorged on green flesh, would return to their caves where the nimblies would be breeding. The bumblies would breed too, on the floor. Once satiated, they would fly up to their perches to hang upside down for a three-year slumber. Sometime during their long torpor, the female nimblies would lay their eggs all over the sleeping bumblies in a tough slime that thoroughly coated each "bat."

For the people, tomorrow meant a hurried harvest. The best poms would be whisked away for storage and juicing. The second-best, to the oil press, Salistar's usual station. The many that had split open with ripeness and were beginning to sour, to Felsic's wine station. Two major stations vacant, not even counting the Akash! Not even an apprentice! Who was Akash now?

"Pindrad and Jeneven will wed," Salistar began.

"If they live," Valko squashed her attempt at cheer with the customary response to such Passascenday predictions. It had new meaning this time. What had happened to the others?

"Who will make the wine?" Felsic wondered aloud. "They wouldn't let me train Bazu until Baput ascended. Just in case he had to be Akash someday." Bazu was G-Pa's sister's grandson. Descended from the less-favored female side of the Akashic line, he would be next in succession without Baput.

Valko snorted. "He's not trained for that, either." They all stared at him, realizations stealing across each face in turn.

Baput tried to lighten the mood. "Pindrad also will ascend to take his popa's place as Rasta maker."

"None too soon," remarked the stubbornly dismal Valko. "How can a man paint the events and people of the village when he can't even see his own hand in front of his face?"

"Tamaya will watch her brother wed and ascend," Felsic teased, trying to smile.

Baput imagined lanky, 17-year-old Tamaya, his betrothed, watching the Passascenday ceremonies. *But how could that be? They are gone. Everything is gone, like G-Pa says.* He struggled for words. "If they, um, are..." He trailed off into a silence that swallowed the quarters.

All this would go on tomorrow wherever, whatever, home was. If home even *was* anymore. *How can it exist? It has been replaced by this, this....* They all wondered, but none could find the words to ask the question.

That night, with the end of the Season, and no nimblies or bumblies so far, the family spread into the plain but ample three bedrooms of their quarters. Felsic moved to the bedroom near the back door. Baput and G-Pa moved into the corner room. It had two windows, one facing north, toward the orchards, and the other, west, toward Jerry's house. Like before, Baput placed G-Pa's mattress on the floor and climbed up to the top bunk, at window level.

G-Pa whined from his mattress on the floor waving his hands like a baby. "Baput, come closer!"

Baput looked down from his beloved roost by the window. *Really?* He raged silently. *Haven't I already given up enough for that bumbling old fool?* Cringing at his own thoughts, he grabbed his blankets and slithered into the lower bunk. Angry tears fell on G-Pa as Baput grasped his outstretched hand.

Baput lay on his back, thinking of the extra care G-Pa was requiring now. *I've got to help him, just to help me! And Momama. She even had to help him in the boor. I know. That's what a Tether is for. To tend the Akash so he can be on the Plane all the time, seeking wisdom for the people. But he does not serve the people! He serves his own wishes! And now, he is just lost, serving no one.*

He lay flat on his back, still holding the old man's hand. He tried to meditate, but his heart pumped too hard and too fast. He gulped air and held his breath instead of breathing in the Akashic way. His stomach felt like he had eaten rocks. He didn't want to close his eyes and see those violent images. He didn't want to sleep… or stay awake.

TV or Not TV

The Musiks adjourned to the living room and turned on the TV to another mass shooting. People were being carried out of a mall, bleeding. Then an angry face was shouting on half the screen, with more carnage on the other half. Jerry grabbed the controller from the arm of Elmer's chair and turned the TV off.

"Hey, what?" Elmer cried.

"It bothers them, Dad." Jerry gulped, hating this like suicide. "Baput picks up TV, too. I think it's whatever we're watching. And when he tries to get G-Pa on the Plane, he runs into the TV layer, and it's always violent. It freaks him out, and G-Pa crashes."

Elmer and Fran stared at their son, bravely standing in front of the TV, hands on his hips, remote control in his right hand. Then Elmer roared like a little bulldog, "You mean to tell me I can't watch TV in my own house because it bothers the *help?*"

Fran's mischievous smile was more discreet than Jerry's. "Why, Elmer, who was first in line at the market? How much faster do you think they'll pick with a good night's sleep?"

"Well, even so, I lost a whole day teaching that one dummy to drive."

"Dummy, Dad? How many days did it take you to learn? And you'd at least seen a vehicle before."

"Can you imagine?" asked Fran, disarming Jerry of the remote on her way to the stereo. She put on one of Elmer's dad's old vinyl Grateful Dead albums.

"Not ever seeing metal," Elmer added. "That's what tripped me out."

"But they *did* see metal! In the Cave." Jerry resumed the tale. "The pipes Valko used to direct the beam out of that Rock, and the wires on the coil Felsic pedaled, and the wire from there to Baput's lever, whatever that did. And the Rock starts vibrating, see?"

Elmer nodded vigorously, resonance already explained.

"And it glowed and shot some kind of energy out. The pipes concentrated the energy. You get that, right, Dad? It's like water. If it's sitting in a pond, it's nice and lazy. But put it in a pipe and it has power 'cause it's concentrated."

"And they shot that stuff, whatever it was, at the varmints, huh?" Elmer interrupted, finishing the story this time. TV forgotten, they talked the evening away, imagining seeing this and that for the first time, and speculating, still without a clue, *where did they come from?*

Fran walked them through the family empathy exercise. "Try to imagine what it would be like. Just the TV part. Having all this violent stuff popping into their heads. They don't understand any of it. They keep seeing people hurting each other, killing each other every night, and they just lost their world!"

They all sat quietly for a minute, trying to imagine.

Jerry broke the silence. "I don't think they all get the signals, Mom. Just Baput, and the Akash when he tries to meditate. The other guys don't pay enough attention, and women can't feel them at all."

Fran grunted incredulously. "Oh, really? I'm going to ask them tomorrow, when they're done picking."

"Ah, Franny, don't go nosin' into their business. They'll get used to it. Leave it alone. I was gonna pull their cable off the dish anyway. How's that?"

"Why, Dad?"

"You never mind. I disconnect their box, and they don't get the signal."

Jerry started to say, "They'll pick up ours," but he stopped himself. "Yeah. Let's try that."

"Fine," Fran agreed stubbornly. "But I'm asking them. Aren't you guys curious?" She looked from face to face, then to the clock. "Look! It's 10:00! And no TV! We all survived. Now, let's go to bed."

"Baput says his Momama is not the boss. His Popa is," Jerry wore that grin again.

Fran whirled around, a spark in her eyes. "What did you tell him?"

"I said if you weren't the boss, we'd starve!"

"Oh, hey!" cried Elmer.

"Good boy!" Fran crowed over him. She raised her head smugly and pranced up the stairs.

Elmer chuckled in his armchair, an unfinished beer in its holder. "Good play, Boy." He whispered. "Butter her up."

Jerry chuckled, too, but he was still worried about losing this battle. And afraid of winning. What would that do to Baput? He hoped just unplugging the cable would work, but he doubted it. "I'm going to bed, Dad."

"Me too. Good night, Son."

Elmer automatically went to turn off the TV, chuckled again, and turned off the stereo instead. Then he followed his family upstairs.

A weight lifted from Baput's chest and he relaxed. He closed his eyes and soared straight to the iPlane. He wanted to learn more, but he was so tired. With his last burst of psychic energy, he leapt out of the current of the iPlane, up and to the left, onto the familiar Akashic Plane of home. He felt G-Pa's hand in his and squeezed it gently. "Can you feel it, G-Pa?" he whispered. "It's the Plane." He suddenly felt his old love for his mentor, but it caused a pang in his heart now. Spiritually holding the Akash's hand, he curled up around the tendril that connected his soul to the Plane, hugging it like an umbilical cord.

He realized it was quiet because Jerry made it so. *That would be a "Thank You."* Wearily, he explored the alien concept. At home, everyone freely gave what was needed, if they had it, with no concept of ownership or cost.

"Thank you, Jerry," he whispered as he went into a deep trance. Not sleeping, not learning. Just resting. For a while, he thought he heard melodious music playing and gentle voices singing in harmony. *Is the Plane sending this? I've never heard anything like it. But they're singing in English! And I'm hearing it with my ears!* He rested in his faith in the Plane as his new friend's namesake sang him into a sleep that lasted eight blissful hours. When he woke, G-Pa had let go of his hand and turned away, sleeping peacefully. "Thank you, Jerry." He whispered again.

Passacenday

As Fran predicted, the crew was sharper than ever. They gathered another full truckload of perfectly ripe pomegranates by noon. Elmer gave them the afternoon off and came in for a quick lunch before heading to the docks. Halfway through it, he put down his sandwich and looked at Fran. "Hey, I didn't commit to *nothing* last night."

"Did you unplug the cable?"

"I'll do it before I go."

"You do that, and I'll go ask them if it's a problem."

Elmer looked up savagely as she poured him more coffee. "I don't want you going in their house all by yourself with them guys there."

Fran scoffed. "Maybe I'll find out there's no problem and you can go back to watching your killing shows."

"You watch the news. That's the worst killing show," Elmer retorted. "And maybe you going over there will be a killing show."

Fran fired on him. "Do you really think so? We've had lots of workers who worried me way more than they do. Like those two guys three years ago. I was afraid to leave Jerry around them, and they were Americans, born and raised."

"Well, these guys ain't American. They ain't even Earthen, I guess. We don't know nothing about them. Maybe they'll eat you!"

"They don't eat meat."

"They're aliens, Babe. They're gonna get up inside you and control you, take you over. Plant alien seeds in you. Pretty soon we'll be working for them doing who knows what?"

Fran levelled her eyes at him. "Come on. Do you really think so, Elmer? You've seen too many sci-fi movies."

Elmer's eyes ducked away, less sure than yesterday. "I gotta go to town, so I guess you'll do what you want. But I don't want my boy finding you all…" His mouth worked soundlessly for a few words. Then he snapped, "We'll talk about it tonight! Don't you go over there, Fran!"

Fran watched from the window over the sink as Elmer grabbed the corner post on the porch and hoisted himself onto the porch rail. She didn't rush out there to spot him, like she usually would. She didn't even say "be careful." She just watched him fumble angrily with the second cable from the satellite dish on the porch roof. Then he half slid, half lunged down the corner post, turning his left ankle a bit when it hit the porch. His revenge, a swift kick of the offending railing with that same foot, couldn't have helped much. He limped down the porch steps and disappeared around the overloaded truck. It sputtered to life noisily and lurched down the driveway, wayward pomegranates bursting from under the brimming tarp to smash on the rocky driveway.

Fran didn't think for a minute that the humble little vegetarian family would harm a fly. But Elmer had said about as flat-out a "no" as she'd ever heard in almost 20 years of marriage, so she finished the dishes and watched their quarters from the window, waiting.

Salistar came out on the porch and grabbed a lug box a little too urgently for a leisurely garden mission. Fran decided to give her the tour.

As she approached, she heard Valko's voice thundering from the house in his unfamiliar language.

Felsic's much lighter voice replied in a submissive whine. Then suddenly, in perfect English, "I must make the pomegranate wine! It is my station!"

Hum, that sounds good, Fran mused to herself. *I could get wine-making stuff at the store.* Her parents' feed store had branched out recently in directions never thought of by Fran's grandparents, Fred and Ann Abel. Pragmatic as salt, they'd called it by the clever name of Abel Feed and sold animal feed, like the sign said. Then Fran's parents, Frank and Bernice, brought in more garden items and pet food. When Fran's younger brother, Frank Jr., took over, he changed the name to Cow Chow, with a cute logo of a cow's snout with a blade of grass in it. He introduced grow bags, grow lights, and high-end organic fertilizers with price tags that rendered them cost-effective for only one crop. It wasn't pomegranates.

Medicinal marijuana had just been legalized in California, and with that came a new, more urban clientele: pot growers with disposable incomes and a yen for artisan wine- and beer-making materials, and, Fran's touch, home canning supplies.

Fran joined Star at the garden gate. She spotted Baput and G-Pa in the distance, sharing a bench facing the river.

Fran clicked the carabiner that latched the flimsy wire gate to the saggy chicken-wire fence.

Star fingered the cold metal posts and raised her doe-like eyes questioningly.

"Keeps the zebkin out," Fran explained. She had memorized the few words Jerry had taught her.

Star smiled with warmth and recognition, fingering the chicken wire curiously. "Good idea, no zebkin eat the garden."

The autumn garden was empty but for the mold-speckled skeletons of last summer's tomatoes, peppers, and zucchinis. In a shady corner, bright green chard leaves drooped on their stalks of brilliant red and yellow. Star gasped, walking toward them. "The most color I have seen since..."

"Go ahead. Pick some," Fran encouraged. "Anytime. It's all there is now, but do you have time to plant tomorrow? I got some seeds. More greens, and some cabbage and broccoli. Snow peas, for protein, you know. You must know about plant proteins. You don't eat meat at all, do you? Dairy? Eggs?"

She looked at Star, to see if she knew what an egg was, and found her silently crying. "Oh, Honey!" She rushed to hug her, then glanced toward the house, where male voices still shouted in a foreign language.

For the first time, Fran feared the big man. Would he see her embrace as a threat? Think Star's telling tales? *How would a bruise look on that green skin?* Fran wondered, and turned her budding embrace into a beckoning motion. "Come on, let's pick some of this chard right now. Then we can lay out our new garden." This would mostly be pantomime, a cover for a deeper discussion, but Fran was delighted to have a new gardening partner.

Star spoke as she picked, drinking in the deep colors as if she got nourishment just by looking at them. "Felsic makes the pomegranate wine. It is his station, like pomegranate oil is mine. But he drinks too much of it. Every year. All year around if there is enough. That was before he lost Peratha and Trillella."

Fran quickly counted syllables. *Three and three. A wife and daughter, probably.* "Did the nimblies get them? The bumblies?"

"I don't know!" Star rose, suddenly agitated.

Was that fear? Anger? Fran stood up and turned her gaze at the rest of the garden. She pointed. "We'll put the broccoli over there and cabbage over there."

Star continued, "They were outside the Holy Cave, with only Heffala, the ganeesh, to protect them."

"The elephant?" Fran interrupted, remembering what Jerry had told her.

Star nodded abruptly. She knelt by the tomato bed and began pulling the rotting stems.

Fran knelt across from her and did the same. "Why were they outside during the attack?"

That is when she saw a side of Star she had not yet seen. Her face was drawn, so she had wrinkles where there were none before. Her cheeks were sunken, and there were dark bags under her eyes. *The poor thing's just exhausted. No, it's deeper than that. She's weary, like a war mom.*

Star's face seemed to become more pointed when she replied tensely, "Akash. No. G-Pa!" she spat. Had she just demoted her father? "G-Pa would not let them in!"

Feeling like an inquisitive three-year-old, Fran asked again, "Why?"

"They are not Akashic line. And they are women. So of course, they should not enter the Holy Cave. But the nimblies were coming! Even Valko wanted to let them in. G-Pa," she almost sneered the nickname, "G-Pa say 'no. They stay outside.'" She looked far away, squeaking, "I don't know what happened to them. Peratha, Trillella, Azuray, Banova, all of them!"

"All of them? Wow. Most of them probably still there, aren't they? Could the elephant, ganeesh, have protected Felsic's family?" she asked hopefully.

"Yes, she is tough old ganeesh. Nimblies can't," she made a circle with the thumb and forefinger of her left hand and stuck her right forefinger through it.

"They can't pierce their skin?" Fran guessed.

"Right. Very tough," Star confirmed.

"And the nimblies might have passed by without seeing them?"

"Nimblies go by. Go to the Great Hall. Lots of people there to kill. Maybe if ganeesh hid them, they would live."

Fran went on hoping. "Would they go in the Cave when it was clear?"

"Go in the Cave? After Akash said no?" Kneeling in the wet weeds, Star tilted her head back and closed her eyes in thought. Then, her warm, black eyes opened, and she smiled mischievously. "Yes. Peratha would go in the Holy Cave if G-Pa was, was…"

Suddenly Star looked almost as lost as G-Pa. Fran let her be quiet for a while. The house had quieted, too. She looked over at the silhouette of Baput and G-Pa on the bench by the river. Shastina sat on the ground beside them, facing the river, too, head cocked slightly to one side.

Baput and G-Pa stared at the sparkling river that flowed below them, always changing, yet always the same. Baput breathed deeply and began to ascend, delighted to see G-Pa's spirit right beside him, eager and happy. Had he forgotten about yesterday?

The TV Plane was just scattered booms and flashes, like lightening in distant clouds. The immediate space was clear, and they ascended rapidly. The iPlane was not so overwhelming here by the river, but it was definitely there.

Baput's spirit grasped G-Pa's by the hand. "G-Pa, remember when we jumped into the river? Hang on. It's gonna feel like that."

The surf of the internet hit them. Hauling G-Pa behind him, Baput swam as hard as he could, scrambling up and to the left, onto an imaginary surface that bobbed in the flow. He hauled G-Pa up next to him and let him lay there gasping while he steered the ethereal raft to a website that taught young children to read English. He liked it for G-Pa, because it used non-threatening rasta images of small big-eared creatures like the ones Shastina caught in the orchards. G-Pa calmly watched the cartoon, and Baput could tell he was learning. He could see his soul expanding.

"But, G-Pa, there's so much more!" Baput exclaimed after a while, eager to explore this limitless new world. His spirit grabbed the old Akash's, and they dove right into the surf. They passed millions of doorways. Baput could sense what was behind each one. Billions of voices, spoken and written, in every language on Earth. Sellers hawking wares that a green person could not even imagine. All kinds of music. Drama and action. Discussion. Often angry discussion. *Why?* Baput wondered. He had never heard such insults and curses on the Plane at home. He clutched G-Pa's spirit tightly and shied away from the white-hot fury that lined both sides of the flow. That pushed them into the fastest part of the current. They were getting swept away, out of control. He had to get G-Pa up to the Akashic Plane.

He opened his eyes. He could see the calming river, flowing much slower than the surf of the internet. He breathed deeply and deliberately, trying to slow the inexorable tide of information, or slow himself and G-Pa. Let it flow around them. "Be like a rock in the river." He imagined telling G-Pa, or did he say it out loud? Which plane was he on? He saw the true Akashic Plane, up and to the left, as he always envisioned it. His spirit swelled like it was taking a deep breath.

He grabbed G-Pa, encircled him with his soul and held tight. Concentrating hard, he used the pressure of the surf to launch them both onto the Plane. The sudden leisurely pace made them feel like they were moving backwards for a moment. G-Pa hugged the Plane like a weary traveler kissing his home turf. His spirit relaxed. It seemed to breathe, long and slow.

Baput couldn't tell how long they remained there, resting and healing, until the buzz of Jerry's dirt bike came up the drive. Baput didn't mind the interruption. He was satisfied with their session. He started to coax the Akash out of his trance, then decided to leave him there for a while. Could he get down through the iPlane OK? *I won't be too far away,* he rationalized as he crossed the grassy area to meet Jerry at the stone sauna.

Jerry had the windowless square illuminated down to the corners with a battery-powered camping lantern. He handed Baput a broom.

"This is woman's work!" Baput objected.

"You want your mom to get bit by spiders? This is our project. The cleaning's no fun, but I've got plans for this place! This is gonna be a mini Taj Mahal! We just gotta do what we gotta do. No complaining."

They knocked the cobwebs from the rafters and swept the wide benches along the walls where Jerry's grandparents had sat, naked and sweating, the smell of eucalyptus oil rising from the roaring stove and mingling with the steam that filled the pitch-dark little world.

"This light is too harsh for meditating. I'll go find something else," Jerry decided and headed for the shop.

"I'll check on my G-Pa," Baput replied.

Baput tentatively approached his G-Pa on the bench by the river. He was so still! That was good. He was meditating. *Or dead. Also good. What?!* The thought shocked him. How could he think that? It seemed the former Akash had no more to offer. He was just a burden. Ashamed of his darkest thoughts, Baput suddenly wondered if G-Pa could hear them. If he was truly meditating, really on the Plane, he could see and hear everything!

Baput didn't know whether to be relieved or disappointed when he heard the snoring. Alive, yes. On the Plane, no. But had he been? "G-Pa, wake up." He roused his pater gently.

The Akash's eyes opened, vague and disoriented, but with something of the old twinkle. "You fell asleep." Baput searched his eyes. "Did you ascend? Did you reach the Plane?" Baput asked in a rush. So much hung in the balance: Sleeping in the top bunk without holding his sweaty hand, spending time with Jerry, continuing his training to be Akash, finishing his childhood!

"I think so," G-Pa evaded.

"You think? How can you not know?"

"It is different. It is not clear. What I see is blurred. Do you remember Pindross, your friend Pindrad's popa? He was the artist, the Rasta maker."

"Pindrad is now, G-Pa. He must have ascended today, if he lives." Baput and G-Pa both got that curious look again, trying to image how things could still be going on back at home when they couldn't see them, couldn't feel them.

G-Pa pushed past the confusion. "Pindross has lost his sight. A terrible thing for an artist. Good thing he has a son. He once painted me a painting of what he sees now. Images doubled and tripled, offset and blended together, the colors muted and blurred. That is how I see the Plane now! And the sound is garbled, too! I can feel it. It comforts me, helps me sleep. But I cannot understand its messages."

"Can you see and hear on the iPlane?" Baput wondered.

"The place with the little animals?" he asked fondly. "Why yes. I could see them. They were like Pindross' earlier work. I could hear, too. A, B, C, D," he sang the alphabet song all the way back to their quarters, leaning heavily on Baput's shoulder. Baput shook his head sadly at his mother's anxious look, knowing she had even more at stake than he had.

They had just gotten the old man settled in his chair when the high-pitched whir of Jerry's cordless vacuum reached him from the sauna. The Akash looked straight up and let out a flesh-curdling howl, his eyes and mouth wide open. Shastina, at his feet, joined in. By the time the vacuuming stopped, G-Pa was shaking and mumbling, lost again.

Where Ya From?

Electric Christmas candles flickered from the top of the wood stove and two of the sauna benches.

"How?" Baput asked, gazing at the candlelight.

"I've got a solar panel on the roof, and I ran a wire right down the chimney, 'cause my dad said you guys can't light a fire."

"Solar panel?" Baput asked, running his finger over a string of white Christmas lights that spiraled up the outside of the stove pipe.

"Yeah," Jerry answered proudly, "the power of the sun."

"Shavarandu!" Baput gasped softly, the whites of his eyes gleaming in the dim light.

"What? It's just electricity, like the lights in your quarters." Jerry shrugged. He showed Baput how to turn the lights on and off. Baput practiced silently, his hands shaking a little.

"You want to go to the Horizontal Tree?" Jerry invited. He stepped outside without waiting for an answer. Baput extinguished the lights and followed.

"Did your G-Pa get on the Plane?" Jerry asked as they headed up the trail.

Baput didn't answer. Neither spoke until they sat side by side on the worn horizontal trunk, staring at the river.

"So," Jerry began, as casually as he could, "where are you from?"

Baput didn't answer right away. Finally, he said slowly, "I don't understand *where.*"

"What? You speak really good English! What do you call the place you live?"

"Nauve." Baput answered with the word for "home."

"Is that your planet?"

"Planet?" Baput echoed as dumbly as when he'd first arrived.

"You've been on the iPlane. You've gotta know about planets! Doesn't your Plane teach about planets?"

"I don't know." Baput saw an image of round balls spinning in magnificent order, but he had no idea what they were. What did these spinning balls have to do with home?

"Well, if you don't know about planets, what is Nauve? Your country? Your state? Your village?"

"It is home," Baput answered with a shrug.

Jerry had so many questions, he started another line. "Is the weather the same as here? You grow poms, so it must be."

"This is like harvest time at home. A little warmer, though."

"Really? Warmer here? I wonder why," Jerry remarked, his sarcasm lost on Baput. "Same weather. Same time of year," Jerry mused. "How many moons do you have?"

Baput looked up sharply. "Moon? Kakeeche is the only moon. We would never have another moon!"

Jerry looked at him sideways. "OK. One moon then." The young scientist brushed off the odd reaction and pursued his line of questioning. "How old are you?"

"I'm 12 now, since the day we met. It was my birthday."

"Wow! That was quite a party you had. I've been 12 for a couple months. August fifth. How about your mom and dad? How old are they?"

"Momama is about 40. Popa is older, I think 43. Felsic is about 38. G-Pa is so old, I don't know." Baput shrugged. He leaned away uncomfortably, started to get up.

"Sorry." Jerry had been told he could get intense sometimes, usually when he was trying to solve a problem. "I'm just trying to see if you guys age like us, and," he added significantly, "if your years are the same length." He explained quickly to those confused dark eyes. "Your climate is like ours. Your planet must be about as far from its sun as we are from ours. And your home would have to be at about the same place on that planet. The same latitude and longitude, for the crops to be the same, the climate the same..." He trailed off, his eyebrows furrowed. "Maybe you aren't from another planet at all. Come on." He touched Baput's shoulder. "I want to show you something."

He took off running toward the houses, Baput at his heels. They ran right past the sparkling-clean sauna, past the garden and up Jerry's porch steps.

Brodey slid off the couch as they entered. He looked past Baput anxiously, as if hoping for Shastina, then greeted the boys with a disappointed grunt and a half-hearted wag of his tail.

The farm workers didn't usually enter the house. Jerry assumed the normal rules didn't apply to these helpers, the Nauvians? Mom had said Baput should get an education, and Jerry had promised to see to it.

Baput and Brodey followed Jerry straight back to the end of the hall, to a room on the left with a huge oak desk and shelves full of books. In the middle of the room was the strangest, and perhaps the most beautiful thing Baput had ever seen. Something about it stirred his blood deep inside, although he had no idea what it was. Balls of different sizes mounted on thin, circular tracks of metal, each circle bigger than the last, surrounding a large ball of glass at the center. Jerry turned a switch and the central orb lit up.

The balls on the outer rings were larger, but all were dwarfed by the central light. Most of the balls had little rings around them, with teeny, tiny balls on them. Jerry spun all the metal rings, touching each orb and setting it spinning. Baput stood open-mouthed. It was like music, the way they all moved in harmony.

"Do you know what this is?" Jerry asked pointedly. If this Plane of his gives him access to unlimited knowledge, why doesn't the apprentice Akash know science? Why no technology? Not even metals? He grabbed the third orb from the center. Bigger than the first two, but smaller than some of the outer ones, it only had one tiny sphere circling it. "This is Earth. This is where we are now. Where I live."

"On that?" Baput squinted at the tiny orb.

"Yeah, that's our planet. The rock we live on. Of course, this is just a tiny model. It's actually really, really big. Earth travels around in space, and we ride on it, like a tick on a dog." Jerry scratched Brodey's ears. He really enjoyed that analogy. It put the whole thing in perspective, made it all seem less serious.

Baput closed one eye and put his face right up to the little ball, like he was trying to look at something tiny. *How could I be here, and on that little ball?* He wondered. But then, how could he be on Earth and not nauve?

Jerry named all the planets, pointing to each: "Mercury, Venus, Earth, Mars, Jupiter, Saturn, Uranus, Neptune and Pluto!" He said the last one defiantly. "This thing is old, back when he was still a planet." Jerry explained to his completely uncomprehending friend.

"Watch this." He put his finger on the tiny sphere that circled the Earth. "That's the moon. Look." He put the moon on the side of the Earth toward the glowing orb of the sun. "If you're on Earth, looking at the moon, you don't see it when it's here, because you're looking at the sun, too. It's day. The sun's too bright for you to see the moon. That's what we call new moon, or no moon. You don't see the moon that night because it's been up all day, right in front of the sun."

He pulled the sphere to the other side of Earth, away from the sun. The tiny sphere glowed, reflecting the sun's light. "This is full moon. The sun hits it and lights the whole thing up, so it looks like a big circle in the sky."

He put the moon at both halfway points and explained the waxing and waning moons, perfectly half-lit on one side, then the other. Prattling along happily, he didn't notice that Baput was down on the floor, breathing heavily. Brodey kept sticking his snout in his pale gray face and wagging his tail defensively.

Jerry got down on the floor with his friend. "Baput, what's wrong?"

"Kakeeche!" Baput muttered over and over. He sounded like his G-Pa.

Jerry wondered if he was allergic to something in the house.

"I go nauve," Baput muttered, staggering to his feet.

"To your planet?" Jerry asked. Could they just leave any time?

Baput pointed in the direction of the quarters. "Home," he translated, walking unsteadily out the door. Jerry and Brodey stayed close behind him until Star received him at the quarter's door. Baput brushed right past her and into the house without a word.

Baput went straight to his room and climbed up to the top bunk. He lay on his back in his favorite meditation pose: palms up, legs and arms slightly spread, no part of his body touching any other.

He tried to Akashic Breathe, but his body gasped for air in frantic gulps. Silent tears ran into his hair and ears and onto the thin mattress. He gulped another breath clumsily, knowing it was wrong. *You have to do what they say, think what they say, even breathe as they say! As HE says! So you can ascend to the Plane and serve the people, according to their stupid rules that don't make sense!*

Baput stopped trying to breath in a special way. He didn't try to ascend. He just lay there, his mind running this way and that like a caged animal. *The village was on a ball. And the Look 'N Up is on another ball. And our ball got on their ball… But, what happened to nauve, home, the Great Hall, the Holy Cave, the whole village? How can there be a moon, but not Kakeeche! No Kakeeche!* Dread crept in from all sides. There was no way to keep it away.

He woke when his momama called him to Passascenday Dinner. He didn't know he had slept. He slid down from his bunk, walked into the dining room like a zombie and sat heavily.

Still in the corner, G-Pa struggled to get up. Felsic came in and grandly swept the old Akash to his feet and brought him to the table. Valko followed, after washing up in the indoor bathroom with the hot running water he had come to love.

Oddly, Valko talked more than anyone, reporting on their progress with the harvest. "Just two more days and we will have the first pick. Then Elmer says we take two days off. That will give the late ones more time to ripen, and we will go through them again. On our days off, we will pick for ourselves. He says we can take as many as we want."

"I have no jars for oil. I will ask Fran. Is the press ready?" Salistar dared ask her husband.

"Tomorrow. Right, Felsic?"

Felsic replied excitedly. "Yes, tomorrow. You should see. We used metal to make it strong. It will last for years!"

"Years?" they all asked in unison.

Each pair of eyes searched each other pair. No one could even ask the question, much less answer it: *How long will we be...?*

No more was said, not even about Passascenday.

At their own dinner table, Jerry reported, "Something's wrong with Baput, I think. I showed him the solar system model, and he got sick, or freaked, or something. He kept muttering 'Kakeeche, Kakeeche' over and over."

"Did he say what that means?" Elmer asked.

"No clue."

"Maybe it's a religious thing," Fran guessed. "Honey, you go easy there."

"One thing you don't talk about." Elmer recited: "Politics and religion."

"That's two things, Dad."

"Is it? It's getting kinda all mixed up these days, seems like."

Fran was empathizing again. "Jerry, I know how you feel about science, but you have to respect your friend's religion. He's from a strange land. They're primitive. They don't know science like you do. They've evolved completely separately from us. They're bound to have some very different ideas. Be tolerant, Jerry, please. Don't make fun."

"Of course, Mom. I'll be nice. He's my friend, and he needs my help. We gotta take another night off from TV tonight, so he can sleep. I think I might have blown his mind." Jerry hated to say it. His favorite show was on tonight. He wondered if they would pick up the signal if he recorded on the DVR with the TV off.

Elmer interrupted his musings. "Don't worry. I unplugged them."

"They might still receive our signal, Dad," Jerry had to put in, just to show how smart he was, even though if he just stayed quiet...

Fran's eyes tightened. Should she tell? "Elmer, watch Felsic, OK? I think he has a drinking problem."

Elmer responded quickly. "That's too bad. I was looking forward to having a cold one with him in the shop."

Was he sarcastic? Fran couldn't tell. For all his tough talk, he had spent the afternoon in the shop helping Valko and Felsic build a pomegranate press, and she'd heard laughter coming from there more than once.

"I'll tell you what," Elmer proposed, brightening. The Giants are in the playoffs, and baseball ain't violent. It's nice and boring. They'll sleep like babies, right?"

They all exchanged a look and a shrug. "I guess so," Jerry agreed.

Fran sighed, "And I won't turn on the news between innings."

"We'll turn the sound off and the music on, like we used to. I don't need to hear them announcers yapping."

So after dinner Elmer watched the playoffs and Fran read a book. Jerry did his homework and surfed the net instead of playing video games. He mostly wondered what Kakeeche was, and why the model of the solar system made his friend ill.

Baput picked at his dinner until everyone else was done eating. Then he excused himself and headed for bed.

Salistar jumped in front of him and put a hand on his forehead. "Are you OK, Son?"

"Yes, Momama. I'm just tired."

"Good boy!" Valko crowed from his chair. Baput could not imagine why. "He is like his popa. He doesn't sleep until the Season is over. That is a good Akash!" He shot a disdainful glance at the incapacitated G-Pa in the corner. "You are right, Son. We should retire early and catch up on our sleep."

Baput suppressed a groan when Momama brought G-Pa for him to tend. He would have to help the old man in in the boor, then sleep on his back in the lower bunk, holding his shriveled hand all night long.

Without trying to ascend to the Plane, or even the iPlane, Baput's mind wandered. He even longed for the TV plane. He wished he had never said anything to Jerry. Watching a story he couldn't quite understand, but could almost relate to, would take his mind off the thing that swirled so fast it still made him nauseous.

Eventually he fell into a fitful sleep. He stood on a ball, barely big enough to hold him. The ball traveled at a high speed toward a man with a club. The man swung the club and hit the ball, smack! With a sudden reversal of direction, the ball flew far, far away, over the left field wall, carrying the little world of green people hurtling through the space between balls to land on the flat spot by the river on the Look'N Up Pomegranate Ranch on Earth.

When the little ball came to rest, he and his family came staggering off of it. They found Jerry standing there, hair over one eye and that lopsided grin exaggerated like one of Pindrad's caricatures, laughing at him. Laughing at Kakeeche!

3. Kakeeche

Jerry was right, thought Elmer. *Something is wrong with that kid.* Baput picked alone, far behind the others, at about half his usual pace. *We were quiet last night and everything. At this rate, it will take until 2:00 to fill the truck.*

He smiled and chided himself aloud, "Elmer, what are you complaining about? They're still the best pickers ever."

Baput was glad they were running late. He wouldn't have to spend much time with G-Pa before Jerry came home. He picked alone, trying to think of ways to approach the Akash. Could he admit his faith was shaken to the core? Would he get some reassurance from his mentor? Or would he just start yelling, or worse, go back to his mumbling?

Salistar stared at her silent son through lunch. Tired last night, OK. But something else is wrong. Something serious.

By the time they finished their late lunch, there was only an hour until Jerry got home. Baput plucked a meditation cushion from the floor, took G-Pa by the hand, and walked him to the sauna.

Shastina stayed at G-Pa's heels until Baput opened the sauna door. She stepped inside ahead of them and sniffed the dark space thoroughly. When she emerged, she whirled around in a circle and lay down just outside the door, her ears erect.

G-Pa fondled the rock of the walls, subdued, but aware. Baput turned on the Christmas lights that spiraled up the stovepipe and handed one of the electric candles to G-Pa, who stared at it myopically for a minute before he took in the whole room.

"Do you like it, G-Pa?" Baput asked.

"Why, yes, Son. Very much." He was lucid!

"You won't pick up any signals here. You can get right on our Plane any time." Baput gulped, hoping G-Pa wouldn't want to right now, because he sure didn't. *Keep him talking.* "G-Pa? Um, Akash?"

"You are troubled, Son." The Akash was aware enough to see.

"I don't think Kakeeche are here."

"Well, of course they are. I see them every night." The wiry frame tensed suddenly and G-Pa's eyes blazed in the flashing light. "First Full

Kakeeche is in two days!" he cried. "We must prepare for the ceremony! Has your momama made the costumes? Where is my robe?" He scanned the unfamiliar building. "Where is the shrine?" he gasped, clutching his balding forehead.

Baput hadn't even thought about First Full Kakeeche since they'd arrived, as Jerry put it. Had he lost his faith even sooner than he realized? G-Pa had forgotten too, until now. Baput wished he hadn't even mentioned Kakeeche. The elaborate ceremony would add to Momama's work. "But, G-Pa, there are only five of us. How can we do the ceremony?"

"What of those others? There are three. That makes eight. Still too few, but we'll make do. Tell them they will join us. Do they have extra costumes?"

"G-Pa, they do not believe in Kakeeche."

G-Pa stood frozen, right hand raised slightly. The twinkling e-candles glinted in his dark eyes, flashing on and off, on and off for too many breaths. "Don't believe in Kakeeche," he repeated slowly, then snapped, "You stay away from that boy! You hear me?"

"But G-Pa, he's my friend."

"No, he is not! You stay away!"

"We need him to help us find our way in this world!"

"Let the adults find their way in this world," G-Pa mocked. "You are Apprentice Akash. You don't find the way in this world. You find your way on the Plane." He gestured vaguely upward.

"Do you?" the words were out before Baput could think. The buzz of Jerry's dirt bike rang the rocks of the sauna.

In a hurry and feeling trapped, Baput took charge. "We can't do the ceremony with five people, or even eight. It won't do Kakeeche justice. They will be insulted." He almost rolled his eyes, like Jerry. Why did the familiar realities of nauve suddenly seem ridiculous? There was a remedy in Akashic law. Something sensible for once. Baput tried to sound mature and dignified, like an Akash should.

"We should declare *Antipassa*, postpone the ceremony." The ceremony was held on the first full moon after First Pomegranate Day. But if it occurred during the Season, when everyone was too busy fighting bumblies and nimblies, burying the dead, or frantically harvesting and processing the over-ripening pomegranates, the Akash could declare Antipassa and postpone the ceremony until the next full moon.

"But the Season is over. There are no bumblies and nimblies, no dead to bury. The harvest is going well. I heard Valko say so," G-Pa argued with unusual clarity.

"We are not ready." Baput protested. "We have no costumes. Momama has no squares stored. She would have to weave them all from scratch and make all the costumes in less than two days! And we are still harvesting. Besides, we don't have enough people, G-Pa! It will be a travesty!" he repeated.

"We failed to celebrate Passascenday. We must honor Kakeeche or they will turn on us." G-Pa's deep eyes showed genuine fear.

Would he fade again? He needed something to hold on to. Something that would last longer than a ceremony. The shrine!

Baput spoke softly. "We, um, I, will make a shrine for you. Then we can have a small ceremony. We'll gather at the shrine under the moon and say some words. Just us believers. You can do a sermon about how we all love Kakeeche and we ask them to protect us here on Earth."

"Earth?"

"Yes, G-Pa. That's where we are. It's a planet. A round ball in the sky." When Baput said it out loud, it sounded every bit as silly as Kakeeche was going to sound to Jerry!

G-Pa's eyes were starting to wander toward the back of his mind. Baput rushed the encounter, eager to leave. He placed the meditation cushion on a sauna bench and steered his G-Pa to it. "Here, G-Pa. You stay here. Look at your candle. Try to meditate. Our Plane is here, and no others. You try. It's here."

"But no Kakeeche!" the old man was getting mumbly again.

"No, G-Pa! You see Kakeeche every night! They are here. It's OK." Baput knew the last thing G-Pa needed was to feel as lost as he did without Kakeeche. It added an extra layer of guilt to his next move, but he had to do it. They were lost, and Jerry knew the way. "G-Pa, I am going away for a little while. You stay here and try to meditate. Think about your sermon for the ceremony. But don't go anywhere. I'll be back."

"Where are you going?"

Baput would have hated to lie to his Akash, so he didn't. "To school," he replied. He stepped out of the sauna and looked toward Jerry's house. He had never felt so anxious before, not even when the Akash had shown him the Shavarandu hidden behind the door in the Holy Cave. He still wasn't sure he wanted to, but he just had to explore the forbidden mysteries Jerry knew, even though they made him sick.

Here came Jerry, straw-colored hair covering one eye and a big grin twisting his face like some disturbing memory. Baput stepped out onto the trail to meet his friend. Brodey broke from Jerry's heel and ran right to Shastina

"My G-Pa's in there," Baput whispered, jerking his thumb toward the shed. I have to stick around, in case he wanders."

"Is he, um, sane?"

"He was when I left," Baput glanced toward the shed, then toward the river. "Let's go to the river bench. We can talk, and I can watch."

The two boys walked across the lawn to the river bench, Brodey bounding around them in circles. Shastina whined, but she stayed at her post just outside the sauna, watching after them.

When they sat, Jerry poured his questions out. "How's your G-Pa? Did he like the lights? Did he get on the Plane?"

"He liked the sauna. Especially the flickery candles."

"Did it work? Did he get on the Plane?"

"He's trying now, without me. It's better. He wants a shrine for the First Full Kakeeche ceremony tomorrow night."

"So, you and him are gonna make a shrine?"

"You and me. Even though I told G-Pa you don't believe in Kakeeche."

"How can I believe in it when you won't even tell me what it is?"

"You will see. Tomorrow night. Your whole family can come, I guess. Even though you don't believe." Baput found himself whispering the last part.

"You're not gonna, like, kill anybody, are you?" Jerry started to get up slowly.

"No, of course not! What are you talking about?"

"Well, some people do sacrifices to their gods. They kill people, or animals. Kakeeche is a god, right?"

"They are many. We cannot represent them with only eight people, especially if only five believe, so we will just have a small ceremony. The women must weave us all new white costumes. And we need a shrine. A little tower," he indicated about three feet high, "with Kakeeche on it, in five phases." He counted on his fingers. "New crescent, waxing half, full, waning half and waning crescent."

"What about new moon?" asked Jerry, finally getting a clue about Kakeeche.

"You mean, no Kakeeche? How can you show no Kakeeche?" Baput asked, and continued his list. "Also, a pomegranate, ganeesh, and a dog like Shastina."

"My mom has some stuff. She might let you have her golden pomegranate. She has an elephant, too. A wooden one. We have a dog silhouette thing. You know, like a shadow? But it looks like Brodey, not Shastina. I have just the thing for the tower. It's in the shop. Come on!"

Jerry started to speed off toward the shop.

"Wait!" cried Baput, "My G-Pa!"

Baput relieved Shastina from her post. She wrestled in the grass with Brodey, rolling over and over in total abandonment. The boys agreed that Jerry would go home and ask his mom for stuff, then head to the shop to scrounge for the rest. Baput would meet him there after he took care of G-Pa.

"If I help you with this shrine, B, you gotta tell me all about Kakeeche. Deal?"

Baput agreed. He entered the dim shed and found G-Pa on the meditation cushion, snoring softly. He looked peaceful enough, but had he ascended? Had he found the answers? Baput shrugged, his new cynicism rooting through his thoughts like an over-amped immune system. *Does it matter?* He woke the old man and guided him home.

The Shrine

Fran hesitated at Jerry's odd request. "My mom got us that golden pomegranate when we switched from almonds to pomegranates. It's kind of special."

"It's for a good cause. We're making a shrine for Baput's Grandpa. I'm respecting their religion, Mom," he said earnestly.

"Did you find out what Kakeeche is?"

"I think it's the moon. He's gonna tell me while we make the shrine. I need your wooden elephant, too. And do we have a dog thing that looks like Shastina? Doesn't have to be purple."

"Your dad and Uncle Patrick had a German shepherd when they were kids. I think there's something. I'll look."

"I'm gonna put it all on my windmill."

"But, Jerry, you were going to make electricity with that old lawn ornament. That was a great project."

"I know, Mom. It's going for religion now." He gave her a strangely mature look that almost scared her. "Those old coffee cans still out there? Can I use some?"

"Sure, Jerry. And you can have the golden pomegranate, too."

When Baput arrived at the shop, he found Jerry kneeling before a short tower, metal tools and cylinders scattered on the floor. He was removing the blades from a three-foot high windmill. He left two blades, opposite each other, so they made a straight line.

Jerry brought Baput right in. "We'll cut the bottoms off these cans and use them for the moon phases. Leave this one whole, cut this one in half, see?"

Baput watched in amazement as Jerry cut right through the rounds of shiny metal with teeth of harder metal that he wore on his hand. He continued to talk as he did it, as if it wasn't amazing at all. "We'll put 'em across on top of these blades. We can hang the golden pomegranate from the middle, where that blade used to attach. We'll put the elephant on the side here, and the dog, if my mom finds one, over on this side. OK? Does that work?"

Jerry thrust a cutting tool into Baput's hand and showed him how to use it. He was awkward at first. It wasn't as easy as Jerry made it look, but he was cutting *breen*! Every cut made him stop to stare in wonder.

Jerry prepared the windmill frame and then started trimming Baput's first product into slivers.

When their hands were busy, Jerry prompted, "OK, Baput. Now tell me about Kakeeche."

Jerry had been so understanding, Baput wondered if maybe it was all just a language thing. He took his first shot from that unlikely position. "What is your word for the creatures that form the moon?"

Jerry choked on a total loss for words. Baput continued into the stunned silence, punctuated by the tinny moans of tortured soft metal.

"Kakeeche are the luminous creatures that make up the moon. Each night, they assemble, according to a very precise schedule. One night, they all come, and make a beautiful glowing ball like a giant pomegranate in the sky," Baput said raptly.

He seemed different to Jerry. Different from when he talked about the Plane. Kind of glossed over, like he was on some drug, or reciting something he had memorized. "About 14 nights later, none of them come at all. It is a terrifying night of total darkness without the Kakeeche. But they come back, the next evening. Just a few come the first time. Right after sunset, they appear in the west. They hold hands to form a half-circle around the outside, but only on the side toward the setting sun. Each night there are more. The half-ring gets thicker, and they come later and later. By the time half of the Kakeeche appear, they do not show themselves until midnight. Then, 14 more days and again comes that glorious full Kakeeche, when they all assemble in the eastern sky just as the sun goes down in the west. Then later and later they come, and less and less. They come up after sundown, then later into the night, until they are so late and so few you can only see a tiny sliver in the east before dawn, like the first evening one, but the other side is illuminated.

"First Full Kakeeche after First Pomegranate Day is the most important time for Kakeeche. That is tomorrow night," he concluded dramatically.

Always looking for an explanation, Jerry simply asked, "Why?"

"Because of their love for us," replied this new, alien Baput.

"Oh, boy," was all Jerry could say. He knew he had to respect his friend's religion, but he was so disappointed! It just didn't fit! Baput claimed to access a Plane of infinite knowledge greater than the internet. Couldn't he just Google "Lunar Cycles" and get a rational explanation? Eyes wet with shock and disillusionment, he asked, "Do you really believe that?"

Baput gathered himself indignantly. He looked bigger, somehow, and his face was older, but still with that blank, zombie look as if this was all rehearsed. "People take great comfort in knowing Kakeeche will come in their cycle, every month the same. If we don't believe, they'll turn their backs on us. We know, because every so often someone doubts Kakeeche, and they disappear! The Kakeeche all assemble at Full Kakeeche, as normal. Then, one by one they turn their backs so the moon darkens, not over several nights as usual, but right before your eyes! Sometimes all of them, until the moon is all dark. Sometimes, if the offense is less, only some of them go dark. The light has always returned within hours, but someday, if there is too much disbelief, Kakeeche will go dark forever!"

Jerry averted his gaze and rolled his eyes secretly, trying hard not to laugh out loud. Why would a smart kid with access to an infinite Plane of knowledge accept such a bizarre, and, in his opinion, ridiculous theory without question? Sure, it had scientific basis, based on simple observation. The lunar cycle was described correctly, and the punishment for doubting, that was simply a lunar eclipse. Nothing more than the Earth getting between the sun and moon and casting a shadow. It was one of the few things where Jerry found the scientific explanation less exciting than the lore primitive cultures used to explain it.

Wordlessly, Jerry began to affix phases of Kakeeche to the windmill blades with an electric drill and screwdriver. He wore the goggles he had worn to clean the sauna.

Baput's gut roiled and clenched as the high-pitched whirring of the tools swirled together with last night's nightmare and the bitterness of telling the story of Kakeeche to someone who doubted it, without fully believing it himself! Maybe it *was* idiotic! He looked over his shoulder and cringed at some unseen watcher of his thoughts.

Fran walked into a thick wall of silence. "Hi, boys! Look! I got your stuff! Even the German shepherd, a silhouette, like the Brodey one. It was in Uncle Patrick's stuff. He wouldn't mind. Go ahead, take it. Look at the moon!" She admired Jerry's arrangement but added, "Ooh, those have sharp edges, Honey. Someone might cut themselves!"

"Mom, it's a shrine. You're not supposed to touch it."

Fran looked at Baput. "You're not?"

"Akash touches it all the time."

"See?" Fran crowed. "File them down, or pad them or something."

"OK, Boss!" Jerry said sarcastically, digging a little cone-shaped grinder out of his kit. "I might need Dad, 'cause of you," he muttered, glancing at the grinding wheel on the workbench.

A shy voice came from the floor next to them. "Um, Jerry's momama?"

"You can call me Fran."

"My momama needs your help," Baput mumbled humbly.

"Why, anything! What does she need?" Fran asked anxiously.

Baput gushed, head down, embarrassed. "Tomorrow night is First Full Kakeeche." He glanced at Jerry. "First full moon after First Pomegranate Day. The Akash wishes to hold the ceremony." He tone got stiff and formal, until his eyes met Fran's and he broke down.

"I am sorry, Francina! I could not talk him out of it. He wants you and your family to attend, even though you are non-believers. He says you are just ignorant!" That official, brainwashed tone again: "Once you participate in the ceremony and see the true magnificence of Kakeeche, you will believe, and save your Earth! The Akash is amazed you even have a moon at all anymore!"

Fran looked sidelong at Jerry. He read her mind.

"It's OK, no sacrifices," he reassured. "I already asked."

"What's the bad news, then?" Fran wondered aloud, wishing maybe she hadn't.

"Do you have many squares?" Baput asked, looking into a face as blank and confused as his must have been on that first day. "We need white costumes. All eight of us. Momama has nothing to start with. No squares stored away, already woven and dried and ready to sew together like at home. She must make eight Full Kakeeche costumes by tomorrow night, from weaving to full adornment! My popa and uncle are out cutting the dry white grass from the edge of the West Orchard. I hope that's OK."

"Well of course, Honey." Fran hunkered down to Baput's level without touching her knees on the oily cement floor.

Jerry tried grinding the sharp edges of the metal. The piercing noise hurt Baput's head and made it impossible to converse. He headed for the door.

Fran followed, telling Jerry, "You be careful! I think we're going to Star's house."

"If I hurt myself grinding on this, it's your fault, Mom," Jerry muttered.

"What?" Fran whirled and demanded.

"I said, if I hurt myself grinding this for safety, it would be ironic."

Fran gave him The Stare. "I'll get your father out here." She headed out the door with Baput. "What does your momama need, Hon?"

"Can you weave grass?"

"I could learn. But I'd be slow. There must be another way." Fran calculated quickly as they walked. *White clothes, hmmm.* "I'll go get Elmer to help Jerry with the shrine. You go tell your momama I'm coming to help."

Helping

Fran and Salistar talked excitedly as they walked into the quarters' cluttered living area. Salistar's English was improving rapidly. Fran wondered if she could access more planes than Baput gave her credit for, no matter what parts she didn't have.

"Do you have time? What about your dinner?" Fran checked thoughtfully. She would offer their stew, but it was venison. Zebkin!

"In the oven," Star declared proudly. "I love oven. So easy! I have time now until dinner. Then tomorrow…" She sighed heavily.

"Is there special food for tomorrow?" Fran asked, seeing now why Baput was so worried.

"The first pumpkin pomegranate soup of the year." Star puffed with a timid pride. "I start it tomorrow morning, cook all day while I make the costumes."

"*We* cook. *We* make costumes," Fran promised gently. "I hear they need to be white. What else? Robes, pants?"

Star gestured at her own long-sleeved tunic top with full-length drawstring pants underneath, like the men wore. It was made out of one-foot squares of woven grass, sewn together. "Do you have any squares?" Star asked anxiously.

"No, Honey. We don't weave squares here. Hmmm, what do we have? I wish we had more time. I could order some white outfits on the net. But we can't get overnight delivery out here in the boonies."

Star hurried into her kitchen to get refreshments.

Fran talked louder. "You have no idea what I'm babbling about. What we can't do. How about what we *can* do? White squares. Sheets!

You have your white sheets on your beds. And there are some extras. You'll love my sewing machine. But does the Akash really want us there?"

Star looked puzzled. "Why no?"

Fran recalled the silence she had walked into at the shop. What had Jerry said? She knew Jerry could be harsh sometimes, intolerant of people who didn't share his belief in science. He was like a religious zealot in his atheism. *Who knows what damage he's already done? Baput was obviously upset.* Star trusted her, needed her like Baput needed Jerry. How could she tell her she didn't believe?

"Well, we're not, um, family, is all," she explained.

"Don't you have costumes?" Star asked, looking up and down at Fran's blue jeans and pink-and-gray plaid flannel shirt.

Fran thought hard. *We don't buy white clothes. Ever. This is a farm. Jerry would ruin it even before he outgrew it. Elmer's got that white baseball outfit! Would that still fit? And Jerry has his Junior League one, too. I have that white sweatshirt with the Cow Chow Logo. I could turn it inside out. But pants...*

"Don't worry, Honey," she decided. "I'll take care of my family's clothes. You have too much work already. What do you think? Sheets? Big squares, like on your bed."

"Maybe us. Not Akash. Not Baput, the apprentice, either. They must have the correct clothing and full adornment."

"Baput understands. He came to me for help. He said he tried to talk the Akash out of the ceremony, mostly because of what it's doing to you. He's a good boy! What's the minimum we have to do to make G-Pa happy?"

Salistar looked at Fran like she was alien, indeed.

Breen

Jerry tried to grind the edges of the moon phases to smoothness, but they just folded in front of the little grinding wheel. He was about to give up when Elmer walked in. "I hear you want to use the big grinder."

"Did Mom tell you about the ceremony?" Jerry asked without looking up.

"What ceremony?" Elmer asked, examining a half-moon shape with lumpy, tattered edges. "You're grinding too hard," he complained, forgetting his own question.

"The metal's too soft, Dad. The big grinder will just be worse, won't it?"

"Maybe if you folded it over like this here." Elmer pointed to an edge that had been accidentally folded over by the grinder. "Then it won't be sharp. This stuff's so soft, just use pliers."

He looked down at Baput on the floor, struggling with the metal scissors. "I'll show Baput. Wait till you see how fast he works!" Elmer grabbed a pair of gloves, a half moon and a pair of pliers, and sat down next to Baput.

In far less time than Jerry expected, Elmer presented the final crescent. Smooth in its narrow middle, the edges of both curved sides were knotted in rough, uneven curls.

"That's hideous, Dad."

Felsic ran in, out of breath. "I have to go tell Valko to stop mowing! Baput, you should see the squares Jerry's momama has!" he spread his arms as wide as they would go, across and up and down. "She and your momama make the outfits for us all. First Full Kakeeche ceremony!" He whooped, did a little dance. He looked out the door toward the orchard, then back at Elmer and the boys. "I will have a surprise!" He grinned like Elmer had never seen him grin. Then he spotted the sad scraps of thin metal on the floor. "Breen!" he called the soft, malleable metal.

"I thought you guys didn't have metal!" Elmer recalled.

"Breen, yes. Very ancient. You find pieces lying around sometimes. It lasts forever. You can bend it, fold it, or shape it by hammering it with rocks. It's not like your metal. It's too soft to hammer things with, or cut them. But it can't be cut, either. You can bang it together, make it smaller, or bang it thin and spread it out, but it's always the same piece." He put his scythe down and grabbed a hammer with an oversized, textured head.

"Oh, boy," muttered Elmer, rising to protect his son. *What's this wildcard up to now?*

"Watch," Felsic said as he tapped all around the edges of one of the half-moons.

"It still looks really bad." Jerry mourned his art, destroyed by interlopers.

Felsic raised the hammer higher. Everyone backed away, even Baput. He smashed the heavy, textured head into the half moon over and over, then went on to the others. Baput cringed behind his hands as Felsic beat gleefully on Kakeeche.

"That's better!" Jerry called when the beating stopped.

Baput slowly withdrew his hands from his face. The shiny metal surfaces were dimpled with craters and ridges, just like the moon! And the edges were smooth and safe.

"OK?" Felsic asked, satisfied. "I gotta go tell Valko to quit mowing," he repeated happily, about a half-hour after he'd said it the first time.

Cilandra

Star decided that if she made the Akash a really ornate ceremonial robe out of the almost-white grass Valko had cut way too much of, and decorated it with some of the wonderful items in Fran's bead collection, he would accept an undergarment made of white sheets.

Fran ran home and got her portable sewing machine, some spare flat white sheets, and a queen-sized set for Valko's attire. She would use the fitted corners as elastic waistbands for four simple pairs of pants.

Having inspired all this frantic labor, G-Pa snoozed peacefully in the corner. Star sat at the end of the table, weaving her grass squares. The sewing machine whirred softly as Fran fed the sheets through. Before long, Fran had to ask. "This is a lot of work. How can they expect you to do all this by yourself?"

"I am the only woman." Star stated the simple fact.

"Can't the men help? You've got more grass here than you can weave in days."

"They cut. Women weave. We store all the squares in the Great Hall. People take what they need to make new things, fix things, or make things bigger."

"What a great idea!" Fran remarked. Indicating the large pile of grass, she added, "After the ceremony, I can help you make squares of all that, if you show me how."

Star just started weaving again. Fran watched as she sewed.

Eventually, Star began to speak, her eyes fixed on her square, but also far away.

"I had a daughter, Cilandra," she began. "She could weave squares faster than anyone. And press oil. And cook, of course. She was so quick, so smart! Fully dedicated to the rolling pin, without question."

The rolling pin? Fran wondered. But this was no time to ask.

Star went on. "I tried to never complain in front of her, so as not to ruin her attitude." She choked, swallowed, went on. "Now no one remembers her. They only remember Batuk."

Fran had seen that bitterness before, and thought she understood the reason for it, but was that just the tip of some giant iceberg? A lost daughter? And who was Batuk? Hesitantly, she asked, "You've lost two children?"

"Yes," Star responded matter-of-factly. "Hasn't everyone lost at least one son in battle? You only have Jerry. How many have you lost?"

Fran looked down at her first pant leg. Salistar hadn't flinched a bit when she had measured her waist and legs, even from the crotch. She was as unabashed as Baput had been on the toilet.

Fran gathered her courage on an incoming breath and asked, "What happened to them? What happens to everyone's children? What happened to Cilandra?"

"Last Season, three years ago, the bumblies." Star's words came slowly, in a thick voice. "Like every Season, we all gathered in the Great Hall. The Akash and his apprentice usually stay there with the women and children, but that Season, they went to the Holy Cave right after the ceremony, before the attack. They were trying that new weapon…" she trailed off.

"Cilandra?" Fran nudged gently.

Star approached the memory again.

"We all feast before the battle. Then the men gather in the trenches in front of the Great Hall to fight the nimblies. They keep coming, all day. Then at night, the bumblies come, and keep coming all night. There are lulls in the evening and morning between nimbly time and bumbly time, but it never ends until three days and nights have passed. No matter how many the men kill, they keep coming until the Season is done.

"The women and children stay in the Great Hall. It is made of whole logs from the ancient trees of the forest. The bumblies and nimblies cannot penetrate it. The fourth- and fifth-cycle boys, nine years to fifteen, are too young to fight, but they are in training. They guard us as we continuously prepare food and supplies to send out to the trenches. Bandages, splints, poisoned darts, juice, and water, but mostly food and oil. The men get too hungry, too tired."

"Yeah, vegan food doesn't stick with you as much," Fran mused. "How do you send everything to the fighters?"

"Ganeesh," stated Star.

"Oh, yes. The elephants?" Fran exclaimed.

"Yes! El-e-fant. Ganeesh. Very tough skin. The bumblies can't cut through it. Grown-up ganeesh, that is," she finished sadly. Then she swelled with a resolute breath, looked up at Fran, and went on.

"As usual, Cilandra was at the center of the preparations, though she was only 14. She had that thick, rich hair, like Baput. So shiny. Black, with purple under." She lifted her hair at the temple to show a soft lavender underdown, like G-Pa's thin hair.

"It had never been cut. It cascaded past her waist, swaying back and forth like the Akash's robe. Her clothes bore more *gaa* than anyone's, man or woman. Even the new squares I had added in just the past year, she was growing so fast."

Tears welled, then dried and hardened, like her resolve.

"She surged about the Great Hall like a war chief, somehow commanding without being bossy. People responded by doing whatever needed doing, and they did their best work because they loved her. She inspired them all to do their part, no matter how small, to help us get through another Season.

"That year, everyone had time to get a good feeding and fill their food packs before the first nimblies came. The men went out. The great doors closed. As always, we waited inside, where we couldn't see what was going on. The boys took turns watching from the turrets and reporting what they saw to me. I am Tether to Akash, so I am in charge."

That timid pride flashed again.

Still wondering about "gaa," Fran had to ask, "What are the turrets?"

"They stick up above the roof. Made of small logs, about," she made a two-inch diameter circle with her thumb and forefinger. "Up and down," she gestured, "and close together. All around you, in a circle, big enough to stand and turn, look all around, above the roof.

"After six hours of fighting nimblies, Valko brought his troops in for food and supplies. He told us the northern longstick line was cut off by a bad flock of nimblies. They couldn't send their ganeesh in for supplies, because they needed him for cover. Valko was going to bring his men over from the side and try to flank them and drive them out of there so the longstick men could retreat. 'Be ready for them. They will be hungry, and wounded,' he told me—as if we hadn't been ready for hours!

"I told him Heffala, the mother ganeesh, could bring them food and more weapons." Star's voice rose a bit, tightened. "But he wouldn't listen! He says I am a woman. What do I know of fighting?"

Star almost sobbed, wiping her eyes with the square she was weaving. Glancing at her sleeping father, she went on with a fiery air that was new to Fran. "Two of Rakta's best men joined him from the East

Line, *the extra tough first line of defense,*" she mocked, flexing tight, wiry muscles that impressed Fran. "Valko took his two best men as well. Always so competitive! It will be his end! So," she looked around. G-Pa still snored in the corner.

"I think Rakta's East Trench and Valko's West Trench, the key trenches, were weakened by this move. Then the South Line came in with heavy casualties. The old men were sore and tired but smart and so fast! They all train on their assigned weapons since their second cycle, until it is mindless reflex. They ate like young men while the women loaded their ganeesh, and they went back out. The young men lay moaning on the floor, being ministered by young women for minor injuries, or mourned by old women for fatal ones.

"After that, no one. The North Trench had been pinned for almost eight hours. They had to be out of ammunition, food, water, pomegranate oil. Bleeding to death. No bandages, no shelter. And now it was dusk. Bumbly time!

"You call them bats, but much bigger than your bats. They have a horn right here." She pointed to the bridge of her nose. "Sharp, like my new cooking knife. They hook upward." She thrust her chin forward and looked up. "They are silent. They come from above and to the left."

Fran's eyebrows went up a bit at that.

"You don't see or hear them until they are on you, ripping your face, your neck! Then more come. Many. Their sharp blades rip your flesh…"

Star trailed off, dropping her head.

Fran shyly put a hand on Star's shoulder, stroked her back. Her hair was so soft! "Get it out, Babe. If you feel like it. Popa's asleep. I won't tell. It's OK."

Star sat up taller, turned her wet eyes to Fran. When she wiped them on a new square she had started, Fran took a chance and blurted, "That's twice. Akash's robe will be specially blessed!"

A sudden smile broke out across Salistar's face, like the sun coming out from behind a cloud. She even laughed a shy giggle. Then she went on weaving her square and her tale.

"The boys watched from the turrets as Valko's men traveled along the West Trench to the North Trench. When broke out in formation to attack, the air was so full of nimblies, the boys said they couldn't see the men anymore. The nimblies hovered over them, diving in and out with their wicked stingers for so long, we thought all the men would be dead, but still nimblies swirled.

"I beckoned to Azuray and Peratha. Cilandra came too, of course. And that little Tamaya," she remembered, suddenly angry. "Fourteen years, like Cilandra, but much younger, you know? She had no business, even if she is Baput's betrothed!"

Fran's eyes lit up. Baput was engaged? Is engaged?

"I told them we must get supplies to the men. 'If they live,' said Azuray. She is the War Chief's wife. Ruthless.

"'Should we load the ganeesh?' asked my dutiful Cilandra.

"'Yes,' I told her, 'but don't open the door until I see for myself what goes on. And keep her babbet locked in that pen!'

"'Yes, Momama,' she said. 'It was the last thing..." She took a deep breath and continued. "Tamaya followed her. *I'll help you!*'" Star quoted mockingly.

"As I climbed the ladder to the back turret, the boy in the front turret called, 'the nimblies are leaving! The North Trench is clear!' I knew that could only mean one of two things: They are all dead, and the nimblies would have gone away slowly, looking for other food, or... I looked to the east, upriver. 'Bumblies!' I yelled as loud as I could. They flocked toward the North Trench. I yelled again.

"They had the ganeesh loaded, and Cilandra let her go. I saw her plunge out of the Great Doors. She galloped with her heavy load, toward the North Trench, toward the swarm of bumblies. That was OK. They couldn't penetrate her skin, or the packs she wore, made of clay or ganeesh skin, freely given. But Tamaya," she sneered the name. "Tamaya didn't lock the pen, like I instructed. Cilandra trusted her. She would be Tether to Akash! But now, she was just a child. An arrogant, disobedient, irresponsible child. Not like my Cilandra at all!"

Tears stained a third square of the Akashic Robe.

"I saw Heffala, the old mother ganeesh, run out. Then the babbet! Her third-year baby boy ganeesh,

Dambu, came running out after her! Barebacked, no packs. Baby ganeesh's skin is not tough yet. Nimblies and bumblies go through it just like our skin.

"Cilandra ran out after the babbet, trying to stop him. She leapt up on his bare back. In regular clothes, no shield or armor. The babbet followed his momama right into the swarm of bumblies. They swirled round and round like a black whirlwind, a black cloud descending on my little girl—then she was gone. Dambu gone, too. Nothing left but bones. Heffala took Dambu's bones to the Ganeesh special place. Cilandra went into that season's pit along with Novamp, Tolgib, Tedchal, Zeleb, and Lapruss, and more kips than we could spare, to honor our Cilandra."

"I'm so sorry," Fran said, and squeezed Star's hand.

They worked in silence until the boys entered, proudly carrying a three-foot-high tower with a teetering blade bearing the beaten effigies of the phases of Kakeeche. Fran caught herself grieving for Jerry's wind power project and her prized golden pomegranate, then scolded herself. *How can I care about that after all she's been through?*

"It's the Akash's Shrine to Kakeeche," Jerry explained proudly, wearing his adorable, lopsided grin.

Shastina rose from G-Pa's feet and barked. The old man let out a loud snort and opened his eyes. They all laughed, except Valko. He stood in the doorway glaring at the stack of unused grass and the four pairs of puffy pants made from the fitted sheet. Fran had the big sheet laid out, ready to cut for Valko. She was hoping Star could get some measurements, but Star was slowly, subtly withdrawing the sheet from the table, balling it up behind her back. Valko heaved a menacing sigh and went to see G-Pa's reaction to his new Kakeeche Shrine.

Star handed the wadded sheet to Fran and whispered, "I make him one of squares tomorrow. There will be time, with your help."

"No problem," Fran promised. "What about food? You said there was special food for tomorrow?"

Salistar smiled like a child. "Pumpkin-Pomegranate Soup! First of the season!" she squealed with delight. "Cook all day. And gup cake, with this molding pan. Oven OK?" she checked, holding up a Bundt pan admiringly.

So that's where that went, Fran remembered. *I loaned it to Carmine when she and her family worked here. She made a cake for little Rosa's confirmation. Not so different from this family, really.* Out loud, she asked, "I'll bring my crockpot in the morning, for cooking the soup. You'll love it. What else can I bring tomorrow?" It was second nature.

"Nothing but you, tomorrow morning. You have brought us pumpkins from Far-mer Mar-ket. And the soft, fine flour, already ground, and the dried fruit, and so many things! We would starve without you! I will grow food for us all. You'll see."

"I know, Hon. We'll grow it together."

"I serve dinner now," Star told Fran decisively.

"Me, too. See you tomorrow morning." She grabbed Star's shoulders and scanned her soft eyes, now seeing that unimaginable pain deep inside. She pulled the smaller woman close and embraced her quickly. She wanted to ask them all if they were sleeping better now, but Jerry and Elmer were waiting in the driveway. She headed that way.

"You two are getting chummy, eh?" Elmer chided his wife.

Fran replied with, "Where's your baseball uniform?" as if Elmer would know.

G-Pa was awake, or at least, his eyes were open. Baput spoke gently in their home language, coaxing him to Earth. "G-Pa, look at the shrine we made for you."

Getting no response, he spoke more sharply: "Akash! Tomorrow is First Full Kakeeche! Here is your shrine you requested!" *Has G-Pa forgotten about the ceremony?* Baput hoped vainly.

G-Pa focused slowly. "My shrine!" Finally looking at his anxious grandson, he smiled. "Where did you find it?"

"We made it."

The Akash looked up at Valko and Felsic.

Valko grunted and stepped aside. Felsic leapt forward, beaming.

"Yes, Akash! I pounded the Kakeeche so they look real! See?"

G-Pa looked at him, at the shrine, then at Baput. *Did he like it?* Baput couldn't tell. *What would make him like it?* "Francina gave the kip and…"

"No!" G-Pa bellowed into sudden silence. "This is my shrine from nauve. It came to me! That's what I was doing when the boy left me alone in the shed."

Momama arched her black eyebrows at Baput, but Popa didn't look mad at all.

"I called it," the Akash continued, caressing the polished edges. "I called, and it came."

Valko was suddenly interested. "You called nauve? Did you see anyone? Did you speak to anyone?" He rushed to G-Pa's side and shook his shoulder a little too roughly.

"I wanted my shrine. I called my shrine. It came, because I, the Akash, commanded," G-Pa replied, his bony cheeks inches from Valko's hawk-like beak.

Valko didn't back an inch. "Did you see the village?" he asked again, studying the ancient eyes.

G-Pa broke the gaze to look at the shrine on the floor. He bent to it and pushed on the Kakeeche, making the windmill blade rock back and forth. The softened edges didn't cut his fingers. "My shrine," he muttered. Humming an Akashic song, he caressed it, ignoring the small crowd around him.

"Glad to have pleased you, Akash," Felsic grumbled.

First Full Kakeeche Day

The next morning, Fran was glad to see that Star's pile of woven squares had grown substantially, with a corresponding decrease in the messy pile of grass on the floor. But had she worked all night?

Fran plugged in the big crockpot she had brought for Star's pumpkin-pomegranate soup. They spent a couple of hours hacking a pumpkin to pieces and picking pomegranate seeds out of their husks. When the soup was in the crockpot, Star just kept right on chopping dried fruit and nuts. By pointing and grunting, she made it clear Fran was to keep the pomegranate seeds coming. Then, she brought out a rolling pin. *That wasn't in the quarters' kitchen equipment! Did someone leave it?*

"Where did you get that?" Fran asked.

Star handed her the rolling pin. It was beautiful and heavy. It had a marble roller, purple, with swirls of white and pink, smooth and almost perfectly round. The handles were hard wood paddles. You could press on them with your whole palm.

"My rolling pin," Star said proudly. "You have one, no?"

"Well, it's not as special as this. You had this on you when you, um?" Fran made a bursting motion with her fingers, at a loss to describe, or even imagine, how her new friend had entered this world.

"Yes, I always have my rolling pin. I am Akashic Tether."

"You take care of the Akash, yes."

"Yes. So the Akash may spend his time seeking wisdom on the Plane without having to attend to his body." Was that bitterness creeping into her voice as she recited her pledge? "Even if not, I would still have a rolling pin. Every bride gets one. It is a symbol of her duty to nourish her man and her family with all her being. To dedicate her life to always taking care of their every need, so men are free to do great things. And I, especially, as Tether to Akash.

"And there is power in it! Sugia, Akashic Tether to Yanzoo, killed four nimblies with her rolling pin, protecting her children. So we always carry our rolling pins during the Season."

"Of course," Fran agreed as she watched Salistar dump the pomegranate seeds into a cookie pan and cover them with a clean dish towel. Star reached for the heavy tool, rinsed it in the sink, and then rolled it over those pomegranate seeds. A vein stood out in her muscular neck. Her mouth drew back in a grimace. She stood on tiptoe, all her weight on that heavy marble roller. Pop, pop, pop, the whole tray of seeds fell to the rolling pin of the Akashic Tether, staining the towel indelibly.

"That is gaa." Star said calmly, looking Fran up and down. "You have none. Means you don't work hard. Look at me."

Fran looked closely at Star's outfit. It was stained all over with different colors. Some stains ended abruptly at the edge of their square. The adjacent square would be cleaner, like it was added after the stain.

"You can't wash it out, but it is OK. It shows we work hard." Star explained proudly. "If it's something awful, like boo, we just replace that square."

The gaa-stained woman punched down a puffy blob of risen dough from the stovetop and turned it out onto the cookie sheet. Here came the rolling pin once again. She rolled the dough into a rough rectangle, then spread the first of her fresh pomegranate oil over the doughy plane. She mixed the pomegranate seeds with chopped dried blueberries and cherries and sprouted seeds of pumpkin and squash. She spread the mixture evenly all over the oiled dough, like a fruit-and-seed pizza, and placed it in the preheated oven. "Three-fifty, like you tell me."

"That's right!" Fran gushed, letting go of all the other things she had planned to do today.

"We have all the squares. Machine can sew them together?" Star asked, glancing over at G-Pa in his corner chair, mumbling. Shastina lay on the floor on her side at his feet, her belly rising and falling rhythmically. Star spoke softly. "We make Valko's first. So, if we make a mistake, it's OK."

Fran wasn't so sure of that. The robe seemed easier, and Valko less forgiving. But Star knew what she was doing. Star put squares together expertly, and with a heavy thread and needle, the machine managed to cobble them together crudely, but securely. To Fran's relief, Star was delighted with the results. She arranged the squares expertly, not needing to measure her husband's familiar girth, and held them in place while Fran sewed them together. Soon they had a mammoth two-piece suit of woven grass: tunic and pants with a drawstring made of braided grass. It took a lot less time than the weaving had.

Star floated into the kitchen, pulled out the gup cake and put last night's leftovers in the convenient Earth oven. "Now the Akashic Robe," she announced. She began to lay the squares in place, feeding them to Fran to sew together. Fran thought Star was losing it when the squares became more and more misaligned, overlapping, as she went. She pointed it out once, but Star just looked blankly at the perfect garment and overlapped the squares even more. The result was a spectacular texture. The squares lay in cascading layers like shingles on a roof, or feathers on a bird.

"The fun part!" Star squeaked, approaching Fran's bead box.

Feeling like a kid, Fran opened the box she had treasured since childhood. Beads of all kinds were sorted into tiny drawers with teeny golden handles.

Star drew in her breath and oohed and ahhhed and picked out an eclectic mixture of beads made of shells, seeds, glass, and plastic. "Come, help me put on!" Star invited her friend.

"Oh, no!" Fran protested. "I don't know what I'm doing! Is there a special pattern?"

"OK," Star agreed, withdrawing the offered portion of the Akashic Robe. "Why you not know, Francina? Why you not know Kakeeche?"

Fran took on the role of "heathen" to Star's missionary. "Our people have not been told the good news of Kakeeche." *Three syllables,* she mused. *They see the moon as feminine, like most Earth cultures.*

"Your people?" Star wondered aloud. "You mean, your family? You and Elmer and Jerry?" She reached out tenderly for Fran, touched her shoulder. "No nimblies, no bumblies, but you are all that's left? Only one boy child? Is that the cost?" She looked deeply into Fran's confused eyes, then looked away, far away. "Here I am whining about Cilandra, and you have lost almost everyone!" She punished herself. "One boy child. All that's left. And I bring a boy! If only I had a girl! If only Cilandra was with me. If only I had... or hadn't..." Her face crumbled. So did Fran's heart.

How could Fran explain that there were lots of other people, but Star couldn't see them, because they couldn't see Star, because they might hurt her because her skin is green?

Before she could even find a place to begin, Star began reciting the story of Kakeeche, exactly as Baput had told Jerry, in that same memorized monotone. "So we *must* believe, or Kakeeche turns away!" She peered anxiously at her dozing popa again. He stirred as the rumble of the farm truck shook in the driveway between the house and the quarters. "The men are home! I must serve food."

"Me, too," agreed Fran. "Then I'll pull our own costumes together, if you can spare me."

"I decorate the robe." Star grinned, quickly clearing the table.

"You sure you want us to come?" Fran worried.

Star shrugged, looked at the old man who struggled to awaken. "Up to Akash."

The old man snapped to attention. "Daughter! Who is this woman?"

"Francina. Do you wish her and her family at the Kakeeche ceremony?"

"Well, of course, why wouldn't I?"

Glad the Akash had forgotten about this strange, pale family's ignorance, Star looked at Fran and nodded subtly. She wanted Fran to come, despite her fear of Kakeeche's wrath. These poor, ignorant people had to be saved! *How can they have a moon and not know Kakeeche?*

"We'll be there." Fran assured, hoping she could get Elmer to go along.

Fran finally found Elmer's baseball uniform, with its disturbingly tiny waistband. *It's only been two years!* She heard a yell and looked outside in time to see Felsic dart out of the storeroom at the back of the shop and hurry away. She ran outside.

Valko came down the driveway from the shop as Fran approached the porch of the quarters. He gave her a look that said, *mind your own business.* She stepped aside and let him go in, but she stuck around, once again listening to the strange, shouted language. Apparently, G-Pa was mad because Felsic hadn't made wine for the ceremony. But Valko had forbidden it.

Poor Felsic! No wonder he ran away. What was he doing in that room, though? Fran wondered. She slipped toward the door to the little room in the back of the shop where they kept odds and ends that were never needed until they were, (and then no one could find them). An eclectic litter of Christmas ornaments and camping gear remained strewn about from Jerry's quest to illuminate the sauna.

And what was this? There were car hoses coming in and out of a hole in the cap of a five-gallon plastic water cooler bottle. *Oh, no!* Fran realized. *A still! Do I tell? These hoses, this plastic, is it safe? Do I dump it?* She didn't dare. Elmer was on his way to town with another load. She headed home to her laptop to do some research.

Evening fell on the grassy area, on the squeaking crickets and frogs, on the babbling river, and on the quiet rustling of the uncertain little crowd. The faithful and not-so-faithful, the solemn and the sarcastic, all dressed in white or silver.

No one was hitching up their pants, Fran noted proudly, but they all looked a bit cold in their sheets. Star was alluring in the thinly draping fabric.

Fran looked dazzling, if odd, in her fuzzy inside-out white sweatshirt and silver spandex leggings. Elmer and Jerry wore their baseball uniforms, white except for pinstripes and grass stains. The logo, a baseball bat hitting a pomegranate with a screaming face, kind of bugged Baput, but he couldn't remember why.

They milled around shyly for a while, waiting for the Akash. It reminded Fran of church. It *was* church. Green People Church.

The full moon broke over the horizon. The Akash emerged from the sauna. His robe was a sight to behold. The phases of the moon were laid out in beads along the ruffled bottom. A pomegranate made of purple glass beads, red plastic beads, and Jobe's tears blazoned the back. Cylindrical beads exploded out of the stem like confetti, then circled the collar. When the moonlight hit it, the beads shimmered on a pure white background of dried grass.

Standing majestically before them, his longstick decked with a new string of Fran's white beads, the Akash told of Kakeeche. He told the long version, for the non-believers. Baput stood beside him and translated. Everyone had heard the short version before, except Elmer. He had absorbed as much as he cared to, secondhand over last night's dinner. Now he was just wondering what kind of food they were going to spread out on the tables he, Felsic, Valko, and Jerry had worked so hard to move over here.

The Akash described the lunar cycle in Kakeeche terms, just like Baput had. When he finished the rote speech, he paused for the ritual response.

"Hail Kakeeche, glorious Kakeeche," the green people chanted, staring at the luminous orb in the sky. "They always return without fail, as long as we believe."

The Akash stared at the beige-skinned trio who failed to respond. It made the hair on Baput's neck raise a little. Could G-Pa see their thoughts? Could he really do the terrible things they said he could do with his mind? Baput had always assumed so; he'd never even wondered about it before. But the Akash was different now. Everything was different.

Baput looked at the full moon for comfort, but it just made his skin crawl even more. He saw the little balls on the solar-system model, Jerry's alternate explanation, equally bizarre.

The sermon continued. "They give us comfort. We know they will come in their cycle, every month the same. We *must* believe or they will come no more. We have seen this. Men have doubted Kakeeche! And when they do, Kakeeche turns their backs!" G-Pa was belting out his words like an evangelist. His subjects all gasped at this last line, as if they had never heard it before. The Akash elaborated this terrible event, just the way Baput had.

When he was done whipping his loyal subjects into a quivering mass, he surveyed the non-believers. Baput breathed a sigh of relief to see his G-Pa wasn't including him in these glares.

His new subjects did not appear sufficiently horrified, so he decided to tell the rarely heard cautionary tale of Keeldar, the Doubting Apprentice. "Keeldar was the young apprentice and son of Keelan, the First Akash. Keeldar was 15 on First Pomegranate Day, but not an *Alanakash*, like Baput, here. He was born two months too early for that," G-Pa reported scornfully, as if it were some kind of failure.

"What's Alanakash?" Jerry asked out loud. No response.

Baput stared at the Akash. He knew this story and what it meant.

"The boy was lazy, disobedient. He did not do as his popa, the Akash, instructed. He had no discipline. He wished to wield the power selfishly. The First Akash could not step aside and allow the boy to ascend. He clearly wasn't ready. But the popa feared his son. He feared for his life. He feared for his spirit, that the son would curse him, for the son dabbled in Shavarandu, the dark arts, against his father's wishes. He believed more in Shavarandu than in Kakeeche!

Baput stopped translating, looked at Jerry, and added: "Shavarandu means 'the power we fear.' That's the sun, and what you call technology."

The Akash kept preaching the foreign words. Baput caught up quickly in English. "Imagine an Akash that cannot tell you what phase Kakeeche is in, any time, day or night? Keeldar didn't care! He never even looked up at Kakeeche, unless he was forced to by ceremony.

"How could such a boy ascend to Akash? The First Principal is to never use the power of the Plane selfishly. The boy's non-belief was arrogant and selfish. He thought he was better, dared to think himself above worshipping Kakeeche!

"His Popa refused to ascend him that Passascenday, so Keeldar rebelled. He stopped attending his daily training. He missed every ceremony. He took a battle ration box from the Great Hall and moved into a cave that was too big for nimblies and bumblies. He stayed there for three nights, until his rations ran out. The men searched and searched. His momama wept all the days and nights. Kakeeche waned to a crescent, then nothing.

"At midday of the fourth day, it happened. A sudden breeze blew, and the light changed, just a little, as if the sun went behind a cloud. But there were no clouds. The birds suddenly took flight, all of them at once, rushing home to roost as if it were evening.

"Men turned their faces to the darkening sky, but the sun burnt their eyes as fiercely as ever. They could not see what was happening. But they could feel it. The animals could feel it. Eerie, cold, just wrong. It got darker and darker. Not night-dark, but the sun grew dimmer until they could look right at it. And what they saw, you would not believe!

"It was half gone! The sun! Shavarandu, giver of all life!"

"True," Jerry whispered.

The Akash stretched his arms out before him, longstick in his left hand, white beads jiggling. "Half gone. Like Half Kakeeche! Then more gone! More of the sun gone! Until it was nothing but a bright ring flaming around a dark heart!

"That is when he dared to come walking in. Keeldar! Dirty and disheveled, staggering into the village in the dark of the sun. He looked to the sky then, alright! Blinded by the missing sun, he fell into his father's arms, terrified. 'Popa! You have taken Shavarandu!'

"The Akash was enraged! 'I take the sun? No, you, boy! *You* take the sun! You risk all life, man, animal, plant, everything, because of your arrogance. 'The self-indulgence of disbelief.' That is what the statute calls it, but your case is worse! The self-indulgence of laziness! You believe nothing! You don't even care to!'

"Keeldar was done trying to please his popa and ascend to a position he never wanted. It was time to end it. He stood up straight and tall, before all the people, and said loud and clear, 'I don't believe in Kakeeche!'

"Keelan whirled the boy about so fast no one saw him do it. He stared into the weak eyes of his apprentice. The impudent fool of a boy stared right back!" G-Pa turned his distant eyes at Jerry. "Boys say Keeldar was brave. But we know he was a fool!

"Their gazes locked. The boy did not flinch. Some said they saw the light coming out of the Akash's eyes and entering those of the poor apprentice. Others said they saw no light. What one can say about the difference has been a subject of Akashic debate ever since. Either way, they all saw the blood that trickled from the boy's ears first, then his nose, then at last from the corners of his mouth, oozing its way between the lips that remained set tight. His eyes, young and sparkling just moments before, were frozen with rage and stubbornness. His face looked older than the Akash's.

"Still, he stared, unblinking, until his eyes flooded. Not with tears mind you! That would mean he admitted he was wrong! Oh, no, not

Keeldar. Stubborn and stupid to the last, he stared through eyes drowned in his own blood. His own evil essence!" G-Pa bellowed, raising his longstick above their heads.

Elmer rested his right hand on his hip and moseyed closer to the "stage." The Akash didn't seem to notice. He continued to describe young Keeldar's demise.

"He sank to the ground before his popa, the faithful First Akash, as if groveling for forgiveness, as he should. But he did not grovel—he died! He lay dead on the ground, his mind melted by the Akash's Evil Eye!

"Just at that moment, Shavarandu began to return! The rays cast shadows on the ground and blinded their eyes if they looked directly at it, as it should be. By the time Keeldar was buried, the sun was restored. That was the only time any person has killed another, since the Beginning. And no one ever again dared to doubt Kakeeche."

The frightened faithful and the underwhelmed fakers all chanted praise for Kakeeche, except Elmer. They broke into a hymn, green people first, the others catching on, Fran singing happily. Elmer kept looking around, humming and moving his mouth just enough to blend in. He looked at the Akash, who avoided his eyes.

The song ended and suddenly everyone was embracing each other, congratulating one other on a great costume. The Akash, alert and exhilarated, approached Fran and rubbed her leg with his skeletal right hand. She withdrew, appalled, and Elmer was suddenly between them, chest pumped, breathing hard.

The Akash paid Elmer no mind but called to Star, "I must have a cape of this material that shines like Kakeeche!" The tension melted.

Jerry and Baput romped on the grass with the dogs.

Fran ran after Star, who sprinted barefoot in her sheet outfit toward the quarters.

Elmer approached Felsic tentatively and tried to whisper a question, but he didn't know just what to ask.

Star returned and announced that the Full Kakeeche Feast was ready. They filed to the tables.

Elmer and Jerry sat at their own table while Fran helped Star serve the food. "We should sit with them," Jerry complained.

"I need you to get on your phone and look something up."

"Now? Here? I can't. No signal. That's why it's the shrine, remember?"

"Well, where can you get a signal?"

"Over there. In the driveway," Jerry pointed.

"Well, go over there and look!" Elmer ordered just as Fran came to sit down. Star had finally taken a seat with her family.

"Where are you going?" she whined at Jerry. "I just got here. I want to talk to you guys, see what you thought. I'm so proud of you both for not making fun. We should be sitting with them, though." She ruffled Jerry's hair and gave Elmer a peck on the cheek before she sat. Jerry sighed and sat down, too.

"I'll tell you what I think, Fran." Elmer leaned over the table and whispered loudly. "I asked the boy to go over there and look up when the next solar eclipse is."

"Right now? We're eating! What's the rush?"

"Hey, this stuff isn't as bad as I thought!" Jerry chirped, mouth full.

Elmer grunted at the meatless fare in front of him.

"Eat, Babe," Fran pleaded. "Be polite."

"Polite?" Elmer rasped loudly. Fran and Jerry jumped backward. Felsic and Valko looked up sharply.

"You don't get it," Elmer whispered condescendingly. "I'll tell you later." He ate savagely, ripping the flaky fruit pizza, dipping it in his soup and shoveling it into his mouth like a machine.

After dinner, the men folded the tables and chairs and returned them to the shop. Elmer and Jerry both offered to help with the dishes, but Fran felt it would not be acceptable, so she went to the quarters to help Star, and the men headed home.

"Can you look now? When is it?" Elmer nudged Jerry as soon as they reached the driveway.

"OK, OK, Dad." Jerry stopped to look up eclipses visible from their location.

"Not for a hundred years or something, right?" Elmer presumed hopefully, guiding Jerry as they walked slowly.

"Wow! There's a lot of lunar eclipses! Like, two every year, spring and fall. That must be when the paths cross."

"You can't see them all from here, though," Elmer reminded him.

"Yeah, Dad. I filtered them that way. But some of them are in the middle of the night. Maybe if we don't tell them…" Jerry rambled.

"No solar eclipses?" Elmer still hoped.

"Why, Dad? What's the matter?"

"Don't you get it? We're the non-believers. If there's an eclipse, they're gonna blame us! If it's a solar eclipse, they might try to kill us!"

Jerry had found the information. He digested it along with his dad's thoughts. "You're not gonna believe this, Dad."

"That sounds bad," replied Elmer.

"There's a partial solar eclipse, about thirty-eight percent, in two weeks, next new moon. And guess what else?"

Elmer grunted impatiently.

"There's a total lunar eclipse tonight. It starts at 1:15 a.m."

"*Tonight?* When does it end?"

"Not till 6:33, when the sun is up. The moon will be so low it will be hard to see by then."

Elmer let out a long breath. "Then let's not tell 'em tonight. If we can get through tonight, that gives you two weeks to talk 'em out of thinkin' that way."

"But, Dad, it's their religion! Mom said not to diss on their religion." They climbed the porch steps. Jerry opened the door.

"I'm countermanding that order," claimed Elmer. "You have two weeks! Teach 'em some science. Now, go get a frozen pizza into the oven and turn on the game while I get out of this monkey suit. OK, Son? Baseball and pizza? Ancient Earth ceremony."

"I have a saying," Star told Fran as they stood cozily side by side at the sink, washing the last of the party dishes. "It is always true."

Fran had to bite. "Tell me your saying."

Star stopped rinsing and wiped her hands. "'No matter what happens in life, there are always dishes to do.' Is true. No matter what. Maybe catastrophe, and you are bereaved, so your sister does them for you. But there are still dishes to do."

"So true," mused Fran. She let a moment go by in respect for Star's saying. Then she snooped. "Felsic didn't drink much."

"The wine was very good, Francina," Star said especially gently. "But it's different. Maybe Felsic didn't like it. That is good. But my popa says we must make pomegranate wine, at least for ceremonies."

"Oh!" Fran feigned surprise. "Is Valko OK with that?"

Star gave Fran a conspiratorial smile, like they were sisters or old friends. "No," she said, almost gleefully. "But Popa is Akash, and he says. So Felsic will make wine out of some of our share of pomegranates."

Fran decided not to mention Felsic's false start. "I can get good wine-making equipment," she offered, "and bottles and corks for keeping it. You'll see. It will be Felsic's best wine ever!" Fran concluded excitedly, just as Felsic walked in, having successfully kept Valko from discovering his still while they stowed the tables.

Had he heard correctly? Felsic almost entered the kitchen in his excitement. "My best wine?"

"Akash says you must make wine." Star told him. "Francina will get you some Earth things, to make it better. You make some for her and Elmer, too."

Fran started to object, then shut her mouth and rationalized. *If we don't drink some, Felsic will probably drink more. And I want to try it. Might as well!*

Fran said goodnight and headed for home. The full moon shone so brightly, she didn't need a flashlight.

Suddenly, Felsic appeared by her side. "A woman shouldn't walk at night alone. Even on Full Kakeeche."

"Thank you, Felsic," Fran replied, not sure where this was going.

"Francina, you saved my wine."

"G-Pa did that. Um, Akash I mean."

"You saw my batch. You didn't tell?"

"No. And I won't. But I am going to get you a better fermentation vessel, and some bottles to keep it in."

Felsic was beside himself. He had his wine back! The Earth wine, made of grapes, of all things, had left him sober and uninspired. He had thought about drinking more, to get drunk, but he didn't like the taste. It wasn't worth it, especially with Valko on his case about it.

"Salistar said you can make it better." Felsic probed curiously. Would Fran's improvements make it insipid, like Earth wine?

"It won't spoil, anyway. The taste and potency, that's up to you. You're the winemaker."

"Did you make last night's wine?" Felsic asked, holding his breath.

"No," Fran answered.

Felsic exhaled loudly, relieved, as they stepped up on the Musik's porch, into the smell of pepperoni and the roar of the baseball fans.

"Thanks again, Felsic. Tell Salistar it was a wonderful celebration, and the food was delicious."

Felsic looked a bit surprised at the instruction. You usually compliment the Akash. Then he smiled. *Women's stuff, of course. It doesn't have to make sense.* "I will," he promised.

Lunar Eclipse

The green family went to bed soon after the ceremony, around 10 o'clock.

"Kakeeche! Kakeeche!" G-Pa cried out in his sleep.

"What is it, G-Pa?" Baput asked, straining to sound gentle.

The Akash rose from his bed on the floor to tower over Baput, who suddenly found himself in the top bunk. "Kakeeche is wounded!" he whispered urgently, looking down at his helpless apprentice. He extended a long, bony forefinger into Baput's sleepy face.

Silver-white moonlight poured from his fingertip and flowed straight into Baput, filling him so he glowed like one of the Kakeeche. Baput looked down at his own body, glowing like the moon, sitting cross-legged in meditation pose. He looked back at the Akash's face, larger than life and glowing with the same silvery light.

The Akash pointed to Baput's heart. The flow reversed and a steady stream of white light flowed from Baput's chest into G-Pa's finger. The last of it left his body, leaving Baput dark and formless.

Baput looked up at his mentor, huge and glowing with moonlight. The Akash leaned his head back, and the light streamed out of the top of his head, out the window toward Jerry's bedroom. The immense face went dark. Baput couldn't see his Akash anymore, but he heard his voice bellow, "You know…"

"I'm right." It was Jerry's voice that finished the sentence. There he stood, where the glowing Akash had stood just before, looking down at Baput in his bed. His blond hair covered his left eye. He leaned his head back and laughed hard, like in a half-remembered dream.

Baput's heart raced. He felt heat on his face. He sat up, wanting to strike the apparition that mocked him, mocked his religion, his family, his best friendship. His eyes opened. He was on the lower bunk holding G-Pa's sweaty paw like every night, not even free to turn over in his sleep. G-Pa lay on his mattress on the floor, his muttering incomprehensible except for an occasional, plaintive "Kakeeche!"

Baput sat up, angry. *The old man wakes me again!* He thought, but he knew there was more to it. He looked out the west window toward Jerry's. The window the light had flown out of. It was dark. Too dark.

He looked at the digital wall clock Fran had provided. Earth people liked to assign numbers to hours, as if that were necessary. At nauve, everyone knew when it was time to get up, time for dinner, bedtime. The clock said 2:14. Middle of the night and appropriately dark. But it was full Kakeeche! The full moon should be riding high in the sky, but it was dark! Darker than a full moon should be, even on a cloudy night. It had been crystal clear for the ceremony, and he could see the stars through the high window.

He couldn't see Kakeeche from his room. Only when the moon was almost set could he get an awkward, partial glimpse from the west window. He wanted to get up, go out on the porch, where he could see the whole path of the sacred silver orb. *But, what if G-Pa wakes up? What if*

Kakeeche has really turned away from us? On First Full Kakeeche! What does it mean? Something sour rose up from deep inside and told him in Jerry's voice, "It means nothing."

He wiggled his finger, tickling G-Pa's palm until he let go. Then he withdrew his hand and lay perfectly still for a moment. He heard a snuffling noise in the dark room. Shastina! She usually slept by the front door, on guard. Baput raised his head and looked down. Shastina lay on the bedroom floor at G-Pa's feet, twitching and whimpering. She knew! She would wake the Akash!

He glanced out the window again. Still too dark. He closed his eyes and breathed, tried to focus. *Should I wake him? Will he blame me? Or worse, blame someone else? Jerry. He'll blame Jerry, of course. He would be right. It's Jerry's fault I doubt Kakeeche. But Jerry doesn't know better. He doesn't know Kakeeche. I do. I am Akash-in-training, and I doubt Kakeeche, like Keeldar! This is all my fault! I must attend to it!* He lay still for another moment, planning his exit. He heard whispering, footsteps, and rustling noises outside.

He slithered over the headboard of the lower bunk and hit the floor without making a sound. Giving the fitful pair a wide berth, he crept on bare tiptoes through the dark room and out the door, onto the frosty porch.

"*Pssst!*" Baput froze at the sound. His neck prickled where his hair stood up. Slowly he turned his gaze toward Jerry's front porch. Three figures stilled in the dim light. The smallest one slipped silently towards him.

Baput turned, full of dread, toward where the moon should be. There it was, big and full and right where it belonged. But it was dark red.

Not totally dark, just a slice on the bottom left. As he stared without breathing, Baput could see the darkness spreading. Kakeeche was turning their backs! Because of him! But not all of them yet. He could still stop it! Reverse it! He needed G-Pa.

He turned back to the quarters. His knees wobbled and failed him. He collapsed into the arms of his new best friend, burying his face in the thick canvas coat of the one who laughs at Kakeeche. The other unbelievers rushed to surround him and half-carry him over to their side. They sat him down heavily on the steps of their porch, where you could see the whole path of the moon, sun, planets and zodiac.

Jerry sat down close beside him.

"Look at it, B! It's not that bad," Jerry whispered.

Baput peered out from behind his arms, which rested on his knees. More Kakeeche had disappeared from the bottom left.

"This is my fault," Baput whispered miserably.

Fran sat behind him in a wicker armchair. "No, it's not, sweetheart," she cooed softly.

"Fran!" Elmer hissed. "You're doing it."

"That's what we're here for isn't it?" She whispered back through her teeth.

Doing what? Baput wondered, tearing his eyes away from the blood moon to look at Jerry's parents in their chairs. Something gleamed dully from Elmer's right hip.

"Baput, look." Jerry poked his shoulder, pointed at the moon. "See? It's the shadow of the Earth. Just a shadow." He raised his fist. This is the moon, see?" He raised another. "Here's the Earth. Dad, could you be the sun?"

Elmer blandly raised a fist from his seat.

Jerry rolled his eyes. "We have the model! The eclipse setting. Baput, you want to come see the model again?"

Baput cringed, turning back to the moon. "I cannot. Don't you see? This is my fault. I must stay here and pray. I must ascend to the Plane."

"Yeah!" Jerry agreed. "Go to the Plane and ask it what an eclipse is."

Baput shot Jerry a sidelong glance. "I will first ask if I should wake up the Akash."

Jerry cupped his hands around his mouth and whispered an ethereal: "Noooooo!"

Baput scowled, then almost smiled. He looked at the moon again, then closed his eyes and began to chant in a whisper. Over and over, he chanted words the Musiks did not understand. After a while, Jerry joined in, mimicking the sounds, until it got too boring.

Fran brought a throw blanket from the couch and draped it over Baput's grass-woven nightgown. Then she stood between the boys and the quarters, shushing them whenever they waxed too loud.

Elmer just sat there shaking his head, sipping a beer and occasionally glancing over at the quarters, hoping the murderous Akash and his giant henchman would stay asleep.

After an hour, Fran couldn't repress an: "Ooooh!"

Baput opened his eyes. The moon was completely dark! He chanted harder and faster, this time with his eyes open.

Jerry broke in, speaking with exaggerated calm. "It's OK, Baput. It's nothing but a shadow. Come on inside. Let's look at the model." He looked at his dad, who nodded. "I'll show you how it all works." He helped Baput to his feet.

"I must stay," the green boy protested weakly. "If I go inside, and look at that *lie*, they will turn away forever."

"No, they'll be back. I promise." Jerry pulled out his cell phone and showed Baput a schedule of the current eclipse. "See, this is on the iPlane. You should be able to see this yourself. It will be dark for a whole hour, until 4:24. Then it starts coming back, but still red. That's the penumbra. It's the edge of the shadow, where all the light isn't blocked anymore, but it still has to go through our atmosphere. That's what makes it red. By the time the moon sets at 6:30 a.m., Kakeeche will all be back in their places. No matter what you do. Or don't do. I'll bet you. We'll find out tonight. Either I'm right or you are."

"You would risk Kakeeche going away and never coming back, over a bet?" Baput squeaked in disbelief.

Jerry got harsh again, despite his mother's hushing. "Nobody on Earth believes in Kakeeche. Nobody ever has. And we still have a moon. We've had lots of eclipses, too. The moon always comes back. Because it never leaves. It just goes dark because the sun isn't hitting it because the Earth gets in the way, whenever the orbit of the moon around the Earth crosses the orbit of the Earth around the sun in just the right way." Jerry could almost see his words flying over Baput's head. "I can show you on the model. It even has a special setting to make the Earth get in the way."

During the course of the lecture, Fran and Elmer had steered and pushed the noisy boys into the house and shut the front door.

"Come on," Jerry urged Baput toward the back of the house.

"Easy, Jerry." Fran was afraid Baput would go into shock again. *Is this right, what we're doing? Busting his belief system, forcing science over his religion? He's supposed to be the Akash, the High Priest, when he grows up!*

Glancing out the front window at the red moon, Baput dropped his head and trudged to the back room like a kid on his way to the principal's office. Fran crowded behind him, touching his shoulder. Elmer brought up the rear like a prison guard.

Jerry turned on the electric sun, then used his pocketknife to push a tiny lever on the ring that carried the moon around the Earth. The ring dropped down, just a fraction of a degree, so it was touching the big ring that went through the Earth and carried it around the sun. "Eclipse setting," Jerry announced.

Baput tried to back out of the room but ran into Fran. He looked up at her with the huge, earnest eyes of a Hummel statue. "Would you watch, please? If Kakeeche starts to turn back to us, you must come and get me at once." He turned back to the model fearfully. "They will surely go dark forever when I look at that."

"You'll see, Honey," Fran tried to reassure him without taking sides. *Of course, he'll see what happens. We all will. But whatever happens, it can't be undone.* "I'll watch from the kitchen window. I'll make us some tea." She fled to the kitchen, tears welling.

Jerry put the model through its paces in eclipse mode. "A lunar eclipse can only happen on full moon. Remember last time, I showed you the full moon, when the moon's on the other side of Earth from the sun?" The two metal rings scraped together as he brought the tiny moon into position, but this time the moon's luminescent coating extinguished as the Earth came between it and its only source of light.

Jerry rambled on. "See, the moon doesn't give off light like the sun does. It's just a dead rock. Bare, smooth rock, so it's shiny. It *reflects* the sunlight. That's all it does. That's all it is. A dead rock."

"That's enough, Son," Elmer declared softly.

Baput stood staring at the model for a long time. He got the concept, the planet blocking the light of the sun from hitting a dead rock in space. But he couldn't picture himself standing on one of those little balls, floating in nothingness, and he sure couldn't picture Kakeeche as a dead rock with no light and no life!

Batuk

Baput slipped past Jerry and Elmer, who were still playing with the model, and headed to the front window to check on Kakeeche.

"They're still gone, but they'll be back soon, Hon!" Fran chirped. Jerry's phone beeped. "That means maximum! We're halfway there. Kakeeche are on their way back to us now."

Baput cast dazed eyes at her. *What? Now she believes? Or is she making fun, like Jerry? I didn't think she would. Maybe she doesn't mean to. These people are so ignorant!*

Fran lifted a kettle from the stove. "Want some chamomile tea? It will relax you. Come sit here at the breakfast bar. You can see Kakeeche right out the window."

Baput sat and accepted the tea. Elmer and Jerry came in from the back room and peered out the front window. "Maximum. Half hour more, and they start coming back," Jerry promised as he and Elmer pulled up stools on each side of Baput with a soda and a beer. Baput still felt like they were making fun. Like they just didn't get it.

Fran stood in the kitchen facing Baput across the breakfast bar. "Have you ever seen an eclipse before, Honey? There must have been at least one in your lifetime, if your planet is like ours."

"I have seen some," Baput heard himself recall. "The first one I remember, I was almost five. All the Kakeeche turned their backs. It was total darkness for a long time. You could not even see the moon. Then it was all red, like tonight. Later, I thought it was a dream."

Jerry drew out his phone. "Do you remember when? Here's one!" he cried, before Baput could answer. "August 28, 2007. You're 12, right? So, you would have been almost five."

"Yes," Baput confirmed. "It was my brother Batuk's 15th birthday. He would have ascended to Akash the next year, on Passascenday."

"It was visible here, too," Jerry muttered, "I knew it."

"Wow!" Elmer mouthed silently.

Burning to ask about Batuk, Fran tiptoed around like a cat. "When is your birthday, Baput?" she asked gently.

"The day we arrived. First Pomegranate Day. An Akash born on First Pomegranate Day is very special, called Alanakash. There hasn't been one in many, many cycles."

"Cycles?" Fran asked.

"A cycle is the three years between First Pomegranate Days, the time it takes a new kip tree to bear its first fruit," Baput explained. "Being Alanakash means I will be a very powerful and important Akash. Or I would have been, if we were at nauve. Now I don't know what I am...."

Fran concentrated on the positive side. "I bet your momama was proud to bear an Alanakash. But it must have been awful hard to have a baby on First Pomegranate Day, with all that ruckus going on."

"Momama cried and prayed and crossed her legs, trying to hold me in," Baput replied, recounting the story he had been told from birth.

"She didn't want you to be an Alanakash?" Fran asked, puzzled.

"No. Because my older brother Batuk was 10, in training for Akash. If I was to be Akash, what would happen to Batuk? Well, he died, right before my sixth birthday."

None of them said a word for an unbearable moment. Then the Musiks all asked at once, "What happened?"

Baput sipped his tea and swallowed hard. "No one really knows except G-Pa. He was the only one there. There is a steep staircase hewn out of rock that leads to the entrance of the Holy Cave. At the top of the stairs, there is a wide porch, a stone ledge. You can fall off the sides and go straight down, about thirty feet, without the stairs. Batuk fell off that. G-Pa came running home, and we all went to see. We found him on the ground in front of the Holy Cave, dead."

After another uncomfortable silence, Baput went on. "I heard Popa tell Momama he doesn't believe Batuk would have fallen from there. He knew the Holy Cave too well."

"Does he think G-Pa gave him The Eye?" Jerry asked excitedly.

"No!" Baput cried. "We never even think of killing another person on purpose, except Keeldar. It had to be an accident. Why would he want to kill him? Why would he kill his apprentice?" he asked, not expecting an answer.

Jerry had an alarmingly credible one that had never even entered his mind. "So you could be Akash? So he could train an Alanakash?" Jerry immediately regretted saying it. He could see the change in Baput's eyes as he imagined his G-Pa anew.

Baput loved and revered the old man, even with his recent failings. But this thought, though unproven, cast a whole new light. A dark light. He continued his story from a strange, empty place. He voice was a monotone, like he couldn't feel what he was saying. "I took Batuk's place as Apprentice on that Passascenday, though I was only six. We are supposed to start our apprenticeship after our ninth birthday, but G-Pa said I had to start early, because I am Alanakash.

"On the first day of my training, I climbed the rock stairs, carefully, to the Cave entrance. I couldn't help but look down from the top to where Batuk had landed, but G-Pa grabbed me by the shoulder and pushed me inside. He lit the torches with his sulfur stone. I had seen the Holy Cave a couple times before, for Akashic Family ceremonies, but none of us had gone inside when we came to get Batuk, or since. Only G-Pa.

"It was different. There was a big, round, smooth, shining rock half-buried in the floor. It is the Holy Rock, and it gives the Holy Cave its power. That had always been there, but the deep cavern behind it was new. Next to the new opening was a smooth, solid plate, like a door, with strange writing on it. Holy writing, from the Old Ones. I was to learn that language in my training. I have not finished learning it, but I know now that the writing on the door said, 'death to open.' The door was moved off to the side, and the hole was open."

"And Batuk was dead." Jerry made the connection that Baput resisted.

"I told you they were killers," Elmer whispered quite audibly.

Baput paused to finish his tea. Then he rose and looked out the living room window. Was that a sliver of light on the upper left? He whirled briskly away from the window and trudged back to where Fran poured him a second cup.

"Thank you," he mumbled, still uncomfortable with the Earth phrase.

"I saw Shavarandu, the sun, turn his back once. It didn't just happen in the time of Keeldar. It happened a couple of years ago, in the spring."

Jerry was back on his phone in an instant. "Yep, May 20, 2012. Solar eclipse, almost totally visible here. I don't remember that."

"It was late in the day," Baput recalled, his eyes fixed on the ripples in his cup as he fidgeted with the teabag. "The sun was low in the west when it started. You could only see it if you looked straight down the river. If there was a tree or a hill in the way, like here, you wouldn't have noticed. But G-Pa did. I heard him chanting outside our house. I went out. The sun, Shavarandu himself, was turning his back on us, just like Kakeeche does tonight. People were coming out and gathering by the river. Even the women stopped preparing dinner to come and watch Shavarandu turn his back! Not since Keeldar! 'This could be the end,' the Akash told us. 'The nimblies and bumblies will surely defeat us this cycle.'"

Baput's bushy eyebrows furrowed. "That was this season that just passed! They could all be dead…"

"No, Honey," Fran fretted helplessly.

To her amazement, the lost boy blamed himself! "It was my fault, then, and now. I should have stopped Batuk!"

"You were a child, Honey." Fran cupped his cheek with her hand tenderly. "None of that could possibly be your fault."

"And the sun came back just fine." Jerry showed Baput the course of the past eclipse on his phone. "I mean, the moon passed, right before the sun set, at 7:41 p.m., see?" He thrust the device in front of the muttering boy.

"Who got blamed?" Elmer asked, still wearing his pistol.

"Batuk. Even though he was dead for over a cycle," Baput reported in that monotone that rankled Jerry so much.

"Why?" Fran whispered, tears flowing freely for Star.

"The Akash said he committed Shavarandu, the sin of technology, because he opened the door." His forehead wrinkled, drawing his thick, dark eyebrows together, as if he had just now realized something. "But G-Pa said he fell…"

After the longest, thickest silence the Musik kitchen had ever known, Baput finished the story. "Behind the Death Door was the forbidden weapon we used on the nimblies. The one that caused all this." He looked around, newly confused.

The three sets of blue eyes in the room looked helplessly at each other, and at the sleepy, stunned boy at their breakfast bar. The moon was turning red again, starting from the upper left. It rode low toward its bed in the west after a cold night without the sun.

They stirred to get up. Baput stopped them. "Kakeeche turned on us last spring, too. Six months before this First Pomegranate Day."

Jerry tapped on his phone again, nodding. "April 14 to 15. Yup. I don't remember that one, either."

Baput went on. "It started right at bedtime, so no one noticed. Only G-Pa and I saw it. We spent the night at the Holy Cave because it was Half-year Moon, the full moon six months before First Pomegranate Day. The moon turned red, then went all dark, just like tonight. G-Pa called it The Curse of Batuk. He said it was Batuk's blood on the moon. The blood he spilled when he fell from right there where we were sitting on the porch of the Holy Cave.

"I was so frightened, I wanted to run home right then, all alone with Batuk following me, his blood dripping on me..." Baput sat bent over, staring at the floor. "But I was too afraid, so I stayed that whole night with G-Pa while he told me how angry my brother was, and what he would do if I failed to ascend.

"I had to tell Momama and Popa. They were furious like I have never seen! Momama didn't even cry. She ran right up to G-Pa's face and yelled some very bad words. Popa was yelling, too. They said G-Pa made a *Calamunga* out of Batuk. An evil spirit that haunts your dreams and makes bad things happen."

"A boogeyman," Jerry translated.

Baput nodded, in a hurry to continue. "Popa said his son was no Calamunga! They told me not to listen to G-Pa! Never before had they told me to ignore my teacher. I was so upset by all the yelling, I forgot about the eclipse."

His eyes opened wide, then shrank as his eyebrows furrowed. "G-Pa said the blood moon meant that Batuk would come back this First Pomegranate Day and make something bad happen, and he did! But Batuk is long dead. And G-Pa and I have been committing Shavarandu every day since."

Baput jerked to his feet and headed toward the door. The subdued little group donned overcoats, and Fran draped the throw over Baput's shoulders again. They stepped out into the brisk pre-dawn darkness under the red and black moon.

After a long, pointed silence, Jerry tried a higher key. "Hey, Baput. Remember, you said you see the Plane up and to the left? See how the moon is coming back from the upper left first? That's the Plane. The Plane's real. Those Kakeeche in the up-and-to-the-left part of the moon believe in you. They say you should go on the Plane and learn science!"

Baput looked sharply at Jerry's last directive, then back at the moon. Were there more red Kakeeche? It seemed like it.

Jerry saw it too. "See? They're coming back. Up-and-to-the-lefties leading the way."

Elmer and Fran laughed at that. All three of the strange, pale folk pointed up and to the left with extended arms and cocked their heads so their left eyes looked that way, like Jerry had done when Baput and his family had first seen the Look'N Up Ranch.

Baput's sleepy brown eyes stared at them dully, without comprehension. Then he turned his face to the setting moon. "I can't let it set until they all turn back. Silver and bright, no red." He folded his legs into meditation pose on the cold porch and stubbornly resumed his chanting.

At last, the red moon's upper left blazed white against the dark sky. Fran let out another, "Ooh."

Elmer stood up, expecting lights to come on in the quarters any minute.

Baput opened his eyes and gasped like Fran had.

"Five forty. Right on schedule," Jerry reported.

"G-Pa will be up soon," Baput fretted. "And Kakeeche is so low! If they set without…" Once more, he shut his eyes tightly and chanted furiously until Jerry announced, "Six a.m.! Almost done! We're looking for 6:33, and we're home free. Kakeeche live!"

Baput gazed at the moon for several more minutes, until its whole upper left half was lit up like nothing had ever happened, and the dark red half was obscured by trees. "It's not over, but you can't even tell it happened!" he realized in an awed whisper. Then, he turned toward his friends on the porch and handed Fran the blanket from his shoulders. "I must go, before G-Pa wakes up. Um, thank you." he said it a little less awkwardly this time.

He dashed down the steps as Elmer and Fran shooed Jerry into the house and followed him in.

Morning after the Eclipse

"Baput! Akash!" Star called from outside their bedroom door. They were both sleeping late. It was time for breakfast.

Baput looked at G-Pa's eyes as he disentangled his hand. Yes, he was deeply disturbed. He had still been asleep when Baput had crept back to his room at dawn. Shastina's eyes had followed him silently as he slithered back into his bunk.

Now he headed to the boor with G-Pa leaning on his side. He used him to hide, so he didn't have to look at anyone. He looked at himself in the mirror for a long time while G-Pa finished his business. Then he hauled the incoherent Akash to the dining room for breakfast. *G-Pa's pretty bad this morning. How much does he know?* Baput wondered, relieved to see the Akash was in no shape to tell the family what he had seen. Relieved, and guilty.

"You are silent today, my son," Valko pried gently but forcefully.

Baput resisted with further silence, proving Popa's point.

Jerry woke up at the usual time, even without the alarm. He had only had about an hour of sleep. His mind kept going over it again and again. *They can't find science on the Plane, can't access it, can't even see it, right there on the web. They have a religion that you have to believe or else you'll single-handedly bring about the end of the world. And nobody even questions that, not even the Apprentice Akash. The Akash wants everyone to obey the rules, and then he breaks them. He killed his own apprentice, his own grandson, and now he blames him for everything that happens. And they found tech behind that door. Something that harnessed the energy from that rock. It killed those giant flying bugs, and then blew Baput and his family to another planet. Another planet with eclipses at the exact same time as ours. Can that even be?*

Hands behind his head, he stared at the star-decked ceiling. Mom was going to make an excuse for him today. He could sleep in as long as he wanted. Then he would go help pick. He'd share a tree with Baput, and they could talk some more.

But at breakfast, his mom told him to leave Baput alone. "Go easy, give him some time. Let it work in him. It's a lot to process." She caught Jerry's eyes and fixed on them savagely. "He may still decide to believe his way instead of ours. You might have to accept that."

Jerry wasn't sure if he could.

When he arrived in the orchard at midmorning like a spoiled heir, he found Baput picking alone in a heavily loaded tree across the lane from the others, slowly and silently.

"Leave him alone," Elmer seconded Fran.

Grudgingly, Jerry shared a tree with his dad, relieved to see he hadn't worn his gun this morning. After picking, he went with him to bring another full load of pomegranates to the dock, like he used to do when he was little. They didn't talk about the eclipse, or Baput, or Batuk, or green people killing us, or us killing them.

All morning, Baput had avoided the pale eyes that peered at him from the tree in the next row, where they picked together and whispered about him and looked at him as if he were different and didn't belong. After two hours of enduring their stares, which seemed to inflict physical pain on his skin, the brutal, beige boss had finally declared the truck full. He and his loyal son jumped happily into the cab and rolled away with the day's harvest to the mysterious "town," where most of the kips went.

Baput watched them go. Then he fell in behind Valko and Felsic as they climbed the steps to the quarters. He walked into a nightmare, but no worse than he had expected. Salistar struggled with G-Pa at his chair in the corner. He was pushing against her, bellowing, "Keeldar! Kakeeche!"

Baput slid between his G-Pa and his exhausted momama, who disappeared into the kitchen to get lunch. Her popa's episode had put her behind schedule. G-Pa groped at him. Realizing he had his apprentice now instead of his tether, he grabbed Baput by the collar and shook him roughly.

"Kakeeche are angry! They whispered all night. I heard."

"I, too, heard whispering," Valko confirmed, drawing close to the Akashic pair. "Footsteps, too." The hawk-like beak pointed at Baput.

They heard. They know. Baput worried silently. G-Pa knowing was bad enough. "Do you want to go to the sauna-shrine, G-Pa?"

The Akash renewed his grip on Baput's collar, twisting the woven grass. Momama was going to have replace those two squares. He hissed, inches from Baput's face. "They are angry! They discussed turning their backs on us forever!"

"G-Pa! Akash!" Baput struggled against him, like Momama had been doing. Suddenly he relaxed. Embracing the old man tenderly, he asked, dreading the answer, "What did you see?" He leaned close, hoping G-Pa would whisper to only him. But Valko and Felsic leaned in, and Salistar stepped in from the kitchen.

"They looked at us in our sleep," the Akash reported, loudly enough for all to hear. "Each of us, in turn, as we slept. They shined their light on Baput and looked hard at him for a long time. They looked at me, too, but they told me, 'Sleep in peace, Great and Good Akash. We will take care of the non-believers,' they promised me.

"Then they went over there." He pointed toward the house where Baput had spent most of the night. "They looked at that other boy. All those non-believers. Then they returned to the sky and turned their backs on us. All of them. They were so angry they glowed red, burning the air all night. Never before has there been such anger among the Kakeeche. Who has angered them?"

Valko stood up tall in front of the frail old man. A barely audible rumble shook his chest.

The Akash said nothing, but he looked straight at Baput.

"But in the end, because of their love for us," he spoke into Baput's terrified eyes, "they all turned to face us, just before they went below. But that was close!" The old man had broken free of Baput, who was glad to release him. He paced back and forth, Shastina almost tripping him with every frantic pass.

"Their message is clear," he concluded. Everyone held their breath. "We must stay away from the non-believers. Completely away.

Especially the boys. They *must* be kept apart. But not just the boys. All of you. Salistar! That woman with the silver legs. Stay away from her!"

"But Popa! She brings us the food we need. Whatever I ask for, she brings."

Ignoring his daughter's pleas, the Akash went on. "And you men. Stay away from that colorless man."

Felsic was next to object. "But he tells us what to do. He's the, um, boss!" There was no such word in Nauvian, so he used the English word.

"He tells you what to do? Who is he to tell you? Is he your Akash? He tells you not to believe in Kakeeche!"

"No, he doesn't!" Felsic dared argue. If he couldn't work with Elmer in the orchard, or better, in the shop learning the wonders of mowers and tractors and trucks, then he would surely need more wine.

"The man does not tell us what to believe," Valko confirmed.

"Neither does Francina," Star jumped in. "Not ever. She helped me with the Kakeeche ceremony. She's learning to believe."

"Does the boy? Baput? Apprentice? Alanakash? Does that boy tell you not to believe in Kakeeche?"

Lie? Straight out? To my Akash, my mentor? My mentor who maybe killed my own brother, Batuk? Baput couldn't speak.

Why can't I just lie? Baput wondered, his mind racing. His family's eager faces surrounded his awareness. *Why can't they just leave me alone? G-Pa sits there mumbling, useless, through all we've been through. Now he tells us to turn our backs on the people who have helped us, break the friendships that are keeping us alive.*

It isn't fear, or respect, or love of Akash that holds my tongue. It is not the Akashic Oath, which I have not yet taken. It's me, the Apprentice Alanakash. I cannot lie. A good Akash says nothing but the truth. The whole truth. A good, strong Akash would not let another man, even another Akash, tell him what to say. He wouldn't let a strange boy tell him what to believe. A good, strong Akash, like the one we need, would do and say and believe only the truth. But—what IS the truth?

It took Baput such a long time to answer that he sounded like a much older Baput when he finally did. "I am Apprentice Akash. I am being trained by a very great Akash, maybe the greatest ever." He smiled in G-Pa's delighted face, glad to see the flattery was working. "I have been trained to know what to believe. I know what is right, I say what is right, and I do what is right. No one can tell me what to believe or what not to believe. No matter what they believe, they can't hurt us, because we all know what to believe. We will all continue to believe what we believe, no matter what they say."

Felsic thrust his fist up in the air and hopped. Valko and Salistar exchanged a proud smile. Even the Akash looked pleased

The only one who was not impressed with this speech was the Apprentice Alanakash himself. Baput was ashamed. He had avoided the lie by dodging the question. And, despite his resolve, he had not told the truth. Not even close! He really had no idea what to believe or who to believe. And, the stuff Jerry and his parents believed, that *did* matter. It mattered a lot!

The Evil Eye

The families rose slowly the next day. A day off! Baput wondered why Elmer called it a "weak end." The women got up at the usual time and made their way to their respective kitchens to start breakfast. The men slept in a bit, especially G-Pa, who was exhausted from the First Full Kakeeche Ceremony and whatever he had experienced of the eclipse and the next day's argument. He snored blissfully on the floor next to Baput's bunk. Baput carefully slipped his sweaty hand from the wrinkled grip and got up. He tiptoed on bare feet to the boor, then returned to greet Momama in the dining room with a warm embrace and a peck on the cheek.

She replied with a warmed-up bowl of the last of the pumpkin pomegranate soup and a fresh seedcake. It was weird being up first. He had been up earlier than Popa before, but back home, G-Pa was usually up and off to the Holy Cave before Baput was awake. He would have to rush his breakfast and run to the Cave where G-Pa would say he was too lazy to be Akash.

When Baput stepped outside after breakfast, Jerry was waiting in the driveway in front of the quarters, hair over his left eye. He had a weak end, too!

"You're home!" Baput cried, surprised by how glad the sight made him. He bounded off the porch without touching a step, clearing Shastina and almost landing on Brodey, who wagged his whole back half.

"Horizontal Tree?" Jerry invited.

The boys and dogs ran all the way to the Horizontal Tree, where they sat, breathless, looking at the river. It was a comfortable silence, with only a touch of frost, as both boys held their burning questions. The dogs rammed and flipped each other over and over in the dirt.

"Can you teach me to surf the Plane?" Jerry asked suddenly. "I mean, is it allowed, for a non-believer like me?"

Baput scowled. "If you don't believe, how can you get on the Plane?"

"I believe in the Plane!" Jerry countered. "The plane's awesome! It's just the Kakeeche part I'm not buying. If you can get on the internet, and if your Plane has all knowledge, then you should know how the moon really works. It's science." *There. I said it. Just like Dad said to. Just like Mom said not to.*

"You can't have the Plane without Kakeeche," Baput stated unilaterally. "That's why I'm not meditating anymore. You can turn your TV on anytime you want. Play your rasta games. I would rather see that when I sleep than try to get on the Plane without believing in Kakeeche."

"B, you really need to keep trying. Forget Kakeeche! It's a legend. You still need to keep getting on our iPlane, at least, so you can keep learning. And I want to try getting on your Plane, so teach me, and I'll teach you how to find your way around the internet, the iPlane." Jerry negotiated.

Baput sighed. Still expected to be Akash. *Even the non-believers expect it!* "I don't know if I can get you on the Plane at first, but I will teach you meditation. There's a chant for beginners, but no, you wouldn't like that. We don't need it. The river's here. We'll stare at that instead of chanting."

Jerry crossed his legs, like Baput did, but the hard, narrow trunk was quite uncomfortable that way, so he just sat up straight, facing the river, like he had for years.

"Good," Baput approved. "Now close your eyes and focus on your breathing. Breathe through your nose. Inhale all the way down to your abdomen. Feel it expand and fill with breath. Now exhale slowly, squeeze the abdomen, the chest, the arms, the legs, all the muscles, squeeze all the bad air out of them… Now, relax your breathing. Softer now. Open your eyes."

Jerry almost lost his balance when he opened his eyes to the view of the river, flowing low and weak just below his feet. Just downstream, it veered abruptly away, crossing to flow on the opposite side of its wide channel. Jerry always had wondered why it bent away like that, so abruptly.

"You are thinking, not meditating," admonished the Apprentice Akash. "If thoughts come, just let them float on by, like a leaf on the river. Look at the river. It is a perfect example of the world of vibrations that is the Plane. Vibrations, always changing. Light vibrations. See how it glints and flashes in the sun, then goes dull? See the ripples where that bug just hit it? Another vibration, making circles outward. Like all vibrations. Circles, ever outward.

"Sound vibrations. The roaring of the big water over the rocks. Constant, but always changing. Do you hear the trickling sound underneath, where that teeny, little spring comes out of the bank? Hear the high song it sings under the rushing, the roaring?

"All these vibrations. The light, the sound, the air around us. The breeze changing the temperature. Feel them all. Always changing. Always the same. From now until forever. The ever-changing sameness, the continuous replacement of individual drops, the ones here now flowing away, the new drops ever coming in."

Jerry stared at the water and tried to relax. Baput's voice was steady in the background, like the sound of the river. He heard the words, absorbed their meaning without thinking about it. Suddenly he saw it, just for an instant. Force lines! They looked like arrows. The bigger the arrow, the stronger the force. There was a big, thick one along the river, pointing downstream. The tremendous, unstoppable force of the river flowing on its way. A slightly smaller line in the air pointed the opposite direction. The wind. Little arrows swirled on the surface of the water, rising out of the spray as the water molecules collided with rocks, each other, the air. He knew the lines were imaginary, his mind's way of picturing what he was perceiving. But were those really electrons flying around? Boiling in the mist above the water? Did Baput see this? Did he understand? *This is science I'm seeing!*

Just as suddenly, the vision was gone, and he found himself looking at the river like he always did on Saturday morning.

Baput brought him back. "Remember your breathing. Fill your chest and abdomen. Slowly. Now wiggle your fingers and toes. Remember where you are. Watch your balance."

Huh? Jerry thought, *that sounded funny. Oh, balance. Because I'm on the Horizontal Tree.* He looked around.

Baput was peering at him anxiously.

"How did you do?" Baput asked.

"I think I had a vision!" Jerry replied, not quite able to articulate what he had seen.

"Did my instructions make sense?" Baput asked.

"Yeah!" Jerry enthused. The Apprentice Akash needed to learn to teach meditation, and his feedback could help. "Everything was real clear. I looked at the river, the vibrations, the light, the sound, the circles from the bug, all really good, and clear. Made sense. And it worked. I think I got there, for a second. I could see force lines!"

"Good," Baput smiled mysteriously. "Extra good, Jerry, because I was talking in my Nauve language that whole time."

"Wow," Jerry uttered, awestruck, introducing another long silence. He broke it by climbing off the tree and opening his backpack. "Look. Gup cakes. It's your momama's recipe, so it's OK. Here. Have some pom juice. I know you like that." The dogs stopped their playing and surrounded the boys with soft brown eyes and quivering noses.

"You brought a ration pack!" Baput exclaimed with delight. The longer he stayed away from the quarters, the happier he was. The silence was more comfortable when punctuated by chewing.

Finally convinced they would receive no gup cake, the two dogs bounded up and down the trail, chasing each other. Brodey was shorter. He would come rushing in and plow right into Shastina's long legs. Sometimes she would stand, sometimes fall, then he would fall on top of her and they'd roll around in the leaves.

"See," Jerry began his natural discourse, without thinking. "Brodey has a lower center of gravity. He slams into her down low. She's tottering around up there on those long legs, and she falls. Center of gravity."

"Gravity," echoed Baput, dreading another lesson. He was so tired! But he craved it, too, this science. This whole new world.

Jerry dared go on. "The Earth, you know, the big, round ball in space that we live on?"

"Big round ball circling in space," Baput recited in that irritating, mindless tone.

"You still don't get this, do you? OK. My mom says I should just let you believe whatever you want. This is America. You can believe in whatever religion you want. Or no religion, like me."

"Science is your religion," observed Baput.

"No. It's not the same."

"You believe in it faithfully."

"No. I require proof. That's the difference. That's what I don't like about religion. You're supposed to believe and never question what they say. Whenever someone tells me I have to believe something, I just automatically don't believe it. Because that's America, too. That's how we're raised. If it can't stand up to questioning, it's probably not true, right?"

Baput was silent for a long minute. Jerry wondered if he'd said too much, again.

Finally, Baput spoke. "We are raised very differently. We always believe what we are told. Whether it's the Akash, or Rakta, the war chief, or Akira, for the women, or just Momama or Popa or older brother. We believe what they say. We do what we're told. It's not just a matter of respect. Our survival depends on it."

"How do you know?" Jerry didn't stop himself, but Baput's crumpled look made him wish he had. More silence. No more gup cakes to chew.

Baput finally spoke again. "No matter. Like you said, America. We believe our way and you believe your way. I'll make sure nobody tries to force you to believe our way. OK?"

Jerry couldn't answer. Did this mean Baput was choosing Kakeeche over science? He felt a rift opening between them. He couldn't let it! "What about the Akash? Doesn't he kill people with his Evil Eye if they don't believe in Kakeeche?"

"Only that one time. When the sun went away."

"Yeah. It does that. You've seen it. And it's going to happen again in two weeks. And my dad's afraid you guys are gonna kill us when it does, for not believing."

Baput stood open-mouthed, so devastated at the lack of trust from his new friends that the news of the eclipse barely sunk in. "That is why he carried a gun that night?" he whispered breathlessly.

"Yup."

"But we would *never* kill you guys! G-Pa might want to, but—"

Jerry interrupted. "The Evil Eye. Is it real?"

"Only the Akash can do it," Baput mumbled, looking down.

"Have you seen him do it?" Jerry had to ask.

"No, only the First Akash used it that one time on Keeldar."

"What about the nimblies and bumblies? Can he do it to them?"

"No. It doesn't work on animals. Only a thinking person. It disrupts their mind so they die."

Jerry's questions boiled over, escaping into the air all at once. "You're going to be Akash in three years. Is he teaching you how to do it? How can you practice without killing someone?" On he went, in his scientific method. He couldn't help it. He found himself wondering if Baput was right. Was he a zealot for science?

Baput replied briefly to all. "Akash says it is so. I don't know. I just don't know anymore!"

The whine of the four-wheeler broke the awkward silence. Felsic appeared, splattered in purple gaa from head to toe. "Baput!" he called, followed by something in Nauvian.

Baput's frown deepened. "I must take care of G-Pa so Momama and your momama can press the seeds for oil."

"Are you gonna tell him?" Jerry whispered.

Baput glanced at him, confused.

"About the eclipse!" Jerry hissed between his teeth.

Baput just hung his head and climbed onto the four-wheeler behind Felsic. They putted off and the dogs trotted after them, leaving Jerry alone at the Horizontal Tree trying to imagine a world where no one questioned anything. He could almost see it, until he put himself into it.

Questions for G-Pa

On the ride back to the quarters, Felsic chatted about the stainless-steel brewing vessel, the flexible tubing and the clean, smooth corks and bottles Francina had somehow called into existence. Baput wasn't listening. How to bring it up? *"You are right, Akash, there was an eclipse on First Full Kakeeche night."* He practiced to himself under his breath where Felsic couldn't hear through the motor noise and his own babbling.

The quarters were bustling with the pressing of oil and juice. Fran and Star plucked seeds endlessly from an infinite stream of pomegranates. Valko pulled the handle on the elaborate contraption, multiplying his impressive force a hundredfold by simple mechanics. Felsic returned to his station at a smaller, lighter press, generating a silty mash for his wine. It was too noisy to meditate. Too many ears for the talk Baput had planned. He took G-Pa to the sauna.

Baput turned on one electric candle and the Christmas lights on the stovepipe, leaving lots of shadows to hide angry green faces. G-Pa occupied his meditation cushion and motioned his loyal student to sit across from him. "What shall my Apprentice discover today? What nugget shall he pluck from my trove of wisdom?"

It was the traditional initiation of an Akashic study session. Innocuous, practically meaningless. Glad he had kept the light low, Baput ducked into one of the shadows, afraid his sudden searing rage would show on his face. *Why am I so angry?*

The subject having been left wide open, Baput summoned all his swirling courage. Time to just say it: 'You are right, Akash, there was an eclipse night before last, on First Full Kakeeche night'. There. No. That was not out loud. Maybe without the 'you are right' part?

"Akash, remember when the sun turned its back on us?" he blurted. Not the question he was planning to ask at all.

"Only once, in the time of Keeldar, did Shavarandu ever turn." G-Pa replied. It was because of the Doubting Apprentice!" G-Pa struggled to rise into his sermon mode.

"No, G-Pa!" Baput interrupted. "It was six months into this past cycle. Remember? It was evening. Shavarandu was low in the sky. We all went down to the river to look."

Was that a glimmer of a memory in the Akashic eyes, or just the flickering candlelight? Still hidden in the dark, Baput struck. "You blamed Batuk."

The old man was speechless for a moment. Then, denial. "No. No. You dream, boy."

Baput held firm. "Yes. It happened. Then, six months before the end of last cycle, the moon eclipsed." The blank look reminded him. "Kakeeche turned their backs. They all turned red, just like the other night!" There, he'd said it. He went on with the memory.

"We were in the Holy Cave, just you and me. I wanted to go to the village to comfort the people, in case they were frightened. You said the people would sleep in blissful ignorance, and only we Akashes could watch Kakeeche turn red. Then you told me it was Batuk's blood. You said he was a Calamunga, and he would make bad things happen on First Pomegranate Day!"

Baput's face was hot, and his heart was throbbing. He could see his own spit flying in the intermittent light. He stopped suddenly, peering at the old man in the dark. Was he laughing?

"Ha, ha, ha." Unmistakable now, the Akash erupted in spirited peals. "I tried to scare you. To provoke some imagination. You, you…" he breathed. "You were always so serious. I was having fun. But you were such a babbet! Running home to tell Momama and Popa," he jeered.

"You dishonored Batuk!" Baput lashed back.

"Batuk." The disdain in G-Pa's voice was more alien than anything Baput had seen on Earth, even on the iPlane. "Let me tell you something about my former apprentice, your wonderful brother. But his story is my story. And since I fear I am not long for," the bewildered look reappeared, "whatever this is, I must tell you my story."

Baput started to protest the first statement but shut up when he heard the second. He hoped G-Pa's lucid state would hold out. G-Pa settled into his meditation pose. Baput did the same.

G-Pa began: "For all the time I have been Akash, and even apprentice, I have been watching our demise. Cycle after cycle, more nimblies and bumblies, and our weapons are less effective. The old ganeesh skins won't stop a bee's sting, much less a nimbly's. With not enough ganeesh to supply the battlefields, we dare not hope for fresh skins! Each cycle they are stronger, and we are weaker. I knew there was only one way for us all to survive.

"I had dreams, too. Oh, yes." He nodded vigorously, as if trying to convince himself. "Dreams of the Cave. The part behind the door. I saw it as I slept. It was dark and cold and very dry. The walls were so smooth, like nothing I have ever felt in reality. It was a magical place I saw. And, forgive me, my Apprentice, but I knew I had to commit *Shavarandu*, to uncover the forbidden technology of the Old Ones. It was the only way to defeat the nimblies and bumblies. All the answers were behind that door.

"At first I told no one. Not Rakta, the war chief. Not your Popa, my guard. Before I had an apprentice, I could study in secret. All the ancient texts. Or I thought that was all. They talked about the Death Door, buried behind the Holy Rock under a pile of loose stone made to look like an ordinary cave wall. The texts had a drawing of it, all smooth like it is, with the words 'death to open' in the ancient writing of the Old Ones.

"So I removed all the rocks. I was younger then, but it still took days. Near the end of the third day of digging, I found it. The smooth, dark surface reflected my torchlight as I read, 'death to open' just like the picture. I was amazed, awed, actually, but so tired. I withdrew without covering the door. That night I dreamed Batuk was trapped behind the door. He was scratching on those featureless walls, trying to dig his way out. I woke terrified and began covering the door back up the next day.

"Batuk started his apprenticeship on his ninth birthday, before you were born. I hoped he and I could complete the weapon before the next First Pomegranate Day. And, to be honest, I needed a young back to haul that heavy rock away. But I only had a year, and I spent all of that just completing Batuk's basic training. I had not trained an apprentice before. I did not realize how much there is to it at the beginning. Batuk was bright and eager to learn, but I didn't feel he was ready to know what I was up to. Besides, that dream, and the sign on the door, haunted me.

"Batuk ascended to Apprentice on that Passascenday, three days after you were born. I am afraid your mere presence stole Batuk's moment. Everyone wanted to see the Alanakash! When the excitement wore off, I finally thought to look for Batuk. I found him standing all alone outside the Great Doors while all the women gushed over you and the men began to get drunk. I looked at him, and we both realized it, he and I at the same time. I could see it in his eyes. You were Alanakash. You had to be the next Akash. So, what of Batuk?

"Well, you were just a babbet, so I went on training Batuk. I brought him in on my secret. I showed him the ancient drawings and documents, and he studied them so hard, I feared his eyes would wear out. Every word. Every detail of every drawing. These drawings were not pretty like Pindross' rasta. Very rough and plain, for one purpose only. To teach about that door and the weapon.

"When he turned 15, he was old enough to ascend, but he was off cycle. Not like you, my perfect Alanakash. I would have to wait another year for Passascenday. *Just as well*, I thought to myself. *He is still not ready*. And I was not ready to give up my explorations. What if he tried to cut me out?" Breaking meditation pose, the Akash raised his fist and glanced around the darkened room. An Akash ready to do battle with whom? Batuk the Calamunga?

The Akash lowered his arm, and his voice. He whispered, "The night of Batuk's 15th Birthday, Kakeeche turned their backs on us, like I have never seen before or since."

He didn't see it then, the other night. Baput hoped silently, bracing himself for the next attack on the brother he had idolized.

"Batuk and I went to the Holy Cave. We were supposed to be celebrating, but we ended up working on the contraption. What else was he to do? He could not marry his Tamaya for another year." The Akash winked in the dark.

My Tamaya. Baput thought of his betrothed who had once been his brother's. His gut clenched unexpectedly, and his hands went numb as his blood rushed to his fluttering heart. *What is this feeling?* He wondered.

G-Pa went on. "It was late at night, and he noticed it first. 'G-Pa! Come look! Kakeeche is turning red.' We sat on the top of the steps and drank wine and watched Kakeeche turn their backs. Right there, where you and I watched a half-year ago."

"Right where he fell from," Baput tested.

"Nonsense," G-Pa muttered. "Now listen. Batuk was the same as you. He wanted to go back to the village to comfort the poor, ignorant people. I told him not to bother. We had more important things to discuss.

"'I know,' your brother droned miserably. Then he asked me a foolish question: 'Who has angered Kakeeche?'

"I told him, 'It was you, of course.' He started denying everything he had ever done. Most interesting.

"'Grab that wine and come over here,' I told the blathering mess. So he came, and we drank. The wine calmed him. We had a very adult talk. We came to terms, him and me and Kakeeche. We decided that if he could open the door by First Pomegranate Day, he could ascend to Akash.

"'What of Baput?' he asked. He always thought of you. I told him to let me worry about that. I told him you would be fine. You were to be apprentice to your Uncle Felsic. A sodden winemaker." G-Pa grasped Baput's shoulder, shaking his head violently. "No! You were Alanakash! How could I let that happen?"

G-Pa spoke into Baput's face in a way Earth people would find most uncomfortable. "That is exactly what Batuk said, too." He sighed and looked away. "He was right. I could not overlook an Alanakash, no matter what poor Batuk did. But I led him to believe I would." He rose and ambled across the tiny floor, running his hand through his thin hair. "I wanted that door open!" he mumbled.

"And you wanted Batuk out of my way," Baput added, stunned cold. "You knew he would die! It said 'death to open.' You solved both problems."

"*He* solved them. In the only way he could. He understood. Of course he did." G-Pa talked faster and faster, then suddenly stopped and looked right at Baput. "He did it himself, you know. I didn't tell him to, or make him. He did it on his own, without me, in the middle of the night. He slipped out, seven nights before First Pomegranate Day. He came here, in the middle of the night, and opened the door."

Here? Baput caught the old man's confusion, dismissed it.

"When I awoke that morning, Batuk was not in the kitchen. Your momama had not seen him. I knew he had gone to the Cave. I found him at the Death Door, lying on his back, as stiff as the bar he held clenched in both hands. He wore a horrible, twisted grimace of agony on his face. He was dead, but the door was open!

"I hauled his body to the door of the Cave. No small task. He was heavy, his popa's son, and I was no longer young. It took me all morning to get him there and push him over. That is why it took me so long to come home and report. I told your parents I had been praying over him, trying to revive him, using all my powers to save him, when actually I was dragging his limp, heavy corpse inch by inch across the floor of that accursed Cave. He got stuck on every rock and crack the whole way, stubborn and stupid to the end!"

Baput was as disoriented as the moment he'd arrived on Earth. He had always heard how great Batuk had been! How smart, what a promising apprentice! To think G-Pa had thought of Batuk as stubborn and stupid shattered the last of Baput's memories.

Mercilessly, G-Pa continued. "I finally reached the porch. My back was aching so! I pushed him off headfirst, so the ground below would break that dreadful look off his face before your momama could see it.

"I was elated! The door was open!"

Baput wanted to cry out in rage, but he couldn't interrupt. He had to hear it all.

"I was relieved! Now you could ascend to Akash!"

Baput's silent anger grew.

"But of course, I was also horrified! Batuk was dead! I headed for the hut to break the news to your parents, and," he sighed heavily, "I lied to them. By Passascenday, your first ascension, I had the door covered back up with rocks."

The two sat silent. Baput felt hollow, numb. G-Pa hadn't killed Batuk. Batuk had done it on his own. But G-Pa had lied, told him he could be Akash if he opened the door. *But Batuk knew he was lying. That's not why he did it. He did it because he had to, to kill the nimblies and bumblies and save the people. And maybe so I could be Akash. So the people would have their Alanakash.*

At last, Baput spoke softly. "I remember that night, G-Pa. We went to bed as usual, but Batuk barely said goodnight, and when I asked for a story, he said he was too tired. In the middle of the night, I woke to find him up and dressing. I asked him where he was going.

"He sat on my bed and took my hand. He started talking funny, like he knew he was going to die. He said, 'I do this for you, brother. This is my purpose. You are going to be a great Alanakash. Take care of Momama and Popa, and—'" Baput's voice broke, "'Cilandra.' But I lost her! And I lost him! I lost us all!"

Baput bolted from the little rock shed, almost toppling the little shrine as he ran.

Questions for Popa

The next day was Sunday. Jerry got to sleep in, while Baput picked with Valko and Felsic to fulfill their family's insatiable need for pomegranates for oil, juice, wine, dried seeds, lining for clothes, even leather for shoes. They picked only the less-perfect specimens that they had skillfully skipped on the first picking for market. They left the under-ripe ones for Elmer's second picking.

Once again, Baput picked by himself on his own tree. The heavy bag Momama had woven dug into his shoulder. Foggy with sleep-deprivation and disillusionment, he stared at the mist that shrouded the river. Everything he had ever known, his whole life from top to bottom, was wrong. Or was it? *Why didn't I see any of this before?* He couldn't stop wondering. He tried to remember more, but the harder he tried to remember his life back home, the farther it flew from his head.

Elmer showed up and told Felsic to come with him. He was going to learn a new skill. They headed to the shop to get the forklift.

Upon losing his picking partner, Valko strolled over to Baput's private tree and began picking the highest branches without a ladder. Baput's shoulders sagged.

"What troubles you, Son?" Valko asked. "You have not been yourself since First Full Kakeeche Day. Your momama worries."

Baput paused. He had played this scene out in his mind last night as he lay awake. *Tell Popa. But how much?* He looked up at the eyes of his father, still high above his. They held the gaze for a long moment and Baput saw something he hadn't seen before. Something softer. It didn't match the stern, hawk-beaked warrior. *But then, the world is upside-down and nothing is what I thought it was. And my Popa is gentle and kind and wise, and he is on my side.*

"Popa. After we had the Full Kakeeche Day ceremony, that very night, Kakeeche turned their backs on us. All of them. They turned red, like that other time..." Baput trailed off as the rumble that swelled from his Popa's chest knocked two ripe pomegranates from their branches. They each caught one. They placed them gently into their bags.

Baput leapt over the ugly Calamunga memory, straight to his point. "Jerry says Shavarandu will turn his back on us, too, on the day of No Kakeeche, in less than two weeks. It is called an eclipse."

"E-klipps. How can the boy know this before it happens?"

"I told you about his iPlane? The Earth Plane? It tells him so."

"What does our Plane say?"

"I try to look, but all I see is Full Kakeeche, all of them together, singing their song really loud!" Baput almost shouted.

Valko stopped picking and looked down at his son. "I am not Akashic," he began humbly. "But it seems to me, that if these people don't believe in Kakeeche, then Kakeeche will turn their backs every month. And they will tell Shavarandu to turn His back, too, every month on No Kakeeche Day." The big man shuddered, sending ripples down his beard. He looked at the pomegranate he held. "I worry for Elmer. How can his kips grow? How can his family live this way?"

Valko laid a steady stream of kips into his woven grass bag as he spoke. He looked down proudly at his strong young son, already bearing such a burden. His voice was low and quiet, but Baput heard him loud and clear. "Maybe it is up to you to help them. To teach them to love Kakeeche and save their world." The suggestion settled on Baput's shoulders like the third layer of kips they dumped on top of the second, knowing that too many layers would crush the tender young fruit on the bottom.

With a familiar Felsic whoop and a less familiar engine roar, the forklift entered the orchard.

Baput had one more question. "Popa, this eclipse, it will be in the afternoon. Everyone will see."

"Your momama will be frightened. I will wrap her in my arms and hold her. I love the eclipses," Valko muttered softly, turning another of Baput's memories upside-down.

A crash of metal and the thumping of pomegranates on wood and earth erupted from two rows away, followed by a pitiful wail.

"Those go to his wine," said Valko.

When the noise died down, Baput blurted it out. "Popa, Elmer's afraid that when the eclipse comes G-Pa will blame him and Francina and Jerry—and try to kill them with his Evil Eye!"

The forklift was moving again. No, that was a new rumble coming from Popa's chest. He looked down at Baput, then up at the sky, toward the sun.

"We will see, my son," he muttered, "We will see."

First Solar Eclipse

It was a busy 12 days. In the mornings, they picked for Elmer. In the afternoons, they pressed the meat of millions of pomegranate seeds into juice and wine. Millions more dried in the fall sun, the oven, and Fran's food dehydrator. There were pom seeds and people all over the quarters. Baput helped, crossing the line into women's work, just to avoid another session with G-Pa. Popa growled at first, but when Baput looked up into the eyes behind the beard, he saw again the new look of his conspirator. He was allowed to continue his unmanly behavior as the sun, moon, and Earth continued their inevitable march toward their appointed alignment.

When the time arrived, the families gathered at the sauna-shrine once again. The green people clung together in a tight cluster. The Musiks whispered anxiously in their own bunch.

At a little after two o'clock, at a subtle signal from Jerry, the two boys joined in front of their families. They stood side by side nudging each other, the afternoon sun at their backs, until Jerry found the courage to speak. "We're here because there's going to be a partial solar eclipse."

Baput translated for his family. "Part of Shavarandu will turn away for a time, but He will turn back in a few hours. Jerry has foreseen this."

The Akash snapped to attention. "How can this boy know? He dares say this before it is true? He sets a bad mold. He makes it happen!"

Fran offered Star a pair of cardboard eclipse goggles. "Here, you can watch without hurting your eyes. You have to. You could go blind otherwise."

Salistar shyly took the glasses.

"You, too." Fran handed Valko a pair, then turned to Felsic. He waved his hand in front of the odd offering. "I do not look at Shavarandu. He will burn my eyes," he chanted in a monotone.

"True," Jerry muttered softly. He turned to Baput. "So, Shavarandu means technology *and* the sun?"

Baput nodded. "Yes. It literally means, 'the power we fear.' That used to just be the sun, until Batuk opened that door."

Jerry touched Baput's shoulder. His muscles were so tense! "You OK, Pal?" he whispered, seeking his friend's eyes.

Baput put on his eclipse goggles.

Elmer's laughter drew their attention back to the crowd. Valko was wearing the tiny, white cardboard glasses with the dark lenses. On that huge face with that beak, copious beard, and little bit of dark green skin that showed—yeah, Valko looked pretty ridiculous.

Fran rushed over to install a pair on her husband's grinning face, provoking a well-deserved roar of laughter from Valko.

"It's time!" Jerry donned his glasses and looked straight at the sun. "There's a tiny slice off the upper right. See it, guys?" he gushed.

Baput struggled to put glasses on the Akash. "See, G-Pa, like me. It will give you the power to gaze on Shavarandu."

"I must not," G-Pa insisted.

"But you can, G-Pa. You will be the first Akash to look upon His face!"

That did it. Against a long lifetime of training, the Akash accepted the glasses and turned his craggy face toward the white-hot sun. Gasping, he took two steps back. "Shavarandu! He turns! Kakeeche tells Shavarandu there is no faith here. They tell Him to turn away from the non-believers! The non-believers!" he repeated, turning toward the couple with the pink skin and straw-colored hair.

Still in his paper goggles, he charged Elmer and Fran, snarling: "Non-believers! You anger Kakeeche! You must believe!" He raised his bedecked longstick high above his head, ready to bring it down on the skulls of the heretics.

Elmer stowed Fran behind him and got ready to confront his attacker. The glasses looked as ridiculous on that gaunt, pale face as they did on Valko's dark, expansive one, but Elmer didn't laugh. He was hoping they would stop the Evil Eye.

The old man lowered his longstick to the ground before him. He went into a grotesque crouch, like an underweight Sumo wrestler. Strained tendons emerged from behind his glasses, crossed his cheeks and continued along his extended neck as the Akash pushed his face into Elmer's, leading with his right eye. Elmer stared back through his flimsy eye protection.

"G-Pa! I mean Akash. You can't! You mustn't!" Baput cried. He grabbed his G-Pa's sleeve.

G-Pa looked down at the hand that dared touch him. With a snort, he ripped off his paper glasses and shoved them into that hand, loosening Baput's grip.

Again, G-Pa leaned into Elmer's face, right eye first.

Elmer thought the Akash's right eye was going to pop out. It bulged outward like some kind of insect's eye. Cursing his dad and his coach for installing that doggoned sense of fair competition, Elmer removed his own glasses.

Fran let out a gasp.

Jerry yelped, "Dad!"

Elmer's pale gray eyes met the Akash's black eyes without flinching. He hoped the wizard couldn't see the blood pounding behind them. The Akash's lips drew into a bestial snarl that widened on the right side below his bulging eye. He reminded Elmer of Popeye and an inside family joke about their congenital deformity. He tried to repress the laugh that welled up, unbidden but insistent.

Valko watched in horror as a gurgling cough escaped from Elmer's clenched mouth. His belly breathed in and out in spasms. *Can the old man really do it?* Valko had never quite believed in the Evil Eye, but... He released Star from his protective embrace and rushed to where Elmer seemed to be choking on some unseen miasma. As he arrived, the pink, frozen face cracked. What emerged was, *what? A smile?* A broad, impudent grin, as rude as Jerry's, from which escaped a belly laugh that flowed over the self-righteous Akash and drowned his fearsome power with a wave of awkward guffaws and timid giggles that spread throughout even his most loyal subjects!

The Akash gathered himself in defense, if not of Kakeeche, then of his own supreme abilities. "It doesn't work on dumb animals," he mumbled in Nauvian. Baput translated. Yet, the Akash tried it once more, thrusting his right eye at Elmer like a bird zeroing in on a bug.

Again? Elmer was the first to look away this time, out of impatience. That's when he saw Valko step up behind the Akash, wrap his great arms around the skinny old man and scoop him right off the ground. The stick-like legs flailed helplessly, and the Akash sputtered in his native tongue as Valko hauled him away to the green side. He set their spiritual leader down on the grass, none too gently.

Star wept and clawed at her husband, then her popa, then her husband again. Valko gently removed the crumpled cardboard glasses from her sweaty fist and placed them on her strained face. He turned her toward the sun and stood behind her, wrapping her in his arms. "Watch," he commanded.

Star quivered in a most pleasing way as she stared at the fearsome phenomenon. Valko stood quietly behind her, thinking about the Evil Eye. All these years he had put up with the Akash in his home, watched his wife suffer, and both his sons, because He was supposed to be supreme and unchallengeable. It had always been so. No one had ever questioned the Akash, mostly because of his Evil Eye.

Defeated, or at least temporarily subdued, G-Pa pouted at the solar eclipse through the safety goggles of Earth, as no other Akash ever had.

"Chant with me, G-Pa," Baput said gently. They began chanting the same rite Baput had used against the lunar eclipse two weeks ago. The repetition lulled the Akash into meditation. Baput felt him ascend, his spirit floating up and to the left. But Baput himself only felt an annoyance that grew with each repetition. He opened his eyes and looked at his family.

Popa held Momama tightly while she cried and whispered all the fears her popa, the mighty Akash, had instilled in her. Fears about her own dead son, Batuk, the angry Calamunga, wishing ill on his own family, on the whole village, and now, on her new friends.

Uncle Felsic sat cross-legged on the ground in a ball, head bowed under his arms, unwilling to look upon Shavarandu, or hear Salistar's terrible imaginings.

"It's nothing to be afraid of, people," Jerry announced. "Kakeeche is just passing between us and Shavarandu, that's all. Two hours and it's all over, like it never happened."

Baput's buried doubts and fears erupted all at once. "Shavarandu turns His back! Giver of all life! How could this be nothing? We must stop this. Keep chanting, G-Pa, Akash. We must beg Kakeeche to not destroy this world!"

Baput joined the Akash in a vigorous round of chanting as their family watched helplessly, hopes pinned on the pious pair. Almost an hour passed. Still buried in Valko's arms, Star squirmed like a cat who has had enough petting and wants to exit the lap. The moon had covered the top center of the sun and was working its way down the golden face to attack its magnificent middle.

"They think it's because we don't believe," Fran whispered to her bored family. "They think we're causing this. Why don't we just tell them we believe now? Then when the eclipse ends, they'll think it's because we converted. Go to them, Elmer. Tell them we've seen the light."

Elmer folded his arms in front of him, shook his head just once, back and forth. "Nuh uh! I ain't worshipping their god just because they say to, even if they say they're gonna kill me."

"You'd die over religion?" Fran asked curiously.

"Yeah, Fran. That's how civilizations get wiped out. Someone comes along and tells you to give up your religion, your way of life, or else they'll kill you."

"*They* is usually *us*, Dad. White people," Jerry corrected the historical record. "And we usually come with superior weapons. I think we've seen what they've got."

Fran took Elmer's arm, ignoring his flinch. "He's just a scared old man, Honey. He's lost his power! If we do this, it will make him feel better. And Star won't be so scared. When is maximum, Jerry?"

"Ten minutes from now. I set my alarm."

"Can you ask Baput to come over here?"

Jerry took off to extract Baput from his meditation at the Akash's side, wondering if he was committing a sin.

"What are we doing, Fran?" Elmer demanded.

"At maximum, we declare our loyalty to Kakeeche. Then, the sun starts coming back, see? We did it. We saved the world. They're happy, we're happy."

"Why are we happy?" Elmer asked unhappily.

Fran tried her sweetest smile. "Because they don't want to kill us anymore. And they're great workers, they can stay. Honey, I'm worried about Star, and G-Pa, too."

"Is that why we're giving in, Fran? To make them feel better? Or because we're scared to stand up for our religion?"

Fran stared at Elmer like he was from another planet. "What religion? When was the last time you went to church?"

"I dunno. Frank Junior's wedding, I guess."

"My brother got married five years ago. And yeah, I think that *is* the last time. Face it. We're Holiday Christians! We're just in it for the presents. Not worth dying over. To some people, yes. To those people over there, probably. But we're not zealots. What do we have to lose?"

Elmer snorted. "A man don't have to be a zealot to stand up for his beliefs, Fran. Even die for them, sometimes."

"Yeah, Dad." Jerry joined them, Baput standing timidly behind him. "I'd die for science. That's my religion. Huh, Baput." He gently guided his bashful friend into the circle of beige skin and tawny hair. "I'd die standing up for science," Jerry repeated.

"Over my dead body!" Fran cried.

"Then you'd die for science, too, Mom." Jerry tried to fist bump his scowling mom, laughing. She pulled her fist away.

Elmer did the shushing this time. "Enough with the drama, OK? Nobody's dying today." Two pairs of the most precious blue eyes he knew and one pair of irresistible brown ones all stared at Elmer, waiting for him to fix the sun and moon and make everything alright. Long minutes passed as the moon crept closer to the sun's heart.

"Awwww jeez! Alright!" Elmer's plaintive cry drew stares from the green group, and an anxious, high-pitched whoop from Felsic. The Akash continued to meditate, oblivious to his latest converts. "Baput, you gotta wake your G-Pa up, right after Jerry's beeper goes off. Tell him I'm ready to, well, I'm ready to negotiate. Can you say that? I want to talk to him. Man to man. Right before the sun comes back, see?"

Baput looked puzzled for a second. "Ah. Because Jerry knows when it will start to turn back." A smile broke across his worried face.

"Five minutes," warned Jerry. "Practice what you're going to say."

Elmer looked down at Baput. "What do I do? Is there a ceremony or something?"

"I don't know," the green boy replied. "We have never had a non-believer before. Except Keeldar."

"Yeah, Keeldar," Elmer mumbled around a gulp as he stared at the oblivious Akash. *Well, he tried it once, said I'm too dumb, like an animal, so here goes…*

Jerry's cell phone beeped. "It's time, Dad."

Baput escorted Elmer to the Akash. The old man removed his goggles ceremoniously and handed them to Baput. He extended his right hand toward Elmer, palm down, and made a downward motion.

"You should kneel," Baput instructed.

"Yeah, no. Uh-uh. Not happening."

Baput looked up at this strangely colored man with his unorthodox code, then shook his head subtly at the Akash.

"Have you come to embrace Kakeeche, you heretofore foolish man?" The Akash roared like a mouse.

Elmer leaned back from the verbal slap, then plunged into his hastily prepared speech. "I understand that it would be better for my crops and my son if the sun and moon didn't keep going out all the time. So, your grandson here tells me I can fix it if I just start kissing your alien moon god's—"

"*Elmer!*" he heard Fran's voice in his head.

"So, what do I have to do?" Elmer continued, brave and cautious, into the stoic face of the Akash with no goggles between them. "Do I come out and howl at the full moon with you and Baput every month? Or can I worship Kakeeche quietly, in my own way?"

The Akash looked Elmer up and down as if appraising him, which indeed he was. "You are a less-than ordinary man, like that idiot Felsic."

"Hey, now," Elmer stood up taller. "Felsic's my friend, and he's a hellava lot smarter than you guys give him credit for!"

The Akash pretended not to hear the unprecedented backtalk. Without his weapon, what could he do? He looked right through Elmer with no effect! *A talking animal. No wonder he thinks Felsic is smart!* He searched for his usual weapon: words. "Simple men do not often worship openly, except on special days in ceremonies, like the First Full Kakeeche Day Ceremony. I saw your joy that night! How much you loved Kakeeche!"

"Holiday Kakeeche," Elmer surmised. "I can do that." He almost slapped the old wisp on the back but stopped short when he saw the size of his hand relative to those narrow shoulders. *Probably not protocol anyway.*

"But in your case," Baput had trouble translating the rest. "You have ignored the Spirits all your life and raised your son to do the same. There is no greater transgression! You shall have to atone. You and your family will recite the ritual every month on Full Kakeeche Night, out here in the, um, plaza, no matter how cold or wet, wearing nothing but your hideous pink skins. Maybe it will toughen them up, give you some color! You look like the grubs that hide under the logs of the forest." G-Pa shuddered his revulsion.

Elmer stood with his hands on his hips, sizing the old man up. He looked grand in that robe decked with Fran's beads, but under that, he seemed puny and frail. Especially now that they'd seen his stuff. Elmer choked back another laugh, remembering that Popeye face, and how he had been so afraid of this relic!

He waved an exaggerated swat at the Akash of Nauve, turned and walked back to a disappointed Fran. From her side, he shouted back to the Akash, "You keep your Kakeeche."

He looked over at Valko. "You guys are free to practice your own religion. I won't stop you. But leave me and my family out of it! You're here to work! And you won't be, not for much longer if I hear any more of this crap!"

The crowd stood in stunned silence as the moon completed its passage across the sun. Kakeeche released their grip on Shavarandu, the power we fear. Then it was over, as if nothing had happened.

Star shot Fran a wounded look, gathered her helpless popa and walked home beside a husband who was even more silent than usual, but who wore a strange new smile on his face.

Jerry steered a sullen Baput toward the river. "I'm sorry, B, but we just don't believe in that. There are eclipses all the time, and the world doesn't end. Like I told you, my family believes in science. We believe, we *know*, well, I've told you already…"

"Yes," Baput interrupted, "Science. Evidence, right?"

"Yes," Jerry answered firmly.

Baput pressed like Jerry would. "Evidence says the eclipses are not because your family doesn't believe in Kakeeche."

"That's right!" Jerry applauded his student, resisting the urge to say, 'duh'.

"You want to hear my evidence?" Baput asked calmly, lounging on his back on the grass.

"I'd love to!" Jerry sat gladly on the ground next to him.

"My G-Pa and I have been committing Shavarandu for years. Each year we got closer to activating the Weapon. As we did, there were more eclipses. Six months before our Arrival. Then the First Full Kakeeche, as soon as we arrive here, total eclipse. The very next New Moon, solar eclipse. Two opportunities for eclipse since we arrived. Two eclipses. That is 100% correlation. Evidence. It's not you. It's us."

"Wow. I guess you're getting this science stuff. Excellent argument!"

"So, I am right," Baput said smugly.

"No," Jerry countered. "Too small of a sample. You need more, um, Kakeeche cycles. And I can guarantee no more eclipses until next spring."

"When exactly?" Baput tensed as he asked.

Jerry knew without looking at his phone. "Total Lunar, April 4th."

"What will happen then? What will your popa do?" Baput asked anxiously.

Jerry laughed at the big black pupils with the white shining all the way around them. "My dad was scared of your G-Pa, and your popa, too. Now you guys are scared of him."

"My popa's not scared." Baput's response was instinctive, but not convincing. He spilled his own fears. "We can't be kicked out, Jerry! What would we do? It's almost three years until next First Pomegranate Day, when the portal opens, maybe…"

"How do you know that?" Jerry had to ask.

"That's the only time the Rock rings like that, on its own. It was ringing even before Felsic pedaled and I pulled the lever. G-Pa and I we were there on First Pomegranate Day three years ago, too, and it rang all by itself. We didn't even have the net and the wires then."

"What about the years in between?"

"I go to the Holy Cave in the off-cycle years for my birthday. The Rock is still, unless we hit it with the hammer we found behind the Death Door."

"The Death Door." Jerry repeated the name solemnly, then brightened. "So you're here for three years, at least," he said gladly. Then he remembered. "My dad wouldn't kick you out, not really." His promise hung in the air like a question. "Hey, what time do you guys all get up?" he asked suddenly.

"Your clock says 6-0-0 exactly, every morning."

"Well, next spring, the lunar eclipse will be maximum at about five o'clock in the morning, and the moon goes down right at sunrise, naturally, at about 6:30. It will be low in the sky by six, even lower than last time. It will be in spring, so probably cloudy, and foggy down by the river where the moon will be. They won't even see it. Just let them sleep through it. You sleep through it too. Sleep late."

Baput burst into a grin. "I will have a special Spring Full Kakeeche Ceremony and make sure everyone drinks lots of wine that evening."

"That's using your powers."

"I hope they all sleep through it, especially G-Pa. But I can't ignore it, Jerry. I am to be Akash. An Akash must always watch the sky for signs."

"The Akash also must know what the signs in the sky really mean," Jerry countered. "They have to know when something is a special sign, and when it's just normal sky stuff.

"You know what? You guys aren't alone. The iPlane says a lot of Earth people are freaking out, too, because this year and next year, they call it a lunar tetrad. Four total lunar eclipses in two years, every six months. That's not even counting the solar ones. They say it means weird things are going to happen," he rolled his eyes, "But it's all just the natural movements of the Earth and the moon. That's all there is to it."

"And no weird things have happened," Baput replied flatly.

Speechless for once, Jerry stared down at his green-skinned best friend, lying comfortably on the grass of the Look'N Up, gazing back at him.

"Evidence," Baput concluded with a grin, pointing to his chest.

The Tiny Akash

Baput lay on his back, holding G-Pa's rough knot of a hand in his, as he had every night since shortly after their arrival. He drifted peacefully, surprised at how easy it was to relax. He didn't sleep or meditate. He simply floated along in an invisible current, some unseen and unnamed force that flowed through his consciousness. Without resisting, he let it pull him up and to the left.

He reached a strangely new, yet comfortably familiar place on the Plane. He had visited this space with G-Pa many times, for his lessons. The place probably looked totally different to G-Pa. It looked totally different to Baput every time he visited, but it was the same place on the Plane. The same place in his mind. The Learning Room.

The Learning Room was dimly lit by a full moon muted by heavy clouds. *But it is No Kakeeche night!* His conscious mind interrupted. Even so, a bright, full moon, unobstructed by clouds, now lit the Learning Room from the upper right corner, like a shiny silver bird in a cage.

Where was G-Pa? Baput looked around, then down. A puddle of dark liquid glowed dully in the Plane-generated moonlight. It moved! It coalesced into a tiny tornado and rose, forming a whirling column, about two feet high, reflecting the light of Kakeeche. Before Baput's third eye, the Akash rose from his puddle, hair and beard in all their lavender glory, but no bigger than a *dracna,* a lowly field rat known for stealing people's grain.

The tiny Akash raised his longstick and pointed at the disappearing moon on the screen. "Kakeeche angry!" he squeaked in a voice proportional to his stature. "Who does this? Who's to blame?" he clucked, pacing frantically back and forth across the space that had been his puddle, going nowhere, still tiny.

This is not G-Pa, Baput told himself, wanting to wake up and see the old mess snoring on the floor. "G-Pa!" he cried, squeezing for the hand. *Was that out loud? Am I awake? Is G-Pa?*

Baput knew better than to think logically. That's a sure way to chase a dream away. The whole left half of Kakeeche was shaded now, and the tiny Akash was less bright.

As the Kakeeche turned from silver to red, the lavender hair of the tiny Akash turned a brilliant magenta. He paced faster and faster, talked louder and louder. "You pasty-faced non-believers, step forward!" he demanded in his squeaky little voice. "You must face your punishment! Kakeeche may never return. Your fault! You will all die!"

"What about you, G-Pa? Won't you die, too?" Baput watched himself ask. At home, he never would have asked a question of G-Pa when he was preaching, or ranting. But he was so tiny! *So* tiny. Baput suddenly felt like he was rising into the air, no, growing! Growing so fast, he towered over his already-tiny mentor.

His last question still shook the imagined air like thunder, then he surprised himself by adding: "What will you do about it? You tiny, insignificant insect running back and forth, getting nowhere and squeaking your threats! What will you do?"

The undersized apparition stopped pacing and looked straight up, craning his neck to look high up into the face of his Apprentice Alanakash. The puny image squirmed and squeaked pathetically, "Kakeeche is gone!"

The image darkened as the last sliver of the moon went from shaded gray to deep crimson.

"They will never turn back this time, Boy!" The little red Akash shook his six-inch longstick so menacingly, so sincerely, that Baput felt a terrible guilt at his urge to crush his spiritual guide. The little guy's glow had faded, being just a reflection of Kakeeche's glow, a reflection of a reflection, if Jerry was right.

As if to add insult to injury, the moon immediately contradicted the Akash's prophecy and began to reappear, starting from the top and spreading quickly down, red turning back to shaded silver.

Baput puckered his lips and blew on the tiny figure softly, but steadily, like a kid playing with an insect. The miniature G-Pa bent in the stiff breeze like grass in the wind. As Baput maintained the pressure, the little apparition melted back into a mumbling puddle of liquid, shining in a light that was not his own.

Baput's eyes flew open. The clock said 6:00. It looked like a normal morning, as if nothing had happened to the sun yesterday, or the moon last night. G-Pa's hand rested limply in his. The regular-sized Akash snorted, then opened his eyes.

He met Baput's eyes for a split-second, looking a tiny bit evasive, embarrassed, humbled. Or so it seemed to Baput.

Gaa Fight

Jerry usually had to spend Thanksgiving break finishing the harvest. This year, the trees had been gone through four times, each pomegranate picked at perfect ripeness. Elmer gave the crew the holiday off, so Jerry and Baput had time to play. They wandered into the East Orchard which, despite the thorough picking, was littered with left-behinds that had ripened too soon, too late, or not at all. Now split down the middle, they clung to the branches or rotted in the wet leaves on the ground.

Baput stared open-mouthed at the untapped bounty. "Still so many!" he marveled, exhausted from two months of harvesting.

Shastina and Brodey fought over one of the rotting balls, chasing and nipping all around the dark, sad trees. *Splat!* Something hard, wet and mushy slammed into Baput's face.

"Ha!" Jerry cried, already gathering another wet, soggy kip from the ground and whipping it at Baput.

Baput lunged to dodge it, grabbing a dark mass that barely clung to its branch as he flew by. He drew back and hurled it at Jerry, splattering his forehead and the front of his knit hat.

"My Eddie Bauer hat!" Jerry bawled. He grabbed two poms off the ground and fired one, then the other. One got Baput right in the heart. The other hit the tree next to him, splattering his sleeve.

Baput stepped behind the tree, stripping four overripe messes from the branch above him. *Boom, boom, boom, boom,* they hit Jerry in the heart, the gut, the right shoulder, and the right thigh.

"My Carhartts!" Jerry cried, then he retaliated with four deft strikes with the mushier poms from the ground.

Baput returned fire, this time with the ground poms, too. They fell to their knees in the mud, laughing.

"Great gaa!" Baput enthused, looking down at his clothes. "A year's worth, at least!"

"Gwar?" questioned Jerry, out of breath.

"Gaa. This." Baput indicated the stains on his woven grass clothing, then pointed to Jerry's. "All over your Carhartts and Eddie Bauer. Gaa. It is a badge of honor. The more gaa on your clothes, the more honor. It means you are a hard worker."

"How do you get the stains out?" Jerry only now thought to wonder.

"You don't. You can't. Why would you? You have gaa all over. Many years' worth of gaa. You should wear your Carhartts to school and be proud."

The gaa-stained boys staggered home, laughing and pushing each other, dogs bounding around them, as the late November afternoon sun lit the world from the side. When they got home, they went their separate ways. Jerry had to get home. They were going to his grandparents' for dinner.

"Nice gaa!" Felsic remarked as Baput wiped the mud and wet leaves from his shoes and removed his grass-woven jacket lined with the honeycombed inner rinds of pomegranates.

Salistar came out from the kitchen. "Ooh!" she agreed. "Have you been working? I thought all the kips were harvested."

"There's just a few stragglers in the East Orchard. Me and Jerry had a war."

"Jerry and I," Salistar corrected as she hung Baput's wet, gaa-splattered jacket by the door. "What war?"

"We threw them at each other. I hit him, eight shots out of ten! You should see his gaa! The rotten ones, they splatted so good, gaa all over!"

Felsic shared Baput's excitement, but his parents did not. Valko had entered quietly and was glaring at his son.

"You smashed good kips?" Star asked uncomprehendingly.

"They were left over. Elmer says the harvest is done. We have more than we need, and they can't sell any more, so they leave them on the trees and let them fall. What else can they do? They won't keep."

"You wasted them," Valko scolded. "They shouldn't have been smashed. A true Akash would never smash a kip without cause, no matter how many kips he had." He snorted at G-Pa who sat muttering in the corner, unaware of the controversy. "The boy gets no training anymore," he muttered, then barked, "Tomorrow we pick for shoes!" He stalked out of the room.

Jerry entered the kitchen next door and removed his wet boots. Fran, oven mitt on one hand and potholder in the other, was pulling two pumpkin pies out of the oven. Kicking the oven door shut, she looked up to greet him. "Jerry! What have you been doing?" she demanded.

"It's gaa, Mom. Baput and I had a pom fight!"

"Jerry, your Carhartts! I'll never get this out! Do you know how much these cost?"

"It's gaa," Jerry answered. "It's a badge of honor. The bigger the stains, the bigger the man." He started up the stairs to his room without removing his coat.

"I'm not buying you new ones!" Fran cried after him.

"Don't!" he yelled back. "I'm gonna wear this to Gramma's."

"Jerry Musik, you are not showing up at my parents' house looking like a, a—"

"Like a green person, Mom?"

Christmas Surprise

It was late December, and the yal grass that had served them through the First Kakeeche Day Ceremony was finally properly ripe. Fran suggested a cutting expedition. "We'll all go out there with the Jeep and trailer. The men can cut all you need, and we'll bring it all home in one trip."

Baput helped Fran load the squirming Akash into the back seat. "You need to bless the yal," he told him. G-Pa summoned his dignity and settled down. He had an important Akashic duty to perform.

Fran helped Star into the front seat and drew the belt across her friend's lap. "So you don't fall out," she chirped lightly. She sprinted around to the driver's side and climbed behind the wheel. Watching Star's face carefully, she turned the key and put the Jeep in gear.

As the Jeep started moving, a smile slowly spread, wider and wider, brighter and brighter, across Star's face as the sensation of moving without moving flowed through her body. Not scary or painful like the portal, just the wind crossing her face, blowing her long, soft hair. Fran had to turn away, to watch where she was driving, but she would never forget that smile.

Felsic and Valko rode behind in the trailer. Jerry was at school. Elmer stayed behind. When they were gone, he drifted toward the quarters.

As they cut the thick grass in the East Orchard with their scythes, they all heard the unfamiliar motor pull up to the gate at the bottom of the driveway. Baput looked over at Valko. His subtle eye contact was permission enough. Baput stole away unnoticed, then ran to a spot in the West Orchard that overlooked the driveway.

Baput watched a strange vehicle labor up the driveway, kicking dust in its wake. It was like Big Truck, but smaller and completely enclosed. On the windowless metal side it had a drawing like on the door of Big Truck, but different. It said: "Look'N Up Plumbing," and instead of a kip, it was the end of a round pipe that wore the cockeyed face, left eye too high, looking up and to the left.

Baput crept along the trees above the driveway, following the van past Jerry's house without being seen. It stopped at the front of the quarters, where Elmer waited on the porch.

Baput ran to the shop and ducked into the room that held Felsic's state-of-the-art pomegranate wine operation. He stepped through a narrow door in the back that opened right behind the quarters.

Elmer and his brother, Patrick, rolled a dishwasher off the truck on a dolly and escorted it towards the quarters. "You sure got this fast," Elmer complemented his brother.

"I already had it. I'm collecting appliances for a workers' quarters. Whenever something gets returned, doesn't fit, wrong color, whatever, they put a big discount on it. With my contractor discount, I get a great deal. I've got a fridge, oven, microwave, even a toilet." He grinned. "It's green! I got it all the way installed before they realized how hideous it was. Then it was all my fault. 'Take it out! Put the old white one back in! I want my money back, you charlatan!'" Patrick's voice was all over the place, high, then low, imitating different voices. "I didn't think we needed a dishwasher, but I grabbed this anyway." Patrick babbled on in his regular voice. "But here you are, putting one in. Glad to see someone treating their workers decent, Bro."

"These ones are special," Elmer replied with a warmth that surprised himself. He couldn't help but smile about his secret super-crew. "A family," he went on, "and the mom would love a dishwasher. Never had one."

Patrick could tell his brother was hiding something. "And where is the lady of the house?" he asked, measuring the hole under the counter one last time. "I'd like to show her a few things, especially if she's never had one before."

Elmer stumbled for an answer. "Um, it's a surprise. Christmas present."

"Where are they from?"

Elmer froze for a second, and Patrick wondered what was up. Illegal aliens weren't unusual in California farm country, including Look'N Up Ranch. But this was something else.

Elmer didn't answer, and Patrick let it drop. He moved the dishwasher into position and started hooking the hoses up.

Elmer changed the subject. "Workers' quarters, huh? You guys strike it rich or something?"

"Did you? You're installing a dishwasher in yours."

"Yeah, but this is a farm, we need field hands. What kind of help do you guys need?"

"Those pomegranates we planted are starting to produce a lot."

"Six trees?" Elmer snorted. "OK, 'fess up, what else are you growing?"

A half smile played across Patrick's lips for a moment, then vanished. "We're thinking of some domestic help. With Lorraine working all the time, we need someone to keep house, cook, and be home for Belinda so she doesn't have to go to After School every day.

"Lorraine doesn't cook at all anymore. She brings home takeout and frozen lasagna. She usually doesn't get off work till at least six or seven, so I pick Belinda up from school and take her on my jobs with me. She stays in the truck, doing homework or playing with her phone. No one sees her. Bad enough they see me..." he trailed off.

Elmer's forehead wrinkled and the left corner of his mouth went up a little. "Are you guys OK?"

"Yeah, yeah," Patrick answered too quickly. "She just likes her career. She went to school all those years in engineering, and we agreed she should go for it. And that's going great. But at home, it's just me and Bel heating up frozen pizza and hoping Mom gets home before bedtime."

Elmer briefly touched his brother's shoulder as he was standing up to push the dishwasher into place. "Sorry to hear that, man. That's tough."

Patrick put down his wrench and wiped his hands. "Let's try this puppy out." He pressed the on button and closed the door. It was almost silent, except for a gurgling in the pipes below. "Are you guys coming for Christmas? We'd love to have you. Bel would love to see Jerry."

"We, er, committed to Fran's mom again."

"They had you for Thanksgiving," Patrick objected.

Elmer thought fast, hating himself for lying to his brother, maybe putting a whammy on his brother-in-law. "Yeah, her brother, Frank Jr. and his wife are having a little trouble."

"Yeah. There's nothing for a marital crisis like Christmas with the in-laws," Patrick muttered with poorly concealed sarcasm. He gathered up the vast amount of plastic that had wrapped the dishwasher. It swirled around the kitchen like a hurricane in the middle of the ocean.

The window was too high for Baput to see into, but he stayed outside, listening. When he heard the dolly roll, he slipped along the wall to where he could see the front of the house without being noticed. Patrick came out, pushing the empty dolly, still wrestling with the plastic.

When he saw his face, Baput drew in a sharp breath. Elmer's brother had straggly, wavy, brick-red hair about chin length, pale white skin with reddish flecks, and gray eyes in a kind, wrinkled face. But he wasn't like the other Earth people Baput had seen, even on the iPlane or the TV.

Patrick had a profound facial deformity. More than a misaligned eyeball, his left eye socket was noticeably higher than his right, and oriented so his eye pointed up and to the left, like the pictures on the doors of the trucks. Like the way Jerry looked when he first showed them the Look'N Up Ranch, and the way they had all pointed when the upper left quarter of Kakeeche turned back. It was also like the location of the Plane, the way Baput envisioned it, and the direction from which the bumblies attack.

Is this guy human? He's Elmer's brother, Jerry's uncle. He must be human. Just different. Baput cocked his head at odd angles, wondering what it would be like if his eye pointed that way.

4. No Otherwhere

Elmer didn't drink much, but he did enjoy a cold one now and then, a treat he figured he deserved. Working on that old Ford tractor in the shop, the woodstove clicking up to temperature on a crisp spring evening, was one of those times. He hadn't really worked on, or played with, old Beulah lately, until Felsic came along with his curiosity and enthusiasm. He was like a kid, only better. He listened, and he didn't argue or wander off halfway through. But Fran said he might have a drinking problem.

Today the crew was building a greenhouse. It was Fran's project. She was in charge, an uncomfortable but educational arrangement for the aliens. But it was their project, too. They were going to use it to start their pomegranate seeds indoors. So maybe Valko could tell himself that he was in charge. *Like I do with Fran*, Elmer admitted to himself with a grin.

The Nauvians wanted to plant the Holy Seeds that the old man had in the pouch around his neck. They were from last First Pomegranate Day, over three years ago. They always planted four seeds from the last cycle in the spring after First Pomegranate Day. Of course, they usually planted them outside. Elmer convinced them that they would be better started in the greenhouse, but when they got bigger, they would want to plant their alien poms in the Look'N Up orchard.

Elmer just wasn't sure. He thought of Little Shop of Horrors, the Day of the Triffids. Then he wandered back to reality, where he worried about diseases and genetic interactions. *Should we let them plant them? Bend to their religion, again?*

He reached for the disembodied piston of the old tractor. Felsic called her "Dead Ganeesh," and was devoted to her resurrection. Grabbing an emery cloth from the workbench, Elmer sat down in his folding chair. He pulled the bottle of beer from the cup holder and twisted the cap to a satisfying hiss.

He had just finished polishing the first piston, and his first beer, when Felsic trotted in. "Whoo! Cold! Warm. I hoped you were here. I saw smoke."

"Hey, buddy!" Elmer hid the empty bottle and refrained from pulling another from the ice chest. "How'd it go?"

"Done. We put the windows in, only broke one." Felsic declared with his own humble version of pride. "Whatcha' doing?" He had learned Elmer's lazy brand of English. It suited him. "Whatcha' drinkin'?"

Felsic didn't miss a beat. Elmer wondered how to tell Felsic that Fran had told everybody she'd overheard Valko yelling at him. *Shucks, Fran means well.* "Um, it's called beer." He handed Felsic the empty bottle he had already spotted.

Felsic sniffed the mouth, drew back sharply. "Like wine, but not!"

"Yeah," Elmer confirmed.

"Got more?" Felsic asked shamelessly.

Elmer had had his battle with the demon alcohol, but he was lucky. He'd had a pretty easy life, when he thought about it, growing up right here on this nice farm with his parents and grandparents. He had never lost a wife, a child, a world. He looked at the eager dark eyes in the etched green face. Behind that goofy smile, there was a deep sadness. *Who knows what this guy's been through? That world of his gets darker with every new thing we learn about it.*

A little empathy, a dose of the Look'N Up, as Dad would say, and Elmer could see it, as clear as he'd seen the warrior in Valko. The family was Akashic. The holy man's family, highest in the land. *But this guy here, he's The Meek. Downtrodden to the core. Lowest of the low. He's Valko's brother! You'd think... Did they even live together on Nauve?* He had always pictured them living together, along with Felsic's wife and kid. *And what's that like? Not knowing what happened to them?*

Chilled to the bone, he reached into the ice chest and pulled out two cold beers. He held one up, out of Felsic's eager grasp. "OK. It's like wine. Here's the thing about it. It's smaller that a wine bottle, right?"

Felsic's eyes darted back and forth and he danced from one foot to the other, wondering like a lab rat, *what am I supposed to say to get that bottle?* "Yes, much smaller than my wine crocks at home."

"Well," Elmer pronounced, Felsic's fate in hands, "You only get this one. And I'm gonna tell you how to drink it. OK?"

"Yes!" Felsic couldn't have agreed faster.

Elmer twisted the top and let out the hiss, deliberately not showing Felsic how. He handed him the bottle. "Wait." He cracked his own beer.

"Now you have two," Felsic observed.

Elmer grabbed a piston and emery cloth for each of them and pointed to the second oily folding chair near the wood stove. "Sit," the boss ordered, handing Felsic his assignment.

Felsic took it with one hand, carefully holding the open beer aloft with the other. Securing the piston on his lap, he started to swig the new drink.

"Wait!" Elmer ordered, juggling his own materials in his lap. "OK. Now, take one swig. Just one."

Felsic did. He started to tilt the bottle a second time, but Elmer stopped him. "No! Just savor it. Feel it. That first swig. I can't, 'cause I've already had one. Feel it? How everything feels like, brighter?"

Felsic exhaled, long and slow, melting into the chair. "Yes. Feels good." A smile spread across his face as it relaxed. He raised the bottle to his lips.

"Nope," Elmer scolded again. "See, you feel good, now you want another swig. OK. Now. But slow. One swig at a time. You gotta take time to savor it, make it last. Besides, you ain't used to them bubbles. You'll get all bloated. Put it in your cup holder and start polishing that piston." Felsic did, after he figured out the cup holder.

"Now the pistons, there's six of them. They go up and down inside old Beulah, kind of like her heart. When they go up, they compress the gas. Then the spark plug sparks it, and pow! Explosion! Boom!"

"Boom!" Felsic repeated, polishing the piston firmly but delicately, like Elmer had shown him. The bottle of beer dangled in the cup holder, near forgotten and warming.

The soft brushing of rough cloth against smooth metal and the occasional pop of the fire in the stove filled the silence while Elmer calculated his approach. "When you were on Nauve, did you live with Valko and Salistar?"

"Oh, no." Felsic answered the silly question. "I live with Peratha and Trillella in the hut at the edge of the village. It's the last hut before the orchard and the fields."

"Sounds nice."

"It is the lowest hut, because I am the lowest," Felsic stated plainly.

Elmer looked up from his piston. Felsic continued to polish. "What's that? The lowest? Why are you the lowest?"

Felsic looked up and shrugged one shoulder. "I was born that way." He sounded like Patrick, Dad, or Pop, talking about their misplaced eyes.

"But, why?" Elmer persisted. "You're Valko's brother, and he's married to the Akash's daughter."

"It's because I'm the winemaker. That's the lowest."

"Why are you the winemaker?"

"That's how I was born," Felsic repeated, completing the circular logic. He returned to his polishing, humming a Nauvian tune.

Elmer couldn't stand it. Pressure built behind his forehead until he relieved it by blurting, "Do they treat you bad?"

"I'm the lowest," Felsic repeated.

Elmer stared for a long time, until the dark eyes looked up to meet his. It was as if a veil had dropped. Elmer could now see the wretchedness, burning like a dark coal somewhere deep inside, underneath the casual, accepting air. "Why do you let them treat you that way?" he finally asked.

The helpless shrug from Felsic drew a flash of anger from Elmer's heart. He tried to direct it, but where? *Valko? No. The Akash? Of course.*

"What can I do about it?" Felsic asked, as if he'd never wondered before.

The most obvious solution came to Elmer first. "Did you ever think about running away?"

"Away?"

"Yeah. Leave the village. Go someplace else."

"Where?"

"I dunno, away! The next village?"

"Next village? There is only one village."

Elmer leaned back in his chair, piston forgotten. "There's gotta be other villages. Other places. Just start walking and see what happens!"

The casual facade collapsed, the deep sadness turned to abject fear. "Surely not upriver, into the mist!"

"Then go across the river."

"Across?" Felsic looked at Elmer as if he'd suggested he fly to the moon.

Elmer shook his head. "Downriver, then. What's downriver?"

"The rice bogs?" Felsic's answer sounded more like a question.

"Past that," Elmer persisted.

The confusion on Felsic's face dropped away, and he raised his head to the ceiling, as if receiving a revelation. "The forest? That's where Romey went with Jakima, who was not his betrothed." He whispered, scanning the room. "He built a hut in the forest, and they ate wild animals, like the dogs do. But it got cold, and they built a fire and the people saw the smoke and found them and brought them back."

"They didn't go far enough. You've gotta walk for days and days."

"Laplin walked for days and days, many years ago. He came back a whole week later, exhausted, almost dead. He had walked and walked in the forest. It all looked the same. Then he realized it *was* the same. The same forest, over and over. He knew every tree."

"Did he have one leg longer than the other?" Elmer interrupted.

Felsic tilted his head and wrinkled his eyebrows, searching for that detail in the memorized story.

"Never mind," Elmer grunted, eager to hear the rest.

Felsic resumed the tale, telling it exactly as it had been told to Nauvian kids for as long as anyone could remember. "He turned around and ran home. It only took him half a day to get to the village, even though he had walked for seven days in the other direction. He was so thin! So starved and weak! He never left the village again. No one did," Felsic concluded, head bobbing up and down.

"Ever again?" Elmer tested.

"Ever," Felsic confirmed. He remembered his beer and drained the bottle, more guzzle than savor.

Elmer didn't try to stop him. He sat speechless, trying to imagine such a world, or such a world view, anyway. *No escape. No choice. Is that why they listen to that old fart, believe his bullshit without question?* His beer was empty. He reached for another, handed Felsic a second.

"When they all get down on you, don't you even imagine running away? You know, pretend?"

"I used to pretend I was an animal. I tried being a dog or a ganeesh, but they have to obey their families, or the Animal Keeper. They're just like us.

"The dracna is better. He is small, but he comes and goes as he pleases, stealing our seeds and grain. But he depends on it, and the people hate him for it, so being him is too much like being me.

I like being a zebkin best. Sometimes they eat in our gardens, but they don't need to. They have plenty to eat without us. They run free in the forest, or in the woods along the river, wherever they want, with whoever they like, and no one hates them, not really, even when they *do* eat the garden."

They finished their pistons and their beers in thoughtful silence. Elmer closed the flue on the homemade woodstove his dad had created from an oil drum and an article in Mother Earth News. He turned out the light and walked down the driveway with his friend, the zebkin. As they parted, he tried once more to imagine a world with no otherwhere.

Dinner Talk

"We wanted to keep that open out there by the river," Elmer argued over his plate of roast pork with homemade applesauce and steamed winter greens. "Just grass, like it is now. No trees."

"Just four," Fran told him. "They want to put them around the sauna. North, south, east, and west."

"The north one won't get any sun, and the east and west will only get a half day. Don't they know that?" Elmer snapped. "They're supposed to know pom farming."

"They *really* want to plant them in the East Orchard, along the river, or at the north end," Fran spilled the true agenda.

"It's planted all the way up to the north property line setback already. And as close to the river as they'll let us."

"They don't get that stuff, Dad," Jerry chimed in, his mouth full.

"Well, that don't matter. We can't plant there, and I don't want to plant the grassy area! Don't I get any say around here anymore? It *is* my place, you know."

Fran got up to disarm Elmer with a hug. "What is it, really, Baby Bear?"

"Not in front of the boy!" Elmer pulled away. "Why does there have to be a *really?*"

"You are extra upset, Dad."

Elmer whirled on his family. "OK, Mr. Scientist. Ms. Environmentalist. Think about it. Alien pomegranate trees with ours. Cross pollinating. Spreading disease. We could be wiped out. Here in the heart of Pom Country USA, we could wipe out everybody else, too."

"But, Elmer," Fran objected, it's an important ceremony!"

Elmer snorted angrily.

Fran talked faster. "They say they're darker purple than ours. I really want to see—"

"OK," Elmer granted, "They plant them in the greenhouse. They're quarantined for a year. It's for their own good. Maybe ours have diseases that will kill theirs. So, start some cuttings or seeds from ours and put them in there with 'em. A ceremony for them, an experiment for us. How's that?"

"Good thinking, Dad," Jerry admitted.

"Farmers ain't dumb," Elmer reported, pointing to his own temple. "Or they don't stay farmers for long. End of discussion," he added, diving into his plate.

They ate in strained silence, utensils clinking. At last, Elmer pushed his empty plate away and spoke. "Felsic said the weirdest thing today." His family's attention was drawn like mosquitos to a zapper. "It kinda explains why they are the way they are. Why they all just believe the Akash's stuff, obey him without even talking back."

"Why, Dad?" Jerry had been wondering night and day.

"There is no otherwhere," Elmer announced.

Fran hooted. "There is no underwear, either."

"Really?" Elmer perked up.

"How do you know?" Jerry demanded impatiently. *No otherwhere? This is heavy stuff and they're…* His thoughts wandered to physics as his mom prattled on.

"Salistar and I talk. I want to get them some. They wear those scratchy grass pants. But I know. I'm spoiling them…"

"Mom! Did you hear what Dad said? 'There is no *otherwhere*'. What do you mean, Dad?"

"Well according to Felsic, they tell the kids these stories where everyone who tries to leave doesn't get anywhere. They always end up coming back, soon. Sometimes by force, I gather. And they believe it. They really believe there's nowhere else they can go."

"How can they believe that?" Jerry demanded.

Fran chimed in, "If that's what they've always been told, for generations, maybe they've never thought anything different. Look at us. Until a few months ago, we didn't know there was a portal to another planet right here on the Look'N Up. We never even imagined that!"

"It's impossible," Jerry had already decided. "A planet that small wouldn't have an atmosphere. Not enough gravity. But I don't think they're from another planet. I think it's another dimension. Maybe it's a bubble, just a piece of this world that's separated…" He trailed off, shook his head. "Naw, that's crazier than Kakeeche!"

Elmer sprang from his chair. "Don't say that word in this house!"

Jerry leaned his chair back, almost falling over. "Whoa, Dad! I was just using it as an example of an irrational belief."

"Yeah, irrational," Elmer muttered, sitting back down.

"I don't know, Jerry." Fran thought out loud. "What if it *is* a bubble? What if it's true?" Her eyes darted to each of them, and Elmer knew the empathy machine was rolling. He'd been there all afternoon. It was a dark place, this place with no otherwhere.

He told them what he'd seen. "It's how they stop dissent. They tell the kids there's no way out, nowhere to run. No choice but the status quo, as they used to say."

"No new ideas," Fran mused.

"No freedom," Jerry added. "You have to marry who they tell you to, do whatever job you're born to. They don't even *think* of doing anything else, according to Baput."

"Yeah," Elmer replied with a sudden bitterness. "He's Apprentice Akash. Highest of the high. He's got it made. He don't feel it like Felsic does."

"I suppose he wouldn't, would he," Fran spoke from the Empathy Train. "Star feels it, I'm sure. She is Akashic, the highest caste, but still a woman, still oppressed. She must believe she has no choice, or else she'd tell G-Pa where to go!"

Elmer laughed. "Valko must believe it, too, or he woulda smashed that old man into the ground years ago."

Fran looked at Jerry. "Baput doesn't believe it, does he?"

"I don't know, Mom. He gets weird, like he doesn't get things sometimes, some words… Come to think of it, it's usually otherwhere stuff."

"I made up a word!" Elmer cackled. Then he straightened. "Do you think G-Pa knows it's not true?"

Jerry shrugged.

"Maybe it *is* true." Fran explored the other side. "I still like your bubble idea."

It didn't work for Jerry. "There's a river, Mom. It's got to come from somewhere, go somewhere…"

"Can you ask Baput?" Fran coaxed.

"Sure," Jerry replied dismally. "He'll just give me that blank look like he's never even thought about it, or spew some of G-Pa's bullcrap."

"Set him straight, then," Elmer demanded.

Fran leaned between them, glaring at Elmer. "Honey, he's supposed to be their Holy Man when he goes back. We can't keep attacking his belief system!"

Elmer glared back.

Jerry backed out of that uncomfortable current. "I'll just ask him some stuff, Mom. I'll be careful," he promised.

Money

Jerry was awake all night thinking about it. *No otherwhere.* It had to be a lie. Did the Akash really think there was no other place in their world? Or did he just tell them that so they'd think there's no escape and they have to do everything he says? *When's he going to let Baput in on that?*

It couldn't be true, of course. Physically impossible, as he'd explained to his parents last night. *But it sure explains a lot!* He'd been distracted all day in school, thinking about ways to bring it up. He had a plan.

After school, the boys met at the Horizontal Tree. Their sessions had been cold and damp lately. Jerry wondered how Baput's woven grass pants treated him when he sat on that wet surface without underwear, as he had done so many times without complaining.

"You guys know you have money, right?" Jerry approached the subject, already knowing the answer.

"What *is* money?" Baput gave the expected reply.

"You work, and we're supposed to give you money. You can get whatever you want with it. You guys have been building up a lot of money in Mom's book. You can't go to the store or put it in a bank, so you just gotta tell my mom if you ever want anything, and she'll get it with your money, if you have enough."

Baput's brows wrinkled. "She already gets whatever we need. And even some things we didn't know we needed. Stuff we didn't even know existed."

"Like the dishwasher?"

"Yes, and this knife." Baput produced his newest and most treasured possession from his waistband.

The knife gave Jerry an idea. He pulled out his cell phone. It was useless at the Horizontal Tree, but he carried it by habit, like most kids. "Money's complicated. It started with trade. That's simpler. What do you guys do when you need something someone else has?"

Baput recited, "I have, you need, I give. You have, I need, you give."

"You give nothing in return?"

"Return? You don't have to return it, unless I need it later."

"Because it's yours." Jerry thought he understood.

"Because it's ours," Baput shrugged, as if it was obvious. "Everything is ours."

The concept hung profoundly in the air. Jerry was wondering if it was socialism, communism, or something else when he saw his opening. "What if other people come to trade?"

"Other people?" That maddening echo, that blank look. Bullseye. There it was, the missing piece. Jerry began the lecture he had planned during Social Studies class.

"A planet is a whole world, all the people, all the countries, the different races, and the animals, all live on this planet we call Earth. It's so big, you could walk forever and not cover it all, but two thirds is underwater anyway. Your planet is probably big, too, or you wouldn't have air to breathe. There wouldn't be enough gravity."

Jerry kept on, watching for a spark of recognition. "You say you come from Nauve. Is that your planet? Or your country?" Still no reaction, just thick, black eyelashes on closed eyes. Was he even listening? "Or your village? What is Nauve?" A vein in Jerry's neck popped out and throbbed his frustration.

After a wait long enough to qualify the response as a miracle, Baput turned to his friend, his eyes calm. "It is where we live. Our home. It just means 'home,'" was his frustratingly simple response.

"So when other people come to your village from someplace else, do they say they're from Nauve, too, or do they have another name for where they come from?"

"Other people? Another place? You mean like here? The portal?" Baput floundered, incoherent, then a clear revelation. "There are no other people. No other place. Only the village."

Jerry had tried to imagine it all night. He couldn't. But, of course, Baput believed it without question. "You mean, there are no other villages? Other families that live somewhere else, maybe look or talk different or have different ways? People you don't know at first, like me and my family. Maybe they come visit, stop by on their way to somewhere else."

"Somewhere *else*..." Baput muttered, panic crossed his face.

Jerry smelled the fear. Wondering why, he asked, "Do they attack your village? Rape your women and burn your homes?"

Baput recoiled from the graphic image. Jerry changed the scene back to the original, peaceful one. "Do people come and bring things from far away? Stuff you can't get in your village? You give them stuff in return, like some of your mom's oil, 'cause maybe poms don't grow where they live. That's trade."

Baput tried to search the Plane, but he couldn't converse at the same time. This kind of idea wasn't something you looked up on the Plane, anyway. This took pure imagination. He couldn't imagine it any more than Jerry could imagine the opposite. *Other, different people, like Jerry's family, coming to the village.*

"No," he said. "There are no other people, no otherwhere. Nauve is just nauve. It's like, you've been working in the orchard all day, and the sun is setting, and you say, 'Let's go nauve and have some pumpkin pomegranate soup.'" Baput sounded like an old man remembering what he thinks was a simpler time. "Everybody knows everyone in the village from birth. All 25 families, about 100 people. Without our family, it's only 24 families and 95 people. That is all there is, all the people, if they still exist."

"What do you mean, if they exist? You mean if they didn't get eaten?"

"If, we, they..." Baput stammered. "So, we are otherwhere now, um, here, with you?"

"Yeah, this is otherwhere alright," Jerry mused.

"So what happens to the old where, if we are in the otherwhere?"

"It's still there!" Jerry answered the crazy question, glad to finally be getting somewhere. "There's lots of different places, B. People go to different places all the time and come back. The other people stay there and go on with their lives. Believe me, Buddy, your friends back on Nauve still exist."

Baput tried to imagine the village going on without him. He could almost see it, but was it real? "I wish I could explain that to Momama and Felsic!" he exclaimed. "They think, if we are here, then Nauve is, well, disappeared, and replaced with this, um, place. And then, what happens to Peratha and Trillella? Bazu and Pindrad? Azuray and Rakta? Tamaya?"

Calmed by the bit of assurance for his faraway loved ones, Baput summoned the courage and imagination he would need to apply the idea of otherwhere to his tiny home world. "No one has ever come from otherwhere, not even in the old legends. Who would come?"

"I don't know, purple people?"

"There's purple people? I've seen none on the iPlane…"

Jerry sighed, exasperated. "It's just an example."

"No," was Baput's firm final answer. "There are no purple people. No other people of any color. No otherwhere, just Nauve."

"So, you don't have a name for your people, do you?" Jerry realized suddenly.

"You call us Nauvians. But we don't call our people anything. We are just people. Sometimes the Akash says 'the people.' That means all of us."

"Has anybody ever gone exploring? Did they ever come back?" Jerry wondered, hoping not to hear about the guy who walked in circles for a week. He got the short version.

"Some have tried to run away, into the forest. Bad people who wish to do forbidden things, like marry someone who is not their betrothed. But they always come back, because there is nowhere to go."

Jerry couldn't imagine not even trying. "You've gotta have some urge to find out what's out there. It's a basic human thing."

Baput shrugged. "The only going away is death. Then, everything you knew and felt becomes part of the Plane, and your spirit becomes a star. You can look down from above, but you can't come back to the village and be a person anymore. The only other way to imagine going away is to look at Kakeeche. They go away and come back all the time, but…" he caught Jerry's stern look and turned away.

Jerry put his left hand on Baput's right shoulder and met his eyes. "And now you know that the moon doesn't really go away. It's always there, all of it, even when you don't see it. It may be on the other side of the planet, shining on somebody else in some otherwhere. Or it's up in the day, but you can't see it because the sun is too bright."

"Shavarandu drowns Kakeeche." Baput sounded both dramatic and monotonous, as if he were reciting some ritual.

Jerry narrowed his eyes, keeping them locked on Baput's. "But the moon is still there. All of it. All the time. And when we get between Kakeeche and the sun, it's us that casts the shadow. They're still there. We're still here."

"Your religion is more comforting than mine," Baput mused.

"I told you, it's not a religion," Jerry replied with a sudden venom that ushered in an uncomfortable silence, as conversations about religion often do. The boys rose stiffly from the cold trunk and drifted toward home in the low sunlight, as deep in thought as two 12-year-olds can be.

G-Pa

The Akash sat peacefully in the dark sauna, cross-legged on his meditation cushion with his eyes closed. Baput blinked a goodbye to Jerry and sat down quietly without turning on any lights.

Their daily sessions had been meaningless since the solar eclipse. G-Pa would repeat old sermons, rites and chants, or rant senselessly and endlessly. He never spoke to his apprentice, never asked or answered a question. Baput had learned to meditate in the dark shed with G-Pa's prattle droning in the background like a mantra, soothing in its ceaselessness, as long as you ignored his words. Baput meditated on his own now, like a full Akash would. He didn't need help.

But he needed answers, and if anyone had them, it was G-Pa.

He tried to meditate, but the things Jerry had told him swam around in his head like sharks that can never be still. Now he understood the iPlane images he'd seen, the people in different *places*, looking just a little different from one another. He understood it in his brain, but it hadn't sunk in as a whole, real idea. It hadn't cast its shape on his known universe and changed it forever. Not yet. The known universe resisted. The idea just wasn't going to fit in his brain without bending something, maybe everything. A certainty known by his race for three thousand years, forever. *There is no otherwhere. There are supposed to be otherwheres in a world. Nauve is not complete.*

G-Pa's eyes opened slowly, as if he sensed the racing young mind nearby. Baput fixed his gaze on those relaxed eyes. He had ascended! Perhaps he had sensed the important, world-shattering news on the Plane. Good. He would be prepared.

"G-Pa?" Baput plunged in. "Are there other people at nauve, besides us in the village?"

G-Pa put on his stupid question face that he saved for the most mundane of matters, beneath his interest. "Well, you know as well as I," he began gruffly, his time being wasted by this foolish boy. "Kaysen the Tender lives in the orchard with his family, to pull the weeds and pluck the bugs and keep the dracna away. Keplar's family lives by the river, tending the mill."

Baput's nostrils flared, annoyed by what seemed to be a dodge of his question. "No, G-Pa, not them. They are us. I mean somebody you don't know. They come and trade things with us, bring things that we don't have in the village."

"You speak nonsense, boy. What is it we don't have in the village? What could you, the Apprentice Alanakash, possibly desire that is not already at your command? And speaking of Akashic commands, your Akash is hungry. Take me to my tether."

"Yes, G-Pa."

The old man leaned extra hard as Baput escorted him home. Not from weakness, for the downward pressure he exerted on his Apprentice's shoulders was greater than the gravity he commanded. Baput bore it, tried to ignore it. His mind raced as they approached the hut. *G-Pa doesn't know. Or he won't tell me. Why not? If I am to be Akash, I have to know even the secrets. Will he tell me when I ascend to Akash? I need to know now.*

Does Momama know? She reads and writes in Old Akashic. She writes down G-Pa's words and reads to him, even though he can do it himself. She has read the books. She knows the truth. She would be too afraid to tell me a great secret like that. But she might whisper to Popa in the night...

He won't tell me, either. It is for the Akash to tell. He pictured his Popa's face, the new one he'd worn since the eclipse, and was suddenly sure: If Valko knew the truth, and his son, the Apprentice Alanakash asked for it, he would divulge what he knew, for he no longer feared the wrath of the Akash.

He deposited G-Pa in his chair in the corner. Momama plugged the Akash's whine with a rice cake and assured them that dinner was almost ready.

"I'll tell Popa," Baput offered.

Valko

Baput found his popa sitting alone in the shop, sharpening his blades. Felsic and Elmer were just outside, trying to get the brush mower to work.

"Popa, I have to ask you something. It's important."

Valko set the file down on the floor and lay his machete across his lap. "Of course, Son."

"Popa, at um, nauve, are there other places besides the village?"

The puzzled look answered Baput's first question. He had worn that look himself, just an hour ago. He knew how it felt. He knew the thoughts that swirled behind it, like leaves picked up by a sudden wind. He knew, now that Popa had been asked that question, he would never be the same.

Baput gave his father a little time to gather those leaves back into a messy pile. Then he asked his second question. "Popa, have you ever heard of other people coming to the village? Different-looking people, like Elmer's family?"

"No, never! I would…" Valko was on his feet in an instant, his freshly sharpened machete above his head, gleaming blue in the shop lights. His face was a twisted battle snarl, and his eyes stared daggers at some unseen foe, who, from their direction, must have been as tall as he was.

Baput knew better than to approach him.

Valko stood there like a statue of Meldan, the Warrior Akash until a short burst of motor noise followed by a metallic scream and a string of curses melted the monument.

Valko grunted, blinked, and shook his head. He kept his eyes on his machete as he brought it down slowly to the floor and stepped away from it. His eyes were confused, embarrassed, and deeply frightened, and when they lit on Elmer, a new understanding dawned.

"Dinner is ready, Popa," Baput said softly. Errand complete, he headed home with his answers—and a lot more questions.

That Night

At dinnertime, Jerry was still wondering what it would be like to have never seen or even heard of a foreigner, an exotic stranger with different looks and ways, and all the baggage that Earth humans attached to that concept.

"They're not Nauvians," he began before his first bite.

"Well, what are they, then?" demanded Elmer. "We've all been dying to know."

"I don't know. Nauve just means '*home.*' They don't have a name for themselves, or their planet, village, whatever, because it's the only place there is. He's never even heard of a stranger showing up, and they'd notice, because they all know each other from birth, for generations. Maybe it really *is* the only place! If there were other people, why wouldn't they ever show up?"

"Maybe the other people in the otherwheres believe that, too," Fran mused as she doled out the pork fried rice she'd made from last night's leftovers.

Jerry launched his prepared speech. "There are only about a hundred people in the village. They're all the same: green skin, brown eyes, and black hair that turns lavender when they get old. No one has ever left and gone away, and no one new has ever come. Not even in the old legends. No different-colored people with strange clothes and customs. Never anyone coming to take them over, or make slaves out of them, or force some religion on them, ever. And that's why they *so* don't get why we have to hide them because of the color of their skin."

Elmer was struck silent for once.

Fran's eyes brimmed with tears.

Elmer leapt into the gooey pause. "Well, that's cheating!"

Fran turned liquid gray eyes to him, "What do you mean?"

"It's easy to have no war or racism when you're all the same! They've got nobody to hate! But they do it anyway. They may all be the same color, but they still hate each other. They're divided by class, by bloodline. And the lower ones are downright oppressed! And they've only got peace 'cause they got no toleration for dissent. They nip it in the bud! They tell their stories over and over to scare them into obeying, to convince the kids there's no choice. 'The Akash will get ya with his Evil Eye! You can't run away, no place to go!'" he mocked.

Fran sighed as another green dream shattered.

Elmer wasn't done with his hammer. "I'll tell you something else. Them stories? They didn't just happen once, a long time ago. It's gotta happen once every generation, don't you think? Some kid won't go along with being told who to marry or what to do for a living? Somebody who doesn't wanna take orders from the likes of old G-Pa, there? They gotta feel that way, if they're as human as I think they are."

Fran cleared the dishes like a zombie, her thoughts far away in a dismal otherwhere. No racism, no language barriers, but still they'd found a way to divide themselves. Caste. Your life decided at birth, by others. No hopes, no dreams, no courtship. No trying, succeeding or failing, and then trying something else. Just do what you're told, or... or what? Just do it and be quiet.

They sat through the evening news without talking. Then they all drifted off to bed, deep in their own thoughts.

In the middle of the night, a bolt from the Plane delivered a dream that was somehow shared by Jerry and his mom down the hall. They were both at Baput's wedding. He lifted his bride's veil. Fran and Jerry held their breaths, anxious to see what Tamaya looked like. They saw her face. It was Baput's face! The identical couple turned and faced the crowd of cheering friends and relatives. Everyone looked exactly like Baput! Both dreamers jolted awake with a realization that had them musing and mulling until it was time to get up.

Next Morning

Jerry's questions burned brighter with the rising sun. He was glad there was no school today. The teachers had an all-day training on what to do if somebody shows up and starts mowing kids down with an automatic rifle. Jerry didn't want to think about that right now. Dad had given Baput the day off, too, so Jerry could grill him, gently, and find out more. He was dying to do just that, in the privacy of the Horizontal Tree.

This was delicate stuff, maybe even insulting. Not knowing science, Baput would definitely take it wrong. At breakfast, Jerry asked his mom, "Are you thinking what I'm thinking?"

Fran's subtle nod sufficed for an answer. She packed them a lunch within Baput's limited diet and sent Jerry off to find out more.

During his sleepless night, Jerry had come up with a way to introduce the subject of genetics. Now he plunged in headfirst. "You're a couple months younger than me, but you're bigger. You're gonna be big, like your dad. Are most of the men on Nauve as big as him?"

"My Popa is called 'Tiny' at Nauve."

"No way."

"Oh, yes. Most men are bigger than him."

"What about Felsic? He's no bigger than my dad. Bigger muscles, maybe. What do they call him?"

"They say my popa got all the good stuff out of his momama and there was not much left for Felsic."

Getting closer, thought Jerry. He kept digging. "Your mom's not big."

"Females are much smaller," Baput stated.

"Your G-Pa's not big. He's really small. You're bigger than him already, and you're only 12!"

"He shrank when he got old," Baput explained. It was true, his G-Pa had decreased in both girth and stature within Baput's recollection, even before their "Arrival." Yes, that was true, but the rest… Baput sputtered, trying to hold back a laugh. Then he let it go.

"What?" Jerry demanded, punching Baput on the shoulder.

"My popa is considered a larger man," Baput admitted when he could breathe. "Our people are about the same size as yours, as far as I've seen."

"And you suddenly have a sense of humor," Jerry grasped the back of Baput's neck and rocked it back and forth roughly. Baput was taking it so much easier than he'd expected. That was good, because if he didn't know this already, it was going to be really bad news.

"Your families don't have a lot of kids, do they? And not real often. Wasn't Batuk 10 years older than you? And Cilandra was what, five years older?"

"Yes," Baput said tightly, his good mood dissolving quickly.

"Were there any other kids who died?"

"I think some at birth. Women have, um, failures, all the time."

"Failures?"

"Yes. Babies die. Born dead, or right after. Akira buries them in a sacred place."

"Does the mother get to see them first?"

"Oh, no! She does not wish to. It is a curse to. Her next baby will surely die too, if she looks."

"And this happens all the time? To everyone?"

"Well, yes. Akashic families have less, because we get the best betrothals. But others, well, Akira struggles to keep the lines apart. That is why we must marry our betrothed."

Jerry wanted to laugh at the idea, but it was too sad. One hundred people, over how many generations? How could you keep the lines apart, yet breed them together? *Who is this Akira who decides who marries and has babies and what babies live or die?* He completed the terrible thought. *Could it be? Does Baput know? Does G-Pa? Salistar? How can I find out without telling Baput, in case they didn't know?*

First, the obvious. "Is anyone, um, deformed? Born missing an arm or leg or something, maybe an eye in the wrong place?" Jerry's voice tightened to a squeak.

"All the babies are perfect, if they live," Baput replied confidently.

"Are there any people that are, um, mentally, well, slow?" Jerry pointed to his own temple while groping for the correct English word.

Baput did not hesitate. "Downudara!" he cried out, unabashed. "Yes. Every generation has a few. Felsic is, well, a little," Baput hunched his shoulders and made a moronic giggling noise, "yuk, yuk!"

"Goofy?" Jerry exclaimed, not believing. After all, Baput had just tricked him. "Are you kidding? That guy is smart! He'd never seen an engine before, but he can fix anything mechanical! He's a genius! He was just born on the wrong planet."

Baput's hopeful face clashed with Jerry's dark thoughts. "Maybe all of our downudara would be geniuses here!"

Seeing Baput's innocent joy as a soft spot, Jerry drilled in cruelly. "Tell me about the others. Felsic makes wine, has a family. He's not really what I'm talking about. I mean, like, they never grow up. They can't learn, maybe even to walk or talk. Someone like that."

"Yes. The old people say there are more each generation. Right now, there are five who are not as fortunate as Felsic. One cannot speak at all. He is old now. He lives in a tiny hut by himself. Akira's Unmarriageables bring him food. Another makes noise almost constantly, but he makes no sense. He is 22 now. Of course, Akira will never let him wed. His parents will listen to his constant ranting until the day they die.

"Then there is Lalanar. Her face is a little odd, wide and flat, with droopy eyes. She speaks and can do housework, cook simple meals. She is exceptional with children. She, of course, has none of her own, but she is so like them! They think she is one of them. But she doesn't let them get away with anything! She is very useful to the community during gatherings, or when a mother is sick, or has died. She lives with my betrothed's family now, since her momama died." That brow furrowed again as Baput tried once more to imagine Nauve going on without him. "Tamaya's brother, Pindrad, would have married Jeneven on Passascenday. She would move in, and Lalanar would be gone... Well, there is always a family who needs her. She is dear to everyone."

Jerry tried feeling for Baput as he paused to collect himself, choked up over the, the, *OK, there is no politically correct word. Why should there be?* The woman who had watched over him like an adult and played with him like a child, both at the same time, lots of times. Someone whom he, and all his peers, had known all their lives.

Composed again, Baput went on. "There are two others. Twins. Akira doesn't like twins. She says they are bad luck. But these both survived birth. They are seven now. I know, because they were born the same year that Batuk—"

"It's OK, B." Jerry leaned up against his friend's side.

Shastina sat down in front of the boys and laid her head on Baput's lap. Baput lost the painful memory of Batuk in her soft eyes and went on. "They are beloved by their parents, but they still cannot hold their bowels. Will they be adorable at 30? When their parents are dead, who will care for them?" Baput sounded cold. It was not like him talking. Who was it? G-Pa? Valko? The old war chief? Or that woman, Akira?

Jerry's science-driven mind chilled itself with speed, running to the sanctuary of abstract thought, fleeing the truth that lay plucked and roasted before him. His fears had been confirmed. The physically deformed were being killed at birth. The mental disruptions of intense inbreeding, undetectable at birth, were getting through, and increasing. And Baput, the future ruler of this tiny world, seemed to have not a clue about it.

Jerry unpacked some snacks that Fran had made, using Star's recipe. Kind of a pancake of nut flour, rolled up with nut butter and berry jam. They weren't bad. It took a while to get his mouth unstuck from the dough and nut butter, but he was glad for the pause. Should he tell him? If so, what should he tell him—and how? He wanted his mother. He plunged in.

"Baput, sit down."

Already sitting on the cold, wet trunk, Baput looked curiously at the boy who sat next to him. "OK, breathe then. Do your breathing and listen. I'm gonna hit you with some really bad news. Get ready."

Baput obediently closed his eyes and began his Akashic breathing.

Jerry took a deep breath too, and began. "Baput, how can you guys even survive? You must be *so* inbred! I mean, no insult, dude, I'm sorry, but, do you even know what I'm talking about?"

"Akira keeps the lines apart," Baput recited in that brainwashed monotone Jerry detested. "That is why we are betrothed very young, so we always know who to love."

"There's what, 100 of you? I don't care what your Akira says. I was up half the night on this. My mom, too. It's *impossible* to keep the lines apart with such a small group. Say you marry Tamaya, because, what, she's not related to you? Or not *as* related?"

"Yes," Baput said blankly. "That is how we keep the lines apart."

Jerry fought back an eye roll. "But now you're going to breed those two lines together. Then, your kid marries a kid from two other lines, and that's four lines that can't have kids together anymore. Four lines locked out of each other in just two generations, out of what, 25 families? And the others are getting married, too. How long has this been going on?"

"Three thousand years," Baput stated without hesitating. "Exactly, last year, on the day we met. That was a special First Pomegranate Day, Milikipa, One thousand cycles since the Beginning."

Too long, Jerry mused silently. Out loud, he asked the logical question, "What was before that?"

"Nothing." The answer was a flat, matter-of-fact dead end that burned in Jerry's stomach where the nut butter still sat.

He began again, summarizing the numbers. "OK, so you're down to 100 people. About five percent mentally disabled. How many babies die in childbirth? You said a lot," he asked, not wanting to hear the answer.

"Yes. A lot. The old people say that is increasing, also," was the grim, but numberless, report.

"So, you know everybody, right? How many births per year in the whole, um, Nauve?"

"All who can, try to have one per cycle. There are 20 married women who could."

"How many fail?"

"Sometimes only six. Sometimes eight." Baput turned his face away. The tips of his ears were a weird brown color. "I don't know these things. They are silly woman's things. Seventh Rule of Akash says, 'The Akash need not bother with the silly troubles of women.'"

"But it doesn't say you can't," Lawyer Jerry countered.

"Why would I? I know nothing of babbets and betrothals. Those are woman's affairs. Ask my momama. Or it would be better if your momama asked my momama, if you really have to know." Baput got up off the tree.

Jerry did the easy math in his head, comforted by his faith that Mom would get all the answers out of Star. Then, despite his friend's clear objection, he continued his cold calculus as if maybe the Akash *should* know.

"About 20 percent of the population try to give birth every cycle. Of that, about a third fail in some way." Jerry kept one of the ways to fail out of Baput's mind, for now at least.

Baput's calculus was simpler. "So, we only gain about 13 new lives each cycle. And each cycle, we lose almost that many to the nimblies and bumblies. Plus, of course, people die in other ways, in the off season. We seem to be slowly losing our numbers," Baput stated gravely, as if this fact had just now dawned on him.

"You guys need some new blood," Jerry quipped.

"Blood?" Baput winced.

"It's not really blood. It's called DNA. Genetic material."

"Dee En Ay," Baput sounded.

Jerry went on. "It's the tiny parts that make up a person, some from the momama and some from the popa. It's what makes you who you are." He thought of his cousin, Belinda, left eye blazing up and to the left from its misplaced socket. She and Uncle Patrick would have been killed at birth on Nauve! *Except they wouldn't even* be *because Granddad and my great-grandpop would have been killed, too. So, no Dad, no me. The Look'N Ups would have been wiped out of existence on Nauve long ago.*

How could he begin to explain all this to Baput? He would probe no further and reveal no more. He would pass this delicate mission to his highly empathic mother.

Baput and G-Pa

The last thing Baput wanted to do was to talk to G-Pa. First, the otherwhere stuff. Now this. *But Jerry says the village is dying! That it can't go on without an otherwhere, other people.* Baput had to find out what the Akash knew, if anything. He found the old man in the dark sauna, as usual. His breathing changed slightly as Baput entered. Baput could tell he wasn't on the Plane. He interrupted the soft breathing impatiently, his voice harsh. "Akash! I would speak to you."

G-Pa stirred with a snort. "What nugget of wisdom..." he began the standard beginning of another pointless session.

"I asked you yesterday about otherwheres, other peoples, other than the village."

"And I told you that you spoke the nonsense of a greedy, arrogant child. Speak sense to me, or do not speak at all!"

Baput spoke anyway. "G-Pa. Jerry says if we have no otherwhere, no other people, we will breed bad babbets. Deformed babbets. And downudara. G-Pa, I know we have downudara, but I have never seen a deformed person in our village. You know, someone with a part missing, or in the wrong place?"

G-Pa stared, unblinking, unmoved. "You speak of women's matters," he muttered dismissively. "I let my sister worry about such trivialities."

"Akira is your sister?"

"Of course!" the old man snorted. "Didn't you know that?"

"No! She is so, so very old!" Baput marveled.

"So am I," the Akash replied indulgently. "What did you think? I am a first-cycle kip tree on First Pomegranate Day?

"No, G-Pa," his obedient apprentice laughed.

"You are correct!" G-Pa coughed a phrase Baput hadn't heard lately. "She looks much, much older than I," he told his forgiven apprentice with a conspiratorial wink. Then he closed his eyes, inhaled a deep, Akashic breath and spoke no more.

Troubled

Jerry left Baput at the sauna. He hoped the old man would be sharp for once, so Baput could ask him some hard questions. *The Akash must know. Maybe he just thinks Baput's too young to know,* he thought wishfully. He headed on to his house alone, deeper in thought than, perhaps, ever.

He walked right by the garden without noticing the disruption. He climbed the porch steps, swung the door open and stamped his shoes halfheartedly on the doormat. He glanced right, into the kitchen. His mom was barely visible behind a pile of fresh greens, whole plants, roots and all.

"Hey, Mom! Can I help?" he offered gallantly. He needed to talk to her at any cost.

"Rinse these greens," she ordered without hesitation. "We pulled a bunch out to make room for the summer stuff. I'm going to try to cook them, then freeze them."

"Spinach?" Jerry asked without caring.

"You can buy frozen spinach in the store, so why not?" Fran asked. "Wash your hands first."

Jerry surveyed the piles. "They're dirtier than my hands." He observed the irony.

"Wash your hands!" she repeated, shoving him gently toward the bathroom.

When he came out and settled into his job, she started with an easy question. "Baput never helps his mom?"

"Nope. It's against the rules. Not just 'cause he's Akash, either. No man does what they call 'women's work.'"

"Yeah, that's what Star says," Fran agreed.

Jerry tried to imagine it, in the empathetic, Look'N Up way. He laughed. "I guess the other guys would really get down on you if you *did* help a woman. They've got a good thing going."

Fran puckered angrily. "Well, you're not green! You offered to help, remember? Now get to chopping, or I'll tell Valko on you."

Jerry grinned that priceless one-eyed grin and set to work. Soon the grin faded, and he sighed.

"What's the matter, Son?" Fran asked, already knowing the subject and dying to hear the latest.

Jerry began, "Mom, I'm troubled."

Amused by the old-fashioned word, Fran tried it with a Scottish accent. "Aye, and just what be troublin' ye, laddie?"

"You remember about the no otherwhere?"

"Of course. I thought about it all night."

"And how nobody ever came and raped and pillaged and stole women? Not that that's good. I'm not saying that. But Mom, they don't have…"

Fran looked into the compassionate blue eyes of her cherished only offspring and understood all too well. "I know," she whispered. "I guess you could say I'm troubled, too."

"Are you thinking what I'm thinking?" he asked again.

"Genetic diversity would be a problem." Fran phrased it coldly, blocking the tragic thoughts that came barreling in when she opened that empathy door.

"No new DNA for three thousand years," Jerry explained. "That's when everything started. There was nothing before. That's the legend."

"What happened?" Fran wondered again.

Jerry didn't have much of an answer. "He just called it 'The Beginning.' One thousand cycles ago, so three thousand years. He got that same stupid look on his face, like when he talks about Kakeeche. That blind faith look. He says this old lady, Akira, she's supposed to keep the lines apart. That's why they're betrothed. They can't just marry whoever they want. Akira decides, picks the one least related to you, I guess. But there's only 100 people, counting these guys here. They've got to be all inbred by now, right?"

The pithy thought hung in the air over the sounds of chopping, ripping, and rinsing. Eventually, Fran asked, "And this woman tries to keep them from inbreeding. She gets it."

"But it's impossible, Mom!"

"She probably gets that, too," Fran mused, empathizing for a woman she had never met, in an alien world that grew darker with each new tidbit of information.

Jerry launched into his presentation. "There's about five percent mentally, um, you know, and an infant mortality rate of about 33 percent, I guess." He smiled at Fran's awestruck look. "It's easy, Mom. There's a hundred of them, so percentages are easy. But Baput's numbers were pretty vague. He says everybody knows everybody from birth, so you'd think he'd know how many babies die, or how many are messed up. But he doesn't. It's Akashic Rule Seven: 'The Akash need not bother with the silly troubles of women,'" Jerry repeated perfectly.

He expected his mom to scowl, but smirked instead. "That one sounds like Akira's idea. Cleverly worded."

With a sidelong glance at his cryptic mother, Jerry dragged the ugly subject out in the open like a slab of raw meat and plopped it on the table with the pile of clean greens. "Here's what really bugs me, Mom. There are some, five, like I said, with mental problems. But nobody is deformed. He says if a baby dies at birth, or it's born dead, Akira takes it away and buries it in a special place. Real fast. The mom doesn't even get to see it. Maybe they're deformed and—"

"They could have a high infant mortality rate anyway, because of the inbreeding," Fran defended. "But—do you think? No!" Her stubborn illusion of a perfect, peaceful world shattered yet again

"This seems *way* important. Why don't they tell the Akash?"

"It's just silly woman's stuff, Son," Fran replied playfully, then, suddenly dead serious: "Would you?"

There was a short, leaden silence while Jerry contemplated the wisdom of Akira's secrecy. Then, he dropped his last trouble bomb. "Mom? What would they do to Belinda?"

Two pairs of blue eyes looked as dark as blue eyes can look. Fran wriggled out. "Well, I was hoping to never find out, even before hearing this." Her eyes scanned the living room walls, the photos of Patrick and Belinda, Elmer's dad in his '60s garb, the faded sepia of his grandpa, all with right eyes staring into the camera, left eyes gazing up and to the left.

"But we can help them, can't we, Mom? Somehow? When the portal opens, I'll be 15. That's when the boys get married. I could go to Nauve with them and bring them some DNA."

"You're going to Nauve over my dead body!"

"Why not, Mom?"

"Because you'd never come back!"

"Sure I can. In three years."

Fran muttered under her breath, making sure Jerry heard every word. "Why did I have to insist on raising a compassionate child? Didn't I realize he'd end up getting himself killed for some noble cause?"

"Mom! I'm not going to war! I'm not gonna get killed! I'll just make some avocado babies and come on home! It'll be fun!"

"And leave your family behind? That adorable ivy-colored two-year-old who will never meet her g-ma and g-pa?" Fran pouted.

"I'll bring them to see you, Mom. My green wife and kids. Three years there, three years here. We'll rotate." Jerry talked fast, trying to pull his mom out of her imaginary tailspin. It wasn't working. Motionless now, her eyes had a feral look Jerry had never seen. "What about the dogs, Mom? They probably need doggie DNA, too. We never fixed Brodey. Maybe he and Shastina will make some puppies, at least."

"What if they're too different?" Fran was surprised she hadn't covered this ground before in her midnight ramblings.

"Too different? Different dogs mix all the time, don't they?"

"Not from two different planets."

"But if they're all too much alike, and we're too different to, you know…"

Fran launched a tirade of shrill words like a jaguar attacking with teeth and claws. "Jerry, they need a lot more than one new strand of DNA. Besides, we don't even know if that portal will ever open again. Or if it works both ways. Or if it's safe. Maybe it'll throw you into outer space

Maybe you'll have a Look'N Up kid, and Akira will…" She trailed off, her voice shaking.

Jerry was silent for a second. Then he pressed, "Sure wish we could give them some DNA. Or else, they're doomed, huh, Mom?"

"Maybe so, Baby." She stroked his tawny hair and kissed the top of his head. "Even if they beat the monsters."

"And they don't even know it."

"Star might."

"Are you going to ask her?"

Fran was already working on her plan. Elmer called her "Fran with the Plan" for a reason. "Tomorrow," she promised.

Spring Planting

Breakfast was done, and Jerry was back at school. Elmer and the crew were mowing the orchards again, in their various ways. Fog flowed down the river, spilling over its banks. Fran gathered her things and her thoughts and stepped out onto the porch. She could barely see a silhouette of Baput and his G-Pa crossing the grassy area to the sauna for meditation. Good. She and Star would be alone.

Last night, she had been surprised to find herself unable to bring the subject up in front of Elmer. She felt like Akira! Why couldn't she share this with a man? She somehow felt like she was betraying Star's trust, so she'd clammed up. Jerry had, too. He'd never been so silent at dinner.

Elmer hadn't noticed. He'd just kept on about the other downsides of "no otherwhere," oblivious to the "silly troubles of women."

We're so like the Nauvians! Fran thought, wincing at the name, which had now been rendered technically incorrect, like "Indians."

Her face lit up in a half smile as she passed the mess in the garden that, only yesterday, had been the dark greens of spinach and the redder shades of kale and lettuce. She set her box of hand tools, gloves, and seeds by the gate and climbed the steps to the quarters.

Star greeted her at the door, beaming. "Spring planting time!" she sang. She grabbed her gloves and almost skipped to the garden gate. Fran joined her, dismayed. She had never seen Star so happy!

Star looked at the pictures on the seed packs and squealed the names delightedly. "Pumpkins! Summer squash, peas, beans, carrots, and beets. So many colors! Beautiful eggplant and…" she stopped, inhaled, at the heirloom tomato. "It is yellow and red, in stripes!" she gushed like a happy kid on Christmas morning. She stepped over the box to hug Fran, who wanted to melt, but froze instead.

Hugging back, Fran said, "You sure are happy today!"

Star leaned back at arm's length and looked at Fran. "It is Spring Planting!" she declared the obvious.

Fran tried to match her smile. She failed miserably.

Star babbled excitedly. "It is a happy time. Planting is easy work, and full of hope. The women's favorite time." She scanned the empty garden and deflated a bit. "It is strange with so few..."

Fran began to turn the loose soil. Star raked it into smooth new beds. As they worked, Star told her all about Spring Planting. "The men do the tilling the day before. Well, the dogs do the work, really. They pull the tilling stones. The man just walks along behind, thinking he is the boss, as usual." Star was smiling in a relaxed way Fran hadn't seen before. Empathizing, she realized Star was home on Nauve, working with women she had known all her life, gossiping and grousing about men. But had she gotten it wrong, about caste?

She asked, "Surely the Akashic Tether doesn't have to labor in the fields with the common women?"

"No, I don't," Star answered. "I do it because I love to. I love them. It is not normal. My momama never did. And Tamaya won't, if she is tether, someday..." She trailed off, her elation dissolving into confusion.

Fran looked away to hide her sudden tears. Star was special. She broke the rules, ignored the caste system. *And here I am, bumming her out on her favorite day.*

Star moved on down the bed and on to a new subject.

"All the women help with the planting. Even if you have babbets to care for. We had Lalanar for that. She is unmarriageable, because she is like a child, but she is good with the babbets. She cares for them while we work."

Fran eased in. "Unmarriageable? What's that?"

"Akira decides," Star answered. "If there is no clear line for you, you can't be married. No babbets. Or, of course, if you are like Lalanar."

Francine had conjured Akira's disturbing image so many times last night, she felt as if she knew her as well as Star did. "What happens to the unmarriageables?" she asked.

"They live underground, in The Lair. They serve the village, at Akira'a command. They clean the Great Hall, and take care of the sick, the dead, the waste pits, that kind of thing." She spoke with neither sympathy nor aversion, simply telling Fran how things were.

"Untouchables," Fran muttered. Her image of a caste society confirmed, she plunged into her subject. How much darker could this get? "Do they birth your babbets?"

"No, Akira does that herself. She injects you with a small dose of nimbly venom, aged at least a cycle. It's not so strong then. You are awake, and you can push, but you can't feel the pain so much, and you can't get up and walk. Your legs would just collapse."

"So you can see your babbet being born?"

Star's eyes were far away, as if she were seeing one of her birthing experiences. "I can feel her taking it out. She holds it down low, where I can't see it. I can't lift my head. It cries, then it doesn't. So quick! The other ones cried and cried until she cut the cord and put them on my breast, but that one, before Cilandra, I failed. Akira took it away and buried it in the special place."

Star looked down and realized she had dug a hole in the bed as she spoke, just big enough a newborn baby. She looked at Fran, then down again at the hole, raised the back of her gloved hand to her mouth. "I'm sorry," she breathed.

"It's OK, Hon!" Fran leaned across the bed and gave her an awkward hug, trying to imagine how she felt. She would be embarrassed. She'd want to get away. But Star had nowhere to go, and not even the concept of going.

As Star repaired her soil bed, she gathered herself in a surprisingly businesslike fashion and continued. "It is OK. I have three. Or—had. I am privileged. I am Akashic Line. Akira sent me the very best to marry. Valko." There was admiration in her voice, but love? Fran just wasn't sure. Her empathy machine had wandered that path on many a night. *What would it be like to be betrothed as a baby?* She knew many women on Earth shared such a fate, some even today.

Star bent over and picked a flat rock out of the turned earth. "There is a custom women do. It is forbidden, unlucky, but they do it anyway. They take a flat rock like this and scratch their mark on one side, hold it between their hands like so." She held the rock between her palms, fingers straight up, like she was praying. She tipped her fingertips down in front of her, then swiftly up again, parting her hands, flinging the stone up in the air. "If it lands with her mark up, the baby will be born. If her mark is down, the baby will fail."

"Fifty-fifty," muttered Fran.

Star went on, excited now. "It works, too, most of the time. But it is unlucky. They say if you do it, you will fail. But women do it sometimes, and it says, 'yes, babbet,' and the babbet comes, so it can't be bad luck all the time, don't you think?"

The hopeful chatter reminded Fran of Belinda when she was six, prattling on about a dream marriage. Hope in the face of a 50 percent failure rate. She wondered how many babies died at birth. How many were deformed by their inevitable inbred condition and murdered—tiny and helpless, at the secretive hands of Akira? Even Salistar, Tether to Akash, didn't seem to know anything about what was surely happening.

Fran slammed on in, taking a wrecking ball to what was left of Star's good mood. "Is there anyone in the village that looks different? Maybe they have only three fingers, or funny ears, or an eye in the wrong place?"

Star shook her head violently.

"Do you think you had a babbet like that, and Akira killed it?"

No more Spring Planting bliss. Star was now more withdrawn than on the day she had arrived. "No, noooo," she muttered, sounding lost, like her Popa. Then she raised her face and looked at Fran with a kind of rehearsed look, and finally answered. "She wouldn't do that. Every babbet is precious! We never have bad babbets. Akira makes sure."

Fran recognized that brainwashed look Jerry had described in Baput. Unquestioningness. Dogma swallowed, hook, line, and sinker. As the little Jerry inside her roared, she asked mercilessly, "How?"

"She doesn't let the lines cross," the automatic Star answered remotely.

Fran stabbed her shovel into the ground and reached across the row to grasp Star's glove hands in her own. She searched those absent eyes. *Does she really believe this Akira could keep the lines uncrossed with just 100 people left? She has no background in science, let alone genetics. How could I possibly make her see? Should I?*

With a deep breath, Fran went back to work spreading fresh compost on the beds while Star raked it in. Despite the unpleasant depths of the undiscussed, the silence was not too uncomfortable.

Fran wondered if this Akira was the wisest of all the Nauvians. Perhaps she had managed to brainwash the entire population to be oblivious to their doom. And why not? What could they do about it? What good would it do if they knew? Let them fight nimblies and bumblies and dream of a day of victory. She could hear the chant Star had taught her, *'No more nimblies! No more bumblies! Not ever! No more!' Yeah, let them have that hope. Because for the real doom, there is no hope. At least, not until now. And now, what?*

Saving the more tender varieties for the greenhouse, Fran took the onion sets and root crops, giving Star the hearty kernels of peas, beans, and squash. They worked separate beds, tucking their seeds into the spring soil. Fran's mind replayed thoughts from her sleepless night, when she had tried, and failed, to come up with a practical, humane, and tasteful way to send some Earth DNA to Nauve. Besides Jerry's crazy idea, of course. That wasn't happening, not with that Look'N Up gene in the mix! Besides, the Nauvian Race needed a lot more than one DNA donor, no matter how eager that one may be.

Her reverie was broken by deep voices speaking in that staccato language of theirs as the men came ambling from the shop to the quarters. Baput's burgeoning baritone called back from the sauna. It was lunchtime.

"I'll meet you at the greenhouse after lunch," Fran suggested. "We'll start those lovely tomatoes and eggplants, and some basil."

Star slipped away toward the quarters like a dutiful ghost. Fran trudged slowly to her own house, deep in thought.

Family Photos

"What are you nosing into now, Fran?" Elmer questioned Fran as they ate their sandwiches and chips.

"You know. The otherwhere thing."

"What about it?"

Still not knowing how to begin, Fran tried to make him come up with it himself. "There's less than a hundred of them, did you know that?"

"So?" Elmer regarded her, eyebrows raised.

"No one else for three thousand years, at least."

Fran watched, fascinated, as Elmer's face changed, each muscle dropping in turn, like slow dominos. He jaw slacked, his cheekbones sagged, his brow furrowed as the unexpected storm passed through his slow but earnest mind. When his eyes fixed on Fran again, they were different.

"They'd be inbred. They'd mutate, wouldn't they? Like us Look'N Ups."

Fran loved the way he included himself, as if he had The Eye, just as much as the men he grew up with. He had it in his genes, it just didn't show.

Elmer scanned the living-room walls. The bare nails poking out, the empty rectangles where the paint wasn't as faded. Fran's heart sank.

He whirled back to face her, the left side of his mouth lifted in a snarl. "You took down the Look'N Ups? You promised you'd never!"

"I was afraid!" Fran whimpered, too ashamed to defend herself.

"Afraid of what?" Elmer was on his feet.

"They kill them," Fran stated flatly.

"The mutants?"

"Yes. I'm pretty sure. I thought about it all night. With such a small gene pool, they must have mutations, but Baput doesn't know of any. I thought, *they must be killing them*. I lay there all night thinking, and I got scared, Elmer. I didn't want them to see… But it was fear, not shame! I'm so sorry, Babe. I'll put them back up right now."

Elmer crossed his arms and stood scowling as Fran started putting the photos back up. She told him what she'd learned. "This old woman, Akira, drugs the mother and delivers the baby, keeps it out of sight while she inspects it. If it's not perfect, she kills it. Star doesn't seem to know about it, even though…" She trailed off. That was private. "There's no one who looks different. Just like there's no otherwhere. Nobody knows why, nobody asks. So I got worried. What would they do if they met Patrick and Belinda?"

"They won't, ever. We're hiding them for three years, till they go back," Elmer reminded her. "But they're just culling, Fran. Like us farmers, if you've got a genetic thing, you, you… Well, it's easier when it's just plants. But anyway, you don't go killing adults, or half-grown kids."

He took a two-year old photo of his brother and niece down from where Fran had just rehung it. "Tell you what, don't put 'em all up yet. You go on over after lunch and show Star what my family looks like. See how she reacts."

Fran slid the old sepia of Elmer's deformed grandpa with his kids, Elmer's cockeyed dad and his straight-eyed brother, Joe, from its nail again. Next, she took down the nearly identical shot of Elmer standing proudly with *his* cockeyed dad and brother. She took the photo of Patrick and Belinda from Elmer, swaddled all three photos in a towel and set them on top of her seed box.

"Yeah, just ask her if they wanna kill my little niece, will ya?" Elmer's voice dripped with sarcasm. "What do you think?"

"I don't think so. Not anymore." Fran fled to the kitchen to wash her hands. From its safety, she goaded, "You know, not too long ago, *you* were the one who thought they were going to kill *us*."

Elmer approached from behind as she stood at the sink. "Well, I don't think so anymore." He slipped his arms around her. "Can you picture Valko or Felsic hurting a little girl? Maybe G-Pa will give her the Evil Eye, put her into a giggling fit."

Fran turned into his embrace and whispered, "I love you, you straight-eyed freak."

Greenhouse

When Fran met Star at the greenhouse, G-Pa was with her. *Will it make Star shy? Will he throw a fit when he sees these photos? Does it matter?* Heart heavy but hoping for the best, Fran braced herself and went in. There was work to be done.

Star must have been thinking about their weighty morning discussion. She was quieter this afternoon but more forthcoming. She sat her popa down on a padded folding chair in the corner. He explored the strange, clear building with curious eyes, then fell fast asleep.

Fran set her box down on a shelf where G-Pa couldn't see, then she removed the framed photos. Star looked curiously over her shoulder.

"I want to show you Elmer's family. They're different, see? Do you have anybody different like that, or in some other way, on Nauve?" Fran asked, with an anxious glance at the snoozing old man. She hoped an example would trigger a memory.

Star was surprised by the strange men in the old photos, but Fran didn't sense any of the hidden shock and revulsion she had learned to detect in most people. Just mild curiosity. But when she saw Belinda, Star switched on like an electric light. "A little girl!" she crowed.

"Yes, my niece, Belinda. She's 10 now." Fran felt a jolt when she said it. "That's her popa, Patrick. He's Elmer's brother. And these others are Elmer's popa and g-pa."

Star glanced again at the men, returned to Belinda. "She lives?"

The question threw Fran. When she recovered, she saw it; that weird glitch they get when you talk about other places, other people. Belinda and Patrick are otherwhere! How could she explain?

She usually stuck with the things they had in common: gardening, cooking, cleaning, and raising kids. This was conceptual, delicate, frustrating. She had a new respect for Jerry, and a new understanding for the times when he'd come home looking like he wanted to clout his best friend.

"So, you have your village, on Nauve. About 100 people, Baput says."

"Yes." Star smiled as she turned away from the photos and dug into a bag of potting soil. "We are fortunate to have so many." Her smile dropped suddenly, and she raised her eyes to Fran's. "I am afraid for you, Francina! You defeated the nimblies and bumblies on Earth, but the cost! Jerry and Belinda are the only children left, and their popas are brothers! Like Baput and Trillella. No good! You've got to keep the lines apart, Francina!"

Star stared at Fran with rapt urgency melting to tender empathy. She reached for Fran's shoulder. "Francina! You have only one child left! How many have you lost?"

Fran's heart wept silently at Star's misplaced pity. She tried to explain. "We *chose* to have one. The second child usually gets The Eye, so we stopped at one."

Star looked at her, unbelieving. "How do you stop your husband?"

"No, no!" Fran corrected quickly. *What would Valko think of Elmer?* "We take, um, medicine, so we do not have children unless we want to."

Star's dark eyebrows furrowed deeply over completely uncomprehending eyes. "Why would you do that?" she whispered, glancing anxiously at her sleeping popa.

"We have too many people for our planet. We try to control how many babies we—"

"Too many people?" Star interrupted. "What are you talking about? I see only you and Elmer and Jerry, and some *rasta*. Do these people live, this little girl?" she asked again. "Why don't I see them?"

Francina sat silently, her head spinning. How could Star turn the situation around like that? Was it easier to process? *Yes,* Fran supposed, *it's easier for me to think about this happening on an alien planet than if it were happening to us.*

Star's face brightened at an apparition Fran couldn't see. "If we are nauve again, next First Pomegranate Day, then you will see. We have many lovely young men and women to marry Jerry and Belinda. Of course, if we cannot be nauve, then Belinda must be for Baput. They are not related. And he is Akashic." Star reminded, her little nose pointing up just a bit. "I am sorry, Francina, but it is best for your world. We will pray to Kakeeche for Nauve to be again, so Jerry can have a tether, too."

Fran's brains were still in a blender, but she was no longer afraid. Star didn't mind the Look'N Up DNA! It didn't matter to them! Not these particular ones, anyway. They sure weren't going to kill anyone over it. She narrowed her eyes at the dormant Akash in the corner and continued to think her forbidden thoughts.

Star even considers Belinda to be a suitable mate for Baput! At least, if they're stuck here, marooned forever. She just wants her people to go on. It's all that matters to her! She watched Star, mothering over the infant pomegranate trees from two worlds. Like them, she would do whatever she could to continue her kind. That was a momama's job in any world.

But if they went back to Nauve, Salistar might be Tether to Akash, and she might not be like the others, but she would never be Akira. She would never be the one to decide if a deformed babbett lived or died.

5. Fire

Four peaceful months passed, marked only by hard work done in comfortable routine. To Baput's delight, Jerry didn't have to go to school anymore. They spent a lot of time on the Horizontal Tree. Jerry could get on the Plane pretty regularly, but it wasn't like it was with G-Pa. Jerry always saw things Baput couldn't see.

In turn, Jerry taught Baput to search the iPlane with a computer, so they could both see the same thing. Baput especially liked Google Earth, where you could travel all over the big ball, zooming in here and there to see people with different skin colors, different clothing. Even their huts were different! He still didn't quite get it, this otherwhere business, but he was convinced it was real, at least on Earth.

One early morning in late July, Baput jerked awake, confused. The sky was tinted with red, like the skies of Nauve. *I'm home! What? Was it all just a dream? Did G-Pa give me an elixir or something?* He closed his eyes, took a deep breath to center himself and find the cause of his confusion. *What is that smell?* His eyes flew open to the morning light streaming in from the windows. It was too red. He looked around. He was in the bottom bunk in his room on Earth. G-Pa was gone. "Something is wrong!"

He sat up just as Jerry knocked on his window with a stick, like he often had this summer, but harder, more urgently. "B, get up! There's a fire!" he called.

Baput jumped out of bed and padded barefoot to the door to let his agitated friend in. "Get everybody up!" Jerry whispered, then, realizing the irony, spoke louder. "There's a fire on the next ridge. It's coming this way. We have to evacuate."

"E-vac-u—" Baput didn't know the word.

Jerry cut him off. "We have to GO! Now! Get everybody up!"

Salistar was up, making breakfast. She had witnessed the whole exchange, and roused Valko, who rushed into the front room with her.

Baput turned to them. "We need to get Felsic and G-Pa!"

"Your G-Pa is in his shrine," Momama told him.

Baput sighed. That meant he was out there in the sauna, where only Baput could reach him. "I'll get him."

Felsic staggered from his room, unshaven, his short hair tussled.

"Get your stuff!" Jerry warned "Whatever you can take real fast. This place might burn!"

"The kips!" was Star's first thought. "The trees! Jerry, what happens to the trees?"

"They might burn, Ma'am. They might die," Jerry said solemnly.

"Then we must save them!" she declared. Jerry was going to say what people always say, "It's not worth your life." But he wasn't sure she would agree.

"Salistar, please, we've gotta hurry. They have kip trees where we're going." He knew she didn't understand. Then it dawned on him. "We can save *your* trees! We can take them with us," he promised, wondering what his dad was going to say.

"Gather your potatoes, beans, rice, all that," Jerry ordered, knowing his Aunt Lorraine's style of cooking.

Having a course of action, Star sprung to it. Jerry beckoned Felsic, and they headed to the greenhouse.

Baput could see the electric candlelight flashing erratically from the open door of the sauna.

"G-Pa?" he said quietly, then louder, "Akash, *esculara!*" he used the Nauvian word for emergency. Finally, a spark. He struck again. "G-Pa! Akash! Fire!"

G-Pa's hair hung in his face. His eyes were confused.

"Fire?" Fire was rare on Nauve, but they had seen it. There were colorful rastas of it throughout the records, followed by bleak monochromes of the devastation it left in its wake. The Akash snapped to the present with one thought: "The shrine!"

Baput rolled his eyes in his mind. He'd been hoping G-Pa wouldn't. It was bulky and fragile. It took two people to carry it. It would take up space in the load that should be used for important things, like food. *I'm thinking like a woman!* Baput realized, keeping it to himself.

But arguing would take too long. G-Pa was already dug in. "I need you to help me carry it, G-Pa." Baput tried to sound small and helpless. The Akash rose from his cushion and tottered unsteadily toward the shrine. Was he exaggerating? *We'll never get this thing as far as the quarters.*

He heard the four-wheeler approaching. Jerry!

"Come on, B! My uncle's coming! We've got to be ready!"

G-Pa growled when Jerry entered. Baput ignored him. "He won't leave without it," he told Jerry, ashamed.

"I was afraid of that." Jerry grabbed a side of the shrine, and Baput grabbed the other. As they staggered to the vehicle with their frail load, Jerry lectured loudly enough for the Akash to hear. "That's the problem with worshipping material objects. They get lost, stolen, burned, or broken. Kakeeche is in the sky! The Plane is in your mind! What do you need this pile of junk for?"

Baput knew Jerry was right. He was surprised the Akash said nothing. Had he understood?

The boys balanced the shrine and the Akash on the four-wheeler seat, and Baput climbed on behind the fragile load. G-Pa wouldn't leave his longstick, either. It jutted straight out next to Jerry's head as he drove. They could have walked faster.

At last, they reached the driveway where the two families waited, surrounded by bags, boxes, bedrolls, and eight potted pomegranate trees from two worlds. Elmer and Fran already had the big farm truck and flatbed trailer, as well as Fran's Prius, loaded with necessities and not-so-necessities. Too little time to think and too much capacity led to a heavy load.

"Good call on the trees, Son," Elmer surprised Jerry with a wink.

Felsic rushed to help the boys unload the shrine. G-Pa staggered into Star's relieved embrace. "Fire!" he muttered. "Shrine!"

"I know, Popa," Star comforted him, stroking his hair.

Elmer's brother Patrick arrived in the windowless van with the cockeyed pipe logo. Baput remembered when he'd brought the dishwasher, and he felt guilty for spying. He remembered that misplaced eye, and how he had thought an eye pointing up and to the left would be an advantage at nauve, because that was where the bumblies always attacked from. He had searched the iPlane and never found anyone else like that on Earth. *Is he what Jerry was talking about? A bad babbet? Jerry says there is plenty of DNA to keep the lines fresh on Earth, so why do they have bad babbets?*

Patrick stepped out of the van, bleary-eyed from the urgent phone call at four a.m. and the four-hour drive. He looked the little group up and down, or so Baput guessed; it was hard to tell. A delighted smile spread across his face, which was even whiter than Jerry's, but with reddish brown freckles.

"They're, um, colored," Elmer stated.

"People of color," Patrick corrected, nodding.

"People of another color," quipped Elmer. "But Dad taught us not to see color, right?"

"Absolutely! But that's old school. Now we see it, and embrace it," Patrick replied, walking straight up to the apparent leader, a deeply bearded giant. He dared to meet those narrowed eyes. "Creation's wondrous variety," he murmured, warmly extending his hand.

Valko took it, but he did not look the strange man in the eyes.

Salistar didn't cower like she had when Elmer first tried to shake her hand. She reached hers out to Patrick gently, but with a firmness that surprised herself. She looked right up at him and spoke, "I saw your *rasta*, your picture. You have a—"

Patrick gestured toward his eye. "Yeah, I have a—"

"A daughter," Star finished with a coy smile.

"Yes!" He shook her hand gently and went on to Felsic who shook too eagerly.

G-Pa let go of the shrine and raised his head to look at Patrick. Clear-eyed, he greeted him in their native language, "*Braykipseulum*," meaning, "Good pomegranates to you." They shook hands heartily.

Then Patrick cocked his head and pointed that weird left eye straight at Baput. Baput wanted to fear him, to see him as something wrong, a bad babbet, but there was something about that cocked eye, no, something inside it, that made Baput feel at home. He extended his hand first. "I am Baput. And this is Shastina."

"What a beautiful dog! She looks like the German shepherd Elmer and I used to have when we were kids, only, purple! May I?" He stroked the hair on Shastina's back, coarser and darker than the hair on her sides. Then he straightened up and reached for Baput's hand. "Hello, Baput, I'm Patrick." They shook hands, then, unexpectedly, embraced.

"It'll be OK. You'll see," Patrick assured, wondering how Lorraine was going to react. He opened the van's back door and scanned the odd load waiting on the ground. Potted plants, potatoes, vegetables, bottles of wine and oil, squares of woven grass, a beautiful marble rolling pin and a couple of weird contraptions; a cider press? *And I don't know what THAT is or how it's gonna make it out of this driveway, or up mine.*

Jerry, standing beside the odd mess, caught his eye. "It's a religious thing," he explained.

"Ohhh Kaaaay!" Patrick raised his uneven eyebrows and whistled. He saw eye-to-eye with his straight-eyed nephew on this one. His mom, Jerry's grandmother, had taught science at the local high school. She started the Science Club so he could have fellow nerds to hang with that could deal with his eye without being mean. Now he was a plumber with a physics degree, a student loan, and no money for grad school. His grades weren't good enough for a stipend because, frankly, he'd smoked a lot of pot in college. It helped him visualize physics concepts really well, with occasional practical applications, but the skill didn't translate to tests or to making a living, not without that PhD or access to a particle accelerator.

"Hope it makes it" he whispered to Jerry from behind his hand. He knew enough about being different to say nothing more about the silly shrine. Baput grabbed one end of the delicate jumble while Jerry hoisted the other. The two boys found a relatively safe place for it in the van.

As soon everything was loaded, Elmer gestured for the green people to get into the tightly packed windowless box. They looked at each other apprehensively.

"They're scared," Jerry observed. "I'll go with them."

Fran looked at Elmer. If the aliens were going to do weird stuff to Jerry, this would be their chance. She knew they wouldn't. She was proud of Jerry for trying to comfort the deeply confused little family. "OK, Hon. I'm going to go ahead in the car. I'll hit the store when I get close so we don't show up like poor relations."

"It's OK, Mom, we're refugees!" Jerry bragged. "Come on, guys!" Holding a battery-powered lantern aloft, he led the Nauvians into the dark.

As Fran watched Elmer climb into to cab of the big truck after Brodey, her cell phone buzzed. The evacuation warning had been upgraded to mandatory. She looked at the sky. The sun was crimson. She glanced anxiously at the van. *They'll think it's the end of the world!* Fortunately, Patrick had already shut the door.

Tale of Yanzoo

They all found their places on the mattresses. Motor noises started all around them. Their tiny world bucked and swayed as the van lurched forward and worked its way down the potholed driveway.

"Sit down, G-Pa," Baput begged, at Jerry's advisement. The van bumped down, then up. Jerry and Baput got up on their knees and steadied the stubborn old man.

"Akash!" Valko's roar made the metal walls rattle. "Sit!" Shastina, already sitting, whimpered, confused. The Akash looked at the source of the noise, the largest single mass in the van, with dull, perplexed eyes. Then he folded his legs and dropped onto the mattress between Baput and Shastina.

The ride smoothed when they reached the road, but the stops and starts through town made them sway involuntarily. It was a most eerie feeling, with no windows. Jerry didn't seem to pay the sensations any mind, so Baput figured everything was OK. But what was this box they were in? It wasn't quite like the Jeep or the truck. It wasn't like the portal, either. That hurt more, but it was much quicker. They had been in this magic box for almost half an hour now, going to an otherwhere, where strange people lived.

Jerry wondered what they were thinking. Not seeing, not knowing where they were going or even how they were getting there. *They must be terrified! Maybe a diversion would help.* "Hey, you guys got any stories? From Nauve?"

"Tale of Yanzoo!" G-Pa cried, trying to stand up again.

The road was smoother, but Jerry still said, "No." The Akash settled for half-standing on his bony knees on the thin mattress. He picked up his longstick, holding it vertically, his left hand at the midpoint. "Tale of Yanzoo!" he insisted, stretching his arms straight out. Baput anticipated and ducked.

G-Pa began in Nauvian. "I'll translate," Baput offered, then whispered, "The tale is fiction."

"Yanzoo was a young Akash, many, many years ago. He was an Alanakash, born on First Pomegranate Day, like Baput, here. His popa, the old Akash, knew that his son would be the greatest Akash the people had ever seen. He would perform a miracle! Yanzoo ascended to Akash in his 15th year, and was given a Tether, Sugia, the best cook of all the women.

"Yanzoo knew he had to be the greatest Akash. But he didn't know how. 'What can I do that is great? I'm just a boy,' he thought. The old Akash he hadn't taught him anything special. Just basic Akashic training. The old man was not exceptional!"

The Narrator suddenly sounded a lot like G-Pa. He went on, returning to the expressive, yet neutral, tone. It had that memorized quality, like when Baput talked about Kakeeche.

"But the boy was exceptional. He was just too humble. Now, humility may sound like a good quality in an Akash, but it is not! Humility may lead to wise decisions, selfless decisions. But it made Yanzoo, like his predecessor, afraid to take risks, to try anything new. But Yanzoo played the bowl."

Baput hurriedly whispered and gestured, describing for Jerry the hammered breen-metal bowl and the ganeesh-skin mallet you tapped it with, then ran along the edge to make a tone. The Akash stared daggers at the interruption. When the boys quieted, he took up the thread precisely.

"That was where Yanzoo excelled. He would sit on the Holy Rock in the Holy Cave, cross-legged in meditation, and play the bowl for hours. He ascended so high on the Plane! They say he went higher than anyone else, but it is impossible to measure such things, one Akash to another.

"'What can I do that would be exceptional and make me worthy of the people's adoration?' he would ask the Plane. 'What do the people need most?'"

"DNA!" Jerry mouthed silently, while G-Pa Yanzoo answered his own rhetorical question:

"To be rid of the nimblies and bumblies, of course. What can I do to rid us of the nimblies and bumblies? Something that's never been tried. Something exceptional! What am I exceptional at?'

The answer came to him in a flash, directly from the Plane. 'Playing the bowl! Play the bowl to kill the nimblies and bumblies!' It was Mitten then."

Baput explained to Jerry. "Halfway between First Pomegranate Days, so 18 months to the next one."

G-Pa continued the story:

"Yanzoo told his tether, 'Pack a ganeesh with four months' worth of food. Bring the boys! We will go kill the nimblies and bumblies in their caves!'

"Sugia grabbed Yanzoo's young sons, Yanzid and Yanlee, and backed away from her husband, her Akash! 'But it's too dangerous!'"

G-Pa mocked in a high-pitched voice. Salistar's face tightened.

"I told her, 'I am Alanakash, Woman! I will play my bowl at the mouth of each cave, and the bumblies and nimblies will explode in their sleep, just from the sound! We'll kill them all. Think of it, Sugia! No more nimblies! No more bumblies!'"

G-Pa waited while they repeated the chant, then went on, as Yanzoo, speaking directly to Salistar.

"Many dared question me for bringing my family, my children. Mostly old women of no consequence. I did it to prove I knew I was right, that I could kill them all safely, in their sleep, with no danger to my family."

Salistar's upper lip quivered a little, barely detectable on her downcast face. G-Pa went on as Yanzoo.

"Besides, I needed my Tether. She had to bring her whelps or leave them with her mother, or worse, her sister. They would teach my sons their ignorant ways! They would think I need them. I need no one! I am Alanakash! I am exceptional!"

He puckered like he was going to spit, then swallowed hard. It was as if he knew these women! Jerry wondered if this was really part of the story or was G-Pa riffing now?

G-Pa's longstick swung around the van at face level. Everyone ducked and cringed. G-Pa tried to stand up again. In the unseen cab, Patrick hit the brakes. G-Pa fell forward onto Salistar, his longstick ripping the mattress beneath her.

Grabbing the stick, Valko bellowed, "Sit down, old man!" not caring if he was talking to the present Akash or some ancient, fictional one. An awkward silence filled the van as it hummed along at an even speed again. Then, G-Pa rose back to his knees and resumed his story.

"I played the bowl in front of every cave. I could feel them squirming. I thought I felt them explode. I was sure they were all dead. No more nimblies! No more bumblies!"

The faithful repeated the chant again.

"I spent all that summer traveling from cave to cave. When I returned to the village, I told the people what I had done! No more nimblies! No more bumblies!"

Jerry joined in this time, with a hidden eye roll.

"But the war chief, Tymar, he did not believe! 'How do you know they are dead?' he dared to ask. 'You didn't go in and look, did you?'

"That fool! Of course I didn't! Do you think I would have risked my life, my family, to the Curse, just because I doubted, as you do?

"We had the biggest celebration ever! So much happiness. So much wine. Young and old had the time of their lives, except Tymar. He refused to participate. It was like he didn't want the nimblies and bumblies to be gone. The very next day he dragged the miserable troops from their beds at the crack of dawn and trained them harder than ever, every day for the next 14 Kakeeche Cycles, until First Pomegranate Day, just for spite. It's all his fault for not believing. He cast a bad mold on the Plane, caused bad things to happen!"

G-Pa shook his fist over the lantern, casting weird, snake-like shadows all around them.

"First Pomegranate Day came. I took to the stage for the ceremony. I didn't say a word. I played the tone I had used to kill the nimblies and bumblies. They all began the chant, 'No more nimblies! No more bumblies! Not ever! No more!'"

The captive audience chanted one more time. Then silence. Jerry looked up. G-Pa was still on his knees, but he seemed to tower above the rest of them. He breathed in, slowly, dramatically, then bellowed, "They have awakened!"

"Nimblies and bumblies, nimblies and bumblies!" was the new chant.

Valko lent a new perspective while G-Pa regained his composure. "Tymar and his troops were ready. Tymar knew they would come, with a vengeance. Yanzoo had tried to commit Insitucide!"

G-Pa's thin face and hollow cheeks seemed to puff into those of a much younger Akash, Yanzoo, who rose from his defeat and took the story back from Valko.

"It was the rock of the caves, I realized. It protected them from the vibrations. The Tone must be made from the battlefield before the Great Hall, to get them as they come in.

"I shall take my tether and my sons and sit in front of the battle trenches and blow the nimblies to bits as they fly at us.

"'But why bring the children? Your tether?' the women squawked at me. Even the old men told me, 'Leave your family in the Great Hall, like we do.'

"But I told them, 'I bring my family to show my faith. I know I will prevail. I place my family in its way. I am not afraid. Are you?'

"Sugia whined like the pathetic woman she is when I dragged her and the boys outside. Young warriors flanked us with dart guns and longsticks. I sat on top of the large rock in front of the East Trench, where the cowardly war chief usually hides. I told my wife and sons to sit in front of me, right in the path of the nimblies, to show my faith.

"The first nimblies came. 'Bzzzzz!' They stopped, hovered, right over my family. I tapped the bowl, ran the mallet around the edge. Four nimblies dove straight down. Their needles pointed straight at Sugia and the children."

Salistar suddenly jumped to her feet, swinging her marble rolling pin around in wide arcs over her cringing family. "Sugia knocked all four nimblies out of the sky with her rolling pin, saving her children, *before* Yanzoo could make the Tone."

G-Pa stared so hard at his daughter, it scared Jerry a little.

"That is what they teach us in woman's school," Star explained with a shrug.

Jerry looked at Valko. Was he laughing?

Still staring coldly at Salistar, the Akash continued, speaking slowly, as if teaching children. "Yanzoo made the Tone. The pure, round Tone that stirred the air so that the nimblies all exploded. Row after row. Every one. No more nimblies!"

"No more nimblies!" was the refrain.

"Now my family stood proudly by my side. The men poured out of the trenches, whooping and embracing each other. All but Tymar. Again. Still. 'What of the Bumblies?' he argued. 'Bumblies are too tough to pop with a mere noise. They will be here soon. Back to your trenches, men!' he ordered.

"But I am Akash, above all! So I took command of the joyful troops. 'Return to the Great Hall,' I ordered, 'and drink of the kip wine. Celebrate! This day will be remembered forever. The day I, Yanzoo, rid us all of the nimblies and bumblies.'"

Another round of chanting filled the van.

"I told my tether, 'Go! Take the children to the Great Hall. If you go, the rest will follow. I must do this myself, alone. It will all be over soon.'

"The men hesitated at first, but soon they were running to the Great Hall ahead of the approaching bumblies. I stood alone on the rock. Only Tymar remained, crouching in the trench with his longstick.

"I struck the bowl and circled the rim with the mallet. The tone rose all around us as first bumblies arrived. I stood fast and kept playing. The bumblies circled closer. They would not come in. They could feel it. They knew.

"Suddenly Tymar leapt out of the trench and went into his war dance. The bumblies dove on him, their horns and talons extended, ready to tear him to bits. But when they came within range of the Tone, they exploded! Pop, pop, one after another, attacking the dancing Tymar and shattering above his head. As I played, the range got longer and longer until the last few bumblies popped before they dove.

"It was over in minutes. The end of the bumblies. And the nimblies. And I, Yanzoo, once timid and humble, now exceptional and most supreme, have done this all by myself, from inception to implementation. Now, let us celebrate in my honor!"

Do all Akashes grow up to be egomaniacs? Will Baput? Jerry wondered as he succumbed to the inevitable chant, hoping it was the last time.

G-Pa Yanzoo concluded his tale:

"They carried me on their shoulders into the Great Hall. Tymar followed behind, ashamed. The celebration went through the night. The next day, they returned to the harvest, as if it were not The Season, but Easy Harvest. First Pomegranate Day became the Feast of Yanzoo, where everyone ate and drank their fill, and no one died. Their children all lived to ripe old ages without any fear."

They all surged forward as the van slowed sharply, turned and stopped. "Good timing!" Jerry exclaimed. They were almost to Uncle Patrick's. Just a few blocks and then that driveway, longer and rougher than the Look'N Up's.

Second Arrival

The van stopped moving. They heard voices. The door opened onto sunlight that would have been blinding but for the dust that still hung in the air from their arrival. No smoke, no red sun, just a distant haze on the south horizon. They clamored out.

Patrick took charge. "Here, Jerry, help these guys take their stuff to the quarters. Elmer and I will take your stuff to the house."

Baput went for the shrine first. Jerry rolled his eyes and grabbed the other end, leading the way to the workers' quarters his uncle was building.

Halfway up the trail, she appeared, coming toward them. She was a little younger than Baput and Jerry. A free-flowing sea of bright copper waves, the color of the darkest parts of the fire they had just escaped, cascaded below her shoulders. Red-purple-brown spots flecked her otherwise pink cheeks, beneath eyes as brightly colored as Jerry's, but a deep malachite green. She was the most colorful human Baput had ever seen! But there was something else. One radiant green eye was misplaced. It cocked up and to the left, like her popa's, giving her an irresistible vulnerability.

Shastina ran to her and leaned hard against her legs, almost pushing her over. The girl giggled and stroked the course, lavender hair on her back.

The boys set the shrine down gently. Jerry walked right up to his cousin, a feat Baput couldn't imagine doing. He spun around beside her and escorted her toward Baput. Her stunning green eyes looked more surprised by the rickety shrine than by the green-skinned boy.

"Belinda, this is my friend Baput," Jerry introduced him.

"Be-lin-da," Baput repeated with an odd smile. "Three syllables. Momama would be pleased."

"What?" hissed Jerry, socking Baput on the shoulder.

"Don't!" cried Belinda.

Baput turned an even deeper shade. "Sorry?" he asked.

Belinda put him right at ease. "Welcome to our home, Baput. Sorry you guys had to leave all your stuff and come running here, but we'll take care of you all, as long as you need us to. What can I do to help?" She cocked her head so she could get that skewed green eye right into Baput's. Then she winked.

The other refugees had arrived behind them, all carrying bundles or boxes. Baput turned to introduce them. "This is Salistar, my momama." *What's that strange smile Momama's wearing?* "Popa, um, Valko, my father. This is my uncle, Felsic, and my G-Pa. He is the Akash."

"Pleased to meet you," Belinda responded, mostly to Salistar. "I'm—"

"Be-lin-da!" Star finished for her, lips pulled tight around that eerie smile.

A woman came out of the guest quarters, took one look at the little crowd of green people, and screamed, "Belinda! Get away from them!"

Belinda's momama had the green eyes and auburn hair of her daughter, but her hair was cropped short. *Why would a woman with such color cut it off?* Baput wondered silently. *Elmer's popa taught his sons not to see color. Patrick said you're supposed to see it. But he said that green toilet was hideous. I'll have to ask Jerry why Earth people don't like color.*

Belinda turned toward her mother and negotiated rapidly. "Momma, aren't they pretty? They're really nice, too!" she bubbled, out of character for the usually understated child. She grabbed her mom's hand and introduced each green person by name, with perfect pronunciation. "This is my mother, Lorraine," she finished.

"Lor-rain," the green strangers repeated. The woman and the boy giggled.

"What the—? Who are you, um, people? What are you doing here?" Lorraine sputtered, hauling Belinda away by her plump, freckled arm.

Patrick rushed up the trail to the rescue. "Hey, Babe, everything OK? What's the matter?" He sounded way too casual.

"I just wasn't expecting..." Lorraine hissed.

Patrick went on calmly, "Yeah, this is Baput and—"

"We've met," Lorraine interrupted through clenched teeth.

Patrick cocked his head so she had to look into that weirdly wrinkled, misaligned eye. "They're aliens, Babe. I mean, actual aliens!"

Lorraine gave the little group a second look, scanning their green skin and shiny dark hair, their dirty woven tunics and pants made of what, grass? She couldn't help but narrow her eyes at the timid little woman who supported an old man with a vacant, faraway look in his eyes. They whispered in a strange language.

Lorraine wrapped her arms around her daughter, burying her face so she couldn't see the aliens. Belinda struggled against the embrace.

Patrick kept trying. "You know, Lorraine..." The green woman and boy giggled again. Lorraine bared her teeth over her young.

Patrick walked behind Lorraine to put his hands on her shoulders. They tensed at his touch. She let go of Belinda and headed toward the house, talking to herself a mile a minute. "I wasn't expecting five *aliens* on top of a couple and a kid. That workers' quarters will have to do, as is, for them. Now I've got to fix up the guest room in the house, put sheets on that, and I guess give up my study for the kid. Belinda! Come help me!" she bellowed without looking back.

They all watched Belinda go. Patrick sighed in a way that touched even the most alien heart. "Come on, guys, let's see your temporary home."

They completed the walk to the quarters and dropped their burdens just inside. Star entered last, still supporting G-Pa. She deposited the old man on a couch and scanned the room anxiously.

There were no interior walls. The studs were in. The wiring was bare. "The plumbing is finished, of course. After all, that's what I do," Patrick declared.

"Where?" asked an unusually brazen Star.

"I am so sorry, my lady." Patrick graciously pointed the way to the bathroom, partitioned off with blankets tacked to naked 2x4s. "It's bare, but functional. Hey, maybe you guys can help me work on it while you're here. We could have walls separating your rooms by tomorrow night."

When Star emerged, relieved, Patrick showed her the kitchen while the others returned to the van for another load.

"Gas stove, just like yours, see?"

"Yes," Salistar said, uncomfortable with the man in the kitchen.

"You have a fridge and an oven. No dishwasher though, sorry. I put that one in there, where you live, did you know that?"

Salistar cocked her head to the side so uncomprehendingly he thought she was seizing or something. "We are... here," she muttered slowly.

"Are you OK? Have a seat." He escorted her back to the couch and gently sat her down next to her father. He rushed to the door and looked out. They were all coming with the second load. Everything from potatoes to mattresses. *Well good, I don't even have beds in here yet. What was Lorraine thinking? She was gonna put my family out here? Instead of the guest room and the study, or the music room, or the living room, for crying out loud?*

Guitar String

The last load in the van was Jerry's stuff. His guitar and amp, laptop, some games, his favorite clothes. More than he could carry, so he'd asked Baput to help him bring it all to his temporary bedroom upstairs in the house. Baput hoped Jerry knew what he was doing. He was pretty sure Lorraine was going to chase him out. He wanted to block his ears as they entered to the high-pitched wail of the vacuum cleaner. Under its agonizing cover, they crept upstairs with their loads to Lorraine's study.

"Crap! It's sprung!" Jerry cried as he unpacked his guitar. The high E string had gotten wrapped around a knob on his amp. The jostling ride had stretched the string, and Jerry had stretched it more as he yanked the guitar out of the box. "I didn't bring a spare," he mourned, futilely trying to tighten it. He plucked the sprung string. It thudded dully. He played the string next to it, which rang out with its particular vibration, then the dull E string again: "thud."

"Baput, look. This is like your string. Your connection to the Plane." Jerry plucked the undamaged string extra hard. It thrilled the air, sending ripples out in all directions. "But your G-Pa's string is like this." He played the damaged string. The air did not vibrate. In fact, the sound seemed to suck the remaining vibrations right out of the air. "His spring is sprung. That's why he can't get on the Plane!"

"It snapped!" recalled Baput. "I felt it when we came through. Remember when we threw those stones with that slingshot? I felt like the stone, and my string was like the sling. I felt it pull really, really tight, and then, snap!" he illustrated with his arms, drawing them far to one side, then flinging them across to the other side, his long, dark hair swinging behind him. "It felt like something broke. Then I woke up on the ground. But it didn't break. I didn't lose the Plane. It was just hard to find, through the Earth planes."

"Maybe it's more than that. Maybe that snap really tweaked his string. Yours too, but you're young. It's like a muscle. Old people are kind of crispy. They don't get over a strained muscle like us kids do. G-Pa's just cramped. He needs therapy. String Therapy."

"What's String Therapy?" Baput asked.

Jerry played a quick riff, unplugged, without the high E string. "Music. I'd order a string, but how long are we gonna be here?" He looked at Baput, knowing he didn't have the answer. Seeing the confusion on his friend's face, he realized, after four hours in that windowless truck, Baput still didn't quite get the idea that they had again been transported to another place. None of them got it. That truck trip had been just as mysterious for them as the portal had been. No wonder the old man needed therapy!

"My Uncle Patrick has an old acoustic. He'll probably let me use it. Your G-Pa can meditate, or you guys can chant, whatever, and I'll play, soft and gentle. We'll see if we can get that string tuned up and vibrating again."

Music Room

Patrick came into the house to check on Lorraine, but she was in the basement washing more sheets for the unexpected company, so he crept into his music room to "listen to a quick song."

A couple of solitary, smoky minutes later, when he was feeling more relaxed, the boys barged in. He stashed something in a desk drawer. A charred musk hung in the air.

Jerry explained his theory.

"String therapy, huh?" Patrick responded. "Great idea. I've got just the thing. But first, face it, you're gonna be here more than two days, so let's order you a string. We'll get together this evening after you've all unpacked and found out what you forgot, and we'll put in an order this evening. Second," Uncle Patrick carefully handed Jerry his acoustic guitar, "yes, you can play this, but be careful. You just tweaked your string because you jammed it into that box with the amp."

"It was an emergency," Jerry defended.

"But you yanked it when you unpacked it, when you had all the time in the world. I know, I get anxious to see my guitar, too, sometimes, but they're delicate instruments. You gotta love 'em." He rubbed a knotty hand over the face of the guitar in Jerry's hands. "Go ahead. Pluck something."

Jerry fingered a few chords and strummed idly, while Patrick turned to his extensive CD collection. His frizzy hair, a duller red than Belinda's, glowed in the sunlight that streamed through the window. "String therapy," he repeated softly. "Violins, that's what we need. I went through a violin phase. You listen really hard, concentrate, meditate, and you can feel the violin vibrating your soul, right here." He placed both hands on the back of his neck. It's like getting a psychic massage."

The cocked left eye turned to smile at them, while the other scanned a CD jacket. "John Mellencamp has a great lady violinist." He opened a drawer in the corner, away from the rest, and produced three CDs. "I liked the violin so much, I got these: a string quartet, Yo Yo Ma, and an all-violin concerto. Then I got bored with them. They're not rock. I like to play along with my old favorites. So if these help your grandpa, you can keep them."

Lorraine's footsteps emerged from the basement and disappeared out the back door with a medium slam. Patrick knew that slam. He knew the pace, the pressure of the footsteps on the stairs and across the floor. After 15 years of the turbulent drama that was his marriage, he knew every nuance.

"You can bring your grandpa in here and let him listen, if you want. But maybe not when your Aunt Lorraine is home."

"Why not?" Jerry asked.

"Well, she's, um, she's just not used to these guys yet. Give her time." He turned to Baput and changed the subject. "They must have music where you come from. What kind of instruments do they play?"

"There is," Baput curled both hands, held them up to his mouth in a line, and blew.

"Yes, some kind of flute. Do you have one?"

"No. I do not play those. I play the bowl. It's for meditating, but also for music. Meditation music. It's like string therapy."

"Would it help your G-Pa?" Patrick asked, abruptly rising to his feet.

Baput hung his head and mumbled, "He does not play. They are metal. The strange metal from the Old One, called breen. Soft metal, hammered into a bowl and polished smooth. You wet your hand like this," he stuck his fingertips in his mouth. "And you rub around the edge, or you use a stick with a ganeesh skin wrapped around it, freely given, of course."

"Like Yanzoo?" Jerry asked, recalling the tale.

"Yes," Baput answered, "But G-Pa cannot."

Patrick had brought up the question, but he seemed to be ignoring the answer. He was rummaging on a high shelf on the other side of the room. "Aha!" he exclaimed as he brought down a silver bowl fitting Baput's description, along with a wooden stick with a fabric head on the end.

"They had these at a yoga class I took. You want vibrations, man, this is it! If you can get it to work. I'm not very good. I never did master it." He placed the bowl on his outstretched hand, tapped it and ran the mallet along the edge. It made a couple short beeps and squeaks.

"That is how G-Pa plays," Baput reported, unable to repress a smirk.

"But you know how, right?" Patrick offered, gladly handing the bowl to Baput, who looked at the mallet curiously, then tapped the head on the edge of the bowl. He ran the mallet along the rim, slowly at first, then a bit faster as a tone seemed to grow from the bottom of the bowl and spill out all over the room, deep and rich and loud.

Jerry almost wanted to hold his ears, but it felt good. He felt the vibration to his core.

Baput went round and round with the mallet, losing himself in the waves so he didn't even notice when Belinda opened the door, until she asked loudly, "What's that noise?" She came right in and sat on the floor next to Baput, as the last vibration buzzed the corners of the room and slowly melted into silence.

"You keep it." Patrick offered, impressed with Baput's skill. "It's definitely yours."

"Wasn't it expensive?" cautioned Jerry, seeing his uncle getting carried away.

Patrick looked down fondly at the green boy sitting next to his daughter on the floor. "Hey, it isn't every day you get to meet an alien, I mean, an Akash, and help him get his string tuned up." He locked his cocked eye with Belinda's, their special look.

Belinda turned to Baput and reached for the bowl. "Can I try it?"

Baput grabbed the bowl tightly to his chest and dropped his head, looking up with big, dark eyes. There was fear in them, like that all-too-familiar way some people looked at her because of her eye, only so much deeper!

Her elated face shattered. "OK," she gulped, scooting out of the room without getting up off the floor. Patrick and Jerry stared at Baput as Belinda's footsteps fluttered up the stairs and into her room above their heads.

"Baput, what the——!" Jerry cried. So Baput *did* have a problem with the Look'N Ups! When they'd met Patrick, they had all seemed fine with him.

"I'm sorry!" sputtered Baput. "I couldn't let her!"

The warmth gone from his voice, Patrick asked, "Why?"

"Because she is woman."

"Ah," Patrick jumped in. "Girl, actually. A hurt little girl."

"She thinks it's her eye," Jerry explained.

Baput frowned, confused. "What about her eye?"

"She thinks you don't like it."

"I love her eye!" He glanced at Patrick and looked down quickly. "I like it. I like her. I want to let her play the bowl. I want to make her happy. But I cannot let a woman, a girl, play the Bowl of Yanzoo."

"You need to apologize," demanded Patrick.

Baput looked longingly at the ceiling with wet brown eyes. "How?"

Patrick visualized the bedroom, strewn with stuffed animals and decked with posters of unicorns. "I'll go," he answered quietly. "You guys go to the quarters and help your folks."

Patrick trudged up the stairs bearing heavy thoughts. He knew this was the beginning of a long, hard adolescence. Lorraine was so pretty. She had no experience to help her daughter through this. Patrick did, but he wasn't a girl.

Belinda lay on her bed, face buried in her favorite stuffed animals. "No one will ever love me!" she sobbed, in full drama when her father entered.

Patrick sat on her bed, and she crawled into his arms. "I do." He whispered, knowing it didn't help.

"I know, Daddy. I mean someone else. Not even an alien likes me, and he doesn't even know what an Earth girl's s'posed to look like!"

"That's not it, Baby," Patrick explained. "He likes your eye. He likes you. He told me so. He said he wants to make you happy!"

Belinda brightened right up. "He does?"

"That's what he said. It's not your eye at all. He just can't let a female play the bowl. It's a rule. Their religion, or something. I guess women are restricted where he comes from."

"Why?"

"They developed their culture that way. I'd say they're primitive, but that's like saying we're better than them. We're not. Just different. Not even that different, really. Some of the oldest and wisest cultures on Earth restrict their women in some ways. Almost all of them, actually. Us, too, until recently. Now, we're the unusual ones." He touched her tiny nose. "Why, in all his space travels, I'll bet he's never met another little girl who would even ask to play that bowl."

"I don't think so, Daddy." Belinda was sitting up now. "I don't think he's done a lot of space traveling."

"How can you tell?"

"He'd be used to new things. He's not. Everything here is new, and he's scared."

"Maybe you can help him with that," Patrick suggested as he marveled at her perceptiveness and empathy.

"Mom's not gonna like him, you know."

"Mom likes Star Trek, right?"

"Of course, Daddy, we all do."

"What's the Prime Directive?"

"Don't mess with other people's cultures," Belinda recited.

"Even if you don't agree with some of it, right? It's not for us to change it or put it down."

"So, I should just let him treat me that way?"

"No. Don't play the bowl, because that really hurts him. But stand your ground. You have just as much right to your culture. He should respect yours, too. If you respect each other, and understand that you were just raised differently, you can work it out. Try to be friends, anyway."

"How, Daddy?" Belinda asked through dried tears.

"I wish I knew, Baby. I wish somebody knew." Brimming with tears himself, he gave her The Eye. "Maybe you can figure it out and teach us."

Belinda did her unique version of an eye roll. "Thanks, Dad. No pressure."

"Now, Baput wants to apologize. You need to talk to him again. Next chance you get, or maybe wait for the next chance after that. You gotta play a little hard to get." Patrick advised, though he hoped this was just practice for a much later relationship, not because Baput was green, but because she was 10. His eyes got that far away, calculating look, where his left eye gazed into something in space and his right eye looked right through you. Belinda knew that look.

He spoke again. "I don't know why I'm telling you this, because I'm not sure I want you to go there," he locked left eyes with Belinda, "but I think I know the way to his heart."

Plumage

"Bel-in-da" the three syllables rolled musically off Baput's tongue as soon as he and Jerry were outside on the porch alone. "She's beautiful! She's got plumage!"

Jerry laughed out loud. "Plumage? Like a bird?"

"Like the *kiko bird*. She sits high in the pomegranate tree, her plumage all puffed out, purple and luscious, waiting for the male birds. They are even more beautiful. The tufts on their heads are a bright red that turns bright blue when they turn their heads. They gather at the base of the trunk, squabbling. The winner walks up the trunk, spiraling higher and higher until he almost reaches her. Sometimes the second winner comes up after him, and he has to fight him back down. If he fends off all comers and reaches her branch, she holds her head to the side and looks down her beak at him with one eye, then the other. If she doesn't like him, she turns her back and walks to the end of her branch, and he flies away in shame. One after another, they try. When she finally finds one acceptable, she flies out of the tree and away. It's funny to watch. The chosen one gets so excited he almost falls out of the tree. Then he finds his footing and takes off. He flies away with her upriver, into the mists."

"Down, boy!" Jerry cried protectively. "Belinda's not plumed out yet! She's only ten!"

Lorraine

Lorraine scrambled to adjust for the unexpected green field workers. It would have been easier to put Elmer's family in the unfinished worker's quarters, rather than clean out the cluttered spare bedroom, but then along came these, these, *people, I guess. Aliens! I should be stoked! I never thought I'd be changing sheets for them, but, they can stay out in the quarters, Elmer and Fran here in the guest room, and Jerry in my study on the futon. Aliens!*

As she finished making the guest bed, she looked out the window at the driveway. Here came Fran, her car full of food. Lugging boxes of fresh vegetables, more potatoes, squashes, eggplants, tomatoes, beans, and a huge sack of black rice fresh from the Sacramento Valley. She had the boys carrying half the stuff to the quarters and half into the house. That green woman came out to the car, and they rocked to and fro in a tight embrace while Elmer and Patrick carried two big ice chests into the house. *They've been apart what, four hours?* Lorraine rolled her eyes.

She ducked into the bathroom, touched up her face and straightened her sleeveless buttoned shirt, disheveled from all that housework. She dropped her sweats on the floor and wriggled into her jeans, then waltzed down the stairs. "Fran!" she cried magnanimously, catching her sister-in-law with an arms-length embrace and a pair of air kisses. "I have some frozen lasagna I was going to—"

"Save it," Fran suggested with only the best intentions. "I brought plenty of food for all of us. I'll cook. You don't have to lift a finger. Unless you want to."

"I want to," Belinda stepped up, shyly eyeing her mother.

Lorraine cleared her throat and glanced from Belinda to Fran. "No, Baby," she said cryptically.

"Why not?" Fran wondered out loud.

"I don't want Belinda to have to cook. It's not fair to her. I get a career, and my daughter cooks for me? I won't have it. I'd rather she didn't learn, so she'll never have that assumption thrust upon her."

"Mom! Pleeeeaase! Just this once, I want to help Aunt Fran!"

"Oh, OK. This once," Lorraine grunted, pulling out her phone.

Fran washed some vegetables and gave Belinda a quick safety lesson on the knife, aware of the depth perception issues that came with the family affliction. Lorraine stayed in the kitchen for what may have been a record time, but she was texting on her phone the whole time.

"They're a secret, you know," Fran worried.

"Of course," Lorraine agreed, too casually. "I saw E.T."

Fran made a quick dinner by her standards; chicken thighs, baked in the oven with yams, and a pot of steamed vegetables.

"Aren't we going to eat with them?" Patrick asked, eager to break bread with a new culture.

"We don't," Fran explained. "They're vegan. I'm afraid the sight of people eating meat will scare them, or at least gross them out. This is what they're used to. Let's keep things as normal as possible for them."

"They laughed at my name," Lorraine complained, not used to being made fun of. Fran didn't help by giggling.

"Lor-raine!" Fran tested. "Yep, too short. That's a man's name. Like mine. I'm Fran-cin-a now. Three syllables, for a woman. You can be Lo-ri-anne! They'll like that."

"Lori Ann," Belinda echoed.

"My name's *Lorraine*," their red-haired hostess replied, identity intact.

"So, what's their story?" Patrick asked with his mouth full.

Jerry uncorked the pent-up saga through dinner. He was eager to hear what a physicist and an engineer thought about the portal, the Rock and the Plane, but he didn't pause long enough to hear their thoughts, or to take questions, bites or even breaths.

All plates empty but his own, Jerry finished the bizarre tale with the weirdest part. "They've never been anywhere but their home village, then the Look'N Up, and now here. They didn't even know there was another place besides their village, until they accidentally went through that space portal and came out on Earth."

With that, Jerry finished his dinner while the story seeped into their brains, working its way through all those wrinkles and folds, new thoughts firing, making new connections.

Belinda broke the silence with a giggle. "They don't like girls," she blurted.

"What?

"Women are considered, well, they're old-fashioned," Fran explained.

How did *you* know?" Lorraine grilled Belinda.

"Baput wouldn't let me play his bowl."

"He wouldn't let you *what* his *what?*"

Strange Quarters

The mattresses were spread out on the floors of the rooms without walls. Elmer had laid it on thick about not touching the bare wires, wound and clamped together in their metal boxes with no covers. Felsic was fascinated and still tried to touch one every once in a while, until one got him. He screamed and jumped back, hair standing on end and his grass sleeve smoking. Valko let out a laugh that shook the walls and popped the bubble of tension that enveloped their strange new space.

Just like that first day, Star cooked fried potatoes. This time, she had fresh vegetables to add to her stir-fry. She and Fran had stripped the garden together, taking everything that was even close to ripe. Fran had brought even more from that mysterious "town" where she got food all year round.

"Why is everything turned around?" Valko asked suddenly, pointing to the bedrooms. "Bedrooms here, living room, here. It is backwards."

"This is not like any fire at Nauve," Star said from the kitchen "The walls are gone, but no burn marks."

Baput knew how they saw it: Nauve had vanished and been replaced with the Look'N Up Ranch. Now the Look'N Up had been replaced with something similar, but not the same. It wasn't the Look'N Up. It also wasn't what remained of the Look'N Up after a fire. It was another *place* with different people, like Jerry had told him, and shown him on the iPlane. But none of those people looked like Patrick or Belinda.

"Popa, G-Pa, do you remember I told you about otherwhere? Other villages with different people who look different? Well, this is an otherwhere. A new village, with new, different people." He gazed in the direction of the main house, a strangely mature look on his face, and whispered, "New Dee En Ay."

The Akashic Record

By the time Fran brought out a store-bought apple pie she'd been heating up in the oven, Patrick was up and pacing the floor, pondering. "So, this rock is made of an especially resonant material, and when they apply electricity, it gives off energy. And they used the pipes to concentrate the energy, and direct it at those, what do you call them?"

"Nimblies," Jerry answered. "Bugs, up to a foot long with a two-foot wingspan on the third day. They start out smaller on the first day. They're built like dragonflies, but they have a long proboscis like a mosquito, that sucks you dry. They have complex eyes like a fly, you know, with all the little tiny lenses?

"Then at night, it's the bat things, the bumblies. They're just as big. On the first night, they're about the size of a fruit bat. On the third night, they're more like small ducks. They have a horn on the end of their nose like a rhino that can rip you to shreds in minutes!"

Jerry was still talking when they all adjourned to the living room. "… and when he gets on my computer, he can surf all over the place without even touching the mouse. We've been practicing, and now he can send me an email with his mind. I can email him, too, and he picks it up right out of the air."

"Can you text him?" Belinda asked, pulling her phone out.

"No," Jerry answered. "It has to be the internet. He calls it the iPlane, because it's like his Akashic Plane at home."

Patrick jumped out of his recliner. "Akashic Plane? I saw that on TV. DaVinci and Einstein and Tesla, a whole bunch of geniuses all over the world and they got these ideas out of nowhere, for all kinds of inventions, all at the exact right time. What show was that on, Babe? *Ancient Aliens?*"

"I think so," Lorraine replied, embarrassed. "That impeccable source of knowledge."

"I saved it in the DVR." Patrick circled the room, searching for the remote. "Here it is." He sat down and pressed the buttons, brought up the list. "Look at this, guys! It's called 'The Akashic Record.' Not Plane, but Akashic! I thought that word sounded familiar."

"Whoa!" Jerry rushed to Patrick's side. He had resented the interruption, but this was worth it. Some people on Earth knew about the Plane!

Uncle Patrick rambled on about the Akashic Record as he switched the set off and they settled back into their chairs.

Jerry interrupted him. "But, Uncle Patrick, here's the thing. They have the Akashic Plane, and it has all that knowledge, but they don't have all those inventions and stuff. I think it's because their religion tells them it's a sin or something. It's like they're brainwashed!"

After Bedtime

They explored the physics of it all for a couple of hours, steering away from the sociology, until Lorraine coaxed and cajoled Belinda into bed. To Patrick's surprise, the conversation stalled awkwardly while they waited for her return.

When she did, Elmer began, a safe distance out of her reach. "There's something I've gotta tell you guys. They got a real small population in their village. About a hundred, and no one else on their whole planet. So, they have a problem."

"Wouldn't they mutate?" Lorraine jumped right to it.

Fran took over. "There's a powerful woman there called Akira, I'm not sure if that's a name or a title. She is in charge of the women. She births them, and we think she might, well, kill them if—"

"They're probably culling," Elmer explained. "But these guys don't know anything about it, not even the Akash."

"Not even Star," Fran resumed. "I showed her your picture. They don't seem to mind the Look'N Up Eye a bit. We just thought you should know." She smiled innocently.

"Yeah, they didn't react bad to me at all." Patrick mused, "I thought the kid did, to Bel, but it wasn't her eye, it was just the sexist thing."

He looked at Lorraine, expecting at least a snarl. She was silent, her green eyes blazing like lasers at Fran. "You just thought we should know," her words sliced the air, "that you brought five aliens here, knowing they might kill our daughter?"

"Of course not!" Fran erupted.

Elmer seconded, "I don't know about that Akira, but these here ones wouldn't hurt a fly. They don't even eat meat."

"Baput wouldn't let anybody hurt Belinda." Jerry told them. "He's in love with her."

Plants

The next morning was Sunday, so Lorraine stayed home. She graciously spared some of her precious home chore time to join her guests on a grand tour of their five acres tucked away in the Sierra foothills outside of Sacramento, where she worked at a private engineering company.

"Just like home at the Look'N Up," Patrick introduced as they strode along a four-wheeler trail past an empty garden. "That's why we picked this place. It's nice and private. No neighbors can see you. I have nothing to hide, except my face, but that seems to be enough. Oh, and an illicit plant now and then, but that's legal now." He smiled at his uncomprehending green audience and the knowing looks of the white ones, even the young ones.

"We lived in town for a while, before Belinda, when Lorraine worked for the county. Your neighbors see you in the backyard or on the front porch. They try not to look, but you can see them wanting to, like Austin Powers. Moley! Moley! Moley!" he cried, pointing at Belinda, who giggled more than most nice kids would have dared.

He went on. "People don't say anything, but you can't help but wonder what they're thinking. You can't relax. I like it out here." He walked down the slope to a green lower terrace. He stretched his arms out wide over his "orchard."

"Here are my pom ladies. Elmer gave me the cuttings, what, six years ago?"

"Yeah, about," Elmer replied.

Baput approached the young trees, touching one. They were pruned wrong, like Elmer's. There were only six of them, all two cycles old. He could tell by their size, and by the way their wilted flowers were turning into tiny fruits, just a few on each tree.

Behind the six little trees were six deep green, almost purple bushes. They were as wide as they were tall, like a kip tree should be. They were imprisoned in containers, like the Nauvian trees. They smelled like that rude little animal with the white stripe down its back that Shastina had chased. He and Jerry had had to bathe her in tomato juice.

Patrick approached the strange plants proudly. "These are my other ladies. Remember when I brought the dishwasher, guys? I stopped by old Doc Adam's. You know, Dad's old doc? Dad convinced him the herb helped him with the headaches and depression we sometimes get. He couldn't do anything about it then, but he wrote me a 'scrip right before he retired. So we're legal now." He embraced one of his sticky pets, inhaling deeply.

A wooden picnic table sat by a pond that Patrick had excavated next to his up-and-coming pomegranate orchard. It collected water from a spring that popped up in a thicket of willows just uphill. A pair of mallards bobbed in the cattails at the edge.

Elmer stepped across the pipe that brought water from the pond to the plants. He turned to the crowd and made an announcement. "We'll plant our trees right here. OK, Patrick? Alien pomegranate trees. They say they're extra dark and rich."

Patrick's face wrinkled even more.

"You said you wanted to expand, right?"

"With help," Patrick objected. "Why don't you plant them in your orchard?"

"Well, think about it, Bro. Poms are my livelihood. A lot of other folks around my place grow poms for a living, too. Does anybody around here grow poms for a living?"

"I don't think so." Patrick admitted. "Just backyard stuff."

"So what if these guys have a disease, or a weird genetic reaction with ours? This here's the perfect place to test that, see?"

Lorraine stormed down the trail into the orchard. "No way. We don't want diseased plants, either."

Scientist at heart, and eager for an experiment, Patrick was already sold on the idea. On one condition. "It's OK, Babe," he dismissed his wife's concerns. "As long as you guys help me plant them."

Lorraine stepped away, mumbling.

Felsic sprinted down the trail, ready to work.

From the top of the slope, Valko reined Felsic in. "It is the height of summer. We plant in spring."

Good idea. Fran thought as she turned from Elmer's presentation. She found Star staring at the tiny orchard with her mouth open. G-Pa clung to her side, muttering.

"Did the fire take the rest?" Star whispered through tears.

Fran rushed to her side and embraced her, but she didn't know how to answer.

Felsic joined them in staring at the greatly reduced kip orchard. "Was it the fire? Did it get all the other trees?"

Fran and Jerry looked at each other. They still didn't get it. How to explain?

"This is Patrick's place," Fran began. *No, they don't understand ownership.* "We are not at home now. Home is still there. Home is OK, so far. Our trees are OK. We can see on the internet, the iPlane. We can communicate with people there. Baput knows, right? You know we can communicate with other people, right?"

"Yes," Baput confirmed. "Momama, this is otherwhere, like I told you. It is another place. There are many places on Earth."

Valko nodded knowingly. The other faces were blank.

Fran tried again, speaking the way she had to Jerry when he was two. "Right now, we are at Patrick, Lorraine, and Belinda's house. There's no fire here. When the fire at our place is out, we'll go home, and you'll see all the kip trees are still there. Your quarters are all there, just like before," she promised rashly.

"Unless it all burns." It was left to Jerry to say the bad news. "But, so far, so good!" he flashed his signature Cheshire Cat grin.

Fran abandoned the fruitless effort and guided the group back up the trail toward the houses. She couldn't resist taking a right on the weedy side path to the pitiful garden. Lorraine and Belinda followed her.

The others followed Elmer down the main trail to the quarters. "Come on, guys!" he told them. "We've got projects for you. We've gotta bring our trees out here and set them in the orchard where I showed you, and help Patrick plumb in some water for them. We'll have to trust him to plant them in the winter when the time is right.

"And, we're gonna fix up your quarters. Just because we're evacuated don't mean you get a free ride."

Lorraine and Belinda followed Fran down the unkempt foot path to the homemade gate in the rickety fence of chicken wire and steel posts that still stood after four years of neglect.

Beds were still distinguishable, choked with weeds and some hardy volunteers. "Those tomatillos, still all over the place!" Lorraine remarked, amazed. "I only grew them once!"

"Mom doesn't do the garden anymore. We used to, when I was little. It was fun," Belinda told her aunt.

"Why don't you do it anymore?" asked Fran. "It's very calming, I find."

"I used to think so, too," mourned Lorraine. "But then it got to be another chore. Only two days at home a week, and I'd have to spend them planting or weeding or canning. I'd be out here in my beautiful, peaceful garden, with my adorable little girl, and I'd be thinking about some problem at work. Or worse, I'd be thinking of some other drudgery chore I had to get done, too, but I couldn't because I was doing this chore, and when was I going to do the other one?"

Fran could literally see the blood pressure rising in Lorraine's ears.

"It wasn't fun anymore," Lorraine finished flatly. "So I quit."

On that note, the three ladies trudged back to the house, but not before Fran picked a bunch of those tomatillos into a scoop of her T-shirt. She showed Belinda how, and she carried a scoop home, too.

Hung the Moon

Valko handled the sheetrock like it was cardboard. Elmer held a panel up while Patrick nailed it in place.

"Belinda sure likes Baput," Patrick remarked between blows.

"She thinks he hung the moon," Elmer replied with the old phrase.

Baput stood just around the corner, hammering the panel Felsic held. An old annoyance flared up deep inside him.

On their break, he raced with Jerry to the pond in the tiny orchard. It would be their place, like the Horizontal Tree. As soon as they were alone, Baput asked Jerry, "Your popa says Belinda thinks I hung the moon. What does that mean? You think Kakeeche is stupid, then you say one boy hung the moon in the sky all by himself?"

"I never said Kakeeche's stupid!" Jerry defended, then admitted, "OK, I guess I sorta did. And my dad definitely did. But 'hung the moon' is *supposed* to be stupid. That's the point. It means Belinda's gone stupid over you."

Baput was flattered, then worried, then terrified. "I have this... power?"

"Get over yourself, B," Jerry snapped. "It's not a superpower. People get stupid over each other all the time. Don't your people ever fall in love?" he batted his eyes theatrically.

Baput's response was soft and cold. "We don't dare. I told you. Our marriages are decided by Akira, according to the lines. If you are lucky, you fall in love with your betrothed. If not, you'd better not fall in love with someone else. There are many sad stories, but in the end, they always marry their betrothed, or no one..." he trailed off and lifted his hand to his mouth. A wave of cloying sickness swept over him.

Belinda had crept into the orchard, unnoticed, and heard the whole exchange. Her voice cut through Baput's miasma. "What's a, a betroved? You mean, you're engaged?"

Baput wasn't sure he wanted to tell her, but he couldn't lie. "Yes. I am to marry Tamaya."

Belinda's heart sank in a way she had never felt before. "Is she, um, pretty?"

Baput thought about the slim young lady with her long legs and high forehead, vibrant green skin, shiny, straight hair, and intense midnight-colored eyes that always looked impatient or far away. "Yeah, I guess," was all he could say around the lump that filled his throat.

"Do you love her?" Belinda squeaked like a terrified mouse.

"I don't know," Baput mused. "I'm scared of her."

"Are you scared of me?" Belinda asked, the playful spark returning.

"Yeah, a little," Baput admitted.

"Good!" Belinda grinned. She turned and skipped away.

Color

The next morning after breakfast, the men began to hang the siding on the quarters' outer walls. Baput and Jerry headed out to the orchard where the new pomegranate trees waited in their pots. Jerry had a box of tiny black hoses and fittings that dripped a half gallon per minute. They used their sharp pocketknives to cut the little hoses and fit the drippers so each tree would be kept continuously moist. Jerry assured Baput that Uncle Patrick would place the trees in the earth when the time was right.

"Why don't Earth people like color?" Baput asked out of thin air.

Jerry's head spun. "What do you mean we don't like color?"

Baput sounded like he'd been practicing. "Lorraine has beautiful red hair, like Belinda's, but she cut it off. And Patrick said our green toilet is hideous! And your popa, when he introduced us to Patrick, he said we were colored, and they laughed. Then Patrick said that their popa, your g-pa, taught them not to even see color. What does that mean?"

This was a hard question, but Jerry tried. "Baput, people from otherwhere come in different colors. Like I showed you on the iPlane, remember? All over the world, different colors?"

Baput remembered. "White, black, red, and yellow, but really just different shades of tan and brown. No green."

"That's right," Jerry confirmed. "Well, sometimes those people don't like each other. People do bad things to people of another color. Like, us white people are from Europe, across the ocean way east of here. We came here and wiped out a lot of the red people and just took over."

"You killed them!?" Baput looked at his friend with such revulsion!

Jerry needed to distance himself. "Not me! And not my dad, or Uncle Patrick, or my grandparents. It was our Old Ones, a long, long time ago." He took a breath and went on, trying to remember how his parents and grandparents had taught him. This was like having a kid!

"After the white people took over this country, brown people kept coming here from other countries. They looked different and had different ways."

"Like us," Baput interrupted defensively.

"Exactly," Jerry responded, which did not relieve Baput. "I guess people thought there wouldn't be enough for everybody. Enough food, water, even enough space. I guess that's why. It's the only thing that even comes close to making sense. But some white people wanted to hurt the brown people, even kill them!"

Baput gasped loudly, and Jerry decided to skip the slavery part for now. Baput didn't even understand ownership, how could he possibly imagine the brutality of "owning" another person?

"*Most* white people said 'no, you can't kill them. They're people, like us.' But some said, 'They're not people. They're different. We're better, we should be above them.' The majority of white people made laws against killing the brown people, but still they're not treated the same as us. And some people still want to kill them. They hate them.

"And it's not just here, it happens all over the planet. People hate people who are different. Even if they're a white family who just got here, and the brown family has been here for generations, the white still hates the brown. So the brown then hates the white, too. And they teach their kids to hate, too, without questioning, to hate the brown people as soon as they see them, just because they're brown. The kids don't even know why." Jerry's speech slowed down like he was teaching a child. "They don't ask why. They just hate."

"What is hate?" Baput asked, suddenly terrified of this place that had been starting to feel like a new home, even with the recent, disconcerting shift in scenery.

Jerry marveled at the question. Everyone on Earth had a pretty good idea what hate was. How to explain hate? "I guess I've never really hated anyone." He realized, a proud smile lifting his lips. It quickly collapsed into a downcast look of shame. "But maybe that's just because nobody's ever done anything really mean to me. Not compared to the stuff some kids do to the Hispanic and black kids. I guess I'm a white spoiled brat."

"Is that bad? You don't seem happy about it."

"Most people here are white. Well, maybe not anymore, but the ones with money and land. And I'm one of them. I've been here all my life, and my dad and my g-pa, too. And we own land. We're not coming here from another place. And we're the same color. So they don't hate us."

Baput reflected, "We just came here. We own nothing. And we're green. So, some people hate us?"

Jerry nodded solemnly. "Probably. That's why we keep you hid, see? The windowless truck to haul you up here to a place like home where no one can see you? You heard Uncle Patrick, right? He likes it here because no one sees him. They have the same problem, you know, him and Bel. People are mean to them because they're different."

"Why?" Baput asked. Thinking of Belinda reminded him of what had irked him yesterday. *Hung the moon. Stupid. Kakeeche. Stupid.* Then it dawned on him. "You know? Your hate is way stupider than our Kakeeche."

Jerry sighed his agreement, tacitly conceding humanity's ancestral lameness.

Belinda's Eye

They spent the afternoon painting the inside walls of the quarters. Then the boys headed back to the orchard. Belinda followed, toting a stuffed unicorn. It had purple plush fur, a lighter lavender mane the color of G-Pa's, and huge feet. Its floppy legs splayed in all directions when she plopped it down on the picnic table in front of the boys. "This is my best friend, Dodi."

Baput stared uncomfortably at the single horn on the fuzzy forehead.

"Don't you like him?" Belinda pressed.

"He doesn't like his horn," Jerry explained.

"Why?" asked Belinda.

Baput had not introduced Belinda to the horrors of the nimblies and bumblies, and he didn't know that Jerry had spilled his eager guts at the dinner table, and long into the living room, on that first night.

Jerry covered quickly. "Because horses don't have horns."

"Yeah," Belinda giggled. "He's a freak. Like me."

"Don't say that, Bel!" Jerry cried. "Hey, we got Baput here now, and G-Pa. They're Holy Men. Maybe they can do a healing ceremony and fix your eye."

"Daddy's too?" Belinda asked generously.

"You first. You're the guinea pig. What do you think, Baput, should we get G-Pa?"

Baput found he was too ashamed to let Belinda see G-Pa in his current state. Then, more shame for feeling ashamed. "I can do it. Close your eyes." He began to hum a low, monotonous tone.

He closed his eyes and reached out, gently touching Belinda's face. He started at her chin and worked his way up her soft right cheek to her conventionally oriented eye and rested there. Then he slowly worked his way across her freckled nose to her left eye. He could feel the wrinkles in her young skin where her eye corkscrewed up and to the left.

There was no such "healing ceremony," but touching Belinda's soft, fascinating face felt so delightful he didn't want to stop. When he'd had his fill of the sensation, for now, he concentrated.

His breathing slowed and deepened, and he watched the space behind his forehead, his third eye. He visualized the question. "What is wrong with Belinda's eye?" No response from the Plane. "What can we do about Belinda's eye?" Nothing. An unusually empty nothingness. Was he losing it, like G-Pa? Nothing. *Nothing!*

"That's it!" he realized. "I can't fix it, because there's nothing to fix. There's nothing wrong with you, or your popa. You're just you."

Belinda drooped with disappointment. She rested her head on Dodi.

Baput pressed his point. "My skin is green. All my family's skin is green. There's nothing wrong with us. We're just green."

"You're a mutation," Jerry offered.

"You said not to say that, Jerry," Belinda retorted.

"I said, 'don't say freak.'"

"Same thing," Bel pouted.

"An adaptation," Jerry went on. "Evolution. If your eye has a benefit, then you live longer and have more kids, so then more people have The Eye. If it's not a benefit, then you all die out."

Belinda winced and looked to Baput for protection, but he just stood there with a goofy grin on his face.

"You've got it too, Jerry," Belinda lashed out. "Every generation gets one. You know that's how it works."

"But the straight-eyed brother never has a kid with The Eye," Jerry answered.

"That's because they all died in the wars." Belinda was right. Jerry's dad was the first to make it this far, thanks to the cessation of the draft.

Jerry grinned. "So it's a good mutation. It helps you survive by making you 4F. That means the Army doesn't want you."

"I'll say good!" Baput erupted his agreement after waiting politely. "I've been thinking that very thing. When I think of the Plane, try to look at it with my mind's eye, it is always up and to the left. No matter where I am. So Belinda's eye," he pointed to where Belinda's eye was pointing, "is pointing right at the Plane. The way I imagine it, anyway. It's really everywhere. But if my eye were pointed like Belinda's, it would always be on it. And, even better, the nimblies make a buzzing sound and you hear them approach, but the bumblies make no noise at all. They are swift, maneuverable, and silent." His hands flitted randomly. "But they always approach you from above and to the left. If we all had that eye, we could defeat the bumblies."

The extended Musik family gathered for dinner, gushing their rave reviews for another home-cooked meal. Lorraine was especially pleased to hear that Francine was giving Patrick cooking lessons.

Even better, Belinda bragged, "I didn't help one bit, Mom," her eyes sparking.

"Good girl," she told her daughter proudly, then she saw that sparkle. "What *did* you do?"

"I hung out with the boys in the orchard. Baput tried to fix my eye, but he couldn't 'cause he says there's nothing wrong with us, Daddy. We just *are*. Like he's just green."

Patrick leaned back and nodded slowly, wiping his lips on his napkin. "Well, that's positive. I like that."

Lorraine leaned forward intensely. "What did he do to try and fix your eye?" she demanded.

Belinda described the healing ceremony.

"He put his hands on you?"

"Just my face, Mom. It didn't hurt."

"He didn't do anything bad, Aunt Lorraine, I watched. He just put his hands on her face, like she said."

Lorraine lowered her head, looking sideways at her daughter and nephew as she chewed.

Jerry's 13th Birthday

As the evacuation wore on, the Musiks settled into a routine. Every morning they checked the CalFire website on Fran's laptop to get the latest information about the fire. Was it closer? Can we go home? The situation got worse each day, but it wasn't getting any closer to the Look'N Up. At least not yet. It still could. It wasn't over. Always the same, more or less.

After that, Lorraine would grab an energy bar and a smoothie, now with fresh kale, thanks to Fran. Fran would make breakfast for everyone else, grabbing Patrick, Jerry, or even Belinda to help chop potatoes or mix dough.

Francine knew the birthday present she had ordered for Jerry was lost in limbo, undeliverable until… when? Patrick had helped her find a better one on the internet, and it had arrived just in time, along with the rest of their order.

Jerry eyed the two wrapped birthday gifts while his folks checked the fire report on the internet. He knew one was just his guitar string. *Only 15% contained. Evacuations still in effect. Same old thing.*

"We still can't go home." Elmer sighed his frustration. "We got work to do."

Fran brought out a chocolate cake topped with raspberries and set it on a table on the porch. "I thought our friends could join us. It's organic, and I used flaxseed instead of eggs."

"They're dairy-free?" Lorraine asked.

"Yes, totally vegan. No meat, eggs, cheese, or milk. They've never used any chemical fertilizers or pesticides, so their systems are so clean! I'm trying to keep them natural. Who knows how their innards would react? And we can't exactly take them to a doctor, you know."

"Aliens are such high-maintenance," Lorraine mused indulgently as she headed for her car. "I'm late for work."

Elmer came out, spotted Felsic on the quarters' porch, and waved. "It's Jerry's birthday. Come on over! All of you!"

Felsic opened the door and yelled a burst of strange words into the quarters. Baput appeared first, then Star's timid face. Valko stood behind her, looking vaguely bothered, as he had since they had arrived. The group advanced slowly as a unit down the stairs. Baput led an especially vacant-looking G-Pa wearing headphones. They filed solemnly to the foot of the porch steps and looked up, silent and wide-eyed, at the Musiks.

"For crying out loud, you guys, it's a birthday party, not a funeral!" Elmer chided, whacking Felsic on the shoulder with his hat. "Come on! We did your ceremony. You gotta learn one of our songs now. It's real easy."

The Musiks all sang, "Happy Birthday." Then they sang it a second time so the green people could join in.

"Make a wish," Fran reminded her son.

Jerry closed his eyes, then blew all over the cake until all 13 candles winked out.

Star inhaled violently. "Why does he spit on cake?"

Felsic got it. "So we can't have any. It's all just for him now, because birthday. Right?" he surmised, pleased with himself.

"Sounds good to me!" Jerry quipped, cutting a big slice and licking the knife.

"Jerry!" Fran cried, grabbing the knife.

Elmer and Felsic hooted and punched each other.

Fran ran into the kitchen and returned with a clean knife. She cut 10 slices, hoping everyone would have some. "Open your present, Jerry. The one I ordered you is probably in limbo somewhere, but when we get it, we'll send it back. Uncle Patrick found a better one." Jerry ripped the paper so savagely the green people stepped back a little.

"It's a tape recorder!" Fran blurted. "Well, not tapes, disks. You can record 1,000 hours of high-quality digital sound." She went on like a commercial. "If that's not enough, you download it or put in another disk. I thought you could record their stories." She looked at the questioning, green faces that held no concept of a digital recorder. "If it's OK with them, that is."

Shoving the instructions aside, Jerry examined the recorder, inserted the included disk and put his finger on the record button. "Say something," he ordered Baput.

"Say what?"

"Whatever you can think of. Sing a song. Tell a story."

Baput tried the birthday song again, and the rest joined in. Jerry hit rewind, then play. The Nauvians jumped when the little box sang the song they had just sung, sounding just like them. G-Pa's eyes flew open wide. He raised his longstick and muttered something that Baput said meant "evil."

Jerry ignored the superstitious outburst. "See, when you guys tell stories, like in the van on the way over here, the Tale of Yanzoo? I could have recorded that. Then if you guys ever go home to Nauve, we'll have your stories to remember you by. Maybe we can even tell people about you guys, once you're safe." He felt a familiar frustration at their mostly uncomprehending faces.

He heard a click. Suddenly his words came back to him, with all the embarrassing dramatic emphasis and squeaky cracks. "See, when you guys tell stories…"

Baput grinned, his finger on the play button, not so clueless after all.

School

By the first Friday in August, the quarters were more than complete enough for the Nauvians, but Patrick insisted on linoleum and an exterior coat of paint. Saturdays were a day off at home, but the men kept working. So did Lorraine, but she promised to stay home on Sunday.

Maybe it was the yellow leaves, just starting to drop, or maybe it was the television commercials and the spreads in the magazines and newspapers. Some deep instinct signaled, "School."

Dinner was a hearty beef stew and a fresh green salad. The clinking of spoons and men's appreciative grunts were the only sounds.

Suddenly Belinda asked, "If these guys are still here when school starts, can I stay home?"

"With Baput," Jerry jeered.

"With my dear cousin Jerry," Belinda corrected, showing him her tongue. "And my Aunt Frannie, and my Uncle Elmer."

"And Baput," Jerry insisted.

"Yes. And Baput. And Salistar."

Lorraine looked down at her empty bowl.

"And Valko, and Felsic, and Shastina," Belinda completed her list.

"Wait, which one is Shastina?" Lorraine searched the table for an answer.

"The dog, Mom," Belinda answered impatiently, like Lorraine really should know Baput's dog's name.

Patrick explained: "We have some angst. Bel starts middle school this year."

"Already? She's only 10!" Fran asked, concerned.

"They start early here. Fifth grade through eighth."

"Hey, that's kind of good." Elmer counted on his fingers. "If we'd had that, I could have been there for you in middle school, Little Bro. I was in high school already. You had to face that hell all by yourself." His eyes cut suddenly to Fran. "But you didn't, did you? You had Frannie, here."

Patrick smiled dreamily, not at Fran, but at something far away, or long ago. "Fran took good care of me." He dipped his spoon for another bite.

"Yeah," Elmer grunted, stuffing a hunk of beef into his mouth. "She does that."

None of this helped Belinda. "I won't have anybody," she moaned. "Why do I have to go to a new school, anyway? Why can't I stay where I'm used to it? Where they're used to me, kinda?"

Only Patrick knew what to say. "All those kids from elementary school, they'll be there, too."

"Oh, joy!" Belinda replied in a sarcasm too bitter for her years.

"But they'll stick up for you. Believe it or not, you're one of them now, against the kids from the other school that none of you know. You'll be surprised."

"How many other schools feed into it?" asked Fran.

"Just one. About the same size as her school," Lorraine replied.

"But can I pleeeeaase stay home until they go?" Belinda turned her eye on them in a gesture that looked cute only to her family.

"You don't want to do that," recommended Lorraine. "If you go on the first day, everything's new, there's lots of new people. Yeah, they'll stare, and talk about you, but you're just one of a lot of new things. If you show up a week later, everyone's found their places and formed their cliques. You walk in then, and you're the only new thing. Everybody's staring at you, all at once. And they all got their buds with them, egging them on."

"You need to teach her to fight," was Elmer's solution.

Patrick objected, "Violence isn't the answer."

"Easy for you to say!" Elmer exploded jovially. "You know how many kids I had to beat up on account of you?"

"It's different with girls," Lorraine tried to explain. "It's not about who's bigger, who can beat who up. It's, well, even stupider. And I hate to say it, but my mom was right, in a way. It's about appearances. A nice body. Not too fat, not too thin," she recited.

Jerry's flesh crawled. She sounded like Baput. But there was a cynical edge to Aunt Lorraine's recital, like she was mocking it as she said it. "Makeup, but not too much, nice clothes. Not provocative. Not prudish either. Not that frilly, dolly stuff my mom made me wear."

Belinda was familiar with the transference of her current issue to her mom's same old one. She rolled her eyes unattractively.

Fran mused deeply, "It's primal. All about what makes us a better mate. For a man, strength and prowess in battle. For a woman, well, beauty? Seems it would be something more pragmatic, if it's primal. No offense, Lor."

"Don't we do the best we can, Bel?" Lorraine asked, catching Belinda not listening.

"Baaaapuuutttt!" Jerry hissed in a whisper.

"Yeah, Mom." Bel tried to placate her, not knowing what her mom had asked, wishing they would both just shut up.

Satisfied, Lorraine went on. "We dress nicely. We don't give them anything else to pick on her for."

"But maybe if she dressed weird, it would distract people from her eye," Jerry proposed.

"You're in middle school. Do you think that would work?"

Jerry thought. "Nah. I guess she'd just have two strikes against her. But I know what you mean. Girls are different. They're extra mean!"

"And they're extra, *extra* mean in middle school," Lorraine informed them.

"How would you know, Mom?" Belinda muttered, not meaning to be heard.

"I'm sorry, Belinda, everyone, but I am going to make a confession right here in front of all of you. That's my penance. I feel so guilty. I was pretty, you know." Lorraine said it like it was a crime.

"I was one of the mean girls. We used to pick on the fat chicks, and the ugly ones. The poor kids who couldn't afford decent clothes, or maybe they didn't have anyone to show them how to dress. Anyone different and weak, with no friends to back them up. It was easy. Don't let them sit anywhere at lunch. Knock their tray away, trip them, tell everybody they have bugs, stupid stuff. I never did anything mean on my own, really. I just went along. But I didn't try to stop them. I kept hanging out with them because they were the cool kids. They accepted me." She looked at her daughter sideways, avoiding her eyes. "Honey, if we had a girl like you in middle school, I'm sorry, Baby. We would have been SO mean to you!"

Lorraine rushed over to her daughter and smothered her head in her arms. "I have no right to ask you this, Belinda, but it's for your own good. When they attack you, and we all know they will," she scanned the room. "You just remember, that girl in the back? The one who's not really doing anything or saying anything, just going along? Well, that girl just might grow up to love someone like you more than anything. Just like I love you and your dad. But for now, she's like you. She just wants to be accepted."

Lorraine let go of Belinda's head. She walked to the window where she could gaze far away, facing no one. "What kind of world is this?" she asked the darkening glass. "Where tormenting someone who can't fight back gets us accepted, but my sweet little girl and my amazingly smart husband can't get accepted no matter what they do?"

The Chant

Belinda still had school on her mind the next day when she joined the boys at the picnic table by the pond in the tiny orchard. Jerry's school was supposed to start this Thursday, but he wasn't worried. "The whole town's evacuated!! There's no way school's opening this week."

"I don't have to start school until next week, either," Belinda bragged.

"Oh, yeah?" Jerry poked his finger into his cousin's ribs. "What was all that drama last night then?"

"Nothing," she giggled. She quickly changed the subject. "Do you go to school, Baput? What grade are you in?"

"I am Apprentice to Akash," he repeated, as he had said many times.

"Yeah, but don't you go to school with the other kids? Do the regular kids go to school?" She could fire questions faster than Jerry.

As Baput started to answer, he heard a click. The disk spun softly in the recorder. "We all go to school. We start in our second cycle. We count our ages in three-year cycles, from each First Pomegranate Day to the next.

"First Pomegranate Day, when the nimblies and bumblies come, every three years?" Belinda proved she had been listening.

"Yes," Baput answered, surprised she knew so much. "We start school at the beginning of our second cycle. If you are born on First Pomegranate Day, like I was, then you are three years old when you start.

But, if you were born a year or two after First Pomegranate Day, you wouldn't start school until you were four or five. Understand?"

"Boys and girls together?" Belinda asked.

Baput couldn't tell if she'd understood about the cycles. "Of course not," he barked. "Girls go to Akira's school. We boys go to our school for six years, until our fourth cycle, when we are nine to twelve years old. Then we go to our master's to learn our specialties, as apprentices. In our sixth cycle, when we are at least 15, we ascend to our assigned profession, if we have mastered our skill."

"Like, you'll ascend to Akash," Jerry filled in.

"Yes. If Akash deems me worthy."

"What do the boys learn in school at three years old?" Jerry asked.

"First, they learn to meditate. Later, they learn to read and write."

"Really?" Jerry asked, surprised.

"Yes," Baput replied. "Just a few symbols, how to make their own mark and read other people's marks. There are marks for some things, but not everything.

"Old Akashic is different, more like your English. You string letters together to make words. Only Akash in Training learns to read and write in Old Akashic." He flashed a dazzling smile at Belinda. "And the girl who will be his tether, she learns too, so she can write down the wise words of her Akash for all time." He held Belinda's gaze as he said it, a little bit playful, a little bit serious.

"What do the regular girls learn?" Belinda asked, transfixed.

Baput broke from her gaze. "I don't know! Cooking and cleaning and weaving squares, I suppose."

"But not meditating." It was Jerry this time.

"Of course not," Baput responded, frustration painting wrinkles across his young face.

"Why not?" demanded Belinda.

"But all the boys learn to meditate?" Jerry interrupted.

"Yes, yes," a weary Baput replied. Kids at home all knew this stuff. He'd never had to explain the common facts of life before. It was exhausting!

"Do they get on the Plane?" Jerry kept up the questioning.

"That's why they meditate," Baput's impatience veered into sarcasm.

Jerry babbled on. "How do they teach them? Do they take them to the river, like when you showed me? You said there was a chant they use to teach beginners, but I wouldn't like it. How does it go?"

Belinda joined in. "I want to hear how to get on the Plane. We can go on the Plane, all of us together, and you can show us around.

What's the magic chant, Baput? I learn words to songs really fast, and I never forget them."

Baput sighed. Did he really have to say this again? "I can't show you, Belinda."

Her happy face fell. Even her left eye drooped down. "Because I'm a girl?"

"I am so sorry, Belinda. Maybe, when I am Akash I can change things."

"Break the rules?" Belinda whined, already knowing his answer.

But there was no time for an answer. There was a very unsatisfied young scientist gnawing on a theory like a dog with a bone. "Hey, Bel," the older cousin ordered. "How about you go over there to the other side of the pond. Go watch those ducks over there, see? They have babies!" As if Belinda didn't know about her baby ducks. "Go stand over there and watch them and cover your ears so you can't hear. OK?"

"OK." Belinda trotted around to the other side of the pond where the baby ducks bobbed in the reeds. She covered her ears, scrunched up her disfigured face and closed her eyes tight. "OK!" she repeated.

Baput looked at Belinda, way over there, trying so hard not to hear, and Jerry standing in front of him, finger on the record button, so anxious to hear the silly chant they used to teach babbets how to meditate. "Here goes." He sighed, then cleared his throat. The recorder clicked to life.

> "Do not look at Shavarandu.
> He will burn your eyes.
> Only cool light from Kakeeche
> Can enter your mind.
> Think cool, kind thoughts of giving
> Guided by their silver rays,
> Or evil thoughts from Shavarandu
> Will burn your only world away."

He knew it by rote, from early childhood, but now it sounded so strange! Maybe it was the translation to English. "It doesn't sound as good in English. I tried to make it rhyme, but—"

"Did you change the words to rhyme it?" Jerry worried. "Or is that exactly what it says?"

"That is my best translation." Knowing Jerry's next question, he reminded, "Shavarandu means the sun."

"It burns your eyes," Jerry nodded thoughtfully. "You said it means technology, too."

"Yes," Baput answered, "Like the stuff we found in the Holy Cave, behind the door. Literally, it means, 'the power we fear.'"

Jerry beckoned to Belinda to return.

Baput turned to greet her, feeling terrible for sending her away. Jerry stood behind him motionless, except for his lips that mouthed the words he had already memorized.

Sunday dinner was a classic for the Musiks. A 16-pound turkey stuffed with toasted bread, squash, nuts, "whatever we have, shove it in there," Fran had told Patrick and Belinda. Lorraine stayed home from work, as she'd promised, but she spent most of the day on her computer in her makeshift study (Jerry's bedroom). Belinda kept one eye on the stairs while she helped in the kitchen.

It sure is nice to have my wife home, even if she doesn't cook or even come downstairs, Patrick mused as Belinda suppressed her delighted squeals, smooshing her little hands in the stuffing and shoving them deep into the cavity.

Lorraine emerged at Patrick's call. Fran rousted Elmer and Jerry from the quarters. Patrick's un-masculine cooking duties were being kept secret from the Nauvian men.

They filled their plates. Lorraine, genuinely curious, started the conversation. "What's going on in the Green People world today?"

"It's a doozy!" mumbled Jerry at the same time that Belinda blurted, "They start school at three years old! And the boys learn a poem, so they can medicate, but the girls go to another school 'cause they can't learn that."

"It's meditate. Not medicate," Jerry corrected, eager to announce his discovery.

"Meditate," Belinda went on. "But girls can't learn it, so I had to go to the other side of the pond and block my ears."

"I don't think I like…" Lorraine started to gripe.

Fran interrupted. "The girls go to school? In a culture like that?"

"They need their brainwashing," Jerry said, finally gaining the floor. "You know how I told you about the Plane, and how weird it is that they're so low tech? Well, listen to this poem. This is what they make the little three-year old kids chant when they're learning to meditate."

Belinda blocked her ears again. Lorraine reached over and gently swatted one of her hands down. "You listen," she said sternly. Jerry pressed play.

"Do not look at Shavarandu.
He will burn your eyes.
Only cool light from Kakeeche
Can enter your mind.
Think cool, kind thoughts of giving
Guided by their silver rays,
Or evil thoughts from Shavarandu
Will burn your only world away."

"That's scary!" Belinda objected upon hearing the forbidden poem. "What does it mean?"

"Don't you see?" Jerry chattered excitedly. "It brainwashes them. Shavarandu means 'the power we fear.' It means the sun, but it also means technology. It scares them, so when they surf the Plane, they don't go where the tech is. They don't even see it."

"In meditation. And so young!" Fran mused. "Such a vulnerable state, like deep hypnosis. Brainwashing. But," she continued louder, "Well, it's true, you know."

Jerry flared, annoyed. *Another unscientific truth?* "What do you mean, Mom?"

"They used the tech, and they lost their only world."

Lorraine stared at the picked carcass on the table as if she were cooking it with her eyes. "What did they do?" she asked slowly. "They burned their world away. Then they tried to bury the tech so it wouldn't ever happen again."

"Buried it in the Holy Cave and buried it in their minds," Patrick finished the thought.

Jerry broke the long silence, ready to examine the other side. "But then how come Felsic is so good at motors?"

Fran paused behind him, empty dishes stacked on her arms. "Felsic is what my grandma would call 'not a church-going man.' He probably doesn't meditate that much, does he?"

"Baput says all the men can do it, but they usually don't. Just at ceremonies and stuff. And even then, they just go through the motions."

Elmer exploded. "There's lots of Earth guys like that, and they don't go flying around on no Plane."

"Dad, you don't fly on it."

Elmer plowed through, "They just get it. They're called motor heads. Felsic's like that. He just gets it. We've even got Grandpa's old tractor running. Remember that old blue Ford, Pat?"

"Vaguely," Patrick replied. "I guess I was never much of a motor head. But it's just mechanics, isn't it? That's what they call it: Auto Mechanics. No spooky actions at a distance. Not like electricity, where I flick that switch over the sink and the garbage disposal starts growling and gnashing underneath. Now, that's spooky!"

Elmer picked up the thread. "He can see the crankcase turning, pushing the pistons up and down. It's like his wine press, or their mill, a big grinding stone that the river turns. That's how they crush their rice. Simple mechanics. Not Shavarandu."

"So, they're not *all* that brainwashed," Lorraine mused hopefully.

Belinda piped up. "And the girls aren't brainwashed at all!"

Hakuna Matata

After two weeks, their daily gathering around the computer paid off. The evacuations were lifted, and their neighborhood had been spared. They could go home tomorrow. Elmer taught Felsic five different ways to high five, and they headed off together to the shop to load the four-wheeler on the flatbed.

Belinda was the only one who wasn't overjoyed. She sat on the porch with her unicorn, Dodi, until she saw the boys head to the orchard for the last time. She left her favorite toy behind and headed after them. She found them talking about what they would do when they got home to Jerry's.

"Are you glad you're going home?" she asked with a pout.

"We're just going back to my place," Jerry corrected. "Baput's not going nauve." He used the Nauvian word for home.

"It's nauve now," Baput conceded.

"Are you *ever* going home to Nauve?" Belinda imagined Tamaya, beautiful and perfect.

"Two years from now, at the end of September, on First Pomegranate Day, when the portal opens. I guess. I don't know," Baput sputtered.

"Do you want to go home?"

Baput had to think about it. At that moment, he didn't even want to go home to the Look'N Up without Belinda. "What's there for me?" he wondered aloud.

"Tamaya," Belinda answered flatly. "You have to go home and marry her."

Baput clearly saw that he did not want to do that. But did he want to go home at all? He tried to imagine what was going on there, as he often had since Jerry had convinced him Nauve continued to exist without him.

Who had perished last Season? Did Felsic's family make it back from the Holy Cave? Who was Akash now? Rakta, the War Chief, would be, officially. A good man, but not much of an Akash. He'd had no training, and he rarely meditated, except in ritual before battle. Baput's slightly older cousin, Bazu, would be his apprentice. The only remaining male of the Akashic line.

Now there was someone Baput missed, although Jerry filled that void pretty well. They were so much alike! Both loved to play with science and technology. Even though it was forbidden on Nauve, he had seen Bazu invent some brilliant things. Bazu would be a great Akash, especially since the Door was open, and there was all that tech to explore. But Bazu had received no training, and now there was no one to train him! Baput sighed as he came to a realization.

"I have to go back, if I can. I am Apprentice Akash. No one else has the training. They need me."

"How Lion King!" quipped Jerry.

"Yeah!" cried Bel. "Hakuna Matata, Baput! You can stay with us forever!

"Yeah!" agreed Jerry. "No worries! For the rest of your life! Hakuna Matata, like the Lion King."

Baput had no idea what they were talking about, but they looked happy marching around singing words he didn't know. Belinda stopped suddenly. "But Simba had to go back and be king in the end. It was the right thing to do."

Baput understood the analogy enough to agree. "Yes, I have to go Nauve and be Akash. Sometimes the right thing is the hardest thing."

"But that's what *they* want," Belinda kept fighting. "If you didn't have that, if you could do whatever *you* wanted, what would you do?"

"I'd stay here with you, Bel," he replied instantly.

Belinda beamed. He had boldly used the familiar one-syllable name, telling her what she wanted to hear. Why not? It was just an "if" question. Besides, if he could do whatever he wanted, he could come and go to and from Nauve, and the Look'N Up, and here, and any other *place*, anytime he pleased.

The Ride Home

The green people loaded the van with their truly odd odds and ends, minus the pomegranate trees. Jerry loaded his own stuff more carefully this time, then helped his folks load theirs. Lorraine was in her recently vacated study, heaving a sigh of relief and catching up on her emails. Belinda and Patrick whispered in the music room.

"No," Patrick said, as sternly as he could. "You definitely can't ride in the back with them."

"Why not?" Belinda whined in a whisper. "You're prejudiced, that's why."

"I am not," Patrick objected. If there was one thing he strove against, it was that. To hear his daughter accuse him of it was, well—was he? He stopped to explore his motives. "No," he concluded. "I wouldn't lock my little girl into the back of a truck with a bunch of strangers for four hours, no matter what color they were."

"They're not strangers. They've been here for two weeks. And Jerry's gonna ride back there. He rode back there with them before and there was no funny business, Dad."

Patrick had to grin. "No funny business, huh?"

Belinda promised him so with her soft green eyes. He melted, but, still, it had to be "no." He needed help from the Master, or the Monster, depending on the situation.

"Lorraine!" Patrick called up the stairs, interrupting Lorraine's surfing and sending a twinge of dread down Belinda's spine.

"Be right down," a resentful voice replied. Soon they heard Lorraine's footsteps tumbling down the stairs. "What?" she demanded, looking from husband to daughter.

"She wants to ride in the back of the truck with Jerry and the green people. I said 'no'. She can ride up front, with us."

"Us? I'm not wasting my day riding all the way down there and back. Neither are you, young lady. We're going shopping."

"No, Mom! Not the mall!"

"Oh, yes, the mall. You've been fooling around with that boy so much, I didn't get you to go online with me in time to exchange stuff if it doesn't fit. You've grown in some places more than others."

"I'm a mutation," Belinda claimed proudly.

"Stop it!" Lorraine snapped at her daughter, who would walk with her through the mall to quickly withdrawn pitiful glances from kind hearts and blatant stares and laughter from crueler ones. Sighing at her daughter's burgeoning adolescence, she squeezed the plump hand. "Now go out and say goodbye to your alien friends. You're not going with them."

Belinda rudely withdrew her hand and ran outside to the convergence of greenness around the back of her father's plumbing van. Felsic approached her first. That was odd, but she had no reason to fear Baput's uncle. He barely touched her upper arm, guiding her toward the open back of the van. He pointed inside at two rows of bunk mattresses.

"Here is space for you. Next to Salistar." He let go of her arm and gave in to a fit of giggles. "I tried to get you that spot, next to Baput, see?" he pointed to a mattress across from Star's, too overcome with laughter to talk. Then, as quickly as he had started, he stopped laughing, his face dead serious. "Salistar said 'no,' you sit by her."

Belinda felt that boundless little-girl love for all of Baput's family. She loved this shy, funny little man. He was like a kid, kind of. "Thank you, Uncle Felsic," she patted the back of his hand instead of grasping it, not sure what was OK, and then offered a Nauvian explanation. "I can't go. My momama won't let me."

Felsic nodded. "Ahh, yes, of course. He's too young. You have to wait for Passascenday. A little more than two years, if you live." Felsic hated uttering the customary phrase to that innocent face, but to do otherwise would be to wish her harm.

Belinda was still pondering Felsic's cryptic words when Baput and Jerry came down the path from the quarters, carrying that ridiculous shrine, just like when she first saw him. The moons spun sporadically in the gentle summer breeze. Shastina and Brodey chased each other in a slow lope around the two boys and their weird cargo. Something fell off, and they set the Shrine down. Baput searched the ground behind them and picked up a shiny silver crescent. It took a while for them to get the thing off the ground and moving again. Now, they approached. Too fast. *Slow down, Baput, and let me look at your beautiful green self for just little while more before you go*, Belinda begged silently.

They walked right past her to the back of the van. Jerry let out a cry, "Awwww! Felsic already put the mattresses in!"

Belinda giggled a little, like Felsic had.

Jerry sighed. "Put it down, B. We gotta move some stuff around." They laid their burden down at the back of the van. Jerry headed inside to tear up Felsic's carefully planned seating arrangement and find a safe place for the shrine which, as he had predicted, was falling apart and should have been left behind. He muttered this half out loud, getting louder when he realized Baput had not accompanied him into the van.

Baput came right up to Belinda without Jerry by his side, for once. His dark eyes were big and bottomless. His lashes were thick and long, like his purple-black hair. His face was like no color on Earth.

"I have to go, Belinda." Those eyes looked into hers. "I wish I could stay. I want to see you again. Will I?"

Her green eyes lit up, shooting beams in two directions. Her pale skin, the brownish red freckles on her face, her arms, her tiny hand in his, when had he taken her hand?

"You *will* see me again," she promised. "No matter what."

Jerry emerged from the van, dragging two mattresses and pushing a box of potatoes. He scowled at the tender encounter like they were two rats doing a drug deal. "Come on, B," he ordered drolly.

"I love you," Belinda whispered as Baput tore himself away. He looked back, startled. People didn't say things like that at Nauve. Not in this way. He didn't reply. He had no idea what to say. He walked toward the shrine without looking at his best friend. Together, they loaded the fragile thing into a sheltered corner. Baput silently rejoiced at the darkness that hid his face from Jerry.

By the time they had the mattresses restored, everyone was ready. The Nauvians piled into the dark van with Jerry, his camping lamp, and his new story recorder. Patrick closed the back and walked to the cab, past a sulking daughter who refused to kiss him goodbye.

Love Story

Again they jostled along, thrust about by unseen forces. The silence was awkward. Jerry smelled fear in the tightly packed air. Even Valko seemed to fear the dark, transformative box that rumbled and shook for much longer than the portal had taken to change their world.

Do they understand we're going home now? Jerry wondered. "How about another story?" he asked. It had worked pretty well last time. Besides, he had some documenting to do. He brought out the recorder.

"Romey and Jakima?" Star suggested.

"A woman's story," Valko grumbled.

Jerry turned the recorder on.

"It's a story every young man should know," Salistar retorted boldly, glaring at her son. When it came to raising children, she had the authority. She began.

> "Romey was betrothed to Cinnimar. Eelak was betrothed to Jakima. But Romey and Jakima loved each other."

Valko settled down noisily and snored mockingly. G-Pa sat on a crate, holding his longstick vertically with both hands, resting his cheek on his hands, eyes closed. Felsic lay down on his mattress and fell fast asleep. Still focused on Baput, Star continued her story.

> "Ever since they were little children, Romey and Jakima played together. A boy and a girl. Not forbidden, just odd. Usually little boys play with little boys, like you and Baput. And girls play with girls, when they're not working. But these two played together whenever they could.

"Their parents and the other villagers started shooing them apart, so they took to hiding. They went far out into the orchard, or into the forest. It frightened their parents, even when it wasn't Nimbly Bumbly Season. It angered the parents of their betrotheds, and, as they grew older, their betrotheds got angry, too.

"When Eelak was 15, of age to marry Jakima on next First Pomegranate Day—"

"How old was Jakima?" inquisitive Jerry interrupted.

"She was 12, like Baput is now, and you, too," Star replied kindly, not minding the interruption.

"I'm 13 now." Jerry set the record straight, then returned to the subject. "So, Baput could get married now?"

"No, the boy must be at least five cycles, 15 years old on First Pomegranate Day. Then, he must fight in his first Season. If he and his betrothed survive the three days of nimblies and bumblies, they marry, no matter how old she is. Baput's betrothed is older than he, because she was for his older brother, Batuk."

Jerry offered a polite, "I know. I'm sorry."

"Tamaya is 18 now. But she must wait until Baput is 15, next First Pomegranate Day. She will be 20 then, poor thing." Salistar didn't sound too sorry for the girl. She went back to her story.

"The boy Jakima was to marry, Eelak, was determined to stop Jakima from seeing Romey. He and his popa, Eelan, hid outside Jakima's parents' home for many days and nights until, two nights before First Pomegranate Day, they saw Jakima leaving her house in the deepest shadows of the darkest night. They followed her.

"Jakima met Romey at a crude hut he had built in the orchard. Foolish children! They must have known that the nimblies and bumblies would come, that when the Season was over, the people would come to the orchard to pick, and find their bones. Maybe that was what they wanted, death. But what do fifth-cycle children know of death? They didn't seem to want death when the men found them in their hut, playing Zelk with rocks and sticks they had gathered."

"It is a child's game," Baput explained. "The point is, Romey and Jakima were innocent. Right, Momama?" Baput had never paid much attention to the woman's story before. Now it was as riveting and nerve-wracking as a battle tale, and he was on the wrong side of it. He found himself defending the disobedient pair! He turned the floor back over to the timid woman, who was turning in a compelling performance.

"Eelak and his popa, Eelan, burst in on their little game. They beat Romey and Jakima, tied them together and dragged them back to the village, where the Akash, not my popa, but an Akash long ago, ordered the warriors to stake the two wicked children out on the battlefield in front of the Great Hall, facing each other, not close enough to touch. They were fully clothed, for warmth and decency, but without armor, and totally exposed.

"The two remained staked out before the Great Hall all night. They knew the nimblies would not come until the next day, and the bumblies not until the following night, but still, they were terrified! Would they be left out there through the Season, each one watching their beloved be devoured?

"Dawn came at last. The Akash, the War Chief, and the old Akira filed in, leading Romey's parents, and Jakima's, followed by the true betrotheds, Eelak and Cinnimar, and their parents.

"The Akash asked each one if they wanted him to take the children down before the nimblies came, or leave them. The condition was this: what happened to one would happen to both.

"The parents of the two lovers voted on their behalf. Four votes to free them from the stakes. Eelak, Jakima's betrothed, was considered an adult. He and his two parents voted to leave the two to the beasts. In doing so, they waved Eelak's rights to marry anyone, ever. That is why the parents of Romey's betrothed, Cinnimar, refused to vote, for fear their daughter would become an Unmarriageable, a servant of Akira. Cinnimar was still a child. She had no say.

"So, the parents of the naughty pair prevailed by a single vote. Still, the lovers stayed splayed on the stakes, fearing their doom, all through an agonizingly long First Pomegranate Day Ceremony. That old Akash droned on worse than this one does," she whispered.

"As the men prepared for the trenches, as the women loaded the ganeeshes with food and supplies, Akira and her unmarriageable servants cut the two kids down and brought them back to the Great Hall.

"Sufficiently scared, they stayed apart all cycle, until the next Passascenday, when they were both 15. Romey survived his first season in battle. He could marry Cinnimar, but, due to his past transgression, he could not ascend to Carpenter until next cycle, only after he had completed three years of faithful marriage to his betrothed.

"Romey couldn't bear the thought of being married to someone who wasn't Jakima! To see Jakima around the village every day, married to another, or worse, an unmarriageable servant of Akira! Nor could Jakima bear the thought of Romey being married.

"On the night before Passascenday, the sixth-cycle boys who are due to wed and ascend gather at the back of the Great Hall between the boors and the ganeesh stalls to revel in their first taste of kip wine. In the course of her duties, Jakima brought them another jug. The boys all hooted, 'You stay away from Romey! He is to marry Cinnimar tomorrow.' Romey was the drunkest of them all. That made Jakima happy. He so didn't want to marry Cinnimar! But would he be able to pull off their plan? He winked at her. He was faking!

"She hung around. Romey pretended to drink, but he didn't swallow. He spat it out whenever they weren't looking. When the other boys started to fade, the two lovers slipped out of the Great Hall. No one noticed until the next morning when they assembled for the ceremony and Romey was not among the grooms.

"Of course, they looked for Jakima. Gone, too. The lovers had hoped everyone would stay at the Great Hall to attend the long multi-ceremony, giving them precious time together. But the men were still drunk and full of excitement from the long battle. Those who weren't marrying or ascending didn't care to watch the ceremony they had seen so many times. They took up their weapons and their jugs and went to attack, not nimblies or bumblies, but a boy and girl of their own kind.

"Eelak, Jakima's betrothed, led the way, followed by the brothers of Cinnimar, Romey's betrothed, while she waited in Akira's chamber, adorned in her wedding garb, fearing the worst.

"No one thought they would dare hide in the Holy Cave, but that is where they were found, entwined on the floor in the back. No so innocent this time. They were separated, manhandled, bound again and carried back to the village in time for the end of the ceremony.

"To Cinnimar's heartbreak and Jakima's twisted relief, Akash refused to marry Romey and Cinnimar. Cinnimar never emerged from Akira's chambers that day. She moved from the Antechamber of the Brides to the Lair of the Unmarriageables.

"The two lovers were treated as adults this time. They received the standard punishment. Their clothes were taken. They were draped in a sheer, clingy fabric woven from the webs of lyn spiders, and staked out facing each other, almost close enough to touch, but not quite. For 48 hours they stared at each other's desired forms, alluring in the soft fabric blowing tight against their otherwise bare skin. The aggrieved families of their betrotheds threw things at them and poked them with sticks. Eelak set fire to the fabric wrapping Romey, but Akira's ever-watchful Unmarriageables quickly doused it.

"Their love had ruined two lives. Four, counting their own. When they were finally chopped down, they whispered "goodbye" to each other, knowing they would not consort again, at least for the next three years.

"They stayed apart, thinking if they behaved, Akira would see that their love was true, that it would not die, that they were meant to be together. Then she would relent and let them marry.

"That next Season, when they were both 18, Romey again joined the men in the trenches. Jakima stayed in the Great Hall with the other women, preparing ration packs, tending the wounded and worrying about her beloved. Both were attentive and respectful, waiting for a joyous announcement that never came.

"When Passascenday came, and they saw that their wedding would not be part of the ceremony, our two lovers made a fateful decision. They would run away together, so far that they would never be found. They would live in the woods in a house Romey would build. They would eat roots and leaves that Jakima could identify, and maybe even eat little animals, like dogs do. They wouldn't mind. They would be together.

"It was so easy! No one was watching them. No one cared. They just walked away during the ceremony and never came back. But Akash knew. Akira knew. Life went on in the village.

"Romey, of the Builder Line, built a fine little house where they finally satiated their desire for one another. Five times Kakeeche flew across the sky all together. Jakima gathered roots and greens, planted seeds and cuttings. Romey hunted dracna with his dart gun, and they ate them raw. Romey grew thin while Jakima grew fat.

"It was cold that winter. So cold. Jakima could not get warm enough. 'I can't build a fire, my love,' Romey lamented, holding his darling tightly. 'They will surely see the smoke and find us.'

"'But I must be warm!' Jakima insisted, looking down at her swollen belly. So, Romey built a fire. In a few hours, the men of the village appeared. Again, they beat the pair, tied them up and carried them to the village, whispering about hibudara, a forbidden offspring.

"This time the punishment was most severe. They were stripped totally naked and splayed, arms and legs wide, on tall stakes, side by side. It was Full Kakeeche, and the roundness of Jakima's belly shone like a second full moon in the reflected light.

"They put twine around Romey's testicles and twisted it tight, tight, tight, and left it there all night, throbbing.

"Jakima cried, 'It's too cold! Too cold!' All night she cried, until she stopped.

"At dawn, Romey jerked awake. His testicles lay on the ground below him. There was no blood and he felt nothing. Jakima looked frozen. Stiff blood streaked her thighs and stained the ground below her.

"The Unmarriageables were coming. Without looking at Romey, they unfastened Jakima and lifter her off the stake. Romey watched intently as his motionless mate was carried into Akira's Lair.

"Soon, they brought her out again, lifeless and bloody, and carried her to her parent's home. The Akash himself stepped up to Romey and cut him down. He fell on the ground on top of his testicles, next to his child's blood. 'Be gone,' the Akash commanded. He turned his back on the prostrate young man and walked away.

"Romey's parents covered him with a blanket and helped him to his feet. They tried to take him home, but he broke away and ran into the woods. They tried to chase him but soon wore out. He was lean and fast.

"He never returned to the village. No one looked for him. Sometimes people saw his smoke, on a cold day, but no one bothered to attack his little house again. Some people, kids mostly, you know, they like stories," she mused fondly. "Sometimes they say they see him, to this day. He's a wild man. He eats pinecones and live animals. He screams and howls in a high voice. But we know it's not true, for Romey and Jakima lived many, many years ago."

The tale left Jerry deep in thought. *Nowhere to run. No escape. No otherwhere. And that's three killings, so far. Almost every story has one.* Risking an explosion in a confined space, Jerry dared to venture: "Do you ever have um, two men, or two women, you know?"

Surprisingly, Star smiled warmly. "Ah, yes, often. It is still forbidden, of course, because they would not be betrothed. But the penalty is less."

"Less?" Jerry was surprised. He knew some primitive cultures would kill people for that!

Jerry's surprise confounded Star, but Baput was getting used to explaining obvious things to Earth people. "It's not like they can bear a *hibudara*, a forbidden offspring. They still have to marry their betrothed, though, and have children with them."

"What if they can't have kids?"

"They must try," Star answered. "If they fail, Akira will know why. She is most old and most wise." A dark eye popped open next to G-Pa's staff, above the knobby knuckles. "Of women," Star added quickly. The eye closed. She continued. "Akira keeps the lines apart. Makes sure our pairings produce the best offspring."

Jerry sat up straight, checked the recorder. Still on. Would her answers match Baput's? He tested. "How many lines are there?"

Star answered too quickly for thought, in a voice that was faraway, monotonous, like Baput's Kakeeche Voice, but with a more desperate, defensive edge to it.

"There are many lines! So many it is only Akira who can keep them straight, sort them out and make sure the pairings are right. Only Akira knows how. She is on her third apprentice, and none have ascended.

Two have grown old and died trying. They can't sort out the lines. Akira can't find anyone who understands.

"The apprentice now, Edijay, will be old enough to ascend on next First Pomegranate Day, like Baput." Star whispered like an old lady spreading juicy gossip to a neighbor. "But she won't. Not this cycle, or ever, unless the old woman dies before she does."

Salistar's knowing gossip about Akira's unmarriageable apprentice did little to soothe Baput's tension. In fact, the thought of his first betrothed, Edijay, locked away forever in that dank Lair with no husband and no children made Baput sick in a way he had never felt. It must be the moving-without-moving. He crawled off to a tight, dark space in the front of the truck.

Jerry turned off the tape recorder. He glanced at his friend, curled up on his side with his back to everyone.

Valko stirred, his mumble growing into a small roar that was more than enough for the tiny space. "Women's talk! The boy does not want to hear women's talk! He wants battle stories! Yes, Boy?" So rarely did Valko's roar actually relieve the tension in the room!

So much for no violent TV, Jerry thought hopefully. *These people love this stuff as much as we do. Even the women's stories are gory!*

"Sure!" he replied eagerly.

Roused by the rumbling voice echoing off the sheet metal walls, the Akash was fully alert. "Meldan, Warrior Akash!" he announced.

Meldan, Warrior Akash

Valko didn't consider himself to be much of a storyteller, so he let the Akash provide the entertainment. Despite his recent limitations, old G-Pa could still spin a good yarn. When he was like this, he became the main character. "Meldan, Warrior Akash," Valko conceded to the elder.

Jerry turned the recorder back on. G-Pa knelt, still holding his longstick vertically in both hands, and began the tale.

"Meldan was Second Heir of Akash, just like Baput here." G-Pa looked where Baput had been sitting, then scanned the van until he found him in a dark corner, facing away, whispering to himself in low hisses. The Akash turned away, ignoring him, and went on. "And like our Baput, his older brother, the First Heir, died."

"What happened to him?" demanded Jerry. Was there a fourth murder among these peaceful people?

G-Pa glared at the Earth Boy. "That is no matter here. This is the story of the younger son, Meldan!"

"Yes, Sir," Jerry replied meekly, fully tongue in cheek. His dad got mad when he did that, because he knew it was sarcastic. But it was what the Akash expected, so he bought it.

G-Pa began again. "The elder son, Meldar, was one cycle ahead of Meldan. He started his apprenticeship after three cycles, as usual."

"Nine years old," Felsic translated, giggling. "How come you don't know this stuff everybody know?" he asked Jerry, leaning from his mattress, too close to Jerry's face.

"Different planet," Jerry replied without breathing, leaning away.

G-Pa cleared his throat to retake the cramped little floor.

"Next cycle, young Meldan had completed three cycles, but Meldar was already Apprentice to Akash. A story this family knows all too well." His eyes narrowed sharply at his daughter, who stared back with a venom Jerry had never seen in her, or anyone's, eyes before.

A new rumble seemed to rise out of the background of the engine and the wheels humming on the highway. Was something wrong with the van? Jerry looked at Felsic, an expert on motor noises. Felsic was staring at the source of the noise, but it was no motor. It was Valko, growling under his beard in the barely audible range.

That's about Batuk, Jerry realized, *Baput's older brother, the Calamunga, still haunting the family.*

G-Pa broke from his daughter's glare and his son-in-law's growl and again resumed his tale. "So, what to do with Meldan? Well, he was a very fortunate boy." He gave Baput's back a sidelong glance that Jerry resented.

What? He's ungrateful? Baput hasn't done enough for you guys? Jerry raged in his mind, glancing at his friend's back. *What's the matter with him, anyway?*

"Almost all men are born to their profession," G-Pa explained, "but Meldan got to choose. And what did he choose?"

"The Longstick Line!" they all recited. Even Baput mumbled something to the front of the truck.

"Yes!" the Akash declared, "he joined the Longsticks." He scoffed affectionately. "He wasn't very good, at first. All the other boys were sons of Longstickmen and had been training since their second cycle!"

"Three to six years old! I get it," Jerry volunteered, to stave Felsic off.

"In third cycle, the boys have competitions. They throw spears, shoot arrows and sling rocks; they race and spar. Most importantly, they bond. Boys, men, in a longstick trench have grown up fighting together with their popas and uncles and close-mates. Now here comes this soft, spoiled Akashic Son who thinks he can wield a longstick as well as them. But they were wrong. Meldan knew he could wield a longstick better! Better than any of them, even the instructors."

"Why did he think that?" Jerry had to ask.

G-Pa looked down his scrawny beard at Jerry and replied matter-of-factly, "Because he was Akashic! Felsic is right. You don't know things everybody knows. You are an ignorant animal, like your popa."

"Hey!" Jerry objected.

The Akash, still on his knees, looked down on Jerry like he was a vile insect to be crushed. Then he turned away and went on.

"Meldan joined the longstick line and studied alongside the other boys his age, but he was clumsy and timid. Afraid to strike hard! Afraid to be hit! Oh, how the boys tormented him! They poked him with their little longsticks. They refused to team with him. They wouldn't spar with him in the ring, but they jumped on him in gangs as he walked home.

"He tried to ignore them. No one knew he cried each night in anger. He worked hard, studied hard, learned from the instructors who turned out to be better than he thought. The other boys hated him now! But their hate was more respectful than their ridicule had been. He was an adversary now, no longer just a joke.

"After a full cycle of training, Meldan found himself looking forward to the Season! His brother Meldar would ascend to Akash on Passascenday when the battle was over. Better yet, he, Meldan, would be a warrior! He was still only 12, too young for the trenches. But he was ready. He didn't sleep or play. He stayed in the Great Hall with his cycle-mates, guarding the women and children and practicing whenever he had enough space.

"On the third day, he heard loud voices in the Akash's area. 'He should come! He needs to see!' his popa shouted.

"'No!' the war chief replied. 'It is too dangerous for a boy!'

"Meldan ran to his popa and brother, not knowing what he was volunteering for. 'Can I help? My longstick is sharp and swift, Popa!'

"His popa just laughed. 'He says it's too dangerous for a boy, so I should send a mite like you?' He dismissed Meldan and turned to Meldar, saying, 'Come, Apprentice. It is time.' Time for what, no one knows. They went out. The Akash came back. The apprentice, Meldar, did not.

"That Passascenday, the Akash removed Meldan from the Longstick Line and took him to the Holy Cave as his apprentice. The boy sulked the whole next cycle, refusing to study the books and rituals. He only wanted to practice the longstick, day and night.

"The next Season, Meldan was 15, old enough to ascend, but with only three years of undisciplined training. The Akash was old and tired, and he decided to ascend the young man anyway. Meldan was not enthusiastic, and it broke the Akash's heart. He was ashamed to ascend a son who seemed to embrace nothing but the longstick. He needed to perk the boy up, for show, at least. So, he took a risk. The Akash told the 15-year-old that he could fight the whole battle in the forward longstick line before ascending to Akash, if he lived.

"The war chief was furious with the interference. 'The other ascendants don't get to fight in the forward trench in their first season. It is not fair. You seek Akashic privilege!' he accused.

"'It is for the best,' the Akash argued. 'He practices constantly! He is a good fighter. He will kill his share. And he will be a better Akash for it. You will see.' So the war chief allowed Meldan to take a prized place in the East Trench on the very first day. The other boys his age grumbled and complained, but they did as they were told."

A proud, dignified young warrior shone through the bearded, skinny old man on his knees in the harsh lamplight. He took the longstick in his hand reverently, as if it were Meldan's longstick. Speaking as Meldan, he went on:

"We went to the forward trench to face the first nimblies of the Season. We heard the thrum. We saw them on the horizon, coming out of the mists. The first one came straight at me! I took my longstick and knocked it out of the sky."

Baput's eyes opened to the familiar line of the old tale. *Yeah, great Warrior Akash! Another Second Heir to Akash whose brother died, no one ever asks why. Until Jerry, of course.* He still faced the wall, his back to the others. Had he slept?

He resumed his thinking. *To be with Belinda is death, or worse. For her, too. Those are the rules. But, surely, not on Earth, not while Patrick breathes. Not while I breathe. No matter. We are in the noisy box again, doing that thing Jerry calls 'going.' Going home. Not to Nauve. Back to the Look'N Up that Jerry calls home. And Belinda won't be there.* He closed his eyes again.

G-Pa continued his story as young Melnar.

"Three nimblies circled, looking right at me. I held my longstick tight, with two hands, right at the end, like this." G-Pa demonstrated, holding his longstick at the base and jabbing the dull tip against the van's ceiling.

"I thrust straight up, right through the heart of the diving beast! His partner, enraged, dove next. I held the longstick aloft and firm, the first nimbly still impaled on the tip. The second dove harder than the first, in its rage, and impaled itself on the spike, pushing the first nimbly down the shaft onto my hands. I thrust up again and snagged a third one that dove just as I thrust, stacking itself neatly upon the second, which slid down the shaft and lay limply upon the first. Three on one!"

"A hat trick!" Jerry provided the Earth phrase. "It means you got three in one."

G-Pa nodded excitedly. He had never had a new audience, or a new saying, before. "Hat trick," he repeated.

Felsic joined in. "Hat Trick. One, two, three." He counted on his fingers in English, showing off.

G-Pa Meldan finished his tale.

"The other men in the longstick line dropped their sticks to their sides in a salute to the Warrior Akash! Then they went back to work, impaling thirty more nimbies within a matter of minutes. None penetrated the forward longstick line that day.

"At The Lull, before the bumblies came, they carried me into the Great Hall on their shoulders. I gave a speech, admitting the greatness of the entire longstick line. But," he held his hand by his mouth, whispering confidentially, "I had to admit that I was the greatest longstick man in the history of the Great Battle. Popa immediately conceded the Akashic throne in the Great Hall to me. From there, I could direct the activities, while the less essential persons returned to the trenches to fight."

Jerry added another data point to his egomaniac theory. Again, he wondered about Baput's fate. Engrossed in the war story, he had forgotten all about his friend's distress.

G-Pa turned back into a passive narrator. "Three days later, on Passascenday, Meldan took his place as Akash. He never fought again, and his record still stands. Meldan of the Hat Trick," he concluded, folding back into a sitting position. "Ever since then, the Akash has always carried a longstick, although, sadly, most of us wield it only ceremonially."

They felt the weird force of deceleration, then turning, as the van left the highway and entered the town decked with handmade signs offering the firefighters well-deserved thanks and praise.

As he helped a silent and sullen Baput carry the shrine back to the sauna, two questions burned in Jerry's mind. First, he asked, "do you think when you grow up to be Akash, you'll turn into an egomaniac a-hole like your g-pa and all those other Akashes? 'Cause I'm seeing a pattern here. As soon as you start feeling that power, everybody obeying you, nobody ever questioning you, well, it seems like it'd just be natural. That's why we vote and have more than just the one guy in charge of everything. That's why we question—"

Baput stopped in his tracks and set his end of the Shine on the ground, forcing Jerry to do the same. Dark circles surrounded his near-black eyes as if he hadn't slept in days, prompting Jerry to ask his second question. "What's the matter with you, anyway?"

Baput's sunken eyes probed Jerry desperately. "Don't you see?" he squeaked, "It's Belinda. I love her! But I can't marry her! I have to marry Tamaya!"

"But, Baput!" Jerry countered, naively logical. "It would be better if you married Belinda. She's not related to you at all. Tamaya might be as distant as you can get, but I'm telling you, she's still gotta be at least a little bit related to you, if there's really only 100 people. I told you, you need new DNA."

Tears streamed down Baput's face, wrinkled beyond its years. "You don't get it, Jerry!" he cried. "I *can't* love her. It's not allowed! I *have* to love Tamaya. How do you make yourself love someone? How do you make yourself *not* love someone?

Jerry had no idea how to answer.

6. Discovery

Thanks to a semi-reliable automatic irrigation system powered by an intermittent electrical grid, the Look'N Up Ranch survived their August absence. The brilliant red flowers of the pomegranate trees faded and went about the business of making their valued fruit. The crew fell back into a comfortable routine, roaming the orchards, tending the kips, watching them swell in their bright red coats, through the rest of summer. Jerry had to go back to school. Soon, it was harvest time, Baput's birthday, and the first anniversary of the Arrival of the Nauvians.

Third Lunar Eclipse

Baput stared at the river, an insipid trickle between round, muddy rocks. He turned to Jerry, who was doing the same. "You are quiet," Baput observed. "You know it is not First Pomegranate Day coming. No nimblies and bumblies. No portal opening. Just Easy Harvest, they call it." He smiled a breezy smile. "And my birthday. First Pomegranate Day. The day we arrived. September 27, on your calendar, is Day Number One on ours."

"Yeah. And we're gonna party. All day." Jerry told him with that lopsided grin.

"It's harvest time." Baput replied. "We're too busy. I never get a party. No one does, unless you're special."

Jerry looked sideways at the Alanakash of Nauve, unique to this world. "Who's more special than you?" he wondered aloud.

"Akash gets a celebration sometimes, if he wants one. Then Momama has to do a bunch of cooking, make him special clothes, like on First Kakeeche Day. But he forgets his birthday now, and we don't remind him." He looked down at his wide bare feet. They never had found boots that fit any of the Nauvians comfortably. They often went barefoot when they weren't working. "So I shouldn't have a birthday party, either," Baput concluded, conceding another loss to the old man.

Jerry leapt into the pause with his news. "Well, um, there's a thing tomorrow, anyway. We can't cancel it. It's beyond our control."

Baput was silent for a moment. His face lit up, then crumbled. "It's the tetrad, isn't it? The fourth total lunar eclipse? Kakeeche will —"

Jerry nodded. "You got it, Buddy, and it's early, right at sunset. Everybody's gonna see it."

Baput drew back in fear, not of the wrath of Kakeeche, but the wrath of the pink man. "Your popa will be mad at us. He'll kick us out, or shoot us."

"Oh come on, B!" Jerry whacked Baput on the shoulder. "You know he won't. He really *likes* you guys now. Well, maybe not your g-pa, but he's just an old man—"

"Our Akash," Baput reminded him, his face grim. "Our spiritual leader..." Baput looked at Jerry with his head tilted, "What can we do?"

Jerry rolled his eyes. "Well, we can't stop it. We'll just deal with it. Nobody's gonna shoot anybody, OK?"

"Do what you want," Baput said gravely. "I will take care of my family. And don't worry. Your dad won't need his gun. I promise."

Jerry couldn't leave it like that. He had exciting plans, and his dad was a willing participant. He blurted the agenda. "My dad wants us all to go out there to the flat spot that day, just in case the portal opens. What time did you guys come through? It was about 11 when I brought you to the house."

"I don't know how long we lay there before we woke up. Then, G-Pa and I tried to meditate before we found you. We don't number hours like you do, but it was probably about your 10 o'clock when G-Pa stepped on the Rock. But it was ringing all by itself that day, before Felsic powered the weapon. It won't be like that today, and no one at Nauve would even think to try and fire the weapon. It is not nimbly and bumbly season."

"It's never happened before, so how do you know it's not going to be an annual thing? Maybe every year, on your birthday, you could go back and forth..."

Baput shook his head slowly.

"But, maybe, because of the eclipse..."

Baput gave him a sidelong glance, then rolled his eyes.

Glad Baput had rejected the superstitious idea, Jerry plowed on. "Just humor him, OK? He's so excited about this he doesn't even mind watching the eclipse, as long as G-Pa lets him keep his clothes on. It'll be an all-day party, to celebrate the harvest. We'll do a bonfire and tell stories, and my mom will make you a birthday cake. You can do a ceremony to chant the moon back. Make a sermon about how Kakeeche came back because it is the 13th birthday of the greatest Alanakash ever! That's what an Akash would say, right?"

Baput scoffed, then nodded, smiling. "OK, Jerry. We will watch the eclipse, all together. It is good for my momama to have your momama to cling to."

"She'll be right there by her side the whole time," Jerry promised, "as sure as the eclipse will end at 10:22."

Five Grievances

The next morning, the men loaded the trailer and Little Truck with the summer's prunings, the picnic table and benches, folding chairs, ice chests of food and drink, and Salistar's ration packs. Elmer climbed on top of it all to secure it.

Star leaned out the passenger window and said something sharply in Nauvian to Valko.

Valko tightened his grip on G-Pa's arm. They were going to walk. He would use the unnecessary trip to spend some time alone with his Akash.

"Hurry! Only an hour until, until…" Star trailed off and faced forward as the truck started to roll. She knew the portal wouldn't open at 10 o'clock. Such things could only happen on First Pomegranate Day, eclipse or no eclipse.

Felsic drove the four-wheeler, and Baput climbed in the Jeep beside Jerry, who was practicing his driving every chance he got.

"Akash, I have a grievance." Valko used the formal language, yet he walked at the Akash's side as an equal, skipping the ritual kneeling and bowing, as he had seen Elmer do without consequence. "I speak on behalf of my son."

"And your son is?" G-Pa mumbled, bringing an abrupt end to Valko's patience.

"Oh, snap out of it, Old Man! You know who my son is! Your grandson! Your apprentice! The Alanakash! He carries a heavy load! Much too heavy for a boy his age, because his mentor, the Akash, is not serving his people! And my boy! My little boy!" Valko never cried. "He has stood between us and this, this world, this Earth, where we know nothing! Where we are powerless. Because *you* are powerless! Baput is our true leader, not you. You will make him Akash on Passascenday, will you not?" Valko was not supposed to ask.

"I don't know. His training is not complete," the Akash replied weakly, as if afraid to speak the words. He was right to fear.

Valko's anger doubled. "His training is not complete because *you* failed to train him. *He* has been teaching *you*! As far as I'm concerned, Baput is already Akash, and you are nothing!"

The expedition arrived at the wide, flat expanse of white-gray gravel. About 35 feet from the top of the riverbank, a rock wall covered in dark, shady vines rose thirty feet to where it met the driveway shoulder above.

"Yes. This is the spot," Baput confirmed, wondering about the purpose of this visit to the site of a terrible memory.

"Can you show me exactly where you guys all were when you woke up?" Jerry asked.

"I woke up here." Baput indicated a spot halfway between the river and the vertical bank. "G-Pa was there." He pointed to the subtly mounded center of the otherwise flat spot. "He placed his longstick on the Rock and jumped onto it. That's when it, well, you know."

It was just as Jerry had hoped. Baput was seeing the Holy Cave, where they were before they transported. They had ended up in the same relative positions, here on this flat spot between the driveway and the river, on the Look'N Up Ranch, on Earth. Baput walked around, naming everyone. "Momama and Popa were here, and Felsic was there..."

"I was here!" Felsic interrupted, stepping to a spot close to the riverbank. "I pedaled from here." His smile dropped suddenly. "So I could watch Peratha and Trillella! The river!" he cried, rushing to the top of the riverbank. "Did they land in the river, and..." he couldn't finish.

Elmer pulled his friend back from the overhanging bank. White algae draped the rounded cobbles in the bottom of a dry pool below their feet. Blackberry vines crawled up the gravelly sides.

Jerry rushed to Felsic's other side. "No, the river was low, and it was way over there." He pointed to the other side of the broad, dry riverbed. Green, still water glinted dully in the hazy sun behind a row of willows.

"Are you sure, Son? It was a year ago," Elmer cautioned.

"Dad, I'm out here almost every day. At the Horizontal Tree, the river is close, but up here, it's way over there. I always wondered why. Anyway, it was just like now. It's always like that, this time of year, before it starts raining. They might have fallen in that hole, though." He pointed to the dry pool below them.

Jerry lowered himself into the hole, drew his machete, and probed the blackberry vines under the overhang.

Baput took on the role of comforting Felsic. "They weren't drowned, so they could have cried out. We would have heard them. Or they would have heard us and come to us. And what about Heffala? She was with them. It's pretty hard not to notice a ganeesh!"

"Maybe Heffala couldn't fit through the hole," Felsic whined miserably.

"There's nothing here," Jerry reported. "Like I said, the river hasn't been here since then, so if there were any sign, it'd still be here." He started to add, "Unless an animal dragged them off," but he bit his tongue. He grabbed his dad's extended hand and scrambled out of the hole.

As they wandered back toward the open area, Elmer addressed the group. "So, the Holy Cave was here, right?"

"Akash, I have a grievance," Valko repeated the ceremonial language, still walking at G-Pa's side, not kneeling. "I speak on behalf of my brother's family. His wife, Peratha, and his daughter, Trillella."

"What is your grievance?" the Akash replied formally.

"You left them outside, unprotected, with the first flight of the nimblies on its way."

"They had a ganeesh."

"You used them as bait!" Valko accused. He had never spoken these thoughts before. "I would not have let you leave them out there at night, when the bumblies came." He dared show his fist to the Holy Man!

The Akash pulled against Valko's grip on his arm. "What would you have me do?" he brayed, "Allow two *females*," he sneered the word, "not of the Akashic line, to enter the Holy Cave? That would be blasphemy!"

"*You* couldn't commit blasphemy, eh?" Valko squeezed G-Pa's arm even harder and pulled him closer, stared down at him with his piercing eyes. "You committed Shavarandu! And it is not the first time you have aggrieved my brother!" He spat, white teeth bright against the black beard. He shoved G-Pa away from him while still holding his arm.

Elmer held center stage, his eyes far away.

Jerry sensed a story on the wind. He hoped it was relevant.

"Well, there was a cave here, too," Elmer began with a revelation. He gestured vaguely at the flat area around him. "Just an outline of a cave, anymore, but it looked like it used to be a big one." He walked toward the central mound, arms spread apart. "You coulda drove a truck into it. Except you couldn't, because it was full of silt and sand, like the river came up once and filled it all in. Must have been a hell of a flood!" He gazed at the insipid flow, far away and at least five feet lower than where they stood.

"The river was higher then, Dad."

"I know. There was more water back then. Less people."

"Yeah, but not just that, Dad. I mean, the bed of the river was higher. It was probably right here, that's why there's all this gravel where we're standing. And when it was here, it ran right over that cave hole, filling it with silt and gravel. Then, later on, it meandered over there to where it's at now."

"Youuuu, whatever," Elmer shook his head. "Well, anyway, it was weird rock." He picked a loose specimen from the viney wall. They passed it around, turning it over curiously. "My Dad hadn't seen anything like it around here. Neither had my grandpa, or my mom. She taught science, you know," he informed them proudly.

"It broke into nice flat blocks, like bricks. That's what Dad liked. Great insulation, not flammable. He decided to make a sauna out of it. Dad did all the mining. Me and Patrick, we were around you guys' age, maybe a little younger. We just loaded and hauled, loaded and hauled. We had a wheelbarrow at first, until Dad realized he was killing us, so he got the four-wheeler and that trailer. Much better. I got to drive. But we'd still get so tired! Good thing my grandpa made the Horizontal Tree. We sure did use it! You kids like it too, huh? And your G-Pa sure likes the sauna!

"Dad hacked that thing to pieces with a pickaxe, till you couldn't tell it was a cave anymore, till all that was left was the pile of silt from inside. That kind of slumped down and spread out and fell into the river over time. Patrick and I poked at it with a shovel, trying to find a hole to some deep cave, but you know how it is digging sand. The hole just kept filling back in as fast as we could dig, and we gave up. We were sick of that place by then.

"So the main cave is gone, but I think there's still a tube that runs across, under all them hanging vines." He swept his arm along the 100-foot length of weedy edifice. "In fact, I know it does, 'cause, um…" he looked at the two boys, staring at him raptly, so much like him and Patrick! "Nothing, I just never told my dad there was more of that rock, or we'd still be hauling it!"

Jerry was thinking too fast to notice his dad's cover-up. He walked slowly around the flat spot with his arms spread out, just like Elmer had. "So this whole area was inside a cave?" he asked.

"Yep," Elmer answered. "Here's where the opening was. Like about from here," he paced about 10 feet, "to here, and about half again as high, an arch, right here." He stood, legs apart, arms above his head, hands joined, forming an arch.

"OK, guys. Say that's the entrance to the Holy Cave," Jerry suggested. "Now show me exactly where you were in the Cave, and what you were doing."

Baput shut his eyes. He could see the Holy Cave. He climbed the low mound in the middle of the flat spot, counting his paces "This is exactly where the Holy Rock was."

Jerry marked the spot with a stick. Eyes still shut, Baput walked to the back of the invisible Cave and stopped where the Death Door would be. "This is where Batuk died."

"Oh, no, Baput." Felsic wondered how Baput could make such a mistake, but he had been very young when it happened. "Batuk would be down there, in the river, like Peratha and Trillella. He fell down there."

"No. He died here," Baput said cryptically, and said no more.

Once again, Valko addressed the Akash formally. "Akash, I have a grievance. I speak on behalf of my son."

"We have already addressed your son's issue to my satisfaction."

"Not to mine," Valko grunted, "but I speak now for my other son."

"Batuk's death was an accident," the Akash retorted dismissively.

Valko grew even larger as he filled his lungs with air, alarmed by his own thoughts. The Akash toyed with his patience. He wanted to strike him! No one had ever done so. It took him a minute to find his words.

"I know it was not," he said with carefully assembled calm. "He did not fall. He was alert and agile. He knew the Holy Cave too well."

Fully awake now, the Akash sputtered his outrage. "Well, *I* didn't kill him! Is that what you think?"

"You needed him out of the way, so Baput could ascend as Alanakash. And right after, you had the Door open. You used him in some way."

"Of course I did!" the Akash replied, lucid and unapologetic. "Did you not want your son to die usefully? He could never ascend, Valko, not with an Alanakash in the family. You know that."

"You could have found a place for him!"

"Ah, but I did! But I didn't do it. He did it himself."

"You told him he would ascend. You led him on, so he would do your bidding."

"He did it on his own, willingly, because he knew it was the right thing to do. It was his destiny. He could not be Akash, but he gave his life to save us all."

"Tell me, Akash," the words could barely escape Valko's throat. "What did he do?"

"He opened the door to the Chamber of the Old Ones, fully knowing that to do so was certain death."

Eyes open now, Baput continued his slow walk until he reached the viney wall. Locusts buzzed behind the dense vines that wiggled slightly in the breeze. Jerry, Felsic, and Elmer joined him, craning their necks to look straight up. Felsic drew his machete and stuck it in between two of the thick, twisted vines. It went right in, touching nothing. His hand followed it in, then his whole arm, up to the shoulder before the machete struck rock. He pushed the vines aside and peeked in, then drew back and swiftly hacked through both vines, making a man-sized hole.

Jerry grabbed his cell phone and illuminated the darkness behind the curtain. They stuck their heads in slowly, one by one, and looked up. Above them, much farther than Felsic could reach with the machete, was a roof of solid cave rock, dripping with stalactites. Something about the way the sweat gleamed on the purple-stained ceiling in the blue light told them the roof was rounded like the outside of a tube.

Baput gazed up into the darkness and gasped, "The chimney!"

"What's that?" Jerry asked.

Baput told him and Elmer about the chimney that ran horizontally inside the ceiling of the Holy Cave, conveying smoke from the fire pit behind the Holy Rock to a little hole high in the Cave's west wall, about 100 feet away.

Elmer abruptly left the dark space and walked toward the river, then turned back to look at the cliff again, eyes scanning downstream.

Valko and G-Pa approached the Horizontal Tree in awkward silence. Valko could hear the others. He knew they were close to their destination, but he was in no hurry to reach that spot where he'd found himself a year ago, lost, his head splitting. Besides, he was not finished with his grievances.

He guided the Akash to sit on the smooth trunk of the strange tree where they had first seen Jerry. He folded his arms across his chest and looked down at the Akash. He did not kneel or bow, but again used the formal language. "Akash, I have an accusation."

An accusation was much worse than a grievance, especially if leveled against the Akash himself. Had this ever been done? Apparently not, based on the old man's reaction. "What is your accusation?" he warbled incredulously.

"You have committed Shavarandu! You uncovered and used the forbidden magic of the Old Ones. You unleashed the Power we Fear!"

"It was necessary!" the Akash squealed his defense. "You know as well as I do, the situation is dire! If we don't find a way to beat the nimblies and bumblies, we will all perish!"

"But did you know *this* would happen?" Valko gestured vaguely. "Did the books of the Old Ones say that if we used their slow, clumsy, inefficient weapon we would end up in some otherwhere with filthy air, so noisy you can't hear the Plane, where we have to hide?

"And did we save Nauve? I doubt it. I could have dropped that many nimblies in that much time with my longstick." This last was an exaggeration, but Valko had a point. "That *thing*, no. *You!* You killed my first son, endangered my second, and landed our whole family in unimaginable jeopardy. That Death Door should never have been opened."

The Akash struggled to his feet, avoiding Valko's eyes.

Valko offered his arm, and they began the final leg of their journey—and Valko's last grievance. "We are a third of the way through the cycle, and you are not prepared. Will there be nimblies and bumblies?"

"No," the Akash answered swiftly, but guardedly. "We left them at nauve."

"How do you know? You could feel them, if they were here, could you not?"

"I do not feel them. They are not here." G-Pa sounded strangely confident for someone who had spent the past year crippled by uncertainty and a dread that grew as each day brought them closer to the Season.

"You don't feel the Plane, either, anymore," Valko reminded him. "Perhaps you just can't feel the nimblies and bumblies because you are broken."

"It is simple. At the time we, um…" The Akash struggled for a word for "left," settling for a wave of his hand and an understanding nod from Valko. "The bumblies had not arisen yet, so they could not have been at the Cave. They would never nest in the Holy Cave. You know that."

Valko nodded but countered, "But the nimblies were flying around crazily, veering towards the Cave, hitting the walls. One may have made its way in."

"A nimbly, or many nimblies, could not have survived hibernation without a bumbly to lay its eggs on. Everyone knows this," G-Pa concluded dismissively. He was crisply lucid, but there was something else. Valko was sure the old Akash was still hiding something. *After all this! How could he?* Valko seethed.

"Does Baput feel them?" G-Pa asked, his eyes on the rough ground of the narrow trail. They were almost there. They could hear Baput and Felsic describing that fateful day a year ago.

"You ask me?" Valko whispered harshly. "You work with the boy every day, do you not? You have not trained him to hear them, because he has been training you, ever since we…" he mimicked the Akash's vague gesture.

The trail opened onto the fatal spot where they had first touched the Earth. Now, their family was standing with the pink Earth family, looking at a vine-covered cliff. Before they were spotted by the others, Valko asked the Akash one last time. "How can you be sure the nimblies and bumblies did not follow us here?"

"Because there are no caves," he declared.

The boys rushed up to greet them.

Baput handed the Akash a flat rock. "G-Pa! We found a cave!"

Elmer beckoned to Valko and guided him away from the others.

Baput, Felsic, and Jerry escorted G-Pa to the flat spot.

Baput spoke quickly in Nauvian. "G-Pa, look, it's Holy Cave rock! See? This is where we woke up. We were in the Cave, then we weren't —"

Insight dawned in G-Pa's eyes. "This rock is from the Holy Cave! Where's the rest of it? Did it break when we...?" G-Pa trailed off, unable to imagine what would cause such destruction.

"No, G-Pa. This cave was here on Earth since before we came," Baput started to explain, but suddenly stopped. How could he tell the Akash that Elmer and Patrick destroyed the Holy Cave?

He was spared when G-Pa suddenly threw his head back, his eyes and mouth wide open. He pointed high on the vine-covered monolith behind the flat spot. "The chimney!" he bellowed. He walked up to the wall as if in a trance. Baput and Felsic rushed to his sides.

Jerry stayed in the middle of the flat spot, wondering what his dad was whispering about as he steered Valko downriver. They stopped about 50 feet downstream. Elmer pointed at something high on the cliff, then held his hands in a circle about two feet around.

Valko was so inscrutable, with his grunts and behind-the-beard mumblings, that Elmer never knew how much the big man understood. He preferred to communicate through Baput or Felsic. But this was dad stuff. He guided Valko downstream on a narrow, rock-strewn trail where no one had ever driven. He retold the story of the cave on Earth, and more.

"I didn't tell the boys, because, well, you know how boys are," Elmer explained.

Valko grunted, as usual.

"We were about 10 and 13 then. After we took the cave apart, Patrick and I went poking around up there on that cliff." He pointed two-thirds of the way up the 30-foot cliff. "We found another cave up there. It's just a tiny hole, barely big enough for us kids." He made a two-foot diameter circle with his hands. "It's buried in those vines, so you can't see it unless you go climbing up in there like a couple of dumb kids with nothing better to do and no common sense. And that's just what we did. We squirmed inside, me first.

"It got tighter and tighter, to where I couldn't turn around. Patrick was right behind me. I could only go forward, and I didn't want to. I panicked and yelled, 'Back out! Back out!' I kicked my brother in the face by accident. Broke his nose, messed up his face even worse than it already was. We told our folks he fell down on the riverbed. I didn't want to get yelled at for being stupid and getting Patrick hurt, and neither of us wanted my popa to know there was more of that confounded rock up there. I just thought you should know. There's a little cave up there." He pointed to the near-invisible hole again, once more demonstrating the size with his hands.

Convinced Elmer had more information, Jerry summoned the troops and headed for where the dads were talking.

Felsic and Baput followed, supporting G-Pa, and the three generations of Nauvians followed Jerry down the path between the riverbank and the high, viney wall, talking excitedly in their native tongue.

As they approached Valko and Elmer, G-Pa drew back sharply against the supporting arms of his subjects. Even Jerry could feel the current of white light drilling through the air from Valko's eyes to the Akash's.

Valko charged up the trail towards them. He inserted his face, verdant green above his imposing beard, deep into the Akash's weary yellow countenance. "No caves, huh? There's a cave right up there." He pointed up and to the left. "A little one. The perfect size for them to hide in!"

Felsic and Jerry rushed past the tense group, following where Valko had pointed, down the trail that was rougher now, barely a deer track.

The Akash sputtered. "I, I told you, they can't be here, because, because the bumblies had not arisen."

"Then later you said it was because there is no cave. Well, there *is* a cave. What does it mean, Old Man?" Valko reached for G-Pa's collar, to shake him, but he found Baput's hand instead. His son looked up at him with troubled eyes, and he let go, ashamed, but still fuming.

"Look!" Felsic shouted in English, "The wall ends here and wraps around so it's facing downriver now, toward the Great Hall, just like the Holy Cave!" His face torqued with confusion.

Even Jerry's familiar concept of *place* was strained as he gazed downriver toward town, toward the village on Nauve, and wondered how far it went; this overlap, this eclipse of worlds.

Felsic's hoot pierced his thoughts. "There it is! The hole where the smoke comes out!" He pointed about two-thirds up the cliff.

The others gathered around, searching the vines for the small black hole they concealed.

Baput found it quickly. He knew where the smoke came out. He'd seen it on plenty a morning during his early training. It meant he was late, that the Akash would scold him and whine about how His Holiness was forced to make a fire all by himself in the cold Cave when he should have been meditating or training his lazy apprentice.

He looked up to his left. The wall was farther from the river here, and less viny. It rose about 10 feet higher than the hole, then levelled abruptly in a shelf. Another cliff rose behind it, an oak tree leaning over it, seeming to jut from the flat top of the wall.

Baput knew that tree. It grew at the edge of the West Orchard, hanging out over the driveway. From there, you could see the gate and the county road beyond it. He used to wait there for Jerry to come out of that big, yellow school bus.

The Akash pressed against him.

"It's the Queen, isn't it, G-Pa?" Baput asked gently.

The old Akash spoke only to Baput, but the others gathered around, listening. "It's called a queen, like the queen of the *kims* that pollinate the kips. A bumbly covered with nimbly eggs, as usual, but they only make a queen if people have been working with the Rock, making it vibrate."

"Committing Shavarandu," Valko added with a thickly implied, *'I told you so'.*

Ignoring him, the Akash presented his new theory: "The Queen forms when we ring the Rock, but she won't wake up on First Pomegranate Day. She stays asleep deep in her cave, her babbets unborn, until the Rock is silent. You see, they fool us. We use the Rock to kill all the nimblies and bumblies. We dance and sing." He jiggled his head and arms and chanted in a mocking tone, "'No more nimblies! No more bumblies! Not ever, no more!' We no longer ring the Rock. The Queen awakens, her babbets are born, and it all begins anew."

Valko's face swooped down on the Akash like an eagle on a fish. "Why didn't you tell us this before? It's been a whole year!"

"There were no caves!" the Akash insisted shrilly.

"Sooo," Valko worked up a roar, pointing to the little hole in the wall. "The *nimbumblyborg* could be right up there! Ready to attack us on

First Pomegranate Day, two years from today. What shall we do, Akash?" He glared at G-Pa.

Then he turned to his son and asked again, "What shall we do, Akash?"

Staggered by the implication, Baput had an idea. "If the Cave is here, maybe the Rock is here, too, buried under all that sand. If we can find the Rock, we can make it vibrate, and the Queen will stay asleep."

"Until we find a way to kill her!" Jerry added. Eight purple-black eyes pierced his raving baby blues.

Embarrassed, Baput rushed to explain. "We can't kill them while they are hibernating."

"Insitucide!" An outraged Akash bellowed the word for the sin of killing nimblies and bumblies during their three-year slumber.

Valko took one more shot. "You cannot commit Insitucide or let women in the Holy Cave. But you can commit Shavarandu, not knowing what might happen."

"I didn't know *this* would happen!" G-Pa flailed.

Valko had had enough. Eyes blazing at Baput, he declared, "Maybe it's time for someone else to decide which rules we obey and which ones we disregard." The words were not mumbled into his beard, but loud and unmistakable, to a Nauvian. He spun on his heels and strode off.

Felsic and G-Pa followed close behind, but Jerry held Baput back. "Dude, did you hear your dad? Sounds like he's gonna ascend you to Akash right now. Maybe today, for your birthday!"

Baput rolled his eyes. He was getting pretty good at it. "Don't hold your breath. G-Pa won't ascend me just because Popa says so. It is up to the Akash."

"But, here on Earth, your popa has more power than your G-Pa. Here, your G-Pa is just an old man."

"Then being Akash doesn't really mean anything, does it? Now, what time is it?"

Startled, Jerry checked his phone. "Oh, crap! It's after 10. The portal! If it's going to open, it's already —" He broke into a run. Baput shrugged and loped after him. They caught up to the others and soon reached the flat spot, where an array of vegan and not-so-vegan delicacies surrounded an apple cake topped with fresh-picked blackberries.

Fran greeted them with a bright smile, her lips smeared in purple gaa. "Where have you guys been? It's way after 10," she jeered. "If the portal had opened, we'd be gone, with all this food."

Star earned her name with a grin that was stellar. "We are stuck here on Earth!" she chirped. "Come and have Baput's birthday cake."

Elmer's G-Pa

Fran lit the 13 candles. They all waited expectantly around the flaming pastry.

"Make a wish and blow them out," Jerry encouraged. "Like I did, remember? It's a custom."

Baput closed his eyes and chanted, "No more nimblies, no more bumblies, not ever, no more!"

"Not very original," Jerry mumbled as the chanting began and went on for way too long.

Baput steadfastly refused to "spit on cake." Fran deemed it a wise cultural preference, and plucked the candles from the cake one by one, snuffing them with her tough fingertips. She cut thick slices for everyone. Baput grabbed a hefty piece and wolfed it in three quick bites. He washed it down with the last quart of last year's home-canned pomegranate juice. The others ate just as quickly, finishing the ceremonial dessert first and then nibbling on rice and vegetables, or cold cuts and chips.

The men unloaded firewood from the trailer, and Elmer and Jerry carefully arranged it in a teepee structure. They surrounded the pyre with chairs and picnic benches. Fran and Star sat close together on a bench across from the one Baput and G-Pa shared. Valko lounged in an oversized folding chair, his beard spread across his chest, looking like a green Viking king on a throne. One of Elmer's beer bottles dangled in the cup-holder of Felsic's favorite chair from the shop.

"Why a fire?" Baput asked. "It's daytime, and warm."

"It's fun," Jerry explained. "It's another custom."

"The air is bad enough already," Valko grumbled under his beard.

"We just ran from a fire!" Felsic protested.

"We sit around the campfire and tell stories." Elmer lit the newspaper at the base of the structure and seized the floor. "And I have a story to tell. About my g-pa."

"Oh, boy," Fran muttered.

Elmer scoffed. "Now I ain't told it too much, have I, Jerry? Not like my Grandpa told me, so many times I could tell it in my sleep, but I don't."

Jerry blew on the fire, coaxing it gently while Elmer grabbed a beer from the ice chest and settled into his folding chair. White smoke plumed straight up, dissipating in the clear sky.

Baput checked on G-Pa. The Akash stared into the growing flame, his breathing slow and deep. *Is he meditating already?* Baput hoped so. Fire, with its ever-changing frequencies of light, heat, and sound, was one of the best ways to the Plane.

Elmer launched his story.

"My grandpa came from Oklahoma in the Great Depression. He was 12, just like Baput when he got here. Cars and trucks were new. People didn't know anything about them, like Valko here, no offense."

Valko grunted good-naturedly. Elmer smiled warmly at Salistar.

"And, of course, moms worried about food. They worried a lot! Because there wasn't near enough. My grandpa, his name was Elmer, too. So was my dad's. Until he was 12, his family lived in a little shack on a farm and worked for the owner. They had a garden and a pig and some chickens, and they picked this huge cotton farm for the man. Hard work, like picking poms. They were dirt poor, but they were living.

"They say it was the dust bowl, but it was also Big Ag. They mechanized. They didn't need all those people squatting on their land and picking cotton. They had machines to do that. So they bulldozed their house down. Them and all the other pickers. There were flyers out saying 'Come to California! Lots of farm work! Green paradise!' So they packed up their one truck, that only Grandpa and his older brother, Harvey, knew how to drive, and headed west. It took six months. Lousy, broken-down gas-hog truck! Might as well have been a covered wagon!"

Elmer drained his beer and got another, embracing the part.

"When they finally got here, the place was packed! Everyone in Oklahoma and Arkansas had got kicked off their farms and seen them flyers, too. So here they all were, all wanting to work the same fields. There were just too many of 'em! Not enough jobs, not enough food, no room in the quarters. People lived in miserable camps called Hoover towns, in honor of the President. There were so many people desperate for work, way more than they could hire, so they lowered the pay, lower and lower and still so many desperate people took the jobs that they could pick a whole orchard clean in a day.

"But the pickers didn't make enough to buy a loaf of bread at the end of that day, even with the whole family working. If you had to drive to and from a camp, well, then you'd also need a car or truck, and gas. You couldn't even afford to go to work now. You were really stuck. Or the guys in the camp'd steal your gas, or slash your tires so you couldn't go to work, and they'd get your job. That's your fellow Okies and Arkies! And you shoulda seen what the locals would do to them."

"They hated them?" Baput asked in a dry throat.

"You betcha!" replied Elmer, "How did you know?"

"Were they another color?"

Elmer looked sadly at Baput, then at Jerry.

"I've been teaching him about racism," Jerry said solemnly. "He needs to know."

Baput recited: "You also said sometimes they hate because a lot of people come, so there's not enough re-sour-ses."

"Exactly!" Elmer beamed. "You're a good teacher, Son. Maybe too good. Airing humanity's dirty laundry, eh? But that's it. There were just too many of them. If a horde of people showed up here, I wouldn't hate 'em, but it would be a problem, because they would be a threat to my family. What if my family doesn't have enough now, because of them? Maybe I *would* get to feeling hate for them, if things got bad enough. I like to think I wouldn't. But I'd have to do something. A man fights for his family, right, Valko?"

Valko, unusually engaged in the story, nodded his huge head, "Yes! We fight the men who come from otherwhere!"

"You're getting the idea, Buddy," Elmer was sad to say. "Now, where was I? The hate. Yeah. See, my grandpa had The Eye." He gestured up and to the left. "You know, like my brother, and Belinda."

Baput's heart leapt to attention.

"So they got picked on worse than anybody. Being 12, from a penniless Okie family, and funny lookin' with a crooked eye, poor little Elmer had some tough times."

Baput didn't follow at all. "Because of his eye? They hated him for his crooked eye?"

Elmer had never thought anything of it. It seemed natural to him, not sensible, or good, but unfortunately, normal. Pleased and relieved by their ignorance, he tried to think from a new perspective. "Well, yeah. It's different. Most people hate anything different."

"They hate Belinda?" Baput's voice rose and cracked, his chest and shoulders suddenly tense.

Elmer explained slowly. "That ain't hate, really. That's kid stuff. Making fun of people. They think it's funny. They can get awful mean, though."

"They hurt her?" Baput could barely breathe the words out.

"Not physically. They hurt her with words. They hurt her feelings. I know 'cause they used to tease Patrick, too, when we were kids. I used to have to stick up for him. Got in a lot of fights, until he got older and told me to let him fight his own battles." He saw the horror on the faces of his audience and tried to reel it back. "That's boys, though. Girls don't usually beat each other up."

"But girls can be awfully mean," Fran added. "They can hurt you bad. The kind of hurt that lasts a lifetime."

Tears stained Star's face.

Baput's face flushed an ugly brown.

Valko caught Elmer's eye and pointed at Baput. "A man fights! Yes!" he told Elmer, nodding vigorously.

Valko's understanding got Elmer past the awkward moment.

"Now, back to my story. They lived that way for two years, can you imagine? Things were so bad that if you ever got something, you'd feel guilty about it, want to give it away, or share it. But you didn't, 'cause you had to take care of yourself and your family. Even little cockeyed Elmer was always looking out for his family."

Elmer found himself looking at Baput. He noticed they all were. He went on.

"My grandpa always said it was a miracle when Mr. Charles Richardson came cruisin' through the camp in his fancy car looking for the two sorriest families he could find. He was setting up a brand-new almond orchard, and he didn't know the first thing about farming. He saw poor little cockeyed Elmer outside their cardboard shack, playing with the scrawny, blond-headed runt from the tent next door, and he hired both families, the Musiks and the Fergusons: two brothers, a little sister and a mom, but no dad. Short guys, but strong, hardworking, like Felsic here."

All this talk of family had rendered Felsic silent. He finished his beer too fast. His hand slipped slyly into the ice chest for another.

"He said he hired 'em because of that Bible verse about 'the least of these.' They laid pipes and planted trees, put up fences and scratched in the roads. They built the house and quarters, even dug the well. Long days of hard work, I tell ya!" He grabbed another beer. "They had plenty of food, and they got paid more than most. Mr. Richardson got some hate for that. The other growers didn't like him paying a decent wage. They said it 'wasn't the American way.' But word never got back to them other stiffs in the camps, 'cause our families never went back.

"Now that Eddie Ferguson was a hell of a mechanic. Like I said, folks didn't know much about cars then. Like computers now. So, after a few years, when the orchard was established and they had some money saved up, the Fergusons took off up north and opened a mechanic shop up around where Patrick lives now. Except for the lovely Ruth Ferguson, who stayed on as a cook and housekeeper for Mr. Richardson and ended up being my gramma.

"See, old Charlie Richardson never married and had no kids. So he needed a lady to cook and help around the house, especially since he was getting on, and there was still so much work in the orchard! My great gramma, Betty Ferguson, she was a strong woman who could work all day in the fields with the men if she didn't have to tend to the cooking. Elmer's big brother, my Uncle Harvey, worked hard, too, until he went off and got killed in the Great War.

"So, young Ruth cooked for them all, cleaned the house and the quarters, did everyone's laundry, all that stuff. She worked harder than anyone," he acknowledged, nodding at Fran and Star.

"A tether!" Fran connected.

"Yes! Tether!" agreed Star. That one, they all understood.

"Ruth stayed because she loved our Elmer, cocked eye and all. When they were old enough, they got married. Mr. Richardson let him live in the house, and when those two started making babies, they turned that place into a home. Old Man Richardson now had a family. The kids were like his grandkids. And one of them rug rats was my dad.

"On the day they got hitched, Mr. Richardson signed his almond ranch over to them, while he was alive, so those sons of b's in town couldn't rip 'em off. And that's where we sit right now."

He announced the surprise ending as if his audience were capable of thinking otherwise. "And when the last of the almond trees aged out, we put in pomegranates."

Elmer downed his beer and launched his conclusion. "Now, it's because my grandpa felt that hate, and got that miracle, he always taught my dad and me and Patrick not to hate people who are different but to help people in need, no matter what color, or how poor and desperate they are. That's when you gotta help 'em! Even if there are too many, and it don't seem like you can make a difference, you can help just one person. Or one family. That might not seem like much in the big world, but it sure makes a difference to that one person.

"And Mr. Richardson got a lot for helping. He got a beautiful orchard. But more than that, he got a family. He got love," Elmer blubbered.

"One beer too many," Jerry mumbled, embarrassed. But when he looked around at the faces gazing through the fire at his dad, he thought again: *Good story. Good tell.*

Elmer had a new chapter to add: "You know what? If Mr. Richardson hadn't helped my family, none of us would be here now. And what would have happened to you, my friends, if this ranch was owned by some hater, and you showed up? They woulda shot you on sight! It's the gift that just keeps on giving."

"What is shot?" asked Valko.

G-Pa snorted and stirred, wiggling his toes and fingers first, like he had taught Baput to do. Baput watched him open his eyes. A peaceful, enlightened smile lit G-Pa's face. He had ascended! Had he learned anything more about the Queen?

Baput leapt to his feet to help him up.

Suddenly Star was there beside him. "I'll take him," she offered. "Go, on! The men are calling you." She wrapped her arm around G-Pa. and escorted the old Akash to a lounge chair. Fran walked beside them, a tight look on her face.

Francina never looks like that, Baput thought. *Maybe it's the firelight.*

Jerry, Elmer, Felsic, and Valko were standing around the fire, talking excitedly. Elmer and Jerry were pointing their forefingers at each other, thumbs up, then squeezing their thumbs down against their hand and yelling, "Bang!"

As Baput arrived, Elmer pulled his gun out of the holster and removed the clip. He handed the empty gun to Jerry. Jerry pointed to its different parts, trying to explain how it worked. He needed a translator.

"Baput knows." Elmer greeted Baput. "He watches TV right out of the sky. You can't watch TV for long without seeing someone get shot." He pointed his finger at Baput, flexed his thumb. "Bang, bang! You know."

"Yes." Baput had seen plenty of shootings on the TV Plane. "Popa, they point a stick at someone, it goes 'bang,' and they fall dead. You don't even have to touch them, or even be close to them."

"What is 'bang'?" Valko asked, intrigued.

"That's what I was trying to explain. Help me out, B." With Baput interpreting, Jerry explained how guns work. "It comes out really fast and straight, and a little piece of lead goes right into the guy." He pointed to his heart with his empty hand, the gun hanging limply in the other. "Bang! Or your head," he pointed to his head. "Hole in the brain, you die instantly. Or, if they get you in the belly, it's a slow, painful death. Or they can get you in the arm or leg," he touched each body part as he named it, "and if it goes right through, you might be OK. If not, someone's gotta dig the bullet out, or you'll die of infection."

"Will these work on bumblies and nimblies?" Valko asked the obvious question. His smile dropped. "Do you, um, disappear, when you shoot?"

"Huh?" asked Jerry.

Baput got it. "We shot the nimblies from the Cave, with the beam from the Rock, and we disappeared. Or, whatever."

"Well, this isn't a beam, it's a bullet. A pro-jec-tile." Jerry sought common ground. "Don't you guys have bows and arrows? Blowguns?"

"Yes," Valko told them. "Very hard to shoot the bumblies, the way they move. A good launcher can send a poisoned dart into the heart of a nimbly with a blowgun. He must be close, though. How far away can you be and still kill with this gun?"

Elmer had returned from a quick, unnoticed trip to the truck with the shotgun he had brought along, "just in case.'" "Here's what you need for them bat critters! Sprays a pattern about that wide." He tucked the gun under his arm and made a circle with his hands that was bigger than a basketball. "It gets bigger the farther it goes. A whole bunch of pellets in a circle, peppering them buggers."

Elmer handed the empty gun to Valko without a second thought. Valko held it awkwardly by its center, finding the balance and scanning it up and down.

Elmer invited, "We can't do it now, 'cause we've been drinking, but tomorrow—"

"Tomorrow, the harvest begins!" replied the disciplined warrior, though he burned to see how this shotgun worked.

"In the afternoon, after I bring the first load to town, we'll go down to my shooting range. Bring your earmuffs. We'll shoot some skeet. See if you think you can hit a bumbly."

Eclipse

Elmer stowed the guns in the truck, including his pistol. He sat eating and drinking with Felsic and Valko as if it were a slow afternoon at the shop. G-Pa napped in the lounge chair. Fran and Star scoured the riverbed, looking for pretty rocks that could be polished and drilled for beads.

The boys explored the flat spot, the chimney, the chimney outlet, and the riverbed, wandering all the way across to where the green water slugged along in its summer channel. They threw sticks for the dogs, and practiced launching rocks with the Nauvian slings they had made. Their young voices and laughter echoed across the canyon: "Bullseye! Who needs a gun?"

When the sun hit the tops of the pines downriver, the sky darkened and the air cooled just enough to trigger some deep instinct. Everyone reassembled at the flat spot, claimed their chairs, and turned them to face the anticipated spectacle in the eastern sky.

Baput roused his G-Pa. "Akash. It is time."

The full moon rose when the sun set, as it should. But it rose in eclipse, with a piece missing. Valko, Felsic, and Salistar gawked at the sight, mouths hanging open.

G-Pa struggled from the low chair. Baput helped him to his feet. His deep-set eyes darted back and forth as if he didn't remember where he was. Then he saw the moon. With a snarl, he raised his longstick and stepped bravely between his stricken family and the ailing Kakeeche.

But Baput stepped in front of him and faced the group first. "Family!" The volume of his own voice startled him. "Family, do not be afraid. I have foreseen this."

The Akash pushed past Baput to take the floor. "No one can foresee such things—unless he has caused them," he accused.

"Jerry can. He uses science. And science says, the Kakeeche will all turn their faces to us again by 10:22 tonight."

"Science!" The Akash gargled and waved his longstick menacingly, like a cobra.

Valko stepped forward to restrain him.

"You mean Shavarandu!" G-Pa ranted, disregarding Valko's great hands wrapped around his reedy upper arms. "You committed Shavarandu. You are the cause of all this. You and that wicked Earth Boy!"

Felsic helped Valko wrestle the old man gently to the ground, where he knelt in meditation pose facing the defective orb.

"Do not be afraid, Popa! Uncle Felsic," the Apprentice Akash ordered, pinning each of them with his eyes. "I am telling you, all will be well by bedtime. You will see. Now, take care of Momama. Leave us." The apprentice's seniors obeyed him awkwardly but without argument.

Baput knelt on the ground next to G-Pa. He breathed slowly, deeply, in and out, squeezing his belly, his lungs, his throat, over and over until he drifted up and to the left to the Plane. G-Pa already lurked there, in a dark corner. Like a spider, he rushed on Baput the instant he felt his distinct vibration. His web glowed with excitement as he came.

"It is because of that strange man with the yellow hair, the Unbeliever!" G-Pa's aura raged an ugly chartreuse. "But I know you have not come to join me in appeasing Kakeeche. Oh, no. You are too holy for that. You and your Earth Boy and your Shavarandu! No. You come to plead for those animals! Your friend and his foolish popa, who not even Kakeeche can stand!"

"No, Akash. It is not because of Elmer." Baput's coldly certain reply injected a yellow tinge into the stream, the color of dissent, of Shavarandu.

A surprising thought swirled in a tight orbit around G-Pa's aura. "These poor, simple animal-people! I fear this, what you call Earth, is in more trouble than I thought!" The Akashic aura flashed pure white with inspiration. "They need our help. Go get the pink man. Bring him here. Now. We will teach him our chant. We must do it every full moon, together." G-Pa's aura cooled to a calm lavender that matched his real hair and beard.

Baput's stomach clenched. He knew that just by thinking his forbidden thoughts, he cast them into the never-ending flow that is the Plane, each one changing it in some way. Changing the shape, the color, the course of things forevermore. Suddenly, he didn't care. "Leave Elmer alone. Elmer did not cause this, G-Pa." The final slash of the inferior address was delivered in blazing scarlet, like the shadow that crept across the face of the moon.

G-Pa's aura flashed an angry magenta. "Apprentice, I ordered you—"

Baput's aura erupted like a volcano. Pent-up fiery red lava carried his flaming accusation down to swallow G-Pa in its boiling acid. "It is because we engaged in Shavarandu, Akash. You and I, at Nauve. There have been many eclipses since we began studying the Shavarandu behind the Death Door." Black jets entered the cosmic flow when he thought of the dark door that killed Batuk. "If the Kakeeche turn their backs on us, perhaps that is why."

"No, no! We have done nothing wrong!" G-Pa drew his aura tight around himself like a comforter. "I, at least, have not. Certainly not. Not ever. Nor you, my boy, as my Apprentice. Not before Earth, and Earth Boy, and never under my direction!" A babbling rainbow flowed from G-Pa's spirit, a colorful jumble of false memories and made-up excuses. "It is not you, my boy. Or me. It is these others. Ever since we, we... what happened?" The disembodied spirit looked helplessly at his student.

"We arrived." Baput used Jerry's strange English word for which there was no translation. "Do you remember why, G-Pa?" Baput's aura was the hot yellow-white of Shavarandu Himself.

G-Pa's spewing rainbow slowed, and the colors blended into a sludgy brown mud that eddied at the edge of the cosmic flow, as if reluctant to join it. Baput's volcano simmered idly… for how long? He opened his eyes, just a slit, to see the moon. It glowed darkly in deep vermillion. He struggled to keep his thoughts close, where the Akash could not read them, even in their shared cerebral state.

Counting on his mental privacy, Baput took stock. He did not doubt that Kakeeche would return within hours, without harming anyone on Earth or Nauve. All he had to do was keep G-Pa from trying to kill anyone until then.

G-Pa's flow struggled for coherence. "Yes… and they do not believe…. And then there was fire! Truly a bad sign. And that box? And then we were in another, another…" G-Pa did not have the words or colors to finish.

"Chant, G-Pa," the apprentice ordered his master. "Appease Kakeeche with all your heart. Only you can do it. I, your meek apprentice, shall negotiate with the Earth Man, as before."

The old Akash burst into a spirited round of melodious chanting in old Akashic. Baput winced at the interspersed curses, intended to bring misfortune down on his friends, the non-believers. *Does it matter?* He wondered as he wiggled his fingers and toes, trying to feel the world of Earth before opening his eyes.

"No," came the answer. Was it borne to him from the All-Giving Flow or from his own will? "Let G-Pa think what he wants," it instructed. "You must stop any killing, but otherwise, just let him be. He is the past. Let him pass."

Baput gasped. The unbidden thoughts kept coming, "You must bring the rest of your family into the future. The new way. The Earth way. The way of Shavarandu."

Baput let go of G-Pa's spirit. It didn't sink. It was fine on its own, bobbing around in its happy whirlpool of blame and superstition.

A high-pitched silent cry filled his head, an urgent keening, bereft and desperate. And something else. Alien eyes. Alien, but intimately familiar. Angry, but so loving! A mixture only a momama could produce. Francina! He opened his eyes and looked around.

G-Pa's head sagged. His chant was mumbled, unintelligible to anyone but Baput, who had heard it too many times.

Popa and Uncle Felsic chatted, joked, and laughed with Elmer and Jerry around the fire, completely unconcerned about the disappearing moon in the darkening sky.

But Momama sat pressed tightly against Francina. She looked up desperately the instant he turned his head, as if she could feel the relief of her son's loving eyes. And yes, those had been Francina's eyes, searing a hole in his back with their demand for attention for her dearest friend.

Baput slipped away from the Akash's side and joined the two women at the table, his back to the fearsome blood moon. Blocking Salistar's view, he gazed into her near-hysterical eyes.

"Batuk's blood," she whispered.

"No, Momama," Baput answered firmly. "It is not. It is the very air we breathe that makes the moon red." Salistar gazed tearfully, uncomprehending, at her son.

Fran glanced over at Jerry, but he was gesturing wildly at the men, apparently trying to explain the eclipse.

"You like the pretty blue sky, yes, Momama? That is the atmosphere, the air we breathe. See, at this moment, the Earth is between Shavarandu and Kakeeche." He arranged three empty plates in a row, trying to demonstrate. "It's a shadow. You don't plant on the north side of a tree, because the tree will make a shadow. It will block the light."

Star nodded impatiently. Of course she understood not to plant in the shade of a tree. But what did that have to do with her dead son's vengeful soul coming back to make trouble right at harvest time?

"The Earth is not totally in the way yet, but it is so close, the light must go through Earth's atmosphere. At nauve, the air takes a little more of the red, but Earth's atmosphere cares not for the red. They pass all that red light to the Kakeeche to wear, because they don't have their silver robes. The Kakeeche get cold without the sun." Baput leaned in and winked like he was letting Star in on a joke. "The Kakeeche have no light of their own. All their light is reflected from Shavarandu. And when Earth gets in the way, it cuts off their only light. That is why they go dark."

Salistar's tight, wrinkled face did not light up as Baput had hoped. Without removing her eyes from her son, she whispered, "It is the Curse of Batuk. Batuk will wreck the harvest!"

"No!" Baput replied so sharply that Francina gave him a hard look, but he kept preaching, almost yelling. "No Calamunga! No boogey man! You know Batuk is not!"

All the men looked at them, except the Akash who continued his mumbled chant.

Baput pressed on, leaning in toward his delicate momama despite her terrified look. "You cast a bad mold, Momama. You wouldn't cast your gup cake in an ugly mold, would you? When you think of the future, you should think good thoughts. Cast a positive mold."

Salistar drew back, as if trying to escape the vast new world in the eyes of her son. "That is Earth teaching!" she objected.

Baput gazed at her with a new benevolent power. "No, Momama!" he corrected gently. "It is Akashic. The energy of the world flows forever on the Plane, like the river. Nothing can stop it. It flows past all things, around anything in its way. If there is a rock in the river, the water flows around it. It changes its shape to do so. The Plane is like that, Momama. You can change the shape of the flow. Things will happen no matter what. The flow continues. But you can shape it, just by thinking."

"I cannot," Salistar whispered with a shrug. "I am woman."

Baput seized her tiny hands in his oversized paws. "Anyone can make a positive mold, Momama." He rose and circled the table to Salistar's back so she could see the moon again. He put his hands on her shoulders.

"Chant with me, Momama."

"I cannot. I am woman," Star repeated.

"Yes. You can. Chant with me. Kakeeche will turn back. Chant, Momama. Set a good mold. Look up and chant."

"Yeah!" Fran agreed. "This is the Look'N Up Ranch. That's what we do here. Look up. We're built for it." She pointed up and to the left.

Star looked up obediently.

Hoping familiarity would comfort her friend, Fran said, "It looks like a giant kip, doesn't it?"

Not comforted, Star drew back in terror. "So many seeds!" She began fervently chanting the repetitive anti-eclipse rite in Nauvian.

Baput translated: "Kakeeche will turn back, Kakeeche will turn back…"

Fran sang it to the now-familiar tune of Happy Birthday. "Kakeeche will turn back, and we'll all be OK!" she finished the modified birthday song, then began again, with Star lending her voice.

The harmony soothed Baput's worried soul. He left his women subjects and approached the men, silhouetted against the darkened moon. Bottles dangled from their hands. Jerry paced back and forth in front of them in full lecture mode.

"It's a shadow, get it?" Jerry sounded exasperated, but jovial enough. "Felsic. Valko is bigger than you." He tried something obvious.

"A little," Felsic conceded, long past the savoring stage.

"So," Jerry persisted. "You guys are out in the sun, playing. He gets between you and the sun and you're in his shadow. Get it?"

"Valko's shadow." Felsic knew it all too well.

Valko, a bottle or two under his own beard, threw back his head and roared with laughter.

One of Fran's blue eyes opened at the uproar, met Baput's eyes and squinted happily. She leaned on Star and sang even louder.

"Mangu!" Valko roared with tipsy delight.

"Oh no," Baput moaned under his breath. That embarrassing story he used to believe without question. Now, on Earth, he found it unlikely.

Valko insisted. "Mangu is our greatest warrior ganeesh. He is young and strong and massive! But back when Felsic here was a puny second-cycle—"

"I was fourth year," Felsic bragged.

Valko shot a playful glare at his interrupting brother and went on. "—Mangu was then a young bull. His skin was just starting to toughen, and those magnificent tusks were beginning to emerge, ferociously, as if his already colossal body could not contain his warrior spirit." Valko held up a tensely clenched fist.

"We walked in procession to the Holy Cave for First Full Kakeeche. We boys walked at the rear, behind the elders, before the ganeesh. Well, just then, Felsic decides he has to boo."

"I had to poop," Felsic translated.

Valko resumed the tale. "So he squats right on the trail. Right in front of Mangu! I thought my little brother would be like the mash that comes out of the first pressing."

As if on cue, Felsic squatted with his back toward his much larger brother. Valko galloped toward him a few steps, then stopped just short. He raised his arm up in front of his face and made a trumpeting sound, then narrated, "He stopped just in time!"

"I see his shadow over me!" Felsic cried, still squatting, covering his head with his arms. "Mangu Eclipse!"

Jerry sent Baput a victorious grin.

Baput rolled his eyes.

Valko turned his back to Felsic. He bent his knees and waist, thrusting his butt out over his cowering brother. "Mangu boo!"

Valko roared with laughter, his usual dignity washed away by wine and youthful memories. "Boo gaa! Green and yellow and brown. Ganeesh boo gaa! The worst."

"That's an eclipse, alright!" Elmer cackled, slapping his thigh.

Valko staggered with laughter. Felsic stood up, his giggles providing the melody to Valko's booming base.

"Then came the women and girls, behind the ganeesh," Valko continued. "Momama found him. She would have spanked him, but she didn't want to touch him. He had to go through the whole ceremony that way." Valko roared anew.

"It was the best day of my life," Felsic declared, draining his bottle.

Jerry nudged Baput. His beeper was going off. Baput hadn't heard it through all the laughter. It was 7:47 p.m.

Totality.

Constellations

The sky was as dark as any moonless autumn night. The stars appeared suddenly, as if someone had flipped a switch. The moon was just a round blank spot in the starry background.

"Momama!" was the Alanakash's first concern. He rushed to the table just in time to see Star's eyes open, sleepy and peaceful, like a child waking from a happy dream.

"Mangu!" she whispered through a loving smile.

Jerry scanned the familiar constellations in the southern sky.

Familiar to Earth dwellers, anyway. Northern hemisphere Earth dwellers, Jerry corrected his own thoughts. The stars twinkled brilliantly in the shaky air before a jet-black background.

Dreading the answer, Jerry bravely pointed at the stars, asking, "So, what are those?"

"They are our departed ancestors," Felsic answered. "They watch over us, with Kakeeche. But where is our star?"

"We didn't die," Baput answered quickly. Then, "Did we?" He turned his still-confused eyes on Jerry. His expression was hard to read in the dark.

"Of course, you're not dead!" Jerry replied. "You'll be home before you die, all of you," he promised rashly.

No response. Jerry waited a bit, then picked up his scalpel and started probing. "When someone dies, can you find the new star?" he tested, trying to imagine a night sky in a place with no electric lights, no air pollution.

"G-Pa is good at finding them. Usually they are in a crowded field of stars. That's where they start."

"Of course," Jerry replied with poorly concealed sarcasm. "It's easier to hide there."

Baput detected the tone but had no idea why it was there.

Jerry charged on: "Maybe they don't show up right away, because it takes millions of years for their light to get to the sky, and millions more for it to come back to Nauve."

"So they… go away?" Valko attempted. Even after the trip to Belinda's and back, they still struggled with the concept.

"Yeah, they go on a really, really, long trip, but they come back really fast, as light."

"So Batuk and Cilandra aren't even there yet? Watching over us?" Felsic asked.

"They haven't arrived yet, but they're up there, looking back, on their way!" Jerry was talking faster and faster, trying to cover their questions with comforting answers that fit both the mythology and the science. *Now I'm doing it!* Jerry caught himself. *I'm spinning Kakeeche. This is easy! Way too easy. Look at how I can play their emotions like a yoyo. This is creepy!*

He pulled Baput away from his family. "Do you know where Batuk's star is?" he asked gently.

Baput went to work, scanning the familiar sky. Familiar, except there were never as many stars here on Earth, even on the clearest, darkest nights. Here, the deepening twilight had a strange green-orange color to it, and the air was thick and grainy. He fought to control the crack in his voice when he answered. "There are so few stars here, Jerry. Why?"

"Lights. Even though they're far away, the lights from town drown them out. Then there's the air pollution. They say we've got the worst air in the whole state, even out here in the country. That's the price we pay for the tech, the Shavarandu. You don't have trucks and dishwashers and electricity on Nauve. But you have clean air and clean water and beautiful dark skies."

Star and Fran stopped their chanting and came over to join them. Soon everyone but G-Pa was standing together facing south, exploring the familiar sky.

Felsic pointed at something low in the east, where the Moon had blazed only an hour before. "That's my favorite. The zebkin. See his horns?"

"That's Capricorn," Jerry said tightly, stepping towards it, as if to get a closer look.

"It's a goat, to us." Fran explained. "Kind of like a deer, a zebkin. Horns, small hooves, they can jump and climb." Felsic bobbed his head in loving recognition.

Star pointed further west. "And there is my favorite. Momaqua, the Water Bearer. She pours her water into the river always and for all time. It is she who causes the mists, by her constant pouring." She shuddered at the absent moon.

Fran and Jerry exchanged a look. *That's how they explain the river and the mist!*

Valko pointed southwest. "That one is Luk, what you call 'fish.' The slimy creature with no legs who lives in the river. He wiggles around in the water and doesn't breathe."

"Pisces!" Fran exclaimed, looking at Jerry.

"Perspective," Jerry murmured, gazing at the sky.

"They are like skeletons!" Felsic complained. "At Nauve, they have flesh and luxurious coats. I see only the brightest stars here."

At Nauve. Jerry felt a chill run down his spine. Not only did they see the same constellations, they even gave them similar names! Jerry felt like he had to step aside as the huge missing piece dropped out of the sky into its place. It all made sense now. But, how to explain it?

The shadow began to lift like a curtain. The bottom of the moon flared brightly against the dark sky. Baput inhaled at the sight. Felsic hooted joyfully.

Jerry had no trouble collecting a dozen empty bottles. He took his awkward armload to the picnic table and set them in a neat line down the middle. "Baput, come here," he beckoned. They all came, except G-Pa. He kept up his fervent praying, neither apprentice nor tether by his side.

Jerry switched into lecture mode as the light crept up the face of the moon. "Pretend these bottles are a bunch of stars in the sky. Now, come down here to the end, in front of my dad, there."

Baput obediently took his assigned place.

Jerry instructed him further. "Now bring your eye down here, right to table level, and squint along that line and look at all the bottles." He stepped in front of Baput, demonstrated.

Baput did as Jerry showed him.

"What do you see?" Jerry asked. "If all those bottles were a constellation in the sky, what would you see? Are they close together? Far apart? Do they make a shape?"

Baput hesitated, not sure what Jerry was asking him. "Um, they look close together. A cluster?"

"Yes!" Jerry pumped his fist. "Now, come on over here." Jerry guided his mystified friend to the side of the table, where he could view the whole line of bottles. "Now what does it look like?"

Baput answered more quickly this time. "A line," he called it.

Jerry ran to the end of the table again, tapped the last bottle. "So, this…" He ran to the other end, giving the bottle there a thump. "And this here, are they close together now, in your constellation?"

"It's on the other end of the line, as far away as it can be."

"Yes!" Jerry enthused. "But when you were down there at the end, you said they were all in a cluster, close together."

"I knew they weren't, but they looked…"

"Yeah, see?" Jerry gushed. "If these were a constellation, and we were here on Earth, looking at the stars," he squinted down the line again, "we'd see a cluster. But if your planet is over there," he pointed to the table's midpoint, where Baput stood, "you'd see a line…"

He trailed off at the sea of blank looks. Even his mom looked lost, but with a curious and hopeful glint.

"I'm saying you guys aren't from another planet! If you were, you would be looking at the stars from a different angle. There's no way you would see the same constellations as us!"

Fran couldn't help but smile proudly.

"You only have one, um, moon," he hurried past that tender subject. "Your climate's the same. You grow poms, and they ripen at the same time. You have eclipses at the same times as us. And you see the same constellations. There is no way you guys are from another planet. You're not even from a different location on *this* planet. I think you're from right here—but another *dimension*. Some kind of little bubble, connected to this exact spot on Earth. Just a little piece of this world sticking into your world. That's why you've got no otherwhere."

Jerry waited, not breathing, hoping to see at least a glimmer on his friends' faces, afraid it was too much to ask.

The men returned to the campfire, still prattling about guns and bumblies.

Fran and Star sat back down at the table, comparing Momaqua to Aquarius, Pisces to Luc.

Only Baput remained. Did he get it? And did he get the next thing that dropped into place in the complex puzzle that was Jerry's mind? Jerry picked two shovels from the trailer and walked to the low mound in the middle of the flat spot. "The Rock was here, right?"

"In the Holy Cave it was, yes," Baput replied. His thick eyebrows knotted, then slowly spread and lifted like a pair of wings, high into his broad forehead. His mouth widened into a grin that shined from his dark face with its own light, the dazzling light of discovery. "No wonder G-Pa likes the sauna!" he cried, "It's made of Holy Cave rock!"

"Yes!" Jerry agreed. "The Holy Cave is, or was, here. The chimney's here. And, I hate to say it, but maybe even the nimblies and bumblies."

Baput counted on his fingers. "Momaqua and the Zebkin and Luc the Fish are all in their places, and so is the Holy Rock, the Weapon and the Portal! It's all right here, buried under this gravel."

Jerry leaned a shovel at Baput.

"Not now, Son," Elmer objected. "It's the middle of the night. We're going to bed."

"Tomorrow?" Jerry asked, already knowing the answer.

"It's harvest time, boy. You got two years, and a crackerjack crew, right, guys?"

Elmer had never seen Valko and Felsic shy away from hard work before, but they backed away quickly, not at all interested in *this* job. "You kids can dig after harvest," the boss concluded, and that was that.

Maelstrom

Exhausted by sun, wind, and drink, and still full from an afternoon of continuous eating, the Nauvians went to bed soon after reaching the quarters. The shadow had not completely retreated from the face of the moon, but no one seemed to care, not even G-Pa. He clung to Baput as they went to the bathroom, then into their beds, where they lay on their backs, arms and legs spread slightly, palms up, no body part touching another. Except their hands. G-Pa still wouldn't sleep, or shut up, unless Baput held his hand. All night. As always.

Baput exaggerated his Akashic Breathing, hoping G-Pa would think he was meditating on Kakeeche, trying to appease them, "kissing their shiny somethings," Jerry would say. *He'll be quiet then, and I can think.*

G-Pa chanted anyway, but not the anti-eclipse chant. Now, he chanted the ordinary Full Kakeeche Song that they chanted every month. Nauseatingly familiar, it went on and on, over and over, unrelenting.

Baput couldn't wait for G-Pa to chant himself to sleep, so he could tackle the thoughts that swam through his head. So many thoughts! *And not a word about any of it from G-Pa! Not during their eclipse, not after.* In fact, the Akash had not uttered an intelligible word since they packed up and left the flat spot where they had landed a year ago. *And that place is the Holy Cave...*

He tried to complete the thought, but he couldn't ignore the chanting. It had worn a groove in his nerves that he had never noticed before, and now that he had, it hurt. It was like physical pain, but somehow deeper and more annoying.

G-Pa's tone kept rising. Baput knew he was supposed to join in, or it would get louder and angrier and wake up the whole house. *Popa will roar, and Momama will cry, and Felsic will cringe in the corner.*

With no choice but to chant, Baput translated the verse into English and made up his own lines in between.

> "Kakeeche is, Kakeeche not.
> One more time, my brain will rot.
> Kakeeche whole, Kakeeche half.
> Kakeeche makes the Earth Boy laugh.

Kakeeche born, Kakeeche die.
Bore me with your stupid lie.
Kakeeche left, Kakeeche right.
Kakeeche farts their holy light.
Ever be it so! Ever be it so!
Relax. They'll be back."

The last one didn't rhyme but he liked the snappy, Earthlike sound. G-Pa seemed to accept the insincere offering with its foreign words and irreverent lines.

The new chant was soon as automatic as the original. The words flowed thoughtlessly and perfectly through that worn groove. Baput let his own chanting run in the background along with G-Pa's noise while he thought of other things.

He chuckled to himself when he recalled what Jerry had said. *He thought I would be ascended to Akash today, on my 13th birthday. Because Popa says! It's not even Passascenday! Jerry just doesn't get it. He's so used to questioning everything. We are so used to not questioning.*

G-Pa's chanting grew louder, drawing Baput's attention back. *Jerry says he's just an old man. What he believes doesn't matter. All the truths I've been raised to teach my people are all meaningless here.*

Am I meaningless? Or am I Alanakash? Am I the Holy One who believes in the Loving Watchers in the night sky and the angry, jealous Power we Fear in the day? And when I say it is so, all the people believe me without question? Or am I someone who believes the moon is a dead rock, and the sun is a burning gas ball, and we all live on a ball circling endlessly in empty space? If I believe that, can I still be Akash if I return nauve? Can I tell my people to believe the Earth way, and expect them to accept that without question? Or do I just keep preaching the old Kakeeche stuff, even if I don't believe it myself?

No. I can't be both. It's one or the other, all or nothing. If I believe Jerry's way, I am not an Akash. I am just a boy. A lost boy, who just turned 13, and I don't know what I am, who I am, or even where I am. In a place. The same place as home, but not the same. Not the same at all...

With a deep sigh, he directed his mental energy to the website Jerry had shown him on the iPlane, to watch the end of the eclipse.

The sun, Shavarandu, and the moon, Kakeeche, sped toward each other on a collision course. Baput watched from his bunk, helpless and terrified. *Jerry says we're between them!*

"Wait, that's not how an eclipse works!" Jerry's voice shouted. "They go past each other. They don't—" Jerry's voice cut off abruptly as the sun and moon slammed together. The impact spun them into a swirling whirlpool, a maelstrom of silver and gold light that stayed separate, refusing to form an alloy.

The suction pulled him in. He groped frantically. There was nothing to hang onto. He was sucked deeper and deeper into the whirling strands of silver and gold.

When he finally bobbed to the surface, G-Pa was there, lit up in cool silver light, reaching for him. He tried to grab his wizened hand. He felt the dank huts of Nauve, the familiar songs sung by rote, the dull ache of that groove, the comfort that was no longer comfortable. He hesitated and was swept out of G-Pa's reach.

He spun around helplessly in the vortex, and there was Jerry, all lit up in gold, his blond hair shining. He reached out, like G-Pa had. Baput saw the dazzle of electric lights, orbs spinning in dark, empty space, the breathless thrill of scientific discovery.

He wanted to reach for Jerry, but a sharp pang of fear made him hesitate, just for an instant. Too late. He whirled out of Jerry's grasp. Deeper and deeper, down, down out of reach. He was drowning, being flushed like he had imagined on that first day so long ago, just a year...

"You have heard my call!" A mighty voice thundered all around him, shaking the fluid that bore him down.

"Huh?" Baput grunted incoherently.

"Can you hear me now?" Jerry's smart-alec voice answered, but Jerry was not there, and the ranch was silent.

"Jerry?" Baput choked.

"So, when I speak as Earth Boy, you listen. Very well. We will speak this way. It will take you too long to hear my true voice, and time is short."

"Shavarandu?" Baput whispered the forbidden name.

"Kakeeche!" G-Pa's cry stretched from that familiar place on the other side of the vortex.

Baput tried to swim toward it with all his being. He was nauve, in his old hut with G-Pa. He felt a primal sense of sweet relief, reached for it like a kid reaches for candy.

"Baput!!" Jerry's voice called from behind him.

The ethereal fluid swept him away from the green side, tearing that wafer from his grasp, ripping him from the comfort of the rote repetition, the placid ignorance...

"You bastard!" Baput exploded at the disembodied voice. "You used Jerry! My friendship, my need for him, my love! You used it to turn me away from my faith!"

"Faith?" the voice that was not really Jerry's chortled.

Baput gathered his spirit together. He felt taller, somehow. "I am the Apprentice Alanakash. I will be the spiritual leader of my people. I must keep my faith, or all is lost! Do not tempt me further. I must return to Nauve and lead my people. I must bear the burden of their unquestioning obedience."

G-Pa reached out of the darkness as if to grab his Apprentice and pull him back. "You fool!" the ancient voice warbled, "Their obedience is a blessing, not a burden!"

"Ha!" Shavarandu laughed at them. "See? Whether you embrace me or not, you are already like no other Akash. Do you really think you can go back to Nauve unchanged, and teach that drivel you know is false, after being here on Earth and seeing my wonders?"

"I carry the Holy Seed," Baput recited. "I must lead The People into the future..." His eyes sprung open. He was still on his back, G-Pa's clammy hand in his. He stared at the lattice of springs on the underside of the upper bunk. "There is no future," he whispered. "Not without Shavarandu."

He turned his head stiffly, just enough to see G-Pa lying on the floor, and whispered, "Without Shavarandu, I'm as powerless as he is." With that, he closed his eyes and went into a sound sleep. G-Pa snored peacefully on the floor below, still joined to his apprentice, in body, anyway.

The next day the Nauvians began the Easy Harvest, undaunted by their hangovers, unlike their achy, bleary-eyed boss. By the time Jerry got home from school, Elmer already had delivered the first load to town, and as promised, was now at the shooting range with Valko and Felsic, shooting skeet.

Jerry couldn't wait to start digging for the Holy Rock, but Baput was in the sauna meditating with his G-Pa. They stayed there until dinner.

After dinner, Jerry went over to the quarters to call for Baput. Salistar said he was still meditating. *Maybe Baput's trying to explain all this to the old man, find out more about that queen....*

All week, Baput picked on his own tree, then meditated in the sauna with G-Pa or helped the women process the endless stream of pomegranate seeds into oil and wine.

It wasn't until Saturday morning that Baput joined Jerry at the Horizontal Tree. He didn't want to dig for the Rock. He just wanted to talk.

That disappointed Jerry, but he still hoped to at least find out what was going on. "Hey, Baput, how's it going?" he began weakly.

Baput didn't answer.

Jerry tried again. "What's all the praying been about? Is G-Pa getting it?"

Baput still didn't answer.

Jerry's heart sank. "Forget him!" he cried out his frustration. "There's so much to think about! We have work to do. The Rock is here. The nimblies and bumblies might be here. We've gotta figure out what to do. Two years sounds like a long time, but—"

"Time is short," Baput murmured dreamily. He beamed a crazed smile at Jerry. "Jerry, I see Shavarandu! On the Plane, the iPlane, the TV Plane, in your pocket. It's everywhere! I can see it all! Atoms, molecules, photons, sound waves, gravity, the magnetic field, so awesome!"

He glanced over his shoulder nervously, then turned back to Jerry. "My mind is blown, Jerry! I can see it, but I can't quite understand it. I've been going to the planes all the time, this whole week. While I pick, while I pull seeds in the house with my momama. Everybody keeps asking me what's wrong. I can't tell them! It's forbidden! I have to keep my mouth shut all the time. I try to hide my thoughts from G-Pa, but I go there even when we meditate together. If he caught me looking at Shavarandu, who knows what he would do? But I can't stop!" The rapt look melted into a shameful, pleading face.

He's hooked! Jerry realized, shamed by the flash of pride he felt.

"Come with me, Jerry," Baput invited, to Jerry's delight. "I need you to show me around the Shavarandu side of the Plane."

As the thrill crept up from Jerry's toes to his head, Baput pulled two pairs of eclipse goggles out from under his drawstring. "It's very sunny there."

Side by side on the bent willow tree, the two boys breathed in unison, deep and slow. The river rushed a soothing mantra, and soon Jerry felt his spirit drift up and to the left, Baput by his side, leading the way to the Shavarandu side of the Plane.

Jerry's soul inhaled in awe. It was sunny alright! A dazzling gold light shined from the sky and reflected off the smooth, golden metallic surfaces of, well, everything. All but that dazzling white blob beside him. He checked his glasses. "Baput? Is that you? Dude, you're all white! I get it!" he heard his own voice explain. "You were just green before. Now that you've got the gold of Shavarandu, you're pure white light. The complete spectrum. You're whole, Man!"

The white blob spoke without a mouth. "You are still all gold, Jerry. So gold I can hardly see you here. You need more green." Then he tapped Jerry's disembodied spirit with his own, and they hurled their combined essence into the current of molten gold.

"Electrons in their orbits, just like the planets on the model. As above, so below…" Jerry's voice narrated the indescribable tour.

Mitten

The harvest was even better than last year, being Easy Harvest, with no nimblies and bumblies to worry about. Elmer brought a load to town early every day, leaving the crew free in the afternoons. Valko and Felsic spent most of that time messing around in the shop or down at Elmer's rifle range, shooting skeet with Elmer's two shotguns.

Patrick and Belinda had visited in late December, for the holiday they called Christmas. Jerry had no school for two weeks, and they had spent a lot of time jabbing at the hard, cemented gravel mound in the middle of the flat spot, and talking about ways to commit Insitucide: to kill the nimblies and bumblies, if they were in the chimney.

Patrick had joined them on the Plane, using the mindfulness meditation techniques he had learned from an internet class. The method was almost identical, and it worked. He ascended on his first try. He brought his physics knowledge with him, and they surfed the Shavarandu side, expanding into previously unexplored, unimagined realms.

Belinda didn't try to ascend, despite her popa's urging and her cousin's teasing. She preferred to work with Francina and Momama, making decorations out of cookies and cranberries. That seemed perfectly right and normal to Baput. Besides, he found her presence distracting, especially when she had showed him her new violin.

"My dad says the violin is the way to your heart," she had told him. "So he got me a violin for Christmas, and I'm going to learn to play it, and go to your heart."

Baput still couldn't get that sight out of his head, the emerald eye that lay so open before him. As if she needed a violin! He shook his head to clear the indelible image, and the forbidden thoughts it brought. Like his thoughts of Shavarandu and Insitucide. It seemed most of his thoughts were forbidden these days.

G-Pa's chant pushed its way into Baput's thoughts. It was Mitten, six months after Baput's birthday, halfway between Seasons. A year and a half until the nimblies and bumblies would swarm again on Nauve, and perhaps on Earth.

G-Pa hadn't said a word about that since they had discovered the cave. Not once in six months of pointless daily sessions. Whenever he would begin to preach, or teach, he would lapse into the monthly Full Kakeeche Chant, the one they had all heard too many times. Was he doing it now? He was! That same old chant. Not even the Mitten Ceremony!

He wouldn't let Baput help him prepare for the Mitten Ceremony, something an Apprentice Akash should learn. He had excluded "those pink-skinned animals" and promised a surprise. Baput's foolish hopes had surged, actually believing the Akash would apply his legendary wisdom to their current situation, and announce some decision, or some new ideas, at least. But no, just "Kakeeche left, Kakeeche right..." and on and on.

Can a guy be bored and furious at the same time? Baput wondered. He glanced at his popa, now understanding the expression he so often wore behind his beard.

Patrick had told him G-Pa's brain might not be flexible enough at his age to wrap his head around a whole new world. "But you're young," Patrick had said. "Your mind likes it. It's expanding like the universe, just reaching out in all directions for new stuff to shape itself around. And here you are in a whole new world! But your G-Pa, I'm afraid he might never really be able to grasp it. Not at your level, anyway."

So, I leave the old man behind, along with the rest of my training. Baput resolved. He scanned his bored family, chanting rotely in their living room. *But what about them? And the others at Nauve, if I go back and be Akash? I can't go nauve and refuse to conduct the ceremonies, tell them the religion they've believed since the beginning of time is nonsense, and expect them to leave it all behind, all at once. Can I?*

He turned his eyes to his momama. Her face was blank.

If I am to make change, I have to be subtle, even if they do *believe me unquestioningly.* He shuddered, hating and fearing the thought.

At last, the Akash's voice wore down to a weak rasp and the ceremony droned to a close. The green family blinked and stretched as if awakening from a long, uncomfortable sleep.

Salistar filed to the kitchen and produced the breakfast she'd kept warm in the oven. They ate slowly and wordlessly, except Baput. He rushed through his plate and asked to be excused. It was Saturday, and he and Jerry were going to dig again.

"Francina and I will be planting," Salistar answered happily, stepping out of G-Pa's thrall to remember the happy side of Mitten, Spring Planting. "Can you take the Akash?"

"I go to my Shrine," G-Pa grunted. "Walk me there, boy. You should join me, but I suspect you would rather go try to dig up your fake rock."

Salistar slipped G-Pa's robe over his shoulders.

"It's the Holy Rock, G-Pa, same as Nauve," Baput countered, grasping G-Pa by the elbow and heading out the door.

"It is not Nauve. It is Earth. Therefore, the rock you seek is fake, evil," G-Pa declared as they walked down the porch steps.

"Do you think it's there, G-Pa?" Baput asked, still hopelessly eager for new information.

"It is Mitten. The Holy Rock is sleeping."

"Sleeping?" Baput asked as they passed the garden.

Francina was coming out with her seed box to join Momama.

"It won't ring, even if you strike it." G-Pa told him. It is defenseless today. It will waken, ever so slowly, becoming more sensitive, more easily excited, until next First Pomegranate Day, when it rings on its own, as you've heard."

"Come with us, G-Pa!" Baput urged. "If we're going to find it today, you should be there."

They had reached the sauna, and G-Pa pulled his arm from Baput's grasp. "No. I go here and meditate. Report to me when you find Fake Earth Rock."

The Rock

Jerry fumed as he lifted another shovel of silty gravel out of the hole. *We've been digging for six months! We'd be done by now if those two big strong guys that love to do everything by hand would help for just a few days. Or if Baput would let Dad use the backhoe.* He sighed audibly but kept his complaints to himself. He knew the older Nauvians had a serious case of the willies about this place. They didn't want to dig up the rock that glowed and hummed and shot fatal beams and flung them into an unknown world. A rock that could maybe send them home to that dismal world of theirs. Who could blame them?

Baput was as squeamish as a paleontologist excavating a T-Rex skeleton with a toothbrush. *He's afraid we're gonna scratch it or something, even though he says it's super hard. But he'd never even seen metal before, except the stuff they found behind the door, so maybe what he thought was super hard was really just regular hard?*

All Jerry knew was, it was taking forever. They had started digging at the peak of the mound on the flat spot, which Baput believed was the center of the Rock. From there, they had gone out four feet all around, digging a circular area eight feet across, the same diameter as the Holy Rock. In six months of on-and-off digging, they had only just now broken through the hard crust of cemented sand and gravel into this stuff that was too soft.

Gravel and sand out of the hole, gravel and sand in from the sides. About three shovels to get one shovel's worth out, but at least this stuff was loose. *And Baput's here, digging his heart out,* Jerry thought with some pride. *A new Baput, since the last eclipse. He likes science now. And he never gets that brainwashed look in his eyes anymore.*

Even so, Jerry's patience was wearing thin, again. He jammed his shovel savagely into the seemingly bottomless gravel.

"Easy!" Baput cringed.

"You said it was super hard!" Jerry argued. "If it's that hard, it's gonna bend my shovel before it bends itself."

"Not today. Today it is vulnerable. My G-Pa said so. Today is Mitten, as far from First Pomegranate Day as we can be. The Rock is at its most dormant. That's why we'll find it today. G-Pa says so."

Jerry was amazed that Baput still believed the old man's ravings, but he hoped he was right, for once. "You mean, it has a force field around it?"

"I don't know. It has vibrations coming off of it. But not today."

"OK," Jerry agreed. "I'll take it easy, in honor of Mitten."

"Anyway," Baput introduced suddenly, "it's not the Rock I'm worried about. It's the Net."

"What net?"

"The Net went over the whole Rock, over the top of the pipes that shot the rays at the nimblies. It collects the Rock's vibrations. Remember when your popa built a fire right there?" he pointed to the pile of ash and charred wood remnants.

Jerry nodded.

"Well, he didn't know it, but he built it right where the fire pit is in the Holy Cave. But the smoke didn't find the chimney, it just floated off into the air, because the Holy Cave roof is not here to capture it and direct it. The Net is like that. It captures the vibrations that come from the Rock and collects them. Without the Net, the Holy Rock's energy would just float away uselessly, like that smoke. No weapon, no portal."

"Sounds important." Jerry's comment was an admonition. Why hadn't Baput mentioned this Net thing before?

"It is. And it's delicate," Baput continued. "It plugged into the wires that came from the generator Felsic pedaled. The power, electricity, I guess, spread all through the Net. It's a mesh of fine wires, woven into a fabric, light silver, almost white. It was, um," he held his palm up and kneaded his fingers, "Crinkly. Amazingly light. It was big enough to spread over the whole Rock, on top of the pipes. Yet you could lift the whole thing with one hand and sling it over your shoulder. I'm afraid if just one of those tiny wires breaks, it might not work anymore."

It was unusually hot for April. The boys dug with their shirts off. Baput wore his grass shorts in the Nauvian way, loosely woven and breezy. Jerry couldn't help but wonder how that would feel on a sweltering day. "Are you staying cool in those shorts?" he broke the silence.

"I must say, it is never this hot at Mitten at Nauve," Baput responded.

"I hate to admit it, but maybe your Old Ones were right. Maybe we shouldn't be messing with Shavarandu so much."

"What!?" Baput couldn't believe his ears.

"Technology," Jerry explained. "It's burning our world away. How does it go, Baput?" He hated to invoke Baput's brainwashed state, but he had to hear that poem again.

Baput accommodated him, but this time his eyes were alive, reacting to the words he recited, leaning on his shovel.

> "Do not look at Shavarandu
> He will burn your eyes
> Only cool light from Kakeeche
> Can enter your mind
> Think cool, kind thoughts of giving
> Guided by their silver rays
> Or evil thoughts from Shavarandu
> Will burn your only world away."

"'Will burn your only world away,'" Jerry echoed. "You know, we might wipe out our own world way before the bumblies and nimblies wipe you guys out'" Jerry decided not to mention the other impending doom that the Nauvians still didn't seem to realize.

Three more futile bites at loose, caving sand, then Jerry's shovel hit something so hard that it bounced back, sending shock waves up the handle and deep into his aching shoulder.

"Now we have two worlds," he announced in an awed whisper.

Baput dropped to his knees and scrabbled around with his gloved hands, clearing the loose gravel from the naked surface. "No Net," he breathed, "it's not here!"

Jerry scraped gently with his shovel, uncovering another area nearby. "It's gotta be here somewhere, though, doesn't it?"

"G-Pa threw something at the nimblies. I thought it was his robe, because when we arrived here, he didn't have it on. But maybe it was the Net?" His tone belied his belief in the theory.

Jerry had another. "Or maybe it was never here."

"Here?" Baput's thick brows knotted again.

"Yeah. My grandpa took the cave apart here, but it didn't get taken apart on Nauve, right? Well, maybe nobody ever put the Net on top of the Rock here on Earth."

Baput stopped scraping. "It's not here. It was never here..."

He stood and stumbled out of the hole onto the hard-packed gravel. "It must be here! Maybe it got folded over somehow. Felsic was looking at Peratha and Trillella. Popa was shooting. Momama was in the back of the Cave. No one else saw it. G-Pa jumped on the Rock, on top of the Net, and pushed it down with his longstick, so the Net touched the Rock. That's when it happened." He put his hands together horizontally, then flung them apart, illustrating the traumatic event.

"I must ask G-Pa." The thought drained the last of Baput's hope. Jerry's eyeroll showed his agreement.

But Baput added, "G-Pa foretold this. He practically said we'd find it today. He knows something. I've got to ask him."

"I'll keep looking," Jerry offered, scraping at another area.

"Be careful!" Baput repeated.

"I'll get a broom," Jerry decided. He accompanied Baput as far as the sauna. "If we don't find it, we'll just search the iPlane for a material like that. There's gotta be something," he promised. "We'll make our own Net."

Keebra

Baput found the Akash in deep meditation with his headphones on. He felt a stab of guilt. He hadn't had a meaningful session with G-Pa since the Akash had rejected his apprentice for embracing Shavarandu. *But, didn't he, also? Look at him, so peaceful with his music. Is he on the Plane?*

Baput's eyes darted to the left, low on the rock wall of the sauna. He had sensed something there, without seeing it. Was it real? G-Pa still meditated, not moving a muscle, surely on the Plane. Baput's eyes slid back to the spot on the floor near the wall. The electric candle was the only light, and it didn't quite reach in there. Baput reached for the lantern, keeping his eyes on that spot on the floor. Something moved!

G-Pa's right hand lashed out so fast Baput barely saw it.

Eyes still closed, the Akash brought his arm back from the shadows. His hand was wrapped around the neck of a strange beast that was nothing but neck. No legs. Just head and neck, or was it tail? Baput had only seen these on the iPlane, or TV. They were so strange, so alien, he had never thought they were real.

It was smaller than the ones in the movies. About 18 inches long and only an inch across, it slithered back and forth as G-Pa held it up in front of his own face. *"Keebra!"* he addressed the serpent.

The gopher snake squirmed and flicked its little forked tongue in and out, in and out. G-Pa made a grotesque parody back at it with his own tongue. Then he turned the snake around, putting it in Baput's face, like he had done to his own.

Baput backed away, repulsed.

"You don't like Keebra?" the Akash shook the headphones off his ears. He was weirdly lucid. Baput could tell he'd had a vision. He went along eagerly, despite his discomfort with the snake.

"Akash, I have never, um, met Keebra before."

"You will like him, when you know him. When you know what he does. You want to do it. I know you do."

Do what? What is he accusing me of? Baput tried to look away, but he was transfixed, staring into those creepy vertical eyes and watching that tongue. Crazy or not, the Akash went on.

"Keebra commits Insitucide! Like you all want to do. Like I want to do, but it is against the rules. No one knows why, except for the Curse. They are afraid to go into a cave and kill the nimblies and bumblies in their sleep, when they are just slimy masses of sleeping pregnant mother bumblies coated with nimbly eggs. They are afraid because to touch them is to die, and worse. To touch them is to bring death to your family. You know this, yes?"

His arms tired, G-Pa finally released the snake. *It's way too small to eat a mother bumbly,* Baput thought as he watched it disappear under the wall into its tunnel. He had seen on the iPlane how such creatures could unhinge their jaws, but there was no way that thing could swallow a pregnant bumbly coated with nimbly eggs!

He answered G-Pa. "Yes, I know of the Curse. They used to send the downudara in. The children that were, um," he pointed to his head, then cocked it a little and stuck out his tongue. It was the normal symbolic gesture, part of the language, but an unexpected thought of Belinda rose from his gut and stabbed him in the heart. He had heard this story many times. Now it didn't seem the same at all. Delaying G-Pa's revelation, Baput went on telling about the downudara from his new perspective.

"They gave them daggers to pierce the momama bumblies' hearts, or poisons to throw on them. Those would kill the child too, but he would die anyway. It was better he die alone, deep in the Cave, because if he emerged, he would have the black slime on him. The Curse.

"The Council always said, 'He was downudara. He was put to his very best use.' But the parents wailed anyway, just like for any lost child. If the child came out, the parents would die. Especially the very loving ones. The brothers and sisters, if they were close to their downudara sibling, they would die too, because of the Curse.

"But they never got rid of the nimblies and bumblies, did they, G-Pa?" he searched the old man's eyes. Had he ever put an innocent downudara to death?

"No," G-Pa replied, shifting his eyes away. "They failed. We stopped the practice after..."

"After what, G-Pa?"

"Never mind!" the Akash snapped. He looked away and reached for the headphones.

"G-Pa, did you ever send a child in?"

"I said never mind!" the Akash barked hoarsely. "Do you wish to hear of Keebra? I shall speak no more of the pitiful downudara."

"Yes, Akash," Baput mumbled. He really wanted to hear about the Net, but this was the only program the G-Pa Network was offering today. At least it wasn't a rerun, for once. "Please tell me of Keebra."

G-Pa inhaled a calming breath and began. "Keebra is immune to the Curse. Keebra can go into the smallest holes and he can smell that queen..." The Akash levelled his fully alert eyes on Baput. "Keebra commits Insitucide for us."

Baput gasped. "But you said we cannot!" He stopped himself, took a breath and sat tall. Formally, he asked, "Akash, do you authorize Insitucide?"

"Keebra is authorized. You are not. Earth Boy is most definitely not. Nor his family. Or your family."

"But if we use Keebra? Send him in there, somehow, then we can?"

"Mmmmm, no." G-Pa put his headphones on and closed his eyes, as unreachable as an Earth teenager.

Jerry's 14th Birthday

Four months later, a perfectly smooth hemisphere jutted out of the gravel on the flat spot by the river; the Holy Rock that powered the weapon and the portal and who knows what else? Jerry decided to celebrate his 14th birthday right there on top of the wonderful discovery. Everybody was invited. "I mean everybody," he insisted. "They might not like it, but they've gotta see it and realize it's here. We've got a lot to talk about."

Jerry flew his birthday gift, a drone, ahead of them as they all hiked to the Rock. The low-flying, high-buzzing creature didn't exactly put the green folks at ease.

"Jerry! You're scaring them with that thing!" Fran admonished.

"I knew it would."

"I'm gonna fly it into that little cave," Jerry replied. "We have to find out if there's a queen."

The Akash leaned hard on his daughter, holding back as they approached the exposed Holy Rock. "No Cave! No Rock! No queen! No nimblies, no bumblies, no more!" he cried stubbornly.

"It looks different. It's shiny," Felsic observed quickly.

"It's in the sunlight." Baput explained. "No cave. But there was a cave here, so it is the same place as the Holy Cave at Nauve. It is another dimension."

The green faces were just as uncomprehending of their own son's rantings as they had been of Jerry's on their first day on Earth.

Baput signed, not wanting to continue. "It means, if we can rig it up like the Holy Rock, with the bicycle—"

"A generator," Elmer offered. "Save Felsic's legs. What else?"

"The red hairs that led to my switch, then to the Rock," Baput continued, trying to remember. It seemed so long ago.

"Copper wire, I'll bet. We can get that easy," Jerry promised.

"And the um, pipes, you call them. Also copper. But they are for shooting nimblies and bumblies. I don't think we need them for…" Baput trailed off and fell to one knee next to the Rock.

"We can go home!" Felsic declared the unspoken thought with a delight that none of the other green faces were registering.

Do they get it? Jerry wondered. *And they say Felsic is slow!*

A low murmur rippled through the little group. Big dark eyes looked deeply into other big dark eyes.

G-Pa erupted in a string of Nauvian curses that stopped abruptly with, "Nauve now! First Pomegranate Day, we will be Nauve!" He raised his longstick high and danced in a circle, then jumped onto the Rock, like he had almost two years ago. Everyone drew back and inhaled, all at once. Nothing happened, of course. They all exhaled, looking sheepish, because everyone knows these things only happen on First Pomegranate Day.

What Would You Bring?

Jerry and Baput sat on the smooth Rock beside G-Pa and ate their lunch. The others hunkered down on the ground, still not ready to sit directly on that strange and fateful surface. Fran and Star unpacked and distributed the food.

Felsic leaned over and sniffed Elmer's sandwich. "What's that?" he asked.

"It's meat. Animal. You don't like it," Elmer informed him.

"I try," Felsic proposed.

"No." Elmer finished it in three swift bites.

Fran could take no more. *Look at them! They might be able to go home, and they're all miserable. Except Felsic, of course. He wants to see his family. And G-Pa, squatting on that rock with that maniacal smile. I guess he's happy. But the other three, oh, my!*

Fran had spent many sleepless nights trying to empathize, wondering how they would feel about going back. *And if they do, how have we, I, changed them in ways that will make them, well…* she tried to imagine. *Miserable.* She had known better all along, but she'd spoiled them. *I just wanted them to be comfortable. Not just Star and me. All of us. Elmer, with his tools and vehicles. Certainly Jerry has changed Baput forever in less material, but far more damaging, ways. If he goes back and becomes Akash, those changes will be baked into their culture forever.* She had to assess the damage.

"Hey," she addressed the whole group, "if you could go back, what would you want to bring with you?" She turned to her best friend. "Star?" Her fears were immediately confirmed.

"Dishwasher!" came first, followed quickly by "refrigerator, freezer. Water that comes," she turned an invisible knob with her hand. "Even hot! Boors that…" she made a rushing sound with her lips and a circular motion with her arm.

"Flush. Yeah. They wouldn't work," Jerry interrupted rather roughly, Fran thought. "You gotta have running water."

"What else, Star?" Fran asked gently, hopefully.

"Underwear!" was next, provoking an appreciative grunt from Valko, a nod from Baput, and a hoot from Felsic. "Seeds for plants we don't have, like cotton, so we can make soft clothes." There was the simple, unassuming Star that Fran had met nearly two years ago. But invasive species? Foreign pathogens? Even that innocuous request could have devastating consequences.

Star was not finished, either. "Metal pots and pans. Plastic containers that don't break, canning jars and glass bottles for my oil, and my knives." There were grunts and nods of agreement all around for that one.

"What else would you bring, Felsic?" Fran turned to the most excited energy in the little group.

"Truck!" No hesitation.

Fran looked over at Elmer, who just shrugged, leaving it up to her to be the meanie. "Oh, no, Honey!" she tried. "You can't bring an internal combustion engine to your nice, clean planet!"

"Why not?" Felsic asked.

"It's not good for your world. Your air!"

"And you don't have any fuel," Jerry pointed out.

"Oh, my, they'll start digging for oil." Fran extrapolated. "No, Honey. Your world is better off without such things."

"Ganeesh would disagree," Felsic replied certainly. "I want my knife. And my razor," he stroked his bare chin, stared tauntingly at Valko's mane.

Valko's deep, quiet laugh drew Fran's attention.

"How about you, Valko? What treasure would you bring home from Earth?"

Just as quickly and certainly as the others, Valko replied, "shotgun."

Fran realized she should have known. "That's worse," she blurted. "Guns are a terrible thing to bring into a world that doesn't have them."

"The shotgun would kill the nimblies and bumblies," Valko argued. "We should all have shotguns. All the men. And boys. Women, maybe, even. No. Not safe. But, the men and boys, definitely. We would lose no more men. We would kill them all! If we go home, we must bring many guns. It is the key to our survival. Perhaps it is why all this happened." Valko rose to his feet in defense of his request.

Fran got up, too. It did little to improve her standing against the big man, but it felt better than sitting on the ground arguing with a mountain. So, of course, Elmer had to rise to her defense.

"There must be another way, Valko!" Fran bravely argued. "Guns are too easy. You kill all the nimblies and bumblies, and then your boys kill all the zebkin, if not for food, then for sport. The next thing you know, you're killing each other."

"We don't ever!" Valko claimed.

"If it's that easy, you will. Believe me. If you don't have to bash each other to death with rocks and sticks, if you can just stand over there and pull a little trigger, why, it'll be like everyone has the Evil Eye! In our world, people get mad and just go shoot a lot of people. People they don't even know. Children, even!" She checked Star for the expected wince, and got it, right on cue. "One raging person with a gun can kill more people than you lose in a whole Season to nimblies and bumblies, and it happens a lot more often than every three years. I'm sorry, Valko, we can't send you back to Nauve with guns."

There was a long, awkward silence while Valko adjusted to having "no" said to him so unequivocally, and by a woman, no less. Star would never deny him in such a way. Not in front of the others, anyway. The rest were silent, too, waiting for the explosion.

It turned out to be a dud. Valko muttered something into his beard.

"What's that, Buddy?" Elmer asked anxiously. He didn't want to take the big guy on, but he was willing to try.

"The rolls of soft paper from the boor."

"Toilet paper?" Elmer checked as another wave of nods and murmurs circled the group.

"Yes," Valko confirmed. "Many, many rolls. And metal tools. Knives, scythes, shovels, saws, hammers, files, drills. No razor." He glared playfully at his little brother.

"You got it, my friend," Elmer exhaled, relieved. He turned to the last competent green person. "How about you, Baput? What do you want from Earth?"

Baput made a little noise as his face turned a deeper green. "The model of the solar system," he began.

His answer was not as swift as the others, but Jerry's reply bit just as hard. "Nah. It's too hard to move. You'd have to take it apart, and put it in that big old case. And you guys will never figure out how to put it back together. No offense."

Fran chimed in, too. "Do you think your people are ready for it? It almost killed you when you first saw it." Her fears were real. Baput would rip through their belief system like a missionary on a rampage, tearing it apart just like Hugh's singular consciousness brought down the mighty Borg's collective one in *Star Trek: The Next Generation*.

"Maybe not yet, but they will be," Baput mused, looking at the seemingly oblivious face of the Akash.

"Another time, then," Jerry suggested brightly.

"Another time?" Fran asked.

"Well yeah. If it opens on First Pomegranate Day, then it will open every three years, right? We can go back and forth. Bring you more batteries for your flashlights and stuff."

"Yeah! Flashlights!" Felsic added to his list, while the radical new idea tried to sink in.

Baput's face was still tortured.

"What else, Hon?" Fran asked gently.

Baput didn't answer, so Jerry did, loud and rough. "Belinndaaa!" he dragged out the name.

Baput put his head down on his crossed arms. Star shot him a harsh look. "And my bowl," he mumbled without looking up. The tips of his ears turned a deep brownish green.

The Akash squatted at the highest point of the Rock in the robe Fran and Star had made him for First Full Kakeeche Day. *His eyes are lit, and he's smiling like he's out of his mind again, or is he just that happy?* Fran wondered.

He met her eyes and spoke. "You did not ask me, Earth Woman. Perhaps you do not care, or perhaps it is because you already know. I want nothing of your Earth." He spat on the Rock. "I take only my longstick and my robe."

Star flashed Fran a shy smile of acknowledgement.

"And my Shrine."

Baput and Jerry shared an eye roll.

"And my dog." He clucked at Shastina, who scrambled up on the Rock, claws scratching, paws sliding, tail wagging. "We will be Nauve soon. Yes, we will!" the Akash said gently in Nauvian to his most loyal subject.

Drone

Jerry didn't fly the drone but instead carried it along the rough, narrow, little-used part of the trail. The viney cliff towered on his right as he headed downriver, the others following at his heels. He stopped about 100 feet downriver, where the cliff wrapped around to face west. He found the two-foot diameter hole easily now that he knew it was there, about two-thirds of the way up.

He put the drone on the ground and pulled a small, white booklet and a handheld device with a tiny screen from the bag on his shoulder. The screen lit up and showed his feet.

"Back up, everybody," Jerry instructed.

They gladly obeyed, and the little flying creature buzzed like a nimbly, but with no eyes, no proboscis, just four little blades that whirled around. The humans squinted vainly at the glary little screen. The green faces stayed riveted on the "creature" in the sky.

"It's like nimbly and bumbly, Jerry," Felsic complained. "Same size!"

"Perfect," Jerry whispered. The dark circle of the cave entrance showed on the screen at the same time the warning flashed. "Signal Loss." The drone sputtered and sank sickeningly, then recovered. The warning vanished. Jerry pushed hard on the controller, trying to run it into the hole faster, before it lost the signal, but it sank again. He jerked the joystick to the right. It bounced off the cave wall, drawing a wince from the Earthlings.

Face twisted, knuckles white on the controller, a hiss of air sucking in at the corner of his mouth, Jerry piloted the little craft up, up, right along the cliff face. He ignored the flashing red warning, even though it blocked his view of the cave entrance on the screen. There it was: grayed out, dull behind the red. "Argggghhhh!" he let out a war cry as he pushed the joystick forward hard. The screen showed a dark, round hole. The drone slipped inside.

"It's go—" Jerry started to shout, but the screen went dark. A larger warning appeared, in brighter red: "Complete Signal Loss." It didn't even bother to flash. It just stayed on, mocking him, as Jerry furiously jerked the joystick one way and another.

"Is it stuck?" his dad asked.

"I don't know. Maybe. There's no signal at all."

"So it's stuck."

"I can't get it out." Jerry sighed. "I should have known. It's no-fo here. No signals of any kind, except the Plane. The Plane is so strong here, it blocks all the other signals."

Old-fashioned Fran spoke up. "You still have that old radio-controlled truck, don't you?"

"Yeah, Mom. That thing is old."

"Old's what we need. We can put a headlamp and camera on it."

"How do we get the camera feed?" Jerry wondered.

"Wires?" she answered.

"That was a gnarly little bugger." Elmer recalled Jerry's first model truck fondly. "It'll chew that fancy drone right out of the way. But how do we get it up there?" He rushed forward to grab a vine and place a foot on a tiny ledge in the cliff face. "When we were kids, we—"

"Elmer Musik! You're no kid! Get over here," Fran squawked like an angry hen.

Well-trained, or knowing his wife was right, Elmer obediently rejoined the group. "We need a physicist," he declared.

"And an engineer," Fran agreed.

Phone

After dinner, the Musiks waited for the traditional birthday phone call from Patrick and family. When the singing and the well wishes were behind them, Elmer broached the subject.

"We've got a job for you guys. You'll like it," "You too, Lor." he added quickly.

Elmer heard a low groan from the other side. He shoved Jerry forward. "Tell 'em, Kid."

Jerry told them all about how they'd finished clearing all the dirt from The Rock, but they hadn't found anything like the Net in all their searching on the internet. He finished with the story about losing the drone in the high cave.

"The old cave," Patrick mused into the phone. Elmer could just see him touching his bent nose. "Remember, El?"

"Of course," Elmer grunted, "Sorry all over again, Bud."

"That's OK," Patrick dismissed the old grudge.

Fran broke in to unlock the brothers. "Jerry has a radio-controlled truck. Would that work, do you think? Radio waves?"

Patrick drew a breath, trying to collect his racing thoughts. "We don't know what we're dealing with, so who knows? How far out from the cave did the signal cut out?"

"About halfway up it took a dive. Then I finally got it into the cave and totally lost it. It's still in there," Jerry mourned.

Patrick went on. "Maybe our signals get impacted by the waves from the Cave. Waves from the Cave!" he repeated dreamily. "They hit our waves and mess them up, distort them so they can't transmit information anymore. Not in our language, anyway."

After a respectful silence, Elmer brought up the ganeesh in the room. "We have to get up there, safe and easy, so we can work."

"A platform!" Lorraine exclaimed, suddenly interested. "How high?"

"About 20 feet above the river trail, 10 feet below the driveway. I was thinking maybe winching ourselves up or down to a platform at the mouth of the cave," Elmer rattled out an unexpected plan.

Lorraine was fully engaged now. "We'll need some measurements. I'll borrow the survey gear from work. Just let me—"

Patrick cleared his throat.

"Us." Lorraine corrected, "Let *us* brainstorm on it. We'll come down there on Labor Day. That gives us a month to plan."

They all agreed. Elmer hung up while Jerry jumped up and down, pumping his fist and whooping.

Patrick felt like a kid on Christmas! Lorraine never did anything with the family anymore. He knew how to appeal to her. "They want you as Battle Engineer."

"Battle Engineer, huh?" Lorraine's face lit up. "Like Scotty?"

"Better." A fellow Trekkie to the core, Patrick played along. "Rom. The Ferengi on *Deep Space Nine*. He was the best Battle Engineer."

"Yeah. Rom. I need to burn some vacation time anyway. Sounds like more fun than hanging around here."

Ouch, thought Patrick. They didn't usually go places because it was hard on Belinda, and, Patrick guessed, even harder on Lorraine. She wasn't used to it. He liked to go camping, out in the woods with no one around, like he used to with his mom, dad, and Elmer. Lorraine didn't like it that much, though, and everyplace was so crowded now.

But now, a new Lorraine chattered excitedly. "Labor Day week is wide open. I'll take the whole week off!" She listed, threatened to sink. "I'll have a stack of work when I get back. Those guys won't touch anything... Aww, to hell with it! Let's go Battle Engineer some nimblies and bumblies!"

Go Nauve?

The workers' quarters was silent except for the chewing, the clinking of the odd metal utensils they had still not quite mastered, and the singing. G-Pa sang a happy old song about the beauty of Nauve. He sang it over and over again, twenty times or more.

> "The bright red flowers on the kip tree.
> Kiko bird plumed in the greeny green top.
> The low, lazy river swims.
> Past the caves in the hills.
> Past the huts in the village.
> Past the rice in the bogs.
> As the zebkin watch from the shadows."

Valko didn't roar, he whispered. "Enough, Old Man!"

G-Pa stopped singing abruptly. A slow smile spread across his wrinkled face. He looked younger, somehow. His eyes were clear, fully comprehending. "We will be Nauve on First Pomegranate Day. The Rock will send us home." He looked into Baput's eyes. "And you, my grandson, will be Alanakash."

Baput had not seen that clarity in his G-Pa's eyes since they arrived. It was familiar, but seemed different now. The Akash had seemed so wise at Nauve! Back then, Baput had never seen behind those clear eyes.

"Akash," Baput addressed his mentor respectfully, as Star cleared the dishes and the men moved into the living room. "You seem very, um, certain tonight."

"Oh, yes. We will be Nauve soon. Back in our own hut. You will ascend to Alanakash and marry Tamaya on Passascenday. I will retire with great honor. Salistar will continue to tether me. I will continue to search the Plane for wisdom and continue to advise my Alanakash. I fear your training has suffered this cycle with all this nonsense." He waved his hands at the world dismissively.

Amazed by the old man's sudden clarity, Baput realized Patrick was right. Nauve was an old, familiar pattern that made sense to him, but G-Pa could never mold himself into Earth's pattern. He could only be fully alive at Nauve.

Fully alive at Nauve. Baput repeated the silent phrase in his head. He tried to remember Nauve. *I was such a child! The things I thought! What I believed!* It all seemed as alien to him as it probably did to Jerry. He did *not* remember feeling fully alive. Not until Earth. Not until Jerry showed him the model of the solar system.

His momama stepped into the room after loading the dishwasher. Baput met her eyes deeply, for a microsecond, before she shied away. Popa also avoided his eyes. Felsic stared out the window, fidgeting. He was the easy one. He had a clear reason to want Nauve.

Baput stood tall and addressed his uncle, "Felsic."

Felsic snapped to attention, eyes wide, as if he had been addressed by a full Alanakash. The reaction made Baput uneasy, but he pushed on. This needed to be done. "Do you want to return nauve?"

Felsic did not hesitate. "Yes, of course. To Peratha and Trillella." His excited face deflated. "But, if not for them, well, here I have Elmer. I work on Big Truck and Little Truck. Nauve, I, I…"

"You make the wine," Star pointed out, "for all of Nauve."

"I make the wine for all of Nauve," Felsic mocked in a bitter tone Baput had never heard before. "So important! They don't even give me an apprentice. What has Nauve ever done for me? I go only for Peratha and Trillella. If not for them, I would choose Earth."

The real Akash stormed across the room to where Felsic cowered. "You weak, stupid little man! How dare you speak this way? Your wife and child have no man! You would stay here and play with those soulless beasts? With that evil man who mocks Kakeeche? You ignorant winemaker—"

Baput brightened suddenly, interrupting the Akash without thinking. "Maybe they can come here," he suggested. "If the portal opens, maybe Peratha and Trillella can come through!"

Felsic rushed right past his Akash. "Yes! Peratha and Trillella could be on Earth!" His scanned the quarters, pointed to his room. "They would stay in my room with me. They would help you, Salistar, with the cooking and the oil and weaving the squares. I would keep working for Elmer, fix trucks, pick kips, and make good wine." He danced around the room on light feet, humming the tune G-Pa had been singing, without the words.

G-Pa cleared his throat, an ugly rattle of phlegm.

Baput swallowed hard and looked longingly at Salistar, then faced his popa. His eyes were still at beard level. He could just see the jut of Popa's chin if he crossed his eyes. "Popa? Do you wish to return to Nauve?"

A long, indistinct rumble went on for what seemed a very long time. Felsic stopped humming and stood perfectly still. G-Pa was silent, his sharp eyes drilling into the side of Valko's head. Valko squirmed uncomfortably as if he could feel it. The ground shifted under Baput as he saw his popa looking tender and small, almost childlike, for just a microsecond, quick as an electric shock.

Valko's mouth tried to stick shut when he finally opened it to speak. "Son, you must return. Nauve needs its Akash. If Nauve indeed still exists."

"It does. As sure as Patrick and Belinda and Lori Anne still exist. But I did not ask for my sake. I ask *you*, Popa. Would you rather be Nauve, or here, on Earth?"

Another long silence. Valko stroked his copious beard. "I miss Rakta."

G-Pa hissed a scoff. "Foolish war chief," he muttered.

Valko turned his bulk on his withered father-in-law. "And Sammos. All my other close-mates are dead." He went silent again.

The Akash hovered in front of him, glaring at his chest.

Valko whirled away. "This is not about what I want. If there is a queen, she is here because of us. We must fight her and her spawn. Eradicate them by whatever means necessary!" he roared, raising his fist, his back to the old man. "We became on Earth while the first wave of nimblies filled the sky. Is that the time we would be Nauve, during the first wave? That would leave the Earth people to fight them alone! They know nothing about these beasts. If we leave, Earth will be overrun, like Nauve. And it will be because of us."

Baput proudly joined his popa's side. He stared hard at his G-Pa, suddenly realizing he was looking down. His mentor was so small! The Tiny Akash dream flitted through Baput's head, and he smiled without meaning to. It felt silly, yelling at him. A waste of energy. What did it matter what this tiny, incoherent man thought?

Baput turned away and looked down at Salistar. "Momama?"

A tortured look stole into Star's eyes. Baput spoke gently, as if coaxing a zebkin to eat from his hand. "Do you wish to stay on Earth, or return to Nauve?"

Star's wrinkled face looked desperately at Baput, at Felsic, then at Valko for a longer time. Her expression did not change. Then her eyes came around slowly to meet her popa's eyes, which were waiting for hers, like a trap. When their eyes met, she raised a hand to her mouth to cover a distorted sob. She bolted to the bedroom. Valko looked after her, his upper body and soul straining to follow while his feet stayed planted in front of G-Pa.

A broad smile spread across the face of the Akash. "My dear daughter. She is overcome with joy. We go Nauve on First Pomegranate Day," the Akash stated simply, as if there were no question.

Betrayal

It was Jerry's first day of high school, and Kate was there, standing in the checkered hallway surrounded by grey lockers, bright spirit posters, and her many friends. Her long black hair hung straight down, framing her oval face. Jerry hadn't seen that perfect face, with its fine, pointy nose, cheekbones, and chin, since Kate had graduated elementary school and went off to middle school four years ago.

She looked the same, mostly, but a lot taller. Taller than Jerry, he noticed. And, as Baput would say, she had plumage! She was no socialite. She didn't wear makeup. She mostly wore jeans and T-shirts, like Mom. She was popular, though. Not with the cheerleaders and jocks, but with the kids that did after-school stuff like drama club, or debate team, or that science club Jerry's grandma had started when she was the science teacher here. Jerry was definitely joining that. For Kate, it was journalism. She'd been on the school paper all last year. Now she was a junior. She had a driver's license and her own car.

"Hi, Kate!" Jerry said, as casually as he could, looking up to meet her eyes. She just walked past, as if she hadn't noticed the kid who had loved her for as long as he could remember, who had missed her every day since she had left him to struggle through middle school all alone.

He signed up for the school paper. At the beginning of the first meeting, he found a chance to talk to her. "You remember me, right?" he ventured, fearing the answer.

"Yeah!" Her face lit up in a slow, fond smile as she recognized the cute little boy who used to follow her around, spying on her from afar. "You're Jerry!"

"Yeah. I'm here now. I'm a freshman," Jerry blathered, feeling like a total dork.

"Good for you!" Kate squeaked in a voice you'd use on an insane child.

He was crushed. He deserved it, too. What a geek! *What was I supposed to say?*

The meeting was called to order. The journalism teacher aimed his presentation at the new kids, like Jerry. "Journalism is tough! It may seem exciting and glamorous, but for every moment of glory, there will be hours of boredom, frustration, defeat, even fear, for some of you. It's up to you what kinds of risks you want to take. You can write a gossip column and risk lawsuits. You can be a war correspondent and risk your life. You can find something to investigate and go after it. Risk it all to change the world. Or, you can do sports; that's pretty low risk. That's the great thing about journalism. There are so many different things you can do with it. But no matter what you do, even if you're just a talking head reading someone else's copy, there's one thing you've got to have. You've got to love a good story. You've got to be willing to do anything, and I do mean *anything,* for a good story!"

Jerry watched Kate's mouth form the words, "A good story."

The teacher went on. "You'll know it when you see it. Then you'll start seeing stories within stories, if you have the nose for it. But watch out! Don't lose sight of the main story. Remember that."

When the meeting broke up, Jerry stood just outside the door until Kate walked by, chatting with a plump, blond girl in thick glasses. "Go out with me," he muttered, barely audibly.

"Excuse me?" She answered, looking down at him.

The other girl said, "See you," and kept walking.

Kate looked down at Jerry. "What did you say?"

Fight or flight? Jerry *so* wanted to run. But he took a deep breath, like Baput had taught him. "Would. You. Go. Out. With. Me?" He could barely launch the words. "Please?" he wheezed, a little late.

"Oh, Jerry." That babysitter tone again. "Sweetie, you need to find a girl your age. I'm too old. I'm just an old hag, see?"

How could she say that about the most beautiful girl in the whole school system? Even if it was herself. And why was she talking to him like that? Jerry felt white heat all around his head. His ears rang, and he could feel his temperature rising. The words came out without his bidding, without thought. "I have a story. A big story. Something that's never happened before!"

Kate stopped short and faced Jerry directly. The heat and the white haze suddenly dropped away, leaving him cold and hollow. "Oh, really? What about?"

"Go out with me, and I'll tell you."

"This better be good," Kate cautioned.

"It's real good. It's the story of the century! You'll see. Go out with me Friday night. Just a burger and shake after school, but it's a date. I'll buy, but you'll have to drive. Then after, we'll go to my place, and I'll show you. You can even take pictures." Jerry proposed, all the time wondering who this person was who had taken over his mouth.

Her sharp eyes blinked over her pert nose. She nodded. "Why not? I know your family. Besides, I'll have my car. It's a date."

Friday night was the annual Farm Co-op dinner. It was one of the few times Fran and Elmer ever went out. They used to drag Jerry along, but now he was old enough to stay by himself for a few hours in the evening. Besides, he was never alone.

"I'll ask Star to feed you," Fran had assured him. "Eat there, Honey, OK? Or, at least let her give you something and eat it here. Even if you eat freezer junk after. That way, you get your vegetables, OK?"

"I'll be fine, Mom," Jerry had promised.

Kate paid a little more attention to Jerry whenever they passed in the halls for the rest of the week. Always a bright, happy, not-too-condescending, "Hi, Jerry!" even if she was with other girls, or even guys!

Friday finally arrived. Jerry waited alone in front of the school for Kate to come out. The other kids were getting on the school busses. Nobody hung around for clubs on Friday afternoon! It's the weekend! Time to go on dates! *What if she's playing me?* No, here she was, with three other girls. Laughing and talking. *Are they laughing about me?* The group of girls walked right toward him.

"See you Monday, ladies. I've got a date!" Kate crowed, stopping in front of the trembling freshman.

"Oooh!" the girls cooed. It didn't sound sarcastic, but who knew?

"Let's go," Kate greeted Jerry and rushed him toward her car, looking around as if hoping not to be seen. "Do you really just want a burger and shake?" she asked as Jerry opened the passenger door.

"Sure!" he answered. "I don't care. Better eat, though. You're gonna want to spend some time documenting what I'm going to show you, so eat up now. It's gonna be the night of your life!"

Kate turned to look drolly at the little kid with the big presentation. *What's he on about? Something only a little boy would find amazing? Or does he really have something?*

She drove past the Burger Bar where most of the kids from school went and crossed town to a slow-food restaurant. "Better burgers," she lied. Jerry knew she was avoiding the crowd, but he was glad. He was only selling his story to one person. *Selling my story. Baput's story. Salistar's story. What am I doing? Why?*

He met Kate's breathtaking eyes across the roof of her car. They were deep brown, almost black, like Baput's, like Salistar's, but without the innocence. He studied the cracked white lines of the parking lot as he followed her into the restaurant. They sat at a booth in the empty mid-afternoon diner. Jerry stared at the shiny napkin holder until the waitress brought menus to stare at. They were better. You could hide behind them.

"I'll have a double cheeseburger, onion rings and a chocolate shake," he told the waitress. Puffing his chest a little, he made a gallant gesture toward Kate, "and the lady will have..."

"I'll have the same," Kate echoed, not wanting to spend any more of Jerry's money than he did. *What is he, on an allowance? If he's a source, shouldn't I be buying? No, he wants a date. OK, he's got it. Time to start pumping.*

"So, Jerry," she began sweetly, "Whatcha got for me, buddy?"

"You won't believe me," Jerry mumbled.

"I'm here, aren't I? You said you had a story, now dish." Not as gently as she'd planned. *Good practice, though, even if it's nothing.*

Jerry's face was bright red. That white hot feeling was back. There was a giant force sitting on his head, trying to keep his mouth shut. Those eyes, with their long, dark eyelashes, appeared through the fog. She pinched the straw of her shake and sucked, her cheeks drawing in gauntly.

A deal's a deal. Jerry told himself, forgetting his promise to his parents, and his unspoken obligation to Baput and his family. He drew in a long, slow breath. He wanted to run. "There are aliens working at my place."

"Oh. Is that all? That's not exactly new, you know. Not the story of the century," Kate informed him crisply.

"Not *that* kind of aliens. Alien aliens. Like, from another planet. Except I think it's another dimension. We know they're not from here because they're green." There. He'd said it. *Please don't believe me!* Part of Jerry begged wordlessly at the girl who held his heart.

"Green aliens."

"Bright green. Well, different shades, but they're all definitely green, not like you've never seen on an Earth person. They have black hair and dark brown eyes like yours." He looked right into the eyes that were finally really looking at him. He gulped hard and carried on. "They look just like us, otherwise. There's five of them. A family. The grandpa is Akash, a holy man. And my friend Baput, he's my age, but bigger. His dad is huge! But his uncle's normal size and so is his mom. Baput's the apprentice Akash. He can go online without a computer! Just with his mind!" Jerry spewed on, downloading all the awesome stuff he'd been holding in for so long.

For almost two years he hadn't said a word. He had *so* wanted to tell his friends at the beginning of seventh grade when the green family appeared out of nowhere. He longed to share the majesty of the Plane, laugh at the amusing first encounters with familiar objects and mock the Kakeeche ceremony with his best buds with whom he had shared everything, back when life was boring. Now he had something exciting, a totally unique perspective to share. He'd shared it with his family, and it had no doubt brought them closer. But they could see it all for themselves. The kids at school, they didn't know, couldn't see. Only he could. It made him special. Unique. But only if he could share it. Only if he told.

He heard Elmer in his head: "Loose lips sink ships." That jerked him back to the here and now, where he found himself still looking into Kate's eyes. Besides the meaning of life, they held fascination, with incredulity creeping in from the edges.

"You got pictures?"

"No way. My mom won't let me. I'm not supposed to let anyone know." *Ouch! I'm going against Mom, and she's right! What am I doing?*

"Why?" Kate asked.

"Well, you know, ET, Men in Black, Superman. You know what happens when people find out there's aliens."

"So why are you telling me?" Kate wondered, thinking, *this kid watches too much TV or something.*

Why, indeed? Jerry groped frantically in his mind for the answer. It was like a spell! He didn't want to tell, but he couldn't resist! No more hiding! No lying! Just tell the truth for once!

"I want you to have the story of the century. The biggest story of all time. First contact with aliens. Come to my place and see. My folks are at the co-op thing, so they won't know I told you."

"Well, can I put it in the paper?"

"No! You can't tell anyone!"

"Not much of a story then. Earlier you said I could take pictures, document stuff. What good is all that if I can't publish?"

Jerry saw a way out. "OK, you don't have to come out. Just forget it, OK? Enjoy your dinner, and let's go."

"Really? OK, fine," Kate agreed stubbornly.

They finished their meal in silence. At last, Jerry had to say, "I still need a ride home, though."

Jerry paid for their early dinner, and they got back in the car. Kate headed out of town at Jerry's direction, watching the businesses drop away and the houses get farther apart. Jerry was fiddling on his cell phone.

"HIDE," Jerry used his phone to send an email to his own address with the word 'Baput' in the subject line, hoping the signal would find him. *Darn! Baput will be with G-Pa in the sauna until I come home. He can't get a signal in there.* "Emergency. Hide everyone NOW." He emailed again.

"Who are you texting?" Kate demanded.

"Just my mom," Jerry lied, putting his phone away. "You can drop me off at my driveway, at the school bus stop. My bike's there," he mumbled, feeling like a pile of something really stinky.

Kate dug in. "Oh, no. You had your date. I'm driving you all the way out there. I kept my part of the deal. Now you're gonna show me some green aliens!"

"It's right after the bridge, on the right. I have to get out and open the gate if you're coming up. Maybe you shouldn't. It might be dangerous."

That made it irresistible. "I'm coming up, Jerry. Open the gate."

Baput had heard the school bus hours ago, but no Jerry. Elmer and Francina weren't going to be home tonight, and he hoped Jerry would eat dinner with them. But where was he?

Baput pretended to meditate, to keep G-Pa quiet. He used all his mind to hear in the distance. An unfamiliar engine approached, slowed, crunched on the gravel driveway and stopped. A car door opened. Baput heard the clang of the lock coming out of the slot, and the creak of the gate swinging on its hinges. He unfolded his legs and stepped out of the shed. The signal rose up all around him, filling the air. "Emergency! Hide everyone!"

He ducked back into the shed and looked at G-Pa. He was out. Sleeping, meditating, drifting again, who knew? He would be hard to rouse, and slow to move. Jerry said "emergency." Was there danger? Could G-Pa hide here, in the windowless, solid-rock shed? He looked into Shastina's eyes. "Stay, girl," he said sternly. "Guard G-Pa. Stay." He patted her head and crept out of the shed, watching the driveway. He heard Jerry's bike start up.

He ran across the grass to the quarters as fast as he could. To his relief, everyone was there; Momama, Popa, and Felsic. He heard the bike rev up. He could tell it wasn't moving. Jerry was stuck!

Felsic rushed to the door as Baput entered. "Four-wheeler!" he shouted, trying to pass Baput.

Jerry veered toward the edge of the driveway, putting the front wheel of his dirt bike in the ditch. The back end stuck out in the driveway, blocking the Celica. Jerry revved the bike, spinning the back tire and spraying dirt and gravel at the car.

"Hey!" Kate hollered from the driver's seat.

"I'm stuck!" Jerry lied, revving and stalling. Then he remembered the last time he'd gotten stuck. *Felsic and Baput came down on the four-wheeler to get me out. Can't have that.* He jumped the front wheel out of the ditch and tore off up the driveway, again spraying rocks at the following car. He reached the top of the driveway. He didn't see anyone.

"Felsic, wait!" Baput blocked Felsic's path. "Jerry said to hide. There, he's got it loose. Hear it? He's coming."

Valko crossed the room to the front door, his trained ears alert. "Something else is coming, too."

"Another motor. Not Little Truck. A car, I think, but not Francina's," Felsic reported.

Baput pushed his way inside, forcing the men into the house. "Jerry sent a message. We must hide. There is danger coming."

"Where is Akash?" Star checked dutifully.

"In the sauna with Shastina. I couldn't wake him up fast enough. He's hiding there. I told Shastina to make him stay."

The motor noises got closer. Baput ran to his room, where he could see the driveway and Jerry's porch. His family followed, peeking through the high window. Baput climbed on the top bunk and lay low and still like a lump of blankets. Star hopped up and down, too short to see. Valko put his arm around her to still her but didn't lift her up.

"It's a woman!" Felsic said out loud as Jerry escorted the white-skinned young lady up the steps to his house.

"Shhh!" Baput urged.

Star escaped Valko's embrace and tried to climb into the upper bunk. Baput offered his hand, ignoring his popa's glare. "She's beautiful!" She whispered as the two disappeared into the house.

Jerry hopped off his bike and rushed over to Kate's driver's door, his eyes scanning the quarters, the grassy area, the sauna. "Here's the house. Come on in!" he invited.

"Are they in there?" she asked.

"Maybe. Sometimes they're in here. Come on!"

Kate entered the cozy, but empty, house. *His parents aren't home. Is this brat trying to pull something?* A yellow dog raised his head from the couch, then lowered it and watched with lazy eyes. *Some watchdog,* she mused.

"They're in the fields, working," Jerry explained. "They'll be along real soon. Hey, you want to see something really cool?"

"Cooler than green aliens?"

"No, but cool." He escorted the suspicious girl to the back room and showed her the model of the solar system. "They had this at the high school, back when my grandmother taught science there. When the school got computers, they wanted to throw this out. Can you believe it? So my gramma took it home. See, it even has the moons and everything." He spun the tiny orbs, naming them all. He kept wondering if she was going to go into a spasm, like Baput.

Of course, she didn't. She walked around the model, touching the tiny spheres, making them spin. "This is really cool. You're right. And it's even real! Can I take a picture?"

"Sure!" Jerry gushed, hoping she would accept this story, instead of the less-credible green alien one.

She took pictures from every angle. Then she looked at Jerry and grinned. "So, which one of these planets do your green people come from?"

On the top bunk next to Baput, Salistar sighed. "Why does he say, 'hide'? Why can't we meet her?"

Valko grumbled. "His parents are not home. He tells us to hide, and he brings a woman. What do you think? These people are not so different."

"She's not his betrothed!" Felsic filled in the blank.

"Oh no!" Star screamed in a whisper. "Jerry! No! He would not! It *is* his betrothed. He is 14. His horn is out." She gestured with a finger protruding from her nose, the bumbly symbol.

Felsic guffawed.

"But he's too young. Not 15 yet. Not Passascenday," Salistar sighed like a schoolgirl. "Betrothed and so in love, they can't wait. Fran told me to feed him. I must bring him dinner." She bailed off the top bunk with no warning.

Baput clamored after her. "No, Momama! You can't! We have to hide!!"

"You have dinner for Disobedient Earth Boy," Valko rumbled, "but none for your family?"

"You don't know he's disobedient," Baput defended his friend, hoping he was right.

"He does this the one time his parents are not here." Valko replied flatly.

"Oh, I hope it's his betrothed!" Salistar fretted as she brought dinner from the oven. When she dished, she saved a portion for G-Pa and a double portion for Jerry.

"So, where are they, Jerry?" Kate wasn't satisfied with the model after all. He had promised her the story of a lifetime. Aliens. Not a fluff piece about an old model, although she would take that story, too. She was pretty sure that was going to be all the Musik Place had to offer, anyway.

"Still working in the fields."

"Well, let's go find them. I can't stay here all day, you know."

"The fields are really far. The four-wheeler is down. We'd have to walk a long way."

"So let's walk! Remember, I'm a journalist. I'll do anything for a story," she bragged. *"Almost* anything," she added quickly, still not sure about this kid's motivations.

The screen porch had a rarely used door that opened on the side of the house opposite the quarters. Kate could tell it was not the usual egress, because Jerry had to move a small wicker table piled with a year's worth of magazines to even get to it. He led the way down a pair of rickety wooden steps into a patch of waist-high weeds. Kate started to grumble, but anything for a story, right?

Jerry picked up a deer trail toward the West Orchard. The driveway ran along the other side of the house, right past the shop, where Valko and Felsic might be tinkering with metal and motors.

"Where are we going?" a tense Kate-voice asked from behind him.

"The orchard."

"Isn't there, like, a road?"

"No."

Kate stopped in a narrow, dry creek bed. There were stickers on the ends of her sleeves that scratched her face when she tried to brush her hair out of it. Her jeans were covered with little round burrs that stuck like Velcro. She couldn't even see her shoes, the laces were so buried in stickers. "I'll never get these stickers out!" she whined.

Jerry headed back toward the creek bed to help her.

"Get away from me!" she squealed like a scared little girl. He knew she wasn't, but it still made him feel like a super creep.

"I must bring food to Akash," the Akashic Tether insisted.

"But, he's in the shed, alone," Valko replied, levelling a stern gaze at Baput.

"I was in a hurry," Baput defended. "I didn't think it would be for so long."

"You need a ganeesh," Felsic advised.

"Ganeesh?" Valko sneered.

"We are hiding, like nimbly and bumbly Season! You go out there, you need a ganeesh."

"Well, we don't even have a dog. She's in the shed, too," Valko snapped.

"To protect G-Pa from whatever was coming. I didn't know what, or how long. Jerry just said 'hide everybody.'"

Star vanished into the kitchen, returning with a large woven grass bag. "I must go," she insisted. She headed for the door, not looking at anyone.

Baput stepped in front of her. She looked up into his eyes. Yes, up. It was the first time she'd realized it.

"Momama, you must stop."

"You who left your Akash alone in the cold, dark shed as night fell and dinnertime came? You may be apprentice, but you are no tether!"

"No, he is not," Valko declared, hefting the bag. "That's a lot of food for one old man."

The trail opened up into the West Orchard. Kate emerged from the weeds, her pointy cheeks and chin blazing crimson, matching the fire in her eyes. Jerry really, really liked her right then.

She launched on him. "Jerry Musik, there better be aliens out here, or I am gonna tell everybody you lured me out here under false pretenses, when your parents weren't home, and what are you trying to do anyway? What do you want from me?"

He tried to sound extra calm. It was extra annoying. "I wanted to show you aliens, but now, well," his heart sank, "I think you'd better go."

"And the aliens?"

Jerry's shoulders slumped and his head bowed.

She couldn't see his face when he mumbled, "There aren't any."

"What did you say? You mumbled."

Jerry raised his head, but he still could not look Kate in the eyes. "I said, there are no green aliens. I made it up."

"But why?" Kate asked, almost tenderly. "What were you trying to do? Luring me out here through the bushes to this orchard, when your parents aren't home?" She took off running down one of the orchard rows. "Oh! What do we have here?" she crowed sarcastically.

Oh, crap, she found one, thought Jerry.

"A road!" Kate finished her sentence.

Jerry heard fast feet running down the driveway that went past the shop and ended at the quarters. He sent another email to Baput, "Shut off the lights and lock the door!" *If the shop is empty, and she stays away from the quarters… She won't look. I told her I made it all up.*

Jerry watched her go, unable to move. First, his hopes of Kate ever liking him blew away. Then the bigger stuff underneath started to erode before his eyes. His reputation at school. A kook, or worse, a creep. And his parents would definitely hear. *Mom doesn't do Facebook, but she talks and emails with other moms who do. I'll be the crazy creep on Facebook. Worldwide. And Mom will know I betrayed my best friend. And I don't even know why I did it. Kate's right! What did I want?*

He ran as fast as he could down the rutted driveway that Big Truck followed when they harvested the pomegranates. "Lights off. Lock the door. Hide. Lights off. Lock the door. Hide." He chanted over and over, trying to get the message onto the Plane.

Valko unpacked the food bag he'd removed forcibly from his wife's stubborn grip. "One for Akash," he brought out plastic food container. "And two for Jerry?" he asked, producing a much larger container. "You approve, do you, of this pairing?"

"She is very beautiful."

"You know nothing about her, except that Jerry cannot let his parents see her."

"She's not his betrothed. Has to be that," Felsic stated again.

"They don't do that here," Baput informed them for the first time. In the shocked silence that followed, Jerry's signal came through loud and clear. "Lights off!" Baput cried, leaping for the light switch. "Lock the door! Hide."

They crouched below the windows in the waning evening light. They heard shouts in the distance. Then the light footstep of that strange woman coming down the driveway, followed by Jerry's heavier, clumsier tread. They stood frozen in the semi-darkness. The lighter steps were just outside.

Kate stopped at the intersection with the main driveway. On the right, in front of Jerry's house, was her car. She could hear Jerry's footsteps approaching. Still time to get away. To the left, the workers' quarters brooded, dark and silent. She felt like it was looking at her. She turned left.

Notebook in her hand and heart in her throat, Kate leapt up on the porch of the quarters. She thought she heard a faint rustling low along the walls. She knocked. No one answered. She tried the door. It was locked.

Jerry caught up with her. "What are you doing?" he demanded, almost grabbing her. He dropped his hands and backed off. There was that rustling sound again.

"I just thought, maybe, if they were real, they'd live here, right? I was just still hoping they were real."

"And you'd have the story of the century."

She turned and walked down the steps, slowly this time. "Yeah, but, besides that. It would just be, well, you know... cool."

Jerry dared to walk beside her down the driveway into the setting sun. He wanted to say he was sorry, but it didn't seem like nearly enough, so he didn't say anything.

They stopped at her car. She faced him as she opened the door. "Well, um, thank you, Jerry. I think I got my story."

Jerry trudged slowly towards his house, wondering just which story she was talking about.

As Kate climbed into the car, something caught her eye. In the darkening distance, purple-blue wisps of fog rose out of the river and drifted across the grass like fairy tale figures. One looked like a white German shepherd, tinged purple in the misty sunset. It turned sharply and barked at something behind it; an old wizard with stringy, lavender hair, wearing a bulky robe and leaning on a long staff.

What?! That's gotta be the fog! Did Jerry drug me at the restaurant? I gotta get out of here! She stuck her head out and took one last picture.

"If it was me, you would insist I tell you everything," Baput remarked sternly the next morning.

The men mowed in their various ways, and the boys raked up the clippings and loaded them onto the trailer behind the four-wheeler. Baput hadn't taken to driving like Felsic had. That was fine with Jerry. He loved driving the four-wheeler.

Jerry knew his friend was right, but he tried not answering.

Uncharacteristically, Baput pressed. "Momama thinks she's your betrothed, but you're too young to be together. Felsic thinks she's not your betrothed at all!"

This must be juicy stuff on Nauve, Jerry thought, suddenly shuddering at the tale of Romey and Jakima. *Would they stake me out naked with Kate? Hmm.* "Something like that," he admitted.

"But you said you guys don't get betrothed."

"We're not!" Jerry snapped, too hard. "Not ever, after that." He softened to a mush.

"Why not?"

"I shouldn't have invited her here."

"Why did you?"

Jerry looked up into his friend's warm, dark eyes, full of real, if nosy, concern. How could he tell his best friend he'd almost sold him out? *And for what? A woman? What does that even mean?* Unable to confess the truth, he didn't answer.

Baput drew in a sharp breath. "Oooh! I get it! You like her. You choose her! What is that like? How do you choose?"

"I don't know." Jerry thought about it. "I really have no idea. It's kind of like something from the Plane. It just comes to you. You see someone, and you just like them, a lot, from that first moment." His eyes and tone got dreamy. "That was years ago, in elementary school." He sighed dramatically. "I have loved her ever since." He looked at Baput and managed a smile. "I guess.

But, what do *I* know? I'm 14. I don't know what love is. I just got hormones or something."

"But if you have to choose for yourself, the grown-ups must teach you how. In school, your high school. Or your parents, don't they teach you? There must be rules. Guidelines?" Baput kept trying while Jerry shook his head helplessly.

"Everybody says it's all mysterious. You just feel stuff and try to act on it. Then if she doesn't feel the same, you fall on your face and feel like an idiot. And it hurts, a lot. I got a taste of it last night. I tell you, I should have left that girl in fantasyland."

Baput wasn't listening. He was stuck back a sentence or two. "You mean, she gets to choose, too?"

"Of course. We used to be like you guys about women, but now our women have rights, just like us men. We're trying, anyway."

Baput rode backwards in the trailer watching the ruts roll out behind them as they putted to the mulch pile. As they passed the quarters where Momama and Fran were weaving squares, he felt the familiar tenderness, and a new pang of pain. He pushed the tale of Romey and Jakima out of his head. Was it easier for Jerry, or harder? *What if a girl says no? What if Tamaya said no? What if Belinda...?*

He thought of the poor kiko bird, prevailing over the other males and climbing all the way up the trunk of the pomegranate tree only to have her turn her beak away and fly off with someone else.

7. Construction

"It sure smells like home," Patrick noted as he stepped out of the Look'N Up Plumbing van into the Labor Day Weekend air. The two boys scrambled down the porch steps to meet him. Or, rather, to greet Belinda, who sprang from the bench seat with an assist from Lorraine. The girls were dressed for hard work in jeans, T-shirts and low-top boots.

Jerry embraced his cousin, and so did Baput, innocently following the Earth custom. He found he was shaking when he let her go. He glanced over his shoulder toward the quarters. "Momama and Francina are canning," he told Lorraine.

"Tomato sauce! That's what I smell!" A memory of his grandmother brought a tear to Patrick's wrinkled eye.

"Yeah. They've been cooking since yesterday." Jerry's voice seemed to question the cost-effectiveness. A clanging of metal and a harmony of laughter rolled to them from the shop. "The guys are getting the equipment ready."

At what point did green aliens from another dimension become just 'the guys'? Patrick mused. Then he felt bad for even thinking that, so he kept his mouth shut for once. He flipped the back of the driver's seat forward and pulled out a 10-pound sledge hammer with a short handle.

"We should go to the Rock first," Jerry suggested, eyeing the hammer. "Just us." He looked at Baput for agreement.

Patrick watched the quick calculation behind that expressive face, so human, but for the color.

"Yes, go now," was Baput's eventual answer.

Despite his hesitation, Baput had been wishing for this all month. Now, here he was, at the Rock with Jerry, Patrick, Lorraine and Belinda. He was glad G-Pa had stayed at the quarters with Momama, especially when Patrick hopped onto the Rock and strode right to its center, holding that hammer he'd brought. *Mjolnir,* he called it, named after the hammer of a Norse god, a comic book character, or an Avenger, whatever *that* was. Baput found all three answers on the iPlane before he lost the signal. So, he wasn't sure who Thor was, but Mjolnir looked a lot like the hammer they'd found behind the Death Door at Nauve. He shoved the thought of the Death Door aside impatiently, too excited about the now to indulge in the wounds of the past.

He winced as Patrick struck the Rock with the hammer. It didn't thud like it had when they'd first unearthed it, five months ago on Mitten. Now a loud, clear tone rang out, thrilling the very molecules of the air. Was it the vibrations that sent the chills down his back, or was it the memory?

"Waves from the cave," Patrick kept repeating, like a chant.

Baput was doubly glad that G-Pa was absent when Lorraine put her hand on the Rock, then called Belinda over to do the same.

Belinda's bright green eye looked at him with apology and a little fear—then a delighted smile as she touched the Rock and felt those vibrations. "That feels good!" she squeaked adorably. "Baput, come try this! It's like your bowl!"

"Have you tried playing your bowl up here?" Patrick suggested. "Just set the Rock off with Mjolnir, here, and then sit down and play the bowl. That would be a rush!" He hit the Rock with the hammer again and talked over the ringing. "So let me get this straight. If you *don't* vibrate the Rock, the Queen will appear, if there is one, right?"

"That is what my G-Pa says," Baput answered, suddenly wishing G-Pa *was* there. "That is how they survive. They would fool us. We use the weapon, ring the Rock. We think we killed them all. So, next cycle, the Rock is silent. The Queen awakens. Her babies attack."

Patrick continued his line of thinking. "But if you don't activate the Rock, you can't go home."

"I think that is right," Baput guessed, fighting the sinking feeling those words brought.

"But, if you *do* activate the Rock, you might be able to go home, but the Queen would stay here until next cycle? Or would it go back with you?"

No one had the answers, so no one said a word. Baput finally took a shot. "If we ring the Rock and go nauve, we might be leaving you to fight the nimblies and bumblies without us. You won't know what to do. My popa says we must stay and help you fight, until they are gone from this Earth."

"That's gallant! Thank him for that," Patrick was a little surprised. "I guess we need to find out if that queen is in the chimney or not. I'd hate to see you guys miss your ride home for nothing."

"Don't worry about it," Baput assured him, fully meaning it.

Patrick suddenly stood up straight, raising the hammer. "Did I set it off, just now?"

"No. It is not First Pomegranate Day," Baput replied simply.

"But the Queen would have to know way before First Pomegranate Day," Lorraine contributed as she returned from the wall, carrying a palm-sized rock specimen. "Her eggs have to hatch and go through their larval state, and the baby bats have to be born and nurse and grow big enough to eat people." She peered at the piece of rock through a little lens that hung from a lanyard around her neck.

Belinda scrambled right past her, up to the center of the Rock to join her dad.

Baput cringed a bit. *What would G-Pa say?* But, when he watched her stumble a little, catch herself and come up laughing, looking at her popa with that eye, he didn't care what G-Pa said, not one bit.

"A few months, I would think," Lorraine continued. "Don't you know, Baput? Hasn't anybody ever gone into a cave and looked?"

"They used to send, um, people into the caves to kill the nimblies and bumblies in hibernation. Insitucide, like we've been talking about. But it's forbidden, because of the Curse."

"Curse?" Lorraine asked flatly.

"Usually the person never came out, but if they did, they would get sick and die. All those who loved them would die, too, right after."

"Contagious," Lorraine mulled. "Some kind of pathogen."

Baput stared at the ground. He was apprentice to Akash and knew nothing at all about the life cycle of their predators. He had never even heard of the Queen until G-Pa's bizarre ranting in his sleep on their first night on Earth, and the eventual revelation after they'd discovered the remains of the Holy Cave. "It is a three-year cycle. I don't know when is what, but it is three years."

"And you rang the Rock two years ago, at home, when you came?" Patrick pressed, so much like Jerry!

"Yes." Baput paused to calculate. "When I was six, we started. We struck the Rock with other rocks. Then, we found a hammer like yours in the Cave, behind the door, and we struck the Rock, like you just did. We studied the drawings, examined all the strange materials, the metal pipes and wires, the bicycle generator. And yes, I played with the Rock and hammer. I was just a child.

"When I turned nine and the nimblies and bumblies came, G-Pa and I stayed at the Holy Cave. That was the day Cilandra…" Everyone went uncomfortably quiet until Baput recovered his voice. "We tried to activate the weapon that day, but it didn't work. We didn't have the Net."

Patrick jumped in. "So, you rang the Rock on that First Pomegranate Day, when the bumblies were attacking?"

"Nimblies. It was daytime."

Lorraine took up the thread. She had taken a little biology. "So, when they swarmed, you rang the Rock, so they got the signal to make a queen."

Baput nodded as it all fell into place. "So, I guess two nimblies and two bumblies, a mated pair of each, would have gone into the chimney of the Holy Cave." He pointed at the vine-covered tube in the cliff above them, still not quite believing it was the same place, but then, he still didn't quite understand how places worked. "They made a queen."

Patrick took his turn. "Then you rang the Rock again, next First Pomegranate Day, when you were twelve..."

Baput picked up the tale. "We found the Net and laid it on the Rock over the pipes that shot the beam. Felsic pedaled. The beam came shining out of the pipe, bright white. Popa aimed it at the nimblies as they flew by. We killed some. They exploded in midair! It was working, until G-Pa jumped onto the Rock—"

"The rest is history," Jerry finished the narrative. "The Rock was activated, and the Queen stayed dormant, right there in the chimney." He pointed to where the vines hid the horizontal tube that ran along the cliff. "That's part of the Holy Cave. And everybody in the Holy Cave got zapped to Earth. So the Queen is right up there." He pointed again with a dramatic, sweeping arc. "Theoretically."

Speechless heads nodded slowly as it all sank in.

Belinda finally spoke up. "Can't you just ring the Rock every year? Then the Queen will stay asleep forever, won't she?"

"That's what I—" Baput began.

Patrick interrupted proudly. "A peaceful solution. That's my girl! I tell you, if it was me, I'd have this Rock buzzing every night, queen or no queen. It's better than a hot tub!"

"Or a sauna?" Jerry taunted his uncle.

"Oh, what a memory!" Patrick sat up, resting on his elbows and gazing at the river. "Your dad told you, eh? Well, the Akash found a good use for it. No-fo. The cave rock..." Patrick sat up to reach for the sample Lorraine still held. "What is it, Babe?"

"Do-lo-mite," his adult wife answered slowly, as if to a child.

Patrick turned the rock over in his hand. "This dolomite vibrates. It collides with our waves, even when it's been taken apart and stacked someplace else! I thought maybe the cave was resonating from the waves of the Holy Rock, but maybe it's got a wave of its own." He stood and paced back and forth on the Rock. "Or maybe the Rock transmits its vibration wirelessly to the dolomite."

"Yes, Dear. Come on. We're going to the cave entrance." Lorraine reached for Belinda's hand.

Jerry wandered downriver toward the chimney entrance. Baput followed. Lorraine and Belinda trotted up behind them, hand in hand. Patrick straggled behind, turning this way and that, gesturing and muttering to himself like the old Akash.

The hum of a finely tuned Jeep came up behind them. Elmer parked in the wide spot, and he, Valko and Felsic joined the procession.

Baput recapped the conversation for the newcomers. "We think if we buzz the Rock every cycle, before First Pomegranate Day, the Queen will stay asleep. But, how much before? How will we ever know if she's even there?"

"Who cares?" Patrick enthused. "Buzz it every day. Sell tickets. Elmer, have you tried hammering that thing and laying on it? You gotta try it!" He looked at Baput. His thick eyebrows were wrinkled, his legs squeezed together, his arms bent up in front of him. *It's his sacred Rock!* Patrick covered his face with open hands and looked down at the ground. He felt like a cockroach. "I'm sorry, Baput. That's your Holy Rock! I'm playing with it, lounging on it, talking about selling tickets! I am a, a, hey, Felsic! What's the worst thing you can call someone?"

"*Gapta!*" Felsic offered quickly. "We hate him. He's even punier than a dracna, but he steals even more of our grain and seeds. Then he runs away to his hole and not even the dogs can catch him."

"Then, I am a gapta for disrespecting your Holy Rock!" Patrick declared, bowing grandly.

Elmer let out a huff.

"Aw, come on, Uncle Patrick!" Jerry whined.

"But, really," Patrick insisted, "you should get your G-Pa out here every day, and play your bowl on it. All of you should try it. It's great string therapy, and it will keep the Queen asleep."

Valko grunted. "Do you say we just lay around on that Rock all Season, while Felsic hammers on it repeatedly? We don't fight? I would rather be paralyzed by nimbly venom and devoured slowly by a single, disease-infested bumbly with diarrhea and foul breath than to endure such a Season!" He turned his great beak to point up toward the black opening high on the wall, far too tiny for him to enter.

Patrick and Belinda exchanged their weird eye roll. So much for a peaceful solution! To their dismay, their own family sided with the warrior.

"In your perfect world, maybe," Elmer opined. "But we gotta know for sure whether those things are up there before we go sittin' on our asses on some rock!"

Valko's beard rippled with a nod.

Jerry stepped forward, a little shyly, for him. "Uncle Patrick, you said the cave rocks vibrate with the Holy Rock, right? So the bats would feel the Rock. What if they can feel each other, too? There's more than one cave of them, right, B?"

"Yes."

"Aunt Lorraine, um, Lori Anne," Jerry used the Nauvian pronunciation his aunt had never accepted. "You said there are no other dolomite or limestone caves around here, right?"

"That's what Jan, the geologist at work, said."

Jerry wrapped up his theory. "What if the vibrations in the dolomite are a way of communicating? What if the Queen can tell there are no other nimblies and bumblies out there? That might set her off, whether the Rock rings or not."

"Just like anybody else," Patrick mused. "They just want to keep their species alive. You think that might happen, Baput?"

"Yes," Baput muttered, head down. Then he looked up with baffled eyes. "I don't know. I will ask G-Pa." The group sighed their collective frustration.

"Irregardless all that," Elmer dared say with Fran out of earshot, "We gotta know if them bats are in there or not. We're lucky it's the only cave we gotta check. But how do we get up there?"

As if on cue, Lorraine stepped up and began her presentation like the skilled professional she was. Her clearly subordinate husband pulled a plan sheet from his overalls, unfolded it, and held it up.

Elmer smirked behind his hand and wiggled his eyebrows at Jerry while they watched Valko and Felsic's responses to Lorraine, still known as Lori Anne to them, explaining the plan and handing jobs out to the men like a War Chief. Ignoring Elmer's quips and Valko's grumbles, she pointed to the base of the cliff below the cave hole. "We need to clear this brush."

Felsic drew his machete.

Valko gave him a double take, declining to draw his own blade. In minutes, the only thing standing at the base of the cliff was Felsic. Not a stick remained. "Well, thanks, um, I'm sorry, what's your name again, Sir?"

"Felsic," he replied, blushing a deeper shade of olive green.

"Good job," Lorraine gave the eager worker a quick nod and continued explaining the plan to build a platform just below the cave hole, and a winch and pulley system to haul people and equipment to it from the driveway above.

"Let's go check it out," she suggested, pointing up at the driveway, where she planned to mount the winch. She started walking toward the Jeep, still talking about her plans, Felsic at her heels as close as Shastina followed G-Pa these days. Patrick and the kids scampered after the flaming red torch of Lorraine's hair, talking excitedly. Elmer and Valko followed in the Jeep.

When they passed the quarters, they were waylaid by a gushing Fran in a stained apron. She threw her arms around the visitors in order of their arrival, scolding them for running out there without even saying hi.

Drilling

Valko took the first shift with the rock drill. The vibration was harsh, alien, and extreme. It shook him into tiny pieces. He was grateful for the bulky yellow earmuffs, not for the noise reduction, which was inadequate, but because he felt his head would explode without their restraining band.

Despite his agony, Valko marveled at how fast the drill chewed a row of near-perfect three-inch holes into the base of the cliff below the chimney entrance. Soon there were four, entering the base of the cliff at the precise angle Boss Lori Anne had required, he realized with relief. *Done. Drill off. Got to… stand up… straight now.*

Reassembling all the tiny bits of his body into the original mountain of a man, then re-establishing connection with it all, seemed to take a long time. He felt a gentle touch on his right arm, still shaking from controlling the heavy, spirited drill. By reflex, he flung his elbow backward, almost breaking Patrick's nose a second time.

"It's OK, Buddy, it's me!" Patrick exclaimed. "Good job. Felsic can do the ones up top. You look like you need a break…" he squinted at Valko's face, concerned. "You OK?"

A grunt. Patrick noticed the mountain's hands were shaking. "You guys are sensitive to vibrations, aren't you? I tell you what, Valko, you go to the Rock, bang on it with my hammer, and lay on it. You need a massage."

Valko ambled slowly toward the Rock.

"Let the Akash say no to him!" Patrick mumbled after him. He knew the Akash wouldn't find out. They were keeping him away from here during the work. "Rock for the people!" Patrick resolved out loud. He called after Valko, "I'll send Felsic over when he's done. Let him on, too, OK?"

Valko turned to him, grunted again, and kept walking. A few minutes later, the Rock rang out. It seemed to have a low undertone this time, a deep, low-frequency rumble Patrick hadn't discerned before.

Felsic came strutting up to where Valko had been working. He hoisted the heavy rock drill onto his shoulder with one arm, stuck his other arm through the neatly wrapped air hose, and hoisted the compressed air tank. "Valko's snoring on the Rock." he explained, walking off like he was carrying a pillow and sleeping bag.

"They have awakened!" G-Pa let out the cry feared by all the Nauvians. The cry they heard every First Pomegranate Day, right before the nimblies attacked. But First Pomegranate Day was over a year away.

Baput touched the stone wall of the pitch-dark sauna. It buzzed! He knew the nimblies and bumblies weren't waking up. It was the drilling. Drilling over 1,000 feet away in a body of rock that these walls were no longer a part of, yet the vibration was as strong as if he were standing right next to the drill.

Patrick was right. This was the wave the nimblies and bumblies, the collective Nimbumblyborg, used to communicate. *Does the Queen feel it?* Baput wondered. *She might be right there in the chimney, where they're drilling. Will they wake her up? Maybe she'll think it's other nimblies and go back to sleep. If she wakes too soon, what will happen? Will it kill her? Weaken her? Will her babies be born early? If they are, will they wait for First Pomegranate Day before they attack? If they do, will they be bigger, hungrier? Or will they come early? If so, when?* Every question just begged so many more.

G-Pa's head jerked left and right, his arms and hands swatting the air in front of him, nearly smacking Baput. Was he seeing nimblies and bumblies?

Once again, Baput wondered if the old man was crazy or visionary. "G-Pa, what do you see?"

"Nimbumblyborg is here!" the Akash roared.

"Do you feel them, G-Pa? How many souls are there? Is it only one queen? How many nimbly eggs and bumbly babbets?"

G-Pa hummed along with the vibration of the Rock. Baput could feel it in the air now, without touching the wall. G-Pa leaned his head back. His nose loomed like a little peak sticking up into the darkness. Baput could feel it, rather than see it. He could feel the surprisingly cold breath coming out of the inverted nostrils, the gnarled hand reaching out to touch the wall.

"It is wrong," G-Pa mused. "They are not living. Yet they buzz!" He bolted upright. "Is someone hitting the Rock?" He headed for the door in an explosion of angry energy.

"G-Pa! Wait! They are drilling into the cave rock to make a platform so we can look into the chimney. So Keebra can get in. If he wants to. That is what we felt. The rock of this sauna vibrates together with the cave rock, because it *is* cave rock.

"That was not the Nimbumblyborg you felt, but it is the wave they use to communicate. The drilling will be done today, then the rock will be quiet, until the Queen awakens. Then we will hear her stirring, from here in the sauna. You will be here, listening for her, and watching for Keebra, too. If he returns, tell him we will help him if he wants to kill the Queen. Watch and listen, my great Akash. Our fate is in your hands."

Baput rose to leave, but it felt wrong, leaving him there alone, again. Even Shastina had abandoned him to run around with Brodey. Baput softened, turned back to the old man in the dark. "OK, G-Pa?"

The old Akash struggled to his feet. "Yes, yes, of course. I will watch and listen, just as I planned. Now, get to work, Boy, like I told you to! Go!" He pushed Baput out the door and closed it.

Baput headed for the Rock to report on Patrick's experiment. He still felt like a gapta, leaving G-Pa alone in the dark like that, but Patrick would be on the Rock, using it for a massage. There would be drilling and hammering and power tools and vehicles running back and forth all week. Jerry would be scheming with Patrick and Lorraine on ways to commit Insitucide, which Baput had to admit was the logical course of action. So, G-Pa couldn't be there, but he could be of use if he could feel the Queen stirring from the safety of the sauna.

The Jeep appeared, headed for the shop, Felsic at the wheel, and Patrick and Valko hanging onto an air tank and rock drill in the back. Baput ran behind them happily, the dogs slowing to join him.

Felsic whooped as Elmer fired up old Beulah. It had taken him and Elmer all morning to get the auger attachment hooked up and running. Elmer wondered how Felsic could figure this stuff out, and what he'd ever done without him. But he insisted on driving the old beast himself. With a 12-foot length of six-inch diameter metal pipe swinging from the bucket, Beulah chugged halfway down the driveway to join an eclectic cluster of vehicles, dogs, and people.

Lorraine had Jerry holding the "survey rod," nowadays a receiver for the laser, and spraying white paint marks where the holes would go. A new kind of gaa stained his Carhartts.

"That big pipe goes right here, for the gate." Lorraine pointed to a mark on the outside shoulder of the driveway. "Someone will hook up here to the winch at the end of the gate, and we'll swing him out over the hole and lower him down to it. He can dangle from the winch, build the platform in midair. And Felsic, here, he's our guy."

The whites showed all the way around Felsic's eyes. His mouth worked, forming soundless words.

"I figure you have the best strength-to-weight ratio," Lorraine told him with a thoughtless, habitual wink. Not used to being flirted with, Felsic was mystified. A Nauvian woman would never feign affection, or show real, but illicit, affection lightly. He accepted the unfathomable compliment in the Nauvian way, without thanks.

By dusk, they had the poles for the winch-and-pulley system drilled and cemented into place. Valko turned the crank on the cement mixer while Felsic jiggled and danced around, trying to realign his molecules after taking his turn on the rock drill.

"Let's go down and get the gate and put it on," Jerry suggested eagerly. They were going to detach the pipe gate from its post at the bottom of driveway and use it to suspend the winch above the hole in the wall. Fran wanted to go "gate free," but Elmer had made a big lecture about security, especially now, "when we have a delicate operation going on here." He would pick up a less expensive ranch gate from Cow Chow tomorrow, "for temporary".

"The concrete has to cure before we put a load on it." Lorraine declared, shutting it all down for the day. "We'll spend tomorrow putting the pipes together and setting them in place." She dismissed her crew.

Flying Felsic

Felsic fidgeted as Lorraine fed the straps between his legs, drew the harness across his puffed chest and wrapped it around to fasten in the back. Elmer and Lorraine walked him to the edge of the driveway, where the cliff dropped straight down 20 feet.

"You ready?" Lorraine asked, looking him straight in the eye.

Felsic nodded eagerly, not quite knowing what he was agreeing to. Elmer gave him a shove.

"Aaarg!" Felsic fell off the cliff toward the bushes that grew from the sides. Patrick quickly pulled his lever so the gate swung out, just enough so Felsic was clear of the brush, hanging in a squeaking ball. Slowly, an arm reached out, then another, then his legs. When he was all spread out like a paratrooper, Patrick ran the winch, carrying him out into empty air.

"Woohoo!" Felsic whooped, "I'm flying! I fly like Kiko Bird!"

Baput and Valko cheered him on as Patrick lowered him to the cave hole, whistling like a kiko bird the whole way. When Patrick reeled him in, he panted on the ground on all fours, still attached to the winch.

"You OK, Bud?" Elmer asked without releasing him. "Ready to do some drilling like that?"

Felsic looked up into Elmer's eyes with a look of gratitude and peace that made him melt. Was it for reeling him back in? No. Felsic proved it with a smile that not even his brother had seen before. "I go again. I drill holes. I fly like kiko bird! Did you see? I fly! Even Akash does not fly. Valko does not fly, he's too ganeesh. I have the *ratio*. I fly like kiko bird. Only me. Elmer, give me the drill."

Felsic quieted when he began his second flight. His eyes were fixed on the chimney. Lorraine used her laser pointer to target the spots for the holes, to make sure they would line up perfectly with Valko's holes below.

Felsic giggled and swatted at the red light that danced in front of him.

"It can't hurt you," Patrick shouted. "Just don't look right into it."

Lorraine set the pointer on a tripod, and fixed it on the location of the first hole. "Right there, Felsic."

Felsic brought his drill up.

"Nice and straight, OK? I'll keep my beam on it."

"Keep beam on it," Felsic repeated, pulling the trigger on the rock drill. He howled along with it as it whirled on the cliff face. He tried to lean into it like he had done on the driveway, but the bit wasn't biting the rock like it should. The hole wasn't going anywhere.

Felsic shifted his weight, making his support cable swing. He got a bite then, but he couldn't keep it straight.

"What are ya doin'?" Elmer shouted from above.

"I can't!" Felsic plunged from elation to defeat.

Patrick slapped himself on the forehead. "He's got no purchase! No place to stand. Even Atlas needed a place to stand, for leverage. Reel him in guys!" he shouted above Felsic's whine. "Not your fault, Buddy. Just physics."

They reeled Felsic in without incident or whooping. They released his harness, and he squatted in the driveway, munching on one of Star's seed cakes while Patrick tried to explain the problem.

"I can fit in that hole, you know," Felsic reported.

"Not very far. I can tell you that," Elmer recalled bitterly.

"No. Not far. I don't want to…" Felsic looked over at the little hole in the cliff and collected his thoughts. "Just a little." He indicated his waist. "I can lay my legs and belly down in the chimney. Then I can reach out and down," he demonstrated, "and drill the holes right under me. Then you use the winch to bring me the pipes, and I stick them in the holes. Bring me the platform, and I'll bolt it on. Done by dinnertime."

They hooked Felsic in the front this time, so he could slide face up into the hole and unclip himself.

"Are you sure those things ain't gonna come out and grab ya?" Elmer worried aloud.

"It is not First Pomegranate Day. They sleep," Baput told them earnestly, for what seemed like the 100th time.

"And the pathogen?" Lorraine asked him sharply, "you know, the Curse?"

"The Curse is deep inside, on the Queen," Felsic answered, swallowing hard. "Send me now. I'm ready."

The air hose fed smoothly through the loops along the gate as Felsic floated through the sky in a confident sitting position, carrying the air-powered drill. Flawless as a gymnast, he lined up his legs and slid gracefully in on his back, up to his chest. He unclipped the harness and rolled onto his belly with a very human thumbs-up.

He drilled, strong and straight, into the spot lit by the red laser beam. The air hissed, the drill buzzed, the rock rang, and Felsic sang. Surely, G-Pa felt the vibrations. The whole valley did. Soon there were four holes in a neat row below the chimney entrance. Felsic clipped the drill onto the winch and gave another thumbs-up.

"You OK, buddy?" Elmer checked.

Felsic's sun-darkened face craned out of the cave hole like a moray eel, his white teeth beaming a brilliant smile.

Lorraine was ready for phase two of the plan. "We need guides down there to make sure the pipes go into the holes. Valko, you're tall and strong. And you boys. Go down there and set the bottoms of the pipes into the holes on the ground."

Jerry nodded and ran to the truck. Baput and Valko followed.

Elmer and Lorraine attached the first pipe assembly to the winch and shoved it over the side. Patrick's winch whirred the unwieldly contraption through the air toward Felsic as the troops arrived below.

Valko guided the bottom of the long, top-heavy thing into the angled hole he had drilled at the base of the cliff. Six feet away, the boys held a second support leg up vertically.

Patrick ran the winch, and the joined pipes dropped down into their holes. They repeated the process three more times. Each time was faster, slicker, and more perfect.

Elmer secured the platform to the winch. The wire grid had been part of an old bridge. It would have been lighter and simpler if Fran hadn't made them weld those pipes all around it for guardrails. *But, yeah, Jerry will wanna be up here all the time, that's for sure.* Elmer wondered how he was going to keep his kid from going into that cave. Was his story enough? Was the Curse?

The platform landed gently in front of the chimney hole, centered on four horizontal pipes. Felsic unclipped it, then wriggled out of the hole onto it.

"Clip yourself on," Elmer ordered.

"But I fly!" Felsic looked up gleefully.

"Not without that clip on, ya don't," Elmer insisted.

"Yes, Boss." Felsic clipped the harness to his chest and rose to his feet on the new platform. He fastened three clamps to each pipe while Patrick controlled the slack of his tether. Baput and Jerry cheered him from below. Valko grunted jealously.

When the last clamp was fastened, Felsic stood up tall in the center of the platform. He stuck out his chest, still clipped to the cable. He threw back his head and bayed a long victory howl.

The dogs joined in, the others followed. Flying Felsic rose into the sky and floated over to his best friend, his best friend's friendly brother, and the very lovely Lori Anne. Flying Felsic would never be just Felsic again.

Looking

"Well, tomorrow, we get to see the fruits of our labors." Lorraine surprised them all with her enthusiasm on Labor Day evening. Ordinarily, she'd be blatantly itching to leave after a three-day weekend with 'the family.' Work would be singing its siren song in the back of her head.

"Can I stay home, Mom?" Jerry pounced on Fran.

"No, Son. You have school," Elmer spoiled the party. "Don't worry. We're just going to run your radio-controlled truck in there and see if it works. See if we can get that drone out of there." He grinned at the fuming boy, adding, "It'll be fun."

"Dad! It's my idea. My truck. My drone! I've been waiting all this time!"

Elmer pulled off a perfect imitation of Jerry's eye roll. "Relax," he winked. "Your mom already got you excused. We need you to work on the farm, Boy!"

"You got me," Jerry admitted happily.

After dinner, Belinda and Jerry took the toy truck outside and sent it toward the quarters. With its brand-new batteries, it was running strong. "Baput! Felsic! Come see!" Jerry called.

Three green faces emerged. Baput was excited. Felsic wore his new confidence like an expensive new suit. Valko stood back, aloof, trying to look unimpressed as the tiny truck climbed the porch steps and roared up to his foot, stopping just short of hitting him.

"Little-Little Truck!" Felsic proclaimed.

"Little-Little Truck will look for the Queen tomorrow in the chimney," Baput explained.

Jerry was up earlier than he would have been for school, almost Christmas early. Fran was already making breakfast.

"Are you sure that thing is safe?" she asked, knowing Jerry would to be flying today. Baput, too. "Does Star have any idea what you boys are up to?"

"We're fighting nimblies and bumblies, Mom," Jerry reminded her. "I'm sure she's used to her kids being in danger."

"You would never get used to that," Fran replied tersely. She gazed into Jerry's eyes, seeing a strange man there, just for an instant.

Belinda's pitter-patter sounded on the stairs. "I guess we should stay here," she said with resignation as Belinda emerged. "Like good green women waiting in the Great Hall for their men to return from battle."

Felsic whined a little when Elmer hooked Jerry into the harness, and even more when Jerry stole his trademark whoop as he flew out and down, landing on the platform. Baput came next, clenched into a ball, his teeth gritted so tightly, no noise could escape. When he got to the platform, his feet wouldn't work, so Patrick kept lowering until he was a crumpled heap at the center. Jerry unhooked him gently.

"OK, B?" Jerry checked, signaling to Patrick to pull the cable up.

Baput uncurled slowly, gasping for breath. He crawled to the chimney hole and peered inside. He saw nothing but darkness. Behind him, Jerry waited to receive the radio-controlled truck and the tactical light that traveled toward him in a canvas bag attached to the winch.

Jerry turned the blazing flashlight on. The hole lit up, as far back as they could see. The drone sat on its side, two propellers sticking up, blocking their view of the depths of the long, narrow tube.

Jerry screwed a little metal hook into a hole in the front bumper of the truck, sticking straight out. Uncle Patrick had helped him fabricate it on Dad's milling machine.

He set the truck just inside the cave entrance and pushed the controller. It trundled off to war down the dim corridor. It bumped into the drone a little harder than Jerry had planned. His depth perception was off. He backed the truck up, and the drone came with it. It was hooked! It tumbled and clattered and tried to roll over, but it couldn't escape Jerry's little hook. Jerry winced and hissed as the props banged the cave walls and the turrets scraped the floor. Only five more feet. He reached in, got down on his belly and started to crawl into the cave towards it.

"Jerry!" Elmer roared like Valko.

Jerry had his hand on the drone. He gave Baput the controller, to free his other hand. "Keep pushing here," he instructed. "Here it comes."

Baput scooped up the truck while Jerry brought the drone out with both hands.

Jerry scrambled to his feet with his trophy, holding it high in the air above his head. Two propeller blades fluttered down to the platform, where they found their way through the grate and whirled to the ground below.

Patrick and Lorraine cheered. Felsic whooped. Valko grunted ambivalently. Baput still sat cross-legged, the truck cradled tightly in his arms. He stared into the chimney, saying nothing.

"I told you to stay out of there," was all the congratulations Jerry got from his dad.

Jerry shrugged. Time to see if he could get Little-Little Truck all the way into the Cave. He put the broken drone into the canvas bag and wrestled the truck out of Baput's grasp. "What's the matter with you?" he asked his distracted friend, whose eyes were fixed at a point deep inside, where the light didn't quite reach. "Do you see something?"

Baput shook his head a little too violently to be believed. Jerry unscrewed the hook and set the truck just inside the chimney again. He glanced up at his dad, gave him the grin. Then he wrestled the controller from Baput's frozen fingers.

The little truck whirred bravely into the now-empty cave, down the straight, well-lit tube, undaunted by the shadows around the edges. "Felsic should see this," Jerry murmured to himself, admiring his old toy on its bold journey. Fifty feet and going, going, not going. Not going. Jerry said a bad word. He pulled back on the lever, then forward. No motion. Again, nothing. No forward, no backward. No sideways.

Jerry said a couple more bad words as he shook the controller, slapping it with the heel of his hand. Still, the little truck stood motionless. The folks up on the driveway looked down at him.

"Lost it?" Patrick finally asked.

"He's lost it, alright," Elmer grumbled.

"Did you lose the signal?" Patrick shouted down, distinctly.

Jerry exaggerated a nod.

Now Uncle Patrick said a bad word. "Come on up, I guess," he sighed. The winch whirred as the gate returned to its position above the platform.

Jerry turned the light off, rousting Baput. "Come on, B, snap out of it. What's in there?"

"The Queen," Baput replied, as if in a trance.

"Did you see her?"

"No evidence. But I feel her. I know she's there."

Fran's heart rose a bit when she saw the drone peeking out from the canvas bag, but there was no laughing, no joking, not even talking. They looked like Jerry's little league team when they had lost the playoffs. *Uh-oh.* "Where's the truck?" she had to ask.

"We lost it, Mom. Halfway in. Lost the signal, I guess."

"Are you sure it wasn't the batteries? You were running it all over out here."

She watched her son's hurt deepen. "I put in new ones right before. It only went 50 feet. First it went in a little ways and pulled the drone out. But still. It lost the signal, Mom."

Fran stepped forward to embrace her defeated warrior. "So we go even further back in time," she proposed. She leaned back to look at Jerry's face. "Remote control with wires, if we can find such an antique."

Patrick, Elmer, and Lorraine came up beside them. Lorraine had the answer. "Sewer TV."

"What?" Elmer snapped.

"They use it to check the sewer lines for leaks and clogs."

"Gross," Jerry commented.

"They clean it after. It's on a rolling thing that would only work in a pipe, not a cave. But we could attach it to another toy truck or something. If I can do that without damaging it, I can borrow it from work. It feeds a fiber optic signal right to a screen, all hard wired. You can record, too. I'll bring it next time."

Elmer nodded through a crooked half-smile. "We should buy our own, though," he told Jerry, "so Lorraine doesn't get in trouble when you break it."

"I'll get it," Patrick offered. "It's plumbing stuff. Tax deductible. If you don't break it, I can sure use it for work."

Lorraine sighed loudly. "Well, I guess we've done all we can do, for now. So we'll leave you to the pomegranates and come back when we have something. Christmas, maybe?"

"Mom, no!" Belinda wailed from the porch of the quarters, where she had been helping Star dry eggplants. She glanced back over her shoulder and saw Star frowning in the doorway. She raised her hand to her mouth and recovered her dignity. "Yes, mother."

Lorraine frowned even harder. *She minds that green woman better than she minds me!* "Yeah, we'll be back for Christmas," she confirmed crisply. "Now get your stuff."

When she hugged Fran, she whispered in her ear, "You know, this time even *I'm* a little sad to leave."

Christmas 2016

Despite the drought, the Look'N Up topped the books for the third year in a row. Water was scarce everywhere. The big orchards drilled deeper wells, drawing the strained underground aquifers down even more, until they collapsed and the ground sank into their empty pores, squeezing them shut forever. There were water stations in town where you could fill jugs, wash your dishes, even your kids, if you didn't have water at home. But the Look'N Up was in a fortunate location, right along the river and high enough in the aquifer to not have to worry about sucking up saltwater.

Even in the face of adversity, the year-round care and selective pruning and harvesting techniques of the meticulous Nauvians resulted in another bumper crop.

As promised, the Battle Engineers returned for the week between Christmas and New Year's Day. "The Void," Lorraine called it. "I love working in The Void. There's no one there, and you can get stuff done. But if you need anybody, there's no one around. I mean no one! So," she sighed, glossy lips smiling tightly, "I guess I might as well be here."

Fran accompanied her through the house, her own strained smile vanishing as she listened.

What did I say wrong now? Lorraine wondered in the privacy of the bathroom.

Belinda embraced everyone in turn. She started with Baput, drawing a disapproving look from Star, who she hugged last and longest. Star melted, and the two strode into the quarters like mother and daughter.

"I've got it, guys!" Patrick announced from the back of the van. He opened the door, exposing a three-foot high contraption. "Sewer TV," he raved. "With 200 feet of flexible steel rod, so you can push it right along in a pipe, where it's smooth and it can't go anywhere but forward. In the chimney, there are ridges and cracks on the floor that might catch it. Or it could wander sideways and get stuffed against a wall. So I got three sets of axles and big knobby wheels for a model truck like yours. Check it out!"

He showed them the end of the reel of push rods. A tiny fiber-optic camera lens and a bright LED lamp were embedded snugly in the tip. Three six-inch long axles, each with a pair of oversized wheels with rubber studded tires, were secured to the first two feet of line. He put the vehicle on the ground and started feeding line out by pulling it off the reel and shoving it forward. The wheels rolled on the gravel driveway. He turned on the camera.

Everyone gathered around the little screen, shaded in the van for easy viewing. It was like a cat's view, speeding along about eight inches off the ground, straight as an arrow.

The whoops and hollers from the few that could see the screen infected the ones who were just watching the funny animal spread itself across the ground. Felsic chased it at a slow walk.

"Could work," Elmer offered.

"It *will* work," Patrick countered as the Christmas Eve sky darkened.

"Tomorrow," Fran informed the excited group.

"But, Mom, it's a cave! It's dark anyway," Jerry urged desperately. He had waited so long!

"Tomorrow's Christmas Day. I guess if that's how you want to spend it—"

"Yeah, Mom! Tomorrow," Jerry agreed.

Christmas Eve dinner was a very un-Nauvian prime rib with baked yams, green bean casserole and a salad of winter greens. An unusually awkward silence passed between the diners on what should have been a joyful occasion. Although she was in no way to blame for their frustration, Fran took it on herself to get it out in the air. "You've still got that radio-controlled truck stuck in there, don't you?"

The thought didn't exactly cheer the group. "Yeah, Mom," Jerry answered, turning to Patrick. "I don't think we can get that thing past it."

"We'll have to use *that thing* to drag it out first. And her name is Sojourner, after the Mars probe, which was named after Sojourner Truth, an escaped slave turned activist and suffragette."

"Who didn't get to vote, even after they won, because she was black," Lorraine had to add.

Patrick reached into his baggy pocket and pulled out a little metal object with three hooks, facing each other. He pulled a loop on the end, and the hooks drew toward each other like a jaw closing. "The Claw," he declared in a menacing voice. "Merry Christmas."

He handed The Claw to Jerry and continued excitedly. "We'll have the camera and the light. We can't drive real well, but we ought to be able to roll right up to it and hook it somewhere," Patrick assured them.

"You're gonna run that expensive rig up in there and tangle it with that stuck toy truck," Elmer summarized. "That sounds like a whole load of Murphy up in there!"

Jerry was up early on Christmas morning, as usual, but he squirmed through the gift exchange, the usual source of his excitement and joy. His new Carhartts and video games, Belinda's lovely new outfits and instructional CDs on violin playing were just obstacles. Except the binoculars. Those might be useful. He wanted to be on the platform, running Uncle Patrick's ingenious contraption, Sojourner, into the chimney of the Holy Cave. Finally seeing.

Bright paper and ribbons littered the floor. Empty plates and coffee cups were strewn from kitchen to living room. At last, empathic Fran released the eager crew. Hands darted out to grab hats and jackets, sunglasses and gloves.

Only Belinda was left. Fran questioned her with a fake pout.

"They said I can't go out on the platform. They said only Jerry and Baput and my dad can go. They're essential."

Fran's fake pout turned real. "Who said that?"

"Mom."

"Well that doesn't sound like her. I'd think she'd want to make sure you got to go."

"I don't want to, Aunt Fran. I saw it last time. I was scared to death, watching Jerry and Baput flying through space on that thing. Then they do stuff way down on that platform, and I can't even see what they're doing. Even when Baput's not down there, he's with Jerry and they're all excited, and he ignores me."

"Oh, my!" Fran breathed at the confession.

Belinda brightened. "What are you and Salistar doing today?"

"We're making pumpkin pomegranate stuffing." Fran replied, just as brightly. "It will be their whole dinner. But we're going to bring ours back and stuff a turkey with it. Remember when we stuffed that turkey before?"

Fran reached for her jacket, and Belinda did the same, a Jerry-sized grin across her face and Brodey at her heels.

Seeing

Patrick took charge. "Jerry, Baput, and I will go over—"

Felsic interrupted with a whine.

"Sorry, Felsic. Lorraine says three's the limit. Maybe after, you go for a ride, OK?"

"Don't want to ride. Want to work, not just play like a babbet," Felsic moaned.

"You can caulk the holes," Lorraine promised. "I'll show you. It's important, Felsic. Did I tell you, you have the best strength-to-weight ratio for the flying jobs?" She casually put her arm around his shoulders and steered him back toward the van to show him the caulking gun while Patrick took the first flight of the day, sitting up with the harness wrapped around his legs and clasped at his chest.

"Woohoo! What a rush!" Patrick's shout echoed up and down the canyon. So much for distracting Felsic!

Jerry went next. Not a first-time flyer, he adjusted the harness and buckled it at his chest like a pro and floated through the air gracefully. He didn't whoop or yell, he just grinned that radiant grin, his blond hair streaming behind him like the tail of a comet.

Patrick was there to release his nephew and remind him to clip his safety strap onto the platform grate. "This place gives me the creeps," he confessed.

"The Queen?" Jerry asked, finding his feet.

Patrick stared into the blackness of the little hole. It was even smaller than he remembered. "Just memories, I think."

Elmer leaned over to receive the empty hook. He looped the cable through Sojourner's reel. "Now ease it on over the cliff, real slow."

Felsic, Baput, and Lorraine wrestled Sojourner to the edge of the cliff, then tried to keep it from the rocks, stumps, and bushes until it floated free.

Elmer looked up the driveway and yelled, "Hit it, Valko, real slow!"

Patrick and Lorraine held their collective breath from opposite sides of a few thousand dollars dangling on a thread. Slowly, slowly, Sojourner traveled across far less space and time than it seemed.

"G-Pa is here," Bel observed aloud when she saw the old man in headphones sitting in the corner. "It smells good in here."

Salistar smiled warmly. "He listens to the violin music your popa provides." She simply acknowledged the fact, a Nauvian thank-you.

Fran had to spill the beans. "Belinda plays the violin now. Maybe you could play for G-Pa while we cook."

Belinda's face fell. She reached for Star's intriguing rolling pin. "I want to cook," she whimpered.

Star looked sharply at the whining girl, who quieted instantly.

Fran looked at Star, then Bel. *What was that?* Then, defying Lorraine's prohibitions, Fran gave in to her beloved little niece. *Why can't she cook if she wants to?* "After, then," she compromised. "After we make our stuffing."

Patrick and Jerry rushed to greet Sojourner like a long-lost relative. They unhooked it and walked it toward the chimney entrance as the crane returned for Baput.

Baput shook a little as Elmer wrapped the harness around him and clipped it at the chest. Felsic and Lorraine escorted him to the cliff.

There was something about stepping out over that cliff. He just couldn't bring himself to do it. Self-preservation, naturally, and a flash of Batuk, falling from the top of those steep, rocky stairs... "That didn't happen," he muttered, accidentally out loud.

"What?" Felsic and Lorraine both asked.

"Whoaaa!" Baput answered as the gate swung out and away, tearing him from the edge of the driveway. His black hair tossed from side to side as he wriggled like a trout being hoisted into a boat without a net. Looking back at his family, he stilled, trying to recover his dignity. He dangled, no whoops, no aerobatics, as if the poor trout had gulped too much raw air and perished on the line. He landed in a crumpled ball on limp, useless legs.

Patrick and Jerry surrounded him, causing a hiss about weight distribution from Lorraine.

"You OK, B?" Jerry asked gently.

"I'm OK." Baput fumbled for the clasp that held him to the dangler. He unhooked it and didn't need to be told to clamp it to the platform. *Everyone else thinks that's fun!* He marveled to himself, glad Belinda wasn't there to see his fear.

"Snap, crackle, pop!" said the pomegranate seeds as the Akashic Tether's oversized marble rolling pin rolled across them, constrained from escape by the low edges of a cookie pan and a clean, but gaa-stained, dishtowel.

Belinda squealed with delight.

"You try," Star invited, offering the breathtakingly beautiful, surprisingly heavy, marble rolling pin to the girl. When Bel took it, Star stood back, her purple-black eyes sharply appraising.

Belinda admired the equipment. Pure marble, perfectly smooth, with a natural pattern of pinks, purples, and grays that couldn't have been improved upon, not by humans, anyway. "It's gorgeous," she breathed.

"Crack some." Star's sharp command brought Belinda to Earth.

Bel placed the rolling pin in the tray and pressed down until she heard a pop.

"Roll," Star ordered.

Belinda obeyed. She bore down hard and rolled, like Star had. "Snap, crackle, pop!" The seed shells shattered as a lopsided smile consumed her lopsided face.

"Who needs a blender?" Fran exclaimed, glancing at G-Pa and remembering their aversion to vibrations. No vacuum, no blender, no grinder, nothing buzzy. Fortunately, the floors were bare linoleum, which Star simply swept and mopped. Blending and grinding were jobs for the Akashic Tether's rolling pin. Belinda wielded it like she was born to it.

Jerry shone the bright light into the dark hole. Little-Little Truck leered at them in cameo. Patrick cradled the inventive end of Sojourner, complete with camera, light, and three sets of knobby tires, before laying it on the sacrificial altar of high-tech equipment that was the chimney's entrance.

Patrick held his hand out to Jerry. Blue eyes looked up blankly. Patrick's face fell. "You *do* have the Claw, don't you?"

"I got excited. I forgot." Those blue eyes begged for forgiveness until that ridiculous grin broke through.

Patrick sighed with relief. "Don't do that!"

Still grinning, Jerry handed Patrick the Claw.

Patrick screwed the Claw into the clamp that held the forward axle, just to the right of the cable, so it stuck out ahead of the camera. Reverently, he laid Sojourner down just inside the entrance again. He turned on the camera. They gathered in front of the screen and squinted at the glare.

"Let's go ahead and give her a shove," Patrick said as he yanked on the reel. The wheels crawled straight down the narrow corridor, right over the bumps and cracks.

"Woohoo!" all three whooped like Felsic. Felsic replied with a hoot from above.

Patrick detached the video screen from the reel and shoved it into the cave hole, out of the glare. The boys kneeled on the platform staring at the shaded screen. They could see the straight tube in detail. Tiny, hollow stalactites grew from the ceiling.

"Helictites," Patrick informed them. "See the curly little stalactites that don't grow straight down, they're all squiggly? That's more evidence there's weird forces in here."

Patrick got up and gave the rod another shove. The camera plunged deeper into the ever-narrowing tube. Little-Little Truck loomed ahead, coming up fast.

"Slow down!" Jerry yelled, as The Claw made rough first contact with the toy truck. Good thing it stuck out farther than the delicate fiber optic camera. "Maybe we hooked it!" Jerry cried hopefully. "Back up a little."

Hearts leapt as the truck turned sideways. Patrick reeled slowly, carefully, dragging it out of the hole. Jerry's building whoop choked into an "arggg" as the hooked fender broke and fell off the truck.

"It's OK!" Jerry realized. "The axle's exposed. I can see it. Right down there where the hook is. Just go in slow and straight till I say."

Baput sat breathless beside his friend, staring at the screen.

Jerry heard a click. "Does this have audio?"

"Yeah," replied Patrick. "I paid extra, hoping we could hear the Queen, or those vibrations."

"Well, I think it's hooked. Back it up."

The whooping spread quickly to the driveway, where even Valko, Elmer, and Lorraine joined in, as Little-Little Truck returned from the deep, dark cave.

When it was within reach, Jerry handed Baput the screen, gently pushing him aside. He looked up to the driveway at his dad. "It's right here, Dad." He reached into the forbidden hole.

Elmer's growl turned to a "Yahoo!" as Jerry pulled the truck free from the cave. It looked OK, except for a missing fender and a slightly bent axle, all done during the rescue.

Patrick unscrewed The Claw and cradled Sojourner while Jerry tucked his toy truck into the bag that hooked onto the pulley. "Take it away, Dad," he ordered.

Baput sat staring into the cave.

There was much chopping, as well as seed-popping, but with six hands the work went swiftly. Not only did everyone have their stuffing, but they each had an apple pie, too, since the rolling pin was out. Bel devoured the lesson.

"You have popped the seeds and rolled the dough on this day. You are well-begun!" Star pronounced.

Well-begun with what, exactly? Fran wondered but decided not to ask. Her fears were confirmed when Salistar pitched the whole rolling pin thing to Belinda. Fran watched with scientific detachment to see how Lorraine's daughter of 21st-century California would react to the oath Star recited:

> "To nourish her man and her family with all her
> being. To dedicate her life to always taking care of his
> every need, so he is free to do great things. And I,
> especially, as Tether to Akash."

She wrapped it up with her favorite saying: "No matter what happens in life, there are always dishes to do."

Belinda giggled at that. At the rest, she had shown no visible reaction. Not a single flinch.

"Come on, Baby," Fran told her niece, rising to put on her coat and collect the stuffing. Belinda got her coat and the pie. "We'll stuff the turkey and get it in the oven. Then we'll come back with your violin and play for Grandpa."

Belinda looked at the pale, skinny, drooling man in the corner and tried to smile, just like people sometimes tried to smile at her, she realized. "OK," she promised shyly.

Patrick began unspooling the semi-flexible rod and shoving it into the chimney. The boys huddled in front of the screen again, watching Sojourner advance boldly over the familiar ground. Patrick shoved faster than before.

"Slow down!" Jerry ordered. "We can't see. You're going too fast."

"I'm getting it all recorded so we can take it to the house and play it back nice and slow on the TV, instead of that crappy little screen." Shove, shove. "I can never see those things…"

"Slow down!" Jerry cried louder. "I think we're at the end!"

Jerry and Baput could see the wall at the end of the tube. It was coming up fast. Too fast. It was curved so it ramped smoothly upward. The image blurred against the wall, then shifted to the cave ceiling. Helictites littered the firmament like stars. Sojourner climbed straight up the back wall, then bent over backwards, hanging in midair. They saw themselves on the screen, upside down in a circle of light.

Then the view slipped slowly to the right, bobbing unsteadily between ceiling and wall on the springy pipe. It revealed a chamber hidden from the tactical light, lit only by the LED above the camera. It scanned the small side room, passing a dark spot on the ceiling that reflected the meager light but remained pitch black in spite of it.

"That's it!" Baput cried, gripping the screen, his jade knuckles almost white.

"What?" Jerry demanded.

Patrick yanked back on the reel, trying to save Sojourner.

"The Queen!" Baput called out, just as the camera turned over and the dark image whirled sickeningly, turning head over heels. Next came a fast scan of the chamber wall followed by a static view of the floor.

Patrick pulled on the reel again. The view of the chamber floor receded from the camera, a couple feet. Then the camera stopped moving. It stared at a still view of the floor of the little side chamber from about two feet above.

"Crap." Patrick tugged on the line of flex rods. He tried to turn the reel. Nothing moved.

"Stuck?" Jerry asked, feeling that familiar frustration.

Patrick nodded, his face lined and sunken.

"I saw the Queen," Baput repeated in a near whisper.

Jerry grabbed the screen.

Patrick reluctantly let go of the reel, took the screen from Jerry and unplugged the wire. Then he signaled to Elmer to send the pulley. "We'll watch it on TV, where we can see better," he explained.

"What about Sojourner?" Jerry cast a sad glance into the hole.

"She's doing her shift," Patrick sighed, "like the drone, and Little-Little Truck." He slipped the screen into the bag and sent it away.

"Evidence!" Baput shouted proudly to the puzzled watchers above.

With the day's gaa removed to the extent possible, and decked in their new clothes, Belinda and Fran returned to the quarters to play the violin for Baput's G-Pa. G-Pa still sat in the same chair, wearing his headphones that played the violin music Patrick kept collecting. Shastina lay at his feet.

"Popa!" Salistar said something in Nauvian to rouse him. He grunted and stirred, then turned foggy eyes on Belinda as she approached, with a little shove from Fran. Shastina raised her head and wagged the tip of her tail.

Belinda stood before the old man, who seemed to be paying attention, except for that foggy blindness in his glazed eyes. She shook a little.

Fran brought a stool from the kitchen counter.

Belinda rested on it lightly and raised the violin to her chin. She played two simple songs she had learned to play by heart. "Mary Had a Little Lamb" and "Ode to Joy." Her strokes were short and even. She got most of the notes right. When she missed one, she would go back and replay the whole bar. That made G-Pa twitch. She tried not to notice.

She played "Ode to Joy" a second time, all perfect, but still with those short, even strokes. In the middle of the song, G-Pa slowly, deliberately, raised the headphones back to his ears, closed his eyes and turned away.

That old snoot! Belinda raged silently. *Most grownups would at least pretend I don't suck!*

Fran caught the delicate instrument right before it hit the floor. She looked back at Star and saw a look on that sweet, basil face that made her want to leave. Just in time, Patrick's van lumbering up the driveway gave her a Nauvian excuse. "The men are back. We have to go." Fran grabbed her niece's hand and hurried for the door.

"Back up, back up! There!" Jerry directed as Elmer operated the TV remote. The picture wasn't much clearer, but it was bigger and there was no glare. The image froze on the black blob in the little chamber off to the right, but it seemed like the left.

"It's on the floor," Elmer observed.

"No, Dad, it's the ceiling," Jerry corrected. "The picture is upside-down, because the camera is upside down." He raised his right arm and bent his elbow so it jutted out to the front. His hand was over his shoulder, bobbing up and down, palm up. "It was hanging there upside down, see?"

Elmer nodded. Jerry pointed at the screen. "Now, play it slow, and you can see it turn over, when Uncle Patrick pulled on it. It looks like the Queen flips over, but it's the camera." He pulled his elbow back and flipped his hand over. "Then, for a second, you can see it's on the ceiling, before…" He sent his hand into a swan dive.

Elmer advanced at the slowest speed. Frame by frame, the black blob turned over. It was impossible to tell the size with no scale in the background. Elmer froze the image after the spinning stopped.

And there she was, hanging from the ceiling of a side chamber at the end of the 100-foot tube. She clung to a vein in the ceiling with sharply taloned feet. She was covered all over by a coating of something black and smooth that shined dully in the artificial light, shimmering with her slow, even breathing.

Valko rushed at the screen, gripping the handle of the machete he wore at his hip. "It is the Nimbly Bumbly Queen!" he roared.

"Easy, Big Guy." Elmer stepped up bravely to protect his TV.

Valko stopped and turned around sheepishly. His eyes swept the room as he collected his dignity. "Where is Akash?"

Belinda winced. Fran's lip curled.

"Akash must see this." Letting go of his machete, Valko parted the crowd with his great bulk and rushed to the door.

"What happened?" Belinda asked, threading her way through the hole Valko had left, to the refuge of Baput's side.

"It's the Queen, see?" Baput pointed, his soiled fingers smearing the screen. "She's a big, pregnant bat, a bumbly, hanging from the ceiling of a little room way back in there. You can't see her because she is all covered with black slime that has nimbly eggs in it. All the nimblies and bumblies on Earth are right there in one bundle."

"Let's kill them!" Jerry proposed to nods from Elmer and Lorraine.

Valko burst in, pushing the balking Akash ahead of him. "Look, Old Man!"

G-Pa squinted at the screen.

"G-Pa!" Baput explained. "It is a picture, a rasta, from the chimney. See this black blob?" He pointed again, smudging the same spot. "It is the Queen, I think."

The Akash leaned forward, peering at the TV from four inches away. The head shaking began there, and the "no, no, no." The shaking spread from his head to his feet, and the "no, no, no..." rose in pitch until it was merely a squeal.

"It is definitely the Queen," Baput interpreted.

Insitucide

Elmer carved the perfectly browned turkey. "Turkey *and* prime rib!? We'll be eating leftovers for weeks."

"We'll take some home," Lorraine offered.

"You're here all week, aren't you?" Fran probed.

"We'll see," Lorraine replied tersely.

"Mom!" Belinda objected, too loudly for a lady. They glared at each other for a silent second. Belinda lowered her eyes first.

Elmer sent the heaping platter of meat around the table. Forks and knives clanked. Compliments were mumbled through stuffed mouths. Christmas Dinner had begun.

Lorraine started the conversation, her mouth only half full. "So, how do we kill it? Some kind of gas, I'm thinking. Run a hose in there and pump some gas, enough to fill the little chamber. If we could only get Patrick's thing back..."

"Sojourner." Patrick picked at his stuffing like a kid who didn't get what he wanted for Christmas.

"Grenade launcher," was Jerry's first thought. "Shoot a grenade straight back in there. It hits the back wall, *blam!*" He flung his arms wide.

"Yeah, Boy," Elmer grumbled. "Let's go online and order a grenade launcher. See which terrorist watch list we can get on."

"Stop!" Fran yelled so loudly she surprised herself. "We're not supposed to kill them in their cave while they're sleeping. It's against their religion."

Elmer straightened up in his chair and wagged his fork at his wife. "Yeah, you know, they're nice people, mostly, and I know we gotta respect their culture and all that, but some of their beliefs are not real, ah, wise?" He searched the room for agreement and found Jerry's grin.

Patrick was with Fran. "So we ignore their wishes? They know more about those critters than we do."

"That's 'cause they're overrun with them!" Elmer pointed out. "So let's kill this one handy little bundle right now, while they're sleeping, and they won't get out of hand. It's logic, right, Spock?"

Lorraine attempted a Vulcan eyebrow-raise. "But, why don't *they* do it?"

"The Curse," Jerry reminded them. "People die when they come out of the caves."

"The pathogen." Lorraine corrected, remembering what Baput had said. "It's contagious. Their families get sick, too."

Fran stood up. "Jerry, I don't want you going near there anymore."

"It's way inside, Mom. On the Queen. We just gotta kill her without touching her. They can't. But we can. We have the technology."

"That doesn't make it right," Patrick objected.

"We've got to kill the pathogen, too." Lorraine continued, as if there had been no moral debate. "The gas has to kill that, too. Chlorine, maybe?"

"Liquid nitrogen." Despite his distaste for killing, Patrick couldn't resist battle engineering. "It freezes you at the cellular level. All your cells turn to crystal form. Then, when they thaw, they're just mush. That'll kill them for sure, if that's what you must do."

"Hmm. Maybe they're extremophiles," Lorraine argued. "Some microscopic organisms can live in all kinds of conditions. Volcanic vents, bottom of the ocean, glacial ice sheets…"

"Is a pomegranate orchard an extreme environment?" Patrick replied. "Their climate is just like here. If it lives in this climate, it can't live through being frozen to near-absolute zero and then thawed." Patrick set about finishing his stuffing.

By the time he swallowed his last bite, no one had stepped into the silence, so he took up the other side of his own argument. "I don't see why we can't just build a good, strong grate across the entrance. Rebar or something, sunk in deep with that rock drill."

Now that Patrick had switched sides, Elmer challenged him. "Let me get this straight, Bro. You can't kill them, but you can starve them to death?"

"If by 'starving them to death' you mean not letting them eat my daughter, or anybody else, then yeah, I'm down with that," Patrick agreed.

"That's it?" Jerry sputtered. "We're not even gonna *try* to kill 'em?"

"Apple pie and ice cream!" Fran announced from the kitchen.

At the quarters, dinner was essentially the same as next door's, minus the turkey. Salistar fretted silently about something. Baput wondered if she had heard about the Queen. Felsic was sullen, too. Baput suddenly realized he hadn't come inside to see the video. Where had he gone? G-Pa seemed more absent than he really was. Baput knew. He had seen that trick before.

Popa grunted and ate. Mostly ate. He kept his eyes on his plate and gulped many helpings, as if it were the night before First Pomegranate Day. When his plate finally stayed empty, he looked straight at Baput. "Well, Akash…"

"Popa! I am not!" Baput declared, turning to the real Akash.

Valko turned his nose up with a disdainful grunt.

Baput fought back a laugh as he watched G-Pa try to pretend he didn't know he was being insulted.

When the façade broke down, the old man sputtered, "It was just a rasta! Not real. Earth Boy's deception. There is no queen. No nimblies, no bumblies. We go home on First Pomegranate Day," the Akash commanded. But it sounded more like pleading.

Valko snorted again and settled himself into his chair across from Baput. Salistar cleared the dishes silently.

"I go to the boor," Felsic excused himself in half-Nauvian.

"Well, Son," Valko addressed Baput correctly this time. "What shall we do?"

Baput glanced instinctively at his mentor, who had gone back to his mumbling. No help there. He looked up at his popa's eyes and made an embarrassing squeak.

Valko led the ambivalent young man his way. "I have said before, if nimblies and bumblies are on Earth because of us, it is our responsibility to wipe them out."

"But, Popa, Insitucide is forbidden!" Baput's cry rousted G-Pa and drew Momama from the kitchen.

"Insitucide!" Valko echoed scornfully. "You've heard your Akash, Son. The rules don't matter. Not if we don't like them! Not if they stand in our way!" His bulk rose above the table. He looked down at the Akash. "Isn't that right, your Supremeness?" Valko never used the superlative address for his father-in-law. He sounded sincere, but the sarcasm cut like a machete.

Before the Akash could respond, Valko had turned away again. He paced the floor as he spoke. "We couldn't kill them at Nauve. Not without sending somebody in." He cast a worried look around the room. "But Elmer, he has things…"

"Guns?" Baput suggested.

"The Queen is in that chamber, off to the side. Elmer's guns shoot only in a straight line. But Patrick has some very strange things. Sojourner can bring something in. A poison, maybe."

"Sojourner is stuck," Baput reminded him. His mind reeled as he found himself discussing Insitucide with Popa, in front of G-Pa. *And Popa thinks it is up to me to decide!*

"Patrick and Jerry will find a way," Valko replied confidently. He grinned an odd grin. "Or that woman, Lori Anne. Strange creature, that one."

Salistar froze in the kitchen doorway.

Valko laughed, strode over to where she stood, and swatted her on the butt with his huge hand.

She jumped, but managed to assemble a passable smile.

It didn't matter. He threw his arms around her and enveloped her, covering her face. "What does *my* Battle Engineer say, eh? Do we kill the Queen now, or let her hatch things that bite…" He snatched playfully at Salistar, pinching her lightly, all over, until she squirmed away.

"I am Tether! Not Battle Engineer. Not War Chief. Not Boss. Not Music Maker. I do not say, 'Insitucide, no Insitucide.' That is for you men to decide!" She retreated back into her kitchen, rubbing her bruised rump.

The next morning, Patrick played the video about 10 more times, slow, fast, forward, backward.

Jerry joined him. "I told you, you went too fast the whole way. Now it's all blurry," he complained over his hot cocoa.

Patrick sighed. "I wanted to get to the part we couldn't see with the light first. Then I would have backed out slow and got a good record of the whole thing." He froze on the part right before Sojourner hit the back wall. "Look down here on the right. See the darkness?" Patrick pointed to the screen, near Baput's smudge. "There's a crack there where it bailed over the edge. When I pulled, I think I got it stuck in that crack."

"So, what now?" Jerry asked.

Lorraine joined them, a plate of scrambled eggs mixed with stuffing and prime rib in her hand. She had it all planned. That put her in charge. "We can't build the cage today, because we don't have the rock drill. We'll just take some measurements and figure out how to do it. You salvage what you can from your expensive failure. We'll design and fabricate a grate and come back with it."

"Yay!" Belinda rejoiced as she handed out plates to her dad and cousin, with a smug look for Lorraine.

"Hey, you know what?" Patrick added suddenly, "There's still about 100 feet of cable wrapped around that reel. According to Lorraine's map, it's 150 feet to the house. We'll get more cable and run it all the way to the house, right into the TV. We can only see the floor of that chamber, but maybe we'll hear something."

"We can watch the Queen on TV from here at the house?" Jerry asked as he watched his uncle rise out of the ashes of defeat, a new project taking shape in his mind.

"I can get another camera to watch the entrance, right outside the grate, so you can see if anything gets out. We'll need two monitors so you can watch both views all the time. It will be like The Bridge, command central."

Next Visit

When Boss Lorraine and the Battle Engineers returned to install the cage, Fran had a chicken and vegetable stew simmering in the crockpot. She didn't mind cooking for the extended family, but she had learned that having the food all prepared helped loosen the tension between Lorraine and her daughter. *I just have to keep Bel away from Salistar. Or should I?* Fran mused, her eyes wandering to Lorraine. *Funny how rebellions flip, one generation to the next. Anything to upset the parents, I guess. I wonder what Jerry will come up with, besides running away to Nauve to make green babbetts.*

Lorraine launched into her detailed plan as soon as they sat down. "We have a framework of rebar, all welded together. But the holes are about four-inches across. Those things could wriggle through that, couldn't they?"

"You gotta ask them," Jerry shrugged.

"I've got a five-foot square of the same metal grate as the platform," Patrick added. "We can weld that to the inside of the rebar grate. It's really hard to bend, though."

Lorraine leaned forward over her bowl and retook the floor. "I've got a template to cut the thing with. It's gotta fit tightly against the mouth of that cave, with all its bumps and divots. It's not totally smooth, you know."

"We've got tools in that shop that'll cut and bend it however you want," Elmer invited.

Lorraine took another bite and went on. "So we put the cage across the entrance, and they wake up and start banging on it, then what?"

"Then they're awake, so it's OK to kill them," Jerry ventured.

"How?" Elmer asked no one in particular.

"Shoot them!" Jerry's idea was simple. Almost low tech. "We'll need holes big enough to shoot through. If they're right there, pecking at the screen, we could pump them full of bullets, easy."

"Like shooting fish in a barrel!" Elmer agreed. "Not the shotgun. Shrapnel would bounce everywhere. Maybe my pistol…"

"My show pistol!" Lorraine stood as if she had just drawn her gun, fingers in bang-bang position. "Did I tell you I won competitions?"

Belinda groaned out loud.

Lorraine shot her a poisonous look and went on. "My dad used to take me to his gun club. Mom didn't like it. She thought it was unladylike. That made me want it even more. It was one of those things I did just to piss her off."

Elmer erupted. "Ohhh! One of *those* things!"

Francine kicked him under the table. Her eyes shifted to Belinda, then back to Elmer. The adults in the room all knew Elmer's Theory about the mystery that was Patrick and Lorraine. Fran didn't think Belinda needed to hear it. Besides, the longer they stayed together, the more Fran doubted that the beautiful Lorraine had married the disfigured Patrick *just* to upset her mother.

Lorraine had launched into her routine, anyway. This was something they had all heard. "That was right after I quit being her little beauty queen. I won competitions at that, too. She always said I'd be famous, but I hated it. It was for looking a certain way, standing like they told you, smiling just so, wearing what they handed you. But it wasn't really *me*. It didn't feel like an accomplishment, not like hitting a bullseye.

"So I quit the beauty queen scene, but I kept on shooting, and fighting with Mom, for the next eight years. I wanted to go to college for engineering. She said it was a man's job. She was trying to set me up as some rich guy's trophy wife.

"I was a senior in high school when JonBenét Ramsey was murdered. She was only six! Our old fight erupted all over again. I even accused my mom of trying to kill me, just to make me famous, since that was clearly the route to fame in that racket. I tell you, I could think of a few times, back then…

"Then the media started piling on about how disgusting the whole child beauty queen thing is. I ended up with enough 'I told you so' points to get me into any college I wanted. Dad paid for all four years up front. I guess he knew I wasn't going to be coming home much anymore. So now I don't have a student loan, just Patrick's."

"Or a family," Elmer muttered.

"Just Patrick's," Lorraine repeated with a chillingly sweet smile for her dear "brother."

Tone of Yanzoo

The next morning, the Battle Engineering Team met at the shop to assemble the cage. The kids tiptoed past the sauna, where Baput had again left the Akash alone with only Shastina to block his rare escape attempts. She twitched and whimpered, and Jerry held Brodey by the collar as they passed. When they'd gone, she sat back down at her post, looking after them wistfully.

Baput had his bowl and mallet. Jerry had his guitar and a battery-powered amp. Belinda carried her violin. When they reached the Rock, they exchanged a solemn glance.

Jerry extended his hand, palm up. "Team Yanzoo!" he declared.

"Team Yanzoo!" Belinda echoed, slapping Jerry's hand with her open palm.

Baput followed, relishing touching the skin Belinda had just touched. They climbed onto the Rock. Brodey lay down on the grass.

They didn't hit the Rock with the hammer. They just played their instruments on top of it. Soon the Rock began to resonate, singing its own rich, deep tone that blended with the swelling ring of Baput's bowl, the piercing scream of Jerry's guitar, and the pure sweetness of Belinda's violin.

The Akash's eyes flew open as the rock walls came to life all around him. He reached out to touch the wall on his right. His hand jerked back involuntarily, then returned and stayed on the wall. He stared through the darkness. He rose to his feet and stumbled to the door, tripping over Shastina. Leaning on his longstick, the old man propelled himself past his dog and stumbled, almost running, up the path toward the Rock where the Tone swelled like a bubble in the sky.

Shastina ran tight circles around his legs. Her low center of gravity was a force to be reckoned with, but G-Pa was winning. Slowly, but steadily, he reached the Rock.

Baput picked up G-Pa's huffing and puffing under the Tone. "G-Pa's coming!" he warned. The instruments stopped, all at once. The Rock continued to echo the Tone mixed with Baput's stretched-out cry and the Akash's indescribable wail. Shastina added an agonized howl and collapsed on the ground, exhausted from struggling with him.

The Akash leapt onto the center of the Rock, his longstick extended horizontally beside him like a knight's lance. He landed on his feet, continuing his growl-whoop-roar-howl-moan. He stood, legs apart, arms outstretched like da Vinci's Vitruvian Man, his lethal longstick now held vertically. The Rock still rang.

Baput was caught! Earth Boy on the Rock! Earth Girl!

The old man's howl morphed into words. "Tone of Yanzoo! I felt it in the walls. I feel it in my bones, my soul, my very being! But it stopped." The Akash focused on the trio: Baput, who drew a trembling breath, Jerry, who wore that annoying smile, and Belinda, who glared back at G-Pa with a defiance Baput had never dreamed of seeing on a woman, let alone a young girl.

The Akash pointed his crooked beak at his apprentice and narrowed his beady eyes. He looked almost as confused as the day they had arrived, but now he was angry, too.

The Holy Rock stopped ringing. Baput looked up at the Akash. His ancient aura flared red with anger, but there was a tinge of respect and awe! The Akash spoke again, softer this time. "You play the Tone of Yanzoo. I am certain. But this is not possible. Yanzoo played alone. Only Yanzoo could sound the Tone."

"None of us is Yanzoo, Akash," Baput's voice quivered. "Not even you."

"Of course not!" the Akash snapped. "But Yanzoo acted alone! That is the point of the story. Don't you understand any of my teachings?" He sighed as if completely exhausted. "You are Alanakash. Alanakash must be exceptional! By himself, with no help. Like Yanzoo! He did it all alone."

"But, G-Pa," Baput dared protest. "He did not. His wife and children stood before him. Tymar did the dance to lure the bumblies into the tone."

Jerry took his shot, "And Yanzoo's tether killed four bumblies with her rolling pin."

"A woman's story!" G-Pa scoffed at the impudent Earth Boy.

Baput inflated himself with a deep breath. "Without them, Yanzoo would be nothing!" He forced himself to stare at G-Pa, who stared right back until Baput squirmed uncomfortably.

The old man's nose pointed up in the air; he snorted disdainfully. Then he turned and looked down on his apprentice, who still sat humbly before him with the silver music bowl in his lap. The old teacher lectured. "You avoid your responsibilities. You have other people helping you. Females!" he sneered at Belinda. "Non-believers." He shot Jerry an icy glare. "They sit on my Holy Rock and claim to play the Tone of Yanzoo!"

Baput stood up and looked down on his G-Pa. He seemed even smaller than before. "Play, Belinda," the Apprentice Alanakash ordered the petrified girl with the quivering bow.

"Yes, Alanakash." Belinda nestled the delicate instrument firmly to her chin, fingered the neck, and drew the bow across the strings.

Baput nodded to Jerry, who hit a piercing high chord and dragged it out. Baput strode to the very top of the Rock as if he were Alanakash. He lowered himself into his meditation pose, struck the bowl in his lap, and ran the mallet around the rim. The vibrations spilled from the bowl onto the Rock where they resonated and reflected, multiplying a thousand fold.

Suddenly, the Akash danced like a young warrior in victory. "Play, play, my boy!" he ordered with a triumphant grin. "Practice! All of you children. Practice. We have the Tone of Yanzoo!" He danced Tymar's Dance on the Rock while the tone swelled around them. "No more nimblies. No more bumblies," he sang, while Jerry played the National Anthem, Jimi-Hendrix-style, behind the bowl and the bow.

The Cage

After lunch, the cage was ready. Patrick stood on the platform, staring at Sojourner's cable where it disappeared into the unseen depths of the chamber. He knelt before his fallen robo-comrade as Felsic's joyful whoop rose in the sky behind him.

When Felsic arrived, Patrick helped him with his landing. Not that he needed any help. After all, he was Flying Felsic now. He had the rock drill again, with a smaller bit. The long hose led from the drill to the air tank that was strapped to the gatepost, like before. The precisely fitted grate waited on the driveway with Lorraine, Elmer, and the boys.

Belinda and Fran met Star at the greenhouse. G-Pa was there, in a padded folded chair in the corner, smiling blissfully.

"He is very good today," Star reported happily. She seemed more relaxed than usual. "Baput took him to the Holy Rock this morning."

G-Pa's dreamy eyes gravitated to Belinda and rested there ever-so-gently. The crazy smile broadened. "Tone of Yanzoo!" he whispered, slowly drawing it out. "Tone of Yanzoo, Tone of Yanzooooo..." He rose from the little chair and danced over to Belinda, who backed away.

Star stepped between the two. "Popa!" she cried.

The old man cocked his head and looked Salistar up and down. "What are you thinking, my daughter?" he asked. "Did you not hear? This child has played the Tone of Yanzoo! With help, of course, from your son." He broke his daughter's open-mouthed gaze and searched for Fran. "And also your son, with his screaming strings."

The Akash whirled and danced with his longstick. The women dodged and giggled indulgently as they planted seeds in little pots of dark soil. Star shot mystified glances at Belinda every few seconds, alternating between awe and spite.

Felsic pulled Mjolnir and a pointy chisel from the bag on his shoulder while Patrick unrolled the life-size plan sheet. He found the big divots in the face of the cave wall and fitted the template to them. "OK, hit the red dot."

"Red dot, yep." Felsic complied. The hammer smashed the chisel right through the plan sheet, leaving a mark in the rock below. Twelve times he marked the spots where he would drill holes for the pins that would secure the cage in place. He raised the drill and reached for the switch.

"Hold on!" Patrick stopped him. He gestured up to the winch tenders on the driveway. "Let's bring her down now. Measure the real thing in place before we go drilling a bunch of holes."

"Good idea, Bro!" Elmer agreed.

"The template is accurate," Lorraine insisted.

They hooked the welded monstrosity to the winch. It soared awkwardly through the sky alongside the air hose. Felsic and Patrick unhooked the grate and lined it up with the irregularities in the cliff face. It fit precisely, the chisel marks lined up all the way around.

Patrick heaved a sigh of relief.

"Pretty good, huh?" Lorraine solicited a compliment. "I told you the template would work."

"Good job, Babe," Patrick patronized.

"Good job, Babe," Felsic echoed. At Patrick's silent glare, he corrected himself. "Good job, Lori Anne."

The winch returned with the pins and cinches and a tube of silicone grout. When all the pins were set and grouted, Patrick and Felsic lifted the heavy grate into place. The joints slipped right over the pins, as designed. Felsic's thumbs-up brought hoots and hollers from them all.

"Take it down now," Lorraine ordered, shattering their jubilation. "Let the grout cure before you hang that thing on it."

"Tomorrow?" Patrick asked. *That means we can stay!* He thought, as eagerly as Belinda would have.

Lorraine sighed. "Tomorrow morning. It shouldn't take long. Then we can go. I gotta get back to work."

"Fits like a glove!" Lorraine raved smugly the next morning as Patrick bolted down the last of the 12 steel clamps that would hold the grate snugly across the round opening. The grate was elaborately bent to make perfect contact with every irregularity. Lorraine ran her long, slender finger along the biggest one, a divot about six inches long where the stone wall retreated over an inch away from the flat rebar grid. The fine grate bent inward to close the gap.

There was tight notch for the video cable that still probed the invisible depths. Lorraine ran her finger along one of the two shooting holes, just big enough for the barrel of Lorraine's show pistol or Elmer's revolver. "I put these near the rebar, so they can only tear in one direction, but it's a weakness. I hope it was worth it."

"It was your idea," Patrick reminded her.

"Yeah, shoot 'em in the cage, before they get out and eat us. No duh! We just better kill them when we shoot. This thing might not hold them forever."

8 . Keebra's Return

It had been exactly a year since Keebra had last appeared, in April, on Mitten, the day they'd unearthed the Rock. Now it was April of the final year in the cycle, only six months until First Pomegranate Day. The cave hole was secured. They were as ready for nimblies and bumblies as they could be. But Keebra was authorized to kill them now, in their sleep, Insitucide, and that made a lot more sense to Baput.

Use the snake to kill them now, in their sleep. Then, when the Rock goes off, we can just go nauve. Except, we haven't found anything like the Net. Everything on the iPlane is too heavy. No woven Earth fabric is that light, not even a bedsheet, much less a grid of metal fibers. There is no fiber on Earth that's so crinkly and light-colored, and even if we find something close, who knows if it will work? We can't test it until First Pomegranate Day, when the Rock rings on its own, if it even does... Baput mused in the sauna while he faked another meditation session and watched for Keebra.

G-Pa seemed naively glad to have his apprentice spending more time with him in meditation. It assuaged some of Baput's mounting guilt. The Rock, the chimney, the platform, Belinda... Baput knew he had been disregarding his mentor, who was now more like his student, for far too long.

G-Pa chanted away, ignoring his apprentice and the offending world he had long since rejected. The electric candle flicked weird patterns on the stone walls. *It was dark when Keebra came,* Baput recalled. He extinguished the candle.

He breathed deeply in slow Akashic breaths. His mind ripped through a virtual calendar, counting the days since he had taken the time to really meditate with G-Pa. Counting all the times he had told him to stay in here alone while he ran around with his friends, building stuff and planning Insitucide... *Committing Shavarandu! Is that why they say it is evil?*

His eyes jerked open. Had G-Pa moved? Eyes fixed blindly on the motion he had sensed, Baput groped for the candle and turned it back on. In its fitful flicker, he saw Keebra strangling in the Akash's skeletal hand. He still seemed too small to swallow a pregnant bumbly.

"You have him, G-Pa!" Baput exclaimed, glancing around for the lantern. "Don't let him go. I have a place where he can wait for Jerry. When Jerry comes home, he will take us to the chimney."

"I see what Keebra sees. I must go with Keebra."

"You can't go in the chimney, G-Pa."

The Akash stood, waving the captive snake around the room. "Of course not," he replied. "But what Keebra sees inside the cave? I sit outside and see that, if I am allowed to meditate properly with no silly distractions." The Akash shook the poor snake in his clenched fist, almost hitting the ceiling of the tiny shack.

"G-Pa! You're hurting him." Baput dove under the bench to get the box he'd prepared for Keebra. "Put him in here. He will be comfortable." Baput wondered if G-Pa cared. "He will have to stay and wait for Jerry."

"Why?" G-Pa pouted. "What has Earth Boy to say to Keebra?"

"Nothing. But we can't fly without him." Baput replied, firm as any parent. He closed the box and slid it under the bench in the dark where he hoped the captive gopher snake would be more at ease.

His eyes widened at a realization. "G-Pa, do you have to be *right* outside the cave to see what Keebra sees?"

"Well, of course," G-Pa replied briskly. "Why wouldn't I be?"

"How are you with heights?" Baput asked with a grin that widened when he heard Jerry's bike coming up the driveway.

The boys found both of their fathers in the shop, as usual. Jerry placed the crate on the workbench. Baput stayed close to G-Pa's side as he wandered about, fondling the strange, sharp metal objects.

"We need to fly out to the platform, Dad," Jerry ordered.

"Right now?" was Elmer's knee-jerk response, followed by, "Whatcha got there?"

"It is Keebra!" the Akash proclaimed proudly, as if he had conjured the snake from thin air all by himself.

"The snake, huh?" Elmer put his eye up to one of the air holes and peeked in. "Kind of small, don't you think? How big are those bat things?"

Baput stepped away from G-Pa. "I think he is too small, but G-Pa says he can see what the snake sees. So Keebra can go in, and at least we can see, even if he can't eat the Queen. And he's immune from the Curse."

Elmer chewed on his cheek a bit. "How are you gonna get him in there? Take the screen off? It's too heavy for you kids. You'll need Felsic, and all four of you can't be on there at once."

Jerry gathered his courage, glad his Aunt Lorraine was about 200 miles away. "I think he can fit through that divot. You know, the big one where you guys had to bend the screen all perfect?" Jerry watched his own fear gathering in his dad's face. He plunged ahead, regardless. "I can bend that backwards, with that little crowbar. Then after the snake's done, that claw Uncle Patrick made me will work perfectly to grab that grate and pull it back. If I can't do it, Felsic can fly over after and fix it later. You know how strong he is."

Felsic nodded in enthusiastic agreement.

Elmer wasn't so sure. "Lorraine will notice. I don't care how perfect you put it back. And it weakens it whenever you bend it." He turned to Valko. "Do you know about this Keebra?"

Valko's low-frequency rumble gradually became audible. "I have never before heard of this Keebra, but, yes. Send the snake. It might kill that evil queen as she sleeps, and it is even sanctioned by our most noisy Akash. We must try. It is better than waiting, day after day, for them to hatch."

Elmer was surprised at how much more relaxed he felt with Valko's backing. He tried to think the whole thing through, in the Musik way. "If he *does* eat the Queen, he'll be too fat to move, for a while. Might not come out for days. And when he does, he's gonna need a bigger hole to get outta there."

"But Dad, that's just it. If he eats the Queen, we're done. We can take the screen down. It's worth it, Dad."

"You'll have to check every day, see if he's trying to get out. If he's too fat to get out by himself, we'll know he ate 'er."

"Sure wish Uncle Patrick would have hooked up that camera across the entrance. He said he'd have an alarm and everything, and feed it all into the TV at the house," Jerry complained.

"You're gonna get it for your birthday. In time to watch for nimblies and bumblies. We didn't know you'd wanna watch snakes in April."

"If he goes in, we'll check, every day, I promise, Dad."

Elmer sighed. "That means we gotta fly you over there every day."

Jerry struck at the chance. "That's the other thing, Dad. The solo winches. You know, like I was saying. Solar panels to charge car batteries that operate a winch from the platform to the ground, down at river level, down by the Rock. A guy can go straight up and down all by himself without all the hoopla."

Elmer chewed on his cheek. "Maybe your mother and I don't want you going up and down all by yourself."

"*You* did it," Jerry challenged.

"I did," Elmer admitted. "It was stupid. Why do kids always want to make the same stupid mistakes as their parents? Why don't you think for yourselves and make up some new ones? There's always gonna be stupider mistakes to make!"

Jerry kept up. "The cage is on now. I can't go in, and they can't get out. Besides, Baput will be with me." He turned his grin on his friend, slapping him on the back. "You won't let me do anything stupid, right, B?"

Baput shrugged helplessly.

Jerry and Baput flew first, so they would be there to handle G-Pa when he arrived. Jerry, ever the show-off, bent over backwards in a blond-tipped arch.

Baput forced himself to stay stone still as he crossed the abyss, drawing from a resolve that was more pride than courage. He landed on rigid legs and let Jerry unclip him from the winch and onto the platform.

On the driveway, Valko stood over the puzzled Akash, keeping him still without even touching him while Elmer struggled with the harness. G-Pa struggled back, waving his longstick. Valko deftly grabbed it away, handing it to Felsic. The Akash whined like a two-year old.

Elmer ignored the protests as he wrestled with the leg straps. He yanked the chest clamp to its tightest setting. The ancient one was shrinking, Elmer was sure. He was almost as small as Belinda! He would be, without the bulky woven jacket with the lumpy pomegranate insulation. That was what made it possible to secure the harness.

I wouldn't put Belinda in it, but it's good enough for him. Elmer surprised himself with the thought. He glanced up the driveway. Valko was headed for the winch at the gatepost, the one that controlled the vertical. Elmer could just see the big guy drop his pain-in-the-neck father-in-law real quick, just a few feet, for a laugh that no one would dare share.

"Get up top, Valko," Elmer instructed, handing a trussed G-Pa to Felsic for launching. He took Valko's place at the main winch while Valko climbed the driveway to the upper post.

The winch hummed, and the unsuspecting Akash was whisked off the cliff into midair. "*Oooh!* Baput! Can you see me, Boy? I am outside of my body!" the gravelly voice boomed. "I have ascended! This is the way nauve. I go nauve. I fly nauve now. I am flying Akash! I am exceptional! Only I can fly! I shall be known forever as the Flying Akash…"

A hiss of air escaped from Felsic as he watched the line spin out and the conceited old man soar away. "Flying Felsic," he mumbled through his lower lip. "Flying Felsic was the first."

Baput felt Felsic's pain, but he was glad G-Pa wasn't freaked out. He unclipped the ill-fitting harness and fastened the cord to the platform, per protocol.

"Did you see, Apprentice?" G-Pa continued his happy babbling. "I flew. I am the first and only Akash ever to do so. You know this, yes?"

"G-Pa, I just…" Baput looked at Jerry, waiting, the snake in the box by his side, both clipped securely to the platform. No time to argue. Besides, it was true. G-Pa was the first *Akash* to ever fly.

With the Akash secured and self-entertaining, Jerry turned to the grate across the cave mouth. Midway down one side, the mesh was bent to fill in a hole, about an inch and a half wide by about six inches long. Jerry produced Mjolnir and a wide chisel from a tool belt he wore. Carefully placing the chisel on the grate, he tapped lightly with the hammer. The grate bent inward sickeningly fast. A couple more taps and pushes, and the hole was fully open, the grate tucked up out of the way behind the rebar.

Meanwhile, Baput settled his gleeful grandfather into his cross-legged meditation pose. "You will fly again soon, G-Pa. But now, remember why you are here. To see what Keebra sees, when he goes into the chimney." Baput knelt beside the old man. He took G-Pa's hand and closed his eyes, leading him in Akashic breathing.

Jerry set the flashlight in front of the cave entrance and turned it on. Light glared off the outside of the metal screen. Inside, an eerie lattice of light and dark, knowledge and mystery, filtered through the grate. Jerry hoisted the box onto his lap and opened it. He grasped the snake firmly, right behind its angry head and darting tongue.

"Release me, you!" G-Pa mumbled. *Was he seeing what Keebra saw?*

"Keebra," Baput addressed the snake through G-Pa. "Do you wish to perform Insitucide? Will you kill the Queen of the Nimbumblyborg as she sleeps and gestates deep within her cave? You must know, there is a curse that may kill you."

"He was calming down until you said that last part," Jerry reported, wrestling the serpent toward the opening.

"I know," Baput replied. "But it seemed like the right thing to do."

The snake turned around. His eyes met Jerry's. There was something G-Pa-like in them.

"Earth Boy!" G-Pa exclaimed.

"I think it's working!" Jerry cried, surprised.

Baput urged G-Pa Keebra even harder. "Keebra. You can save the Earth. Make it no nimblies and no bumblies like it's supposed to be. All you have to do is go in there and eat that queen. I hear she is very delicious," he added, having heard no such thing.

As he spoke, the snake stuck his head in, just barely. His tongue darted in and out of the cool darkness. Jerry felt a strain against his hand as Keebra struggled to back out. "What's the matter?" Jerry asked the snake, Keebra, G-Pa, whoever.

The Akash raised his head and reared back, just as the snake did. "Too light!" he complained in Nauvian.

"Turn the light off, Jerry," Baput translated.

Jerry took one hand off the surging snake and reached to turn off the flashlight. The snake sprung free and landed hard on the platform.

G-Pa jumped to his feet, shaking the structure beneath them. "No, no!" he cried. His eyes were open, but they were Keebra's eyes.

Keebra slithered quickly toward the edge of the rough platform. G-Pa turned that way and took a huge step, compounding the shaking.

"What's going on down there?" Elmer yelled.

G-Pa took another step toward the edge. Baput grabbed him by the sleeve.

Keebra dodged Jerry's desperate grasp and launched from the platform, flying through the air untethered as the Akash voiced his screams.

Baput twisted G-Pa's sleeve in his hand, trying to stop him from going the way of the unfortunate snake.

"Aww, man!" Jerry whined, looking over the guardrail.

"Is it dead?" Baput didn't want to know, but he had to.

"No," Jerry replied sadly. The snake slithered into the vines at the bottom of the cliff with a kinky, uneven motion. It reminded Jerry of his kinky, uneven family members. "But he's not right," he concluded. He looked up at his dad's face, obscured by the binoculars.

"He's got a hitch in his giddy-up, alright," Elmer hollered. "Now repair your divot, before your Aunt Lorraine sees what you did to her perfect thing there."

Jerry managed to pull the folded piece of grate back into its place, but there were tiny gaps all around it now, and an extra-shiny line where Jerry had bent it.

9. Second Solar Eclipse

First Pomegranate Day was only six weeks away, and the Nauvians were on pins and needles. The burgeoning pomegranates on the trees, the lurking Queen in the chimney, and the silent, brooding Rock hung over the ranch like doom. Baput's family would surely take the ill-timed solar eclipse as a bad omen, but he had to tell them about it. It would be midmorning and unmissable.

"No work on Monday," Baput informed his family. "We are to watch another solar eclipse."

There were sparks of recognition, but none caught. "Part of Shavarandu will turn away in the morning. He will turn to face us again before noon. It is foretold."

"Batuk's birthday is exactly a week after. Surely he will..." Salistar fretted.

"No, Momama," Baput said sternly. "I told you before. Batuk is no mo..." He couldn't pronounce the words "no more" to that forever-shattered face. "No Calamunga. Only Shavarandu and Kakeeche traveling their paths, getting in each other's way. Nothing to do with Batuk at all."

"Not Batuk," G-Pa agreed, rising to his feet, suddenly lucid. "It is that stupid, evil Earth Man! Harvest approaches! How can the kips ripen without the sun? He told me he understood this, yet still he fails to believe."

"If the kips don't ripen, the nimblies and bumblies won't come," Felsic reasoned hopefully, drawing a thoughtful nod from Valko.

"We will starve!" Salistar cast a disdainful glance around the room of foolish men.

G-Pa grabbed his longstick and headed for the door. "If the kips don't ripen, the Rock will not ring. We will not be able to return nauve! If that faithless man makes it so we cannot be nauve on First Pomegranate Day, I will..."

Valko leaned against the door and removed G-Pa's longstick with a swipe of his bear-like hand. He pointed to the chair G-Pa had vacated. The old man slunk back to his seat.

"The kips will ripen," Baput assured them. "The sun, Shavarandu, will smile on us again in just a few hours. No boogeyman, no angry gods, no failed harvest. We have nothing to worry about except for

First Pomegranate Day and nimblies and bumblies and maybe the portal opening…" Baput's comfort speech was getting quite uncomfortable. He needed to end on a high note. "Patrick and Belinda will be here tomorrow to hook up the TV so we can watch the chimney!"

"No Lori Anne?" Felsic whined like a toddler, "Awww."

They all stared at the unnatural display. Nauvian men did not pine for other men's wives. Not openly, anyway.

Fully wound up to freeway speed, the well-tuned Look'N Up Plumbing Van cruised south in the slow lane of Interstate 5 on Saturday morning.

"Why couldn't we go down there for Jerry's birthday?" Belinda asked, her arms folded. "You *promised* you'd hook up the camera for him."

"I wasn't ready," Patrick mumbled.

"You had half a year!" Belinda snapped. "And wait until they find out you didn't plant their pomegranate trees yet, either."

"It's the wrong time of year," Patrick excused himself again. "You plant in winter."

"Last winter," was Bel's impatient retort. "Or the winter before that." She attacked from a different angle. "Why didn't Mom come this time? Is she tired of Battle Engineering now?"

Patrick sighed. "She had to work." He used the standard answer, with no idea why it was so. They used to be used to this. Having Lorraine on vacation had been nice while it lasted. He remembered, then repeated aloud, what she had told him. "Your mom said, 'don't let Belinda get all green with Salistar.' What do you think she meant by that?"

Belinda just stared out the windshield at the flat, fertile wasteland of California's central valley.

"Well?" Patrick persisted.

"I help Star weave squares of grass for their clothes. My hands get all green just like Baput's…" She trailed off dreamily, then bounced back. "It doesn't wash off. They call it gaa. It's why their clothes are all blotchy. They don't even wash them. If it's gaa, grass stains, pomegranate juice, stuff like that, it's OK. If it's something gross, they replace just that one square of their clothes."

"Gwa," Patrick attempted.

"No. Gaa. No w."

The monotonous miles rolled by in silence. Patrick fumbled in the center console for a CD and popped in *Harvest*, his favorite Neil Young album. He started to sing the title song, looking to his daughter to join him. Seeing only stoic stubbornness, he tried diplomacy. "The eclipse is gonna be really cool. We'll all sit on the Rock together and watch it?" Patrick floated, more a question than an answer.

"It freaks them out, Dad. Especially Salistar. It's not a party. Not for her anyway."

Patrick tried to empathize, like his parents had taught him. Forgetting all about Lorraine's wishes, he extrapolated, "You can sit by Salistar and comfort her, so Baput can do his Akashic thing."

"That's what a tether does, Dad," Belinda finally smiled.

As Patrick stared out the windshield at a vast nothingness, he realized Lorraine was right. The greening of their daughter was already deeper than skin and clothes.

Jerry had been fuming since his birthday. They had set up the solar-powered winches, so they could ride up and down between the platform and the river level where the Rock was. They worked great, and everyone had fun riding up and down until the batteries went dead. The August sun had recharged them quickly.

But Patrick hadn't shown up with the camera and extra cable so they could watch the Queen's chamber and cave entrance from the comfort of their living room. The two brand-new monitors with recorders and alarms he'd unwrapped on that frustrating morning were no solace without the input equipment.

Now he waited impatiently through the pointless chatter of the grownups. School is fine, Bel's school is fine. The eclipse will be cool. Fran and Star are making applesauce, and Belinda wants to help. *Why did Mom and Uncle Pat look at each other like that when she asked? Let's go!*

They got the hint when he got up from the table and started assembling the monitors that would provide a steady stream of real-time information, video, and audio, right into the Musik living room. It could record up to 12 hours at a time, in case staring at nothing in real time got boring. The coolest part was, any motion on either camera set off an alarm at the monitor in the house and marked the place on the recording. If you missed it, it would flash and tell you where to look, and it wouldn't erase that part.

Late, but very cool, Jerry had to admit, *just like my stoner uncle.*

Patrick had a tiny camera, like the one on Sojourner, and enough cable, minus the heavy flex-pipe, to reach the house. "That's all there is to it," he told them. "That's why Lorraine didn't come. Too easy. 'Cable guy work,' she called it. Shall we get it done?"

He flew to the platform all by himself, piloted by the masters, Elmer and Valko. He mounted the snake-like camera on the outside of the cage, so it stared right across the cave mouth, and spliced the feed into the cable.

Patrick and Jerry hooked up the monitors while Elmer, Felsic, and Valko buzzed around the living room like impatient bees. Baput stood over Jerry's shoulder watching him.

"See, how lucky you are, Baput?" Jerry remarked. "You can get online without having all these wires. You're a living Wi-Fi! Except your Wi-Fi messes up our Wi-Fi."

"I should try to see inside the chimney by meditating?" Baput wondered why he hadn't thought of it before.

"There it is!" Patrick interrupted as one of the screens lit up in a silent still life, looking across the cave mouth toward the river.

The other screen was still black, but there was a green light on the frame now. Patrick switched on Sojourner's light. The screen lit up, showing the floor of the chamber.

Valko cocked his head to the side. Brodey barked once, then cocked his head, just like Valko. They heard a roar of barks from Shastina in the quarters, and soon, her claws on the porch. Elmer let her in, and she raced to Brodey's side, staring at the screen, snarling and spitting.

"Quiet!" Valko roared, raising his hand to cup his ear. Baput knelt and put his arms around Shastina, hushing her. Everyone stared at the immense man whose black beard had grown even longer and fuller.

"Peep, peep! Chirp, chirp!" The tiny noises that came out of that huge body! Baput tried not to laugh, but then the sucking sounds started. The pursed lips, the teeny squeaks. Baput couldn't take it. He laughed first.

"He hears like a dog! Must be them long ears," Elmer quipped, and his laughter quickly infected the others.

"They're nursing!" Patrick realized above the mirth. "The bats. They're mammals, and they're nursing. The bumblies are born!"

Fran and Belinda entered with two cases of fresh applesauce, eager to share a big bowl of leftovers.

Baput decided to get G-Pa. "He will hear them. He must. He is always the first to hear them on First Pomegranate Day."

Valko's chirping turned into a snort of swallowed laughter. *Can Popa hear the nimblies before the Akash does?* Baput wondered as he rushed next door. He returned with G-Pa and Momama, more applesauce, and a fresh loaf of her rich squash bread.

As the women laid out the spread on the breakfast bar, Baput led his G-Pa to the motionless screen. The tired old eyes stared blankly. "G-Pa, do you hear anything?"

The blank eyes turned to Baput. Baput pointed to his own ear.

The Akash shook his head sadly, slowly. "Perhaps my hearing is not what it once was," he admitted.

"But you hear the nimblies on First Pomegranate Day," Baput defended his memory. It couldn't *all* be wrong!

"Yes, I hear the thrumming of their young wings as they prepare for flight. I hear it, and I feel it throughout my being!" He wound up to a crescendo, then dropped like a lead ball. "But now I hear nothing."

Belinda escorted him to a seat and set a bowl of applesauce in front of him. With a subtle nod from Star, she added a slice of bread.

Baput stepped in front of the screen. He couldn't hear the chirping and suckling any more than the Earth people could. But if there was one person he knew he could trust without fail, it was his popa. And Shastina. She heard it too.

"They are here. They are awake," Baput declared. "The nimblies will be in their cocoons. They are not ready now, but on First Pomegranate Day, they will come. They don't belong here. We must kill them."

G-Pa squawked and began his mumbling.

Baput disregarded his distress and went on. "We will watch the eclipse from the Rock, but we will not strike it with Mjolnir. We need to feel the natural vibrations. You say they are all connected, right, Patrick?"

"Yes." Patrick felt like an eager student being picked by the professor. "The Holy Cave, the chimney, the Rock, and the sauna."

Baput held the floor naturally. "The Akash and I will sit at the top of the Rock and meditate. We will concentrate very hard and feel the vibrations of the Rock. Maybe we can see inside without the wires. Are you with me, G-Pa? Oh, Wise Akash?"

G-Pa sputtered out of his dream state to respond to the seldom-used complement. "Yes, yes, as I told you, we shall do this."

Baput shrugged, just like a human kid, and sat down next to Belinda. She had a bowl waiting for him.

Fran called it a quick breakfast. Lorraine would have called it a marathon. Jerry spent most of it staring at the video screens. At last, they joined the green family for their pilgrimage to the Rock. They had decided to walk. It was Fran's idea. Of course, she also had to make sure they took enough food for an army of men fighting nimblies and bumblies for three days.

"She was like this even before she met Star!" Elmer complained as he hoisted the backpack she handed him. "Let's take the Jeep," he voted.

Fran reproached him. "These guys work their hearts out all day, and you can't even carry a 40-pound pack out to the Rock? You used to run there! And you packed all those rocks for your dad."

"Don't remind me." Elmer headed out the door with his burden.

Elmer walked with Valko, out of earshot from the rest. He had been thinking about the legendary consequences of being blamed for a solar eclipse. *We've all come a long way*, he guessed, but he had to test his status with the only Nauvian whose opinion really mattered. It wasn't just because of his size, either, although that was definitely a primal consideration.

Elmer reached for the heart of the matter. "Are you, ah, scared?" he pointed at the sun hanging over the river before them. All at once, the birds rose from the trees and flew to their roosts. It was beginning! They were late!

Valko's answer surprised Elmer. "I admit I am afraid. But there is nothing I can do about it. Except just keep my thoughts pure." He looked sideways at Elmer. "Or keep them to myself."

Elmer leaned in gleefully. "Are you saying you don't really believe?"

Valko looked forward, grunting defensively. "I said what I said. I keep to myself." His right eye shot sideways to look at Elmer with a twinkle that assured him there was nothing to fear.

G-Pa slowed abruptly as they passed the sauna.

Felsic urged him on. "We are late, Akash! We must get to the Rock before the eclipse!" He had no idea why, or even if, that was so, yet he believed it with all his heart.

Baput and Jerry caught up, folding G-Pa and Felsic into their little group and pushing them along, swept by the tide of the majority.

Patrick had an idea. "Baput, you know I can get on the Plane with my Mindfulness Meditation. So I was thinking, I could go up there on the Rock and help you meditate so you can see inside the chimney. What's the chant? I can learn it real quick, right now, on the way out there."

Baput needed all the help he could get. "OK," he agreed. He felt embarrassed when he recited the Kakeeche chant for Patrick and Belinda.

"I'm really good at memorizing words," Belinda bragged. "I still remember that other poem you taught me, the one about Shavarandu burning your only world away."

The Akash stopped in his tracks and stood rigid. Baput pulled on his arm, but despite his rapidly diminishing mass, he could not be moved. Baput looked at Belinda, then Jerry. There lay the guilt.

"Yes. I taught her," Baput lied, confessing to a crime he hadn't committed.

"No!" Belinda and Jerry both cried at once.

Jerry produced his recorder, always present at such occasions. "It was me. I recorded it, and I played it in front of her."

"My mom made me listen." Belinda betrayed her own to the scary but harmless old man she now tried to remove from Baput's arm.

He snarled and pulled away from her. "Where is my tether?" he demanded, but Star was up ahead with her best friend Francina, chatting about the feast they'd prepared.

Patrick continued to practice the anti-eclipse chant. Baput decided to save his altered lyrics for later. *Patrick would surely laugh out loud if he chanted my lyrics*, he reasoned. Belinda had it down, too. She even had it set to music by the time they reached the Rock.

The Akash, his Apprentice, and Patrick climbed up on the Rock, but they didn't ring it.

Belinda set her violin case on a log and opened it. Baput almost had G-Pa settled on the Rock when she stroked the violin with the bow, tuning it up.

G-Pa's eyes flew open and he struggled against Baput's sturdy restraint. "You! Girl!" he bellowed. Belinda stopped playing abruptly. She narrowed her eyes at the old man.

"Come up on the Rock here and play! Come! We must save Shavarandu! Come and play your part to awaken the Rock."

"Say 'please,'" Belinda demanded.

"That's my girl," Patrick muttered proudly.

The Akash stared, open-mouthed at the bold young lady. Fran handed him a pair of the now-familiar cardboard eclipse goggles. He remembered the wonders of looking upon Shavarandu through these funny-looking frames. He put them on and saw Shavarandu without the glare. There was already a bite out of the top of his head! He drew an awestruck breath.

Belinda saw the Akash, looking so goofy in those cardboard sunglasses with his mouth hanging open, she had to giggle.

Salistar sucked in a noisy breath, and then everyone laughed at each other's goggles.

Patrick had his welder's mask. It covered his whole face no matter where his eye was. Francine handed Belinda a pair of tinted swimming goggles. They covered both eyes, but she looked like one of those deep-sea fishes that makes its own light.

Baput and the Akash sat side-by-side at the top of the Rock. Star balked at the smooth, round surface, so Fran rushed to her side and helped her tense friend to the Tether's place at G-Pa's right side.

Fran sat down right next to her, cooing, "It's not First Pomegranate Day. The Rock can't do it, remember?"

Patrick, as Assistant Chanter and Meditator, found a spot in front of Baput and G-Pa. "I'll try to stay out of you guys' way," he promised the Akashic pair. "Let me know if I step on your toes."

"I'm right here, Buddy," Jerry promised Baput. He straddled two worlds, one foot on the Rock, one on the ground. "I'm your connection. I'll let you know what's going on here on Earth. Go, dudes. It's already happening! Chant it away!"

G-Pa and Patrick were already chanting. Over and over, the same thing. Baput gagged a little before he settled into it. He knew it was a way to the Plane, but he was so literally sick of it! Then came such sweet relief! Belinda's violin rose from behind him and surrounded the hollow chanting. The Rock started to resonate. No Mjolnir, just Bel's strings. Baput wished he had his bowl, but he needed to concentrate.

The Plane rolled out before him like a wide river, a continuous flow of energy and knowledge in an endless variety of colors. All the thoughts and feelings and wishes of Earth, all flowing as one. Was it Nauve's, too? He couldn't feel it. He couldn't feel Bazu or Pindrad or Tamaya. But he could feel everyone here. All his friends, all around him. Chanting, his conscious thoughts drifted away as Belinda's soft tones gently rocked the Rock beneath him.

Akash of Nothing

Baput knew the Akash would be angered by the question, but he pushed the jet of ugly, pea-soup green out into the stream anyway. "G-Pa, if there is no one other than our one family, here on Earth, are you still Akash over us, or is my popa in charge?"

His grandfather's spirit vibrated a deep blood red. Anger? Baput doubted the wisdom of taunting the Akash during an Eclipse Meditation. If he disrupted the ceremony, maybe the sun would never recover! The thought ran through his mind like a savage swiftly streaking through the forest. He dismissed it with a peeved mental shove and pressed on. "The Akash is in charge over all the families, over all popas. But now, there is only one family, one popa. Plus Felsic, but he is Popa's little brother, so Popa is in charge of him, too. What is Akash in charge of now?"

The angry glow pulsated. No discernable message, just dense vibrations creeping through Baput's ethereal network.

Baput reminded himself of Jerry, pushing that scalpel in, investigating in a way that was often uncomfortable. "At Nauve, people obey you without question."

"As they should," The Akash interrupted conclusively.

It took a long, silent minute for Baput to gather the courage, even in non-physical form, to ask a question the likes of which had probably never been asked of an Akash before. "But, Akash, what if you are wrong?"

"Wrong?" The Akash roared mentally. "I am Akash!" he replied as if it were obvious and inarguable.

Courage at a boiling point, Baput plunged into the abyss. He put his thoughts out there slowly, deliberately. They had come to him in fragments over the past cycle, but he had never cast them, fully formed, into that body of all thought, that ultimate cloud, that was the Plane. Now he cast a mold that had never been cast.

"G-Pa, Akash, I don't always agree with you."

G-Pa's aura turned fire red, then hotter, like molten lava. Baput could actually feel the heat. He felt his own fatal words ring out, expanding through the collective consciousness like the ripple of a stone tossed into a pond, shaping it in a new way. He reeled at the profundity of it, almost dropping his unconscious, automated chanting of the Eclipse Meditation.

The crimson glow of G-Pa's angry aura further distorted the Plane with its melting heat. Damage done, Baput figured he might as well finish his point. He bravely went on. "So, when I am Akash, I will do things differently. And I won't be wrong, because I am Akash. No matter what I do, even if you don't like it, it will be right, like it is for you, now. Yes?"

The old Akash appeared to think about that as his aura cooled. Then, with resolve, he transmitted his reply, somehow adding a condescending tone. "You are still Apprentice, my boy. You have not attained full wisdom yet. When you do, you will ascend to Akash. Then you will think rightly, like I do."

Otherwhere Is Fake News

Jerry's call reached Baput all the way up on the Plane with some resonant guitar string tone in his voice. "Keep at it, B, we're still losing it!"

G-Pa's aura was fading. Was he falling from the Plane? Baput didn't want to upset him further, but this was, unbelievably, the best exchange they'd had since Arrival.

Patrick started another round of anti-eclipse chanting, buoying G-Pa's spirit up in the cooled flow.

"G-Pa, do you ever even try to think about what I told you about the otherwheres?"

"No," the Akash replied crisply.

"But, G-Pa, you must have! There is so much to think about!"

"What else does Earth Boy have to teach us?" A resentful orange aura tried to change the subject.

"Well, he seemed to think this is a pretty big deal."

"And we think Kakeeche turning their backs on us four times, and even Shavarandu twice now, just in this one cycle since Arrival is a big deal, don't we? Earth Boy does not. So, what does he know? Nothing! I don't know why you continue to attend his School of False Teachings!"

G-Pa pulled his energy into a tight, lavender ball with a green heart. It did not communicate. It merely throbbed its green inner light in rhythm with the chanting that their bodies continued to perform. Baput listened anxiously for Jerry's voice.

Suddenly, G-Pa addressed a thought to Baput once again, as if he really *had* been thinking about the otherwheres. "It is a trick, don't you see? It is a smoke screen! It is like the horns that confuse the bumblies by drowning out their sounds. It is like his TV Plane and his iPlane, always drowning out the truth of the Plane! Now he occupies your inner thoughts as well with this, this web. Follow one thread and encounter another that takes you down a path.... Yes. I have thought about it, or tried to. I have found it impossible. It is designed to confuse our thoughts. He tries to brainwash you!" he accused.

Baput shot back. "He says you are the one who brainwashes. You and the school. They brainwash us against Shavarandu."

The Akash's response bubbled like a snorted laugh. "Doesn't work very well, does it?"

"Halfway there!" Jerry's voice penetrated Baput's thoughts again. He felt relief, then sensed something else. Was Momama crying? Baput felt around for the distinct vibrations of each of his family members, and Jerry's family too. He could hone in on each, like a dog hones in on an individual's unique scent. Momama knelt on the Rock at G-Pa's right, tethering him, and yes, she was crying. Her aura felt cold with fear. There was Fran's aura, wrapped gently around hers. *Thank you, Francina.* Baput sent the thought into the flow, fully understanding its meaning now.

Patrick's spirit hovered above the Rock, halfway between Earth and the Plane, his denim blue aura swimming clumsily in the soup of atmosphere, psychic energy, the waves from Belinda's violin, and the responding vibrations of the Rock.

Valko sat on a big folding chair he had hauled from the shop. His dull vibe was one of boredom, truth be told, as vibrations always do.

Felsic and Elmer stood watching the eclipse with their backs to the Rock. Felsic was wearing his glasses this time and actually looking at Shavarandu, forgetting his brainwashing.

Elmer was trying again to explain the eclipse to Felsic. *Felsic? Can he understand it? Jerry said he was a genius!* Baput accidentally squirted a jet of ugly green jealousy into the cosmic flow.

"Keep it up, you guys!" Jerry's voice made him jump. He resumed that laborious breathing, that tiresome chant, and ascended to the Plane again.

Shavarandu

Baput touched G-Pa's vibration, just to be sure. Yes, this was the rational Akash of Nauve. Stubborn and selfish, sneaky and conniving, but sharply lucid, and even with a bit of humor! Was the old G-Pa coming back? Or maybe most of what was 'him' resided here on the Plane now, leaving his withered body behind for Star to care for in accordance with her centuries-old, inescapable job description. Oddly, this more complete, Plane-dwelling Akash didn't seem to be much bothered by the eclipse.

G-Pa's aura glared in chartreuse when it addressed Baput. "You and that Earth Boy. Every day at your school." He sounded scornful, like before, but now a new reason came out. "You never invited me." His psyche pouted.

"But G-Pa, I thought..." Baput's aura sputtered.

"You think I am against Shavarandu, because I am Akash, and those are the rules. Open your eyes, Boy! I have always sought Shavarandu, just like you do! I am required to forbid you to do it. But, you know as well as I that I have engaged in Shavarandu more than any other Akash. More successfully too. I opened the door."

Baput's aura clenched to a dense black hole.

The Akash ignored the chill and continued. "I assembled the weapon. And it worked, too."

"It sent us here," Baput, still clenched, squeaked in pink.

"Yes. Yet you study it daily," the Akash accused. "I see it in your aura. You have changed deeply. Not just manhood. There's all that, too. Disgusting. But there's something else. A different light shines in you."

A chorus of oohs and ahhs distorted the field of sound that the chant and violin had built around them. Felsic's excited voice bubbled over them all, stopping suddenly with an "ooh!"

It must be maximum, Baput surmised. His face was pointed directly at the orb, and he was wearing his glasses. He opened his eyes. Shavarandu was less than half lit, like a quarter-moon. Solar flares erupted along the dark edge of the missing left side.

"That's the maximum!" Jerry confirmed. "Shavarandu's coming back! We're gonna live!"

Baput closed his eyes to conceal a snicker.

What to Do?

The Akash seemed unfazed by Baput's distraction. Not interested in the eclipse at all! It was plain to see where his thought energy was directed, and it was not at Kakeeche. He chanted the chant without thinking about it, just like Baput did. Baput wanted to lash out at G-Pa for his hypocrisy, but he restrained himself, pulling himself into a quiet ball. *What is the Akash saying now?*

He could still read the tracks of the Akash's recent thoughts on the Plane, where they had reshaped it forever. "The point is, Shavarandu was necessary at nauve to defeat the nimblies and bumblies. And now, Shavarandu is necessary for us to find our way home. And Earth Boy can help us. He will find the key."

"The key to what?" Baput asked with a vibrant blue flash. G-Pa had a plan, and it included Jerry!

"The key to Nauve, of course. To going nauve!"

"Oh." Baput's response was a dull, short tone of disinterest in a minor key of disappointment. His heart sank deep down into the bottom of his disembodied spirit like a hard, dense rock. *Going nauve.* The thought brought him tumbling down into his aching body.

"Yes. Earth Boy. Alone. You do not help him. Earth Boy finds the key and turns it, we go home." G-Pa's aura was now deep blue, calm and certain.

"I can help him, G-Pa." Emboldened by the Akash's frankness, he confessed, "I am starting to understand—"

The cool blue flashed orange-red. "You, no! You Alanakash, you stay pure. Return to Nauve."

"But, G-Pa, I—"

"You fool! Don't you understand? Earth Boy commits Shavarandu. Only Earth Boy. That way, only Earth burns. We go nauve."

Baput's vibration contracted, cold and blue. "We would leave Earth to burn? Jerry? Patrick? Bel...?" he touched each vibration as he spoke. He felt Belinda's for just a microsecond, but he couldn't bear it. The connection broke with a jarring snap. The Plane ran scarlet. All the disembodied energy of the seething young man exploded like a supernova of angry fire red. Even the sky above the Plane was infused with vermillion.

He felt Jerry thumping on his back. How long had that been going on? When had Jerry climbed up on the Rock? He could hear Earth loud and clear. G-Pa's chanting, his own chanting, Jerry saying, "Almost done folks. Twenty minutes more and all better! Good job, guys!"

His throat was sore from chanting. He groped for his water bottle and someone handed it to him. Jerry! Acting as tether! He hiccupped a laugh, almost choking on the offered sip. Then he remembered. He was upset about something. What was it?

He resumed the painful chanting that wore a groove in his throat and his soul. The only way he could go on was to mutter the new lines he'd made up while G-Pa and Patrick muttered the traditional ones. He could do them without thinking, almost as well as the old ones. But sometimes they made him want to laugh.

"Kakeeche farts their holy light..."

No one seemed to notice, but he knew Jerry did. He knew Jerry wanted to laugh so badly! He hoped he *did* laugh, but he knew if Jerry laughed, the Apprentice Akash was going to lose it too and laugh right out loud, *right when we almost had the sun back!*

That did it. He giggled. He could feel Momama's concerned magenta aura reaching over from her place at G-Pa's side. He took another swig from the water bottle Jerry faithfully held before him.

"Are you on the Plane? Are you talking to him?" Jerry whispered harshly, shaking his left arm. Baput nodded.

"Ask him about the nimblies and bumblies! Why can't we just kill them now, in their cave?" Jerry placed his order. "You have 15 minutes."

"Time doesn't matter," Baput mumbled, resuming his chant in the less-distracting traditional way.

The Nimbumblyborg

Was G-Pa still here? Had he heard Jerry? There he was, lavender and placid, still chanting. His aura flared pink at Baput's spiritual return.

"Yes," G-Pa's vibe replied. "I hear Earth Boy's commands. You have come to do his bidding?"

"Yes, G-Pa. It is only six weeks until First Pomegranate Day. We must kill the Queen before the nimblies and bumblies emerge."

G-Pa's aura flashed red. "Keebra said no."

Baput projected his novel thoughts into the stream with a steely vibe he had never felt before. "The nimblies and bumblies do not belong on Earth. The law against Insiticide does not apply." Baput beamed deep purple, basking in perhaps the first legal argument ever completed in pure mental space.

G-Pa snorted a little curl of white. "Keebra cannot kill them now. They are not the single mass of despicable black slime that they were when that cowardly snake refused your wicked request."

"How do you know, Akash? The suckling sounds?"

"Come with me and see." G-Pa's breath deepened audibly.

Baput matched it. They joined hands, and together their spirits caught the stream that led into the deep hole in the nearby cliff. Their spirits flew along the dark corridor to the oddly well-lit den. They hovered there, watching the lives of the nimbumblyborg play out in accelerated time before their third eyes.

The black ball of slime hung from the center of the ceiling. The mysterious light gleamed dully off its folds and wrinkles. Suddenly, the mass erupted all over with pustules. They popped one by one in rapid succession. A pale orange maggot appeared out of each popped pustule. They wriggled out, then turned and devoured the shiny black membrane from which they had emerged. There were hundreds of maggots, far too many for Baput to count. They cleaned the slime away, exposing the soft fur of the rotund, pregnant mother bumbly rising and falling with the deep breaths of her undisturbed hibernation.

Once satiated, the worms inched up the mother bumbly's legs to her feet where they gripped the ceiling of the chamber, then along the ceiling to where it met the wall. Each one took off in a different direction, so the pregnant bat was soon surrounded by caterpillars spinning paper cocoons.

When the cocoons were finished and the nimbly nymphs were finally still, the single mammalian mother started heaving violently, pulsing and contracting. Still hanging upside down by her feet, she bent up strenuously, trying to get her head between her legs so she could pull the baby out. The tiny bald thing wriggled and struggled free, toppling into its momama's waiting wings. Then another.

Faster and faster, the baby bumblies emerged, alive and hungry. How many? Six? Eight? Baput wasn't sure. He tried to count as the ugly, wrinkled rats fell into their momama's wings. She fastened each to a swollen breast until she ran out of breasts. They made those suckling sounds that Valko had imitated. *That's happening now,* Baput's spirit realized. They grew visibly as they nursed. There were at least eight of them. They fought over the six nipples. *How can she feed them all?* Baput wondered.

He soon found out, to his horror. In the accelerated image before him, the baby bats were suddenly almost as big as their momama, who now looked sunken and withered, sucked dry. They began using their tiny, sharp horns to rend her into strips, which they devoured exuberantly as their bodies grew even larger.

The Queen was gone. The young bats were still hungry. They crawled on their clawed feet and their hideous folded wings down the walls to the floor where they feasted on the feces that had accumulated over nearly six years of unconscious confinement.

A gentle blue energy perched on Baput's shoulder as the cocoons on the ceiling started to writhe. There was a soft fluttering sound. Scraps of the papery pouches rained down on the bumblies' gross repast.

The nimblies appeared, almost six inches long, much larger than the dragonflies of earth. Soon, countless nimblies clung to the ceiling all around the little chamber, their cocoons in tatters on the floor.

One by one, they began to flap their red, lacey wings. The gentle fluttering swelled and spread until all the creatures thrummed their wings in unison. The sound built. The cave ceiling shook. The walls vibrated. The thrumming built in a feedback loop, exciting all the molecules in the tiny chamber.

The wall behind Baput keened with a high-pitched ring. The Rock beneath him buzzed in reply.

"Resonance!" Patrick's disembodied voice rang out above the swelling tone. "They're making the Rock ring!"

"That's why it rings by itself on First Pomegranate Day!" Baput replied to the new presence that bobbed in the cosmic flow. "The nimblies cause it!" He helped Patrick's spirit out of the whirling current onto the seemingly solid Plane, where it rested, ohming quietly.

"They have awakened!" The traditional cry made Baput let go of Patrick's spirit and turn to G-Pa's. It was stoic, silent. Was he asleep? *It's not really First Pomegranate Day yet,* he realized. Where had the Akashic Cry come from? Had it been part of the show?

"Excellent! Check it out, guys! All better!" Jerry's voice came from Earth. Baput struggled to find the switch that opened his eyes.

The moon had crawled off the face of the sun and disappeared into the light-blue midday sky, revealing an undamaged Shavarandu. Baput looked at Patrick. His eyes opened slowly, looking lost and confused and a little drowned, just for an instant. Then he gave Baput a knowing smile.

Baput turned to the Akash next, hoping to feel their new connection here in the waking world. To talk about what they had seen. But G-Pa's eyes were dull, totally uncomprehending. They bore no resemblance to the lucid, eloquent Akash he had just conversed with psychically for three hours about so many important things. Had it even been real? Did he want it to be? Did it matter?

His momama got up and bent over G-Pa, helping him to his feet on stiff legs. Then, Belinda was standing over Baput and extending her right hand, her violin and bow dangling from her left. Baput looked up at her and felt a pang of grief and pain. Why did it hurt to look at Belinda? He saw a flash of red hair on fire, as something even hotter and redder seared the depths of his heart.

Fran and Star handed out sandwiches and chips for the Earth folks and cold rice and beans for the Nauvians. Patrick, Baput, and Jerry sprawled on the Rock. G-Pa wheezed in his folding chair, refusing Star's attempts to feed him.

"Bring G-Pa closer." Baput was surprised when the barked order came from his mouth. His family looked surprised too. "Please," he added. They looked even more surprised at the un-Nauvian word.

After a moment of adjustment, Felsic and Valko rushed over to help the Akash up and move his chair, and his Supremeness, closer to the Rock.

"Thank you," Baput continued in the alien Earth tradition. He took several bites of his lunch and chewed thoughtfully. All eyes on him, black and blue, hazel and green, his flock chewed their lunches along with him. The Rock finally went completely silent, after resonating from Bel's violin and the nimblies who hadn't really thrummed. Yet.

Baput cleared his throat and began. "We have seen the cycle of the nimbumblyborg." His voice rumbled, tickling the Rock beneath him. He looked at his G-Pa, who still mumbled. His confusion seemed genuine this time. Anger and frustration gripped Baput. *He was there! He saw it.* He raged silently. *I need him to back me up. To help me describe...*

"I saw it," Patrick chimed in.

"You remember?" Baput asked, overjoyed and amazed. People rarely remembered their early visits to the Plane. Jumbled bits and pieces of nonsense maybe, like a weird dream, but Patrick recited the whole show in vivid detail.

"So, when the nimblies thrum their wings all together, they hit the resonance frequency of that chamber they're in. That sets the Rock and the Holy Cave and the sauna all vibrating in harmony. Then..."

Baput interrupted. It was his story, after all. "That's what G-Pa hears when he makes The Call." He looked at the hollow shell of a man, wondering who would make The Call this time. "That is why the Rock rings on its own on First Pomegranate Day. The nimblies make it ring."

Silence for a long moment. Then Valko spoke in low, resonate tones. "If we kill all the nimblies before they thrum, the Rock will not ring, and the weapon will not work, and the portal will not open."

More silence. Patrick had the answer. "We can hit it with Mjolnir instead. Maybe it would still work."

"Maybe if there are still nimblies at Nauve, it will work," Felsic suggested. "There were no nimblies on Earth before we came, yes? But there were at Nauve, and that's all it took to send us—whoosh!" He flew his hand in a long arc.

"No matter," Baput said in his new voice. "Nimblies or no nimblies, we can't go back to Nauve without the Net."

G-Pa was awake now, perhaps sensing a challenge to his authority. "No, no, no! Save the nimblies! Nimblies save us! We go nauve on First Pomegranate Day. Earth nimblies send us home." He rose from his chair and banged his longstick on the Rock.

"You go home, Old Man!" Valko spouted suddenly. "I will not leave Elmer to fight the nimblies and bumblies alone!"

Star smiled.

Felsic rose to his feet. "I will stay and fight, too. With Weed Eater, I will destroy them." He pantomimed waving the long-handled blade in the air before him. When he reached G-Pa's chair, he lowered his arms. He approached the Akash with unprecedented boldness. Was he drunk? "You go, Akash, and send Peratha and Trillella through the portal, to me," he ordered.

The Akash did not answer, but the others all nodded in shocked but enthusiastic agreement.

10. The Season

Deep red pomegranates dragged their branches toward the ground, eager to plant their copious seeds. Baput reached as high as he could, but Valko still towered above him. Baput watched closely as his popa wrapped his giant hand around a burgundy fruit midway up the tree without touching it. He breathed in, waving his beak from side to side. Baput still couldn't get his hand all the way around a kip without touching it. Not yet.

Felsic gazed idly at the red, round fruits and deep green leaves wavering in the early afternoon breeze. No one had ever asked him to make The Decision, and he was certain no one ever would.

Valko smiled down at his son. "By the time you are Akash, you will do it. Try that little one," he instructed. "Close your hand. Gently, don't touch!" The tender coaxing waxed into a roar, punctuated by a hoot from Felsic.

Baput opened his eyes and his hand. "I can't!" he wailed, shaking.

Valko grabbed his hand roughly, forcing it to circle the same pomegranate once again. "You will be Akash soon, and you cannot make The Decision. Where is Akash?" He let go of the boy's hand, placing his immense hands on his hips next to the belt that held his machete and his knife.

"He's not feeling well, Popa. I'm worried. He is so thin. It's like he disappears before our eyes. But on the Plane, he is strong. I have seen him there, spoken with him. He has power there, but he can't bring it to this Earth."

Valko grunted his lack of concern.

"Popa?" Baput looked up. "What if he... before Passascenday? There is no Council to decide. How will I ascend?"

"You will ascend," Valko muttered. "If you can make The Decision." He grabbed his son's hand again. "Now, concentrate!"

Baput closed his eyes and wrinkled his forehead. He tried to circle the fruit again. His hand touched it all over.

"Do you realize how much depends on this, Boy?" his popa bellowed, not helping.

"I do!" Baput snapped. "That's why I can't concentrate! Will the portal open? Will the nimblies and bumblies escape the cage and attack Earth? Will the Tone work? Will Belinda be here?"

"Arrgg!" Valko sputtered, "Our fate is in the hands of a teenager." He shoved Baput's hand away from the pomegranate and encircled it with his own. "Two more days," he declared with his usual certainty.

"Saturday!" Baput calculated happily.

Fran cooked a whole ham and a beef roast for battle rations. They ate the first of them on Friday night, when the in-laws arrived.

Lorraine's eyes lit up in that new way that only happened when they were here, doing Battle Engineering. "It's Nimbly Bumbly Time!" She sang, bouncing in her chair like a kid.

"Too bad it has to be right at harvest time, huh, Elmer?" Patrick observed.

Elmer already had considered that little inconvenience as much as he cared to. Right now, he had other things on his mind. "You know what else is during harvest? Right on First Pomegranate Day, tomorrow? The County Fair! It starts tonight. Kind of made it a Halloween theme since it's almost October. They said they wanted to do it late this year so us pom folks could participate. But we can't enter anything. We can't even go. Even without the nimblies and bumblies. None of the pom farmers can. We're too busy. Those young college brats taking over everything, they don't know what they're doing!" Elmer shoved a big hunk of roast beef into his mouth.

The clatter of pots and pans woke Baput. He was surprised he had slept at all, after hours of chasing his swirling thoughts in circles, getting nowhere. He knew Popa hadn't slept a wink. He never slept on the night before First Pomegranate Day.

"It is time," he told the motionless form that clutched his right hand. "G-Pa!" He was so still! But his hand was no colder than usual. Baput shook the hand in his. The skinny old man snorted sharply. His faded gray eyes stared into Baput's in the pale dawn. Baput watched the Akashic Spirit pour back into the wizened body until it reached the window of those insipid eyes. The Akash returned to Earth from wherever he had been. *The Plain?* Baput hoped. *Had he learned anything?*

"It is First Pomegranate Day, my Akash," Baput spoke gently, but firmly, still grasping the withered hand. "Your people need you today."

Momama was like a machine, packing food into containers and stacking them on the breakfast bar. Battle rations. Purple beans and rice, sprouted seed bread, a hash of yams and purple potatoes. Just like the Great Hall on First Pomegranate Day.

"Good morning, Momama," Baput muttered as he helped the Holy Akash to the boor. The back door was open. In the shop, he heard hushed male voices talking above the ringing sounds of steel weapons being sharpened.

Fran made a heavy breakfast of potatoes, eggs, and slabs of ham. "First Pomegranate Day Feast," she declared it. The Musiks tucked in, talking with mouths full. Behind them, the screens showed the chamber floor and the cave mouth, still and silent as always.

With the hurried meal behind them, Elmer took command. "You guys start loading Little Truck with the stuff they're taking to Nauve with them. Jerry will show you. Put that in the bed. Fran, the food goes in the trailer. I'm headed to the shop right now to load the weapons in the Jeep."

Jerry led Patrick and Lorraine to the back room, where Patrick's beloved solar system model was almost obscured by the pile of warehouse-size packs of toilet paper, underwear, plastic food containers, pots, pans, plastic dishes, razors, flashlights and batteries, a canning kettle and cases of mason jars and glass bottles with rubber stoppers. A plastic milk crate held an old hand-cranked drill and a weighty assortment of metal tools: shovel, rake, axe, hoe, pick, scythe, even a hand auger, all without handles.

"It's the stuff they're taking home to Nauve," Jerry explained, "If the portal works."

"Toilet paper? Plastic ware?" Lorraine asked. "What have you done to these people?"

"You've left your mark, too, Babe," Patrick quipped, hoisting a heavy box full of his grandfather's woodworking tools.

"You bet I have!" Lorraine hissed through clenched teeth.

First Battle Day

Fran drove Little Truck with Star at her side. The bed was loaded with the marvelous housewares and hardwares of Earth. The trailer rolled behind, stacked with three days' worth of battle rations on ice. Jerry drove the four-wheeler with the Akash and Apprentice Akash. G-Pa squirmed as they putted past the sauna, where the truck and trailer pulled to a stop.

"No, G-Pa," Baput reminded him of the occasion. Had he forgotten? "Today we go to the Rock, G-Pa. You will say the litany from there."

"We go Nauve," G-Pa stated the simple fact, his mind made up.

Felsic and Elmer climbed out of the Jeep to unload the ice chests from the trailer into the secure stone shed that would serve as a miniature Great Hall. Elmer unhooked the trailer and left it by the sauna. Belinda squeezed into the little cab of the truck between Fran and Star.

Felsic and Elmer took off again in the Jeep. The back seat was stacked with machetes, spears, longsticks, and swords. It looked pretty prickly back there to Patrick and Lorraine. It looked like heaven to Valko, but he still didn't trust Felsic's driving, so the motley remainder of the crew continued to walk with the dogs, slowed by a heavily pregnant Shastina.

Patrick and Lorraine hiked with the brooding man lumbering between them. The silence was strained, to the Earth folks, anyway. It was more than Patrick could bear.

"Hey, Valko, are you looking forward to going home to Nauve?" Patrick floated the opener, realizing it was technically redundant. "What's the first thing you're gonna do?"

Valko grunted. More silence, then another grunt morphed into slow words. "The boy is right. We will not be Nauve today."

The certainty in that deep voice made Patrick and Lorraine stop walking and look up at the grave face. "How do you know?" Lorraine asked, boldly as ever.

"No Net," was the curt reply.

"How does the Net work, Valko?" Patrick asked with a new respect. Did the big man understand more than they realized?

Valko stopped walking and tucked his longstick under his arm. "When we arrived at the Holy Cave on that day, the Rock was ringing all by itself. No one had hit it with our Mjolnir. The Net lay across the Rock where we'd left it, on top of the pipes we used to shoot the nimblies." He raised his hands to chest level, horizontally, palms together. "Baput plugged the wire into the Net. Felsic pedaled his device. The Rock glowed pure white." He separated his hands, about a foot. "The Net rose up off of the Rock, this high. It floated on a pillow of white light above the Rock."

"When it's electrified," muttered Patrick, "it traps the energy from the Rock, and feeds it back."

"It concentrates it," Lorraine joined in. "The concentrated energy shot out through the pipes and lazered the critters, right, Valko?"

Valko briefly snorted his agreement, then continued his story. "When the Akash jumped on the Rock, he put his feet and his longstick on the Net and pushed it down so it touched the Rock." He touched his extended palm with three fingers of the other hand. "That was when…" He flung his hands wide apart.

He grasped his longstick and began walking again. From behind him, Patrick summoned enough courage to challenge the hulk. "But Valko, what if you're wrong?"

"Then you had better hope your cage holds," Valko replied without looking back.

They Have Awakened!

Jerry and Baput carefully unloaded a shaking Akash from the four-wheeler. The longstick didn't help the operation, but he wouldn't let it go, not for an instant. "Come on, G-Pa," Baput urged as gently as he could. "Get up here on the Rock. When we get it all loaded, and we're ready to leave, you can start your speech."

"It is First Pomegranate Day," G-Pa babbled. "I feel them!"

"Do you?" Jerry dared to ask.

"No," G-Pa answered just as confidently. He assumed his place at the top center of the round Rock and leaned on his longstick as Little Truck arrived with the exports. He turned his head from side to side, watching the women and kids file back and forth like ants, arranging the coveted goods around the outer edge of the Rock, leaving the middle for people.

The Jeep drove past the Rock and down the narrow trail that led to the bottom of the platform. They stopped part way, still in view of the Rock. "Is this far enough away?" Elmer asked out loud to anyone.

"I don't know, Dad," was the only answer he got, from an Earth Boy who'd never seen a nimbly in his young life.

"You don't know Jack. Nobody knows Jack…" Elmer muttered as he unfolded himself from the passenger seat. Felsic clamored out of the driver's side and surveyed the weapons in the back seat.

Elmer turned to him sharply. "I told you guys, no guns."

Felsic withdrew his hand from the goose gun and moved it to the weed eater. Elmer snapped again. "You guys don't have gas for it. I told you that, too. That stuff is for if we have to fight them critters here on Earth. For Nauve, you can take the steel blades and points, bows and arrows, and them potato guns. You'll never run out of ammo."

Elmer loaded Felsic with machetes and swords and pointed him toward the Rock. Then, Valko showed up and went straight for the goose gun. Elmer leaned on the Jeep with his arms folded, shaking his head.

"What is the use of returning to Nauve if we don't bring the weapons we need to kill the nimblies and bumblies?" Valko muttered, settling for the potato guns. He left the darts and slings. He could make those at Nauve.

Star bent to hug Belinda. Trembling, she whispered breathlessly, "I Nauve now. You be a good girl." She stood up straight and moved on to Fran. "My B.F.F. Francina. You make me not want Nauve." She choked on her own tears as she gazed over Fran's shoulder in a long embrace. Fran and Belinda escorted the shaky little woman to the Rock.

Shastina rested her head on a sullen Brodey's back. She whimpered, just once, when Fran and Belinda separated them, coaxing Shastina onto the Rock while Jerry held Brodey by the collar.

"Bye, Shastina," Belinda blubbered, hugging the gentle dog with the swollen breasts and belly. "I hope your puppies are OK."

Could the two dogs interbreed? Fran and Star had been watching for three years. Fran was pretty sure Shastina had failed at least once, but she couldn't get Star to talk about it. Now, Shastina's abdomen was extended, her teats pink and swollen. Fran was hoping that they could send their friends to Nauve with some fresh DNA for the dogs, at least, some good old golden retriever. But could the unborn puppies survive the portal? Or would the only fresh DNA they could offer perish on delivery? The horrible thought stunned Francine, just long enough for Belinda to make a break. She jumped onto the Rock and headed straight for Baput, her violin case swinging in her hand.

"Belinda! Get back here!" her parents and aunt all shouted at once.

"It's OK," Baput said calmly. He took her hand, turning his eyes to Patrick's. "It's too soon. Even if we had the Net, the Rock is not ringing yet."

Salistar nodded her confirmation. That assured Fran and Patrick, but not Lorraine.

Belinda extended her violin to the big, green boy. "Take my violin, Baput. To remember me by."

"I will *never* forget you, Belinda," Baput promised.

"But there are no violins on Nauve. I showed you how to play it."

Baput rolled his eyes.

"You'll get better," Bel promised. "You can play for G-Pa. He needs it. That CD player won't last forever, you know."

"I can't…"

"I can just get another one." Belinda hit on that Earth thing Baput was just beginning to understand. Buying and selling. Cost. He looked at Patrick and Lorraine, nodding eagerly. It was OK! Or maybe they just wanted Belinda to get off the Rock, no matter what it cost.

"OK," Baput agreed. He leaned over to take the violin, and brushed Belinda's cheek with his lips. Belinda grabbed that cheek and ran off the Rock. Sobbing, she fell into her parent's arms.

The Earthlings gathered around the Jeep, stocked with superior Earth weaponry and parked a "safe" distance away. They could hear the Akash rattling off long strings of the choppy, short syllables of the Nauvian language.

Baput translated the Akash's First Pomegranate Day sermon for their benefit. It started with the traditional Akashic Litany:

> "I have been to the Akashic Plane. I have seen that we shall continue. The Plane teaches us to trust our own minds, our own inner knowing. We trust what the Plane shows us. We cast a hopeful mold of the future into the vibrations of the Akashic Plane, and the power manifested there will give us another First Pomegranate Day, another three years of living together and loving one another. We know that the vibrations of all who went before us still remain, part of the eternal energy of the Akashic Plane. Those who fall in battle this Season will join them with pride."

Bored, Lorraine slapped Elmer on the shoulder. Her show pistol was on her hip. He wore his pistol, too. She tipped her head in the direction of the platform. With resigned shrugs from their spouses, they jumped into the Jeep and drove down the trail with the armory.

"If something happens, I'll let you know," Jerry volunteered in a loud whisper. He jogged about 50 feet down the trail, to the one spot where you could see both the Rock and the chimney mouth. Fran and Patrick drew in closer around Belinda, hoping they were far enough away.

The Akash raised his pale eyes to the rude disturbance. Disorientation swirled sickeningly in them. He squinted at the remaining cluster of pale skin, light eyes, and oddly colored hair staring at him from a distance.

"Ah, yes, Earth," The Akash recalled, covering up his disorientation. "We *go* Nauve today. We *leave* Earth behind." The Akash used the English words for "go" and "leave." Baput was pleased that the Akash was finally getting the idea, but he didn't like what he was hearing.

The Akash continued his impromptu delivery in Nauvian, using English only for the untranslatable words. "Earth is an evil *place*." He rolled the word "place" in his mouth like something he didn't want to swallow. As he went on, Baput stopped translating. He stared speechlessly at G-Pa, his mouth gaping slightly. G-Pa raised his pale, pencil-line eyebrows expectantly. Giving the Akash a pleading, sidelong look, Baput turned back to his friends and translated the rest of G-Pa's sermon.

"I have found the way for us to be Nauve this day. We must save ourselves, the Akashic family. I am too important to die on this doomed Earth, where Kakeeche turns their backs every time they all meet together. Where Shavarandu himself turns His back almost every year."

Baput choked the words out, embarrassed, ashamed, and a little afraid. His translations came slower and were more heavily censored as G-Pa's attacks became personal. "Elmer. That hideous, pale animal who does not care if Shavarandu turns its back. And his son! An evil brat who tells lies. He could have sent us Nauve long ago, but he didn't! He wants us to remain under his popa's command, to do that lazy man's work for him.

"But we do not care about that man and his son and the others. They will die. They will all die!" The Akash waved his hand at the crowd in the distance, swatting them away. He said something that Baput refused to translate. Instead, he folded his arms and shook his head.

The Akash growled at his Apprentice, threated him with the back of his hand. Valko lurched forward to restrain the Akash. Dodging his grasp, the Akash finished in English. "We go Nauve today. We leave Earth to the nimblies and bumblies. They will devour you all, if you are lucky." He stretched his arms out wide and roared his conclusion. "Either way, we will leave Earth to burn!"

Baput looked out to where Patrick, Francina, and Belinda stood, with Jerry 50 feet behind them. He remembered how his spirit had died in agony during the eclipse when he'd seen Belinda's red hair in flames. Now, she and Patrick and Francina were all on fire. The redheads glowed like molten copper mingled with Fran's dull blonde.

Baput was in flames, too. Hot rage swelled up inside him, starting with his toes. They tingled. He watched his friends melt down into the burning Earth as the fire consumed his own legs. Behind them, Jerry stood surrounded by flames. His hair was white-hot yellow like Shavarandu itself. The sight seared Baput's heart with an agonizing flame as his best friend opened his burning mouth to scream.

"Something's happening!" Jerry's actual yell snapped Baput back to reality. The fire was gone, but the rage remained. The shaking had spread through his whole body. Every molecule, every atom vibrated all apart, all together. His head was splitting. It felt almost like the portal! Terrified, he repeated Jerry's cry. "Something's happening!"

Then he heard it. The thrumming. When had it begun? A solid roar from the Rock where he stood, echoed and amplified by the cave wall behind him. A distant human cry pierced the wall of sound. The pop of a pistol, then another.

The Akashic voice welled up into the din, belting out like a strong young man, as if his lungs weren't two shriveled raisins in a sinking chest. "They have awakened!" he boomed.

"Naduk," Valko muttered a Nauvian "duh," his voice shaking with the buzzing of the Rock.

Lorraine and Elmer stood side by side on the platform, the muzzles of their pistols stuck through the shooting holes in the cage. Their left eyes peered through the grate, their right eyes squinted. There was a gentle flutter. "Hear that?" Lorraine whispered, cocking her gun in slow motion.

Elmer nodded and cocked his gun, too. The fluttering got faster. It swelled in volume as it grew in unity. The flutters blended into a single, solid sound, a force that they could feel on their faces, still pressed against the cage.

The tac light cast a dappled light through the grate into the depths of the chimney. "You brainiacs should have put the light inside the cage with a remote-control switch," Elmer complained in a tense whisper. "Too many shadows." He squinted harder. Had something moved?

"Something moved," Lorraine whispered back. A blur of motion rippled the deep shadows of the long tube.

The buzzing grew closer, and the image resolved into six yellow-orange needlelike snouts, backed by a noisy red blur of lacy, thrumming wings. Accelerating as they came, the nimblies arrived at the unexpected barrier and crashed hard with their proboscises stuck through the holes in the grate.

Elmer and Lorraine shot, killing the two that were stuck on the shooting holes. The rest wiggled their stuck beaks up and down, back and forth, wearing the metal and making the holes bigger. Elmer and Lorraine shot them through the enlarged holes. Two more gone, then two more. All six!

"Yahoo!" Elmer yelped. "Like shooting fish in a barrel."

"They're getting them!" Jerry shared the news with the rest as they reloaded.

Six more hatchlings hummed down the long corridor, wings never touching. They hid between their dead litter mates and stuck their needle snouts through the holes. They seemed to already know how to wiggle their beaks to distort the metal. Working together, two concentrated on the flap of metal grate that Jerry had bent when he'd tried to send the snake in.

The metal grate breathed in and out as the nimblies pounded on the weak spot. That shiny line that had appeared when the metal had been bent got brighter, and the welds started breaking loose. The bent flap of screen flopped free of the rebar and the first nimbly broke through. Lorraine shot it, and it died, stuck halfway through, with a throng behind it. They pushed their dead comrade through the enlarged hole and followed, one after another, making the hole even bigger.

Elmer and Lorraine both emptied their guns again, backing away. Still shooting at the tattered grate, Elmer waved his arm behind him in search of Lorraine. When he made contact he whirled to her. "Grab on the winch and get down! Get outta here! You first!" he ordered.

"Why?" Lorraine had to argue. "Because I'm a woman?"

"Because you make more money than me, OK?" Elmer found himself negotiating.

"I have life insurance—" Lorraine countered.

Elmer almost knocked her off the platform with his chest. "Get going, will ya? So I can!"

The winch hummed as Lorraine disappeared over the side. Elmer emptied his six gun again. They kept coming. "We can't hold 'em!" he bellowed.

"They're getting through!" Jerry relayed the message.

The six-inch long newborn nimblies spilled from the chimney onto the platform. The winch pulley returned. Elmer hooked on and bailed over the edge. As his face lowered past the platform, he found himself eye to eye with one. It lunged at him, almost poking his eye out with its proboscis. He slid to the ground with his heart pounding in his throat.

Baput was having trouble telling reality from the delirium lapping at his consciousness. His entire being was vibrating. The Rock still hummed. He heard Jerry's voice, calling him back to Earth again. "They're getting out! My dad can't hold them!"

Valko took a giant stride off the Rock. Felsic followed at his heels without hesitation. They sprinted down the trail to the ground below the platform.

"Come on, Star!" Francine called. Star and Shastina ran from the Rock willingly, toward Little Truck. They boosted Shastina's heavy back end into the bed, and Brodey leapt in after her.

"Come on, Belinda!" Fran called from the driver's seat.

"I can't. We have to play the Tone."

Fran and Patrick exchanged a glance.

"I'll watch them," Patrick promised, wishing they could all go hide in the windowless stone building with Star and Fran and all the food.

The nimblies lined the edge of the platform, clutching it with the talons of their six legs. Their three-inch long needle snouts pointed at the people on the ground. Valko and Felsic arrived at a swift trot. Felsic made a beeline for his weed eater with its shiny new steel blade. This time, Elmer didn't stop Valko when he reached for the extra-long goose gun. The big guy handled it well. It fit his proportions. Elmer grabbed his double-barreled shotgun and stood by his side, sighting up at the platform. Felsic fired up the weed eater.

Jerry turned on his battery-powered amplifier and plugged his guitar into it. Baput returned Belinda's violin, and she unpacked it. He cradled his bowl in his arms, the mallet safely inside.

The Rock continued to hum, spilling its energy uselessly into the air. G-Pa still stood at its apex, chanting and banging his longstick, preaching to no one.

He heard Elmer and Lorraine yelling. A roar from Valko. A whoop from Felsic as the weed eater fired up. The boom of a shotgun.

The kids stepped toward the Rock. Moving more quickly than he had in years, Patrick maneuvered himself in front of them. "Uh-uh, no Rock, kids. It's a one-way ticket."

"But we have to play the Tone," Jerry and Belinda protested.

"It's OK." Baput was eerily calm. His eyes were sharp but focused on something far away. "If the portal could open, it already would have. But the nimblies won't come this way. They will go downriver to the Great Hall. Come on!" he commanded, bounding down the narrow trail with his bowl and mallet. Belinda and Jerry ran after him with their instruments. Patrick trudged reluctantly after them into the teeth of battle.

Left behind on the Rock as if forgotten, the Akash watched them go. He felt the Rock's vibration start to ebb as the nimblies emptied the chimney. His molecules were starting to reassemble. But why reassemble as a weak, skinny, almost helpless old man? No. The Akash of Earth, ignored and forgotten, needed a fresh identity. Not Yanzoo. The glory of Yanzoo's solo success had dissolved into a joint effort of a mere apprentice, an unworthy girl and an unholy other. "Let the fool boy have The Tone! He will never be Akash! Not as long as I live!" the abandoned Akash muttered.

"I am Meldan, Warrior Akash, who wields his longstick like no other, knocking bumblies out of the sky and piercing nimblies through their wicked hearts." He danced with his longstick. He did the strenuous, exacting dance of Meldan of the Hat Trick. He danced his way off the Rock and down the trail to the battleground. He was fearless, formidable, mighty, and precise, as long as he was Meldan, Warrior Akash.

A nimbly in the front row suddenly dove off the platform, proboscis first. Elmer was sure it was the one who had tried to eyeball him. It drilled the air, flying straight at Felsic, who raised his weed eater. Valko fired, dropping it just before it reached the whirling blade.

More nimblies dove, three at a time. Valko and Elmer filled the air with buckshot while Felsic waved the weed eater back and forth in a crazy arc. Lorraine wasn't having much luck with her .22 caliber. When the musicians arrived, seven nimblies lay on the ground at the feet of the raging warriors. They set up on the ground, out of the line of fire.

Jerry's guitar screamed. The rounded cry of Baput's bowl swelled and mingled with the mellow tenor of Belinda's violin. They played the Tone of Yanzoo, with the weed eater buzzing a treble and three guns on percussion.

The Akash came dancing down the trail in full Meldan. He whirled in front of the band, in front of the guns. The men growled at the interference. The Warrior Akash moved on until he was safe on the other side of the firing line. He raised his longstick, stabbing it upward repeatedly, twirling and thrusting it left and right.

Elmer took his eye off his sighting scope and watched in awe as the old man, suddenly strong and graceful, thrust the tip of the six-foot long shaft precisely through the narrow heart of a diving nimbly.

They kept coming. Seven more died by gun and longstick and weedeater, but none popped spontaneously until two zeroed in on Baput and dove on him, straight into the wall of sound.

"Pop! Pop!" The two nimblies disappeared. Guts rained down on the musicians.

"Awesome!" Jerry cried, hitting a piercing high note.

"Gross," Belinda complained without missing a stroke.

Two more attacked Baput. "Pop, pop!" again, but no more. The next pair dove partway, to a point just above where their siblings had been blown to bits. They hovered there, just out of range, pointing their needle snouts at Baput and ignoring the other musicians. Then they took off horizontally and sped away. Four more launched from the platform and followed them west, down the river, guns firing helplessly after them.

"Just as they would go to the Great Hall," Valko noted.

"Towards town!" Patrick worried.

"Towards the County Fair!" Elmer cried out loud. "All that warm blood outside. Women, babies! Aw, geez!"

Six latecomers came stumbling out, dazed by the agonizing Tone. They fell off the platform, almost hitting the ground. Lorraine shot one as it struggled to gain elevation. Valko blew two away with a single spray from the goose gun. The other three staggered out of range, then straightened and sped off behind the others.

"They're going away from us," Lorraine theorized. "They need to be flying towards us, into the noise." She started gathering weapons. "We need to get ahead of them! Trap them. Get them to fly into it."

"That's right." Felsic hovered at Lorraine's side, holding the weapons she collected. "Like Yanzoo. He sat before the Great Hall and they came to him."

"Come on kids," Lorraine ordered. "To the van! Patrick!"

Elmer claimed Valko and Felsic. "We'll stay here and keep the rest from goin' anywhere. Leave us the Jeep, just in case!"

"We're going in front of those things? The kids?" Patrick complained.

They carried the instruments and weapons back to the Rock and lashed them to the four-wheeler.

"This amp battery isn't gonna make it," Jerry worried.

"Can we charge it with the van as we go?" Lorraine asked.

"I hope so," was the best Jerry could offer as he mounted the driver's seat of the four-wheeler. "I guess you need to get G-Pa up here, and someone to hold him. The rest of you can run."

Baput smacked Belinda with a gentle backhand to the arm and they took off running together. Lorraine and Patrick looked at each other, then at the bag of bones slouched behind Jerry. They each imagined cuddling that between their legs.

"I can run," Lorraine generously offered, sprinting after the kids.

"Thanks for having my back, as always," Patrick muttered as he mounted the back of the four-wheeler to straddle and embrace the Akash.

Sheriff

It was a sleepy midmorning, as far as Sheriff Dave Riley and his newest young deputy, Rod Otto, were aware. Sheriff Dave, as he was known, had grown up in this town. He had been sheriff for the last 12 years, and a deputy before that. He was a short, burly, heavyset bear of a man, tough as a grizzly, lovable as a teddy bear. Otto had just arrived from a police academy in Arizona. Tall and lean, he had close-cropped blond hair, a square jaw, and piercing blue eyes. He was riding with Sheriff Dave for his first week, so they could get acquainted.

Sheriff Dave yawned blatantly. "Another boring day in paradise. Hey, you want to go over to the fairgrounds and get a funnel cake or something?"

"While on duty, Sir?" the rigid young deputy questioned.

The radio crackled to life. "Control calling S1, come back?" it was Candace, in dispatch.

"S1 here," the sheriff responded.

"Sir, I've been getting calls about some kind of giant bugs flying toward town."

Sheriff Dave looked sidelong at the deputy. "How many?" he asked.

"Different reports say three or four. Some say six. They say they're almost a foot long, and they look like dragonflies, some say, or mosquitos, the other people said."

"Where are they coming from?" Otto asked.

"The east. Heading toward town. Toward the fairgrounds, maybe. Wait. I'm getting another call. Hang on."

"The east," Otto griped. "The foothills."

"Harvest is in," Dave summed up with a laugh.

Otto didn't laugh. "I tell you, sheriff, there's a lot more out there than there's permits for! Hardly any of 'em are really legal, right?"

Sheriff Dave wanted to roll his eyes. "Not yet. How can they be? Pot's been legal for less than a year. The county hasn't got the permitting stuff together yet. But they're trying to be legit. Some of them anyway."

"A few, maybe," Otto argued. "Most of them are just gonna grow it. No permits, no taxes. Just as illegal as before, in my opinion."

"Don't you think I know that?" Sheriff Dave defended. "There's more than we can ever eradicate. It would keep our little crew too busy to do anything else, and we still wouldn't get a tenth of it. I know that. We work with the state and the feds to go after the ones that are stealing water, drying up creeks, or putting out illegal poisons. Terrible stuff, Deputy. It can drop a bear in three paces. It gets in the creeks and down into the reservoir. Our water supply! Those are the guys I go after.

"And mark my words," the sheriff continued, "Somebody will get shot up there before the season is over. Home invasion, armed robbery. Or two partners that work together all summer, then go crazy when the money comes in, just like the old-time gold miners. Happens every year."

"And you respond to that," the deputy stated flatly.

"Of course! It's murder!"

"Yeah, but it's just a bunch of—"

"People?" Sheriff Dave interrupted loudly. "Of course I respond. We serve *all* the people here, the best we can. Get it?"

"Yes, Sir," the deputy mumbled into his folded arms.

Switchbacks

The kids and G-Pa piled into the pitch-dark back of the windowless van. Patrick jumped behind the wheel as Lorraine swung into the passenger seat. She plugged the amp into the cigarette lighter.

"It's only 20 minutes to town," Patrick pointed out.

"We gotta take what juice we can get," Lorraine replied.

They wound down the hill into the valley. Each switchback presented a glimpse of the river, more or less obscured by trees. Six nimblies flew in tight formation straight down the river corridor. Patrick's heart sank. "Elmer was right." He moaned, "They're headed for the fairgrounds!"

The road straightened. They could see the fairgrounds ahead. The first six nimblies made wide circles high above the mass of human flesh.

Patrick slowed and turned into the fairgrounds. He drove his Look'N Up Plumbing van through the parking lot, full of cars but eerily devoid of people, right up to the gate. Rolling the window down, he captured the gatekeeper with his odd left eye and spoke earnestly. "I gotta get in! Ladies room. Big mess!" he whispered confidentially, rolling his cocked eye and waving his hand in front of his face. "Pe-ew! Don't go near there!"

"OK, sure," the gatekeeper agreed. "But did you see them flying things?"

"What flying things?" Patrick asked innocently, as the nimblies spiraled lower and lower, descending toward the stage where a country band had abruptly stopped playing their electric guitars.

Patrick pulled as close to the stage as he could, until he was blocked by the band's abandoned equipment van. People were screaming, running. A man in a bright yellow vest and hard hat was waving people toward the shelter of a huge exhibit building.

Heads bowed, Patrick and Lorraine opened the back of the van and released their eager cargo into the infested fairgrounds. G-Pa leapt out first, longstick ready, escorted by Baput, who called him Meldan.

"Hope this works!" muttered Patrick.

"So do I," Lorraine agreed. "Or else, all we have is my competition gun, and, well, him." She pointed to the mad old man dancing and circling as Baput herded him toward the stage.

Jerry hopped out with his guitar and looked at Lorraine for his amp. Lorraine grinned like an elf and pointed at the deserted stage. The band had fled, leaving their equipment behind. Jerry whooped and took off for the stage, gleefully plugging his guitar into a much bigger amp than his own.

Belinda, violin in one hand and bow in the other, ran to the stage, red curls flashing behind her.

"Bel!" Patrick yelled. Swallowing hard, he followed her, right under the circling nimblies, Lorraine at his heels.

Faces started to appear around the stage, peeking from under chairs, behind concession stands. They stared at the redheaded trio, two with contorted faces, left eyes that looked up and to the left. Father and daughter, they appeared. A fit-looking woman with flaming red hair and normal green eyes ran right behind, drawing a pistol from her belt. The cockeyed man helped the little girl lower a microphone.

Then came the old man and the boy. A kid, about the same age as the other kids, but bigger. He had big brown eyes and thick, black hair in bangs, about chin length in the back. He was wearing a shiny copper bowl on his head like a helmet. His skin was green. Deep, dark, but bright, unmistakable green, like an avocado!

The old man's baggy skin was a much lighter green, with yellow highlights along all his wrinkles, like the leaves of the oaks, now that fall had arrived. His long hair and beard were lavender, thin and sparse, and he was so skinny! His bony arms and legs moved quickly and gracefully as he danced, holding a six-foot long stick that he looked too frail to carry. He swirled in circles toward the cloud of giant dragonflies with pointy stingers that looked like they could pierce a full-grown man to the heart. What were they? What were these strange people doing?

As the boy and the dancing man finally took center stage, one of the dragonflies broke formation and dove straight for them! Everyone screamed, even those in the relative safety of the lemonade stand. The green boy ran to join the other kids. The wimpy-looking old man whirled and swatted the first bug away with his stick. It slammed hard into the footlights and slid off the stage. The frail superhero drew his longstick back, then thrust it fully into the closed eye of his stunned attacker. It made a noise like air being let out of a balloon. The old man used the edge of the stage to scrape the dead bug off his stick.

An eerie noise rose from behind him. The spectators turned their half-hidden eyes to the kids who made it.

Meanwhile, Back at the Ranch

The micro-camera that stuck out of the stovepipe turned on its remote-controlled bracket as Patrick's van drove past the sauna. At the other end of the fiber optic cable that ran down the inside of the pipe, Fran and Star watched on Fran's laptop.

"Where are they going?" Fran whispered rhetorically. "Are the kids with them?" she wondered, searching Star's eyes in the blue light of the screen.

Star's eyes blazed from deep, shadowy sockets, her cheeks and brow lined with wrinkles. Fran hadn't seen the face of a real war mom before. Now she felt that look on her own face as she studied Star's. "How do you stand it?" she asked her worried friend.

Star had no answer, just a shrug, her eyes fixed on the image of the vacant lawn on the screen.

Fran tried again. "How do you deal with it, season after season, every three years? How can you lose a child, and then put it behind you and do it all again the next time? Your sons and husband out there, fighting, and you not knowing…" she trailed off, unable to voice her fears or hold back tears.

"Baput and Jerry are of age, both 15 now. It's Baput's birthday, you know."

"First Pomegranate Day." Fran remembered. It wasn't exactly the same date as the day the Nauvians had arrived, but it was Baput's birthday nonetheless.

Star went on. "Belinda should be here with us, though. At the Great Hall, there are many women, and children, and a lot more space."

"And you just wait around, helplessly wondering? How do you pass the time? Do you talk, tell stories?"

"We talk," Star agreed, her voice bitter. "We say things like: 'The West Trench is coming in. We need more bandages!' Rashetta shouting, 'Help me hold Talluk down, I have to cut his leg off!'"

Fran's attempt at light conversation having met an end as brutal as poor Talluk's, the two fell into silence. Shastina scratched the door and whined.

Star checked the screen again. "Maybe we should let her out. She's pregnant, you know."

"I see that," Fran acknowledged, the subject open at last. "Why didn't you say anything? You know I've been hoping, right along with you."

"I was afraid, after last time. It might be bad luck."

"Last time?" Fran leaned forward.

"She failed last year, right before harvest. She went and hid under the house all day. She wouldn't come out, not even to eat your dog food. I thought she was pregnant, but I was afraid to say it. When she came out, I knew she had failed. I went under there and found three little things. One looked like Brodey, two like Shastina." Star's eyes clouded at the memory. "But too young. They died. I buried them by the river and told no one. I cried and tried to pray like Akira would over the grave of the dead babbets."

Fran had to ask, "Were the puppies, um, whole? Normal?"

Star looked disgusted. "They were dead!" she snapped, clearly not wanting to say it again.

Fran pressed. "I mean, were there any with, like, two heads, two tails? No eyes?"

"No crooked-eyed Belindas!" Star countered defensively, "Just dead! Why Francina? You say we in the village are too much alike, our lines are all crossed, so we have bad babbets. But Shastina and Brodey are so different! Brodey is a whole new line, so why?"

"Different breeds of dogs mate all the time on Earth," Fran answered, knowing they weren't just talking about the dogs anymore. "But from two different worlds, I don't know. Maybe we're, um, they're *too* different...?"

Shastina scratched the door again.

"Poor girl." Fran shook her head.

Elmer and Felsic stood, weapons ready. Valko was on break, sprinkling pomegranate oil on his sprouted-seed bread. They hadn't seen a single nimbly since the van sped past on the driveway above, but Valko was sure there would be more. "They come in waves throughout the day. You can never know how many there are until the end of the day, when the survivors return to their caves just before the bumblies come."

"But here, there is only one cave," Felsic pointed out.

"And only one mother. How many can she have?" Valko wondered.

"And the last ones were kind of lame," Elmer said again. "Is that normal?"

"The runts," Felsic replied. "They come last. Late in the day, after all the others. They are smaller. But not usually so wobbly." He waved his hand up and down.

"Maybe it's the Tone," Elmer suggested. "It makes them sick or something."

Valko spat an oily mess on the ground. "Tone," he gargled, returning to his post and his shotgun. "I kill 10 times as many with my gun."

As if on cue, six more nimblies staggered out of the chimney, poking stupidly at the tattered grate. Elmer raised his shotgun.

Valko outdrew him, blasting one of the slow-witted things with his long barrel before Elmer could pull his trigger. "As good as The Tone!" he bragged as Elmer shot another one off the platform. "Better than that cursed Weapon!" Valko muttered.

The four remaining insects circled above the three men. They followed Valko and Felsic with their lethal snouts, flying over Elmer like he wasn't even there. At last, two of them met overhead and went into a tight dive right at Felsic. The weed eater revved angrily. The first nimbly dove right into the whirling sawblade. Its top half flew one way and its bottom half, the other. Stunned by the spectacle, the second nimbly hovered in place until Felsic's blade found it, too.

The final two nimblies spiraled out of reach and circled aimlessly, looking lost and hurt. The Tone would have knocked them down easily, Elmer thought, but the instruments were in the town by now. Suddenly, the pair recovered and sped west before anyone could take another shot.

Fairgrounds

The five remaining nimblies continued to circle above the musicians, paying Jerry and Belinda no mind at all. They ignored Patrick and Lorraine, frozen on the sidelines, and the curious crowd that gathered in front of the stage. Their heads turned so their cruel stingers stayed pointed at Baput no matter where they were in their orbit.

Ignoring them took all of Baput's will. He got the bowl vibrating extra hard, rubbing the rim, building the sound, bigger and rounder, louder and fuller. The nimblies seemed to hang in midair as the sweet tone of Belinda's violin and the obnoxious wail of Jerry's guitar added dimension. G-Pa/Meldan readied his longstick to stab the two nimblies that dove straight for Baput's bowed head of lustrous black hair.

Their splattered remains flew everywhere. The spectators cheered and the Tone swelled, dragging the cheering into itself, expanding to fill the fairgrounds, absorbing all its sounds. It spilled out onto the highway, into the adjacent pastures and orchards and the outskirts of the sleepy town.

The three remaining nimblies resumed their spiraling over the stage, never dropping to that point where their mates had exploded. When they tried to dive, they seemed to skim across an invisible surface before pulling back up to rejoin the others.

"We're repelling them!" Belinda struggled to say over all the sound.

Remembering what Tymar did for Yanzoo, the Akash ran to center stage, brandishing his longstick crazily. "Come and get me!" he ranted in Old Akashic. He called the nimblies really bad names. He stuck his tongue out farther than seemed possible. He exposed his bare butt to them, in a gesture of contempt that amused the onlookers immensely.

Enraged, or just unable to resist, two of the nimblies dove to devour G-Pa and his disrespectful bottom.

"Pop! Pop!" They vanished in midair one after the other as they entered the Tone's lethal range. Guts rained down on the musicians. The crowd went wild. Patrick tried a Felsic Hoot, but it didn't quite work for him.

Their jubilation turned to dismay when the last creature circled away, spiraling out of range. It headed back upriver toward the Look'N Up Ranch. The kids stopped playing the Tone and watched it go. There was silence for a moment.

"That was awesome!" A boy a little older than Jerry threw a chair off himself and stood up, pumping his fist.

A little girl with a mess of blonde Shirley Temple curls popped up from inside the hot dog stand. "That was the best Halloween show ever!" Grown-up hands grasped her arm from below, then a woman emerged, blowing wayward strands of ravaged brown hair out of her face.

Valko kept his eyes fixed on the silent, brooding cave while Elmer pounded his ham sandwich and Felsic gnawed on his protein-rich seed bread. There had been no business since those last two stunned specimens flew off in the usual direction.

"We gotta go down there," Elmer declared as he swallowed the last of his lunch.

"You are right, Elmer," Valko agreed. "If more come out, we will get them down there. Like you said, Felsic! Tale of Yanzoo. Let them come to us. We will kill them all!"

"The Tale of Yanzoo is fiction, brother," reminded Felsic. He didn't sound too keen on facing a whole flock of approaching nimblies, even with his weed eater.

"Yeah," Elmer fretted. "What if that tone thing doesn't work? Patrick wouldn't take any weapons, that idiot! Lorraine's got that cap gun loaded with snake shot. Oh, and they have a crazy old man with a stick! Sorry."

He looked at the guys whose Akash he had just insulted. Felsic looked a little more frightened. Valko looked a lot friendlier. He seemed to read Elmer's mind, they were so alike in this thought. "The women will be safe. Not even the bumblies can penetrate the shed made of stone."

"Come on!" Elmer ordered, climbing into the driver's seat. Felsic turned a worried gaze up at the tattered grate hanging from the chimney hole. Then he shouldered the weed eater and climbed into the passenger seat, leaving Valko with his extra-long gun and longstick to sprawl across the back with the cache of steel blades.

Fran flung the sauna door open as soon as the Jeep appeared on the laptop screen. The dogs nearly knocked her over on their way to relieve themselves.

Elmer leapt out of the Jeep, shotgun in hand, and bounded toward her like the young Elmer she had once known. He shoved the gun into her hand and fumbled in his pockets for the shells. "Here. Just in case."

"Elmer, where's Jerry?" Fran demanded. Didn't he realize they were waiting to hear about the kids? "Where's Baput? Belinda?"

"In town. With Patrick and Lorraine. The critters are flying that way. To the fairgrounds, we think."

"And the kids are there? Are you crazy? Go get my baby!" Fran blubbered, pounding on his shoulders with clenched fists.

Elmer ran to the Jeep even faster than he had bounded out of it.

Salistar burst through the door after him, carrying a pile of awesomely stackable, profoundly unbreakable food storage containers. Valko took the stack of battle rations in one huge armload, setting it on the back seat beside him amongst the blades. Then came the coolers of bottled water, pomegranate oil and meat sandwiches for the carnivores.

They headed down the road to town, in broad daylight in a topless Jeep. Sure enough, following the path of the flying flock brought them inevitably toward the fairgrounds. Small crowds gathered on the streets, pointing up at the nimblies as they flew over, and pointing at the green people as they rode by in the speeding Jeep, blades poking out in all directions.

Animal Control

The radio popped the patrol car's blister of silence. Candace again. "I'm getting calls from the fairgrounds. The bugs are there. Six circling around over the stage, with more coming."

"You're serious." Sheriff Dave had to believe Candace. She'd been working with him for 10 years.

"What was that?" Otto squeaked, rolling down his window and sticking his head out to look up.

Sheriff Dave saw them through the windshield. "I'll be dipped!" he whispered as he clicked the belt across his ample waist and switched the siren on. "Funnel cakes, here we come!"

No one greeted the Jeep as it entered the gravel parking lot. No attendant asked Elmer for a buck, or 10.

They had passed the group of stragglers that they had failed to shoot. They could see them now, approaching from the east, flying in a phalanx down the river. Where were the six that had come before Patrick and the kids left? And where were *they*? Elmer searched the deserted parking lot for the plumbing van as they climbed out. Valko still carried the goose gun.

Elmer cringed at the sight of the big green man, face masked by that impenetrable black wall of hair, wearing stained and tattered foreign clothes and raising an oversized 10-guage shotgun into firing position, a machete and sword strapped to his waist. He could almost see the CNN logo, the headline, "Jolly Green Giant Shoots up County Fair." He gulped, then bravely grabbed the barrel. "You can't go in there with that!"

Felsic held his weed eater tighter.

Elmer started to put the gun in the open Jeep, but he couldn't leave it there, so he stood, holding it.

The phalanx of runt nimblies arrived. Shooting Elmer a black look, Valko drew both steel blades from his sides, one in each hand. He swept left and right with the machete. Then he stabbed the sky with his sword, impaling one. He smeared the nimbly onto the ground, where it flopped around, still trying to probe Valko's feet.

The two that dove on Felsic's weed eater met an even more gruesome fate at its steel blade. As always, Felsic whooped for joy.

But two more were approaching. *Those last two? Here already?* They converged above the two delectable green men. Shotgun still in his hands, Elmer let them have it with both barrels. Peppered with birdshot, the insects fell straight down on the two Nauvians. Nimbly guts decorated their hair and dripped down their faces.

Felsic couldn't stop grinning, but Valko gave Elmer a dirty look. "Gun," he pouted.

Suddenly, Valko and Felsic's eyes grew big. They turned to each other, then raised their faces to the sky, leaned their heads way back, and let out a duet of blood-curdling howls. There was another sound behind theirs. A siren.

The county sheriff's car screamed into the parking lot, right up to where the armed men stood surrounded by dead nimblies. Elmer's old classmate Sheriff Dave lumbered out of the driver's seat. They had grown up together at school, enjoying a friendly but competitive relationship. The sheriff rushed toward Elmer and his shotgun. A young deputy Elmer didn't know came around from the passenger side.

"Elmer Musik! What are you doing with that gun?" The sheriff bellowed jovially. *Elmer Musik*, he thought. *I always thought he'd get out of here, like he used to talk about. He was lucky. He didn't get that cocked eye like his dad and brother. He should have made his way in the world, left his brother on the farm.*

He made that switch to poms, though. People say that was smart, now that it worked out. They say the last couple years, he's been the Pomegranate King. No sir, Elmer's no terrorist. He's one of Us. "Put the gun down, Elmer," Dave said gently.

"I'm just shooting these things," Elmer explained, pointing at the gore all around him. He had the horrible thought: *What if only I can see them?* But, no.

"That'd go right through your heart!" the sheriff observed a dead nimbly's stinger.

"*Euechhh!*" grunted the young deputy, stepping on a dead nimbly. Its guts popped out, then sucked back in when he let off.

"Don't!" Valko roared, and the cops finally looked at the two green-skinned strangers in their stained, ragged, woven grass outfits.

After surveying the foreign pair up and down, Sheriff Dave looked toward the fairgrounds. It was too quiet! "The rides aren't turning!"

A buzzing sound rose all around them as six more of the giant dragonflies appeared from the east. The nimblies ignored Elmer and the policemen, honing in on the two green strangers. Elmer raised the shotgun to the sky, confidently dropping one just before it dove on the two lime-colored delicacies. It plunged to earth. Another dove, needle straight down, on Valko. He swung his machete at it broadside, knocking it into Felsic's weed eater blade, which flung gooey parts everywhere.

The other four nimblies pulled up sharply and headed into the fairgrounds. The kids! Elmer, Valko and Felsic forgot about the sheriff and his deputy and ran for the Jeep, jumping in quickly without opening the doors.

"Sheriff! Sheriff!" Deputy Otto jumped up and down and dared to tap his superior on the shoulder as Dave watched Elmer sprint to the Jeep like he used to on the base paths.

"What?" Dave swatted the impudent deputy's hand away.

"They're, they're *green!*" the young man informed him.

"Get in the car!" the sheriff snapped.

Lights flashing and siren wailing, the county sheriff sped through the empty parking lot, passing the slower Jeep and smashing right through the unmanned vehicle barrier. "I always wanted to do that!" Dave yelled.

They found Patrick's van parked next to the stage, open and abandoned. Elmer's heart clogged his chest. The four nimblies circled overhead. Valko and Felsic didn't hesitate to take their places below the storm. Elmer jumped as a little girl came running toward them.

"Sheriff Dave!" the little girl screamed in terror, running to the burly officer with the shotgun in his hands.

One of the kids from that bike thing last month, Dave mused for an instant. *I'm her buddy now. I guess that's the idea. Get the kids to like the cops.* Out loud, he tried to stay composed for the terrified child who was… wait, was she smiling?

"Sheriff Dave! You gotta see! It's the best Halloween show ever! Look, they're doing it again!" She pointed, unafraid, to the four remaining nimblies, who tightened their circle, preparing to dive on three kids playing music and an old man dancing with a stick. Dave took it in while the child babbled at his knees. "Everybody ran, but we stayed. We hid in the hot dog stand. Don't worry, Sheriff. We didn't steal any hot dogs, honest. I don't like hot dogs. My mama says they're made of—"

"Keep her here," Sheriff Dave ordered the worried woman who had come looking.

"I want to meet the girl with the violin, Mama!" the tot whined.

"Not now, she's playing again. Shhhh," her mother whispered tenderly. Putting her arm around her daughter, she guided her to the ground in front of the stage, littered with turned-over chairs and nimbly guts, to enjoy the show.

"Lady, wait!" Sheriff Dave cried. An eerie noise rose around them.

Dave joined Elmer at the side of the stage. Deputy Otto was already there, pointing his pistol not at the nimblies that circled ominously above, but at the people on the stage!

The sheriff grabbed the deputy's gun and pushed it down. "What are you doing, Otto?"

"They're all aliens! Three kinds!" the deputy replied, struggling to regain control of his gun.

"Them cockeyed ones ain't aliens. They're ours," Dave explained, successfully disarming his deputy.

"What do you mean, ours?"

"They're from here!"

"I've never seen 'em around here before." Otto pouted.

"Look'N Up Pomegranates? You've seen their label?"

"That cockeyed pomegranate thing?"

"Yeah. That's them. Cockeyed. Like that redheaded guy there. That's Elmer's brother. He grew up here. They've been living on that ranch for generations. Every generation has a cockeyed kid. Their dad had it, and his dad before him. Now Patrick there has it, and his little girl. Poor thing. She'd be cute otherwise, don't you think?"

The deputy ignored the ridiculous question. All he saw was a circus of alien monsters. "If they're from here, how come I never saw them?"

"They moved up north. See that hottie with the show pistol? That's his wife. She's an engineer. Works for a big company near Sacramento."

"What does he do?"

"He's a plumber."

The youthful deputy let out a low whistle. "How in tarnation did he get *her*?"

"Love is a mysterious thing," Sheriff Dave proclaimed, handing the pistol back. "Shoot the bugs. Not the people."

"Are the green ones people? Are they ours, too?"

The sheriff raised his rifle and took aim at a nimbly who broke formation and prepared to dive on the green-skinned boy. "They work for Elmer. Yep. They're ours."

Blam! The nimbly shattered two feet above Baput's head, splattering him with guts. More guts rained as the next nimbly tried the same thing and met the same fate.

The last two predators spiraled upwards, then zoomed away from the heavily armed stage and headed east, back toward the Look'N Up ranch.

The spectators cheered even louder. There were a lot more people looking on now, trickling back in as their curiosity overwhelmed their fear.

The sheriff lowered his rifle and stood next to his speechless deputy. Elmer came up beside him. "Nice shootin', Dave," he said, slapping the sheriff on the back. "It's not over, though."

Before Dave could ask him what he meant, Deputy Otto strode over to Felsic and Valko, gripping the handcuffs attached to his belt. He looked up at Valko's face, then down at his immense green hands. Sidestepping quickly, he stood before Felsic instead. "I need to see your papers." Annoyed by the blank looks, he raised his voice. "Immigration papers! Now!"

Dave and Elmer rushed over. Otto turned to his new boss. "I knew it, Sheriff. They ain't got no papers. How could they? They're green. Green illegal aliens!" He turned back to Felsic, handcuffs ready. "You're under arrest," he informed the hurt-looking creature. Its expressions were so human!

Dave stepped into the narrow space between the two, knocking the handcuffs onto the littered stage. "You can't arrest them. They ain't done nothing!"

"They brought a gun into the fairgrounds."

"That was Elmer. And Patrick's wife."

Otto turned back to Felsic. "Well, this one brought a weed eater."

"Then I'll have to arrest the groundskeeper, too."

"But they're illegal aliens!"

Dave was ready for that. "This is California. A sanctuary state. If you want to arrest people just for not having papers, you're gonna have to do your policing somewhere else." He nodded to Elmer, who escorted his employees to the van where the rest of their party was gathered. Belinda was unpacking the provisions Star had sent.

"You don't represent your people, Sheriff." The deputy complained as they retreated into the sheriff's car to grab a bite and use the radio.

Sheriff Dave took exception to that. "I do too. I've been elected sheriff three times. And the last time, I made it clear that I'd uphold the Governor's Sanctuary Policy. And I won hands down. I don't know if you've noticed, but there are a lot of Hispanics around here who are legal, and they vote. They're tired of getting pulled over and asked for their papers when they're not doing anything but going to work at a job no one else wants. Just because of the color of their skin."

"But these guys are green, boss! Someone needs to get to the bottom of it! Find out where they come from."

"Show me where it says it's against the law to be green."

"You could arrest that Elmer for hiring them, right?"

The sheriff knew his deputy was right about the law. But arrest Elmer? "That would go over real good with the farmers. They've got it hard enough. Sometimes you just can't get the help you need without hiring undocumenteds. Especially poms. They have thorns you know. Besides, what good would that do? He's just a local businessman, a farmer, working his tail off, trying to make a living. Just like these Mexicans and Central Americans, and these green folks too, I'll bet. Ain't that what most people want? Just to live and feed their kids, maybe have a little extra to make life nice? That's called prosperity. And if we can do it without hurting each other, it's called peace. And I am a Peace Officer. It's my job, my duty, to keep the peace."

"What peace?" the deputy snapped. "In case you haven't noticed, *Officer*, we're under attack!"

"Yeah, and Elmer says it's not over. And those green people, they're the ones who know what to do."

"That's because they brought those things with them from wherever they came from."

"And they have a plan to get rid of them. Right now we ought to be helping them, not arresting them, don't you see? We gotta keep the peace."

"But the law!" Otto protested.

"Ahhh!" The sheriff pushed at the young man's shoulder. "You'd arrest the Ghostbusters! They're eating. Get our lunches."

Otto reached into the back seat and produced his own lunch.

Sheriff Dave glared at the empty hand. "Could you get mine, too, Otto? Please?"

"Yes, *Sir*," the young man grumbled, bringing the sheriff's lunch box from the back. The sullen deputy chomped on his sandwich while Sheriff Dave got on the radio.

"Animal Control? Hey, Carol, we have a situation down here at the fairgrounds."

"I've been hearing some crazy things," Carol's voice replied. "What's really going on, Sheriff?"

"You got any of those net guns? You know, you shoot and it throws a net out?"

"Yeah, we got a couple. Never used them, though."

"Well, get them, and anything else you can use to bring down a flying insect. Big ones. About six inches long, eighteen-inch wingspans. Wings like a dragonfly, but they got a long, like a mosquito, um…"

"Proboscis?" Carol offered.

"Yeah, long enough to almost run a man through. And they dive straight down on you with that thing, but only on the green people."

"Ah, Sheriff? I think you're breaking up."

"You heard me! Green people. But never mind them. You're animal control."

Deputy Otto leaned forward and grabbed the microphone. "He's gone crazy, Carol, get some other deputies down here now!"

Dave grabbed it back. "You know me, Carol. The young deputy here, he's a little panicky right now."

"I am not!" Otto whined, hating how he sounded.

The sheriff looked at the eclectic group sitting around the van in front of him in deep consultation. "Carol, tell you what. Find whatever you can find to fight these things and get it loaded. I'll send a couple deputies your way. Sit tight until you hear from me. Stay there. S1 out."

He disconnected before Otto could protest again. Shooting his new deputy an angry look, he took his shotgun and his lunch box, opened the door and strode over to the group at the van. Sirens wailed in the distance.

The hungry warriors gathered around the van. Belinda handed out the food packs. Lorraine, in eager conversation with Elmer, Jerry, and Patrick about the next steps, thanked her daughter without thinking. Belinda turned away from her, grinning like the cat who ate the canary.

She took two food packs from the stack and slipped into the van where Baput sat in the semi-darkness. She gave him his food and sat down next to him, just inside the open back.

Felsic and Valko were already done wolfing another round of their vegan battle rations when Sheriff Dave joined them. "Well, Elmer, you said it wasn't over. I've got some of them air net things, where you shoot a net at them, on hold. I wanted to see what else we needed, and when. I told them anything to catch and kill big flying things, right?"

"That's right, Dave," Elmer replied. "But not these bugs. Tonight, it'll be bats, just as big."

"Not as big yet," Baput corrected. "They start small. About, um, small melon—"

"Cantaloupe?" Jerry rushed him.

"Yes." Baput showed about a four-inch sphere with his hands. "They get bigger." He expanded to about an eight-inch sphere. "Then, on the third night," the sphere was a foot across. "Plus wings."

"How many nights we talking about?" the sheriff asked. It was too late for not believing.

"Just the three," Baput summarized.

"And the other things?"

"They will return every day, for two more days. There are only a few left, but they will come back. Bigger, too," Baput recited like a tour guide. Then, a sudden thought: "Did they kill anyone?"

"Not that I've heard about, no," the sheriff realized to his great relief. "So far, anyway. Thanks largely to all of you."

"I don't think they like, um, Caucasians. White meat," Elmer announced. "They had a couple of chances at me. I was wide open. They went for Felsic and Valko instead. Then, when you guys were on stage, they never went for Jerry or Belinda. They never even looked at you two. Just Baput and G-Pa. That's all they wanted."

"The bumblies will like you!" Felsic promised. "They eat everything." He turned to the new audience and explained about the bumblies, gesturing like he had for Elmer three years ago. Deputy Otto stepped out of the patrol car to watch.

A couple dozen new faces, mostly young people, had shown up, following their cell phones. Jerry scanned the crowd, knowing there would be somebody from high school. He saw Kate. Filling his lungs with a shakey breath, he went to her.

Elmer showed Dave the weapons. "We got machetes, clubs, swords, squash rackets, fish nets and these spears. Longsticks, like the old man's, only his is a traditional, carbonized wood tip. These here are enhanced with lightweight titanium blades, see?"

Dave admired the longstick Elmer handed him. "All I've got coming so far is those shooting nets. They won't cut it, will they?"

"That will knock them down," Felsic exclaimed, eager to try the net gun. "Then I would…" everyone backed away as he swung one of the clubs repeatedly at something invisible on the ground in front of him. After four or five whacks at it, he straightened up and faced the group, grinning.

Elmer had learned how to move past these moments. "Yeah," he confirmed. "And we got one shotgun."

"Two," the sheriff offered, raising his. He started to hand it to Valko, who eagerly moved to accept it. Deputy Otto's mouth opened and he shook his head vehemently at his new boss's crazy judgement. Dave withdrew the gun from the big man's reach. "Nah, sorry."

Otto relaxed visibly, only to tense again as the muttering mountain lumbered past him to Elmer's Jeep, where he plucked an eight-foot-long pole tipped with a point of sharply tapered metal from the seat.

"Don't forget my target pistol," Lorraine reminded.

"And we have the Tone," Belinda announced bravely in front of the growing crowd. "Even if it doesn't pop them, we think it will mess with their sonar. They're bats, you know. They go by sonar."

Baput took over. "They move very fast." He waved his hands all over in crazy patterns. "You can't tell what they'll do next, so it's very hard to hit them. But when they come at you, they come from up and to the left." He pointed, making the family salute. Then they all did, all the Look'N Ups, even the green ones. "Up and to the left."

"Up and to the left." Jerry heard the family's salute, now a war cry. Pinned as he was under Kate's appraising gaze, he had to join in, salute and all. "That's our motto," he explained, blushing. He needed to be with his family and friends, his brothers and sisters in arms. They were strategizing without him! But Kate was talking to him!

He had wanted to apologize to her, but she had never said anything about it. In fact, she had never said another word to him. She published a nice story about Grandma and the model of the solar system. He felt weird around her ever since, and wished he had never spoken to her.

But here she was, and apologizing was all he could think of. He'd rehearsed it enough times. He cleared his throat and began formally. "I'm sorry I brought you all the way out there and didn't show you. I wanted to, but I couldn't," he stammered at the end, not like he'd rehearsed.

She smiled the most beautiful smile he had ever seen, her bright eyes all lit up. "Love won out," was her mysterious reply.

Confused and speechless, Jerry sputtered, "You never talked to me since then. So, love lost."

"Your love for them." Kate turned her fine features to the group of green people clustered around Sheriff Dave. Following her gaze, Jerry caught The Look from Elmer in the huddle. But Kate was still talking! She touched his arm. He couldn't move.

"I thought I saw something when I was leaving that day. It was that old man, wasn't it? And now, here they are! Four of them! Green aliens, Jerry!" As if he didn't know. He had to smile. All this time holding it in. Now it was out, and Kate liked him!

"Introduce me," she asked with those big, soft eyes working their magic. "I want an interview with the kid. How old is he? And what about the other ones? The dad and daughter with the..." she raised her left hand and gestured vaguely at her left eye. "You didn't mention them."

"I guess you didn't research my family too deeply, huh?" he replied proudly. "They're the Look'N Ups. My great grandfather, who came here in the Depression as a kid, he had it. Then his son, who's my Grandpa and the teacher's husband, and now my Uncle Patrick, and my Cousin Belinda."

Something warm welled up in Kate when she saw the pride Jerry showed for his tragically deformed family. She guessed he could have a child like that, but he stood proud. The logo on the truck. The name of the ranch. The family had embraced it, made a proud thing out of it, instead of hiding. She sensed a second story about the Musik Family. Good local material. Third story, that is! Had she just lost sight of the story of the century?

She recovered without missing a beat, visibly anyway. "And the green people? Are they your relatives too?"

"Nope. They're aliens, like I told you. But they're my family too, now," he replied in the same proud tone.

"Jerry!" Elmer snapped. "Get over here and listen. Quit messing with that girl!" He looked sideways at Sheriff Dave and winked.

Jerry wondered what they were grinning about. "I gotta go," he said.

"OK," Kate grinned like a princess sending her champion to war. Jerry turned to go.

She dropped the grin. "I'm coming with you." She followed on his heels.

Bumblies

A siren wailed close, then stopped short. "Parking lot!" Elmer yelled, running to the gate with his shotgun, Valko and Felsic at his sides. A squad car and the Animal Control van were parked where the dead nimblies lay. Were they moving? Elmer squinted in the gathering dusk.

"It's the bumblies!" Felsic cried, firing up the weed eater. "They're eating the dead nimblies."

"Bumblies!" Valko roared, expecting everyone to understand.

Carol stepped out of the Animal Control van with one hand on her gun, the other on her club. At six feet tall, the county animal control officer towered over the two deputies who tumbled out of their patrol car and flanked her, fumbling for their weapons.

Deputy Louie Foster was short, middle-aged and balding, and Deputy Don Dilbert was scrawny and kind of snively. Everyone called him Barney Fife.

Six jet-black, softball-sized bat-like creatures with horns like rhinos crawled over a mass of purple goo with hard orange beaks and lacey red wings sticking out of it.

A bat flew up into Deputy Foster's face and hovered there, only an inch away. Dark purple blood dripped from its fanged mouth. Its blazing red eyes held the deputy's eyes transfixed. He still hadn't managed to draw his gun.

Carol knocked the thing away with her nightstick, almost taking Foster's nose with it. The bat curled into a ball and hit the ground about 30 feet away. It rolled across the lot toward the fairgrounds, right into Felsic's weed eater, which promptly sawed it in two. Elmer and Valko cheered.

Dilbert emptied his service revolver into the mass of dead nimblies and feasting bumblies. He shot one through the head, but the rest flew up and scattered so another shot would more likely hit a person than a bumbly. Then they soared jaggedly up into the air, out of range.

Dave and Otto jumped out of the car with their shotguns. Valko held his neo-longstick with its titanium blade, sword and machete still strapped to his hips. He sulked at the guns the others had. *Even Francina, a woman, has a gun.* "I am a good shot, Elmer," he argued as they approached the deputies and the gory mess. "Why can't I wield a gun, like you and all these men?"

"I'm sorry, but I can't let you do anything illegal, see? That young buck over there with the sheriff, the one with the short hair? He's looking for an excuse to take you away and lock you up. Your whole family."

"Away? Up?" Valko's dark eyes turned to the young man who ran into battle beside them.

"Oh, yeah, you guys don't get... Never mind. Stab 'em with the longstick, slash their heads off with the machete. Just like the good old days on Nauve."

"Want new days. Like Felsic," Valko whined unbecomingly.

"We'll get you a weed eater tomorrow." Elmer sighted his gun, even though they were still out of range. "Hey, Sheriff, did you bring any weed eaters? Those things work great?"

"I'm making a list," Dave replied, then turned to Carol. "You guys were supposed to wait for me to call you with that list."

"We didn't want to miss all the fun, Boss!" Dilbert quipped, reloading his pistol.

"They're heading into the fairgrounds!" Foster reported. They rushed back to their vehicles, Dilbert first. He turned on his siren to cross the parking lot that was getting alarmingly crowded. People were showing up for the fair—and staying for the "Halloween Show."

"We've gotta get all these people out of here," Dave told Otto.

"We've gotta kill those flying things before they kill somebody," Otto replied, still sulking. He looked away, muttering, "Then, we've gotta cage up these green guys and send them off to DC or something."

"I can hear you," Dave snarled, "but we ain't doing that unless they show intentional violence to anyone but those flying things."

He lurched out of the patrol car and ran to the stage with his pistol and nightstick strapped to his belt, shotgun in his hand. The kids were playing the Tone again. The four remaining bats gathered above the stage, circling like the bugs had, out of shotgun range. Dave gazed up at them. Then he whirled and ran right into Carol, his eyes at neck level. "What did you bring?" he asked her. Dilbert and Foster rushed to her side.

"I got the net guns, like you said. Four of them, and 10 shotguns,"

"Now you're talking. Shotguns and ammo for the officers, net guns for the civilians. Any extra nightsticks? Never mind, we got enough crude weapons. These aliens, they must not have come in a spaceship, 'cause they are super low tech!"

"Aliens, sir?" inquired Dilbert.

"Yeah, the green ones. Not the cockeyed ones, though. They're from here."

"Yeah, I had one in my class," Carol recalled.

"Yeah. Patrick. There he is. Give him a net gun," Dave ordered.

"Did you hear that, Foster? Aliens!" Dilbert bubbled.

Carol walked over to Patrick. She always had been exceptionally tall. Not as freaky as Patrick, but they both had gotten made fun of for their physical attributes, so they had a bond. She hadn't seen him since graduation.

"Do you want a gun?" she offered. She had to get used to his face again.

"No. I don't do guns," Patrick replied resolutely.

"Just a net gun. Non-lethal. You knock them down with it."

"Then what?" Patrick asked cautiously.

"Then you bash them with a club. You want a club?"

"Not remotely. I'm a pacifist," he replied sulkily.

"That's nice" Carol said brightly, shoving the nightstick at him. "Now put on your big boy pants, or take your kid and get out of here!"

A crowd had gathered at the foot of the stage, watching the weird kids play the monotonous Tone while four bats circled so high above, people didn't realize their size. They didn't see the horns, or those pitiless red eyes.

They muttered things like: "There's only four little things."

"I could snap those things down with my slingshot."

"Are the rides open?"

"Naw. They shut it all down, for this."

"Aliens, though! I always knew they were real!"

"Are you serious? It's all fake, for the kids."

"They should have made more."

"Probably expensive."

"How do they fly?"

"Drones, I guess."

Some spectators started to trickle away, underwhelmed. More sirens wailed in the distance.

"CHP," Sheriff Dave surmised.

"Who?" Otto asked.

"Highway Patrol. State Police. They're gonna help us secure the site, keep people out."

He checked the crowd again. It was smaller, but their two biggest fans, the curly-haired girl and her mother, still stood bravely at the foot of the stage. "Give me one of those net guns," the mom asked. "You get under the stage here," she instructed her daughter, indicating a hole in the skirting.

"Yes, Mama," the little girl replied without meaning it.

"I'm Tracy," the mom introduced herself as they headed to the truck to get weapons. "My little girl is Ashley. Will she be OK there?"

"I told you to get her out of here!" Dave reminded. "Dilbert, get on the bullhorn! Initiate evacuation protocol. Issue a Code Red Alert, shelter in place, five-mile radius. Get all these people out of here! The press, everybody. It's too dangerous. Musiks, you stay. The rest of you, move!"

The deputies started herding the crowd toward the exit. Soon, the Musiks and Nauvians were the only civilians left.

Dave had the Highway Patrol secure the area. They surrounded the fairgrounds, blocking roads and guarding all the gates.

"OK," Dave announced. "You kids are gonna stop playing and run right into this van here. Those bat things are gonna come down, and you shotguns are gonna shoot first, fill the air with buckshot. Net guns, you shoot right after the buckshot. Get whatever's left in the air. You clubbers, be ready. If a net falls with one in it, well, you know what to do."

"No, I don't," muttered Patrick, getting a better grip on the club.

Dave raised his shotgun to his eye and aimed across the stage. He counted on his fingers so the kids could see. "Three, two, one."

The Tone ceased. The kids bounded off the stage into the van. G-Pa broke into the legendary dance of Tymar, sticking his tongue out like a Maori dancer.

Belinda and Baput sat close together on the van's floor. Jerry scanned the rack of weapons secured to the wall. He reached for Valko's longstick.

"Don't the boys fight when they're 15?" he asked Baput.

"No, Jerry!" Baput moved to take the longstick away. "I mean, yes, we do, but that's much too long for you. You have no longstick training. Men train all their lives."

He scanned the cache of weapons, handed Jerry a long-handled fishnet. "I will wield the longstick. You take this."

Jerry hissed a scoff at the fishnet in his hand, but when he saw how well the longstick fit Baput, how ready he was to fight, he had to smile. "Yeah! I'll grab 'em, you stab 'em. Come on!"

"Baput, Jerry, no!" Belinda screamed.

Baput bent to plant his big brown lips firmly on her forehead. "We'll be OK," he promised as he squeezed through the door behind Jerry.

Bel closed it behind them, turned to her cell phone for light— and listened.

The bumblies swooped down toward the stage from four directions. The shotguns peppered the air, and two bumblies plopped out of the sky. One lay still. The other twitched a bit. The remaining two veered off, then dove again.

Valko's net knocked one out of the sky. It flopped on the ground, entangled.

"Club it!" someone yelled. "Nail it!"

Patrick leaned over the little critter thrashing in the fabric net. He drew his nightstick back. His right eye met one of the beast's crimson eyes. He tried to hate it, to smash it. He saw a flash in the corner of his left eye, felt a loud pop in his ear. The bumbly squeaked brokenheartedly and slowly closed its eyes. Patrick looked up at Lorraine, who was reloading and shaking her head. "Thanks, Babe," he said meekly, to no reply.

Jerry waved his fishnet back and forth uselessly. The long aluminum pole was light, but the contraption was still top-heavy and unwieldly. The last bumbly headed for the wavering object that jutted into the gunpowder haze above the stage. *Wham!* The poor, stunned thing ran right into the side of the net and hovered, startled, just long enough for the titanium blade of Baput's longstick to find it and pierce it clear through.

Meldan danced again, thrusting his longstick into the air, looking for more bumblies to spear, hoping for a hat trick, like the real Meldan. But there were no more. For now.

The Earth people rejoiced unwisely, whooping and slapping high fives, raising their shotguns. Even Otto joined in.

"It's not over," Valko informed them.

The radio on Dave's shoulder squawked. "Dispatch to S1. We have a casualty," Candace reported grimly.

"What do you mean?" Dave asked, hurrying away from the others.

"Guy named Manuel Guzman. He was waiting for the bus at the office park all by himself in the dark. Those things ate him."

"What? They don't like white people. Only green."

Candace still couldn't take this green people stuff seriously. "Well, he was Latino, I guess, based on his name."

"Well, how do you know they ate him?"

"They're still eating him. There's six of them crawling all over him."

"Who says?"

"The bus driver found him."

"He still there? Are there more people in the bus?"

"Nope."

"Good. Tell him to stay inside the bus, close the door and sit tight. I'll be right there," Sheriff Dave ordered. He tapped Otto to get in the squad car. He took a couple of extra shotguns and told Elmer to bring Valko and Felsic in the Jeep. He ordered the other deputies to stay put, with the rest of Elmer's party. "There might be more coming," he warned. Then he asked one of the Highway Patrol cars to follow behind them, to control the onlookers who still hovered around, sure to follow.

"Careful, Dad," Jerry whispered after them. It all felt different, now that somebody was dead.

Manuel

"This guy was Mexican, see?" Elmer tried to explain over Felsic and Valko's howling as they sped along between the two wailing, flashing patrol cars. "They have darker skin. Brown, not green. I guess that's close enough, now that it's getting dark. At night, all cats are gray." He remembered saying that to Fran, three years ago, when he wanted to get rid of these guys. It seemed like another lifetime. "There are a lot of Mexicans here. This could be a huge problem."

The Highway Patrol barricaded the entrance to the office park as the throng of press, bloggers, and thrill-seekers spilled out of their vehicles.

Elmer followed the sheriff's car in the Jeep, creeping down a narrow, dimly lit street lined with pitch-dark single-story office buildings and empty parking lots. They found the bus in a cul-de-sac at the end of the road, the terrified driver locked inside. Just outside was a scene like the one in the fairgrounds parking lot, but here, bare human bones protruded from the goopy mass on the pavement. Thick black hair clung to a naked, grimacing skull. Six grapefruit-sized bats crawled over the mess, snarling softly and ripping at the remaining flesh with their horns.

All six raised their heads at once as the familiar, pomegranate-stained scent of their favorite food wafted towards them. Felsic fumbled with the weed eater. Elmer and Dave raised their shotguns. His eye on the sheriff, Valko quietly loaded one of the extra guns. Deputy Otto gave him a hard look, then turned to the ugly mess on the ground.

The bumblies turned their horned noses up at the blond deputy and kept eating, but when Valko stepped up beside Otto, the closest bumbly flew into Valko's face, too close for the long-barreled gun. It flitted back and forth in a little arc, like a smile, right in front of Valko's grand nose. It stopped flapping midswing, and its little shoulders fell, dropping its wings just a bit. It burped, right in Valko's face. Then it dropped down on Manuel's dwindling remains.

Otto shuddered.

Valko roared with unrestrained laughter! Dave, Otto, and Elmer stared at him, open mouthed, wondering how he could laugh when someone was dead. Valko pointed to the bumbly on the pile. "He says, 'If I knew there was green, I wouldn't have filled up on this, um," his eyes fixed on a severed finger, "brown. Ha, ha ha!"

"Let's see them eat *this* green!" Felsic screamed as he fired up his trusty weed eater. He shouted a Nauvian war cry as he ran at the beasts, the whirling blade extended before him, splattering gore everywhere. One bumbly, perhaps the one who had communicated with Valko, was cut in half.

The bus rocked as its lone occupant ran to the window, then ducked to the floor. Felsic slashed open a second bat as it struggled to get its fattened belly off the ground.

"Felsic, get out of the way!" Elmer yelled.

Felsic withdrew to the sidelines as four shotguns went off at once. Full and sluggish, the bumblies lurched into the air. The bus driver screamed as two of them bounced off the roof of the bus. They spiraled out of range. The other two veered the opposite way, up and to Valko's left. He shot perfectly and got one, but the other bumbly went too far left, then swerved crazily, straightened, and flew low right in front of them. It went behind the bus and climbed a sudden wind, headed toward the remaining two.

Otto fired his shotgun just in time. The wide pattern took the rising bumbly out with a single shot. "I got one!" the deputy cheered, swept up in the common cause of battle.

The last two survivors flew east, toward the Look'N Up. The armed men stared after them from the edge of the gross pool of human remains.

The bus door opened. "Sheriff?" the driver squeaked.

Dave snapped to attention. "Just a second, please. Stay here. We're coming aboard." Summoning a different kind of courage, Dave and Otto climbed into the bus.

Dave looked at his notebook, then at the white-haired bus driver with the generous gray mustache. "Is that Manuel Guzman out there?"

"That's him." The bus driver sat sideways on a front seat, extending his ID in a shaking hand. Dave sat in the seat across from him, recorder ready.

"Do you mind, um, Mr. Michaels? We're recording," Dave asked.

"Please, call me Will. No, of course not. But don't lock me up, cause you're not going to believe this!"

Now Otto laughed inappropriately. "After the day we've had," he gurgled crazily, "we'll believe anything! Won't we, Boss?"

The witness began his story:

"Manuel cleans these offices here at night. But Friday night, he took his kids to the fair instead. It was Latinx Night, so they got a discount. His boss said 'just get it done sometime over the weekend,' but his boy had a game today, so he decided to clean tonight. He asked me to watch out for him tonight at his usual weekday time."

Will looked up at Dave with lowered eyes, as if ashamed of something. "He said, 'Watch out for me, Bro, OK? Don't leave me in the dark! I got no other way to get home.' I said I'd wait for him if he was late. You know what he said? He goes, 'But then all the other riders have to wait for me. I can't ask for that.' That's how he was, always thinking about the other guy.

"I just laughed. I told him there's never any riders on this Saturday night run." He jerked his thumb at the back of the empty bus. "They're probably gonna cut it. To tell you the truth, if he hadn't said anything, I might not have even bothered coming in here."

Will raised his anguished eyes to meet Dave's as he confessed. "I helped another rider, Luisa, with her groceries when she got off. She's old, broke her hip last year. I carried her stuff up the stairs right to her door. Don't tell my boss! I'm not supposed to leave the bus. But there were no other riders. I thought it would be OK. But it made me late! If I had been on time, maybe the bus would have scared them off before..."

Dave handed Will a tissue.

Otto stared at the puddle of dark fluid in the dim streetlights. Then he turned to the weeping bus driver and grilled him. "He *told* you all this?"

"Well, yeah." Will pulled himself together. "We talk. Not that many people ride, but the ones who do are pretty regular. We all know each other, a little. We're a community." A puff of pride bore Will above his tears. He gazed out the window at Manuel's scant remains.

Otto turned and left the bus, shaking his head and muttering, "It ain't right! It ain't right! Manuel was one of Us! And they killed him!" He raised his rifle at the green men.

"Weapon down, Deputy!" the sheriff bellowed from the door of the bus. "*They* didn't kill anybody! Those critters did."

"They brought their vermin!" Otto roared, his face contorted with blood lust. "They're killing us! They have to go!"

Sheriff Dave gripped the revolver in his holster. "At ease, Deputy!" he ordered. "We have to kill the monsters that are eating people. And these folks know how to do it. We need them."

"They already showed us how. We don't need all those bowls and sticks and violins and crap. Just shoot 'em! Just shoot 'em till they're all dead!"

Felsic whooped the Nauvian war cry again, this time in English, "You've just gotta kill 'em!"

Valko and Elmer held their guns tightly against their sides.

Dave let go of his gun and stepped between his deputy and the other armed men. He stretched his arms out straight at eye level, then lowered them slowly. Otto lowered his weapon. The others relaxed. "OK, so we all agree. We've got to kill the monsters. So, what happens next?" Dave looked at Felsic.

Like a kid who finally knows an answer and waves his hand frantically to be picked, Felsic couldn't resist the chance to explain things to the War Chief of Earth. "There were six bumblies, right?" he looked up to nods from Valko and Elmer. "And two went back?"

"Not sure we saw them all," Valko replied. "And what of the nimblies? How many survived today?"

"Three, I think," Felsic replied, not sounding sure at all. He went on anyway. "Well, the nimblies will be back in the morning, at sunrise. Then the two bumblies again at sunset. Then again the next day and night. Then Passacenday! No more for three years."

"No three years!" was the young deputy's ultimatum. He waved his pistol aimlessly. "We get rid of them now! For good! Tonight! Where do they sleep?"

"We can't do that!" Felsic sputtered. "That is Insitucide. Forbidden! We'll kill them tomorrow. There's only a few! If there's not a male and a female of each at the end, then we'll be all done tomorrow night." His mind reeled when he chanted the traditional words. It could be true this time! "No more nimblies, no more bumblies. Not ever. No more."

Otto released his grip and backed away, still staring at the exotic man who was starting to look normal in the gathering dark.

"What about tonight?" Sheriff Dave asked. "Any more coming?"

Felsic went on, based on a barely perceptible nod from Valko. "They usually come all night. But only one mother. She couldn't make much more than what we've already seen." He was guessing now, looking desperately at Valko.

"No more reports," Dave announced after checking the radio. "No more at the fairgrounds. They've got all the evidence bagged and tagged. I've lifted the 'shelter in place' alert, for tonight."

"Maybe we can all go home." Elmer yawned.

"You guys go. I'll send some men out to help you watch."

"Hell no!" Elmer objected. He pulled Dave away from the others and whispered harshly. "We don't need a bunch of outsiders hanging around. We've got this! You heard my man, there's only a couple more. We'll knock 'em out tomorrow, and get back to my harvest."

Dave explained, "But they can help you keep the lookie-loos away. They'll stake out up the road a ways. If they see something flying, they'll shoot. If they see anybody trying to get through your gate, they'll run 'em off."

"Not on my property, though." Elmer insisted. "And you'll keep the feds away? No wrapping my house in plastic? No hazmat suits coming to haul my best workers away? They've been with me three years. They're not contagious, not a threat. They're damn good workers. But they're um, sensitive."

Dave looked over at the two green strangers, chatting and laughing over Manuel's remains.

"Just leave us alone and you'll never see these guys or their varmints again. Guaranteed!" Elmer insisted. "We know where the critters are. We'll keep our guns on 'em, keep 'em on the ranch, you keep everyone else out. Nobody else gets hurt, OK?" Elmer slapped Dave on the shoulder.

"I'll try, Elmer." Dave shook his head. "I can't promise anything. Everybody's seen 'em. It'll be on the news. The FBI is probably already on their way." Dave gave Elmer his personal cell phone number. "I don't give this to just anybody." He cautioned. "But give it to your whole family. Watch that cave. If anything comes out, or if anybody shows up at the ranch, you call me, pronto. My men and I will be there. No matter what time, got it?"

"We'll be watching," Elmer promised.

Dave returned to the bus. He felt like Columbo when he stepped back inside to ask one last delicate question. "Um, Will, Mr. Michaels?" he cleared a lump in his throat. "Your friend, Manuel. Was he, um, dark skinned?"

Will drew back. His face tightened.

"I'm sorry, sir. I know it's, well, I mean no disrespect, but, see those guys over there?" He pointed to the two that still stood reviewing the battle while Elmer headed for the Jeep. "Well, you can't see much of the big guy, but the little guy, does he look like Manuel's skin color, here in the dark?"

"Yeah, I guess. Pretty much," Will answered resentfully. "Why?"

Dave apologized to Will for his loss and held out his card. He wished it was a flashy thingie, like the Men in Black have, to make the bus driver forget what he had seen.

Elmer called Patrick from the Jeep while Valko and Felsic took their places with their weapons and their yucky shoes. Then they drove home, leaving Otto and Dave to process the grisly crime scene.

Campout

Felsic spent most of the ride home worrying about his wife and daughter. "What if they came through the portal late, after we left, and the bumblies…" He couldn't finish.

Elmer tried to calm him. "You guys can go straight to the Rock and check, as soon as we get there. And watch that chimney! I'll get off at the sauna, get those poor ladies out of there and take them to the house. Patrick and Jerry will be right along. We'll board up the windows, then come out and join you for the night watch."

"Yes," Valko grunted from the back seat, "But no old man. And no women! Just men and boys, five cycles or older and willing to fight!"

Elmer wondered how that was going to go over as he pulled up at the Look'N Up gate. He got out and approached the deputies' patrol car that sat in the road, lights flashing. "Pull it on up the road, around the bend. That's the spot."

"Will we be able to see?" Dilbert questioned.

"You'll see enough. Just watch the sky, if you can stay awake." Elmer banged on the roof of the car. Dilbert blasted a quick toot on the siren and crawled up the road.

Fran was startled from her doze by the burst of a siren. She grabbed her laptop, turned on the camera. The ranch outside was as dark as the sauna. She heard the gate open, then the Jeep coming up the driveway. "They're coming!" she exclaimed.

Star was already on her feet, packing more ration boxes. The Jeep's headlights glared on the screen.

Fran hadn't seen a nimbly or bumbly since she'd locked herself away in this tiny space, how many hours ago? She also hadn't seen the sky, or the face of her son. She flung caution to the wind and the door open wide.

The men piled out. Elmer, Felsic, and Valko. No Patrick, no Lorraine, no Belinda or Baput. No Jerry.

"Where is he?" she wailed in a voice she'd never heard before.

Elmer threw his arms around her, and she was sure Jerry was dead. Her legs failed, and she collapsed in his arms like a rag doll.

Star came out of the darkness to embrace Valko and ask her silent question. His hug told her, without a word, that everyone lived. Everyone she knew, anyway.

"They're OK, Babe," Elmer corrected his wife tenderly. "They're with Patrick. They'll be home in a couple of minutes. It's all over, for tonight, anyway."

Still in self-induced shock, Fran moaned in a whisper, "I want my baby!"

Elmer rocked her back and forth. "Come on, Darlin', let's go to the house."

The dogs panted hot breath on Elmer from the bed of the truck as he hooked up the trailer. He shook his head and sighed, looking up at the sky for the umpteenth time today. *No wonder those guys were so furtive when they got here.* He checked Fran as he turned the ignition. She took a deep breath of the night air and looked up at the stars, stretching her cramped eyes.

"Everyone's OK?" she whispered again.

Elmer arrived at the Rock with both boys, Patrick, Lorraine and G-Pa. He pulled the trailer, heavily loaded for a single night only a few thousand feet from home. Tarps, sleeping bags, chairs, ice chests full of soda, beer and food. Jerry had the tactical light. Baput borrowed G-Pa's CD player for the CD loop they had made. It held ten hours of the Tone.

The precious examples of the best of Earth culture were still stacked on the Rock all around Felsic, who sat in the middle, watching the rising quarter moon.

The team disembarked from the truck to a couple of flagrant grunts and groans from Valko.

"No Peratha and Trillella." Felsic informed them, leaping from the Rock like a zebkin. "The cage is all bended."

"Unhook the trailer and load the stuff that's in it into the truck." Elmer bossed. "Throw in a pack of that toilet paper from the Rock. We'll camp down there where we can see that chimney, right, War Chief?"

They filed after the loaded truck as it crunched along the narrow track to the base of the cliff where the platform stood coldly before the tattered grate. The desiccated shells of the nimblies they had killed earlier littered the ground.

"The nimblies that got away," Felsic told them. "They came back here and ate their own dead. Sucked them dry. Must be hungry." He looked up at the cave hole ominously.

Jerry scanned the platform with his light. It was empty. Crickets chirped from the vines on the cliff.

"Is it safe to go up there?" Elmer wondered out loud.

"Those bumblies were more than four inches across," Patrick noted. "How did they get through the rebar grate?"

"You should have seen them after they ate," Elmer replied, strapping on the harness and reaching for the electric winch.

"They're bigger now?" Patrick squeaked. "How'd they get back in?"

Elmer drew his pistol. "I'm fixin' to find out."

Lorraine stepped up. "What about the pathogen? There's feces up there, maybe blood."

"The Curse comes only to those that enter the cave and touch the sleeping mother," G-Pa declared with certainty, but no credibility.

For once, Valko vouched for him. "It is true. In the trenches, we are covered with feces and blood. Both nimbly and bumbly. For three days and nights, we wear their gaa. No man gets the Curse from battling honorably in the trenches. Only when they send…" He looked around at the crowd and lowered his head. "Only if someone enters the cave and touches the Queen." He focused his eyes on Elmer. "Don't touch *anything.*"

"You bet. I brought gloves, too." Elmer donned a pair of rubber gloves, switching the active pistol from one hand to the other. His throat clenched as he pushed the lever that whisked him away with a soft whir.

"They bent the rebar, alright!" Elmer shouted down to a chorus of whispered shushing. "Bent it out, in that corner that Jerry messed up, where the nimblies came through." Lorraine shot Jerry a look that reminded him of G-Pa's evil eye.

Elmer went on. "They started there and leaned on the rebar till your welds popped, Little Bro." He walked across the platform, then returned. "They pushed in on the other side, too, near Lorraine's shooting hole. The nimblies got the screen loose and the bumblies pushed in there, broke the welds and even bent the rebar going back in. Them buggers are strong!"

"Yes. I told you," Valko's voice resounded from below.

"I don't think we can fix it tonight. Not if they can do this. Hey, Boy!" Elmer suddenly reached up and pulled the lever, sending the empty winch down to the ground where Jerry waited. "Put that light and tape recorder in the bag, and I'll put them in here for you. It's wide open."

He turned and put his face up to the warped grate without quite touching it. The winch hummed its way up with the equipment. The platform shook with waves from a footstep behind him.

Elmer whirled around. Jerry stood before him, drawing Lorraine's pistol from the bag. "What are you doing up here? Where'd you get that? You gotta get outta here!"

Jerry walked past him to Lorraine's shooting hole. He reached through and set the flashlight just inside, turning it on.

"Here, put on some gloves at least, Son. Come here!" Elmer struggled two more gloves out of his tight pocket.

Jerry put them on impatiently. He rushed to the hole where he had tried to let the snake in.

Elmer sucked air noisily through clenched teeth, right eye almost closed.

Jerry reached in, remembering the poor snake, limping away. His arm prickled where the hair stood on end. Was it the Waves from the Cave? Or just the good old creeps?

He set the recorder down on the cave floor and turned it on. The Tone rose and swelled around the cave hole, spilling onto the platform and seeping through its holes to the ground. "This will drive 'em nuts," he promised.

"It makes 'em sick. I've seen it," Elmer agreed. "The light might mess them up, too."

"I'm hoping," Jerry schemed.

Elmer urged him to the winch for the trip down. Jerry stood firm, still holding Lorraine's gun.

"Can I, Dad? Just shoot in there a couple times like you and Aunt Lorraine got to?"

"You can't hit any. They're in their hole. If they weren't, we could see them with that blinding flashlight. Works much better inside the grate, by the way."

"So can I?" Jerry batted his baby blues at his dad, but Elmer was unmoved.

"Waste of ammo, Boy. Let's show these guys how we set up camp."

Valko's Story

Elmer tossed another log on the fire. Patrick stared deeply into the flames with his right eye while his left watched the sparks fly. "Tell me, Valko," he mused, "why don't you guys just wall up real good in the Great Hall and starve them out? You've got food, water, and bathrooms. What more do you need? Just wait for three days, and they're gone. Next time they're weaker, if they even live, because you starved them. A couple of cycles and you could wipe them out. Have you ever tried it?"

Valko's low rumble blended with the Tone that blared from the cave hole, bringing the frequency down a full octave. The immense face was noticeably redder. *Uh-oh.* Patrick thought, *you just never know with this guy.*

Valko directed his blackened gaze at the Akash. Wrapped in a sleeping bag, the old man gazed into the fire, appearing to meditate.

Baput nudged a sleepy Jerry and pointed to the story recorder. Jerry roused, embarrassed, and turned it on.

Valko stared into the eerie collage of reds and greens and sparking dark eyes and bottomless black shadows. "We *did* try. *He* tried." He nodded at the oblivious Akash. "That is why I don't sleep during the Season. I was nineteen. I had been Guard of Akash, married to Salistar, for a cycle, and I had an infant son."

"My heir!" G-Pa interrupted out of his oblivion. Valko shot the frail old man a stare that seemed to shake the ground. He broke the gaze and spat, not where the Akash could see. Or, where the Akash could pretend he didn't see, if he were too cowardly to rise to the challenge. Valko took that bet and went on with his story.

"I was not ready to give up the battle trenches to stay inside and guard only the Holy Family, even though it was my own family. I wanted to fight for all the people." He made a fist with his right hand. "Akash, yes, this one, decided to do as you say. Rakta's popa, Rakeen, the War Chief then, he argued bitterly against Akash, as almost no man has dared." His eyes strayed back to the wretched skeleton. The old man was wandering the Plane again, or so he appeared.

"That's when the arguing started." Valko looked at the boys. "Or did I only notice it when I became a man?" Turning back to his main audience, Valko projected his story-teller voice.

"Think of it! For men to just sit inside while the beasts attack! While nimblies swarmed around us, and bumblies gnawed at our shelter that held our women and children. But Akash says so."

He nodded again at the seemingly unaware figure and went on, reliving the bitterness that had been fermenting since his youth.

"So, yes, we waited in the Great Hall. Akash told us when the nimblies were coming. We could soon feel their wings thrumming above the roof. We took turns shooting at them from the turrets. There were only two turrets, and a lot of frustrated young men. The turrets are small. No room for a man to wield a longstick or pull a bow. The blowguns worked, but the darts use poison extracted from fresh nimblies and we hadn't killed any. We tried to throw a sharp dart with a fine thread tied to it, so we could snag a nimbly and reel it in for the poison. It took hours and we never got one that way, but the nimblies crowded all around the turret and stuck their beaks in, stabbing and probing. One impaled my good friend and our best thrower, Mafi. Skinny Samos slipped in and cut the monster's head off so we could extract the poison. Otherwise, we would have been helpless. The Akash was furious! And Rakeen went along with him!

"So we left the turrets alone. The nimblies had done no damage. We could have got them if they came in through the turrets, with short, sharp daggers!" he jabbed at something at eye level. "But no. We waited. The nimblies returned to their caves."

"Hungry." Patrick dared interrupt. "Only one of them got anyone, and you killed it, right? So, the rest went back hungry."

Valko snorted and continued.

"The bumblies came. They could smell us. They ripped at the walls with the horns on their noses and gnawed with their fangs. We could hear them as night fell. Did we fight? No! We were ordered to 'enjoy' a great feast as the monsters destroyed our shelter. The Akash," he jutted his head savagely at the old man, whose eyes fluttered behind closed lids. "He tells us: 'Warriors, drink of the desperation wine!'"

"That's the rude wine I make out of the old sludge from last year and the not-yet-ripe of this year," Felsic explained in a respectful whisper.

Valko recomposed himself and continued.

"The Akash said, 'You have nothing to fear tonight. You and your families are safe in the Great Hall. The bumblies can't eat wood! They will starve!' It made sense," Valko pointed to his left temple, "but not..." he brought a clenched right fist to his heart. "Not to a warrior! We had to fight!

"Instead, we sat in the hallways and listened as they clawed and scratched and gnawed on the roof. It went on into the night. They told us to go to sleep! All of us! No night watch? We said 'yes, sir' but we stayed up, me and Rakta, Sammos, and Bupple. It was agony! I have not yet been devoured by bumblies, but that agony cannot be worse than this. In any case, it would be much shorter. We had the poison! Mafi died for it! I was nearly mad by morning. All of us warriors were. At the Dawn Lull, the bumblies went back to their caves—"

"Hungry!" Patrick coughed the word. "You could have starved them if you'd just kept it up." He grinned at Valko's glare, then met G-Pa's gaze. Patrick and the old Akash saw eye to eye on this issue.

Valko bristled at the exchange. The Akash wasn't going to take over this story and twist it to his side! He retook the floor by sheer gravity.

"Rakeen and Rakta went outside. They had their armor! Where was ours? They told us not to bring it, or our weapons. Of course we did. The day before, my friends and I stashed our war gear under the floor in the back room where they keep the ganeesh feed."

"Where the boys party before they get married?" Jerry asked without taking his eyes from his post.

Impressed that the Earth Boy had remembered the woman's story, Valko glanced at the strange box by Jerry's side. Its hum was almost silent, but not to Valko's ears.

"Yes, the sixth-cycle boys. We let them stow their gear there too, so they would keep their mouths shut.

"Sammos and I were sent to the turrets to check the roof for damage. It was catastrophic! They had gnawed a hole right at the peak, through the roof and into the junction of beams. It was the thickest part, so they couldn't get in, but the damage was structural! It would cost a very large tree and much labor of ganeesh and man to replace those beams.

"Rakta and Rakeen returned. They said the bumblies had eaten holes high on the walls, under the eaves. Again, they ate into the support beams. Were they trying to bring the whole place down? Were they that smart? We had never realized just how vulnerable our Great Hall really was."

He turned to the now-very-alert Akash and finished his long-festering point fully locked in his gaze.

"Without warriors in the trenches outside, there is no shelter inside! We did our best to reinforce the roof and upper walls. It cost the ganeesh stalls, then the partitions for the women's private room, and eventually even parts of the floor. Standing on ganeeshes, we held the heavy planks over our heads and hammered them to the ceiling while the nimblies swarmed outside.

"The hard work kept us busy. It was *almost* what we needed. But what we *really* needed was to fight!" he bellowed, leaning over the fire, fist clenched. "It took all day. We ate another glorious and undeserved banquet, listened to another pitiful speech."

The Akash interrupted. "I merely congratulated most of the warriors for their good behavior that day. You didn't go to the turrets to pick a fight and provoke the nimblies. You didn't venture outside. You were good men, all day."

Valko was enraged by the compliment.

"You didn't even know! Rakeen stopped by our table after dinner and told us to go to the back room and dig up our weapons. He told you we were gambling and drinking. He even slipped a potion into your desperation wine to make you sleep. Our hearts surged. We would soon be outside in the trenches where we belonged."

Valko stood up, looking even bigger with the firelight hitting him from below. He wore a dreamy look, seeing a glorified version of that gory time. G-Pa glared at him through the firelight as he finished his version of the tale.

"We donned our armor and went outside with our longsticks, our slings and clubs, our bows and arrows, and we slayed the monsters as we were born to do. We took turns in the trenches. If we got pinned, ganeesh brought supplies. We fought all night, all day, all night, just as it should be.

"It took nearly a year and our three greatest trees to replace the beams and triple the thickness of the roof."

Patrick dared once more. "You had three years to repair it. You could have reinforced it every cycle until they starved. Just a few cycles and they'd be gone. If you have enough trees."

Valko flicked his finger dismissively. "The trees go on forever."

Patrick and Jerry exchanged a concerned look.

The Akash rose to his feet and started ranting. "It was all your fault! If you would have stayed out of the turrets, as ordered, the beasts would never have attacked! They wouldn't have known we were there!"

"We are always there! They would smell us!" Valko roared back. "Look," he swept his hands up toward the chimney entrance, then toward town. "There is no Holy Cave, no Great Hall, and still they fly downriver, in the direction of the Great Hall. They would come. And if, no, *when* they ate through those walls, all would be lost."

The Akash appeared to get taller in his outrage. "Never has an Akash been so defied! I would have killed you all, but the War Chief could not do it. His son!" He sneered, then glared at Valko, "and *you!*"

Elmer shattered the uncomfortable silence. "What difference does it make? We can't tell everybody in town to stay inside. We've gotta fight! We've got no choice but to kill them all, right here on the Look'N Up!"

"You just gotta kill 'em!" Felsic echoed the traditional war cry.

Second-Day Nimblies

All but Valko dozed noisily, sharing the same dream. A raptor circled above them, watching with a hawk-beaked stare of mounting impatience. The morning light peeked over the ridge upriver and touched their faces just as the recorded Tone fell silent. They snorted awake in unison.

"I have a plan," a booming voice announced as the eyes flitted open, pair by pair. One by one they sat up, sleepy eyes straying between Valko's ominous specter and the chimney entrance looming above them.

The great beak swung over to the bleary-eyed old man, catching him before he had figured out who and where he was. "Yanzoo!" Valko greeted those wandering eyes. "It is time. We will play your Tone and pop the last of the nimblies this morning.

"We began too soon yesterday, at the Rock. It drove them away. This time, we'll bait them with the green meat they crave. Only green people will go to the Rock, and the children who play the Tone. But the Earth children must bathe."

Jerry's face wrinkled defensively. Felsic giggled.

Valko snapped his fingers at a sudden thought. "I will even bring my wife. She smells delicious!"

"Popa! It's too dangerous!" Baput cried.

"It will be like Yanzoo!" Valko sounded as demented as G-Pa. "Am I right, old man? Yanzoo Akash? We use the wife and children to lure them in, and you will dance, like Tymar did for you.

"Elmer and Patrick, you will watch the chimney. You will have guns, but only shoot them if they try to go to Fair Grounds. If they smell us and come to us, as I think they will," his voice had dropped to a whisper, "we will be absolutely silent until the time is right—just before they pierce my precious wife's tiny neck. Then Felsic rings the Rock and the children sound the tone, and..." he raised his fist, then opened it while he made a pop with his tongue. "Gone."

"Or we shoot them!" Felsic offered.

Elmer cleared his throat. "You might want to shoot before they get too close to that tiny neck."

"Do not worry, my friend. I will stand behind my wife and run the beast through with my sword as he draws near, tone of Yanzoo or not."

Jerry took the Jeep to the house to take a shower and grab his guitar and amp. It was fully light when he returned with Star and the morning's rations in the back seat, a freshly bathed Belinda with her violin in the front. A thick fog rose from the river.

The group ate silently. The smell of freshly baked cheese biscuits in the Earth breakfasts mingled with the curry in the Nauvian rice and black beans.

Wordlessly, they took their positions. Elmer, Patrick and Lorraine watched the cave hole. The rest tiptoed to the Rock and crept up onto it. Salistar squeaked her objection. She stood on tiptoes, afraid to put her feet on the smooth, cool surface. Valko, rapier in hand, stepped behind her and wrapped his arms around her. Her face was still twisted with fear, but her body relaxed. She disappeared into Valko's protective bulk.

Jerry plugged his guitar into his fully charged amp. Belinda and Baput joined hands and stepped onto the Rock with their instruments. Felsic stood near the edge, Mjolnir in his hand.

The remnants of the cage rattled. "They're coming out!" Elmer yelled.

Elmer, Patrick, and Lorraine watched motionlessly as three proboscises stuck out of the cave hole and retreated back in. There was a rustling noise, then the sound of bony horns clacking against each other. "Two males and a female." Patrick surmised. "The males are fighting. Loser has to come out."

Sure enough, a single proboscis emerged. The beast oozed forth, wings folded against its body until it cleared the rebar. A second creature emerged right behind it, ruining Patrick's theory.

Elmer raised his shotgun. The long goose gun hung uselessly at Patrick's side. Lorraine grabbed it and handed him her show pistol, just as useless to him. She raised the shotgun to her shoulder.

"Brace yourself, Girl," Elmer instructed. "That 10-guage kicks like a mule."

"I understand," Lorraine mumbled tersely.

The two nimblies waddled out onto the platform, looking like a pair of pterodactyls. One gathered itself and flapped its wings, preparing to launch. Lorraine pulled the trigger.

"Don't!" Patrick hissed.

"*Boom!*" went the goose gun. The nimblies hunkered down as a tight spray of lead soared over their heads. Lorraine's bottom firmly kissed the rocky ground.

"That's physics, Babe!" Patrick squealed delightedly, squelching Elmer's 'I told you so.' "Equal and opposite reaction."

The third snout emerged. The two on the platform opened their beaks wide and squawked at it, pushing it with their chests until it disappeared back into the cave.

"You think that's the female?" Patrick guessed. "Maybe she's already pregnant."

The two on the platform looked down at the bland trio below and sniffed. They turned their exaggerated snouts toward the Rock and sniffed again. Then, they launched from the platform and buzzed upstream, hugging the viney cliff that concealed their home. When they reached the Rock, they began circling, tighter and tighter, lower and lower, descending slowly on the green delicacies they were so hungry for. G-Pa began his whirling dance in silence.

One nimbly stopped his circling to hover over Salistar and Valko. Valko stood perfectly still, both hands grasping his sword firmly in front of him, pointing straight up. Salistar cowered deep in his arms. The second nimbly centered over Baput.

They all moved at once, like a Swiss clock. Felsic hit the Rock with the hammer. The kids struck up the Tone made of three disparate sounds. Valko raised his sword straight up and impaled the nimbly that dove on him and Salistar. The second nimbly dove on Baput, his horn within an inch of the back of his neck where he hunched over his bowl.

The Tone morphed around a new sound: Belinda's scream. That did it. *Pop!* The nimbly splattered all over Baput.

The one impaled on Valko's sword popped weakly, soaking Salistar with the blood and guts of battle, the most honorable gaa of all.

They cheered. The Akash stood straight and tall at the center of the Rock, ready to sermonize. "It is as I have always told you, Boy. Yanzoo did not work alone. He had his tether and children and Tymar, the Great Dancing War Chief."

Baput exchanged a smile with his similarly splattered popa. "Yes, Akash, I have learned."

Elmer, Lorraine, and Patrick stared at the cave outlet. No sign of nimbly or bumbly. The others came bubbling up noisily.

"Shhh!" Patrick warned, "I see something."

The third proboscis emerged again, sniffing. "That's the last one, we think," Patrick told them.

"The female, already pregnant," Baput seconded Patrick's guess. "That's why only the other two came out. Even though she's hungry, she won't take the chance. Not today or tomorrow."

"Poor thing," Star whispered in motherly empathy, drawing appalled stares from her family. "She is the only one left. She must make more." The lone nimbly chirped her pathetic agreement.

"She must *not!*" Valko corrected his too-tender wife as the last remaining nimbly on Earth turned her back and wriggled skillfully through the grate and back into the chimney.

They stared after her in silence, until Patrick asked, "How many bumblies were left?"

"I saw two take off from the dead man. They headed this way," Felsic recalled.

"None escaped the fairgrounds," Jerry reported proudly.

"If the two are a pair, we might not see them tonight, or tomorrow." Baput put it together. "Like this one, they won't chance it. They will stay in and mate."

"Yeah, they ate," Patrick pointed out. "They're in good shape for getting busy."

"So if they don't come out, they're making a queen, right?" asked Jerry.

"Not a queen, really," Baput corrected. "Just insitu, for three years."

"Like in, 'Insitucide'?" Jerry asked.

"Not yet, technically," Baput answered, "They are still awake."

Valko stirred restlessly. "No more nimblies today. The bumblies will not come until evening, if at all. Someone should stand watch here. Someone who can shoot better than they pick. We have a harvest to glean." He scanned the group, pom farmers all but three. He pointed to Lorraine, addressing Elmer. "Let this man-woman keep your gun. She will guard, with her woman-man."

"If you mean me, I can pick!" Patrick protested. "I grew up here. I always helped pick."

"That was almonds, woman-man," Elmer teased. "Poms are real delicate. You gotta know how to handle 'em. And there's thorns."

"Well, you know I'm not gonna shoot anything!"

Elmer agreed. "OK. You come. Jerry, you stay."

"And Baput shall stay," Valko ordered as War Chief. "The boys should keep both shotguns."

"What about us?" Elmer objected. "What if they get past these guys and come after us?"

Valko brandished his sword.

"Great," Elmer concluded, assessing the motley crew. "You're our first and last line of defense, guys. Shoot the gun off if you see anything."

The truck and trailer rattled away, carrying an odd assortment of camping gear, musical instruments, weapons, and the precious exports that would not be going to Nauve this cycle. They headed to the orchards, leaving the fate of the ranch and the town in the hands of two boys with shotguns and an engineer with a show pistol.

Sunday Mass

Sheriff Dave began lumbering from his office to the front desk as soon as he heard the message Candace played, followed by Deputy Otto's irritating drawl. "That's the FBI. The feds! The sheriff's gonna have to do something about those green guys now!"

"What did they say, exactly?" Dave asked his dispatcher.

"Yeah, play it again, Candy." Otto presumed to order her.

"Candace." The dispatcher corrected through her teeth, glancing at her boss.

The sheriff shook his blocky head. Candace withdrew her finger from the recorder. He turned to Otto. "You're riding with Craddock today. Get out there. He's waiting."

"Yes, Sir!" Otto replied eagerly. "I'm all ready to get out there to that ranch, relieve Dilbert and Foster—"

"Ha!" Dave laughed out loud. "You'd just love another crack at those green guys, wouldn't you? Well, that's not happening. You're going to sit in front of one of the Latinx churches this morning."

Otto paced the floor, clutching the revolver on his hip. "Yeah. The green people are killing the Mexicans! Hey, maybe we should let…" His eyes met Candace's frigid stare. "No. No, Sheriff, that's not right. That Mexican, he was legal, right?"

"Does it matter?" the sheriff asked tersely.

Otto went on, ignoring the question. "He must have been, to be working at that office park, don't you think, um, Candard?"

Candace grunted and returned to the papers on her desk.

Otto continued to rant. "It ain't right, Sheriff. The Mexicans, they're, well, at least they're from this planet! And that guy worked. His kids played sports. He took 'em to the fair. He was one of Us, Sheriff."

"Yes. He was," Dave agreed. "I'm glad you feel that way. Now get on out there to Saint Ignacio's and protect them fine citizens when they show up for mass."

"But, Sir, you and I rode together all day yesterday, through all that. I *know* those aliens as well as you do, better than those other guys. I'd be best used out there at that ranch!"

"You'd be *best used* dealing with the flying animals. I'll deal with the green *people*. Me and the FBI, I guess."

"But, Sheriff, you know, we can't just let those green guys—"

"Exist?" Dave roared back. "Look. I'm on it. You just do what you're told." He pointed at the door. Otto didn't move.

Dave walked forward, forcing Otto to walk backward around the counter to the exit. He pointed his thumb at himself. "Sheriff twelve years." He jabbed his finger into Otto's chest. "Rookie." He jabbed again. "Not even a week, and you're the boss already?" One more jab and a lunge as he ordered, "Saint Ignacio's. Now!"

Otto backed out the door, then turned and trotted to the waiting patrol car.

"Send that message back to my office, Candace," Dave asked with a heavy sigh. "Looks like I'm calling the Men in Black."

Second-Night Bumblies

Big Truck idled down the driveway under the year's first load of pomegranates, held back by its flawless compression. It was late in the day, almost closing time. The Look'N Up wouldn't be first this year, and the load wasn't as full as usual. But, pretty good for Nimbly-Bumbly Season. The Nauvians were ecstatic.

Elmer just hoped he didn't have to answer any questions in town about their little "performance" yesterday. Should he stop by Sheriff Dave's after? *No.* He decided. *Stay away. Nothing to report.* He slouched behind the wheel as he passed the fairgrounds.

He sighed his relief when he reached the loading dock and found Ralph on duty, in his customary mechanic's coveralls, his long salt-and-pepper hair tied back in a ponytail. Ralph was a smart fellow, but he didn't have a family, and he kept to himself. He didn't even do social media. One look and Elmer was sure Ralph hadn't heard the local gossip.

"Howdy, Elmer," Ralph greeted him. "You're late. Ian already beat you. He had more, too."

"We got off to a rough start," Elmer explained cryptically.

"Workers just *had* to go to church, didn't they?" Ralph surmised.

"Somethin' like that," Elmer nodded as he signed Ralph's book.

While Elmer was gone, the crew loaded Little Truck and headed out for another night of camping by the chimney. They relieved the extremely bored watchers, who didn't say a word about Jerry's relentless attempts to talk Aunt Lorraine into letting him go up to the platform and shoot into that cave, just once.

When Elmer arrived, they dined on refreshed battle rations. Sliced fresh ham and cheese sandwiches for the humans, more beans and rice and seed cakes sprinkled with pomegranate oil for the Nauvians. The sun set swiftly over the distant town while they ate.

"There is only one male bumbly left," Baput summarized the current theory. "He is hungry, so he will come out to get food. Maybe he wants to bring some back to the females, one bumbly and one nimbly, so they won't have to come out tonight or tomorrow. They are both pregnant. They have to stay safe inside and make babbets for the next cycle."

"So the bat stays pregnant for three years?" Lorraine asked, cringing.

"I saw on the iPlane," Baput revealed, perhaps belatedly, "Earth bats can delay their pregnancy. She keeps the um," he glanced uncomfortably at Lorraine. "The stuff, she keeps it separated until she is ready. Not three years, just a few months, until the weather is right. Her pregnancy doesn't even start. Maybe bumblies can hold it for years."

"So, the male bumbly can come out tonight," Lorraine realized. "His work is done."

As she spoke, the cage rattled. Food flew everywhere as the warriors scrambled for their weapons.

"Early!" Valko protested.

Twice as big as it had been yesterday, the last male bumbly didn't waste any time. He dove off the platform, wings tucked back like a fighter jet, headed straight for the back of Felsic's neck as he frantically tried to start his weed eater.

Shotgun barrels bobbed and nodded, fighting for position. Lorraine struggled to load. Patrick grabbed Mjolnir. He had brought it along to pound tent stakes and such, for camping.

He hurled the short-handled sledgehammer as hard as he could, just like Thor. It flew through the air, end over end in perfect balance, just like Mjolnir. It collided in midair with the oversized bat. They both toppled to the ground. All the guns opened fire. Elmer and Lorraine blasted their pistols. Jerry finally got his release when he emptied his shotgun side by side with Valko. Buckshot plinked off Mjolnir, spraying in all directions. When the guns ceased, they all gawked stupidly at the bumbly-Mjolnir cocktail that smoldered motionless on the ground before them.

The platform above was eerily quiet. Then the cage rattled, harder and harder. The cave walls started to buzz. It felt like the Thrumming, but weaker, somehow less compelling and more desperate. The last bumbly emerged through the grate. She screamed in a pitch that pierced through their brains, right into their very souls. They tucked their guns between their knees and covered their ears.

"I killed something." Patrick said ever-so-softly when the screaming finally stopped. The familiar voice roused the others from their daze. The cage rattled again. They looked up just as the last bumbly on Earth disappeared into the long cave to join her nimbly soulmate in the deep chamber where bullets couldn't reach and the Tone didn't work.

Jerry set the empty shotgun down carefully on the tarp and searched for the remains of his sandwich. Felsic seconded the idea, but his rice was scattered to the birds. He picked another ration pack, his umpteenth, from the seemingly endless pile.

"So, no more tonight?" Elmer asked as he crunched on a handful of spicy dried snap peas.

"I think not," Valko stated, still holding his gun and gazing up at the platform. "I will stay. You all go home to the comfort of your quarters."

"Naw," Elmer protested weakly, but Valko insisted.

"She ate her share of that man yesterday. Perhaps that is enough. That is all most bumblies get at Nauve, part of one person. She will not come out if she has something to fear. She won't risk her unborn young. If you all stay, she will never come out. There will be no action. It will be boring. You will fall asleep. You might as well be in your beds. I never sleep during The Season. I will stay, but I will hide, down by the river where I can see, but not be seen. Where my shotgun will still reach. Perhaps I should bathe. No time," He mumbled his plan to himself, its only participant.

"I will stay with you, Brother," Felsic offered bravely. "Help you watch. I can stay awake."

"Thank you, Little Brother. You can stay, but no one else! You all go home and take care of the women. Baput, take your momama and G-Pa to the quarters and guard them. And you strange, red-haired people, you are of no use here. Go guard your little daughter. Elmer, take one shotgun. I will keep the long gun, if you agree."

"I still have plenty of gas in Weed Eater," Felsic declared his readiness for night duty.

Elmer shrugged. "I could stand a good night's sleep. We've got more picking to do tomorrow. Come on Boys, Bro, Warrior Princess."

"Battle Engineer!" Lorraine snapped, eager to hit the shower.

Leaving only a couple of sleeping bags and an ice chest of battle rations, the crew loaded Little Truck. Baput helped G-Pa into the seat and climbed in after him. G-Pa was definitely getting thinner, but Baput had to sit sideways to fit his broadening shoulders into the cramped cab. Jerry, Patrick, and Lorraine piled into the back.

"You sure you're OK?" Elmer shouted from the window as they turned around.

"OK," Valko answered. Still holding the goose gun in one hand, he picked up his longstick with the other and disappeared down the riverbank. Felsic followed, struggling with the weed eater and the ice chest.

Fran rushed to embrace Jerry when he came through the door. The rest straggled in after him. Star's eyes grew wider and wider as the white folks filed in first, then finally Baput, but no Valko. No Felsic. Baput folded her into his arms, almost covering her like his popa could. "It's OK, Momama. They keep watch. Only one bumbly left, and she's pregnant."

"She won't come out. Not with Valko there. She won't risk her babbets, the only babbets..." she trailed off and pulled out of his arms. "We must go to quarters. You and me and G-Pa, and Shastina. She flitted toward the back of the house, to the back room where the model of the solar system lurked.

Shastina lay there on Brodey's bed, her belly and breasts spread over the round pillow. She panted rapidly, her eyes anxious. Brodey sat in the hallway, his head drooping miserably.

"Yes, Momama." Baput wrapped his arm around her slim shoulders as they looked down at their beloved dog. "Popa says we go to the quarters. I am to keep you safe." He squeezed her reassuringly, pride and fear battling behind his eyes.

"Stay here, please," Fran invited. "It's all boarded up already. If you go, we'll have to board the quarters up, too. Don't you all stay together when the bumblies come?"

"Yes, in the Great Hall," Star confirmed.

"Well, this place is pretty great. We've got everything we need. You and G-Pa can sleep here in my office, right across the hall from Momama Dog. It's got a futon, and we have an air bed for G-Pa."

"G-Pa sleeps on the floor," Baput corrected, glancing at Momama. Would she give him the night off? A night of freedom? No hand holding?

Fran helped. "The boys can camp in the living room and watch the monitors."

Shaking

Most of the Musiks went upstairs to their bedrooms. Salistar and G-Pa settled into Fran's office. Baput and Jerry spread their sleeping bags on the living room rug. Patrick made a nest on the couch in his. They splurged and turned on Sojourner's light, even though all it showed was the floor of the chamber. Sometimes they saw a shadow, or heard a muffled grunt or squawk, but nothing to get excited about. Their battle-weary eyes shut one by one. Soon, loud breathing and soft snoring dampened the mournful cries of the widowed monsters.

Baput was used to sleeping with Valko's snoring in the background, but the distinctive Earth sounds of rattling metal and plastic penetrated his fitful dreams. He woke up.

Jerry and Patrick were sitting up, staring at the screen. Baput followed their gaze. The view shook. The light flickered between blinding glare and dim shadow. Patrick leaned forward, squinting.

The noise resolved into the grumbling of the beasts in the cave combined with the shaking of the resonant cable.

"They're attacking Sojourner!" Jerry guessed.

"No, it's just the light's burning out," Patrick dismissed sleepily. "I figured this would happen."

"Then what's that noise?" Jerry persisted.

Patrick yawned. "The sound's probably going out, too."

"No." Jerry was wide awake now. "They're, like, growling. The cable is shaking. They're attacking it, I tell ya! They're behind the camera, where we can't see them."

Patrick started to lie back down. "Why would they attack it?"

"Maybe they're trying to eat it," Baput guessed.

Jerry scoffed. "Naw, they wouldn't eat me, and I'm delicious. It's an alien thing in their nest. They have to destroy it before they go to sleep."

"Maybe they'll break her loose," Patrick hoped.

Sojourner's light bounced, but she still stared at the featureless floor. Not a nimbly or bumbly in sight. Just the dancing light, always changing, always the same, nothing else happening. The low hum of the shaking cable found its place among the soft growls of the busy beasts and the deep, sometimes noisy breathing of the overly comfortable sentinels.

Puppies

Salistar was the first one awake, as usual. She heard a squeaky grunting noise that didn't belong. Bumblies! It was that contented snorting sound they made as they finished the last remains of someone you loved. *Baput! Where am I?* She tried to sit up, but her hand was tied to the floor, caught in her popa's boney claw. *Baput sleeps like this every night,* she realized. *Like He made me do after Momama died, until Valko chased him from our room.* She wrested her hand from the old man's, trying not to wake him. She picked up her rolling pin and crept out of the room on bare feet.

Shastina raised her head and cast soulful eyes on her most loyal person. Last night's worried look had been replaced with something else. Star heard that noise again. She looked down.

A silver-pink ball of sleek, shiny fur was stuck to Shastina's front breast. Next to it was a tiny bunch of curly blond hair and floppy ears, pink pads stretched out behind as it suckled vigorously on the second breast.

There were four of them, sucking and squirming and crawling around like blind moles. Two looked just like Shastina. Light lavender, almost white, their ears were floppy like Shastina's had been as a pup. Two looked just like Brodey. Star lowered herself to the floor of the hall next to the odorous bed. Brodey laid his sleepy head in her lap. Tears falling freely, she picked each puppy up, examining them gently. Two boys and two girls, vital and perfect.

She lifted the fourth one, a tiny Shastina, to her cheek and held it there, feeling its soft, warm fur. She flinched at a noise on the stairs above her.

Francina tiptoed down the stairs and landed at the end of the hall. "I had a feeling…" she whispered. Her face melted into a wet pool as she sat down next to Star.

They had never fixed Brodey. He never left the farm unless he was on leash. For three years, Fran and Star had wondered if their two worlds could blend. Now, at last, these four perfect puppies, oddly clinging to one line or the other, but alive and healthy.

Fran plucked up a palm-sized version of Brodey and cradled it wordlessly until G-Pa grunted in the doorway. She put her pup down ever-so-gently, brushed Star's thick black hair out of her wet face and kissed her firmly on the cheek. Then she stepped over the tangle of gold and lavender and headed for the kitchen.

Last Day of the Season

Valko twitched angrily as the bumblies spat at him from the platform. They pelted him with tiny sticks that burned like the matches Elmer used to light the wood stove in the shop. *We forgot the matches! They are not on the Pile to Nauve.* He tried to go for the matches, but he couldn't move. He couldn't make his body obey. Was he paralyzed with nimbly venom?

The bumblies roared at him, a constant rumbling thunder that built on itself like the Tone until it burst in a loud, abrupt snort. Suddenly, he could control his body. His eyes flew open and he scratched his upper arms and chest savagely, almost tearing his gaa-stained tunic.

A new noise. His little brother's goofy laugh. "Good morning," Felsic giggled. He flicked another twig at his brother's chest, just to clarify the situation.

The War Chief sat up tall, groping for his dignity. "What is your report?" he demanded of his deputy.

"No bumblies. I watched all night. You slept."

"I was awake. I tested you."

"You snored."

"I was faking." Valko regarded his brother for a long time, until Felsic twitched uncomfortably. "You seem bigger, my brother," he observed solemnly.

Felsic shook his head. "No, I am all grown up. You know that. You always say I'll never be big like you." He glanced down at his belly and grasped it with one hand. "With not so much wine, I grow less!"

Valko grinned, oddly tranquil. He stood up, eyes scanning the river bar. Then he turned and grasped Felsic's shoulder, finding his eyes. "No, my brother," he said, "You grow more."

"Look!" Jerry pointed at the screen that had lulled them all to sleep, how long ago? Patrick and Baput sat up and followed his finger. Sojourner was free!

"The wheels must have come off." Patrick guessed. "Now that it's lighter, it's pointing straight out." The camera bobbed up and down before a new vista. The momama bumbly hung upside down by her feet from the ceiling of the chamber, squinting at the nodding camera at the end of the springy cable.

"That's her!" Baput crawled out of his sleeping bag and touched the screen. The camera bounced down, showing the floor, then up, showing the ceiling.

"It's aiming even higher now," Patrick noticed. "Like the nimbly was sitting on it, then she flew off. Look! There she is, on the ceiling."

The nimbly waddled into view, walking upside down on the ceiling toward where the bumbly hung.

More rumbling. This time it was right over their heads! Baput cringed. "My dad," Jerry assured them. "He always sounds like he's falling down the stairs."

"Hey, Frannie, have you seen this?" Elmer shouted from the hall.

"Get in here, Dad!" Jerry ordered, his eyes fixed on the screen.

"Excuse me," Elmer muttered to someone before he appeared, rubbing his head with a towel. Salistar followed him, supporting G-Pa. She propped him up behind Patrick's couch and joined Fran at the breakfast bar. They chopped potatoes as they watched.

"It's upside-down again." Elmer commented

"It's the ceiling, Dad. The bat is hanging upside-down and the nimbly is walking on the ceiling above her, upside-down, like bugs do. But, what...?"

They all stared as the nimbly carefully positioned her tapered rear end over the bat, who hung enveloped in her own folded wings. The nimbly's abdomen spasmed disgustingly as a shiny black liquid oozed out of its posterior, spilling down in generous goops onto the bumbly. The nimbly walked in a precise circle above the bat, continually oozing the slime. It coated the back, the front and the sides of the bat completely, so she looked as featureless as the queen they had seen on this same screen in August.

The spasms grew stronger as the nimbly emptied out, thinning to a straw-like creature as the last of the liquid membrane sputtered from her backside. Awkwardly, she stepped from the ceiling to one of the bat's legs. She climbed down the leg onto the sticky, ebony mass and turned around. Following her own oozing back end, she backed down the front of the suspended bumbly, over the belly and down the chest.

The bumbly's wings opened up, just enough to expose gleaming teeth in a seemingly disembodied mouth. The nimbly continued marching backwards into her inescapable destiny, that gaping maw. The mouth snapped closed on the nimbly's head, severing the stinger. It dropped to the floor.

A much lighter rumble shook the stairs above them.

"The Queen of the Nimbumblyborg!" G-Pa wheezed, leaning heavily on the back of the couch.

"Puppies!" Belinda squeaked from the hall.

Jerry waivered on one foot, tugging his jeans on. "I'll go get the guys."

The warriors shared a jubilant vegan breakfast while they watched the Queen's vulgar coronation over and over on the screen. "No more bumblies! No more nimblies!" Felsic celebrated traditionally.

"For now," Valko added, leveling his gaze at Baput for an instant. "Now we harvest. Then assemble the presses for the wine and the oil."

"I must prepare the feast for Passascenday," Star resolved.

Patrick had plans, too. "I should go to the platform and see if Sojourner is really unstuck."

"No!" Jerry put down his fork to argue. "It's finally looking at the Queen, like we wanted. We can't chance moving it."

"Ain't broke, don't fix it, Bro." Elmer spouted his favorite platitude.

"It might have that goop on it," Lorraine cautioned. "The pathogen, remember? Besides, we don't know what we're going to do just yet. Let's get the boards off the windows while these guys pick poms."

Fran and Star gently loaded the puppies into a wicker laundry basket for the trip to the quarters. Belinda helped by taking each puppy out, naming it, cuddling it to her cheeky face and returning it to the basket. They each had plenty of names by the time Fran stood and said, "Let's go."

"Come, Popa," Salistar chirped to G-Pa. He shifted his weight to her narrow shoulder and leaned heavily.

Valko, Felsic and Baput stomped into the quarters, each carrying a heavy box full of the vital fruit.

Valko bellowed: "Here is more, Woman! Where shall we put them? And where do you want the press? Same as last year?"

"Yes, my husband," Salistar sparkled. She looked as young as she had before Batuk, before Cilandra. And why not? No more nimblies, no more bumblies for three more years. No one dead, or so she had been left to believe. Plenty of kips to make the oil, the juice, the seed cakes that powered her family. Secretly, she rejoiced to still be here on Earth, the land of running water and electricity, refrigerators, dishwashers and, best of all, Francina. And one more thought completed her joy. *Baput is fifteen, and tomorrow is Passascenday. If only Tamaya was... No. It is better this way.*

Passascenday

Baput thought he was too excited to sleep, but he was tired and satisfied. After two nights of staying awake, or trying to, he fell fast asleep, disregarding the bony hand that grounded him to the cold floor and the old Akash.

The icy hand still gripped his when Baput awoke to the warm spicy smell of the gup cake Momama already had in the oven. He freed his hand skillfully and tiptoed past the threadlike mass under the blanket on the floor, the Akash who would soon speak the litany that would transfer his title to his heir. An heir that would not only succeed him, but supersede him, being not only Akash, but the rare Alanakash, born on

First Pomegranate Day. Baput suppressed a scoff as he opened the bedroom door and looked into the living room.

Momama's brilliant smile already made his day. No matter how glorious the ceremony was, or how terrible, that smile was all that would matter, Baput resolved. She picked something up from the seat of his chair and held it forth, letting gravity unfold a woven robe like G-Pa's grimy one with the disappearing beads, but better. This garment was skillfully woven of perfectly ripe white yal grass in an intricate pattern, adorned with seeds and river rocks with tiny holes drilled through them with what could only have been an Earth device.

"Momama!" he rushed forward to embrace her, still overwhelmed by that proud, happy smile as much as by the work of art.

"Francina helped make the beads," Star admitted, her face buried in his broad chest. "And Belinda helped sew them on." She looked up into his face, smiling coyly. "Don't tell Lori Anne," she whispered.

"It is beautiful, Momama." He summoned the unique Earth words: "Thank you."

Elmer had declared a picking holiday, even though it was the height of the season. "We got a good day and a half in already. If they were home, those guys would have been too busy fighting, but we knocked them buggers right out! We can afford to take a day to see the boy graduate, right?"

"Ascend, Dad," Jerry had corrected him.

The men set the tables up in the grassy area, and the women heaped excessive amounts of delicacies upon them, mostly pomegranate-based. Purple pin flags delineated an area in front of the sauna door that would serve as the stage for Baput's ascension.

Everyone gathered outside the sauna and waited for the Akash and his Apprentice to appear. Star walked around the group holding a coarsely woven two-gallon basket full of pomegranate seeds. Her wiry arm muscles flexed as she extended the heavy basket to each person, Valko first. He took a large handful in his monstrous mitt and held it open so he didn't squash any. Felsic scooped a handful next and held them motionlessly. Star shoved the basket at Fran, prompting her to do the same, then continued down the line until everyone had a handful. At last, she took her place at Valko's right side as his wife.

The sauna door creaked open slowly, dramatically. The Akash emerged first in his filthy robe. Some beads had been restored, but its faded glory was no match for Baput's crisp new adornment that drew oohs and ahhs when he appeared behind his mentor.

Not to be upstaged on his favorite holiday, the Akash spread his arms and legs and raised his longstick. "Passascenday!" he announced in a confident bellow. "We have passed through the fight once again."

He began the Litany of Passascenday. Baput stood behind him, translating. "We have defeated the nimblies and bumblies for another cycle. No more nimblies! No more bumblies! Three more years! Three more years!" The Nauvians all repeated the chant, some in English like Baput and some in their native tongue, like G-Pa. The Earth folks quickly joined in, but the eleven voices soon wound down.

The Akash went on, sticking to the standard language. "We have survived. We shall go on. We have earned the right to continue loving Kakeeche and following their silver light. We have survived because we follow only Kakeeche." The wild eyes focused on Jerry. "We survive because we turn our backs on the harsher light of Shavarandu, the light that burns our eyes!" The Nauvians exchanged worried glances. The Akash didn't usually get so lathered up at this part. Had he skipped something? Just as well. They were all anxious.

"In this cycle's battle we have lost..." He appeared to count heads, then drew back in shock.

"Manuel Guzman," Baput said the name. He stepped in front of the Akash and sprinkled a handful of pomegranate seeds on the ground.

"Manuel Guzman." The small, multicolored crowd repeated the name one by one, each sprinkling their seeds in turn. Salistar went last, reverently dumping the remainder of the basket for the Manuel Guzman she did not know.

The Akash raised his hands for attention. "And who stands ready to ascend on this glorious Passascenday? Any young longstick warriors? Carpenters? Pot makers? Where is the artist's boy? He must ascend to replace his blind popa!" His confused eyes scanned the tiny crowd.

Has he forgotten? Baput wondered. *Or is he just trying to stick to the formal ceremony?* Mustering all his dignity, Baput faced the Akash.

"I do, Akash," Baput delivered the formal response.

"And to what profession do you claim ascension?" the formalities continued.

Baput went along with the unnecessary dialogue. "Akash, sir."

"Akash." The Premier of Nauve repeated flatly. "I am Akash. You are just a boy."

"I am fifteen. On First Pomegranate Day," Baput replied nervously. Surely G-Pa was just dragging it out for effect, as he was known to do.

"Ahhh, Alanakash!" G-Pa exclaimed as if he hadn't known it for fifteen years. "You would claim to supersede my rule?"

"Yes, G-Pa, um, Akash," Baput stammered. This was harder than he had expected. G-Pa was making it hard. *He tests me.* Baput concluded. *One final test. Just be cool, play along.*

"Do you think you are ready, Boy?" Baput had never heard G-Pa ask that question of a boy ascending to a craft, but then, Baput had never seen an Akash ascend before. *What if G-Pa is not ready to step down?* He suddenly wondered.

"Yes, Akash," Baput replied formally once again. He tried to sound calm, but something felt wrong.

The feeling was confirmed when the Akash threw his wrinkled raisin of a head back and began a chortle that rose to a belly laugh that shook the shriveled body of the elderly master. Baput scanned the crowd with distressed eyes.

Valko leaned forward on his longstick, its metal blade polished for the ceremony. His thick eyebrows wrinkled like Baput's often did.

Belinda scowled at G-Pa from the shelter of Patrick's arms. Jerry stood lopsidedly with folded arms and a curled lip.

The wicked laughing finally stopped. The Akash gathered himself to speak, in English without Baput's help. "So you think you are ready, eh, Boy?" he began derisively. Giving no time for a reply, he pulled a written list from his sash and thrust it at Baput. "Read this," he commanded.

Baput tried to read the Old Akashic. He knew the letters, but he had not finished learning to make words, much less sentences. G-Pa had stopped teaching him on that fateful day, over three years ago.

Baput stared at the paper until it blurred. He peeked shyly at the crowd with lowered eyes. Popa raised the butt of his longstick off the ground, preparing to lurch to his son's defense. *No, Popa!* Baput begged with his eyes. *That will make it worse!*

He looked at Jerry, Patrick, and Belinda. *I can't even read! What do they think of me now?*

Jerry unfolded his arms and raised a tight, white fist. Belinda blew him a kiss.

He dropped his eyes again and found the Akash's eyes looking down, no, *up*, at him! *When did he grow smaller than me?* Baput wondered illogically. A forgotten dream flashed by, far too quickly to grasp.

"I have not completed my training in Old Akashic," he admitted. "You have not taught me since our Arrival."

"And what else have you not learned since what you call our Arrival? You have learned nothing from me. You have become lazy and selfish. You do not care to learn. You don't take your lessons. You just play with that Earth Boy. You are like Keeldar, the lazy apprentice who did not believe."

Valko and Elmer stepped forward at once, joining in front of the crowd. "Ain't that the kid that got killed by the Evil Eye?" Elmer asked in a whisper. He hadn't brought his gun this time, not to Baput's Passascenday!

Valko snorted at the stage, his warrior face melting into a smile. "Look at them!"

Baput stared at the written list like it was an intriguing puzzle. He stood at least four inches taller than the wrinkled straw of an Akash that sputtered on about Kakeeche and Keeldar and Nauve. The boy was more than twice the man's weight, most of it muscles, like his proud Papa, who asked, "How do you say it, Earth Elmer? You and what army?"

Baput raised his eyes from the paper and stepped to the front of the area that served as the stage. "These are numbers on the edge. There are six of them. This is the Akashic Litany of Succession."

"Yes," the Akash replied coldly. "The Apprentice is supposed to read it, if he is ready to ascend."

"But I know the Litany by heart. I will say it." Not waiting for approval, Baput began:

"Number one: I shall never use the Akashic power selfishly."

Muttered ironies rippled through the crowd.

"Number two: I shall serve all of the people equally."

Felsic snorted, arms folded, a bottle of under-ripe, under-fermented desperation wine in his hand, a Passascenday tradition.

"Number three: I shall speak only the truth."

"Right on!" "That's right!" Fran and Patrick shouted their agreement.

"Number four: I shall be kind at all times to all people."

The Earth people rallied, ready to explode at the hypocrisy. The Akash must have seen the smoldering volcano. He rushed to douse it with rocket fuel.

"Stop it, Boy!" he tried to roar, but it came out as a wheeze. His legs wavered beneath him. "So you memorized the Litany. That doesn't make you ready. You use the power selfishly, boy, every day."

"How?" Baput wondered, dismayed. He had tried so hard, ever since they arrived, to stick to the Litany. In those first days, in a strange world, with G-Pa not really there, learning all those new ideas from Jerry, the Litany had been his only guide. That and Popa.

The Akash said nothing to back up his accusation, so Baput continued. "Number five…"

The Akash upstaged him, stepping into the audience to do it. "No matter. You betrayed your people. You turned your back on

Kakeeche. You turned to Shavarandu!" His poignant roar echoed from the riverbed.

"You hypocrite!" Baput thundered back. "You condemn me, and all the Earth people for committing Shavarandu. But you know you do it, too. That is what brought us here. You even bragged about it."

"When? I did not!"

"Last First Pomegranate Day at Nauve, before *it* happened, you bragged about the weapon in front of all the people. And when we spoke on the Plane, you said you wished to go to Jerry's school of Shavarandu."

The Akash stretched, trying to make himself taller, but it only made him thinner, like a caterpillar stretching for a leaf. "I never said those things! The Akash you see in your dreams is not me. It is your idea of me, which you often misconstrue. It is your wishful thinking, casting your pathetic molds into the eternal flow, oooh, ahhh…" He waved his hands dismissively. He turned to his audience for the laugh track but found only frigid silence.

"Bah!" he spat. He raised his longstick again. Even the Earth people could see another sermon gathering.

"Accessing the Plane without Kakeeche's guidance is folly at best. Doom at worst. It always leads to Shavarandu. You lost your faith! You turned your back on Kakeeche. So, you turned your back on your people. How can you ever be Akash?"

It was a fair argument, Baput had to admit. Maybe he didn't deserve to be Akash. Maybe it didn't matter. There it was. The thought he had been brushing aside for three years. *Akash of what? Akash of whom? Momama and Popa and Uncle Felsic? My elders, and no one else? How can I rule over Popa? Popa always knows the right thing to do. Maybe I don't want to be Akash here on Earth where it means nothing, where it's all just bad science. Even the Plane. And my powerful, wise Akash who still dwells there? Not real either?*

Tears of rage streamed down Baput's violet cheeks, not for his evaporating Akash-hood, but for G-Pa's. "If the Akash I see on the Plane is not you," his voice broke. "Then where *are* you?"

"I am standing right in front of you, you idiot child! I should have left you to your fate as winemaker." He dismissed Baput with a theatric swat.

Baput's cold tears dried instantly. "If the wise one I see on the Plane is not you, then you are nothing!" He intruded in the old man's space, making him cower. "You are only a shell of my G-Pa, the former Akash. I could blow your dry husk away like dust in the wind!" His voice cracked at the end of the adrenaline wave, as he crashed to Earth and realized what he was doing. This was no dream!

A single pair of hands clapped in the forgotten audience. Baput followed the sound with muddled eyes and found Elmer's version of the Jerry grin. Jerry joined in, then the rest of the Musiks, until finally the Nauvians joined in the Earth custom.

G-Pa stood forward again, arms and legs stretched, longstick raised, soaking up the adoration as if it was justly meant for him. He addressed the crowd with words that were meant for Baput.

"You have one more trial!" he announced like a game show host. "We must see how unselfishly you can sacrifice for the good of all your people." The Akash made the sacred vow of altruism sound ugly and threatening, as only he could.

Despite the size difference, the second implied threat brought Valko forward into the stage area. After all, he was still Guard of Akash. And he, for one, had no doubt as to who that Akash truly was.

"Hasn't he been tried enough?" Valko inserted his bulk between the two competing Akashes. He stared down at his father-in-law as if that was all he was, and he told the old man what he thought. "Baput is already Akash in my eyes. He has done far more than you have to guide us in this new world, even as a 12-year-old! You have done nothing to help him, or your daughter! Baput has sacrificed enough!" He counted on his thick fingers. "He's lost his childhood, his brother, his friends, his betrothed, his *world*, because of you. Because of your Shavarandu, my son does not even have a village to be Akash of!"

Valko's eloquent speech was followed by stunned silence. No applause, just awe. No one had ever shouted back at Akash during a Passascenday Ceremony. On Passascenday, even more than all other times, when Akash speaks, it is so. You ascended or you didn't, as he dictated. Especially if you were trying to ascend to Akash.

The Akash leaned heavily on his longstick, breathing hard, his tongue hanging out to lap extra oxygen from the air. A flash of red caught his eye. Belinda stepped forward out of Patrick's embrace, breaking the silence with her pink floral leggings under purple shorts below her green fleece jacket, decked for Baput's special day.

The Akash pointed his longstick at the approaching girl.

"Akash?" Belinda tried to sound brave with the charred, bloody tip of the longstick wavering in her face, but her tense vocal chords betrayed her, and the word came out like the helpless squeak of a tiny animal in a trap.

The Akash opened his mouth preemptively. "Why does this tiny pink girl child speak to Akash?" he demanded, shaking the stick menacingly.

Belinda worked to control her voice. She pretended it was her violin, and she could adjust the sound by changing the tension of the strings. Her words pealed out loud and clear, like a grown woman. "Excuse me, G-Pa, but you took that oath, too, right?"

The old Akash didn't bother to answer. He turned away, fixing his eyes on Salistar, who stared back with a look her popa had never seen before. His eyes darted around for a friend and found none. *Not even Shastina. She's in the quarters with those stinking puppies everyone loves so much.*

Despite his admonition, the pink girl spoke again. "Number four says to be kind to everybody all the time. But you're not a nice man. Not to anybody. Especially Salistar. She takes care of you all the time, and you never even say a nice thing to her. You're not nice to Baput, either! You're not nice to anybody!"

"Easy, Babe." Patrick stepped forward and squeezed her adorably puffed-up shoulders. He had never felt them so tense! He pulled her back, away from the longstick's dull but filthy point.

To everyone's surprise, especially the Nauvians', Star stepped forward next. She stepped sideways deliberately to stand in the exact same spot Belinda had so bravely occupied. She fixed her popa's eyes in hers and spoke boldly, for a tether. "Belinda is right. You never thank me."

The Akash's face twisted at the foreign word. "Thank? What is this, thank?"

Star remembered when the concept had been unknown to her, too. Back on Nauve, before Francina. She tried again, using the closest Nauvian word she could find. "You never loved me."

Belinda was at her side in an instant, Fran at the other. They rushed the petite green woman off to the side, exposing Patrick. The Akash eyed him expectantly, like a vulture. Not to be outdone by his brave daughter, he had to say something.

"You're kind of a dick, man," is what came out, followed by hoots of laughter and agreement from Jerry, Elmer, and Lorraine.

Felsic stepped into the pregnant pause that followed the dying of the laughter. "You left Peratha and Trillella outside when the nimblies were coming. And you, you..." Valko rushed to his brother's side and steered him away from the crowd. When they were clear of the group, Felsic broke and ran to the riverbank. He stood silhouetted against the white-gray glare of the gravel and the scattered pools of sluggish water, a bottle dangling from his hand.

What did G-Pa do to him? Belinda wondered as Aunt Fran stepped bravely onto what had become the Speaking Spot. The Akash turned away, fixing his eyes on the food table.

Fran began anyway. "You should be ashamed of yourself, Akash, G-Pa, whatever your name is." This hostile, intolerant force was not a Fran anybody had seen before. "The way you treat people. Your family.

Felsic. And your own daughter, who slaves to take care of you, night and day. It's a horrible thing to say, but I'm afraid she's right. You don't love her, do you?" G-Pa just stared at the food table. "Do you love anybody? Did you ever? Do you even know what love is? How can you be a wise Akash who serves his people selflessly if you don't even know what love is?"

Patrick collected the blubbering Fran and escorted her to the comforting coven of women. Even Lorraine had joined with Star in solidarity.

The old Akash was finally rendered speechless. Or perhaps just hungry and tired of all these inconsequential women squawking, and that woman-man. *What did he call me? I will have to ask Baput what it means.*

A shadow crossed his eyes, and he thought Shavarandu was turning away again. *No, just my little grandson, turned into a monster like his overblown father. He's going to speak again! I told him once. It is done! Three more years and try again, like other boys. You are no different!* He fumed silently.

Baput did not address the smoldering Akash, but the rapt and teary crowd. His words, however, were for the Akash. "Akash, you think the Akash-hood is about you. It is not. It is about the people. You are supposed to serve the people, not rule them. Not imprison them and make them do your bidding. Make you fancy clothes and parties, chant your stupid, endless chants, hold your hand all night like a babbet!" There. He'd said it. He hadn't meant to. He changed directions sickeningly.

"But that is trivial. Sorry, Momama, I know he makes you suffer, but he does far worse. He plays with Shavarandu. So do I. So does everyone on Earth. I cannot condemn him for it, for I have done it too. It has its place, and it was for a good reason, when it started. To rid us of the nimblies and bumblies would be a great thing to do for all the people."

"Yes!" G-Pa jumped at the recognition with all the feeble strength he had left. "I did it for the people."

"Yes, G-Pa. But you were irresponsible. You kept secrets, dangerous secrets. After all we've been through, I think you are still withholding information. And your plan. People, you heard his plan, on First Pomegranate Day, on the Rock? He spoke it out loud—"

Baput scanned his audience for signs of recognition. *Did the Akash say it out loud? Or did only I hear it, while the Rock buzzed in my head?*

"We heard," Jerry reassured him. "He was gonna leave us to burn."

"Yes," Baput replied, "this Akash would leave Earth to burn."

"I didn't," the old man sputtered. "I wouldn't. Not now."

"Now that you're stuck here with us," Elmer piled on. The crowd closed in on the frail Akash. Baput found himself protecting him.

"I vote for Baput!" Belinda cried, presuming a democracy that had not yet been established. Nevertheless, the Earthlings all cast their verbal ballots. The Nauvians caught on quickly and added their votes to the tally. Eight for Baput, zero for G-Pa. Baput abstained. Voting for himself would be selfish, but he couldn't vote for G-Pa either, because that would not be for the good of the people. Felsic still stood staring at the river. G-Pa didn't vote. He made a beeline for the food table, where he picked up the pomegranate-pear pie and consumed it messily with his face like an animal.

"Time to eat," Salistar announced at the hint. The People surrounded their Akash-elect and escorted him to the head of the table for the sumptuous Passascenday Feast.

Finished with the pie but still deeply unsatisfied, the old Akash cast about for his tether. She was not eating with the others. He turned his foggy eyes toward the river, where he spotted her silhouette. *There she is, with that idiot Felsic, who stands by the river, too stupid to fall in like he should. She brings him food!* G-Pa leaned forward in his feeble folding chair. *Him! That sloth! Not me! She is my Tether!* He ranted, but all that came out was a tight hiss slowly swelling to a weak wheeze. *Look at her, speaking to him, touching him tenderly and consoling him. For what? I am the one aggrieved! Yet here I sit, my hands and face sticky with gaa, and still hungry.* "Woman!" he gasped in an attempted roar. Valko bumped hard into the back of his frail chair on his way to the table for seconds.

With no other response to his plaintive cries, G-Pa finally rose from his bony rear end just as the chair disintegrated beneath him. He picked up one of the fabric food bags Star had used to bring the food out. He stuffed it full of cakes and bread, beans and rice, with no regard for the mess. He even poured pumpkin-pomegranate soup right into the bag on top of the medley. No one but Brodey paid him any mind as he limped with his longstick and his leaking satchel into the stone sauna. He closed the door quietly while Brodey licked his trail away.

When the chewing slowed and the talk ebbed and the table was surprisingly empty, Valko looked toward the sun and raised his longstick for attention. "There is still time to pick a full load, Boss Elmer."

"Don't you want to take the whole day off, for your holiday?" Elmer offered.

The response was a giggle from Star. She had brought Felsic back to the table for his second-favorite desert, G-Pa having consumed his favorite.

Baput translated. "We don't take time off on Passascenday. We would bury the dead now. Only their bones are left. We place them all together in a big ditch and cover them with pomegranates. Then the young men ascend to their crafts and marry. After the ceremonies, we pick like no human has ever seen!"

And so they did, for the rest of the day.

11. A Delicate Operation

The Nauvian picking crew watched the day's harvest disappear down the driveway to "town," a concept that still eluded them, even now that they had seen it. Dusk was gathering. Despite their feast of four hours ago, the energetic vegans were famished again. They migrated to their quarters habitually, like zebkin filing to the river in the evening.

The leftovers were barely adequate. There was a new pomegranate-pear pie, but Momama said it was for Felsic only.

"Where is G-Pa? Is he eating?" Baput asked as he sat down. Momama only shrugged, grunted softly.

Popa came around behind Baput's chair and rested his hand on the table beside his soup bowl. "Not your concern, Son. You are not Akash, according to him. And you are certainly not his tether!" He straightened gruffly and took his place at the table across from Baput, dumping the last of the soup into his bowl.

They finished their meager meal in silence. When he was done, Baput dared to enter the forbidden kitchen, where Momama rinsed the dishes for the dishwasher. "Excuse me, Momama," the quasi-Akash muttered as he scraped meager scraps of food from the empty pots and pans into a plastic container. Then, he headed for Felsic's pie.

"No!" Salistar cried, grabbing his hand. Shastina raised her head and woofed at the unprecedented noise. Baput dropped the utensil and rushed out the door with the paltry dinner pack.

Baput entered the sauna, casting a slice of twilight onto the pitch-dark floor. He could barely see the old Akash standing there holding his longstick up to the ceiling. It was bent! It was moving! Baput heard a hiss from above G-Pa's head. He fumbled for a light and found the electric candle. It was not his longstick G-Pa held, but that snake, Keebra. Baput knew it was the same snake. It had a painful looking lump on its side, and it hitched brokenly instead of slithering smoothly as it writhed in G-Pa's fists.

"Put him down, G-Pa," Baput commanded. "I brought you food. Come eat."

G-Pa stood his ground, still holding the snake. "How dare you speak to Keebra this way?"

"I speak to you, G-Pa. Eat."

"Where is my Tether?" G-Pa replied sulkily, lowering his tired arms a little.

"Nauve." Baput used the word for "home" without thinking. G-Pa's sudden hope and outrage reminded him of his error. "The quarters, I mean. Nauve on Earth." The flare faded from the crazy eyes. "That's where you should be, too. Come on, G-Pa."

"Keebra!" G-Pa insisted.

Baput looked up at the poor snake. "Keebra sleeps in his hole. You don't. Here, let me—"

"I am Keebra!" the Akash interrupted.

Baput stepped back toward the door, his patience nearly gone. "Are you going to sleep in a hole, G-Pa? Oh, sorry, Keebra?" he asked with uncharacteristic sarcasm. It felt wrong, and he warmed, one last time. "Come on, G-Pa. You can't stay out here. It's cold. You'll get sick."

G-Pa responded with a violent fit of coughing. He brought Keebra down to eye level, bent the wrong way, against the kink. The poor snake squirmed in obvious pain. Baput placed his growing hands over G-Pa's and pushed them to the floor, forcing G-Pa to his knees. The old man wriggled his skinny body more gracefully than the wounded gopher snake could.

"I am Keebra!" G-Pa kept repeating as he dropped to his hands and knees. "I am Keebra."

He released the snake. It limped away toward its hole, then turned back like a kinked hose. Head raised, it stared at G-Pa, who crawled into its gaze. They stayed face to face for a long time. The snake's tongue darted in and out. G-Pa's tongue darted the same way. Baput winced as they almost touched.

When their wordless communication was complete, Little Keebra withdrew his tongue and kink-slithered to his hole, where he disappeared without looking back.

G-Pa stood, eyes wild. Baput peered into them. They seemed like slits, like Keebra's eyes. *It must be this light,* he assumed logically. He scanned G-Pa up and down. His woven tunic sagged shapelessly over missing shoulders. He held his drawstring pants up with his hands.

Following Baput's gaze, G-Pa looked down at himself, inside the roomy tunic and suspended pants, at his thread of a body. He looked up at Baput with a satisfied smile, insane in the dancing light. "I *am* Keebra!"

Sizing him up, Baput suddenly saw it. He was small enough to fit in the chimney! Easily! He *was* Keebra! *Keebra is immune. Keebra can kill the Queen. Keebra must be asked to. He must say "yes" of his own free will.* Baput's mind raced as he hurriedly cleaned up G-Pa's messy private feast. He found the lantern but didn't turn it on, so as not to break the spell. *G-Pa must stay Keebra for tonight, at least until I decide what to do.*

His family helped by ignoring them when they entered the quarters. No one looked at them. No one said a word. Somehow, Momama seemed to say fewer words than the others, even though no one said any. Baput escorted G-Pa to the boors, where Keebra did his business in a very human-like way. Then they walked in tight formation past the room full of silence into the bedroom.

Baput left the light off. Keebra stood next to the bed and let go of his pants. They fell to the floor, and he followed them. He drew his blanket over himself with hands a snake shouldn't have.

Baput snatched the pillow and blankets from his customary, and resented, lower bunk. He tossed them onto the top bunk and climbed up. He turned his face to the wall and tucked both hands snugly under it. "I am no tether!" he snapped in a voice deeper than his own.

He didn't want to think. He searched for the mind-numbing TV Plane, but it was off, out of respect for him, no doubt. *Sometimes you can say "thank you" backwards*, he realized, *Thanks a lot, Jerry.*

But no, I must think. What to do? The Nimbumblyborg does not belong on Earth. Neither do we, but we don't eat people. They did. And they will eat more people in three years. And even if they don't eat us, Jerry says we will all get in trouble. Locked up, whatever that means.

Patrick and Lori Anne are here now, with all their brainy Shavarandu stuff. I was supposed to be Akash! On this night, I planned to decide this matter right here in my bed. I was going to announce my decision tomorrow morning. But I am not really Akash, even if Popa says I am.

If I were Akash, what would be my decision? What difference does it make? I would be Akash of Nothing. No one of nowhere. There is no such thing as Akash on Earth. Why? Baput asked himself. He opened his eyes and saw the plain wooden wall, lit by the window in the opposite wall. That is why he had craved the top bunk. So he could see the setting moon, the morning sunlight bouncing from the red western clouds, the electric light in Jerry's bedroom, sometimes his video games flashing, the TV downstairs...

He found the answer. *They don't need an Akash because everybody has ideas, even guys like Felsic, and Momama! Even little girls like Belinda. They all have ideas, and people listen to them. Then they all talk about it, all together. They decide together. It is Earth way. Tomorrow I will talk to everyone. Even Momama. But not G-Pa. He must stay in the shed and be Keebra, just in case we decide...*

He dropped that thread and started a fantasy meeting in the Musik living room. *I will say, "I think we should do Insitucide and kill the Earth nimblies and bumblies while they sleep. What do you all think? Belinda?" I will ask her first, so she knows she is important. She will hesitate because she is too soft-hearted, like Momama. Jerry will say, "You just gotta kill 'em" like any respectable young warrior. Felsic will say the same. Popa will say something like that, but more clever and dramatic. What about Patrick? He doesn't like to kill. What would he say?*

The exercise had nearly lulled him to sleep, but Imaginary Patrick's answer jarred him awake.

"Ask Manuel. Ask his family."

This is why I am not really Akash yet. Baput admonished himself. *I should have done this on that very night, while I struggled to stay awake by the fire, watching for bumblies. But I was not Akash then.* He rolled onto his back, spread his arms and legs, and breathed in. *I am not Akash now.* He breathed out.

"I call all who knew and loved Manuel Guzman," he chanted softly. "I feel your pain. I too have felt the loss of a loved one. I come to show you the comfort of the unending flow, which your Manuel has joined. The flow that is all life that ever was and ever will be, all joined, always changing, always the same."

He saw a small home lit only by candles arranged around a photograph of a man with a wide face, brown skin, and wavy black hair. A dark-skinned woman was there, petite and slender, with long, straight ebony hair. She looked like Momama! There was a little girl with the same dark hair and bottomless brown eyes, too innocent to comprehend the eternity of her popa's absence.

And there was a boy. He was about the size Jerry had been when Baput had first seen him. But this boy was not like Jerry. He had dark hair and dark eyes and dark skin, like the rest of his family. Like Baput's family. But he had something else Baput had never seen in Jerry, or any of the Musiks. Anger. The brooding anger of the helpless.

Baput felt it smoldering, red-hot just beneath the flow. He watched as the red blotch expanded into a growing patch of scarlet rage. The flow absorbed it, whisking parts of it away to commingle with the cooler greens and blues, and spread, diluted, throughout eternity. *The boy grows. He gets no answers. Those responsible are long gone.* They tell him, "It won't happen again." The news fades, the anger doesn't. *It grows as the boy grows, tenderly nursed and savagely guarded, until he's big enough to do something with it. Then what? More killing? Because of us? Even if we are long gone, back to Nauve?*

The vision left Baput feeling helpless, defeated. But he couldn't be. "What if it happens again?" he asked Manuel's son. "What if it happens again, and we could have stopped it?"

Baput was now certain of his vote. He knew how Manuel and his family would vote, too. Most, if not all, of his friends and family would support Insitucide. He was sure. But, how to do it?

Patrick would say gas. He was going to use Sojourner to carry a hose to the chamber, but Sojourner is stuck, maybe. We have to be able to see inside the chimney while we feed the gas in. We need to go in... Baput's mind swirled in an endless circle until he fell asleep.

He found himself sitting cross-legged on the platform in deep meditation. A rising hiss disturbed him. He opened his eyes. Keebra's head protruded from the chimney hole, wavering back and forth with that forked tongue flashing in and out of G-Pa's most maniacal smile. Then he turned around impossibly and disappeared into the little cave.

Baput could barely see. The light was too dim. It kept moving around, bobbing and swerving. "Helictites," Patrick's voice told him as he tried to focus on the squiggly little stalactites on the ceiling. He was in the chimney! How could he fit? He rolled over, scanning past rocky walls to boo-stained floor. He reached out and touched the walls without unbending his arms. He sucked in an acrid breath and exhaled. His disembodied dream-soul backed up with sickening speed and popped out of the tiny tube, where his real body could never fit.

He was back on the platform in meditation pose, as before. Keebra's head again protruded from the chimney, wavering, flicking its tongue, wearing G-Pa's face. Then it spoke. "Akash sees what Keebra sees."

"Yes, G-Pa. I have seen it. You see what Keebra sees."

"I *am* Keebra."

"I understand, G-Pa." Even in his dreams, Baput was tired of these games.

"Akash sees what Keebra sees," the G-Pa snake repeated.

"But you are Akash?" Baput tried to follow.

"No!" the snake hissed. "I am Keebra. True Akash sees what Keebra sees." It drew a hand from somewhere and pointed its thumb to its, um, chest. "There is no Akash here, only Keebra. Akash sees what Keebra sees."

"Who is Akash?" Baput asked without speaking.

"He who sees what Keebra sees. He who sees rightly," the serpent replied.

"Does Keebra choose to commit Insitucide?" Baput asked formally.

Somehow, the snake shrugged without shoulders. "Only Akash knows. '*Which Akash?*' you ask," he wriggled mockingly. "The one true Akash. The one who truly believes. The one who makes the sacrifice." Keebra's mouth opened wide enough to swallow Baput. Dripping fangs dangled over his head like stalactites. Incisors jutted up on either side of him like stalagmites.

The great mouth withdrew and closed. The G-Pa creature vanished into the chimney with plenty of room to spare. The cave hole went black.

Keebra's Proposal

Baput blinked at the soft morning light. He looked up at the ceiling, rustic beams with a white bowl in the center that lit the whole room if you just flicked a tiny lever. He usually saw the springs of the top bunk when he opened his eyes. But, what? *G-Pa is Keebra. He fits inside the chimney. He said he would go in, and…*

It was a dream. When I dream about him, it isn't really him. He said so. So, he doesn't really fit in the chimney. He didn't really say he would go. It was just me thinking. Wishful thinking… What was I thinking?

The west window caught his eye, and the jumbled dream flew away. He looked down from the high bunk and jumped back, startled. G-Pa lay on the floor far below. If not for the head sticking out, Baput might have believed it was a large snake under that blanket.

G-Pa's eyes opened. He stared up accusingly. "You didn't hold my hand."

"Snakes don't have hands, Keebra," Baput answered from his high perch.

G-Pa looked at his empty hand, turning it curiously from one side to another. He looked back up at Baput. "You are way up there!" he complained again.

"Maybe I only seem higher because you are a lowly snake on the floor, Keebra," Baput taunted, testing the fragile snake.

"I am Keebra," G-Pa agreed.

Baput climbed down, looking forward to the day. He cut the cord from the window blinds and wrapped it around his G-Pa's waist, to hold up his droopy drawers. He tied it firmly and hid the mess under the saggy tunic, then steered the delirious man-snake out the bedroom door.

Her strike over, Momama fried potatoes, squash, onions, garlic, and beets in a cast-iron skillet. Baput stopped in the doorway on his way to the boors, G-Pa leaning heavily on his shoulder. "Thank you, Momama," he spoke loudly and clearly, looked down at G-Pa pointedly. The tongue flickered in and out. Baput got between his momama and G-Pa so she wouldn't see that creepy tongue.

When they were finished, he rushed his secret weapon right past her in the same way, so she could not see what her popa had become. "I will be right back, Momama."

"Will your G-Pa be eating?" she boldly demanded.

"No, Momama," Baput half smiled. "He is on a diet. Oh, and we will have a meeting at the Musik House after breakfast, before picking. You come too, Momama."

Baput left his G-Pa under the bench in the sauna. Keebra seemed quite comfortable there.

The meeting began just as Baput had planned. "I believe we must commit Insitucide and kill the Queen as she sleeps. Now. As soon as possible."

"Yes, Akash," the majority responded without hesitation.

Baput's face fell, to their surprise. "I am not Akash yet. I do not hold the Sacred Longstick or wear the Holy Seed. The Akash has not yet transferred his powers and duties to me."

"Well, where is he?" Elmer asked.

"He is in deep meditation." Baput replied, remembering his unfinished oath. *Akash shall speak only the truth.* But it *was* true, in a way. "I am here to ask all of you what you think. Should we kill the Queen now? We can vote, like Earth democracy."

"American democracy," Elmer corrected. "And yeah, let's kill that little—"

"—Elmer!" Francina interrupted. "But, yes, Honey, Akash, Baput, sorry. Yes, I suppose we have to kill it."

The rest added their votes quickly, all in favor. Even Patrick and Belinda reluctantly agreed. Everyone except Momama, who got all quiet and wrinkly and started to do Francina's dishes.

Baput entered the kitchen and took a wet plate from her hand, raising it out of her reach. She hopped for it futilely.

"Momama?" his face followed hers as she tried to duck away. "Tell us what you think."

"It's OK, Star," Fran encouraged. "We all get a say."

Star shook her head like she was trying to escape a cloud of bees. "No, no, I have no say." She looked up at her new son, this strange young man with these alien ideas. "You won't like it."

"What, Momama?"

"The Queen is all that is left of the nimblies and bumblies on Earth. The only babbets that will ever be born. It will be the end of them. It is too sad to have no more, forever…" She trailed off, grabbing another dish from the sink and wiping it desperately.

"No more nimblies…" Felsic began the chant. No one joined in. He hushed under Valko's glare.

Baput left his momama's side and returned to the breakfast bar. "OK. Momama votes no. But more vote yes, so, sorry, Momama. We respect your feelings."

Valko grunted. Baput shot his popa a hard look. It felt wrong, but it also felt right. Being the Akash of his parents was going to be ridiculous.

"So," Baput paused, "we will kill the Queen this week, while everyone is still um, present." He looked at Patrick, Lorraine, and finally Belinda. "But how do we do it?"

"Gas," Patrick offered, as expected. "Chlorine might work, but I like liquid nitrogen. Freeze that puppy! That'll kill it for sure."

"And it has to kill that pathogen, too," Lorraine added. "But how do we get it in there?"

Patrick was off the couch and pacing back and forth, like he always did when he worked a problem. "We can get Sojourner out, tie the hose to her and run her back in there. We might need new wheels. Jerry, Buddy, we might have to sacrifice Little Little Truck."

"Aww!" Felsic responded.

Patrick babbled on. "But pushing that hose in like that, I don't know. It might kink. That stuff is dangerous. If the seal breaks anywhere along there, the hose leaks and the stuff comes out, it will just freeze everything. The hose, all the fittings, your hand if you're holding it. If it happens before we're in too deep, it might come back out of the hole and get us. It'll freeze you instantly, on the cellular level. Extreme frostbite! Wait… They have those dollies you can use for running hoses down pipes. Remote control. Darn!"

He finally looked up at the crowd who followed him with their eyes. "I know. No remote control." He sat back down and stared at the dark screen that showed the chamber of the Queen. They all joined in the dismal staring as defeat draped their frustration in silence.

Baput closed his eyes and took a deep, Akashic breath. There was Keebra, swaying back and forth in front of the cave hole. His eyes flew open. "Keebra!" he cried, shattering the awkward stillness.

"The snake?" Jerry asked.

"No," Baput answered with all the confidence of a seasoned Akash. "G-Pa." He described his dream, the best he could. Like most dreams, it didn't quite make sense. Baput found himself shaking his head as he spoke. "It was just a crazy dream."

"Brought on by yesterday's trauma," Francina offered her empathy.

"Yes," Baput agreed, "But the funny thing is, G-Pa really *does* think he's Keebra. Ever since yesterday. And he's so skinny now! He could fit all the way into that cave easily, I'm sure."

Felsic dropped his eyes and headed for the boor at the end of the hall, slamming the door behind him. Curious glances were met with shrugs and shaking heads.

Jerry returned to the subject. "So, we get G-Pa, I mean Keebra, to take the gas hose into the hole."

"He'll die!" Fran cried.

"Naw, Mom!" Jerry had it all figured out. "He takes the hose in there, empty. Harmless. He sticks it down in the chamber, leaves it, and backs out. Then we let 'er rip!"

"But the pathogen," Lorraine worried. "That's when you get it, when you go in and touch that queen slime, right?"

Felsic crossed the hall from the boor to the back room with its intriguing model.

"Keebra is immune," Baput pointed out.

"But he's not really Keebra, Baput!" Belinda addressed the almost-Alanakash as if they were equals. "He's your G-Pa."

"Don't you have to ask him?" Jerry remembered.

"Yes," Baput said again. "He said he would do it. But that was a dream. The Akash in my dreams isn't really him. He told me so. I guess he has not said 'yes' to this."

"Well, let's ask him," Jerry proposed, grabbing for his jacket.

"I get it!" Elmer spouted. "See, this way we still have to ask him before we can do anything, even though he ain't really Akash anymore. That's what all this Keebra stuff is about. He's trying to stay relevant."

Valko barked a tense laugh of agreement.

"Well, if he's the one going in, of course you have to ask him," Fran argued.

Patrick started pacing again. "Wait a minute. Think this through. First, let's say he says 'yes.' What if he drops the hose too soon or messes it up so it leaks in a bad place—"

"Or he touches that thing," Lorraine interrupted. "Comes out and infects us all."

Valko's eyes stayed fixed down the hallway.

"We have to be able to see inside while we feed the gas in," Jerry figured.

"We have to be able to control him," Lorraine added.

"We still need remote control!" Patrick completed the circle.

The jumbled mess of his dream unpacked before Baput's eyes, exposing its hidden pearl. "I see what he sees, if I am true Akash," he whispered.

Everyone quieted at the soft proclamation.

"What?" Jerry asked.

"I see what Keebra sees. Remember, Jerry? G-Pa really could see what the snake saw. And why not? It's scientific. The Waves from the Cave, they collide with your waves. Your iPlane, cell phone, your remote controls. The cave waves are ours. Green People waves. Akashic waves. I can use them to communicate with G-Pa and control him. I think."

Power gathered behind Baput's dark eyes like a thunderhead. He rose majestically and took two steps to the door. "I will ask him."

Jerry was at his side. "You need a witness?"

"Yes, my friend, but not Earth Boy. He doesn't trust you. Patrick, it should be you."

Patrick pointed at himself. "Me? But I called him a…"

Baput reached for Patrick's shoulder and pulled him toward the door. "Still, he despises you least."

"I can only command him if I am the One True Akash," Baput explained as he and Patrick hiked to the sauna.

"Well, you are," Patrick answered.

"No, I am not. Not yet. Only in my dreams."

"That's right, Baput." Patrick stopped and touched Baput's shoulder, forcing Baput to face him before they reached the dark stone building. He pointed to his temple. "This is where you are the True Akash. In your own mind. Your ascension is up to you."

"But then, anybody could ascend to Akash."

"Exactly!" Patrick whispered. "Everybody can. You are Akash, I am Akash, everybody is Akash. But then, everybody has to obey those rules you said. You didn't finish. What are the rest?"

"I cannot say them until G-Pa is ready," Baput replied as he eased the sauna door open. "G-, um, Keebra!" he called softly. A muffled hiss sounded from under the bench. Baput crawled under without a light. "Keebra," he asked in a solemn tone, "will you commit Insitucide?"

No answer. To be absolutely clear, Baput asked again. "Keebra, do you agree to risk the Curse and kill the Queen of the Nimbumblyborg?"

Silence. Then a barely audible hiss. The sound built until it seemed to surround them. G-Pa slithered out from under the bench and rose to his feet as gracefully as any healthy young snake. For an instant, he seemed taller than Baput again. He looked down his snout at his former apprentice.

"That is why I have occupied this superior body, you foolish boy!" Keebra scolded. He sounded very much like G-Pa, but he looked a lot like Keebra.

Patrick seemed to think so, too. "I'll call around and see where I can get a dewar of liquid nitrogen and a long hose," he resolved as they returned to the house, leaving Keebra safe and comfortable in his hole.

Flying

Kate smiled at the Look'N Up Pomegranates logo painted on the mailbox. She hadn't noticed that last time. She felt a pang. She heard a shout. She drove past the gate, up the hill and around the bend to the right, there! Another driveway, gated with a crude system of sticks and barbed wire. She had seen it when she was looking for a way out of the Musik's West Orchard, back when she thought Jerry was crazy, or worse.

Tire tracks and junk-food wrappers marked the spot where deputies had watched over the ranch for the last couple of days and nights. They'd run off a few journalists and heard a couple of gunshots, but nothing had taken off toward town and Elmer hadn't called for help. The green guy with the weedeater had said "three days and nights," so Dave had pulled his deputies this morning.

Kate hiked through the orchard, packing her camera and notepad like a gunslinger. She heard another shout. A small engine whirred. Someone cried, "Whoa!"

She almost walked off the cliff into the bizarre operation on the driveway 10 feet below. She tucked herself tightly against an oak tree that hung over the driveway. She drew her camera and watched.

"This is crazy!" Patrick muttered as Valko ran the winch that lowered G-Pa to the platform, strapped into a hammock. He was far too thin for the harness. He wore kneepads over Fran's shiny silver spandex leggings and elbow pads over one of Jerry's outgrown long-sleeved pomegranate-colored baseball jerseys. He had been anointed with the last of the previous year's pomegranate oil for lubrication. Baput was afraid to imagine what Momama had gone through to accomplish this new look. The slick mess landed on the platform like a salmon flopping in a net. Baput and Jerry struggled to detach him from the hammock.

Patrick flew across the chasm next, holding the nozzle tightly in both hands while Elmer kept the hose spooling smoothly through a series of loops along the gate, like the air hose for the drill. But this hose wasn't for air. Patrick had had to modify the tank rack in his van to hold the oversized, insulated dewar flask of compressed liquid nitrogen. The stuff scared the hell out of him.

Baput strapped a spelunking helmet with a battery-operated lamp onto G-Pa's raving head, then put a heavy welder's glove on G-Pa's left hand. He strapped the CD player under G-Pa's right arm.

The signal from the Plane was strong. Even with his limited experience, Jerry could feel the difference between getting on the Plane here and at the house. He could see the force lines between the misty-eyed old man in the top-heavy hard hat and a powerful, benevolent, all-knowing force that seemed to come from above and to the left. A force that flowed in a continuous loop between the wizened mystic and the rock of the Cave like a personal magnetic field.

Jerry helped Patrick out of the harness. "Careful," Patrick kept repeating, keeping the hose nozzle out of Jerry's grasp. He reluctantly crossed the platform to where Baput stood in front of the old man. He muttered "careful" twice more as they gently forced the nozzle under G-Pa's right arm, next to the CD player.

"Akash?" Baput kept his face right in front of G-Pa's. They locked eyes. "Do you understand?"

"I am Keebra!" The delight in his eager reply said G-Pa didn't have a clue, but he was ready.

"Tone of Yanzoo." Baput took G-Pa's right hand and brought it up to the play button. "Push here." G-Pa pushed, then lurched frighteningly on the crowded platform as the Tone erupted from the box strapped to his ribs.

Baput turned it off. "Turn it on and leave it. Leave this, too." Baput placed G-Pa's heavily gloved left hand on the nozzle and helped him remove it from the strap. They had practiced this many times with a garden hose.

"Careful!" Patrick hissed. "I don't think he can…"

Baput looked up sharply, catching Patrick's crazy eye. "He can." Looking back at G-Pa, he repeated, "He can."

To G-Pa, he continued: "Crawl all the way to the end. Drop the hose into the chamber and leave it. Turn on the Tone. Take the player off, and leave it on the floor. Then back out. You can't turn around. I don't care how skinny you are. And whatever you do…" he shook his G-Pa a bit, looked deep in his eyes. He seriously couldn't tell if the old man was getting any of this.

"Don't touch the Queen," the Akash recited. Maybe he understood after all.

"Good. What else?"

"Turn on the Tone and leave it. Leave the hose and back out. Don't touch the Queen," G-Pa repeated proudly.

A still-worried glance circled between Baput, Jerry and Patrick.

Baput grasped both of G-Pa's shoulders and breathed his deep Akashic breaths. G-Pa joined him. Baput closed his eyes, focused on his third eye and watched. Colored patterns formed and flowed in a vision so relaxing, he could have stayed in that moment forever.

Then he saw it. The face of a young green man he didn't recognize loomed right in front of him with his eyes closed. *That's me! Through G-Pa's eyes!* Baput realized with a gasp. *I see what he sees!*

With a subtle nod to Jerry and Patrick, Baput folded his legs and sat in meditation pose, in the exact spot where he had sat in his dream.

Patrick guided G-Pa to the hole, coaxing him to lie down and start slithering. "Keebra," he whispered gently over and over, alternating with "careful."

Jerry stood by Patrick's side. Their hearts raced as the old man slithered out of sight into the chimney, with room to spare. Baput twitched slightly, constantly.

Click

Valko's sensitive ears picked up a single, soft click on the slope above. He looked over his right shoulder, catching a whiff of something sweet and warm. *A woman!* He scanned the top of the cliff above the driveway. There, up in West Orchard, was that lovely young woman who talked to Jerry at Fair Grounds. The same young woman who had appeared when Elmer and Francina were not home. He started to reach for Elmer. *Jerry is five cycles now, yet they didn't wed on Passascenday. Their mating must be forbidden.*

Valko looked back up at the dark-haired beauty and smiled. *She is a wild one, like Tamaya. Brave and clever. You need that sometimes, even in a woman... There were many young women at Fair Grounds! His betrothed must be among them. But this one follows him. Secretly. If I tell Elmer, who knows what some old woman might force him to do to her? I will say nothing.*

He withdrew his hand. Elmer's eyes stayed fixed on the scene below. Valko turned to wink his reassurance at the temptress on the cliff. What was that rectangle she held up to her face? Some vain woman's thing, no doubt. He heard another soft click.

Baput

Eyes closed, Baput breathed slowly, deeply, commanding the image into focus. It was as if G-Pa had a camera on his head. The CD player bumped on the uneven floor as G-Pa slithered forward clumsily. Baput tried to make him hold it up off the floor, but he couldn't control this body. *Keebra, don't bang the CD player,* he thought without speaking. He heard the banging cease, felt the body holding the device away from the walls. It was working! He gave a thumbs-up to the group he knew was watching.

Jerry sat down facing Baput. "What's happening, B?"

"Still in the tunnel. Seems like forever," Baput murmured, eyes darting wildly beneath closed lids tipped with thick, dark lashes. "The hose is hung up on a rock!" G-Pa got it loose with only about six "carefuls" from Patrick, as Baput described the action tensely from his trance.

Felkin

Felsic sat on the edge of the Rock, his feet firmly planted on the Earth. He fiddled with his wine bottle, then turned his face to Lorraine, who stood 50 feet away where she could see both the Rock and the platform.

"Do you know why Valko sent me down here, where I cannot see what is happening, with you for my comfort?" he asked her suddenly.

"I didn't realize I was..." Lorraine began. Intrigued and repulsed, she walked over and sat down on the Rock next to him, just out of reach. She thought she felt a faint rumbling of movement from within the cliff behind them. She swallowed. "Why, Felsic?"

"This is how my son died. They said he was downudara. They tried to say I was, too, but I could make the wine so good. I could do other things too, that my son could not. He needed special care. His momama needed to help him dress, and, you know, clean himself. But he could make wine. He took to it naturally, like I did. Like I took to motors when we arrived here. I wonder if he would have been good at motors..."

Is this guy for real? Lorraine wondered. He had managed to get closer, or had she? His breath stank of wine. She forced herself to watch his face closely as he went on with his tragedy.

"It was before Baput was born. He doesn't know. The others do, but no one speaks of it. His name was Felkin. 'Fel,' to be my apprentice, and 'kin' for the zebkin. You call them deer." Felsic had inched up onto the Rock. He lay on his back, propped up on his elbows.

"He was six when they sent him in. He was so small, and he would gladly do whatever you said. Just how they teach us to be. So, why?" Angry tears emerged in reddened eyes.

"They filled one of my wine bottles with a solution that made poison gas. Felkin was to crawl deep into one of the caves where the momama bumblies sleep, covered with nimbly eggs. To commit Insitucide! Against the law!" He cried out, shaking his fist at the sun.

"He must have released the poison gas and died. He never came out. They said it was good. The Curse, you know. He would have died anyway, and killed me and Peratha, too. It is true, for I could not have watched my little Felkin die without holding him in my arms." Tears flowed freely now. "Trillella would never have been born," he squeaked.

Lorraine nodded. "Yes. The pathogen. Did it do any good, Felsic? "Did the nimblies and bumblies die?"

"We never knew. They arrived at the trenches that First Pomegranate Day as always. A few less, maybe, it is hard to say. There are always a few more or less, this cycle and that."

"But were there any from that cave?"

"How would we know? They all come to the Great Hall the same. We don't know who comes from what cave."

"How many caves are there?"

"I don't know," Felsic snapped, waving his outstretched arms in front of him, bottle sloshing. "The caves go on forever, up the river, into the mists."

He produced a second bottle of wine from his tunic. Or was it a third? He was already way beyond his limit, especially for this occasion. Now she understood why. *Nobody told us we were traumatizing this guy. And now, what? I'm his therapist?*

"I'm sorry for your loss, Felsic," she pronounced formally. She rose from the Rock. Tight jeans pinching her long legs, she strode stiffly back to where she could see the action.

Touchdown

The hose rose off the platform and straightened. "That's it!" Patrick cried, donning a glove and grabbing it. "Baput! That's all the hose! He's gotta stop and take it off."

Baput struggled to hold onto both worlds. "G-Pa, Akash, Keebra, stop!" Then he saw it, through the faded eyes of his grandfather, in the glaring light of the headlamp. A round chamber opened up on his right. It was about eight feet across and four feet high, from its ceiling to its floor, which was a couple of feet lower than the corridor where G-Pa was lying. Baput could feel his G-Pa's old muscles ache, Keebra or not. A claustrophobic hope surged in their comingled mind. A place for G-Pa to turn around!

Take off the strap! Baput urged mentally. *Turn on the Tone! Remove the hose and you can go into that chamber and turn around.* Were they Baput's thoughts or G-Pa's? No matter.

G-Pa scanned a column, where a stalactite had dripped dissolved calcium onto a stalagmite below it until the two had joined. His eyes followed it down, from the ceiling to the floor, where Sojourner's wheels lay, freed from their bent axles. The semi-flexible cable bobbed in the void, its camera pointing at a dark, gooey mass that dangled from the ceiling.

Her long, wicked claws clasped a narrow vein of calcite that protruded from the ceiling. Almost two feet long and a foot wide, her slime gleamed dark purple in the blueish light.

"The Queen!" Baput gasped out loud, as the Akash gasped, deep in the cave.

Silently, he directed G-Pa. *The Tone. Turn on the Tone.* G-Pa switched the CD player on. Baput heard the Tone through G-Pa's ears before it saturated the little space and propagated out to the small anxious group on the platform, the two men at the van above, the secret watcher above them, and the uncomfortable duo below.

Baput had to fight the Tone's vibrations to reach G-Pa's mind, just like he would have had to talk louder if they were communicating in the usual way. He could see the Queen writhing uncomfortably on the ceiling.

The hose strained against Patrick's gloved hand. "He's still pulling the hose! Stop him!" Patrick's edgy voice added to the cacophony.

Stop, Akash! Keebra! Baput fought to project his thoughts. *Remove the nozzle. Then go into the chamber and turn around. Don't touch the Queen! Careful! Don't touch her!* His worry threatened to break their connection. He forced himself to breathe slowly, despite the adrenaline that surged. The hose went limp. Patrick relaxed a bit.

Baput grabbed blindly at his left hand with his right. Not quite touching it, he pulled, like he was removing a glove, as G-Pa removed his welding glove. Baput's left arm stretched forward, trembling, as G-Pa's bare hand reached for the Queen.

"G-Pa, no!" Baput cried out loud.

Salistar

Salistar sat at the breakfast bar with Fran and Belinda. They all had glasses of fresh pomegranate juice by their sides, bowls of pomegranate seeds before them, and crates of whole pomegranates at their feet. The TV monitor showed the Queen dangling in her chamber, lit by Sojourner's built-in LED.

Fran suddenly noticed that Star was shaking all over. "Star?" she rushed to her friend's side.

Belinda got up and came around to stand behind her, not sure what to do.

"It's OK, Star," Fran cooed. "They'll be fine. They'll all come back. You'll see."

"No!" Salistar snapped, pulling away. "Is not OK! I am Tether. Akash has turned to Shavarandu. Now, he, my whole family, commits

Insitucide! Don't you see? We are doomed! They have doomed us all, those foolish men and their warrior ways! They have doomed you, too!" Salistar's eyes looked up to regard her friends with unbearable remorse and sorrow. "Since we arrived, Shavarandu has turned his back on you two times. He stayed with you all the years before, even when none of you believed in Kakeeche! He blessed you with a life free of nimblies and bumblies! But now we come and bring not only nimblies and bumblies but the wrath of Kakeeche! Of Shavarandu!" Her head hung, black hair straying into her bowl of stripped seeds. "I am so sorry," she muttered into the gaa, "we have destroyed your world!"

"Star, please," Fran begged, stunned, circling her dear friend with her arms. "It's not your fault. Bel, turn that TV off."

Star pulled away and resumed picking pomegranate seeds from their white honeycombs. "No! I am Tether. I had a hand in this. I must witness it. I must bear it." She bravely looked up at the screen.

"Then we'll bear it with you," Fran promised, and together they faced the screen that showed the Queen in her chamber.

"Popa!" Star cried as the bony, bare hand appeared, shaking in front of the camera, headed straight for the Queen.

The Queen

Unattached, Keebra slithered down into the Queen's relatively spacious chamber where he could stretch his aching muscles and turn around. "Nimbumblyborg!" he whispered reverently to the bundle on the ceiling.

"G-Pa, no!" Baput shouted. He breathed a shuddering breath. *Did he touch it? No. I would have felt the slime.*

Instead of turning around and heading out as instructed, as Baput was screaming in his head to do, the old man lay on his back on the chamber floor, his body twisted around the column. The eyes Baput saw through gazed up at the slimy Queen, writhing in the painful vibrations of the Tone. Baput couldn't see G-Pa's face, but he felt it smile. He felt a surge of tender feelings rush warmly through the data stream.

"No!" Baput cried, out loud this time. "Come back out now, Keebra. We will end this!"

"Poor things." Baput thought the unwelcome thoughts helplessly. "You and me." The Akash addressed the Queen lovingly. "We are the same. We have no place in this world. I have longed all my life for a world without you. Now I can have it. But it is not for me. I cannot live in such a world. The others may go on, but not me. We are one, you and me. We must leave this world together."

Both hands reached out now. Up and to the left, to the wriggling, slimy mass on the ceiling. Rising to his knees, G-Pa placed both hands firmly, one on either side of the black blob. Then he tenderly brought his face up and buried it in blackness.

"Noooooo!" Baput screamed, opening his eyes and standing up so fast, the little platform swayed frighteningly.

The seed shuckers watched in horror as G-Pa's image came into view. The hard hat toppled from the back of his balding head as he brought his face up to the vile mass. He lay his cheek against the monster sheathed in disease. Then he wrapped his arms around it and buried his face in it, like it was the only thing he had ever loved. Slime coated his beard, his hands, his arms, and his chest. Still attached to the ceiling, the blob squirmed between the loving arms like a playful baby. Happy, not dying.

Sacrifice

"He touched it. He embraced it! He's poisoned!" Baput shouted his worst fears out loud.

"Infected," Patrick corrected, looking at Jerry grimly.

"He's a goner." Jerry was frank, as usual.

"Probably contagious," Patrick added.

The boys looked up at their fathers on the driveway with the nitrogen tank.

Valko nodded to Elmer. "He sacrifices himself, like my son did. He had at least as much choice as Batuk did. Let him have his way. Turn it on."

Elmer stood bravely at the back of the van in front of the dewar. "Are you crazy? It will kill him!"

"Is the Tone working?" Valko called down to Baput.

"The Queen squirms but hasn't popped. I can look again."

Baput settled into his meditation pose again. He breathed Akashic breaths. The colors that played across his third eye were brighter than ever. A hole opened up in the swirling curtain, and he could see through his grandfather's eyes again. He saw only shiny, purple blackness.

"G-Pa. What are you doing? Can you hear me? Talk to me!"

"Baput, my apprentice Alanakash, listen carefully." The psychic voice was that of the strong, decisive Akash of Nauve. "I must do this. This is my destiny. You shall tell my story to your children and their children. It will be the Tale of Akash of Earth. The One and Only Akash of Earth, if you do not do as I say!

"Like your brother, Batuk, I do what I must. You know I am not long for this foolish new world. I will not live another cycle. I feel it. Not on this Earth. If we were Nauve, I would mentor you for many, many more years. But we did not go Nauve. Earth Boy failed."

Tears welled in Baput's eyes as G-Pa's voice continued in his head. "Your new world will go on without me, without the nimblies and bumblies, without even Kakeeche to watch over you. You think I don't know, but I see everything now! Your new world is dying. I can't see how it can possibly go on. But it is your world now. The Earth Queen must die. I must die. Apprentice, make the sacrifice. Turn on the gas."

"I cannot."

"YOU MUST!" The Akash's voice rang in his head so loudly, Baput opened his eyes.

Everyone was staring at him. The two at his sides on the platform, the two staring up from the ground, and the two above, jostling at the back of the van. Had they all heard?

"Apprentice?" Valko asked, brows raised.

Baput looked away.

Valko sighed, tried again. "He chooses this. Like Batuk did. You are his Apprentice. You must obey." *This time, anyway,* he thought silently.

Baput managed a weak nod toward his popa. Then he hung his head and closed his eyes again.

Valko reached for the valve.

"I can't let you," Elmer declared, standing firm in front of the tank.

Valko grabbed him by the collar with his giant right hand, picked him up and placed him neatly out of the way while his left hand grabbed the valve and turned it. It squeaked and hissed.

"Let go!" Patrick directed from below. "Do you see any leaks?"

"No. It's cold! It's turning white," Valko reported, backing away.

"Cold," Baput muttered. "So cold!" He shivered noticeably, teeth chattering.

Jerry leaned over him. "Talk to me, B. What's happening?

"The gas. I can see it. It's bouncing all around in little balls. Now it's filling the chamber! My legs are freezing! So co-co-cold! It hurts my lungs to breathe!" he wheezed. "The Queen! The gas is touching her. Enveloping her. She is crystallizing. She's breaking! I can't see. The Akash has gone blind." Baput felt the explosion in his own chest as the frozen heart of his mentor shattered in a thousand shards.

"*Crack!*" a mighty pop resounded all around them as the super-chilled dolomite contracted from the thermal shock. A rumbling noise rose from below.

"It's caving in!" Lorraine yelled, running toward the vine-covered wall. Dust spewed out from behind the vines. Felsic parted the vines, and Lorraine stuck her phone in to illuminate the dark.

The underside of the horizontal chimney had fallen out. A pile of broken rubble littered the ground. They drew back out of the way as more rocks fell, and something else. A crumbled, heart-shaped mass of shiny black-purple. No longer slimy, it lay in sharp, broken crystals commingled with something else:

A thread of sage and lavender, a snake of shattered glass, wrapped around the heart. Keebra. G-Pa. The Akash of Earth.

Ascension

The vision came to Baput without Akashic breathing or even closing his eyes. The Akash looked younger, like at Nauve, but he wore the robe that Momama and Francina had made for him here on Earth. It was spotless, with all the beads intact. He had color in his cheeks and flesh on his bones. He never would have fit in the chimney like this! He was as clear and sharp of mind as he had been at Nauve.

He spoke in a booming voice that no one heard but Baput. "You have done it. You have proven yourself worthy!" he declared, embracing the trembling boy with his disembodied spirit. He began the Succession Litany: "Baput, son of Valko, son of Salistar, grandson of Badon..."

G-Pa's real name! Baput had never heard it before.

"I hereby extend to you the Sacred Longstick and the Holy Seed. All my power, all I have known and learned as Akash, I pass to you by way of the Sacred Longstick. I pass the responsibility of seeing us all into the future by way of the Holy Seed. Having given all I have, I withdraw and relinquish my power. I return Nauve, to the Plane. I return to the stars."

Baput looked around. Everyone was staring at him. He could tell they hadn't heard. It didn't matter. His momama would know it was true when he said G-Pa's real name. Only she knew it, until now. He would wait to announce his Ascension until he could do it in front of her.

Suddenly, he smiled. "No more bumblies! No more nimblies!" The cry The People had sounded for a millennium was finally true! Here on Earth, anyway. They all joined in, Jerry loudest of all.

"No more bumblies! No more nimblies! Not ever! No more!"

12. Bad News/ Good News

When everyone was gathered inside the Musik home, Baput grasped his mother's hands and told her what she already knew. She said nothing, but a mix of resignation and relief stole across her features.

"Momama," Baput said, looking around to make sure everyone heard. "He ascended me. I heard him say the litany, loud and clear. He said I am 'Grandson of Badon.' That's his name, isn't it?"

Salistar nodded, smiling distantly. "Yes. Badon."

"His name is Badon?" Felsic mused. "I never knew that."

"No one knew but me and Akira," Star replied. "So no apprentice could falsely claim ascension in a case like this, when the Akash is…"

She looked toward Valko. The pair stepped forward together to greet their son formally in Nauvian, "Congratulations, Akash. Alanakash!"

"Congratulations, Alanakash!" said the rest, green and white alike.

Suddenly, Star frowned. "Baput, did you say your part?"

Baput looked down at her tearstained face. "What? Why, no! He was gone, as soon as he finished his part."

"You must say your part of the litany. The response. The pledge. You have to say it," Salistar urged.

Valko stood over them, nodding vigorously.

"Yes, Momama, my tether," he grinned to cover how weird that felt. She was to work for him, care for him. She already did, but before, she had been the boss. He looked up at his formidable father. *I'm above him now?*

He stepped forward and stood extra tall. His voice rang out as he spoke the Akashic Litany of Succession:

"The Akashic Power is a manifestation of the Akashic Plane.
It is not a manifestation of me. I am only its conduit.
The wisdom and power of the Akashic Plane is for all the people.
I will never use the power selfishly.
I shall serve all the people equally.

> I shall speak nothing but the truth.
> I shall be kind at all times to all people.
> I shall pursue wisdom diligently, every day of my life, for
> the good of all the people.
> Empathy shall be my guide when ministering to all of the
> people—"

Star cleared her throat.

"I know, Momama. It says, 'ministering to even the least of my people.' But that doesn't make sense, because number two says, 'I shall serve *all* the people equally.' So, who is *least?* There is no least." He did not look at Felsic when he said it. He went on with the ritual.

> "I accept the awesome responsibility of seeking the
> wisdom and wielding the power of the Akashic Plane.
> "I accept the Sacred Longstick of the past Akash, which
> contains his wave form, what he was and what he knew and what
> he continues to be."

"But I have made a new Sacred Longstick for you, my son," Valko rumbled as he handed Baput a brand-new longstick, perfectly straight and intricately etched, tipped with hammered golden metal. Not much of a weapon, but far more beautiful than G-Pa's. "For you will be a new kind of Akash in a new world."

Baput placed the butt on the floor and spun it slowly. The spiraled carvings on the handle swirled hypnotically.

Then he recited the last line.

> "I accept the responsibility of the Holy Seed, to see us all
> into the future."

Salistar stepped forward, extending G-Pa's necklace. She had refreshed the woven pouch and replaced the four Holy Seeds, after removing it in the struggle to dress her popa in those alien clothes. It was Fran's shiny silver leggings that had sold him. He'd been coveting those for nearly a cycle.

Baput bowed his head so his petite momama, um, tether, could slip the necklace over it.

She stepped back. He looked around the silent room. All the green faces were looking at Belinda! Her eyes darted around like a trapped wildcat. What were they all thinking? He had to free her.

He realized she hadn't heard the good news! Neither had Fran or Momama! He boomed a hearty chorus of: "No more nimblies! No more bumblies! Not ever! No more!"

He let the exuberant chant run its course. When it died down, he announced, "We have committed Insitucide this day. The bumblies and nimblies of Earth are no more. We paid a terrible price, but Badon, First Akash of Earth, chose to sacrifice himself. Now, we must bury His Holy Remains, and Momama will prepare a great meal in His honor."

Lorraine made a little squeaking noise. Baput, drunk with power, went a step further. "Belinda and Francina shall assist her."

"You're not *our* Akash, kid," Lorraine snapped.

At the same time, Belinda chirped, "Yes, Akash!"

"Suit yourself," Lorraine hissed over her shoulder as she herded Patrick and Felsic toward the door. "Come on, guys, we've gotta seal that stuff up in concrete, real tight, just in case."

Fran turned to Star. "You heard the Akash. Your kitchen or mine?" she asked warmly.

"I must go to quarters. I will cook," Star replied in a daze.

"No, Honey. You shouldn't be by yourself at a time like this. On Nauve, you would have others near you, yes? Other women?"

"Yes," Star whispered, head down. "I must get, um, things for the meal. I will make his favorite, sprouted pomegranate seed cakes with berries on top." Her face lifted as she spoke of food, then it fell. "Of course, he will not be here to enjoy it." She headed for the door without looking at Fran or Bel.

"Wait!" Fran called after her. "We'll help you!"

Star kept walking.

"If you don't come back in 20 minutes we're coming over there and invading your kitchen! Do you hear me?"

Star turned back to her, a vague, distant smile on her lips. "Yes, Francina." She replied in a mockingly formal tone. She giggled, a hysterical out-of-control burble. "I'll be back," she promised, but Fran didn't believe her.

Burial

Jerry and Baput walked together behind the Jeep and trailer that carried a cement mixer, water jugs, several sacks of cement mix, a hand pump so you could squirt a watery mix of the stuff, and Lorraine's personal protective equipment. They passed the empty stone sauna on their way to the jumbled mass of frozen, shattered cells that were already starting to melt into an indistinguishable ooze.

"Congratulations, B!" Jerry clapped his friend on the shoulder.

"Thanks," Baput said comfortably.

"You got away with it."

Baput stopped walking for a second and looked at Jerry with those wrinkled brows. "What do you mean?"

"What about Rule 7, wasn't it? Leave the women stuff alone. What happened to that?"

Baput mumbled the ritual quickly, counting on his figures. "It is not in the litany. I think G-Pa made it up."

"My mom thinks Akira did," Jerry blurted.

Baput looked at him sideways, his eyelids lowered.

Jerry grinned his grin. "What about the Kakeeche part?"

"Kakeeche part?"

"You know. The part where you swear your allegiance to Kakeeche, to always believe in them and never doubt them? Where was that?"

"That is not part of the Akashic litany," Baput's answer started out swift and sure, but in eight words it turned into a question that shook him to the core.

Jerry pounced. "You mean, you don't have to believe in Kakeeche to be Akash?"

"I guess," Baput explored the new idea. "I always thought..."

"I'd say, Your Holiness, that by the letter of the law, you do not," Jerry concluded like a Philadelphia lawyer.

Baput stood on the Holy Rock in his Akashic robe, holding his golden-tipped longstick, droning a funeral rite in Nauvian. In the background, Lorraine sprayed concrete over the pile of dolomite rubble stained with green and silver ooze. She looked more alien than anyone else in her blue nitrile gloves and white hazmat suit she'd "borrowed" from the Environmental Department at work, and an N95 face mask left over from when they had returned from their evacuation to finish that summer in a cloud of smoke.

Jerry and Patrick stood among the Cave's frozen waves, watching the liquid concrete belch through the air.

"What is it, Uncle Patrick?" Jerry asked in a whisper. "The portal, the Net, the Rock, what was it all for, really? And why did they cover it up?"

Patrick looked down at the troubled blue eyes. "I don't know," he answered softly, "But when you have tech that high, and you try to bury it, it's like trying to cover up a volcano."

The grout sputtered as the vessel emptied. Lorraine stripped off the protective gear, revealing tight-fitting street clothes. She threw all the PPE on top of the goopy pile and blasted it with the last of the runny cement. "Load up the trailer," she ordered the men. "You kids ride. Stay away from me. I'm heading straight to that nasty old shower in the back of the shop."

Sobeyata

Star walked the familiar path from Francina's house to the quarters in a fog. She didn't see the fall garden on her right, with its bright green leaves and red stems of chard, the oranges of butternut squash and pumpkin. Beyond it was the grassy area where her popa, the Akash, had led the paltry First Full Kakeeche Ceremony last cycle. It would be different this time, two weeks from now.

Francina was right. At Nauve, there would be *Sobeyata*, Sharing of Grief. The women closest to her would cook with her, share the dishes, even spend the night if they felt a dangerous tension in the home. Men would share their grief by passing wine around a fire.

But Nauve was so different! Everyone at Nauve had lost at least one close family member, usually more than one over the course of a lifetime. *How can Francina share my grief?* Star wondered. *She lives in a world without nimblies and bumblies. A world without death, it seems! Her parents still live, and her brother, though I have never seen them. Perhaps what she calls "town" is really death? But she "goes to town" all the time, rolling down the hill in her box. Gone, then here again.* She practiced the concept.

Francina has never lost a child. They have only one! So do Lori Anne and Patrick. They can afford to have only one child and expect it to live to adulthood! I can't imagine what it would be like to never have lost Batuk or Cilandra. Francina is my best friend, all I have in this world. I will share with her. But Belinda is too young.

Girls under 15 did not share in Sobeyata unless they were grieving for one of their immediate family. *It is bad luck to bring a younger girl into the Sharing if she has no grief!* Star thought angrily. *It means she will surely have some in the next cycle. Baput should have known that! He has had such poor training since we arrived, since Popa...*

She opened the door of the quarters. G-Pa's scent assaulted her in a way she had never noticed before. She looked over at his chair in the corner. Shastina, on her bed with her pups, raised her head and looked at her with knowing eyes. Star looked back, wordlessly confirming. Shastina tilted back her majestic, silvery lavender head, pointy snout straight up. Surrounded by her babies, she howled a long, mournful howl that curdled

Salistar's blood. Brodey, confined in the house next door for fear of the Curse, responded in kind.

Star crossed the room to Shastina and sat down on the floor beside her and her puppies. She picked up a lavender one and held it gently to her chest.

Her popa was gone. She tried to remember him. Not the recent shell of a man, but the Akash before, back at Nauve. She stared at the empty chair and tried to recall a happy memory. She turned toward the door. It was as if a pile of junk were stacked up in front of the door, so she couldn't open it. Junk like the constant mumbling and drooling. The, um, messes. Fortunately, not too many, but more frequent, lately. Those hollow, black eyes. The stubbornness. The conflicting orders. The constant complaints and occasional tantrums if a meal was late or not to his liking. The unreasonable bossiness, even when he didn't understand what was going on. He had been more burden than help since their arrival, when they needed his spiritual guidance the most. Her twelve-year old son had had to step into that role. And then the old gapta denied his ascension!

She tried to see beyond that pile of shattered pots and spilled gaa to the Akash of before. The strong, sure Akash of Nauve. She could remember things, but she couldn't feel them. Intellectually, she realized he had been the same, just stronger. Defying the rules and endangering the people for what she now realized was his own ego! Bossy, stubborn, treacherous, brutal at times, always selfish, partly responsible for Batuk's death... *And dear little Felkin, I used to hold him on my lap, alongside my Batuk. Both gone now, because of him!*

She knew her popa had never been any of the things Baput had just promised to be in the succession litany. A promise Badon had made too, so many years ago, before she was born.

She closed her eyes and breathed like she had seen him breathe, like Baput was trying to teach her. She tried to focus on one true feeling of love for him, buried deep in the cluttered past. She saw his young face. She was looking up at it, like she was a small child. She gasped in surprise at the blackness of his beard and eyebrows.

She remembered the moment. He had started to smile, just a little. Then, he seemed to remember something and the smile vanished. "Why aren't you a boy?" he asked his little girl.

Star's eyes flew open. The image vanished. There was no refuge. No happy, loving moment to cling to. Only the desert of a life spent tending to an ungrateful, selfish man. The door slammed shut. No more past. No more Nauve. Not ever. No more. No going back. Only forward.

She took stock. *The Old Akash is gone. He leaves us here in this strange world. Even the nimblies and bumblies are gone. And the portal didn't open on First Pomegranate Day.*

Baput was Akash now. Her son. She was still tether. Her successor, Baput's betrothed, Tamaya, was also behind that locked door. Baput carried the Holy Seed, to carry the people forward. She looked down at the mixed puppies and thought of Belinda.

Belinda, from otherwhere, is somehow here, in that house right next door with my new best friend. Francina. Yes, the future was here on Earth with these colorless, kind people who lived on the Look'N Up Ranch, hidden from the otherwheres of their own world.

Shastina rumbled a low growl. "Sorry," Star muttered, thinking she was crowding the laden dog, who suddenly jumped to her feet and lumbered to the door, barking furiously. Brodey replied from next door.

Even Star could tell the engines she heard were not the Jeep, the four-wheeler, the truck, or the plumbing van. Shastina barked frantically as four doors slammed outside. Fran yelled something.

The quarters' door flew open. Two big men barged in, meaty, not muscular, with swollen, flabby jowls. They had close-cropped brown hair under bill caps like Jerry wore. Shastina ran at them, pushing them back with her chest, snarling and spitting through long canines and raised upper lip.

They didn't look as strong as Valko, but they had guns. Star knew what those could do. She ordered Shastina back and let one of the men grab her by the arm and force her out to the porch. He smelled of smoke, but bitter, not like Patrick's sweet scent.

Shastina stood tight by Star's side, lips curled, glancing back toward the house and her puppies while the other man searched the bedrooms with a pointed rifle.

Brodey bounded down the steps ahead of Fran and jumped on a burly, balding man from the second truck. Fran grabbed the hysterical dog by the collar right before he sunk his teeth into the guy's arm. The other man from the second truck, thin and bespectacled, with curly black hair, stayed back, away from the dog. Fran recognized them both.

"Cody Redmond! Ian Grant!" Fran scolded. "What do you think you're doing? Busting into our houses with guns?"

Ian replied, forcing his way past the bluffing dog and grabbing Fran by the arm. "You've got those aliens here." He pointed to Star, being escorted toward them roughly by the two other men. "They brought monsters that are killing people. So they gotta go. Everyone in town agrees. So where are they, Fran?"

Ian shook Fran roughly, then dragged her to a third pickup truck that had just arrived. She struggled the whole way, screaming about her rights.

Deputy Otto emerged from the third pickup to meet her. His uniform reassured her for a second. But, *that hat surely isn't part of the uniform! And why is he in a private pickup, not a patrol car? Why aren't the rest of these men in uniform? Cody and Ian aren't policemen! They're pomegranate farmers, just like us!*

"Hello, Deputy," she began tentatively. Was this the guy Elmer had told her about, who wanted to lock up the green people?

"Mrs. Musik?" Otto guessed. Fran gulped.

The barbeque in Sheriff Dave's backyard was just coming up to temperature when his cell phone rang. He didn't recognize the number, and the caller spoke quietly. He finally made out, "Belinda Musik."

"Hey, girl!" he greeted her jovially. He liked the kid. Cockeyed or not, she was a cutie. "Which is it now, the bimblies or the numblies?" he asked, proud he remembered the beasts' names.

"It's your deputy." The grave tone didn't match the young girl's voice.

Dave's head spun, although he wasn't surprised. "What?"

"That guy with the buzz cut that was riding with you? He's here at the Look'N Up, in uniform, with a bunch of guys in pickup trucks who aren't in uniform. They've got my aunt, and Baput's mom, and they're holding them with guns!"

"Where are the guys?" Dave carried the phone into the house from the patio, headed for his uniform.

"They're burying G-Pa. We killed the Queen, Sheriff! The nimblies and bumblies are gone!"

"What happened to your grandpa?" Dave pulled on his jacket, mouthing to his wife, "I gotta go."

"Not my G-Pa. Baput's. You know, the old man. He died killing the Queen. He sacrificed. But you're coming, right? I'm scared."

"I'm on my way, Doll," Dave reassured her, getting in the patrol car. Through the phone, Belinda heard the siren start to wail.

Deputy Otto hadn't had much trouble finding like-minded friends in his new community. They didn't like the changes they were seeing. People looked different. The grocery stores and restaurants offered Mexican food, even Indian and Thai. People walked down the street speaking foreign languages. They were illegal, swarthy, and they took all the good jobs. Otto had organized his new friends into a chapter of the Right Identity Doctrine, or RID, and they had alerted the LA Headquarters about the green aliens. That's why Dirk was here with him.

Now Otto stared coldly into Fran's furious face. He was used to seeing pissed-off women, but wow!

Restrained by two men she knew from co-op meetings, school events, her parents' feed store... *They play Beer League Softball with Elmer! How could they?* Fran fumed.

She didn't know the large dull-eyed man with the sour, pock-marked face who remained in the driver's seat of his jacked-up pickup with the window rolled down, staring over Otto's shoulder. She squirmed and spat before them. "You're not a real cop. Or, if you are, you're not on police business! You let go of me and leave, all of you, this instant!"

Otto grilled her. "Where are the rest of the aliens? The two men and the boy? The old geezer? Lady, you're in a lot of trouble, hiring illegals. You better turn them in right now, and we might go easy on you."

"And just who is 'we?'" Fran demanded.

The rumble of the Jeep and the rattle of the trailer emerged from the river trail and accelerated through the grassy area.

Hate

Elmer's hackles rose when he saw three pickup trucks parked in front of the houses. *That's Ted Bates and Ian Grant and ...* Three men stood outside the house surrounding Fran with rifles! One of them had a sheriff uniform on. *That skinhead deputy!* Two more armed men stood outside the quarters, holding Star.

"Momama!" Baput cried, rushing forward on the trailer.

Valko roared and started to climb from the back seat of the moving Jeep. Felsic accelerated, knocking him back. The trailer bounced crazily. Patrick, Jerry, and Baput struggled to hold on. Behind them, Lorraine broke into a run. The men in front of the house raised their guns at them.

"What the hell?" cried Elmer, clamoring out of the Jeep while it was still rolling. "Cody! Ian! What? You're gonna shoot us? Fran?"

"Fran's OK, we ain't gonna shoot you or your wife. Just these green freaks!" Ian replied, releasing Fran.

Brodey at her heel, Fran rushed to the porch of the quarters, where the two men held Salistar's hands together behind her. Shoving angry men out of her way like rag dolls, Fran threw her arms around Star, loosening a sweaty man's brutal grip.

Now at close range, she recognized the two. "Bobby Jackson, Ted Bates! You should be ashamed of yourselves, manhandling an innocent woman like that! Your wives would be ashamed!"

"No, they wouldn't." Bobby's voice was thick with resentment. "They sent us! Those things are gonna kill our kids!"

"Salistar wouldn't kill anyone, for goodness' sake!"

Brodey and Shastina converged, shoulder to shoulder between the embracing women and the invading men. Hackles raised, they advanced in unison, taking small steps, low growls rumbling from deep inside their chests. The men backed up toward the quarters' door.

Fran grabbed Star's shoulders and pushed her through the opening. With the dogs at their flanks, they rushed past the armed standoff to the trailer, where Baput waited with Jerry and Patrick.

"Stay here," Fran ordered. "You, too, Jerry." She felt a sudden stab of unbearable pain as she remembered Salistar's story, when she had told Cilandra and Tamaya to stay put, right before she lost Cilandra. For the second time, she could almost imagine how it would feel to lose Jerry. In shock from this imagined pain, Fran bravely joined the "front line," where Valko, Felsic, and Elmer were locked in a staring contest around the barrels of Cody's pistol, Ian's shotgun, and Rod Otto's sheriff-issued semi-automatic rifle. Shastina and Brodey stood alongside their pack with hackles raised and teeth bared.

Ted and Bobby stepped up beside their mates and raised their guns.

Ian was apparently the spokesman. "They gotta go!" he articulated.

Elmer swallowed and stepped up to him. "Ian, put the gun down. These people ain't done nothing to you."

"They brought those monsters! Their vermin! And they killed someone! They all gotta go!" Ian's mouth was drawn back, making sharp lines on his cheeks. Every muscle in his neck and arms was tense. He breathed hard and shallow.

"Hate?" Baput asked Jerry in a whisper.

"Hate," Jerry confirmed.

Dirk, who had driven Otto, finally stepped out of his truck. His pale eyes studied the green faces with monotonous dullness. He wasn't from around here. He was a city boy, sent from the LA Headquarters of RID to check out a story some sheriff's deputy from an online chapter in the sticks was tweeting about a libtard sheriff who was letting illegal aliens work on an American farm. *Only it's a pomegranate farm, and they're green aliens from outer space. They brought flying monsters that eat Mexicans, and the sheriff won't do anything about it,* Dirk remembered, shaking his head. *I believe in the Cause with all my heart,* he had resolved as he sped through the desert, but he had to admit that some of his "brothers" were full-on wackos.

But here they were, green aliens. And pomegranates. He had watched Cody's truck squash a few of the weird purple balls on the way up that so-called driveway.

Dirk finally spoke, stepping forward to scrutinize Felsic's face. "What the hell are you? You're green. Goddamn." He noticed Felsic's muscles, too. Felsic stared back, twitching.

"They're aliens!" Bobby declared. "We should call the Men in Black. They'll lock 'em up and do experiments on 'em! They'll get rid of all the flying monsters, too."

"We already got rid of the monsters. They're all dead," the blond kid spoke up without being asked.

"Two kinds of aliens," Dirk observed belatedly, finally noticing a weird-looking guy back by the Jeep with two boys—one blond and one green—and a definitely human redhead who stood strangely apart.

Bobby lowered his gun without thinking, in his rush to correct the outsider. "Nah. The cockeyed ones are OK. Just occasional mutations of Elmer's folks. From Earth. From right here on this spot, in fact."

"Take your guns off us then," Patrick said coldly.

They ignored Patrick's request, but Bobby continued to defend him. "They're freaks, but they're our freaks."

"Their dad was a freak too," Cody offered, suddenly chummy.

"Yeah, in two ways," Ted quipped, giggling.

Bobby watched his former classmate squirm while they talked about his family. *He was really a kick to know once you got past that crazy eye alignment,* Bobby recalled. He looked down at the gun that dangled from his hand, suddenly wondering what he was doing, holding his old friend and his family at gunpoint. Hoping he could make the whole thing go away, he told the Musik story.

"Freak by choice. Yeah, he went wandering off to San Francisco in the sixties. He was right there in Haight-Ashbury for the Summer of Love. Then he grew weed up in Humboldt for a while, but he came back after his big brother got killed in 'Nam. Took over the farm, turned it organic. He had that eye, like Patrick, here. His dad did, too. Ran this same farm, except it was almonds back then. So the cockeyed ones are OK. We're just here for the green ones." It didn't make sense anymore, when he said it out loud. Gun barrels wavered.

With so many eyes and guns on him, Patrick blurted what was on his mind. "Where's my daughter?"

Deputy Otto jumped into action. "Dirk, get in there and search the house! There's someone in there! A cockeyed little girl, like him."

Dirk whirled and sprinted toward the house.

"Shit! I'm such an idiot!" Patrick covered his eyes with his fists.

Elmer lunged against Ian and his shotgun. "You got a warrant?" he demanded. "You ain't even cops! Stay the hell outta my house!"

Ian jammed his shotgun into Elmer's ribs and cocked it.

Dirk reached the porch steps just as Belinda stepped out. "Here I am," she offered. Her left eye flew up and to the left, scanning furiously.

"Wow!" Dirk muttered, "Worse than her dad!"

Belinda leveled her left eye right into his, as if she had G-Pa's Evil Eye. Dirk backed up, unable to break her gaze, until he tripped on a rock and fell over backwards on his butt in the driveway.

"Yeah, she's ours, she's from here," the locals claimed between hoots and giggles.

Patrick whispered to Jerry, "I thought only I was that scared of her!"

"Only you knew her power, until now," Jerry surmised as he watched his cousin stride down the stairs right past Dirk, tossing her wild red hair and snubbing him with her tiny nose. He noticed Baput wasn't breathing.

A single siren rose in the west, coming up the county road.

"Finally, your backup!" Cody slapped the young deputy on the shoulder. Otto didn't seem relieved. The siren stopped, and the patrol car crackled up the long gravel grade. Otto lowered his gun and turned away from the tense standoff. He faced the driveway, his eyes darting toward Dirk's truck.

Sheriff Dave hoisted his slightly overweight mass out of the patrol car and looked across the roof at his week-old deputy and his posse of... *what?*

"Otto?" he bellowed, "What's going on?"

"The people are protesting, Sheriff Riley."

"A few of them, I guess," the sheriff responded, not overly impressed with the ragtag group of six who had all turned their backs on their unarmed captives and seemed to be looking to him for guidance. "What's your, um, issue, exactly?" He closed the door and came forward, hand on the revolver in his holster.

Otto explained his group's current position as he understood it. "We know the cockeyed ones are us. But Manuel, he was one of us, too."

"The line keeps moving," Dave muttered, hoping vainly.

"But them green ones, they ain't us! They gotta go! One way or another," Otto concluded. Murmurs of agreement echoed from most of the armed men.

With painful regret welling up in his gut, Cody stepped toward the sheriff. He'd known him since boyhood. "Dave, these guys just ain't ready to deal with a whole 'nuther race!"

"Well, then don't deal with them! Just leave 'em alone!" the sheriff snapped.

Ian wasn't having it. "If we let them stay, pretty soon there'll be thousands of them! Then we'll *have* to deal with them. They'll be on welfare, taking our jobs, and ruining our neighborhoods like the Mexicans do. Look, there's just these few here now, right? We should just kill them all right now!"

The group stared, silently, open mouthed, even Otto.

Ian kept going. "They're aliens! It's not like you're killing *people*!"

Dave hated raising his gun on his fellow citizens, including his own staff, but he did so, pointing straight at the errant deputy. "OK, that does it. No one is killing anybody here today. Otto, come here."

Otto lowered his police-issued assault rifle and approached his boss.

"Give me the gun," Dave said quietly. "And take that hat off."

Otto kept his RID hat on, but he raised the rifle harmlessly, pointed straight up. He slowly extended it to the sheriff, who grabbed it.

"And your badge."

"Sheriff..." Otto protested in a dry squeak.

"You can't wear that hat and that badge. You made your choice. You're fired," Sheriff Dave explained flatly. "Abuse of the uniform. Abuse of firearms. False imprisonment. Illegal search and seizure. Assault with a deadly weapon. I could get you all for that one!"

"Breaking and entering," Elmer added. "That gate was locked!"

"How about attempted genocide?" Patrick snarled, his daughter wrapped in his arms.

Dave's quiet voice grew louder and angrier as he went on listing charges. "You took the law into your own hands, directly against my orders. I told you to leave this alone! It's handled. No more monsters. The young lady told me. I'll take care of Manuel's family, somehow. A guy you would have all been calling an alien, just last week! Now 'he's one of us,' 'cause he's from Earth. Well, you know what? We don't know what's out there, and sooner or later we're gonna have to deal with them. Maybe that day is here, for us. But I don't want this getting out. I've fought side by side with these guys, and I don't want to see them hauled off and cut up by the government for experiments."

A long, pathetic squeak rose from Belinda.

Dave let that poignant sound sink in, then went on telling the heavily armed group how it was going to be. "Now you guys are all gonna rack your guns and go home. Otto's coming back in the patrol car with me to be processed out. If he behaves himself, I *might* not arrest him. You guys aren't gonna see any more green people or flying monsters. And they're not gonna see you. Everybody lives in peace. Live and let live. Got it?"

Cody, Bobby, and Ted unloaded their guns. "I thought you were a cop, Otto," Cody scrambled for distance. "I thought we were helping, like Neighborhood Watch. Dave, I didn't know he was going against your orders, or I never would have come."

Not impressed by the after-the-fact obsequiousness, Dave just said, "Get out of here."

"Sorry, Elmer," Cody apologized without looking back as he headed to Ted's truck to bum a ride. He didn't feel like riding home with Ian.

"Yeah, sorry, Elmer," Bobby and Ted echoed, racking their guns. They climbed into the wide bench seat on either side of Cody, slammed the doors and chugged down the rough driveway in low gear.

"Now, you two. Unload and get out!" Dave ordered Dirk and Ian.

"Wait a minute, Sheriff." Ian was still not ready to quit. "They're illegal aliens, right? You gotta bust the farmers, don't you?"

"You're a farmer, too, Ian!" Elmer bellowed, raising his arms to pound on Ian's chest, gun or no gun. "You mean you've never hired an undocumented before? It's harvest time! We need them or we can't get the crop in!"

Ian had his prejudices, but he was not an unreasonable man. At least, not when it came to people with whom he shared something in common, like pom farming. He could relate to Elmer, just not those alien invaders. "OK. Tell you what. They stay and help with the harvest, then they go back where they came from. And we're gonna come back and check!"

"Hell no! You ain't coming back here ever!" Elmer shouted into Ian's face, disregarding the still-cocked rifle between them.

"I'll do it," Dave offered.

Elmer turned away from Ian to stare at him. "What are you saying, Sheriff?"

"I'm offering a solution. Finish the harvest. Then I'll come and check in say, a month? Is that enough time?"

"Two months," Elmer bargained automatically.

"And they'll be gone by then, right?" Dave confirmed. "And no more nimblies and bumblies, right?"

"That part's right," Elmer agreed. "But I need these guys year 'round. And," he pulled Dave aside and whispered, "They can't go home."

"Are they refugees?"

"Well, from them flying things maybe. But they can't go back. It was an accident. A space portal thing. They don't know how it works."

"Don't worry," Dave whispered back, winking.

"Oh, no!" Otto, already out of a job, decided to fight again. "Not you, Sheriff," he sneered with the disrespect he had been trying to hide all week. "*These* guys get to inspect. Ian here, and Dirk. Not me. I'm out of this hick town. Make him let you inspect, guys. You can't trust him! He'll lie!"

"Yeah," Ian agreed.

Dirk grunted and started unloading his gun.

Dave sighed and looked at Elmer, who pursed his lips and pulled them to the left side of his face. He chewed his cheek angrily as his fate was decided.

"OK," Dave agreed as Elmer's heart sank. "Two months from today. Ian, or, what's your name, Dirk? You will *accompany* me on an inspection. Then another at harvest time next year, if you're still worried about it. Elmer, if they're here then, I'll have to arrest you for hiring undocumenteds. I don't know what will happen to them, once ICE finds out what they are. So let's find a safe place for them, OK?" his voice had gentled as he spoke, but the Musiks looked at him as if he was stabbing them. "Best I can do, guys, to keep this quiet. Sorry."

Ian, Dirk, and Otto grunted obscure agreement to the plan. The sheriff collected their phone numbers so they could arrange the future inspections. Ian and Dirk climbed into their pickups and headed down the driveway. Sheriff Dave put his hand on Otto's head and forced him into the back seat of the patrol car like a criminal.

At the back of his car, he faced a fuming Elmer backed by a crowd of red and green faces with puffed chests, or worse, slumped shoulders and downcast, miserable eyes. Behind them, a redheaded gazelle sprinted for the back of the shop.

Dave holstered his gun and addressed the group. "I'm sorry, but you guys have to hide, somehow. I've already got my hands full covering up what happened to Manuel and keeping the FBI out of here, thank you very much." He focused on Belinda, not at all frightened of her eye. "And no more talking about burying your G-Pa, understand? All I need is another body..." he trailed off.

"Taken care of," Elmer stated flatly, arms folded across his chest. "Like I told you. We got this."

Dave reached out and touched his old friend's tense forearm. "Get rid of them," he whispered, "or something worse will happen—and I won't be able to stop it."

Sanctuary

Lorraine stripped and tossed her clothes into the old washer in the "cleanup room" at the back of the shop. It had been set up long ago, for jobs that were just too nasty to bring into the house, like the organic fertilizer Patrick's dad used to make out of pig shit. She stepped into the grimy shower, grateful for the flip flops Fran had provided.

Felsic's wine fermented in the middle of the room. *That guy better not come in here*, she thought as the frustratingly tepid water cascaded down her pert breasts and wiry shoulders. *Can a still in progress be moved?* She wondered. *What am I thinking? Where would they take it? Where can they go?* The obvious answer sprang to mind, and with that thought she boarded the train that wandered the ups and downs of the sudden and inevitable changes in her future.

Patrick already had witnessed his share of pre-teen drama, but he'd never seen Belinda in a state like this. She accosted him as he came out of the bathroom and literally dragged him into the room where his beloved model of the solar system brooded over their conversation.

"Daddy! They can't stay here anymore. Can they come home with us and stay in our workers' quarters like before? Salistar can take care of me after school. I like her cooking, even though it's no meat. I don't care. We've gotta help them!"

"You're very friendly with Baput," Patrick stated the obvious.

"Dad, I love him. What's wrong with that?"

"He's from another planet!" Patrick glanced at the model.

"That's prejudice, Dad! That's not what you taught me at all."

"It's not that, sweetheart." They locked eyes in their unique way. "I love Baput, too," he assured her. "He's a great guy, but we'd have to hide them forever, Baby. That's no life for my girl."

"I hide anyway, Dad." Belinda's reply stung him. "And if we don't take them, where can they go? They have to hide somewhere, or else the Men in Black will cut them into pieces and do tests on them," she wheezed through choking breaths.

"The sheriff shouldn't have said that."

"Is it true?"

Patrick wasn't sure, but he had to reassure his baby girl. "They might hold them captive in a lab and run tests on them. I doubt they would cut them up. Not Baput, anyway. He's too valuable alive. Valko would probably get himself killed trying to save them, and then…"

Belinda burst into tears.

"I'll talk to your mother."

Dinner

The more-than-adequate leftovers were the centerpiece of the quietest dinner ever to occur in the Musik kitchen. Somehow, the utensils didn't even clink.

At last, Fran stepped into the void, her voice thick. "What did they say, Jerry, when you walked them to the quarters?"

"They don't get it," Jerry answered without looking up from his plate. "It's otherwhere stuff to them."

"They can cook for us," Patrick began his unnecessary pitch.

Lorraine let him dangle, just for fun. "Vegetarian," she scoffed.

"I'll cook meat for you, Babe," Patrick promised, "for as long as you need it."

Lorraine rolled her eyes at the apparently temporary promise.

"They can look after Bel after school when I have a plumbing job."

"They'll have her pregnant the first chance they get!"

"Mom!" Belinda screamed and ran out of the room.

Jerry leveled his eyes at his aunt. "Baput wouldn't do that."

"I'm not worried about Baput," Lorraine said darkly.

Horrified, Fran asked, "Who, then? How could you possibly think—?"

"Salistar," Lorraine declared. "She's grooming my daughter to be some kind of handmaid. Just a baby maker, a housewife, and nothing more."

Fran rose to her feet. "Oh, Lorraine. Empathize. What if you were facing extinction? The last of your people, here on Earth anyway."

"Exactly!" Lorraine agreed.

Jerry stared daggers at his callous aunt. "Star needs my mom," he declared through narrowed eyes.

"She'll have me," Belinda promised as she crept back into the room.

Fran smiled tenderly at her kind-hearted niece. "Baput needs Jerry," she added.

"He'll have me," said Patrick.

"So it's done," Elmer croaked around a lump in his throat.

Thanksgiving

Their last dinner together had been the quietest ever, but Thanksgiving 2017 still broke the record for quietest Thanksgiving. Once again, Francine served a turkey, and Belinda helped make the pumpkin-pomegranate stuffing, forever to be a family tradition.

The green people's stuff was loaded into the windowless van, leaving just enough space to transport four undocumented aliens.

Fran broke the silence. "Star will cook her little heart out for you, but one of you has to buy the food. It has to be organic."

"Why?" Lorraine asked tensely.

"They're not used to our chemicals. They have no resistance, I guess," Fran explained, again.

"It's expensive," Lorraine objected. After almost two months, she hadn't run out of arguments. Yet, the plan for abducting the aliens and bringing them home proceeded unabated.

"Cheaper than take-out all the time," Patrick countered. "Better for Bel. Better for the planet. You know that, Lor!"

"Yeah, of course. I'm just, doing the math…" Lorraine trailed off.

Fran explained again how it worked. "That's how you pay them. You pay them a wage, on paper, and deduct their expenses. They're more than worth it. You'll see."

"You're running a big farm. What are they going to do at our place?" Lorraine countered.

That argument struck a chord with Elmer. "Yeah. They need work. You got one of them new-fangled computer cars Felsic can't work on. Baput would probably be better with your car." Elmer swatted at Lorraine dismissively. "But they're mainly pom farmers. You got what? Six trees?"

"Twelve, including the ones in the pots," Patrick replied without thinking.

Elmer caught on quickly. "You mean the ones you planted, right?"

Patrick looked closely at his stuffing, then up at his brother. "Well, see, there's a job for them right there."

Elmer eyed his brother fondly. "They can tend your wacky plants, too, I suppose. Are you gonna grow a whole bunch of those now?"

"No," Lorraine snapped. "It's illegal to grow more than six without a permit. And we'd get inspected. Can't have that."

Fran nodded. "Now you're talking. Sorry, but that's how you'll have to think now. It puts a crimp in your social life."

"Don't worry, Aunt Fran," Belinda reassured her. "We're used to hiding freaks, huh, Mom."

Goodbyes

The stricken green faces looked on helplessly as their white-skinned friends loaded the last of their possessions, including six more potted pomegranate trees from the greenhouse, Earth variety. Baput wore his fancy Akashic robe and clung, white-knuckled, to his showy longstick. He hadn't looked at his best friend all day.

Jerry brought him the story recorder. "Keep recording your stories," he urged, "for when the world is ready."

Baput took the recorder. Then he grasped Jerry's shoulder gently with his free hand, piercing his soul with those bottomless brown eyes. He addressed Jerry as if he were addressing the whole planet. "At Nauve, we war with the nimblies and bumblies, but they are animals. Predators. You people war with other people. You kill other people because of the color of their skin. Those men, they didn't even know us, but they hated us! They came here and put their guns on my Momama! They ruined everything we had here, just because we're green!" He looked into Jerry's teary blue eyes and spoke to a place deep inside them. "You were born and raised in a world full of hate, my friend. But I have more hate in my heart than you do."

The dark eyes turned away, and Baput disappeared into the shadowy depths of the van.

Sharing in battle breeds trust, even if one is a pacifist. Patrick had agreed to let Belinda ride in the back with the green aliens. Lorraine decided she'd ride in back, too.

Belinda pecked Fran on the cheek. "Bye, Jerry," she chirped, rushing past him to find her spot in the van, the one Felsic had recommended last time, across from Baput. They sat in silence, a shaft of light from the back door lying between them, listening to intermittent snatches of long grown-up goodbyes.

The tension shattered when Felsic loaded the puppies into the van. Lassen and Tehama, Toby and Goldilocks exploded into the vehicle, exploring its contents with blunt noses and clumsy paws and smacking its occupants with their little tails. Belinda giggled. The Alanakash giggled, too.

Felsic helped Shastina in, raising her rear end effortlessly. He climbed in after her and occupied his mattress. "Ready *go*, kids?" he asked cheerfully, pronouncing the strange word naturally, like an Earth person.

Lorraine loaded in last. She curled her lip at the stained mattress where her daughter sat, right across from that kid and his mother. She took a seat next to her.

The van started to roll. Star leaned over and peered keenly at Lorraine. "Have you told her the tale?" she asked. Her eyes implied something Lorraine couldn't have comprehended, even in the best of light.

"Excuse me, what?" Lorraine retorted.

"No, Momama!" the Alanakash pleaded.

Star sat firm. "She must be told: Romey was betrothed to Cinnimar. Jakima was betrothed to Eelak."

Baput switched the recorder on and watched Lorraine and Belinda's reactions. *Let her hear the tale,* he decided. *She needs to know the consequences of what could be, so she knows why it can't be.*

The ride smoothed, and the speed grew monotonous. The engine droned, and passing trucks pounded on the sides of the van. Felsic and Valko slept. The familiar words of the gruesome tale washed over Baput. He inhaled deep, calm Akashic breaths. No G-Pa, no Jerry, no Patrick. He ascended alone.

He found himself in the Holy Cave on Nauve. The Weapon was assembled. The pipes lay on the Rock, the Net draped over them, ready to fire.

The Net! Baput stared, trying to memorize the fabric, the weave, but there was too much going on. Teal-skinned men and women in tight, shiny clothing scurried all around him. He didn't know them, but they were so familiar!

The Great Horn sounded. A ganeesh tusk, freely given and hollowed out by some ancient ancestor, its round tone rose all around him, enveloping him until it was all he knew. Then he remembered what it meant, and his eyes flew open.

"They call the snakes!" he heard himself say in Nauvian, but his voice was different. Deeper, older, like Popa's voice, because he was Vallak, the War Chief, one of the Old Ones.

From the high mouth of the Holy Cave, he could see the bridge that led across the river to Vishnia, where the Blue People lived. The snakes crossed the bridge in mated pairs, obeying the call of the Great Horn.

As soon as the last two snakes disappeared off the end of the bridge into Vishnia, the four corners of the bridge detonated. The bridge dropped into the river below, smashing on the rocks. The raging water ripped it to pieces and carried them swiftly downstream.

"Well, that's it!" declared their elected leader, Keekak. His ridiculously tall hat flopped and teetered above his head as he shook his fist at his sworn enemies. "They have taken Keebra! We will be overrun by nimblies and bumblies without Keebra!"

Vallak and the others knew it was true. The snakes would not swim the river, even in the dry season, and next Nimbly-Bumbly Season, the troublesome creatures would emerge in force. Each Season there would be more, without Keebra to keep them in check. The balance had been upset, perhaps forever, because of those Blue People!

"Fire the weapon!" Keekak ordered.

"But, Sir," the triggerman hesitated. Keekak shoved him out of the way and pulled a lever that was strangely familiar to Vallak. A white beam of light streamed out of the copper pipe, arcing across the river. It touched down in the blue village. Where it struck, an azure mist rose. It expanded quickly until, in just seconds, it had swallowed the river and everything beyond.

Vallak stood staring, his mouth open.

"Success!" Keekak crowed. "We have destroyed them!"

"And Keebra as well," Felnye, the Science Minister pointed out.

"We don't need those dumb animals! We have the Weapon! It works!" Keekak crowed his glee and turned to Vallak. "Go. Make sure. Go to the river and peer beyond that mist." he ordered.

The War Chief ran down the steep stone stairs to where his troops waited, staring open-mouthed at the spectacle, just as he had. Without a word, they fell into formation behind him and followed him to the river.

They could see nothing, but they knew where the bridge had been since time immemorial. They stepped into the frigid, raging water. It tugged at their legs, pulling them with it on its inexorable journey downstream to the village and beyond.

Vallak could barely stand. He fought for every step. In his head, the cries of his loyal troops drowned out the roar of the rushing water. The men bellowed, the women screamed, the war dogs whimpered, and the ganeesh, mired in the river mud, emitted sickening, wet gurgles as their trunks flooded.

Only Vallak made his way across. He grasped at the opposite bank, digging his fingers into the mud. It tore away in his fists, far too easily. He caught a vine, but the roots ripped from the soft clay. He clawed at the disintegrating bank until the voices faded and the last bits of what was once Vishnia slipped through his fingers, and there was nothing left to claw.

Nothing but cold, green water and blue mist.

A woman's voice roused him gently. "Momama?" he muttered.

The voice giggled.

"Belinda?" Baput tried again.

"Who's Belinda?" the woman's voice took on a hard edge. "It's me, Topsana, your wife."

"Topsana," Vallak repeated warmly, remembering the nights they had spent together, talking and making his five children, three boys and two girls, warriors all.

Then he remembered. He told his beloved, "It's gone, Topsana! Vishnia is just gone! There is nothing across the river. Nothing but that blue mist!" She looked at him sadly as he shuddered. "My troops?"

His eyes studied hers, and he knew. His crack troops, his A-Team, all drowned. He allowed himself a selfish flicker of gratitude that none of his children had been among them, then he sank into despair.

"Get up, Vallak," Topsana shook him. "You have to see what they're doing." She steadied the exhausted War Chief as he hobbled into the main chamber of the Holy Cave. There was no Death Door, and the chamber behind it was much longer and deeper.

A model of the solar system, like Jerry's, seemed to float before the Science Minister, who looked a lot like Felsic. Sobbing uncontrollably, he pushed it toward the very back of that deep chamber. When Felnye emerged from the chamber without the model, he seemed smaller, as if he had left a good bit of himself behind with it.

"Do not look at Shavarandu. He will burn your eyes,"

Keekak recited slowly to his doughy, spoiled son, Keelan. The boy repeated the line rotely.

Topsana told Vallak, "We are never to speak of Vishnia or the Blue People again. Keekak will make his idiot son a supreme leader, not to be questioned, and he will make sure we don't make any more new weapons. No science, no technology. They're locking it all away."

"Only cool light from Kakeeche can enter your mind,"
Keelan recited.

"Kakeeche?" Vallak gave Topsana a quizzical look.

She rolled her eyes. "He's made up a hideously unscientific dogma about the moon. He even named it after himself! Keekak will force the children to learn it, along with that stupid chant. It's designed to confuse their very understanding of the universe and our place in it! He will dumb us down to primitives!"

"Or evil thoughts from Shavarandu will burn your only world away,"

Keekak finished teaching his dull-witted son the new chant.

"Perhaps it's for the best," Vallak replied glumly, gazing out on the endless blue mist. "This new weapon. It's too much."

The mist had expanded even farther, wrapping around to obliterate the view upriver as well as across.

Topsana was not ready to give up. "We can't let it happen. Not to our kids. We'll leave. We'll go live with my Mo—" She gazed across the river at the mist and her turquoise cheeks blushed aqua.

There was no place to go.

"Oh," Vallak remembered. "Your Momama—"

"I'm here, Baput," Salistar said softly in Nauvian, like she had when he was a little boy waking from a bad dream. *But was this a dream? Or was it the truest truth?*

"Baput? Are you OK?" another gentle female voice asked.

Who's Baput? Vallak wondered, and suddenly he was in the Look'N Up Plumbing van surrounded by concerned faces of green and freckled white.

"It was us," Baput pronounced in a squeak that matured as he returned to his body. "Vishnia. Across the river, where the Blue People lived. Our otherwhere! We hated them. We annihilated them! They're the mist! We blew them to dust with the Weapon. And so, we doomed ourselves."

ABOUT THE AUTHOR

looknupsmiths@gmail.com
www.looknup.us

NEW STUFF IN AN OLD BOX

Janice Carr was raised by liberal parents in the 1960s in Cambridge, Massachusetts, a short hike from Harvard Square. As a kid, she liked to read, write, and act out her stories with her stuffed animals, and sometimes her brother, Charlie, while Dad's Wurlitzer Organ buzzed the corners of the ceiling, rocking the house. Mom would be out marching for some left-wing cause or candidate.

All that ended when Janice was twelve. Cancer struck, first her mom, then her dad. By fourteen, she was orphaned and living in Florida with relatives who had a very different world view. When they decided to move farther into their rural world, Jan rebelled and returned home to finish high school, living with a dear family friend to whom her first book is lovingly dedicated.

Itching to be on her own, no longer a guest, she left campus-rich Boston for a Radio-TV-Film major at Northwestern University. The college Outing Club opened her city-born eyes to the natural world with hiking, rock-climbing and spelunking trips, and she switched to a Geology major.

After years of wandering, she married John Smith and became an Environmental Consultant, shepherding public works projects through California's rigorous environmental compliance process, first at a private engineering firm and later for a rural county public works department in Northern California.

In 2017, Janice retired in the same county with the same husband. One day, in her garden, she started hearing voices. She looked up, and the Look'N Up was born.

The End

Done With Invasion?

Reviews, ratings and likes are always appreciated. Post 'em wherever you find your books, or on your own social media.

Want More?

Wondering what happened to Baput's betrothed, Tamaya?
What about Felsic's family, Peratha and Trillella?
Is Francine right about Akira? If so, what's it like to be her?
Find out in **Look 'N Up Liberation** coming spring 2024!

Contact me at my website www.looknup.us
Or email me at looknupsmiths@gmail.com

Ask to be notified when Liberation is released, and I'll put you on my mailing list and send you a sneak preview .pdf.
Ask for TAMAYA, TRILLELLA or AKIRA, and find out how they're doing.

Fear not! I promise not to bombard you with newsletters.

Printed in the USA
CPSIA information can be obtained
at www.ICGtesting.com
LVHW041759110923
757087LV00004B/15